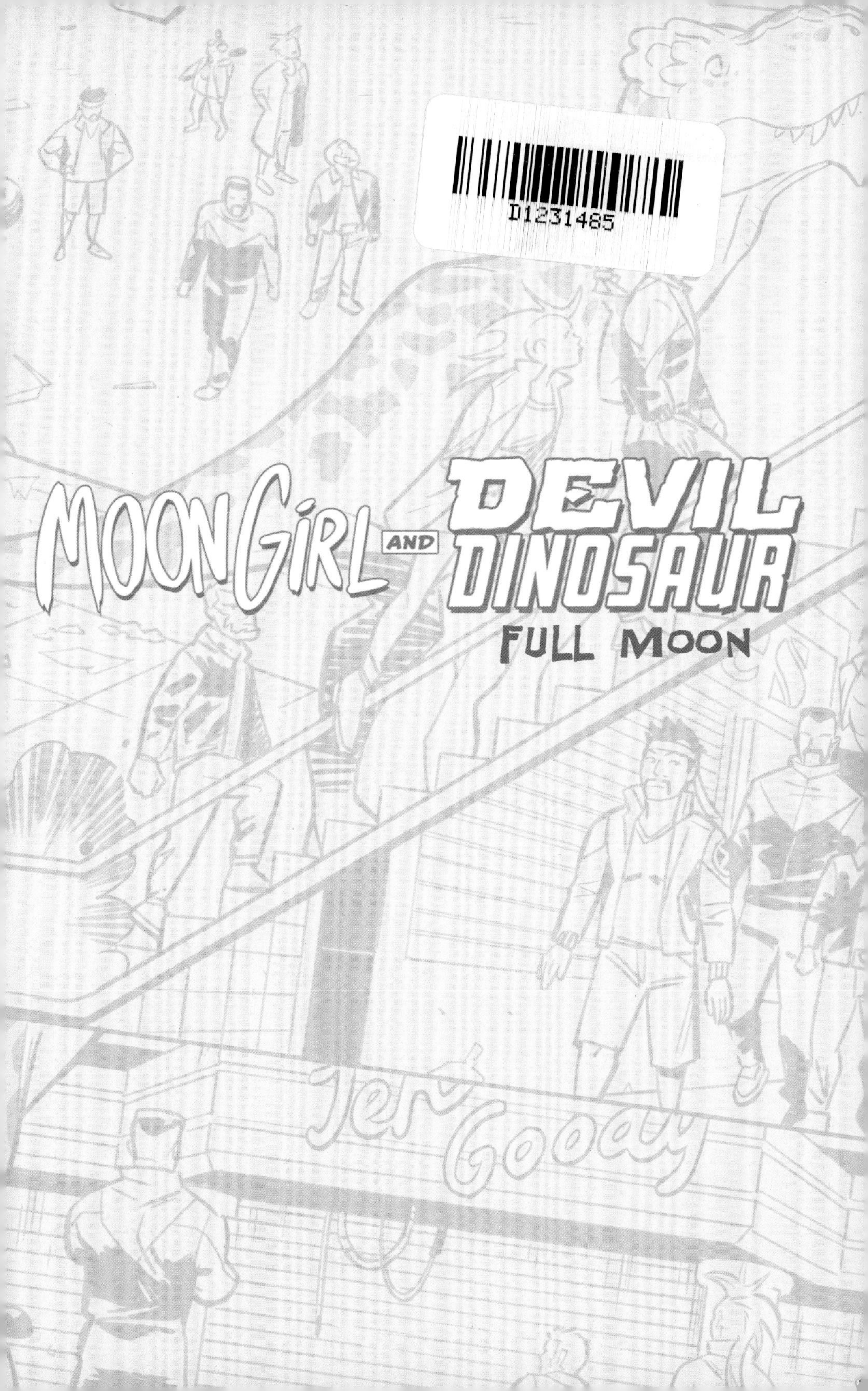

Moon Girl and Devil Dinosaur

Full Moon

CONTENTS

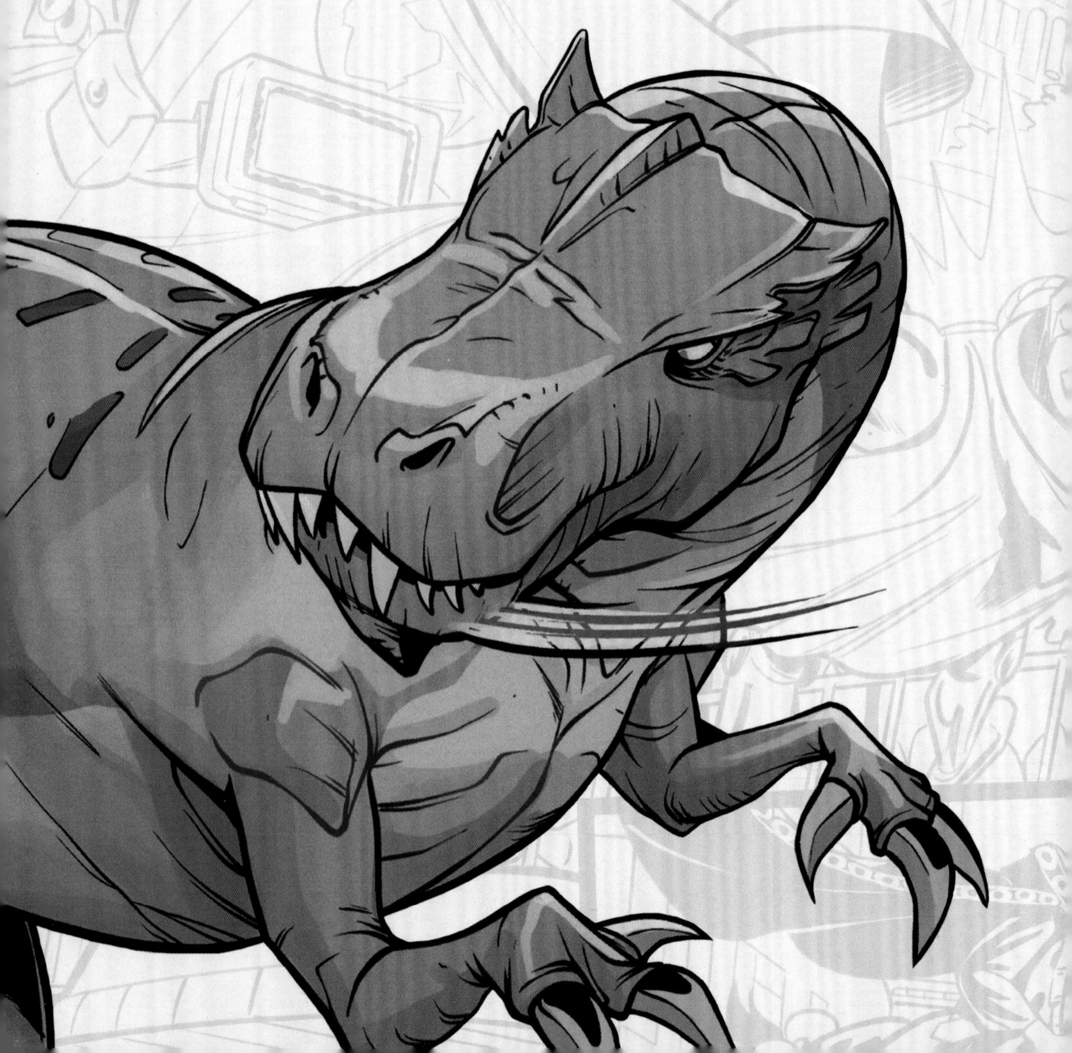

MOON GIRL AND DEVIL DINOSAUR

FULL MOON

writers

BRANDON MONTCLARE (#13-24) & **AMY REEDER** (#13-18)

artists

NATACHA BUSTOS (#13, #15-24) & **RAY-ANTHONY HEIGHT** (#14)

color artist

TAMRA BONVILLAIN

dream art, #13

LEONARD KIRK & TAMRA BONVILLAIN

Artist, "Think Fast"

DOMINIKE "DOMO" STANTON

Artist, "Sign on the Dotted Line"

RAY-ANTHONY HEIGHT

Artist, "Blinds"

MICHAEL SHELFER

letterers

VC's TRAVIS LANHAM (#13-18 & #20-24) & **JOE CARAMAGNA** (#19)

cover art

AMY REEDER (#13-18) & **NATACHA BUSTOS** (#19-24)

assistant editor

CHRIS ROBINSON

editor

MARK PANICCIA

DEVIL DINOSAUR CREATED BY JACK KIRBY

collection editor JENNIFER GRÜNWALD
assistant editor CAITLIN O'CONNELL • associate managing editor KATERI WOODY
editor, special projects MARK D. BEAZLEY • vp production & special projects JEFF YOUNGQUIST

svp print, sales & marketing DAVID GABRIEL • director, licensed publishing SVEN LARSEN
editor in chief C.B. CEBULSKI • chief creative officer JOE QUESADA
president DAN BUCKLEY • executive producer ALAN FINE

MOON GIRL AND DEVIL DINOSAUR: FULL MOON. Contains material originally published in magazine form as MOON GIRL AND DEVIL DINOSAUR (2015) #13-24. First printing 2019. ISBN 978-1-302-92113-2. Published by MARVEL WORLDWIDE, INC., a subsidiary of MARVEL ENTERTAINMENT, LLC. OFFICE OF PUBLICATION: 135 West 50th Street, New York, NY 10020. **Printed in Canada.** DAN BUCKLEY, President, Marvel Entertainment; JOHN NEE, Publisher; JOE QUESADA, Chief Creative Officer; TOM BREVOORT, SVP of Publishing; DAVID BOGART, Associate Publisher & SVP of Talent Affairs; DAVID GABRIEL, VP of Print & Digital Publishing; JEFF YOUNGQUIST, VP of Production & Special Projects; DAN CARR, Executive Director of Publishing Technology; ALEX MORALES, Director of Publishing Operations; DAN EDINGTON, Managing Editor; SUSAN CRESPI, Production Manager; STAN LEE, Chairman Emeritus. For information regarding advertising in Marvel Comics or on Marvel.com, please contact Vit DeBellis, Custom Solutions & Integrated Advertising Manager, at vdebellis@marvel.com. For Marvel subscription inquiries, please call 888-511-5480. **Manufactured between 11/8/2019 and 12/10/2019 by SOLISCO PRINTERS, SCOTT, QC, CANADA.**

10 9 8 7 6 5 4 3 2 1

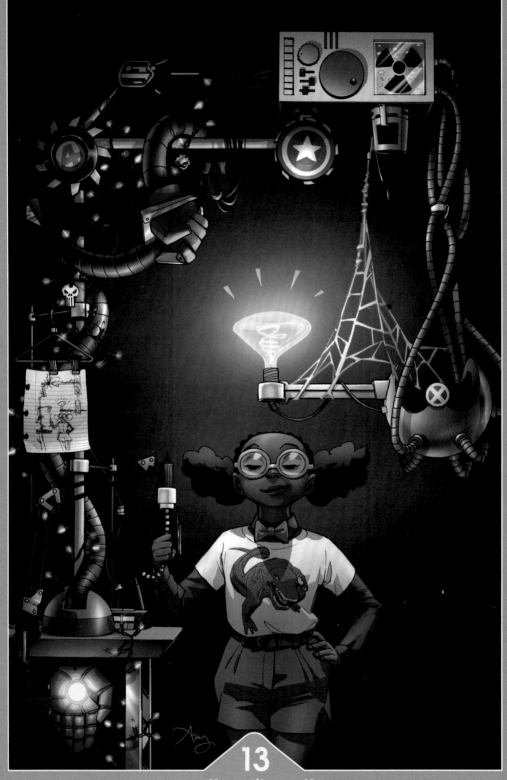

13

"MARVEL NOW OR NEVER"

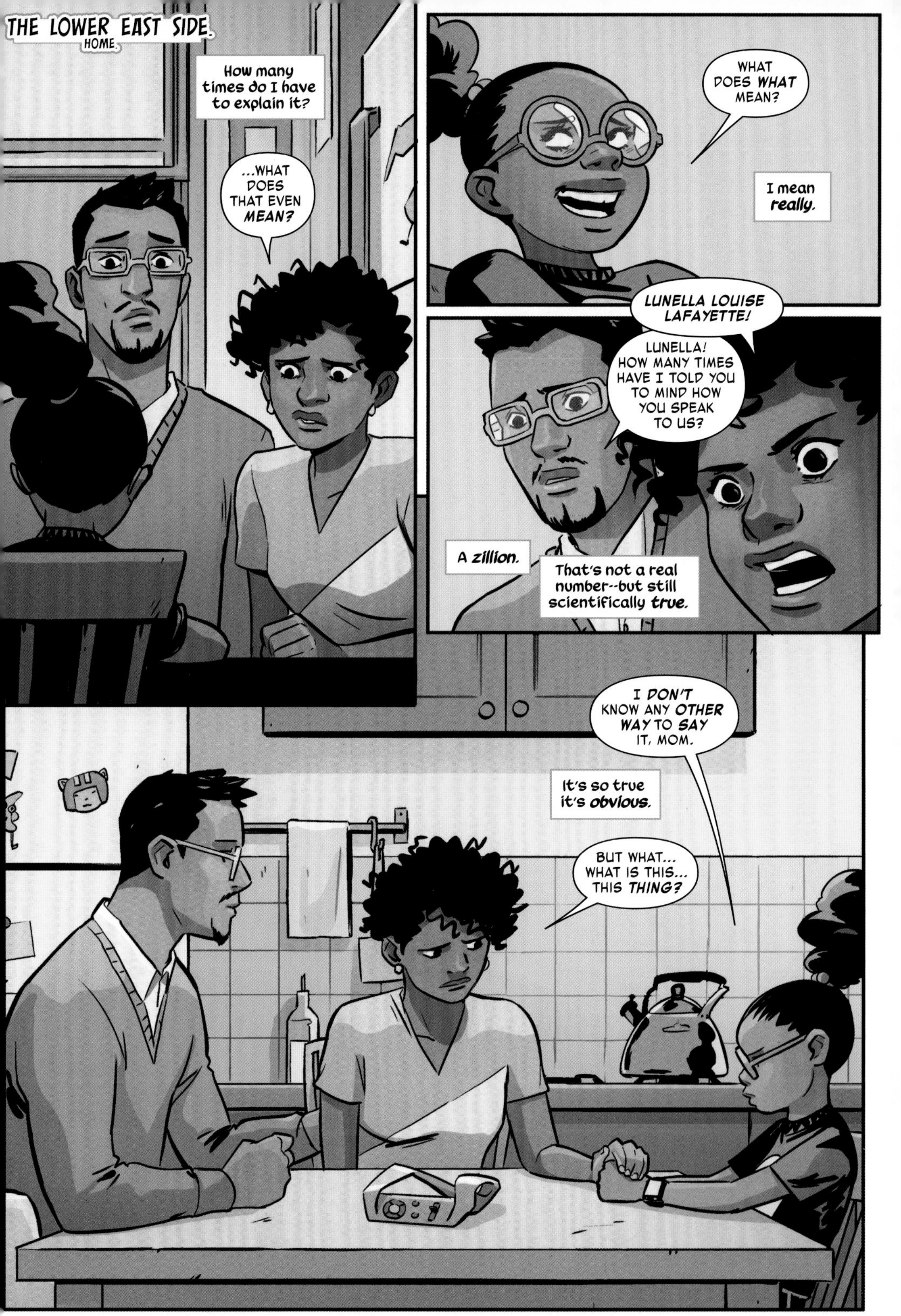
THE LOWER EAST SIDE. HOME.
How many times do I have to explain it?
...WHAT DOES THAT EVEN MEAN?
WHAT DOES WHAT MEAN?
I mean really.
LUNELLA LOUISE LAFAYETTE!
LUNELLA! HOW MANY TIMES HAVE I TOLD YOU TO MIND HOW YOU SPEAK TO US?
A zillion.
That's not a real number--but still scientifically true.
I DON'T KNOW ANY OTHER WAY TO SAY IT, MOM.
It's so true it's obvious.
BUT WHAT... WHAT IS THIS... THIS THING?

THE SMARTEST THERE IS! PART ONE: "MARVEL NOW OR NEVER!"

"My body can do what it wants. I am not the body. I am the mind." --Rita Levi-Montalcini

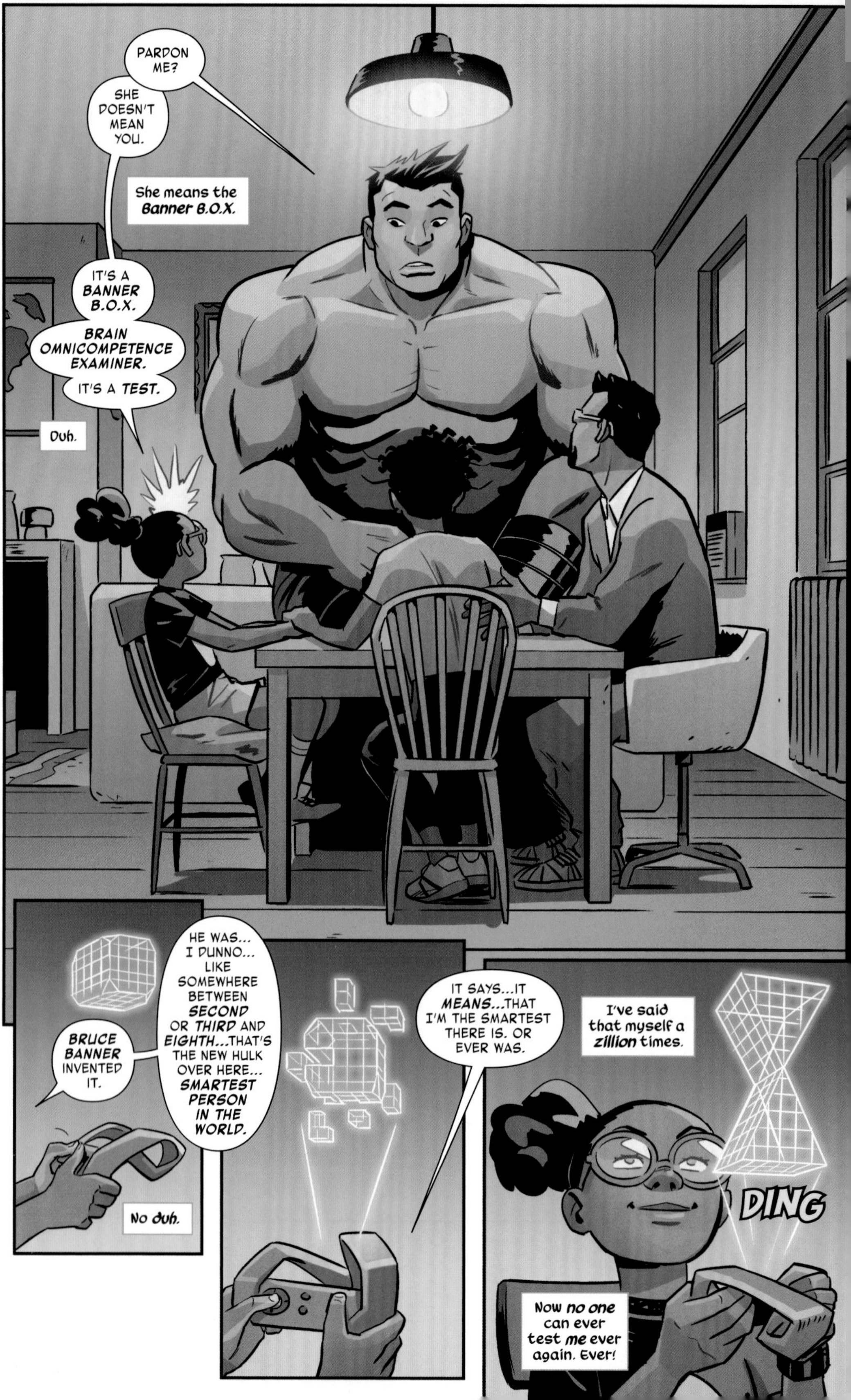

PARDON ME?
SHE DOESN'T MEAN YOU.
She means the Banner B.O.X.
IT'S A BANNER B.O.X.
BRAIN OMNICOMPETENCE EXAMINER.
IT'S A TEST.
Duh.
BRUCE BANNER INVENTED IT.
HE WAS... I DUNNO... LIKE SOMEWHERE BETWEEN SECOND OR THIRD AND EIGHTH...THAT'S THE NEW HULK OVER HERE... SMARTEST PERSON IN THE WORLD.
No duh.
IT SAYS...IT MEANS...THAT I'M THE SMARTEST THERE IS. OR EVER WAS.
I've said that myself a zillion times.
DING
Now no one can ever test me ever again. Ever!

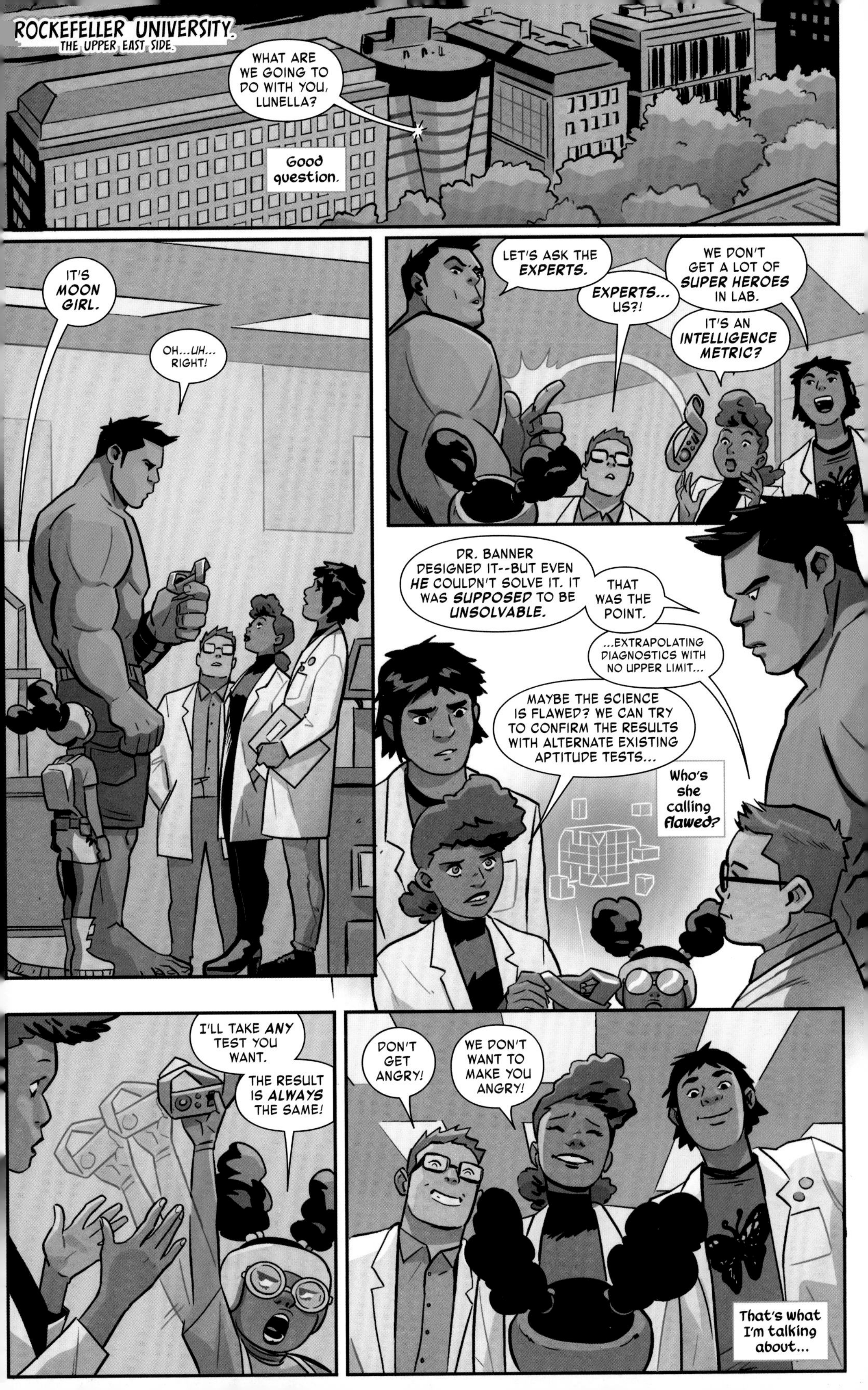
ROCKEFELLER UNIVERSITY. THE UPPER EAST SIDE.
WHAT ARE WE GOING TO DO WITH YOU, LUNELLA?
Good question.
IT'S MOON GIRL.
OH...UH... RIGHT!
LET'S ASK THE EXPERTS.
EXPERTS... US?!
WE DON'T GET A LOT OF SUPER HEROES IN LAB.
IT'S AN INTELLIGENCE METRIC?
DR. BANNER DESIGNED IT--BUT EVEN HE COULDN'T SOLVE IT. IT WAS SUPPOSED TO BE UNSOLVABLE.
THAT WAS THE POINT.
...EXTRAPOLATING DIAGNOSTICS WITH NO UPPER LIMIT...
MAYBE THE SCIENCE IS FLAWED? WE CAN TRY TO CONFIRM THE RESULTS WITH ALTERNATE EXISTING APTITUDE TESTS...
Who's she calling flawed?
I'LL TAKE ANY TEST YOU WANT.
THE RESULT IS ALWAYS THE SAME!
DON'T GET ANGRY!
WE DON'T WANT TO MAKE YOU ANGRY!
That's what I'm talking about...

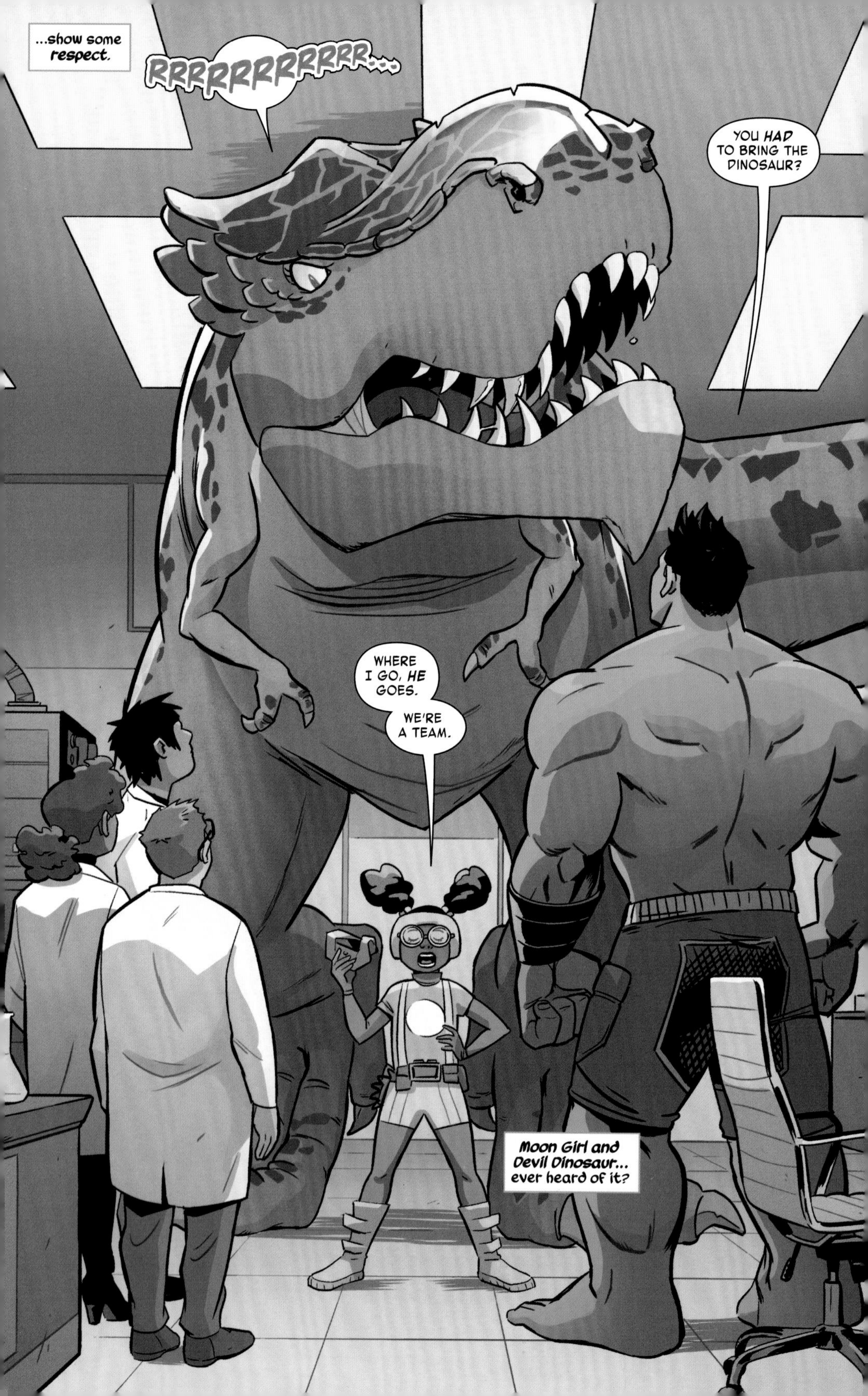

...show some respect.
RRRRRRRRRRR...
YOU HAD TO BRING THE DINOSAUR?
WHERE I GO, HE GOES.
WE'RE A TEAM.
Moon Girl and Devil Dinosaur... ever heard of it?

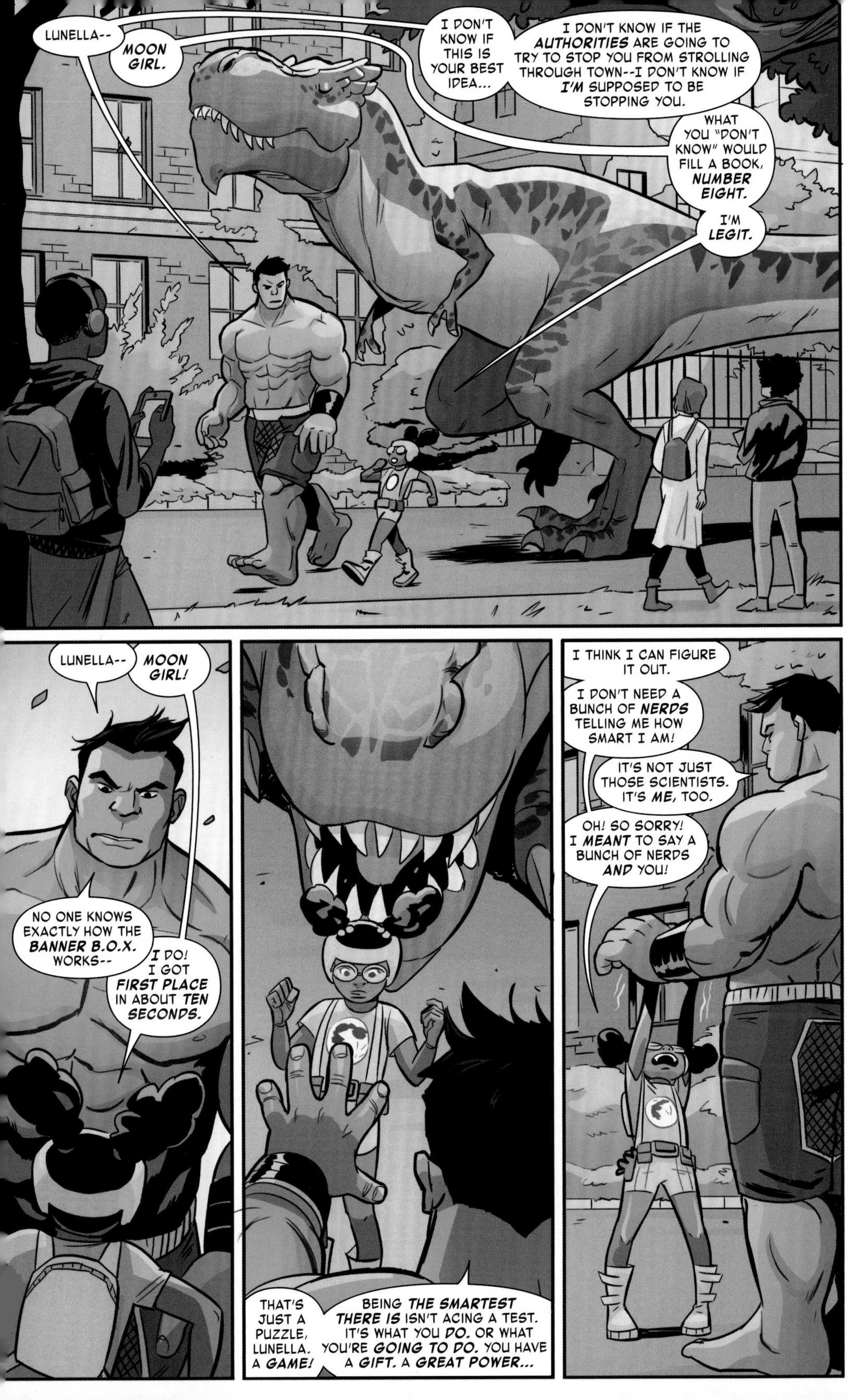
LUNELLA--
MOON GIRL.
I DON'T KNOW IF THIS IS YOUR BEST IDEA...
I DON'T KNOW IF THE AUTHORITIES ARE GOING TO TRY TO STOP YOU FROM STROLLING THROUGH TOWN--I DON'T KNOW IF I'M SUPPOSED TO BE STOPPING YOU.
WHAT YOU "DON'T KNOW" WOULD FILL A BOOK, NUMBER EIGHT.
I'M LEGIT.
LUNELLA--
MOON GIRL!
NO ONE KNOWS EXACTLY HOW THE BANNER B.O.X. WORKS--
I DO! I GOT FIRST PLACE IN ABOUT TEN SECONDS.
THAT'S JUST A PUZZLE, LUNELLA. A GAME!
BEING THE SMARTEST THERE IS ISN'T ACING A TEST. IT'S WHAT YOU DO. OR WHAT YOU'RE GOING TO DO. YOU HAVE A GIFT. A GREAT POWER...
I THINK I CAN FIGURE IT OUT.
I DON'T NEED A BUNCH OF NERDS TELLING ME HOW SMART I AM!
IT'S NOT JUST THOSE SCIENTISTS. IT'S ME, TOO.
OH! SO SORRY! I MEANT TO SAY A BUNCH OF NERDS AND YOU!

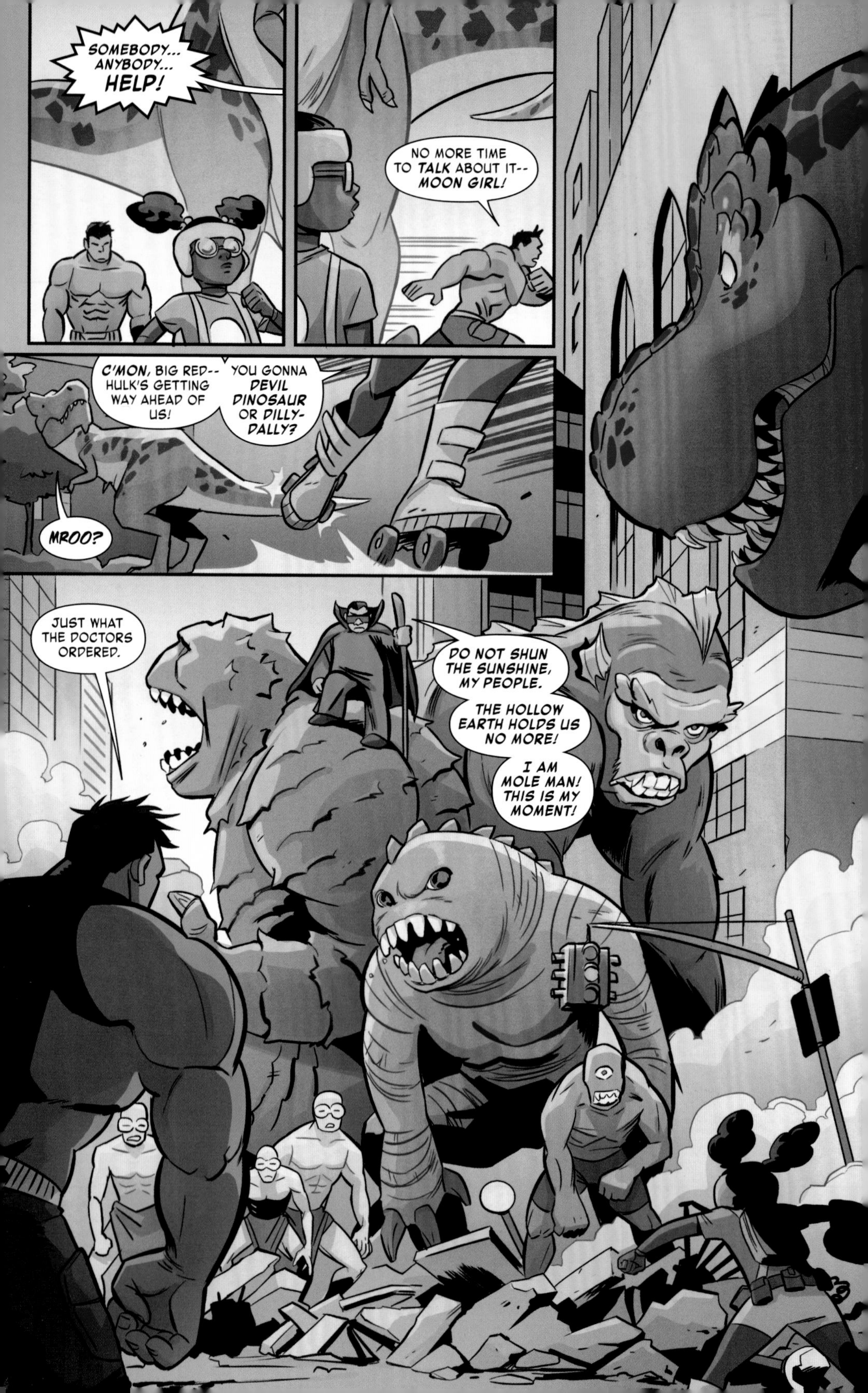
SOMEBODY... ANYBODY... HELP!
NO MORE TIME TO TALK ABOUT IT-- MOON GIRL!
C'MON, BIG RED-- HULK'S GETTING WAY AHEAD OF US!
YOU GONNA DEVIL DINOSAUR OR DILLY-DALLY?
MROO?
JUST WHAT THE DOCTORS ORDERED.
DO NOT SHUN THE SUNSHINE, MY PEOPLE.
THE HOLLOW EARTH HOLDS US NO MORE!
I AM MOLE MAN! THIS IS MY MOMENT!

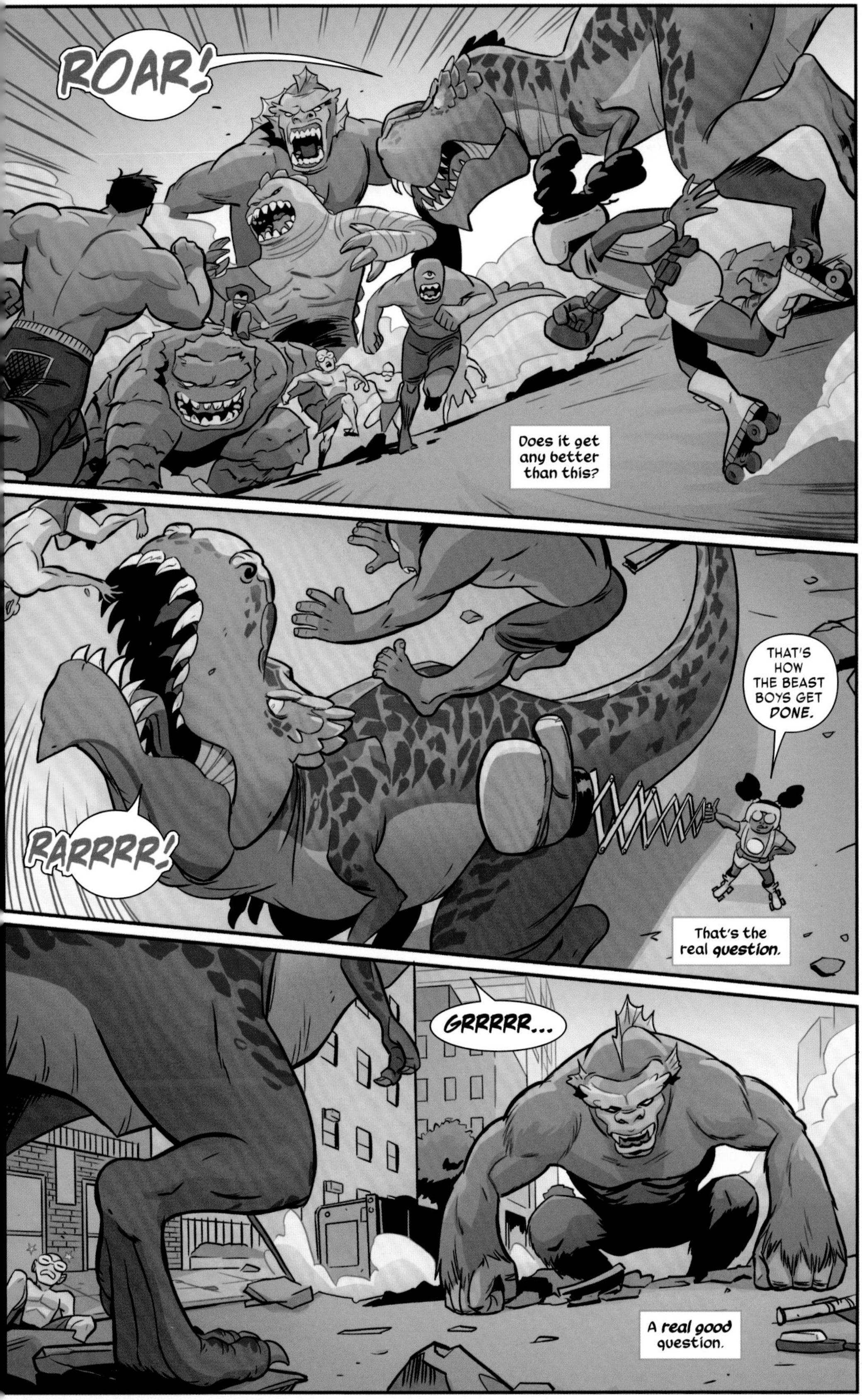
ROAR!
Does it get any better than this?
THAT'S HOW THE BEAST BOYS GET DONE.
RARRRR!
That's the real question.
GRRRRR...
A real good question.

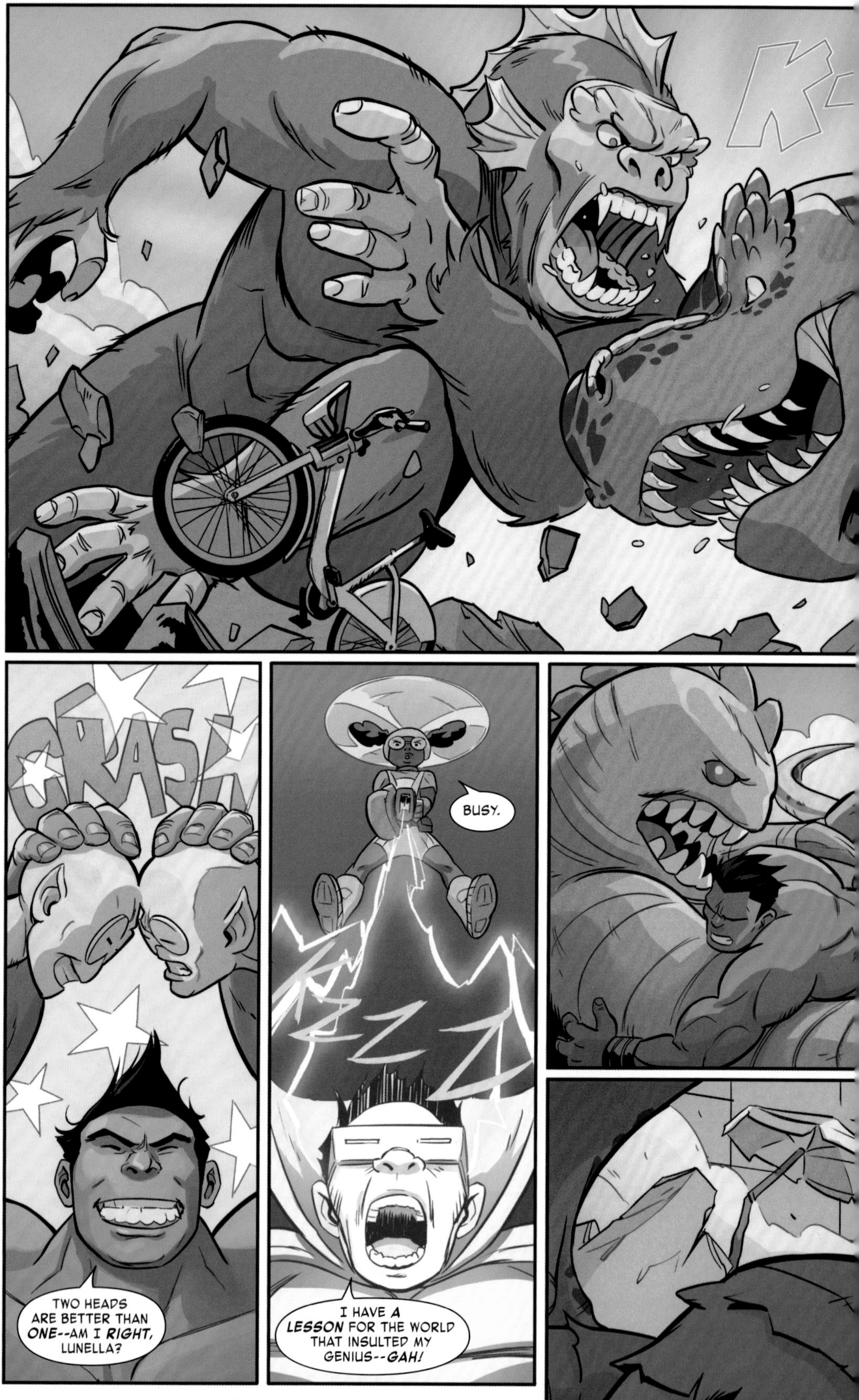

CRASH
BUSY.
TWO HEADS ARE BETTER THAN ONE--AM I RIGHT, LUNELLA?
I HAVE A LESSON FOR THE WORLD THAT INSULTED MY GENIUS--GAH!

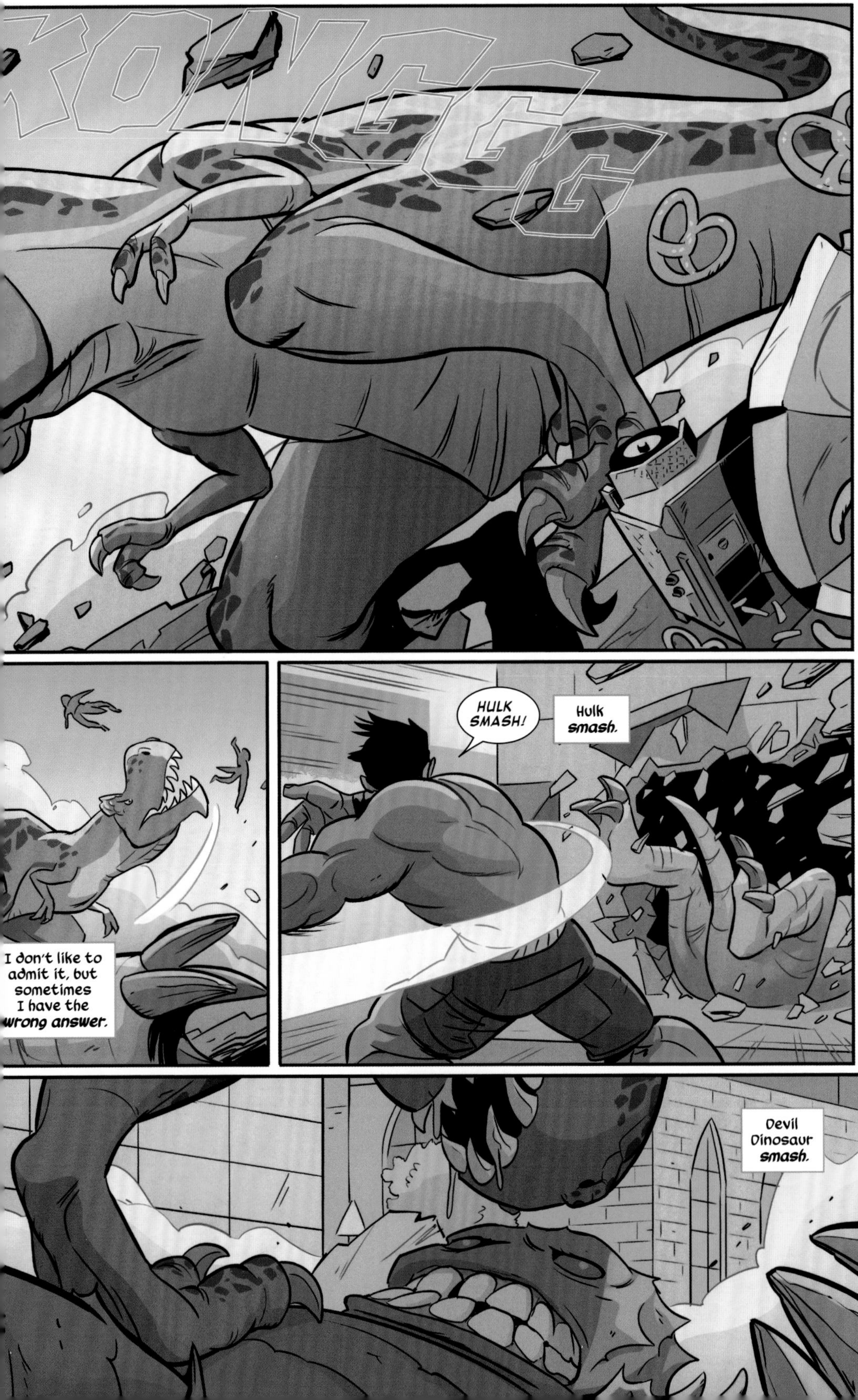
I don't like to admit it, but sometimes I have the **wrong answer.**
HULK SMASH!
Hulk **smash.**
Devil Dinosaur **smash.**

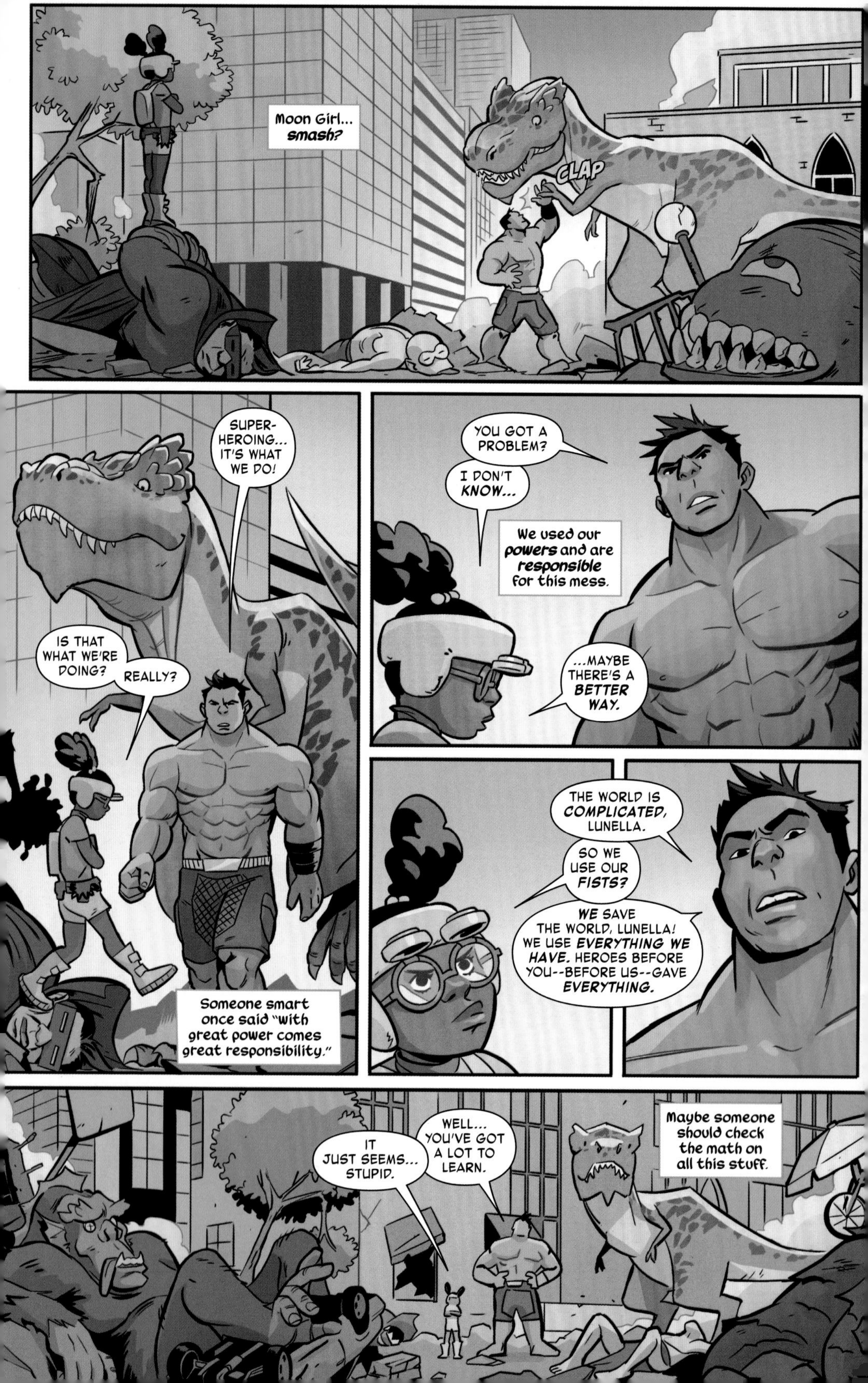

Moon Girl... smash?
CLAP
SUPER-HEROING... IT'S WHAT WE DO!
IS THAT WHAT WE'RE DOING?
REALLY?
Someone smart once said "with great power comes great responsibility."
YOU GOT A PROBLEM?
I DON'T KNOW...
We used our powers and are responsible for this mess.
...MAYBE THERE'S A BETTER WAY.
THE WORLD IS COMPLICATED, LUNELLA.
SO WE USE OUR FISTS?
WE SAVE THE WORLD, LUNELLA! WE USE EVERYTHING WE HAVE. HEROES BEFORE YOU--BEFORE US--GAVE EVERYTHING.
IT JUST SEEMS... STUPID.
WELL... YOU'VE GOT A LOT TO LEARN.
Maybe someone should check the math on all this stuff.

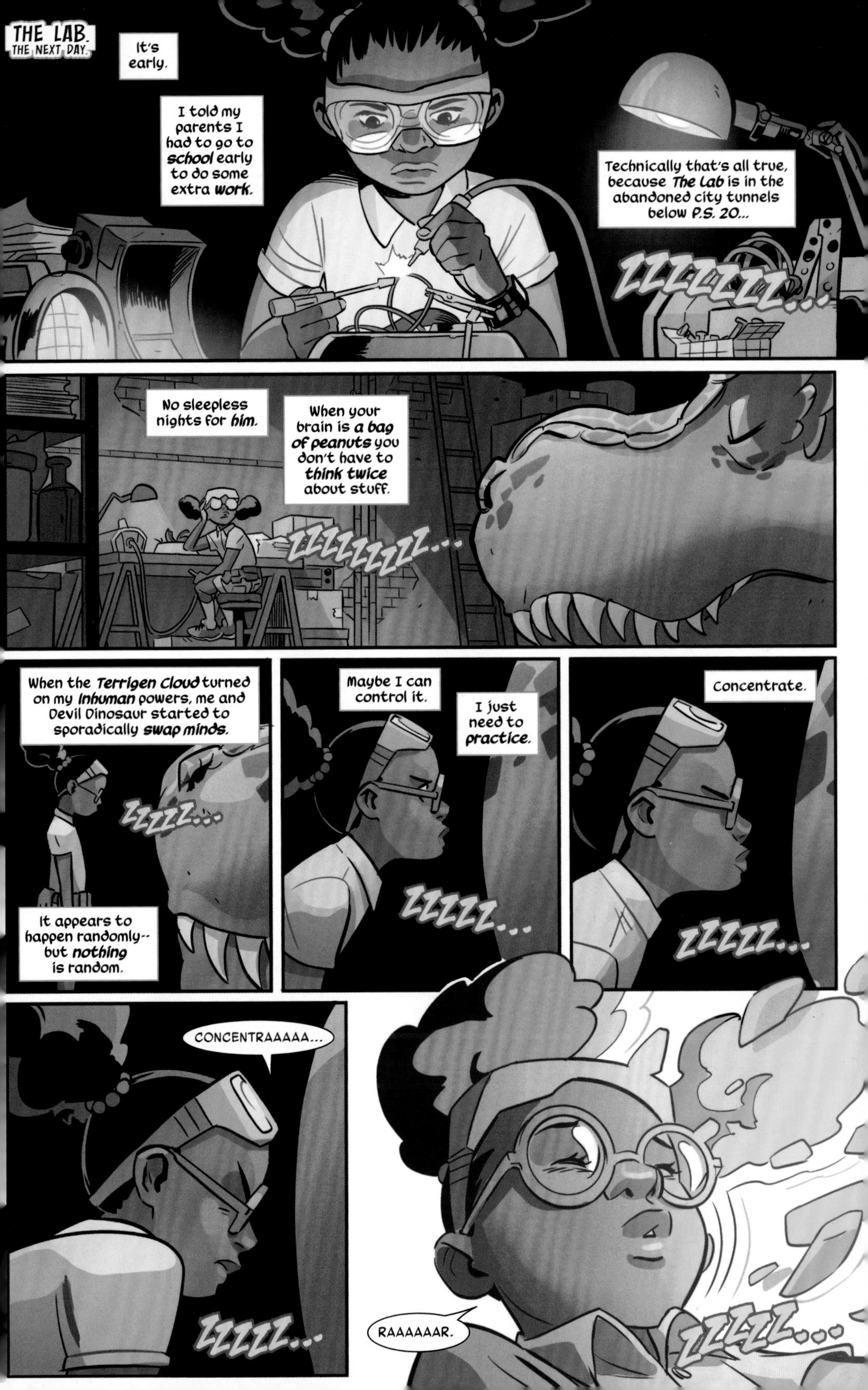

THE LAB. THE NEXT DAY.
It's early.
I told my parents I had to go to school early to do some extra work.
Technically that's all true, because The Lab is in the abandoned city tunnels below P.S. 20...
ZZZZZZZZ...
No sleepless nights for him.
When your brain is a bag of peanuts you don't have to think twice about stuff.
ZZZZZZZZZ...
When the Terrigen Cloud turned on my Inhuman powers, me and Devil Dinosaur started to sporadically swap minds.
ZZZZZ...
It appears to happen randomly-- but nothing is random.
Maybe I can control it.
I just need to practice.
ZZZZZ...
Concentrate.
ZZZZZ...
CONCENTRAAAAA...
ZZZZZ...
RAAAAAAR.
ZZZZZ...

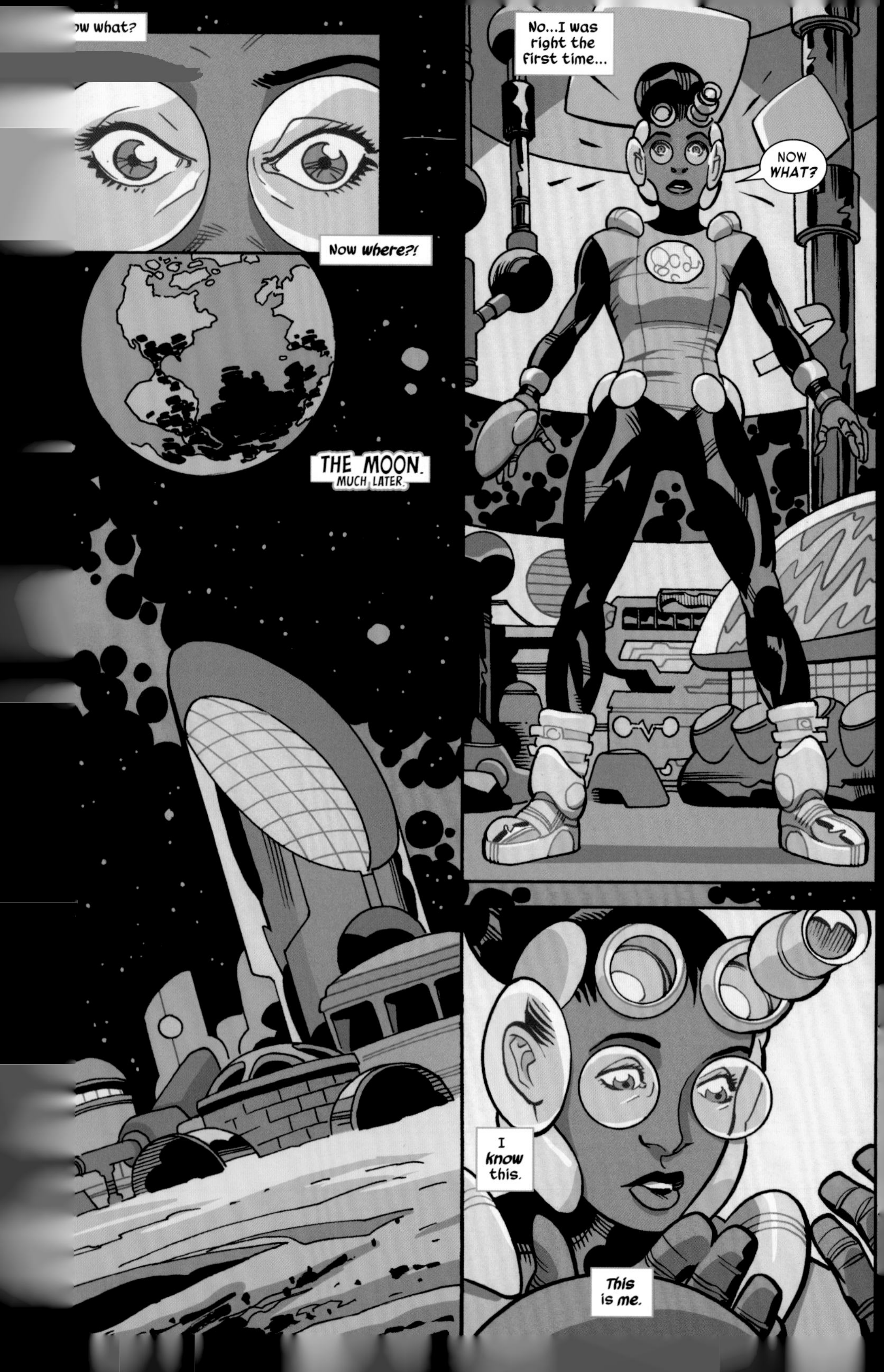
ow what?
Now where?!
THE MOON.
MUCH LATER.
No...I was right the first time...
NOW WHAT?
I know this.
This is me.

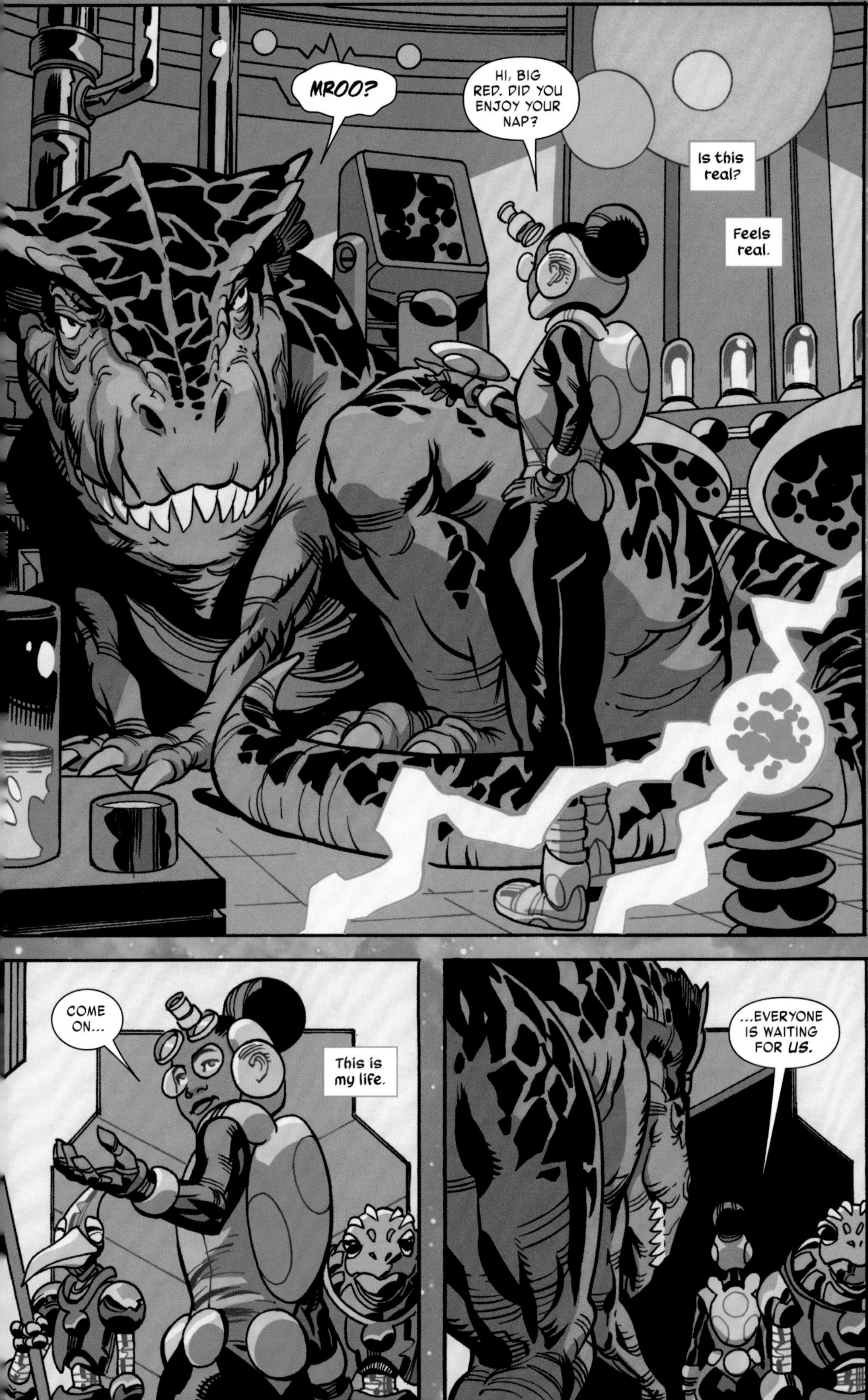
MROO?
HI, BIG RED. DID YOU ENJOY YOUR NAP?
Is this real?
Feels real.
COME ON...
This is my life.
...EVERYONE IS WAITING FOR *US*.

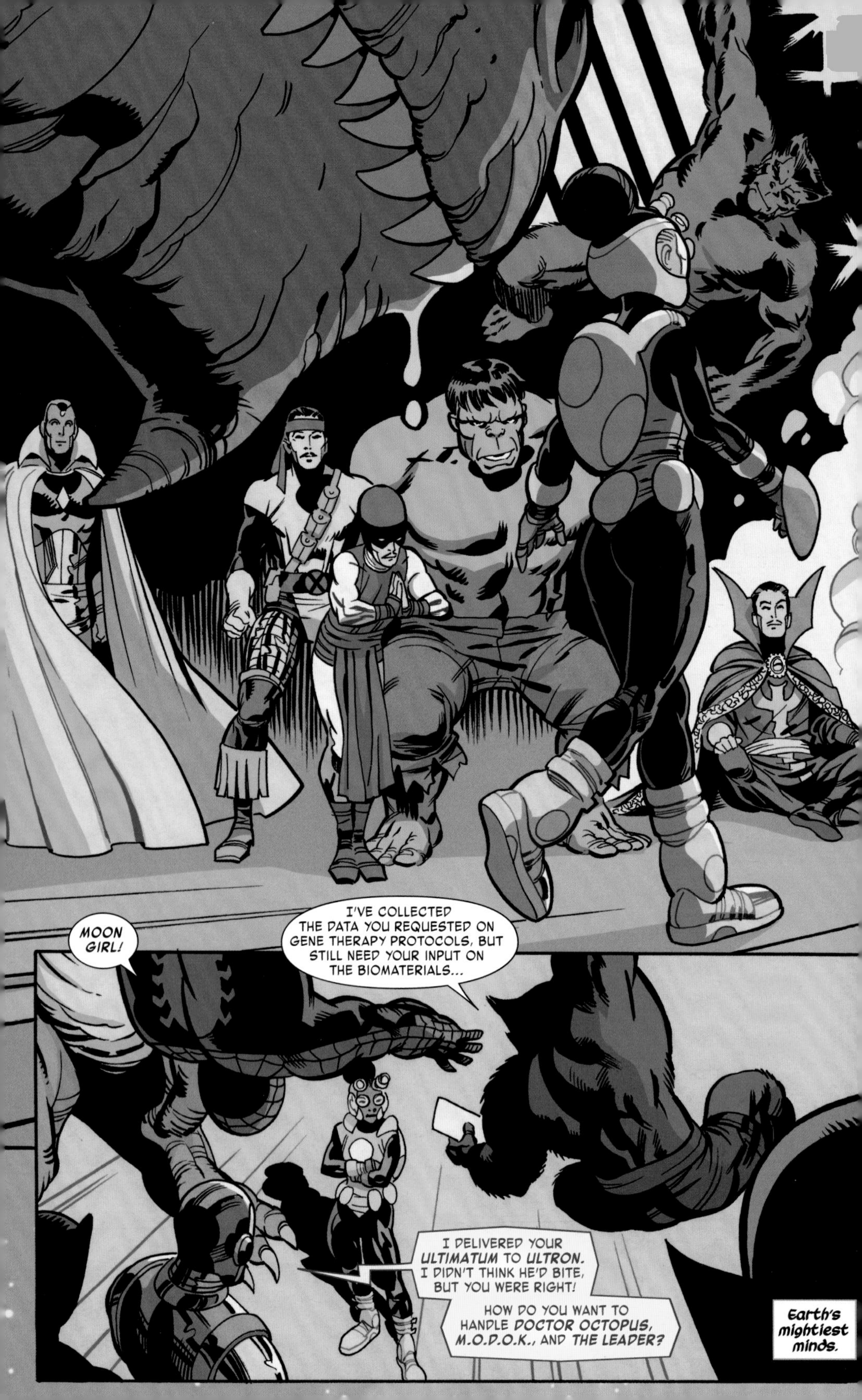
MOON GIRL!
I'VE COLLECTED THE DATA YOU REQUESTED ON GENE THERAPY PROTOCOLS, BUT STILL NEED YOUR INPUT ON THE BIOMATERIALS...
I DELIVERED YOUR ULTIMATUM TO ULTRON. I DIDN'T THINK HE'D BITE, BUT YOU WERE RIGHT!
HOW DO YOU WANT TO HANDLE DOCTOR OCTOPUS, M.O.D.O.K., AND THE LEADER?
Earth's mightiest minds.

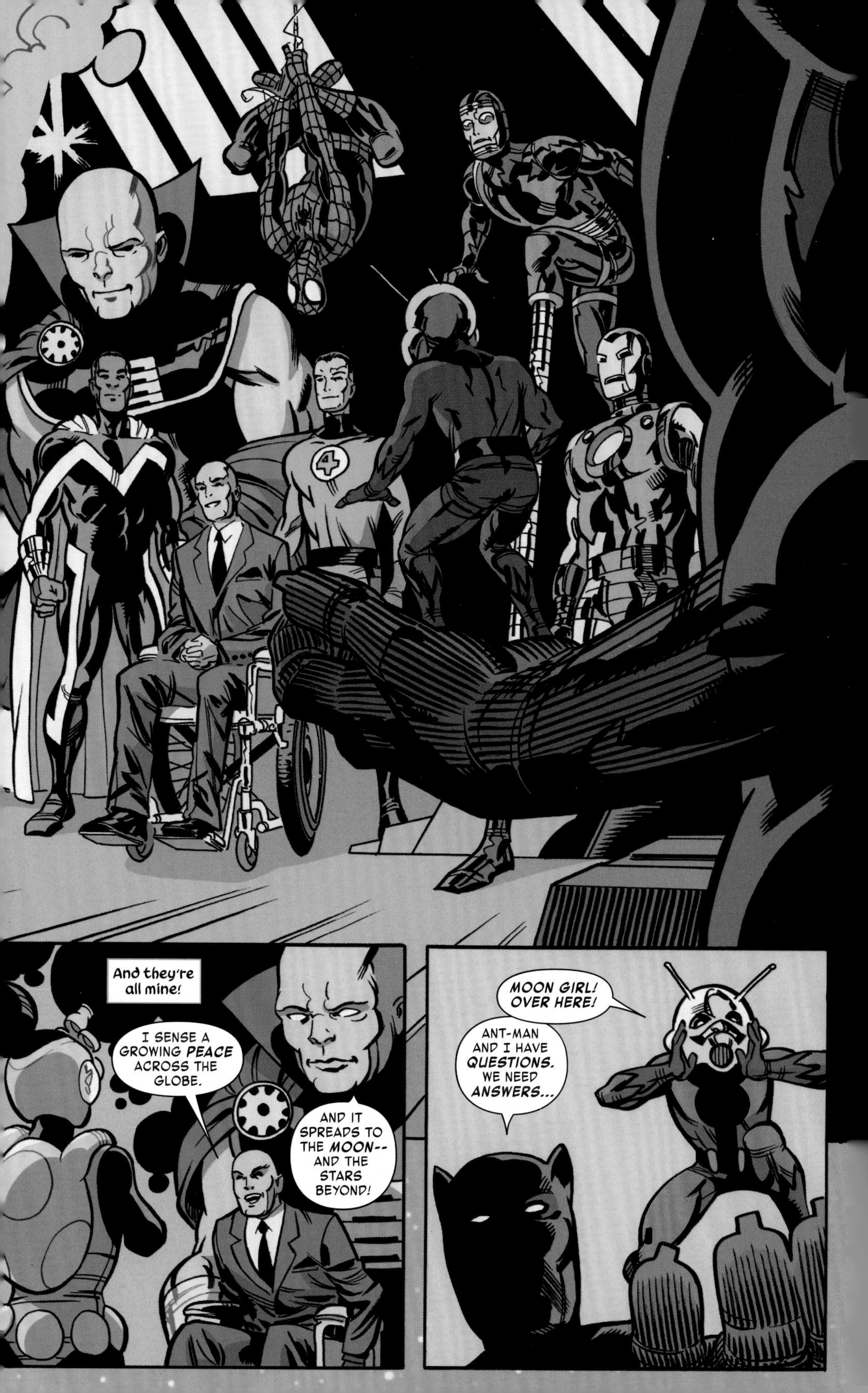

And they're all mine!
I SENSE A GROWING PEACE ACROSS THE GLOBE.
AND IT SPREADS TO THE MOON-- AND THE STARS BEYOND!
MOON GIRL! OVER HERE!
ANT-MAN AND I HAVE QUESTIONS. WE NEED ANSWERS...

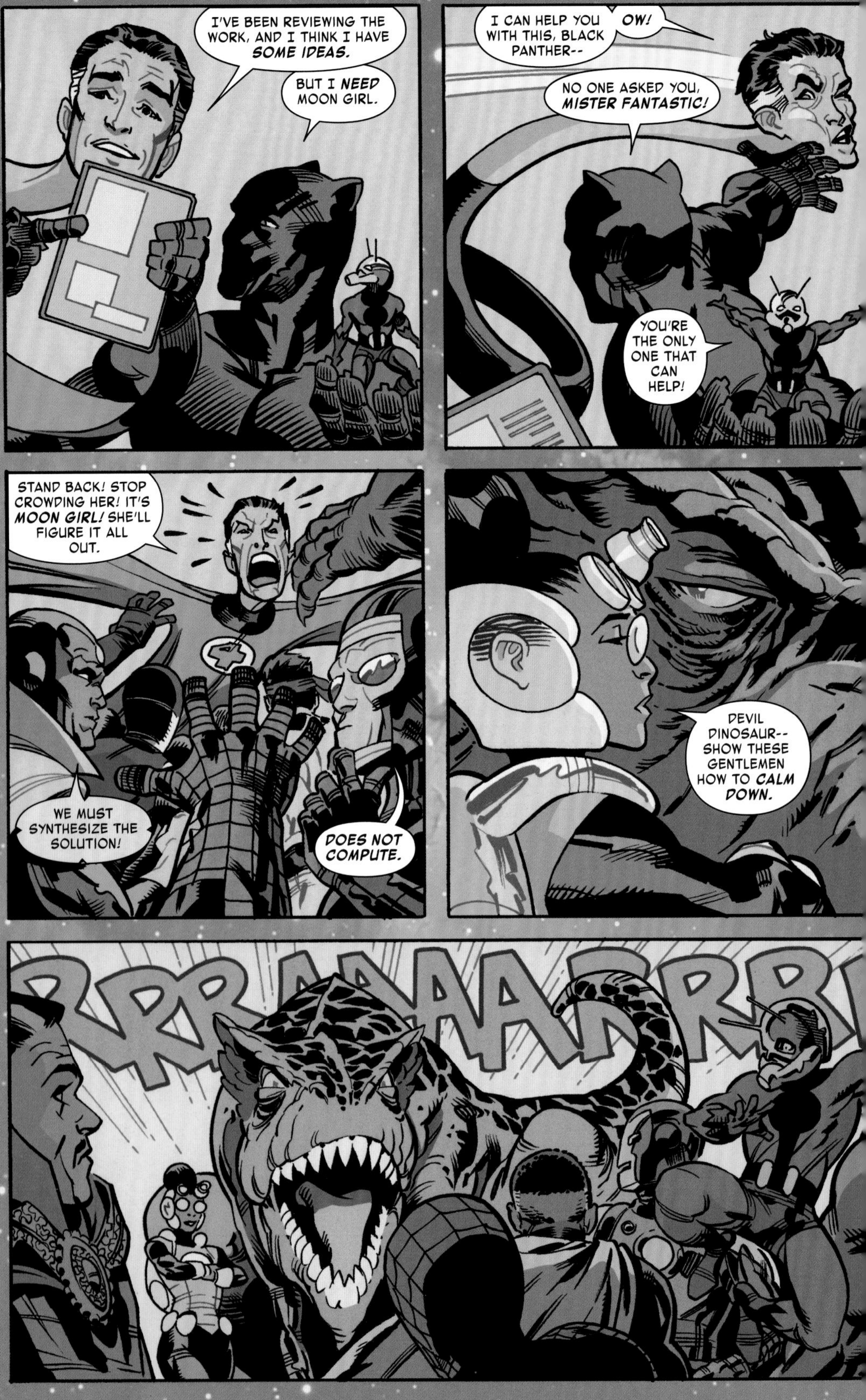
I'VE BEEN REVIEWING THE WORK, AND I THINK I HAVE SOME IDEAS.
BUT I NEED MOON GIRL.
I CAN HELP YOU WITH THIS, BLACK PANTHER--
OW!
NO ONE ASKED YOU, MISTER FANTASTIC!
YOU'RE THE ONLY ONE THAT CAN HELP!
STAND BACK! STOP CROWDING HER! IT'S MOON GIRL! SHE'LL FIGURE IT ALL OUT.
WE MUST SYNTHESIZE THE SOLUTION!
DOES NOT COMPUTE.
DEVIL DINOSAUR-- SHOW THESE GENTLEMEN HOW TO CALM DOWN.
RRRAAAARRR

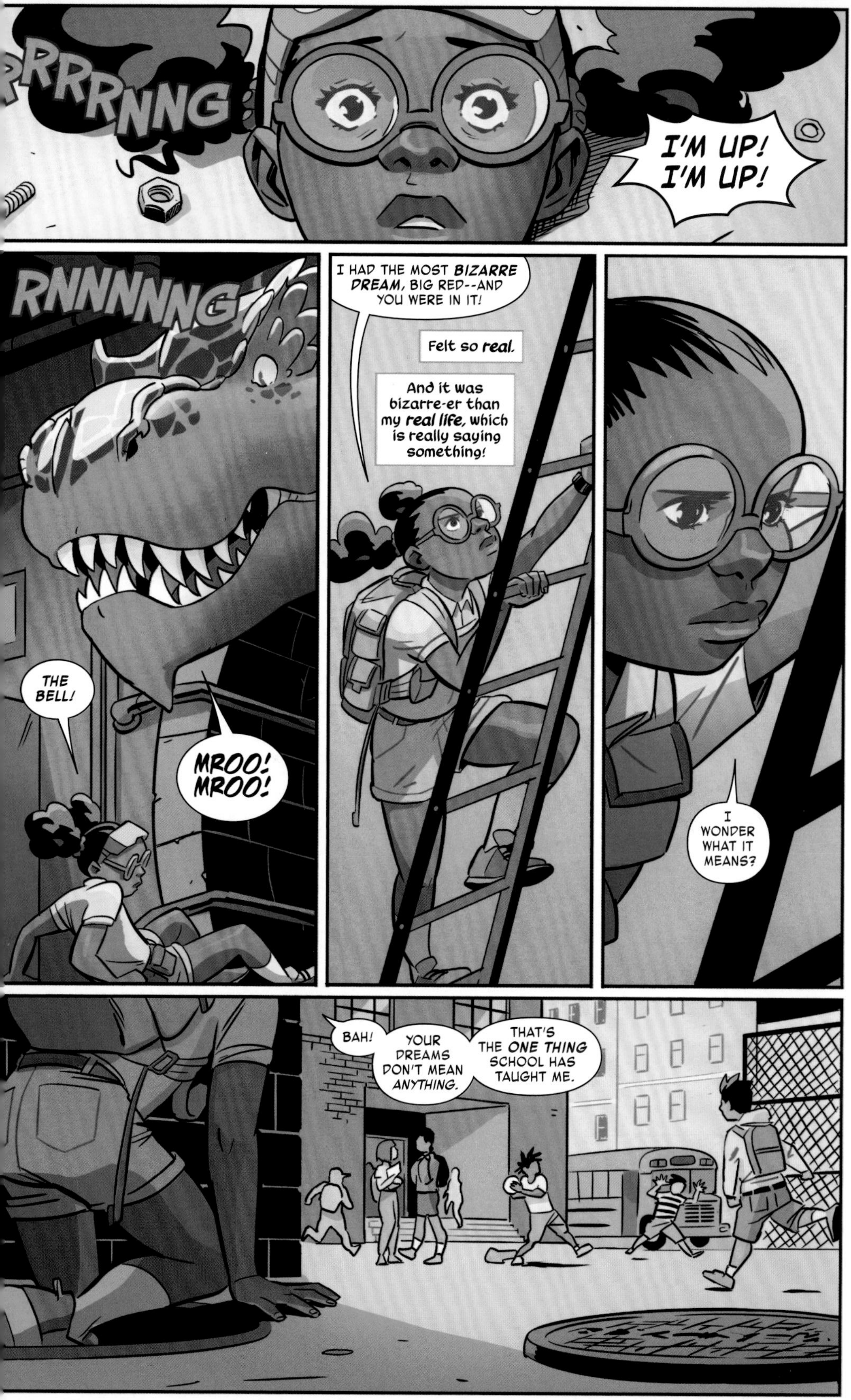
RRRRNNG
I'M UP! I'M UP!
RNNNNNG
THE BELL!
MROO! MROO!
I HAD THE MOST BIZARRE DREAM, BIG RED--AND YOU WERE IN IT!
Felt so real.
And it was bizarre-er than my real life, which is really saying something!
I WONDER WHAT IT MEANS?
BAH!
YOUR DREAMS DON'T MEAN ANYTHING.
THAT'S THE ONE THING SCHOOL HAS TAUGHT ME.

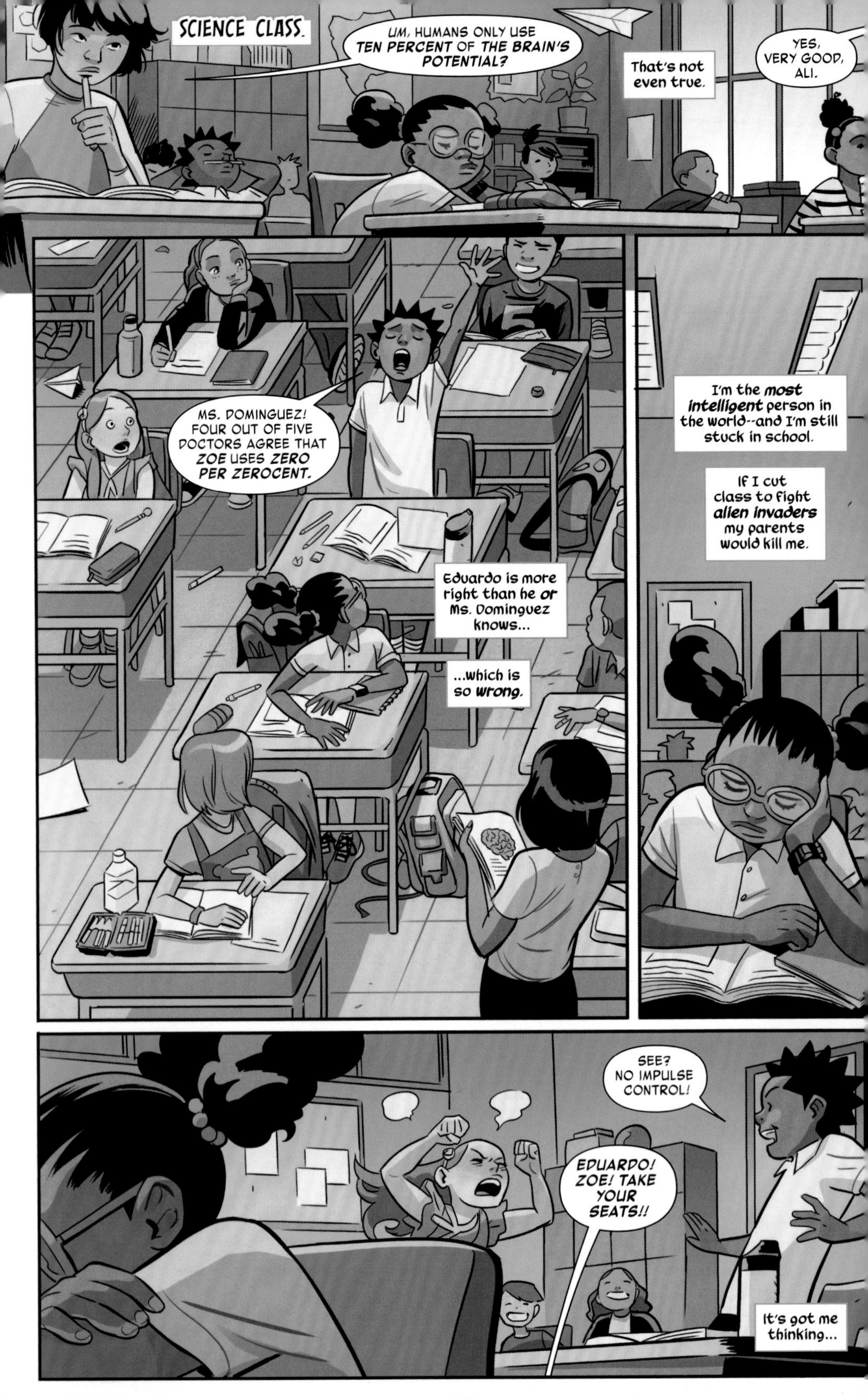
SCIENCE CLASS.
UM, HUMANS ONLY USE TEN PERCENT OF THE BRAIN'S POTENTIAL?
That's not even true.
YES, VERY GOOD, ALI.
MS. DOMINGUEZ! FOUR OUT OF FIVE DOCTORS AGREE THAT ZOE USES ZERO PER ZEROCENT.
Eduardo is more right than he or Ms. Dominguez knows...
...which is so wrong.
I'm the most intelligent person in the world--and I'm still stuck in school.
If I cut class to fight alien invaders my parents would kill me.
SEE? NO IMPULSE CONTROL!
EDUARDO! ZOE! TAKE YOUR SEATS!!
It's got me thinking...

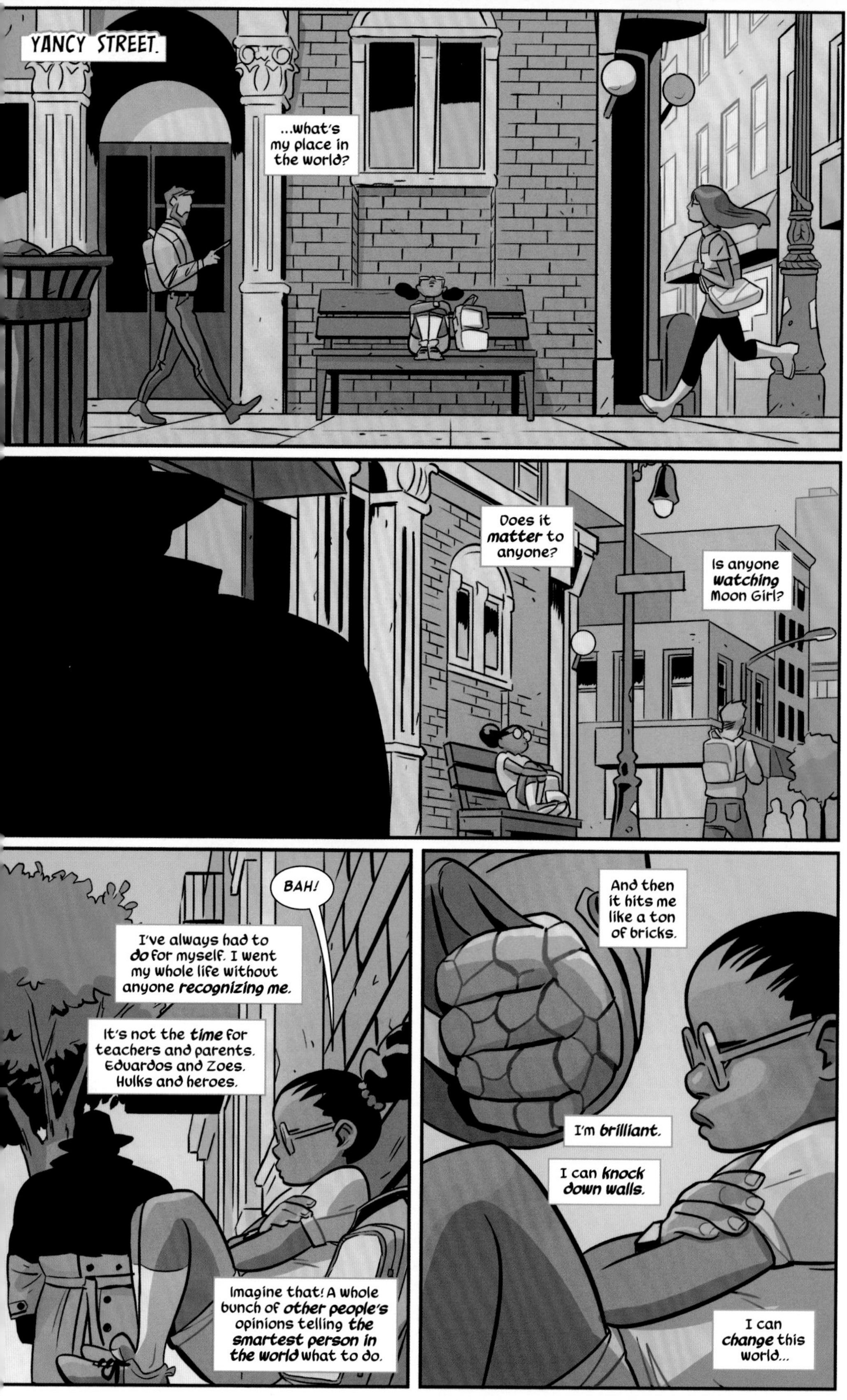
YANCY STREET.
...what's my place in the world?
Does it matter to anyone?
Is anyone watching Moon Girl?
BAH!
I've always had to do for myself. I went my whole life without anyone recognizing me.
It's not the time for teachers and parents. Eduardos and Zoes. Hulks and heroes.
Imagine that! A whole bunch of other people's opinions telling the smartest person in the world what to do.
And then it hits me like a ton of bricks.
I'm brilliant.
I can knock down walls.
I can change this world...

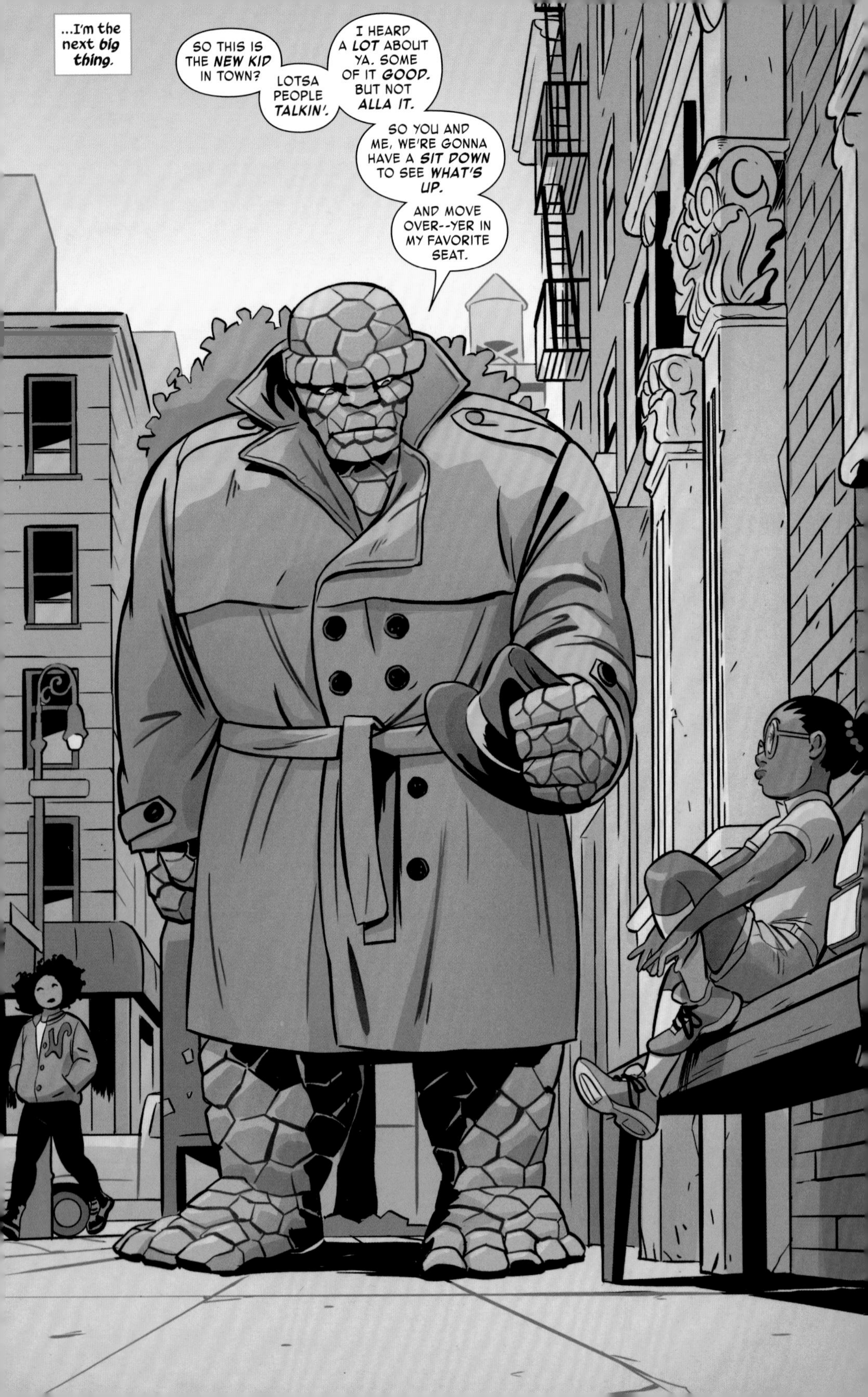
...I'm the next *big thing.*
SO THIS IS THE *NEW KID* IN TOWN?
LOTSA PEOPLE *TALKIN'.*
I HEARD A *LOT* ABOUT YA. SOME OF IT *GOOD.* BUT NOT *ALLA IT.*
SO YOU AND ME, WE'RE GONNA HAVE A *SIT DOWN* TO SEE *WHAT'S UP.*
AND MOVE OVER--YER IN MY FAVORITE SEAT.

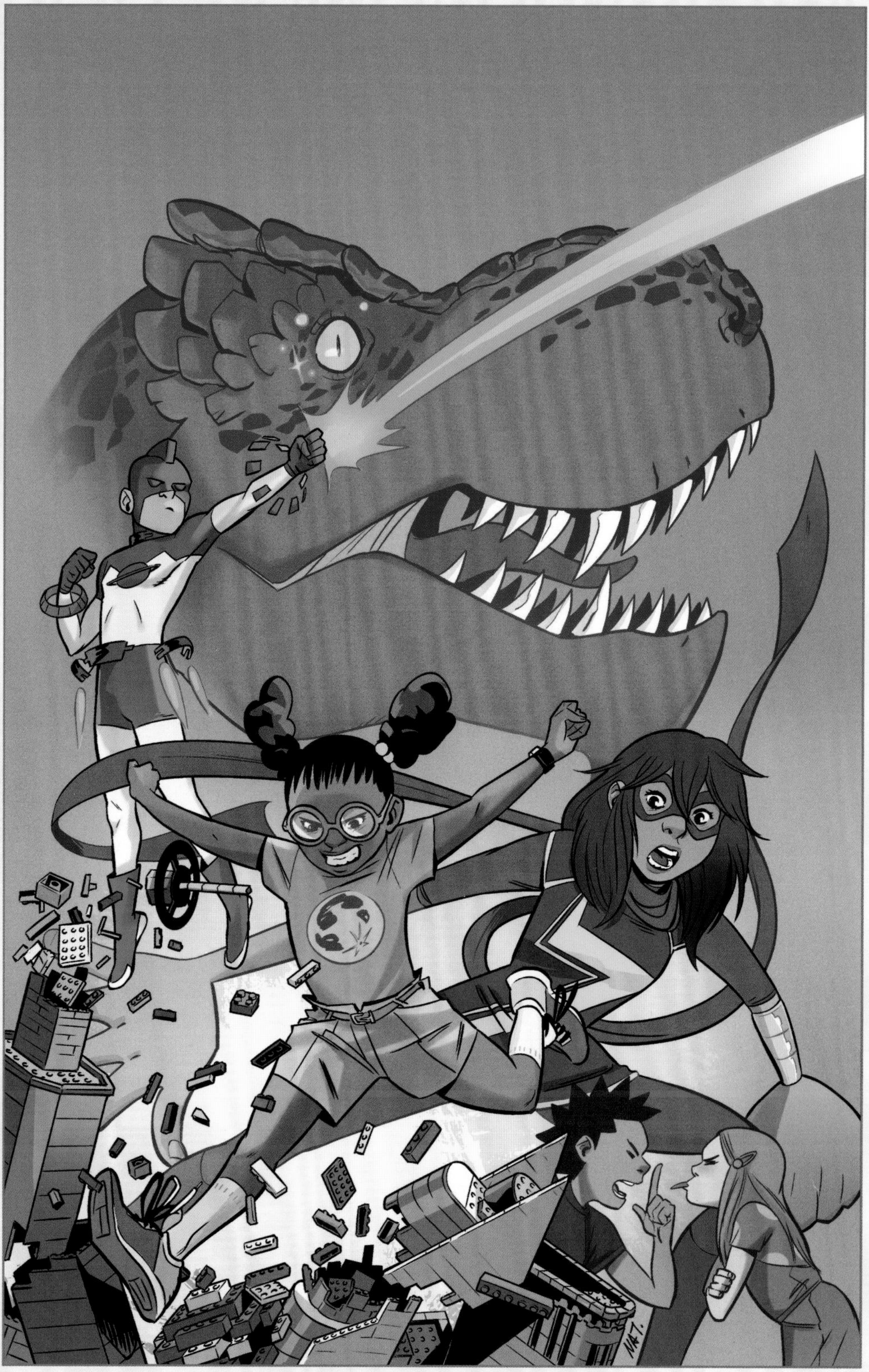

#13 STORY THUS FAR VARIANT
BY NATACHA BUSTOS

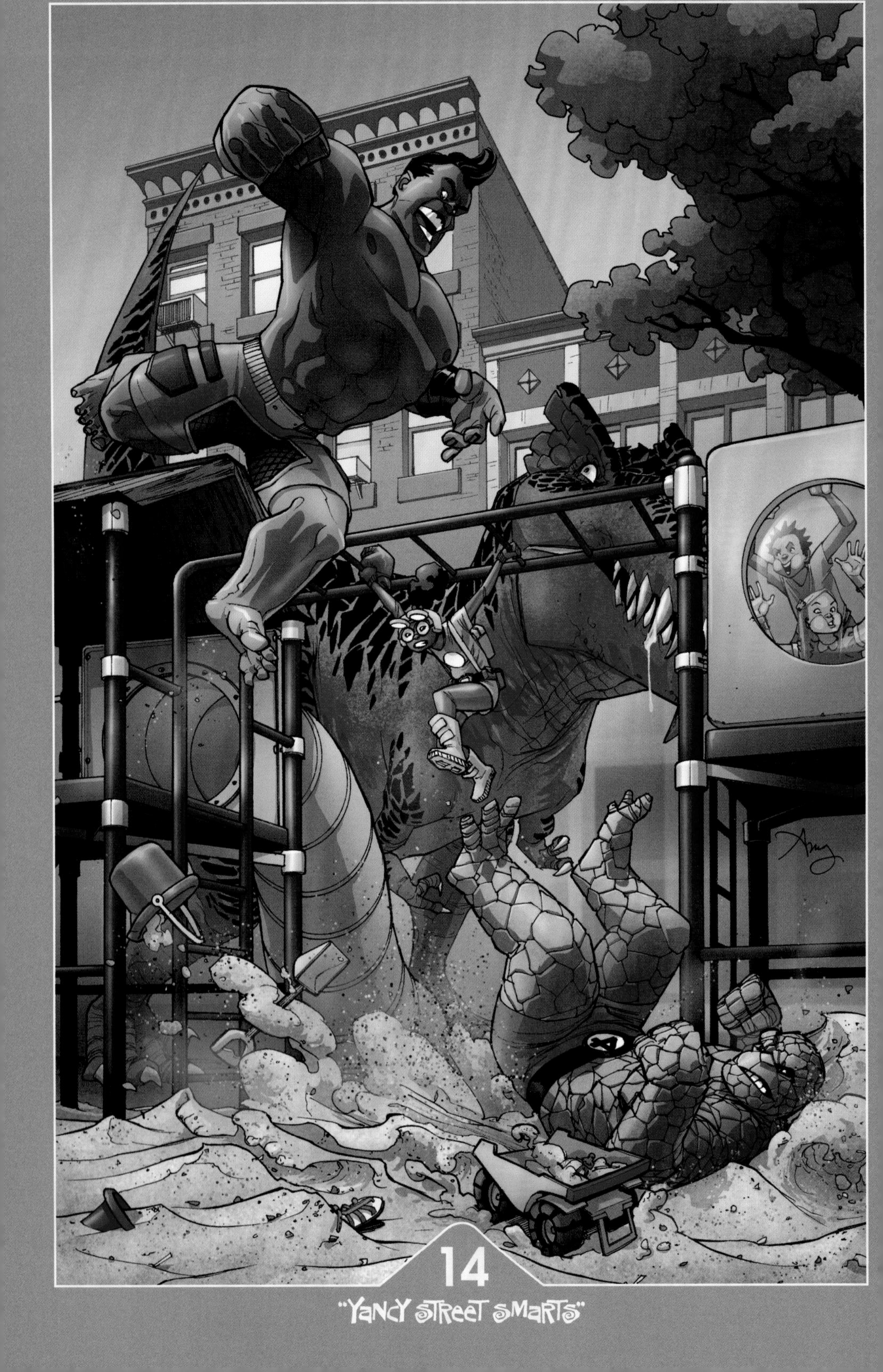

14

"YANCY STREET SMARTS"

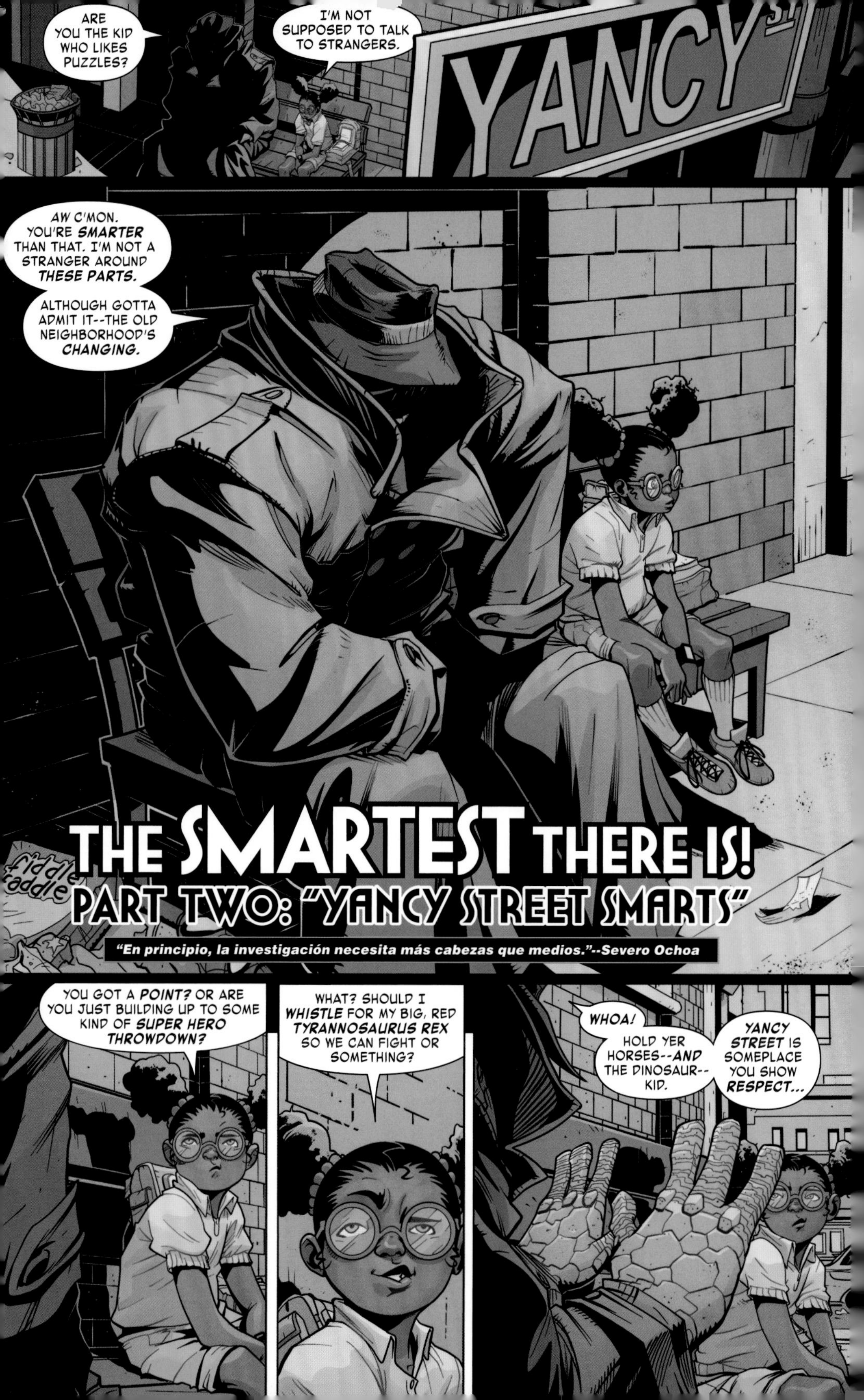
ARE YOU THE KID WHO LIKES PUZZLES?
I'M NOT SUPPOSED TO TALK TO STRANGERS.
YANCY ST
AW C'MON. YOU'RE SMARTER THAN THAT. I'M NOT A STRANGER AROUND THESE PARTS.
ALTHOUGH GOTTA ADMIT IT--THE OLD NEIGHBORHOOD'S CHANGING.
THE SMARTEST THERE IS!
PART TWO: "YANCY STREET SMARTS"
"En principio, la investigación necesita más cabezas que medios."--Severo Ochoa
fiddle faddle
YOU GOT A POINT? OR ARE YOU JUST BUILDING UP TO SOME KIND OF SUPER HERO THROWDOWN?
WHAT? SHOULD I WHISTLE FOR MY BIG, RED TYRANNOSAURUS REX SO WE CAN FIGHT OR SOMETHING?
WHOA!
HOLD YER HORSES--AND THE DINOSAUR--KID.
YANCY STREET IS SOMEPLACE YOU SHOW RESPECT...

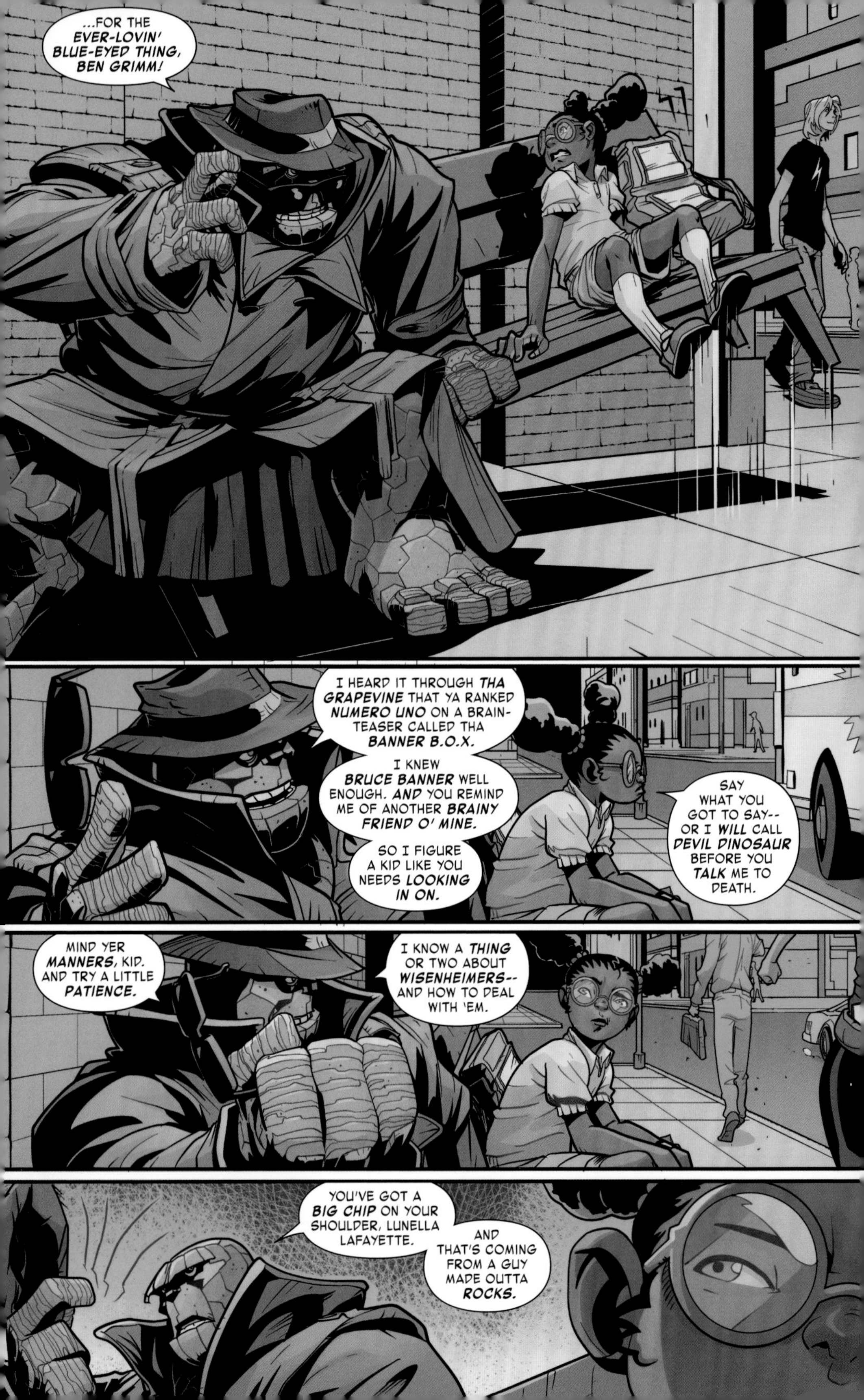
...FOR THE EVER-LOVIN' BLUE-EYED THING, BEN GRIMM!
I HEARD IT THROUGH THA GRAPEVINE THAT YA RANKED NUMERO UNO ON A BRAIN-TEASER CALLED THA BANNER B.O.X.
I KNEW BRUCE BANNER WELL ENOUGH. AND YOU REMIND ME OF ANOTHER BRAINY FRIEND O' MINE.
SO I FIGURE A KID LIKE YOU NEEDS LOOKING IN ON.
SAY WHAT YOU GOT TO SAY-- OR I WILL CALL DEVIL DINOSAUR BEFORE YOU TALK ME TO DEATH.
MIND YER MANNERS, KID. AND TRY A LITTLE PATIENCE.
I KNOW A THING OR TWO ABOUT WISENHEIMERS-- AND HOW TO DEAL WITH 'EM.
YOU'VE GOT A BIG CHIP ON YOUR SHOULDER, LUNELLA LAFAYETTE.
AND THAT'S COMING FROM A GUY MADE OUTTA ROCKS.

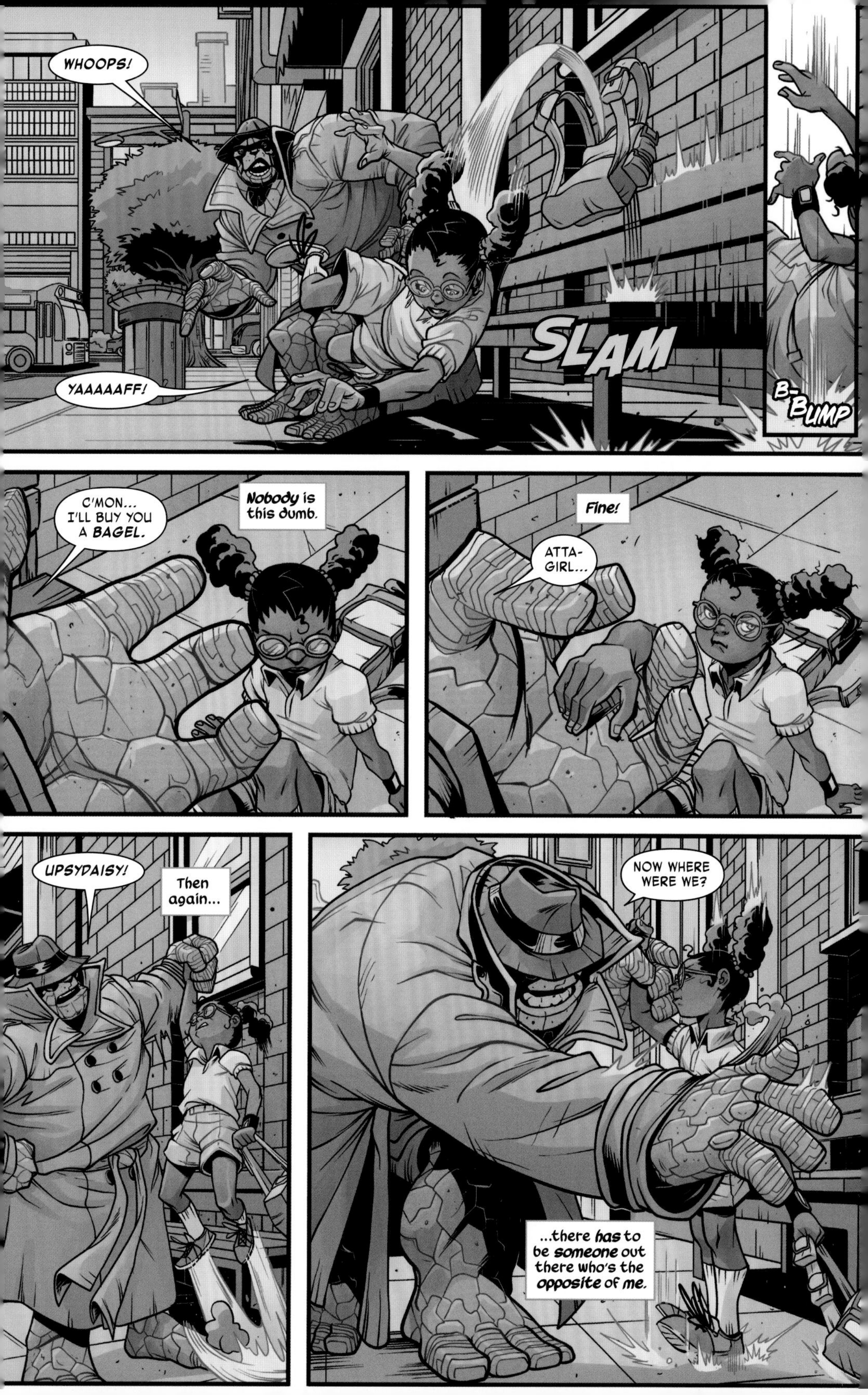
WHOOPS!
YAAAAAFF!
SLAM
B-BUMP
C'MON... I'LL BUY YOU A BAGEL.
Nobody is this dumb.
Fine!
ATTA-GIRL...
UPSYDAISY!
Then again...
NOW WHERE WERE WE?
...there has to be someone out there who's the opposite of me.

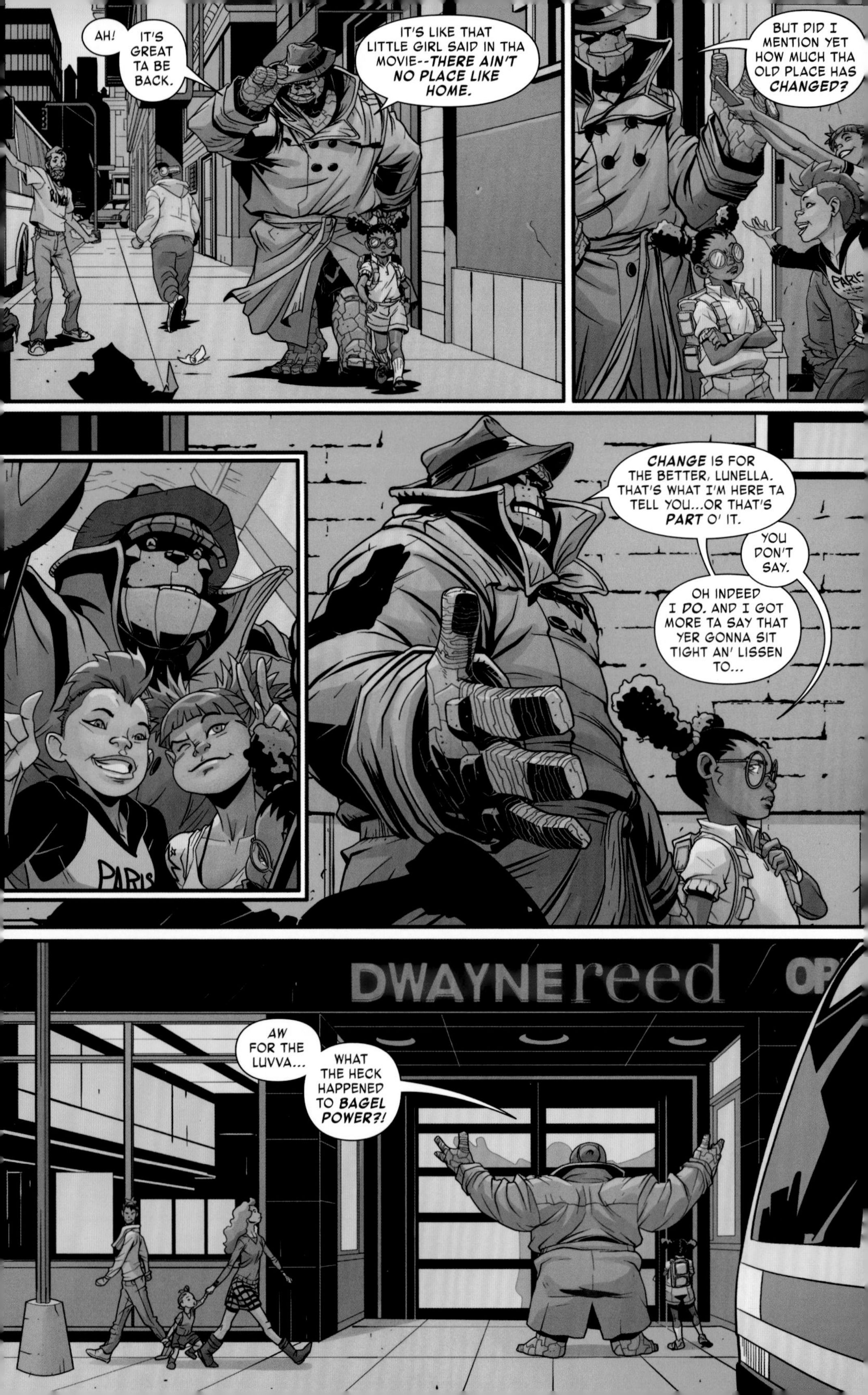
AH!
IT'S GREAT TA BE BACK.
IT'S LIKE THAT LITTLE GIRL SAID IN THA MOVIE--THERE AIN'T NO PLACE LIKE HOME.
BUT DID I MENTION YET HOW MUCH THA OLD PLACE HAS CHANGED?
CHANGE IS FOR THE BETTER, LUNELLA. THAT'S WHAT I'M HERE TA TELL YOU...OR THAT'S PART O' IT.
YOU DON'T SAY.
OH INDEED I DO. AND I GOT MORE TA SAY THAT YER GONNA SIT TIGHT AN' LISSEN TO...
DWAYNE reed
AW FOR THE LUVVA...
WHAT THE HECK HAPPENED TO BAGEL POWER?!

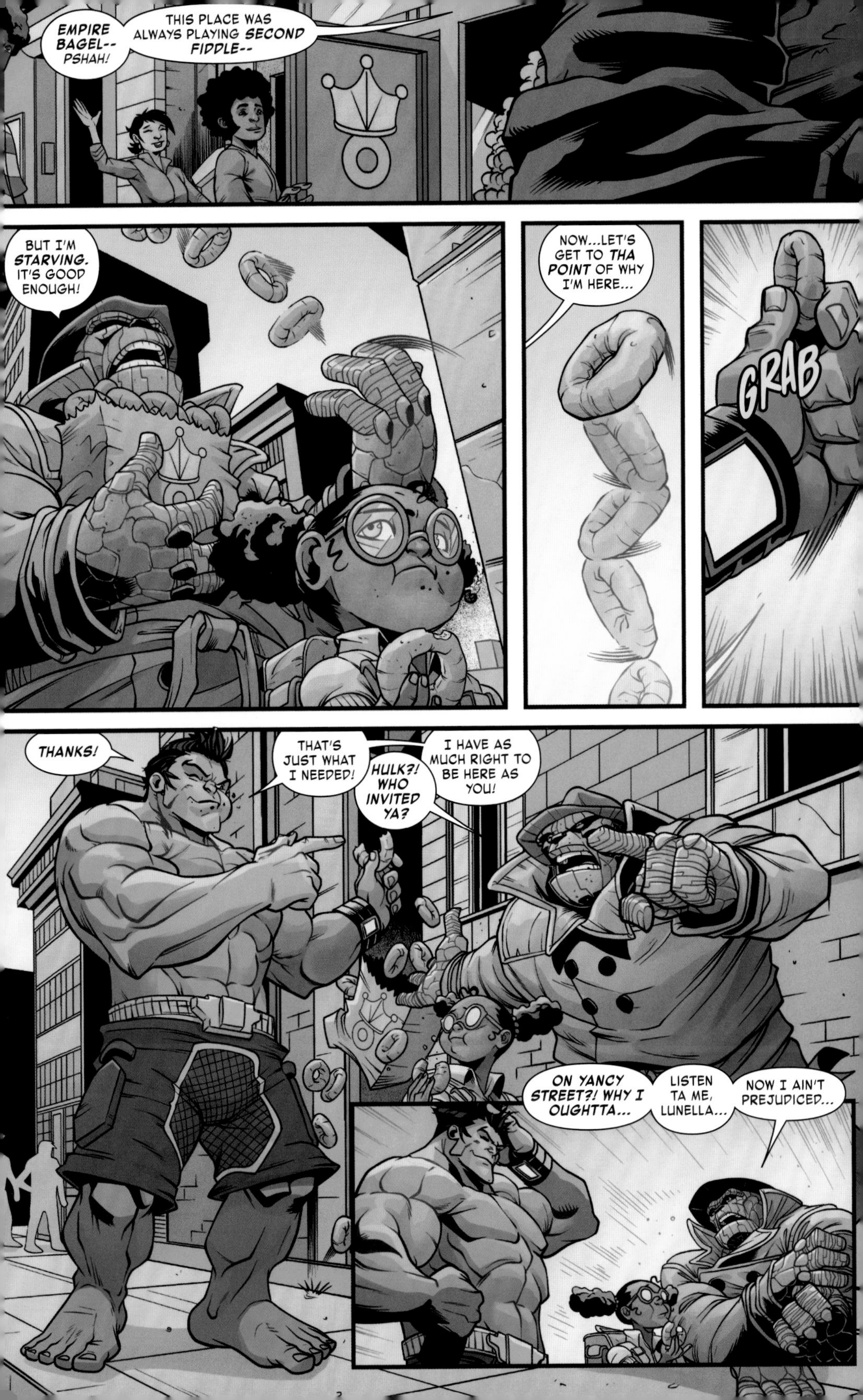
EMPIRE BAGEL-- PSHAH!
THIS PLACE WAS ALWAYS PLAYING SECOND FIDDLE--
BUT I'M STARVING. IT'S GOOD ENOUGH!
NOW...LET'S GET TO THA POINT OF WHY I'M HERE...
GRAB
THANKS!
THAT'S JUST WHAT I NEEDED!
HULK?! WHO INVITED YA?
I HAVE AS MUCH RIGHT TO BE HERE AS YOU!
ON YANCY STREET?! WHY I OUGHTTA...
LISTEN TA ME, LUNELLA...
NOW I AIN'T PREJUDICED...

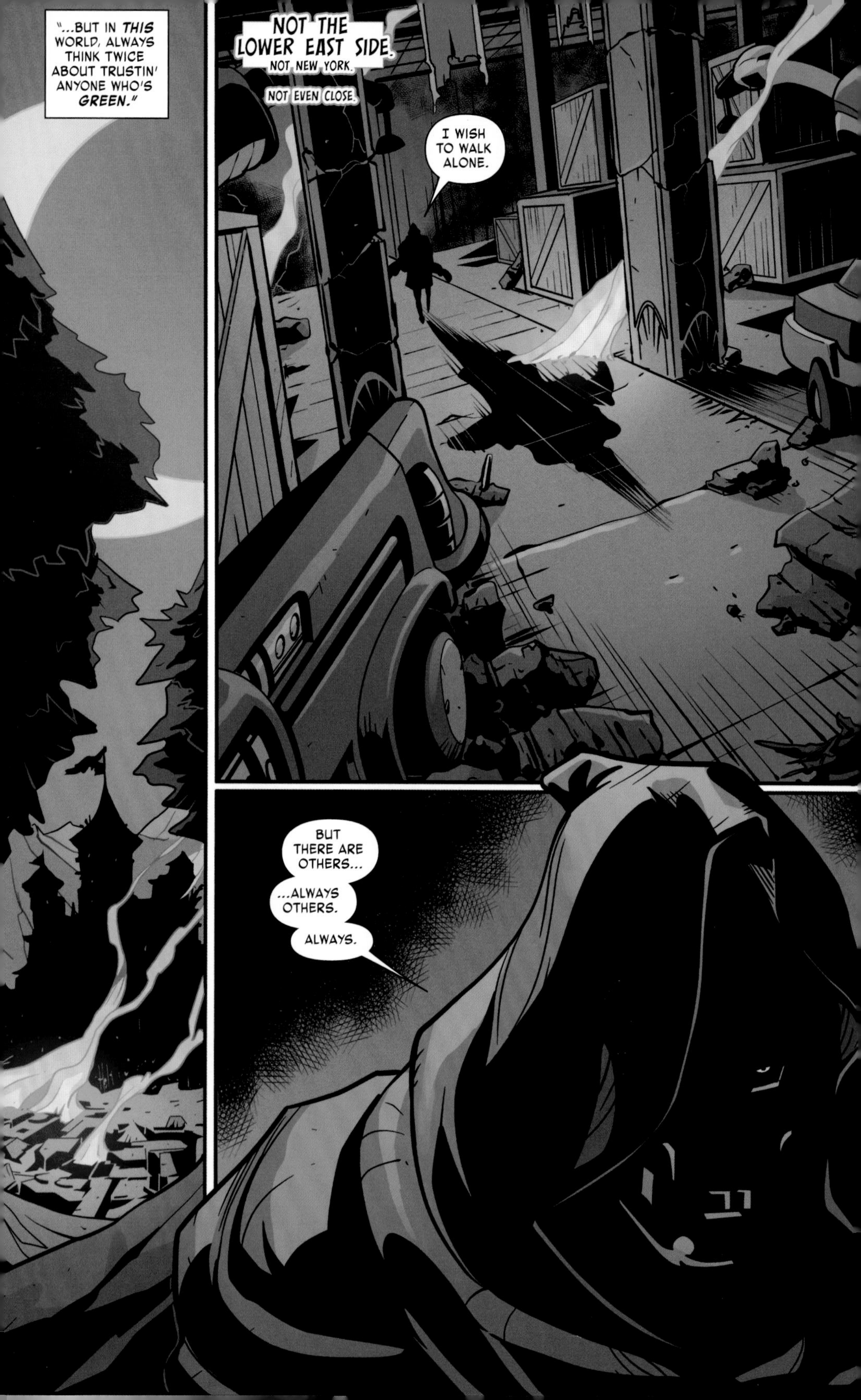
"...BUT IN THIS WORLD, ALWAYS THINK TWICE ABOUT TRUSTIN' ANYONE WHO'S GREEN."
NOT THE LOWER EAST SIDE.
NOT NEW YORK.
NOT EVEN CLOSE.
I WISH TO WALK ALONE.
BUT THERE ARE OTHERS...
...ALWAYS OTHERS.
ALWAYS.

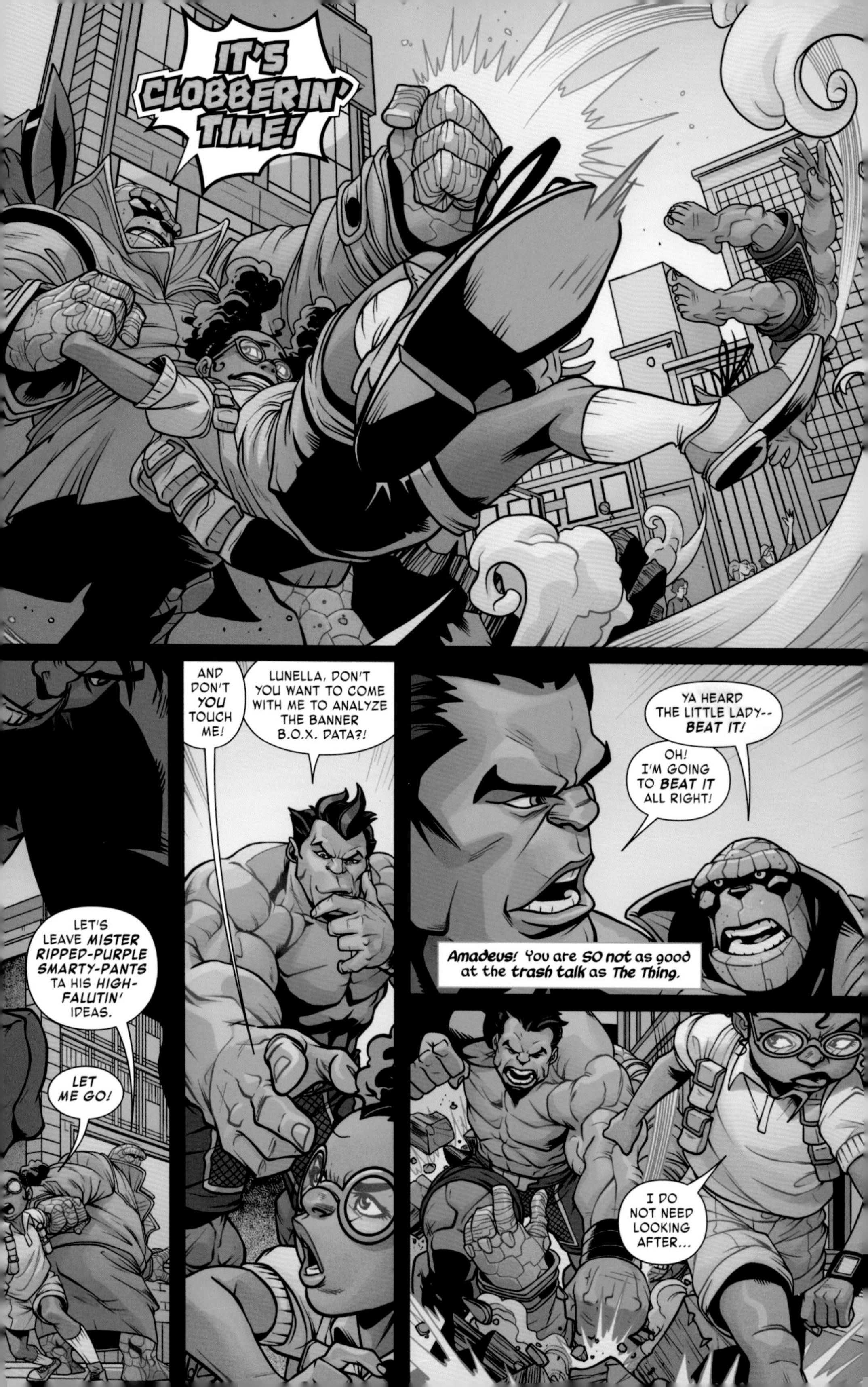
IT'S CLOBBERIN' TIME!
LET'S LEAVE MISTER RIPPED-PURPLE SMARTY-PANTS TA HIS HIGH-FALUTIN' IDEAS.
LET ME GO!
AND DON'T YOU TOUCH ME!
LUNELLA, DON'T YOU WANT TO COME WITH ME TO ANALYZE THE BANNER B.O.X. DATA?!
YA HEARD THE LITTLE LADY-- BEAT IT!
OH! I'M GOING TO BEAT IT ALL RIGHT!
Amadeus! You are SO not as good at the trash talk as The Thing.
I DO NOT NEED LOOKING AFTER...

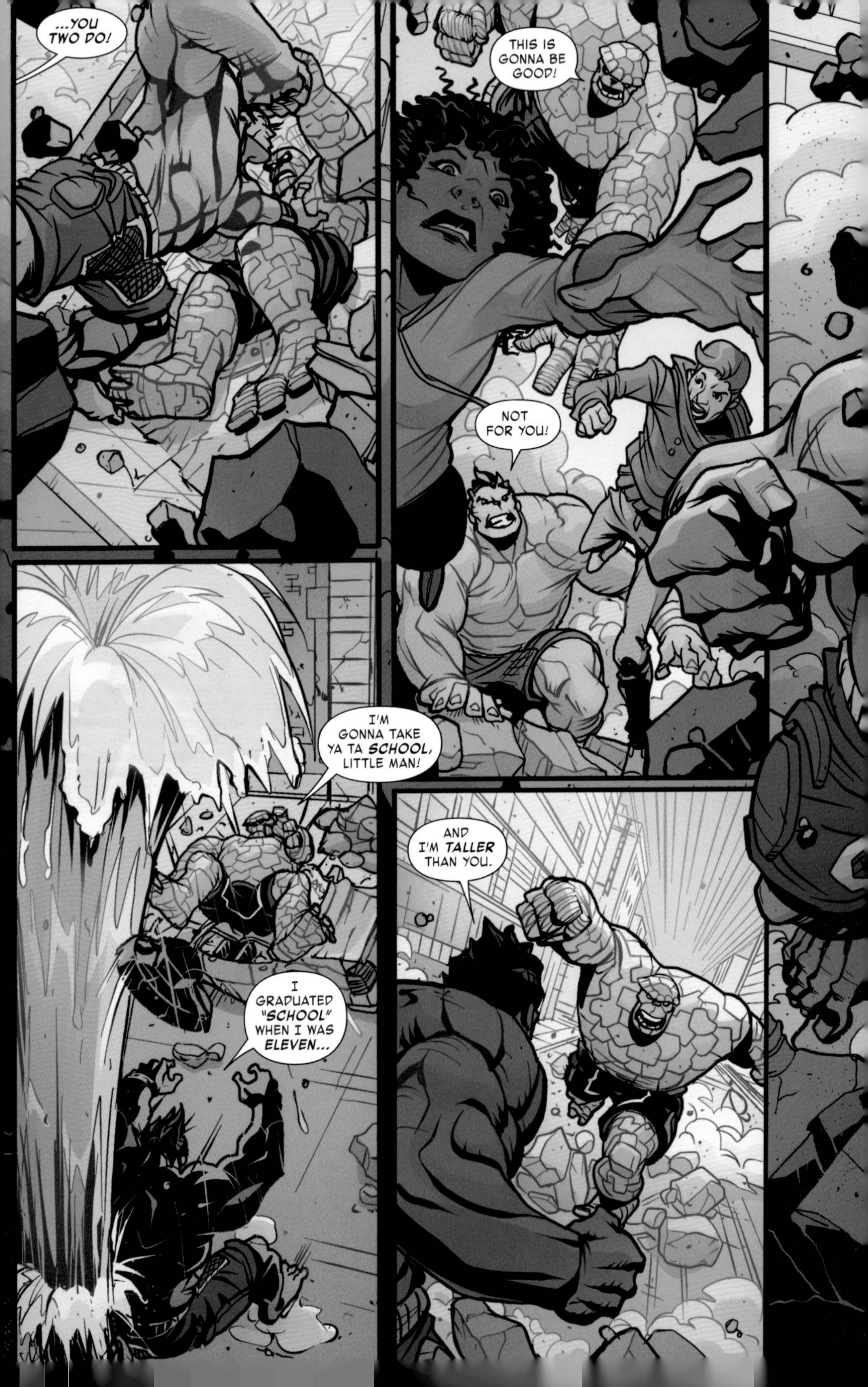
...YOU TWO DO!
THIS IS GONNA BE GOOD!
NOT FOR YOU!
I'M GONNA TAKE YA TA SCHOOL, LITTLE MAN!
I GRADUATED "SCHOOL" WHEN I WAS ELEVEN...
AND I'M TALLER THAN YOU.

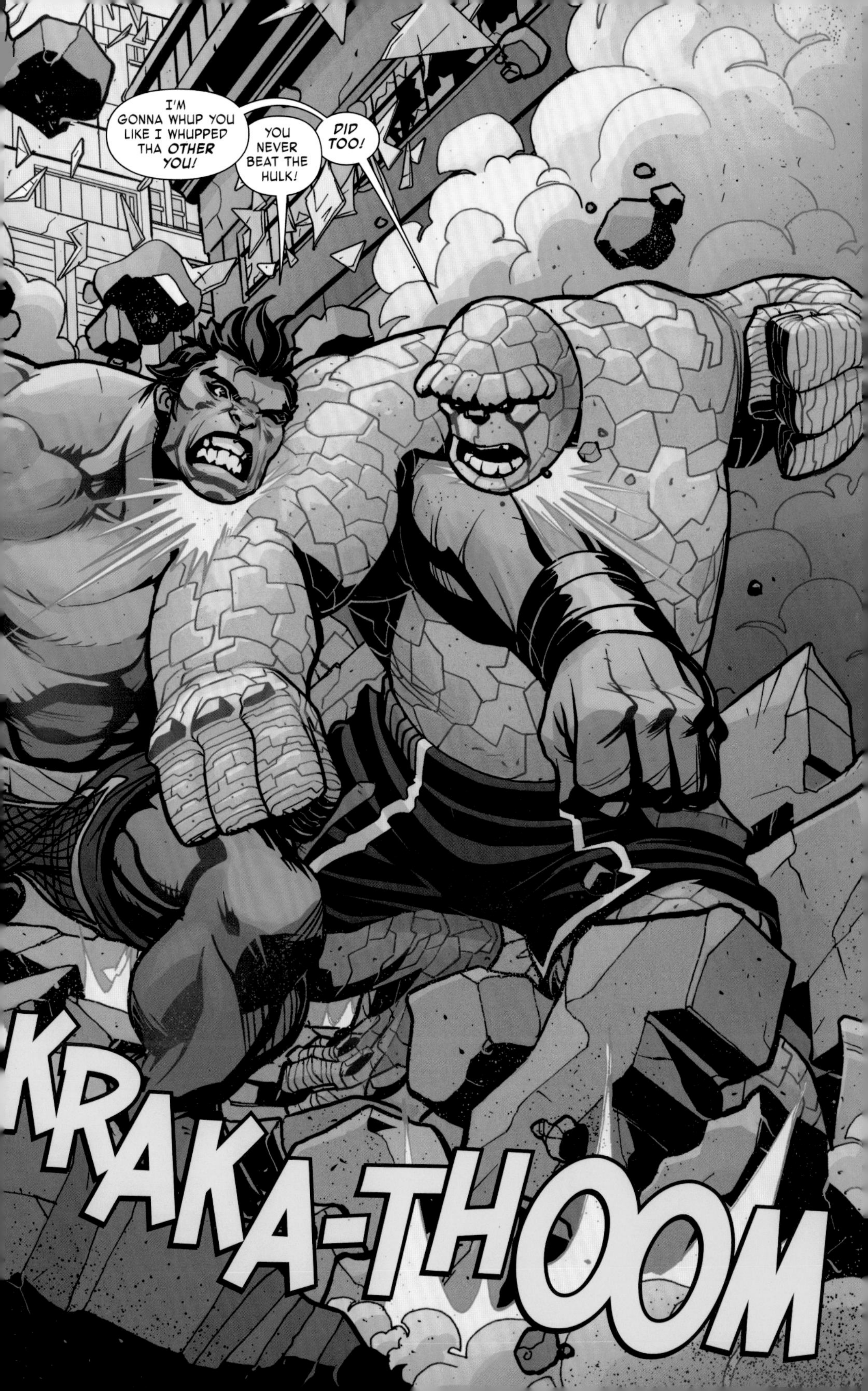
I'M GONNA WHUP YOU LIKE I WHUPPED THA *OTHER YOU!*
YOU NEVER BEAT THE HULK!
DID TOO!
KRAKA-THOOM

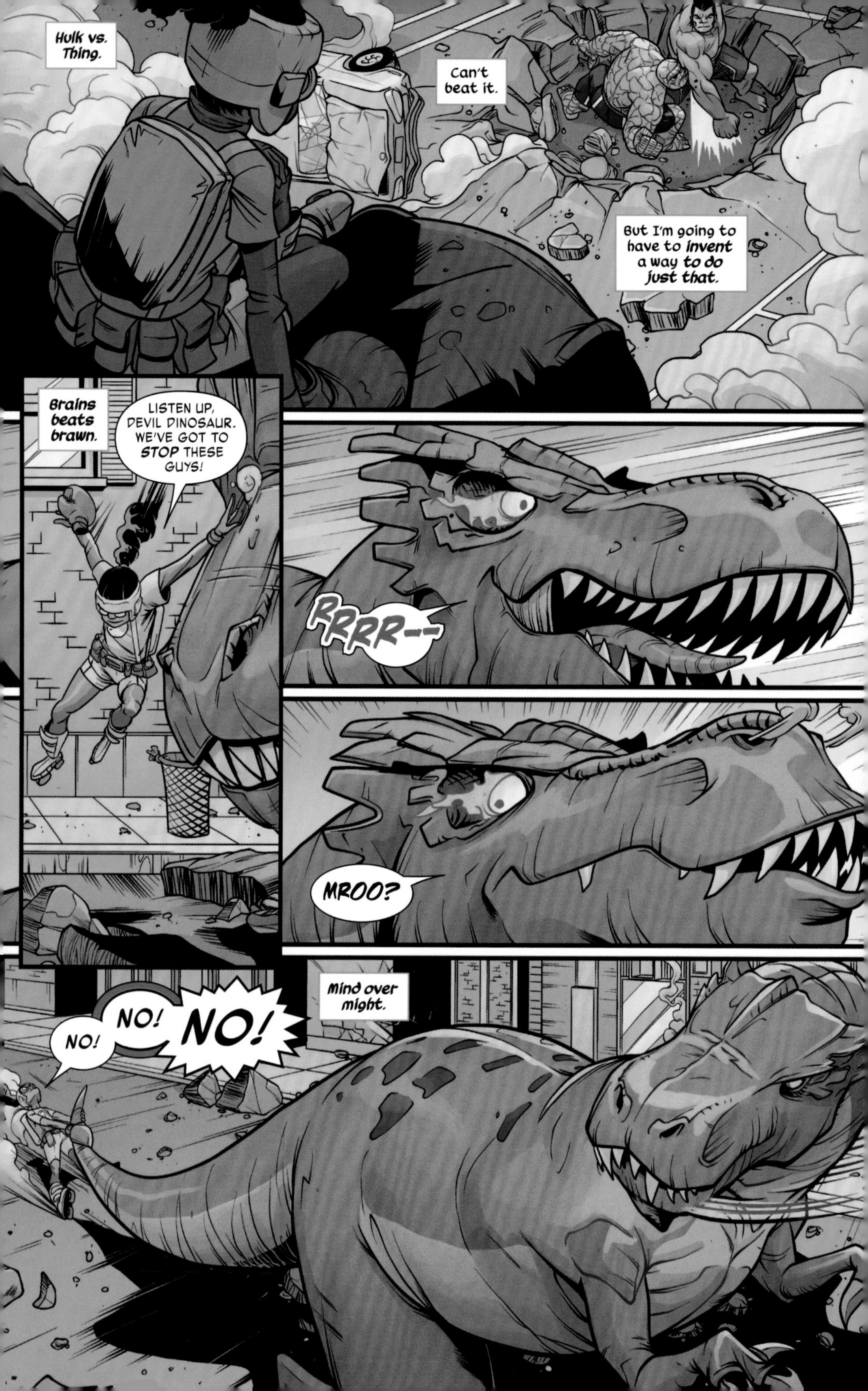
Hulk vs. Thing.
Can't beat it.
But I'm going to have to invent a way to do just that.
Brains beats brawn.
LISTEN UP, DEVIL DINOSAUR. WE'VE GOT TO STOP THESE GUYS!
RRRR--
MROO?
Mind over might.
NO!
NO!
NO!

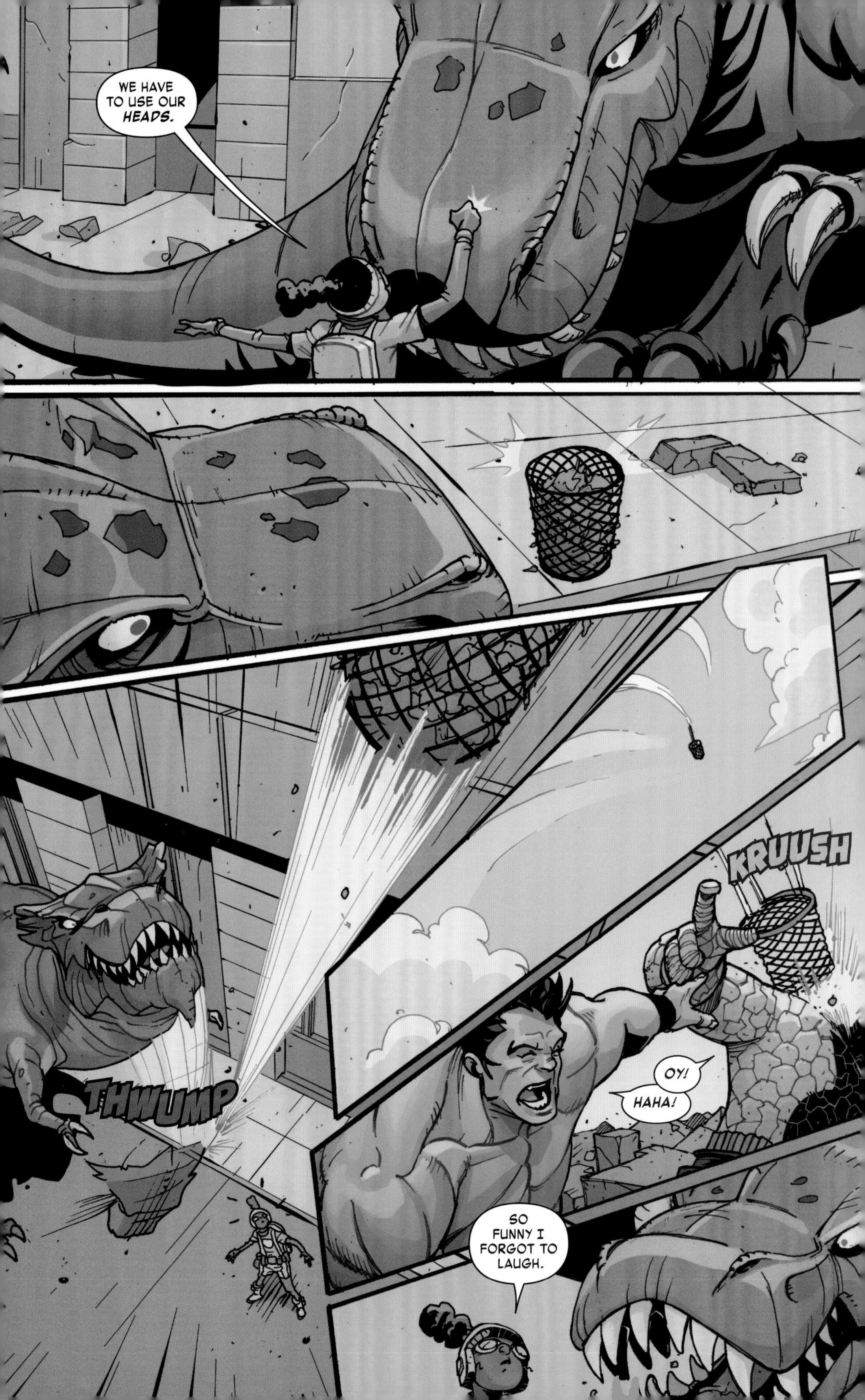
WE HAVE TO USE OUR HEADS.
THWUMP
KRUUSH
OY!
HAHA!
SO FUNNY I FORGOT TO LAUGH.

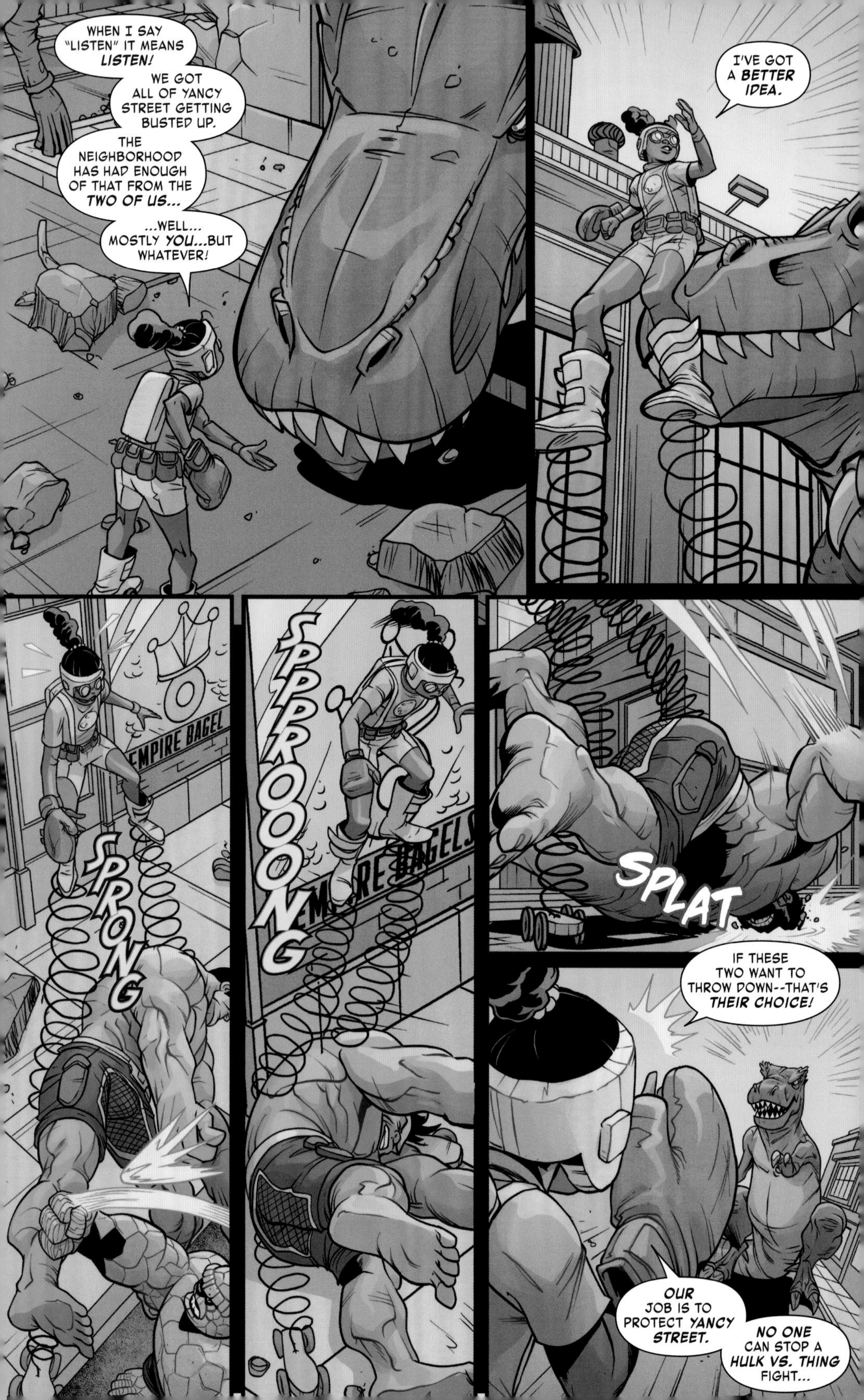

WHEN I SAY "LISTEN" IT MEANS LISTEN!
WE GOT ALL OF YANCY STREET GETTING BUSTED UP.
THE NEIGHBORHOOD HAS HAD ENOUGH OF THAT FROM THE TWO OF US...
...WELL... MOSTLY YOU...BUT WHATEVER!
I'VE GOT A BETTER IDEA.
EMPIRE BAGEL
SPRONG
SPPROOOONG
EMPIRE BAGELS
SPLAT
IF THESE TWO WANT TO THROW DOWN--THAT'S THEIR CHOICE!
OUR JOB IS TO PROTECT YANCY STREET.
NO ONE CAN STOP A HULK VS. THING FIGHT...

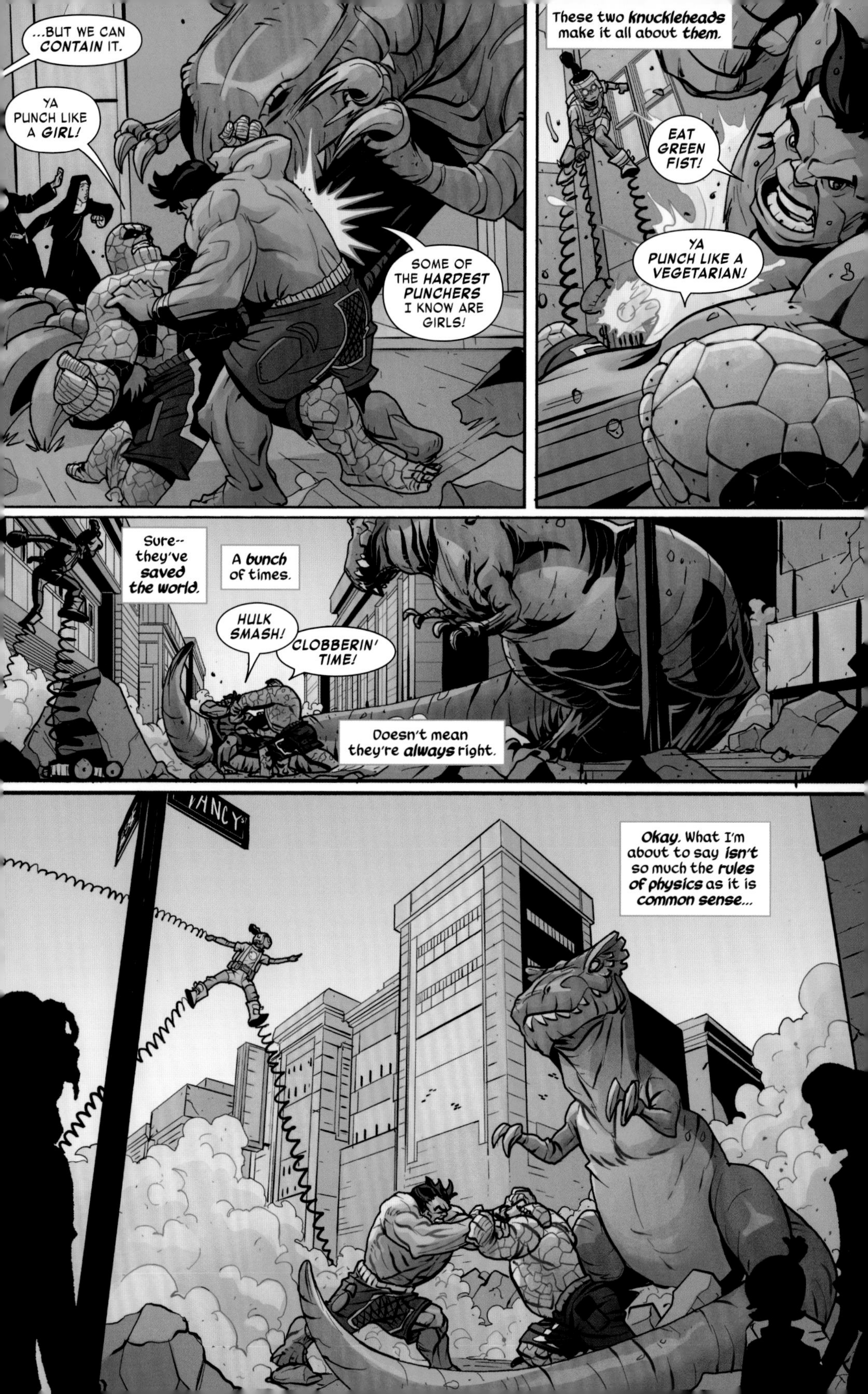
...BUT WE CAN CONTAIN IT.
YA PUNCH LIKE A GIRL!
SOME OF THE HARDEST PUNCHERS I KNOW ARE GIRLS!
These two knuckleheads make it all about them.
EAT GREEN FIST!
YA PUNCH LIKE A VEGETARIAN!
Sure-- they've saved the world.
A bunch of times.
HULK SMASH!
CLOBBERIN' TIME!
Doesn't mean they're always right.
Okay. What I'm about to say isn't so much the rules of physics as it is common sense...

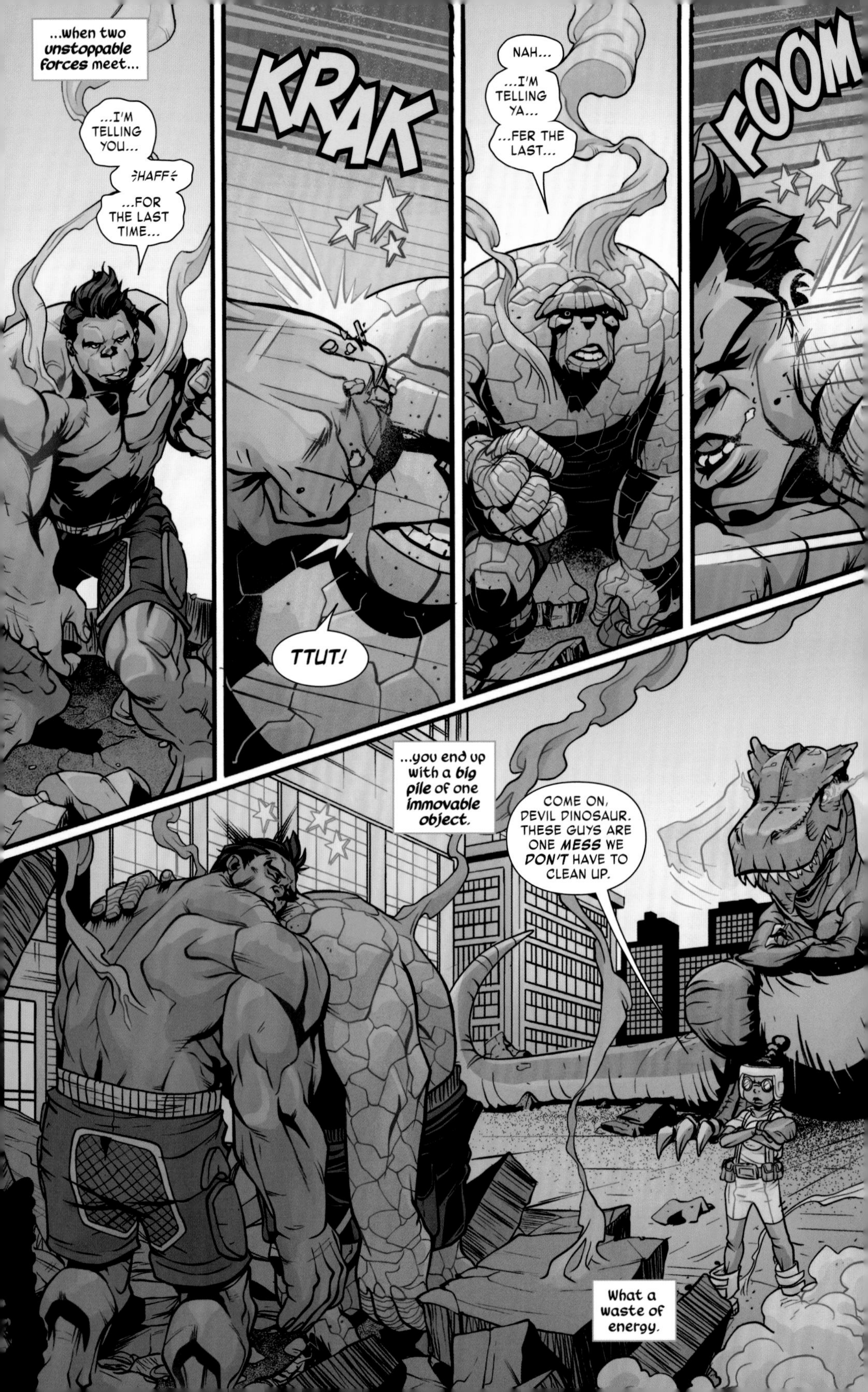

...when two unstoppable forces meet...
...I'M TELLING YOU...
HAFF
...FOR THE LAST TIME...
KRAK
TTUT!
NAH...
...I'M TELLING YA...
...FER THE LAST...
FOOM
...you end up with a big pile of one immovable object.
COME ON, DEVIL DINOSAUR. THESE GUYS ARE ONE MESS WE DON'T HAVE TO CLEAN UP.
What a waste of energy.

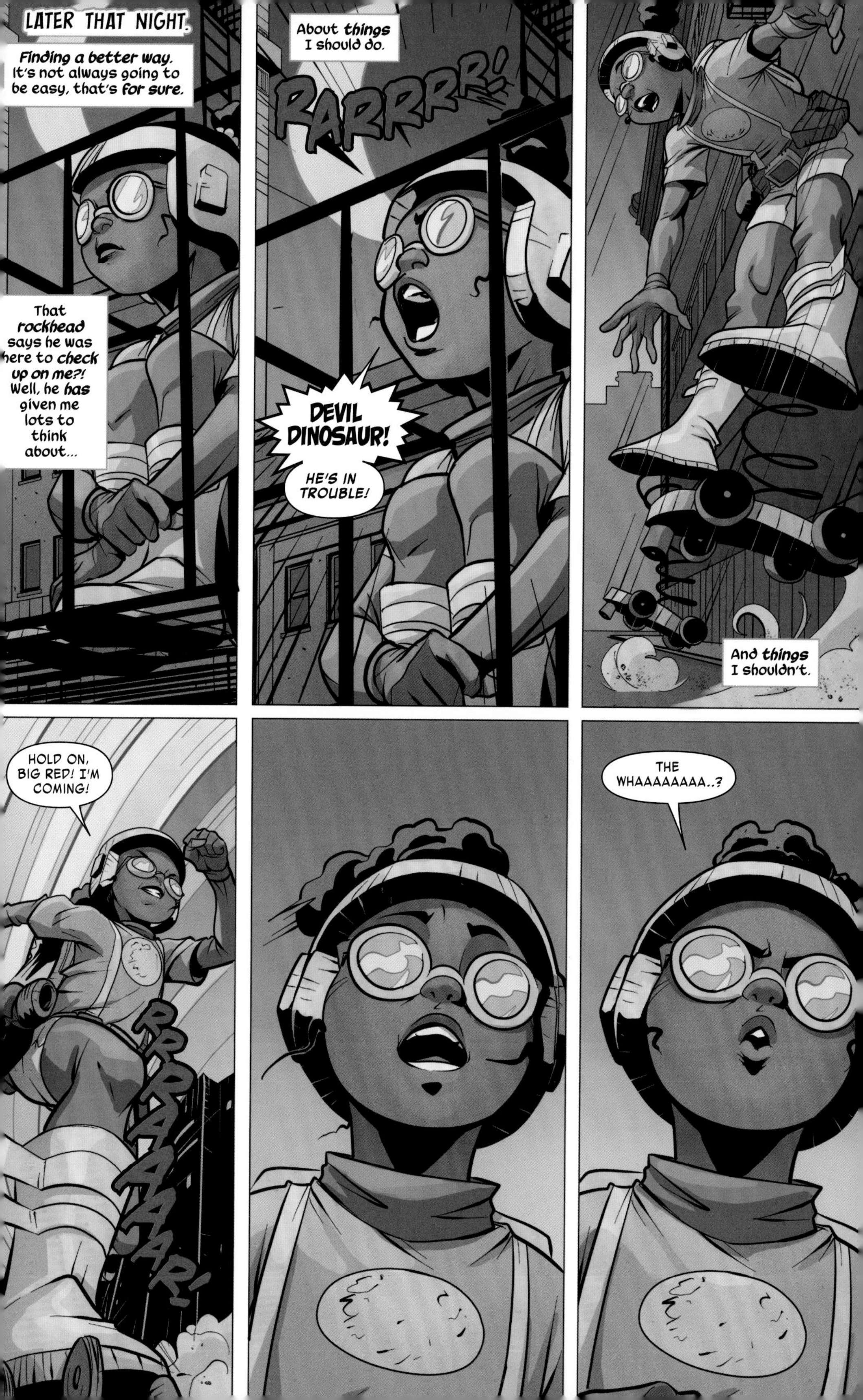

LATER THAT NIGHT.
Finding a better way. It's not always going to be easy, that's for sure.
That rockhead says he was here to check up on me?! Well, he has given me lots to think about...
About things I should do.
RARRRR!
DEVIL DINOSAUR!
HE'S IN TROUBLE!
And things I shouldn't.
HOLD ON, BIG RED! I'M COMING!
RRRAAAAAR!
THE WHAAAAAAAA..?

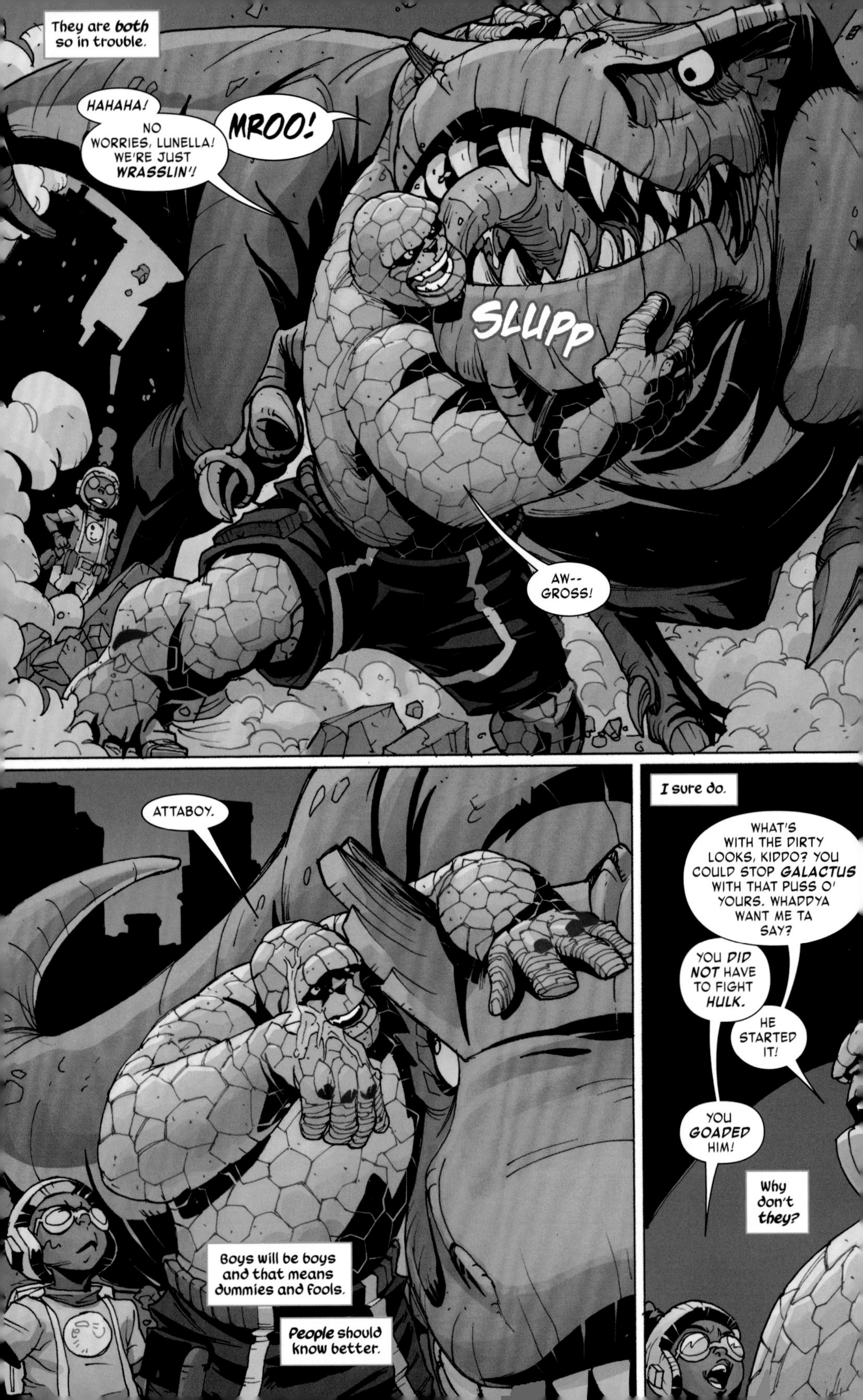
They are *both* so in trouble.
HAHAHA!
NO WORRIES, LUNELLA! WE'RE JUST *WRASSLIN'!*
MROO!
SLUPP
AW-- GROSS!
ATTABOY.
Boys will be boys and that means dummies and fools.
People should know better.
I sure do.
WHAT'S WITH THE DIRTY LOOKS, KIDDO? YOU COULD STOP *GALACTUS* WITH THAT PUSS O' YOURS. WHADDYA WANT ME TA SAY?
YOU *DID NOT* HAVE TO FIGHT *HULK.*
HE STARTED IT!
YOU *GOADED* HIM!
Why don't *they?*

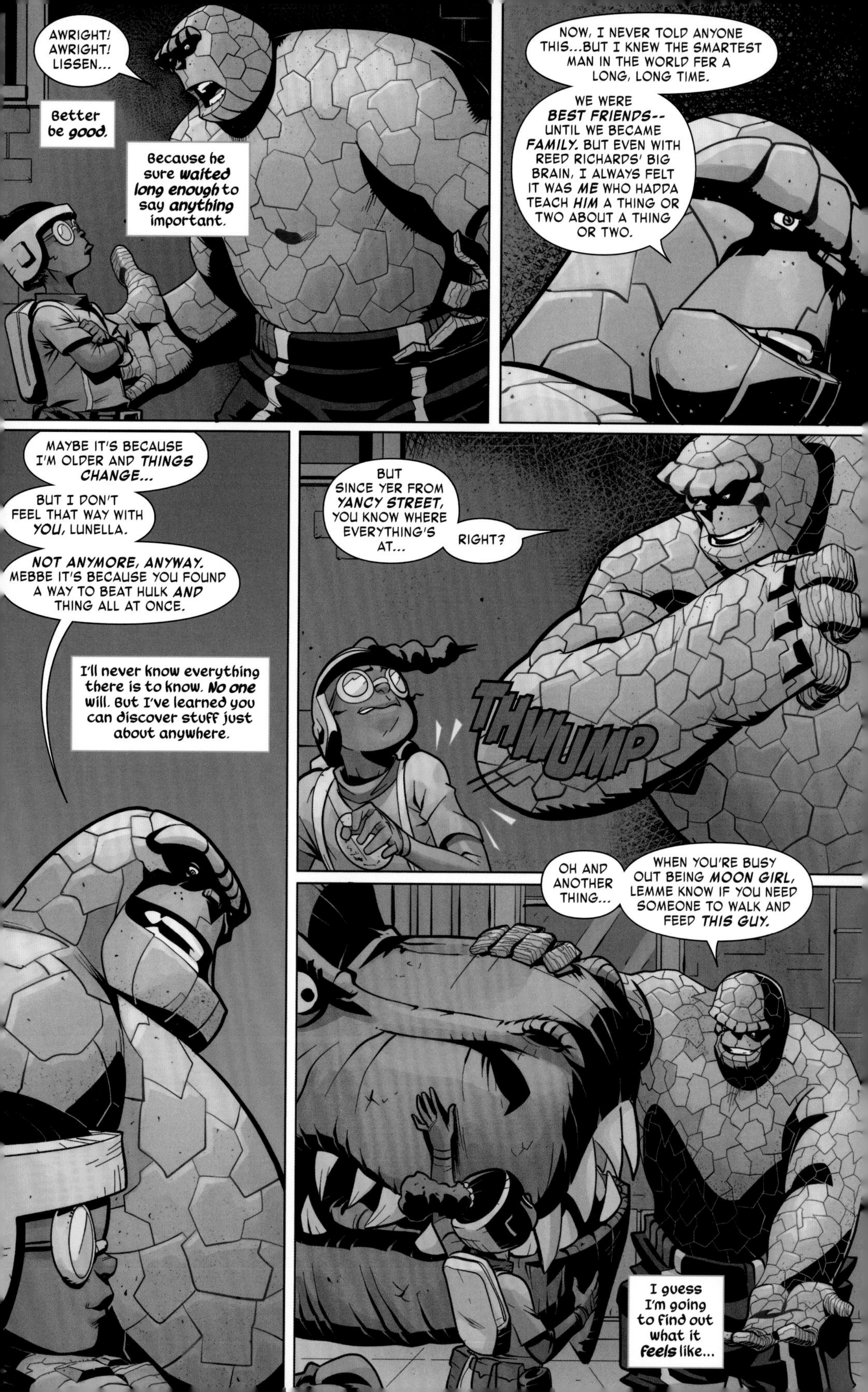
AWRIGHT! AWRIGHT! LISSEN...
Better be good.
Because he sure waited long enough to say anything important.
NOW, I NEVER TOLD ANYONE THIS...BUT I KNEW THE SMARTEST MAN IN THE WORLD FER A LONG, LONG TIME.
WE WERE BEST FRIENDS-- UNTIL WE BECAME FAMILY. BUT EVEN WITH REED RICHARDS' BIG BRAIN, I ALWAYS FELT IT WAS ME WHO HADDA TEACH HIM A THING OR TWO ABOUT A THING OR TWO.
MAYBE IT'S BECAUSE I'M OLDER AND THINGS CHANGE...
BUT I DON'T FEEL THAT WAY WITH YOU, LUNELLA.
NOT ANYMORE, ANYWAY. MEBBE IT'S BECAUSE YOU FOUND A WAY TO BEAT HULK AND THING ALL AT ONCE.
I'll never know everything there is to know. No one will. But I've learned you can discover stuff just about anywhere.
BUT SINCE YER FROM YANCY STREET, YOU KNOW WHERE EVERYTHING'S AT...
RIGHT?
THWUMP
OH AND ANOTHER THING...
WHEN YOU'RE BUSY OUT BEING MOON GIRL, LEMME KNOW IF YOU NEED SOMEONE TO WALK AND FEED THIS GUY.
I guess I'm going to find out what it feels like...

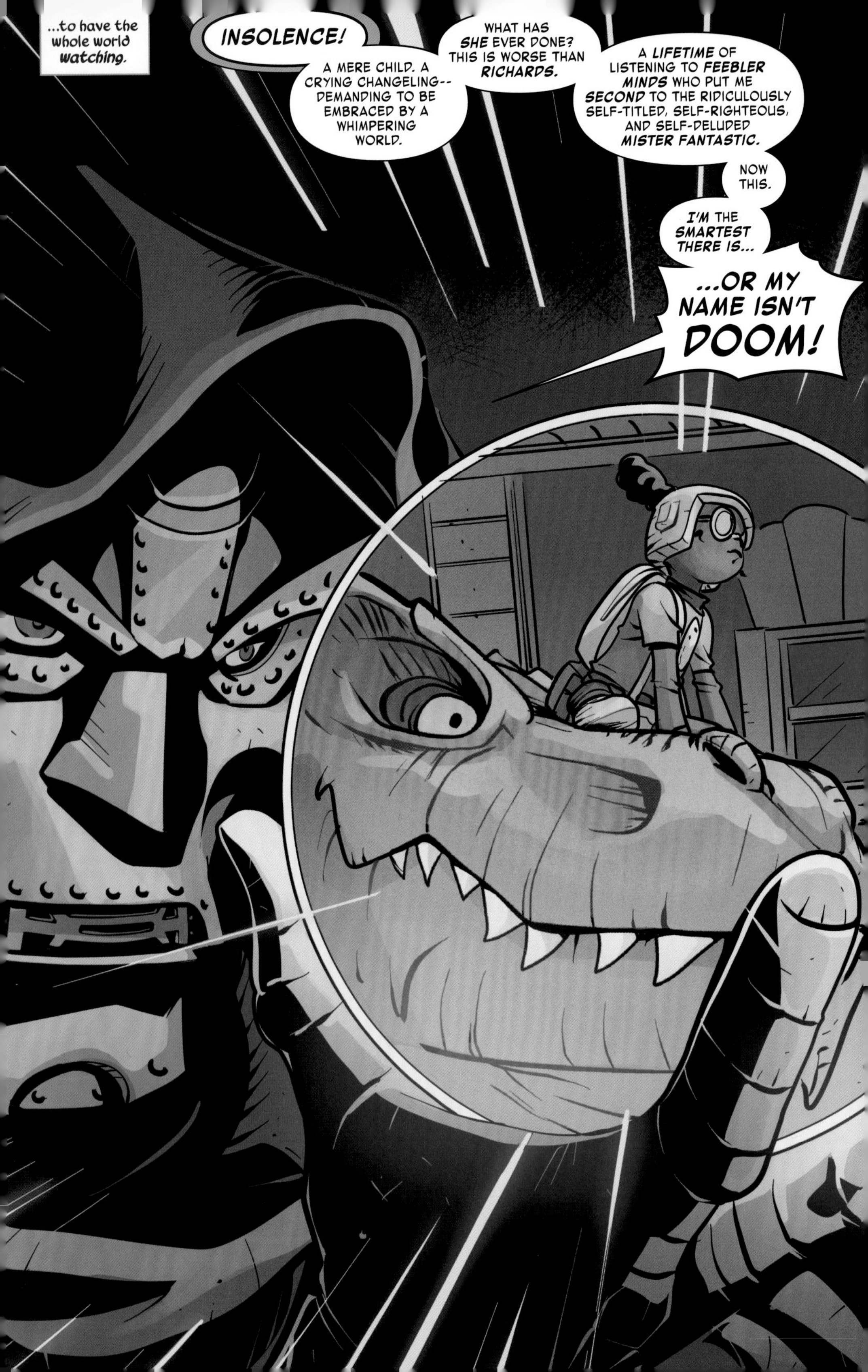
...to have the whole world *watching.*
INSOLENCE!
A MERE CHILD. A CRYING CHANGELING--DEMANDING TO BE EMBRACED BY A WHIMPERING WORLD.
WHAT HAS *SHE* EVER DONE? THIS IS WORSE THAN *RICHARDS.*
A *LIFETIME* OF LISTENING TO *FEEBLER MINDS* WHO PUT ME *SECOND* TO THE RIDICULOUSLY SELF-TITLED, SELF-RIGHTEOUS, AND SELF-DELUDED *MISTER FANTASTIC.*
NOW THIS.
I'M THE *SMARTEST* THERE IS...
...OR MY NAME ISN'T DOOM!

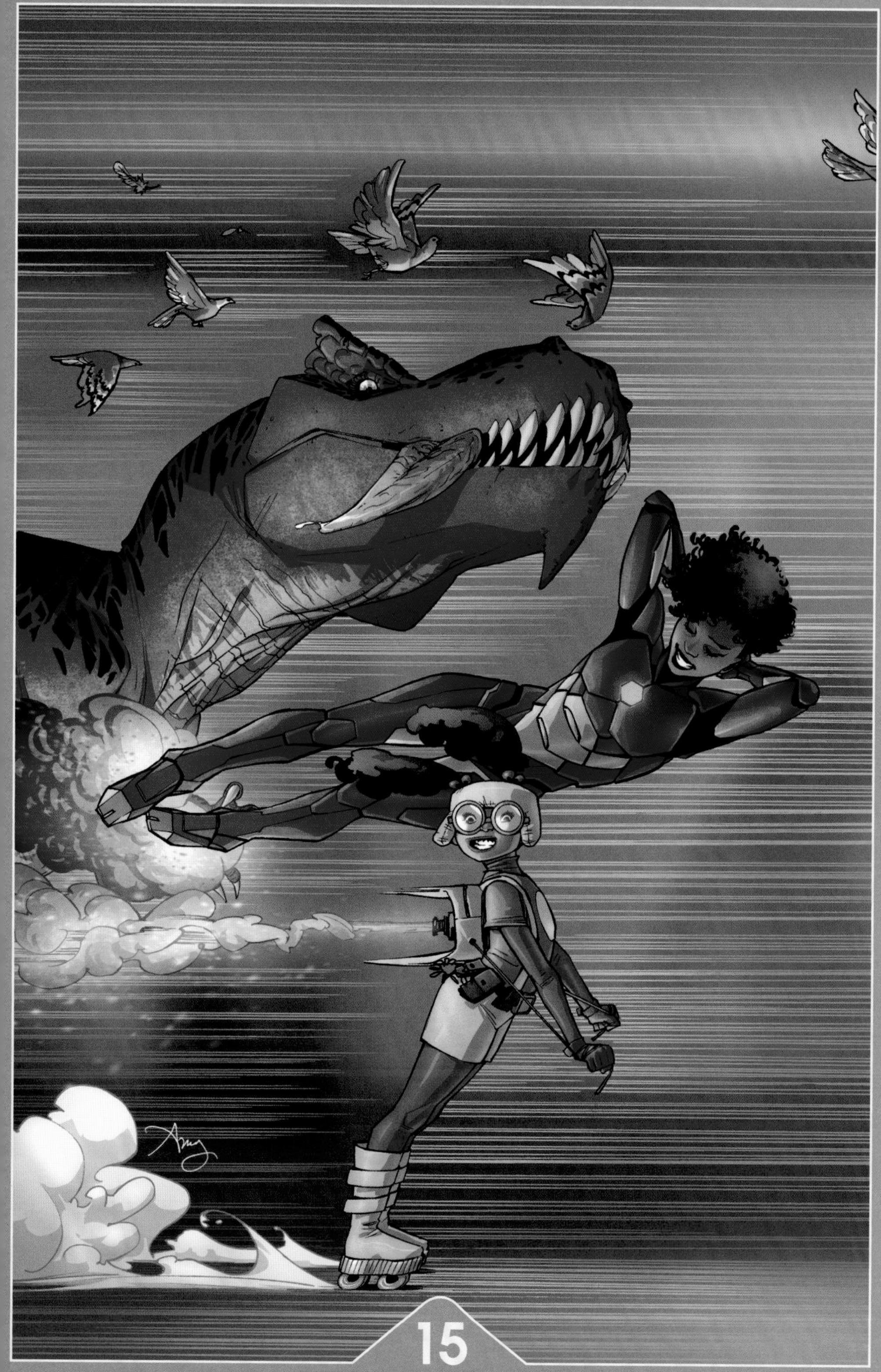

15

"CODE"

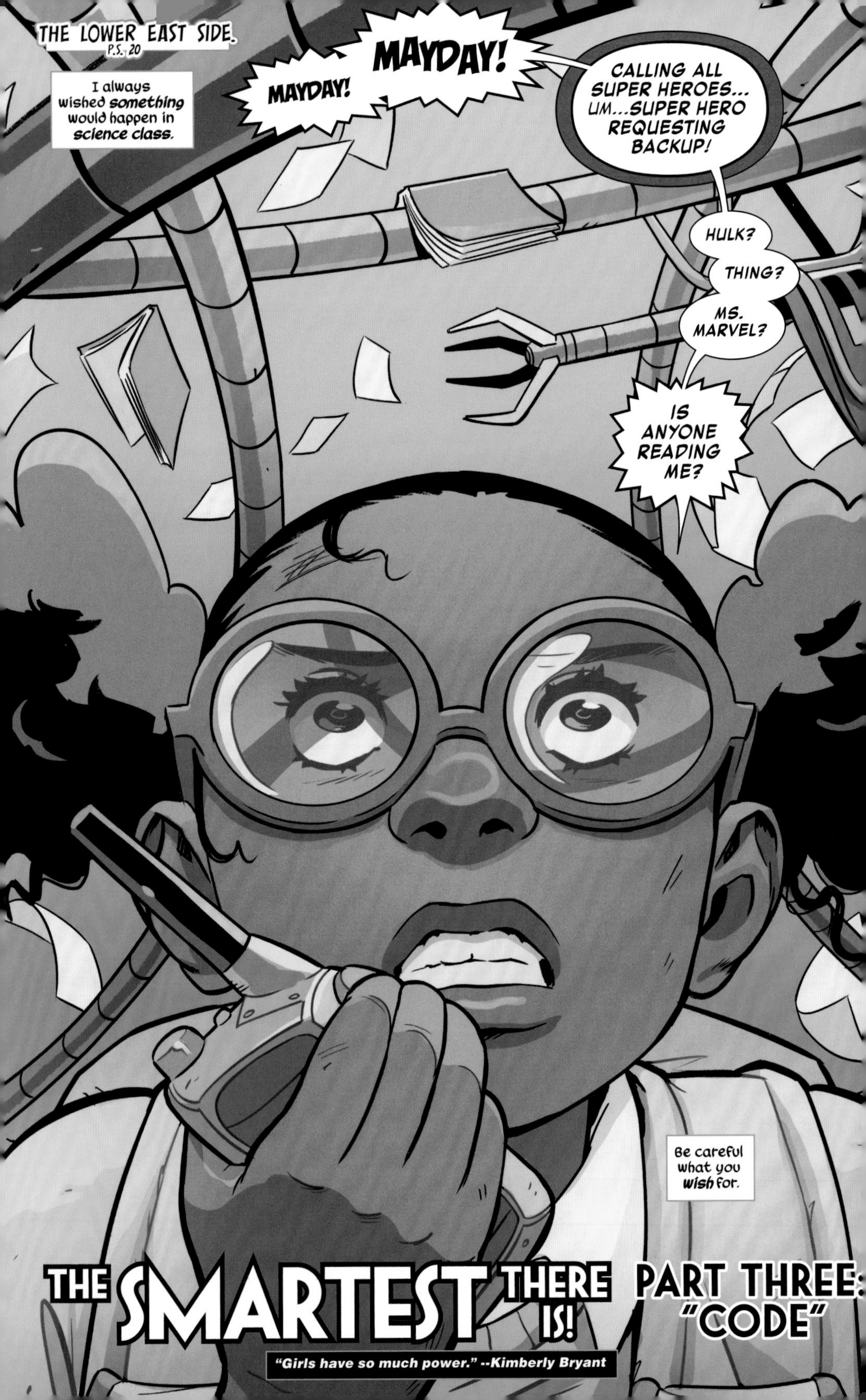
THE LOWER EAST SIDE.
P.S. 20
I always wished something would happen in science class.
MAYDAY!
MAYDAY!
CALLING ALL SUPER HEROES... UM...SUPER HERO REQUESTING BACKUP!
HULK?
THING?
MS. MARVEL?
IS ANYONE READING ME?
Be careful what you wish for.
THE SMARTEST THERE IS!
PART THREE: "CODE"
"Girls have so much power." --Kimberly Bryant

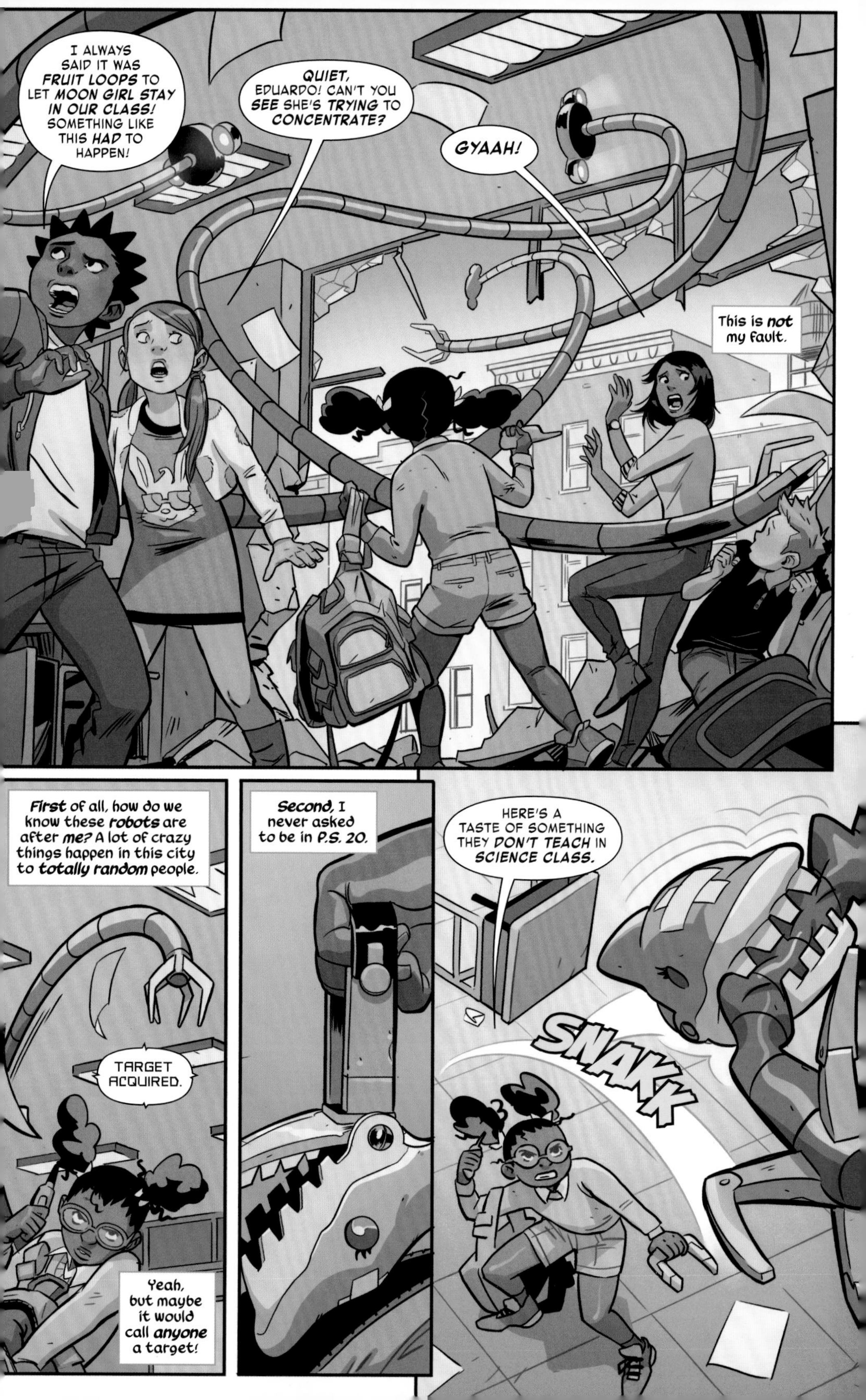
I ALWAYS SAID IT WAS FRUIT LOOPS TO LET MOON GIRL STAY IN OUR CLASS! SOMETHING LIKE THIS HAD TO HAPPEN!
QUIET, EDUARDO! CAN'T YOU SEE SHE'S TRYING TO CONCENTRATE?
GYAAH!
This is not my fault.
First of all, how do we know these robots are after me? A lot of crazy things happen in this city to totally random people.
TARGET ACQUIRED.
Yeah, but maybe it would call anyone a target!
Second, I never asked to be in P.S. 20.
HERE'S A TASTE OF SOMETHING THEY DON'T TEACH IN SCIENCE CLASS.
SNAKK

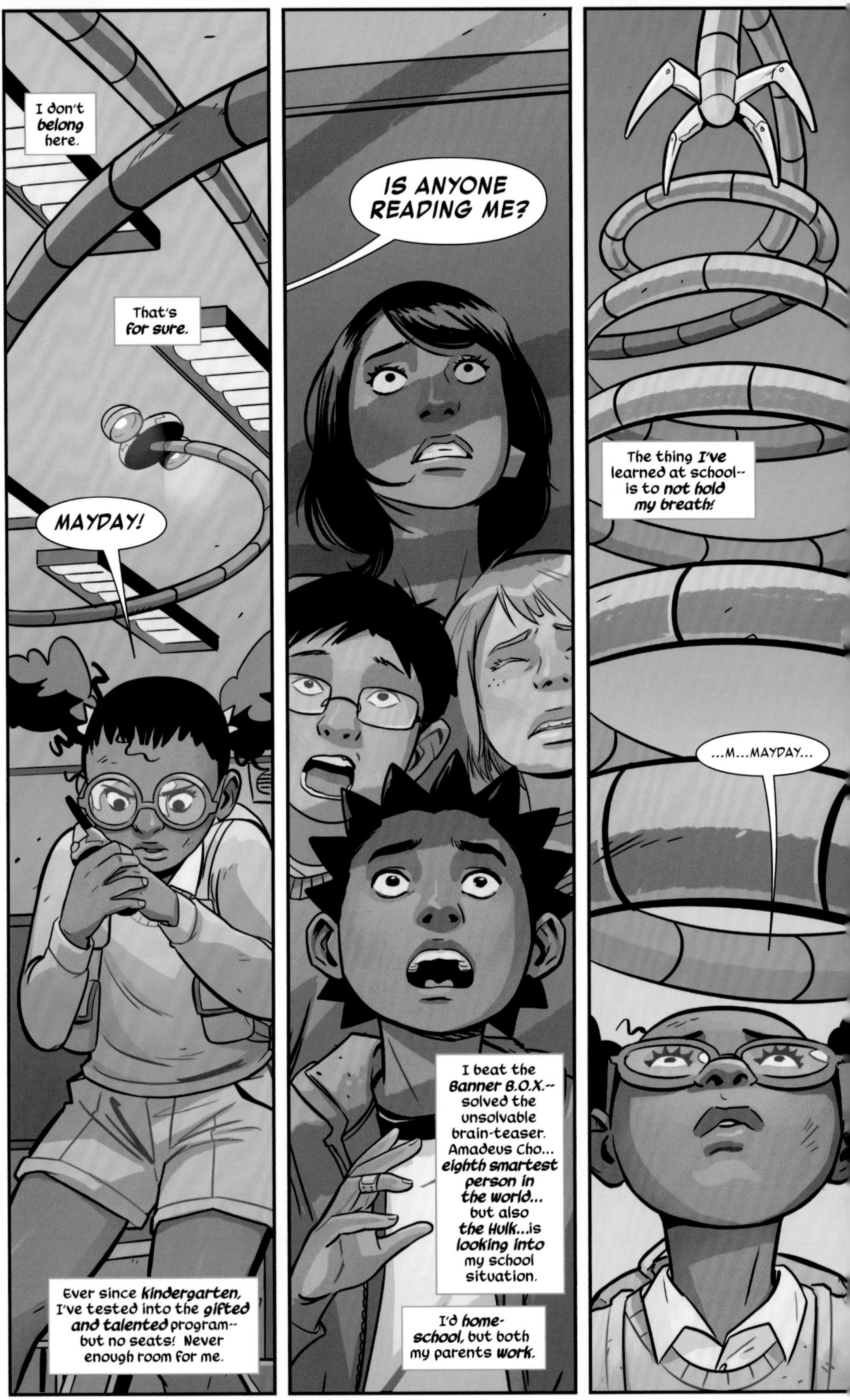
I don't belong here.
That's for sure.
MAYDAY!
Ever since kindergarten, I've tested into the gifted and talented program--but no seats! Never enough room for me.
IS ANYONE READING ME?
I beat the Banner B.O.X.--solved the unsolvable brain-teaser. Amadeus Cho... eighth smartest person in the world... but also the Hulk...is looking into my school situation.
I'd home-school, but both my parents work.
The thing I've learned at school--is to not hold my breath!
...M...MAYDAY...

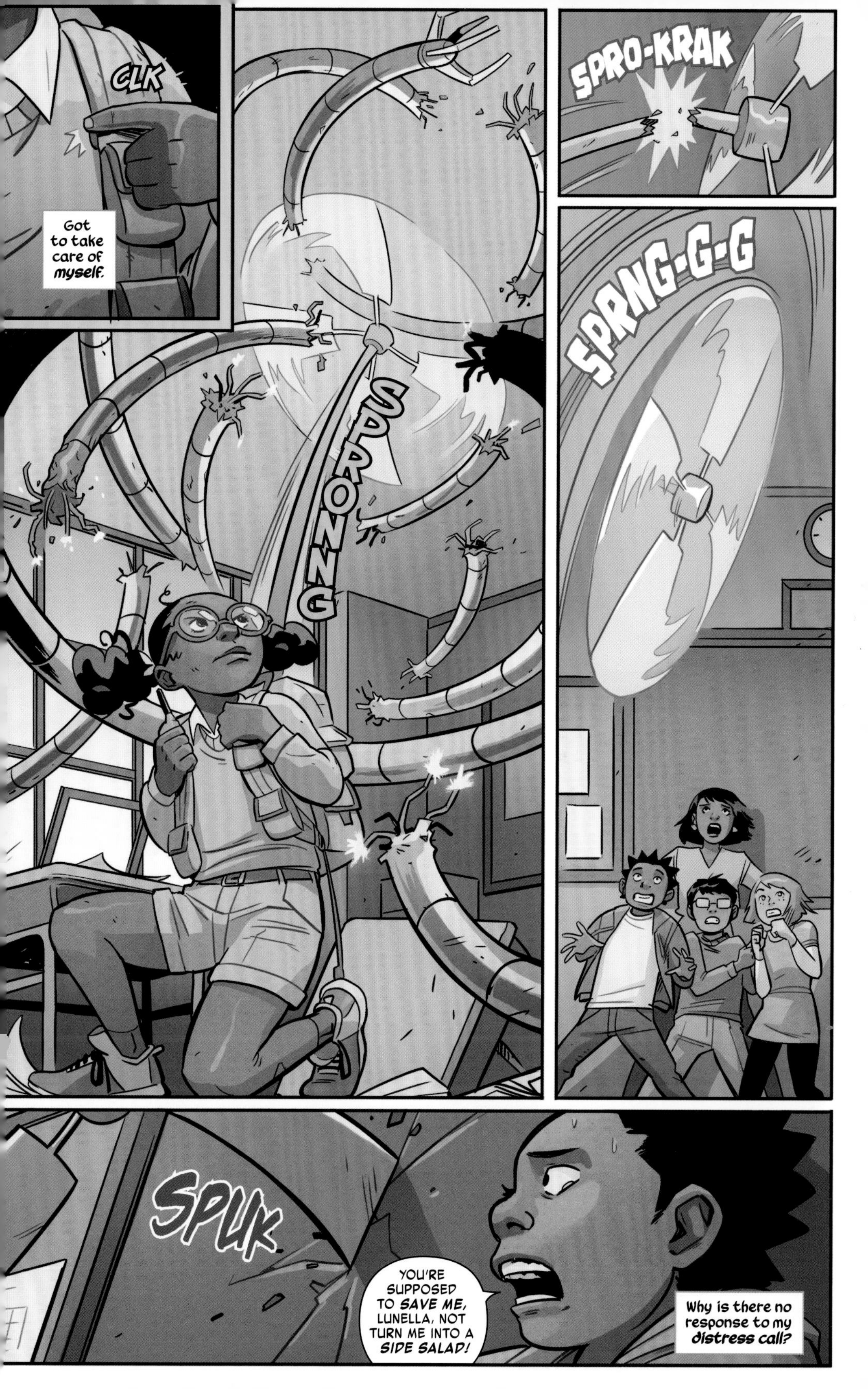
CLK
Got to take care of *myself.*
SPRONNG
SPRO-KRAK
SPRNG-G-G
SPUK
YOU'RE SUPPOSED TO *SAVE ME,* LUNELLA, NOT TURN ME INTO A *SIDE SALAD!*
Why is there no response to my *distress call?*

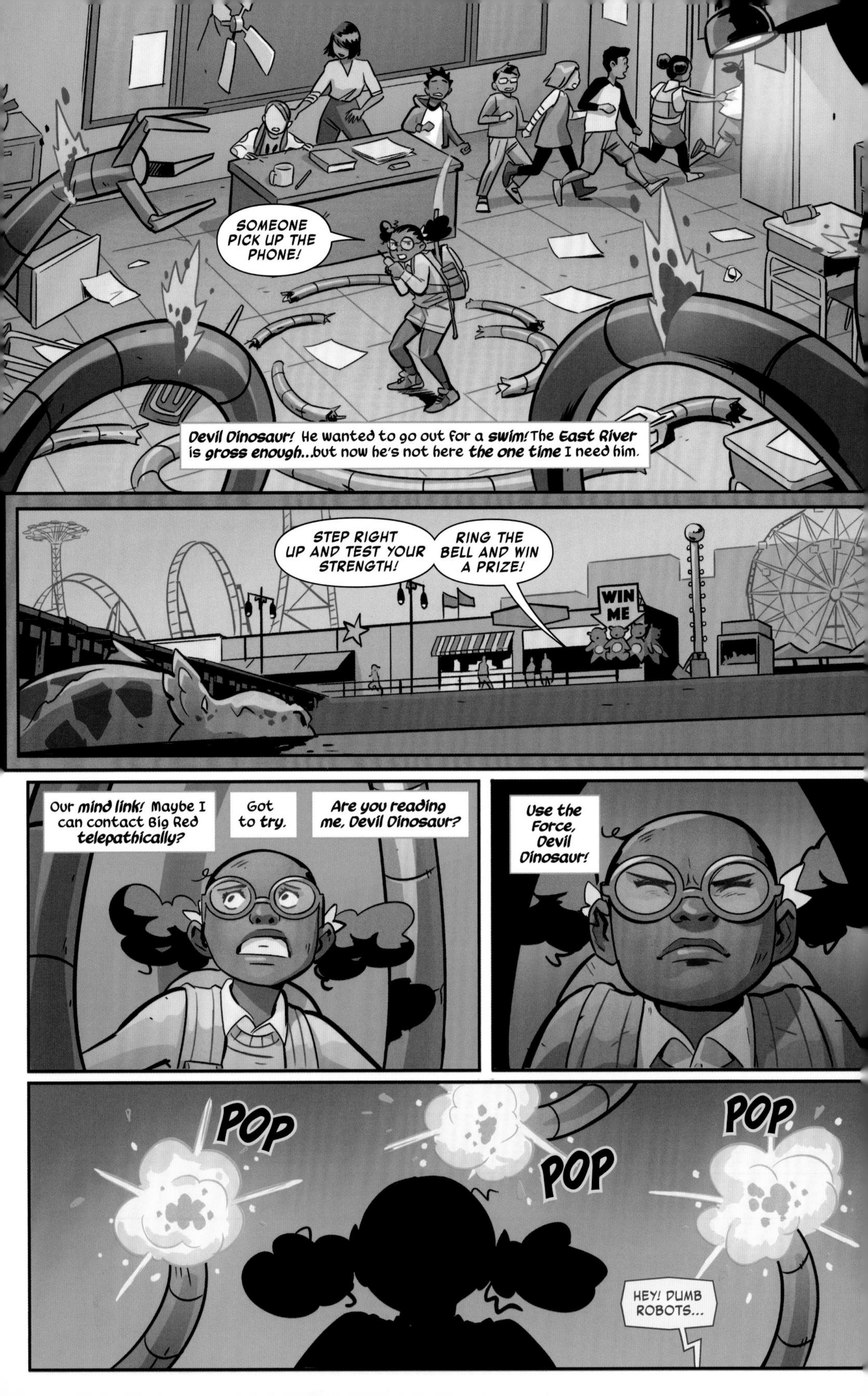

SOMEONE PICK UP THE PHONE!
Devil Dinosaur! He wanted to go out for a swim! The East River is gross enough...but now he's not here the one time I need him.
STEP RIGHT UP AND TEST YOUR STRENGTH!
RING THE BELL AND WIN A PRIZE!
WIN ME
Our mind link! Maybe I can contact Big Red telepathically?
Got to try.
Are you reading me, Devil Dinosaur?
Use the Force, Devil Dinosaur!
POP
POP
POP
HEY! DUMB ROBOTS...

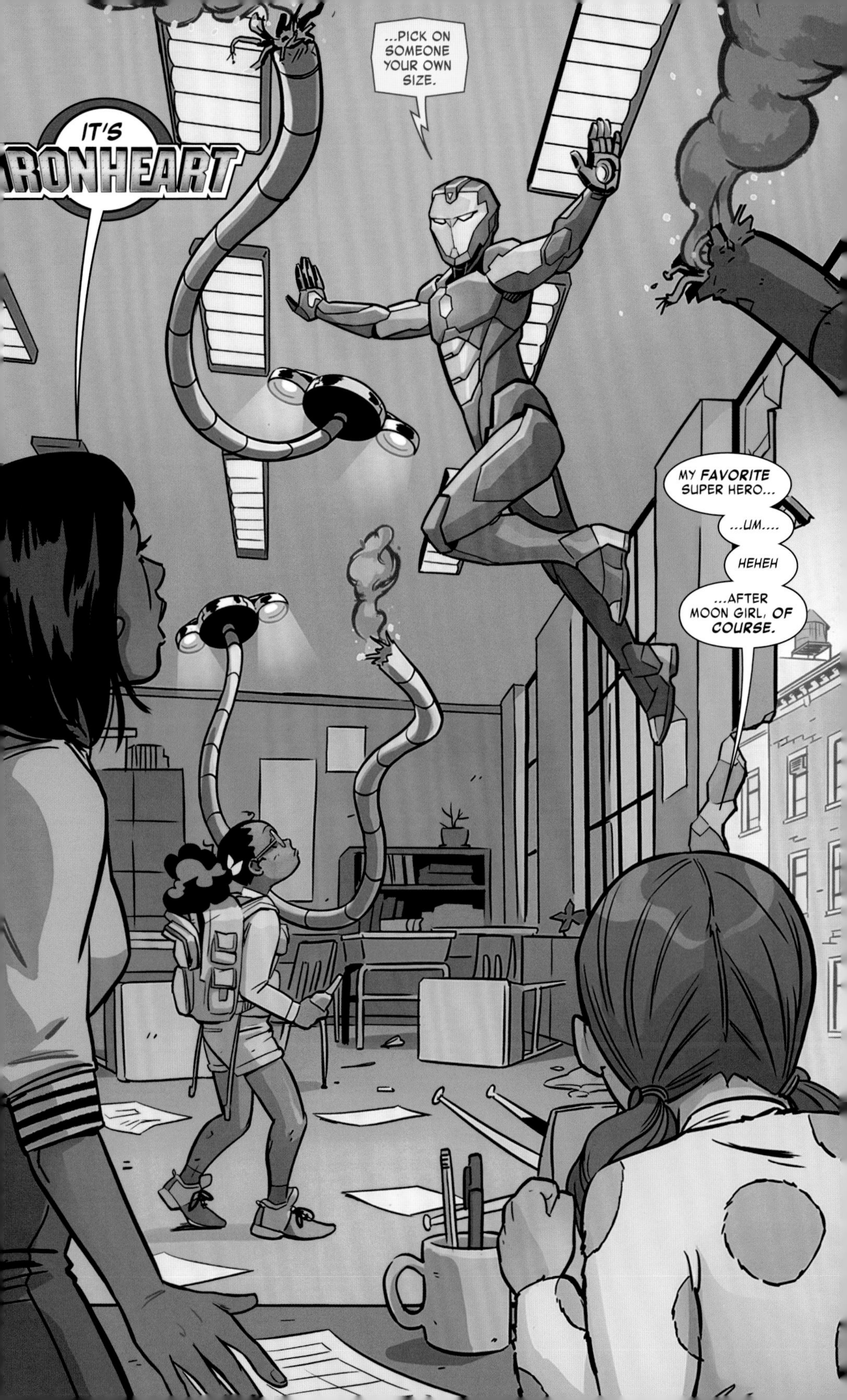
IT'S
IRONHEART
...PICK ON SOMEONE YOUR OWN SIZE.
MY **FAVORITE** SUPER HERO...
...UM....
HEHEH
...AFTER MOON GIRL, **OF COURSE.**

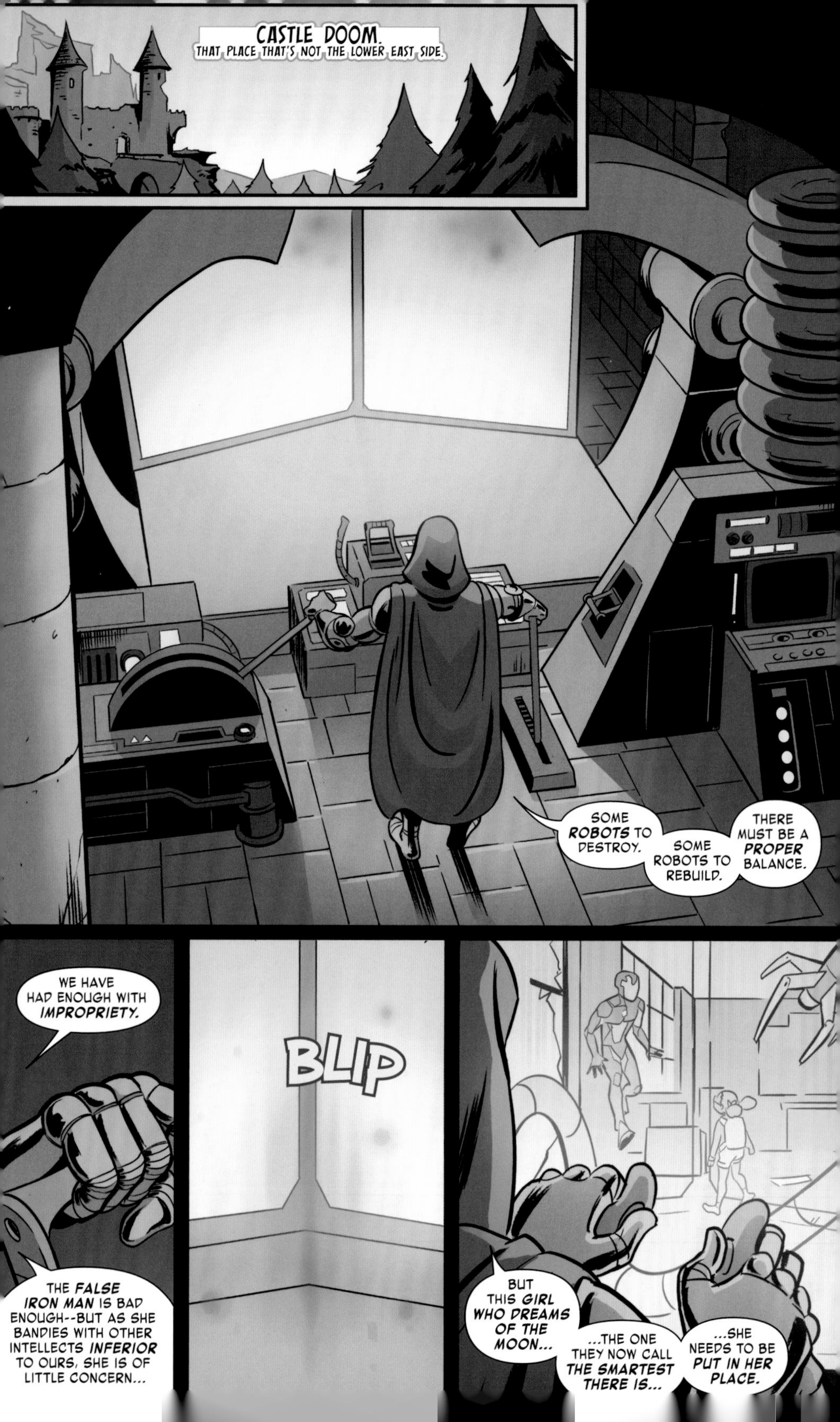
CASTLE DOOM.
THAT PLACE THAT'S NOT THE LOWER EAST SIDE.
SOME ROBOTS TO DESTROY.
SOME ROBOTS TO REBUILD.
THERE MUST BE A PROPER BALANCE.
WE HAVE HAD ENOUGH WITH IMPROPRIETY.
THE FALSE IRON MAN IS BAD ENOUGH--BUT AS SHE BANDIES WITH OTHER INTELLECTS INFERIOR TO OURS, SHE IS OF LITTLE CONCERN...
BLIP
BUT THIS GIRL WHO DREAMS OF THE MOON...
...THE ONE THEY NOW CALL THE SMARTEST THERE IS...
...SHE NEEDS TO BE PUT IN HER PLACE.

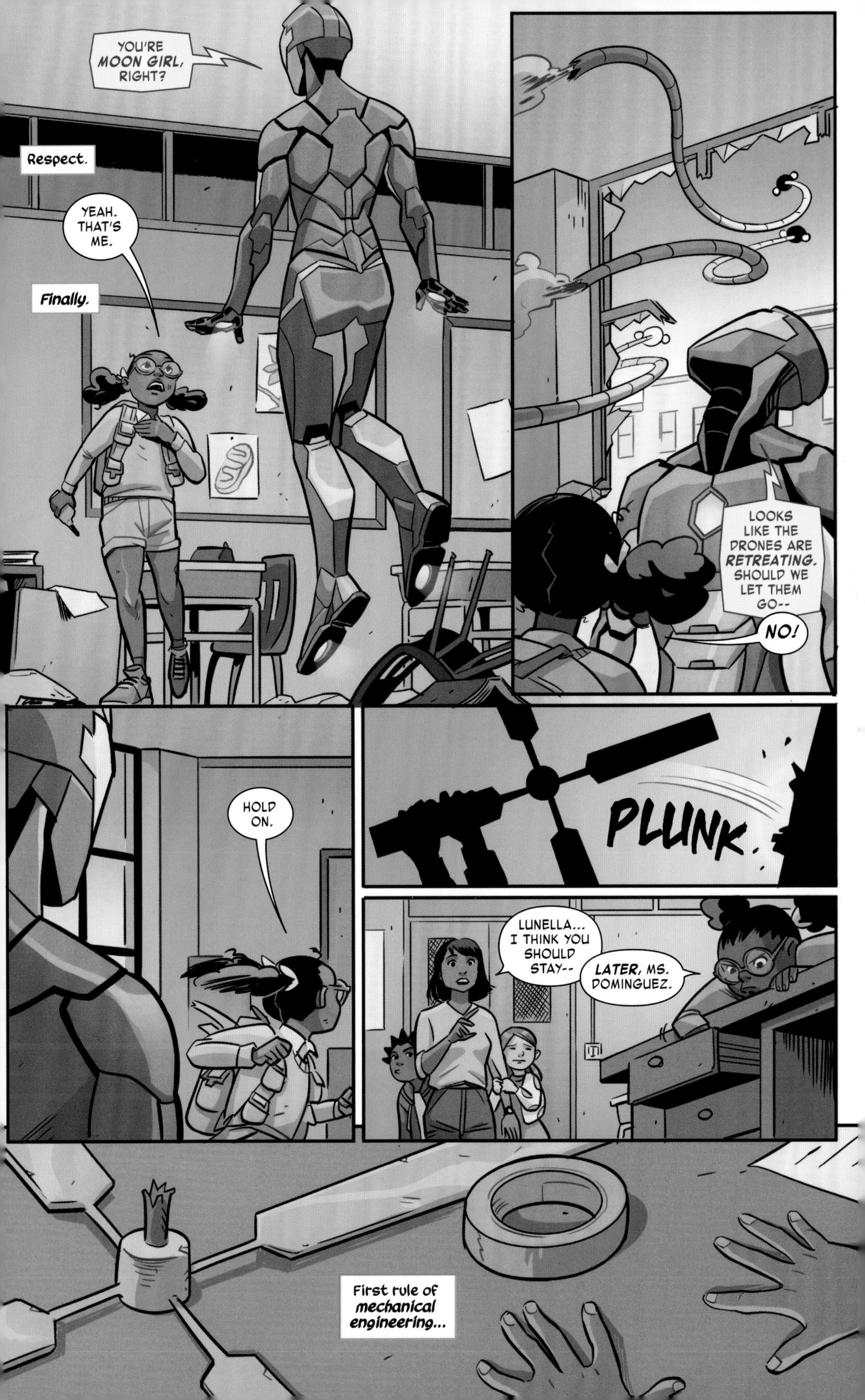
YOU'RE MOON GIRL, RIGHT?
Respect.
YEAH. THAT'S ME.
Finally.
LOOKS LIKE THE DRONES ARE RETREATING. SHOULD WE LET THEM GO--
NO!
HOLD ON.
PLUNK.
LUNELLA... I THINK YOU SHOULD STAY--
LATER, MS. DOMINGUEZ.
First rule of mechanical engineering...

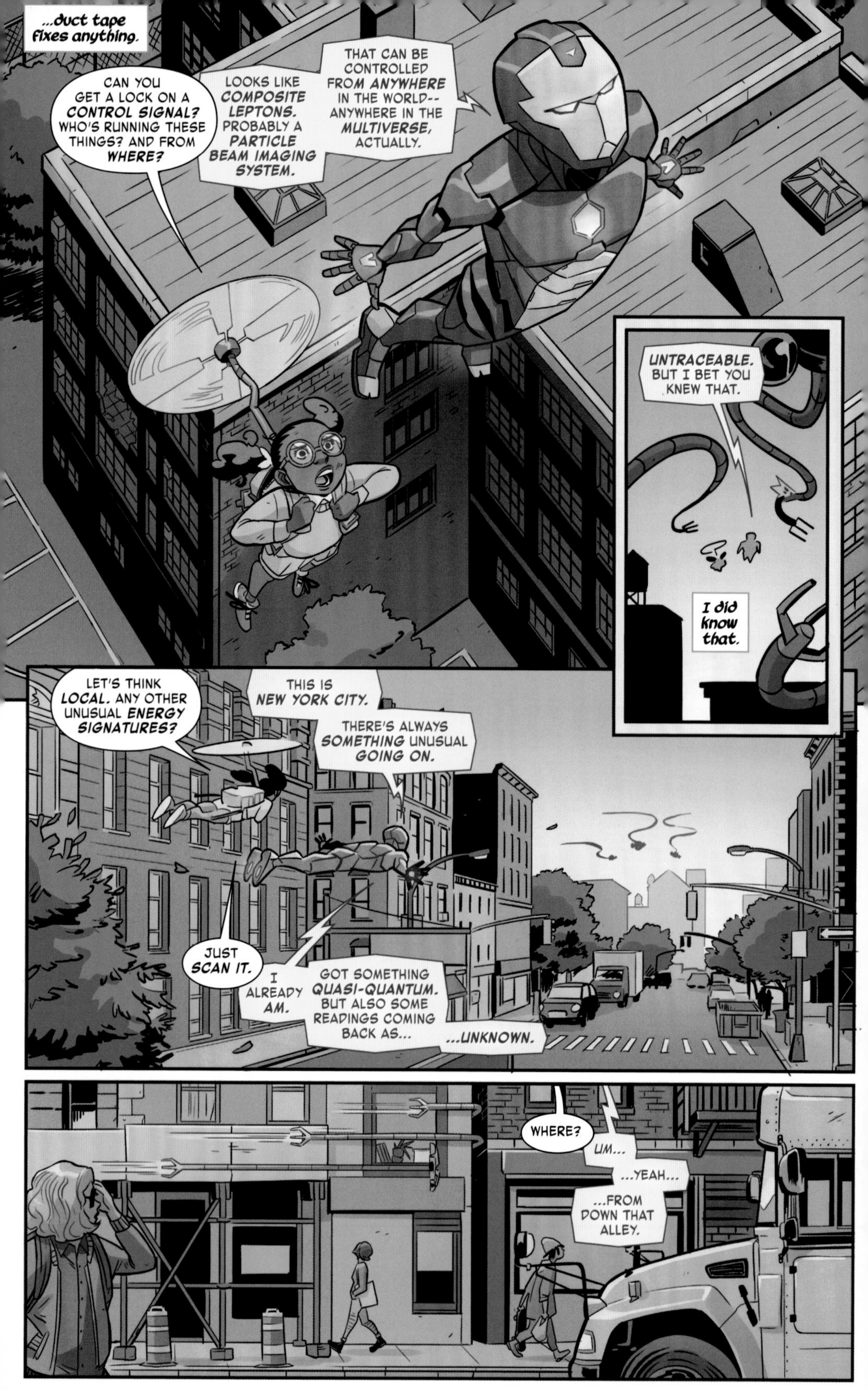

...duct tape fixes anything.
CAN YOU GET A LOCK ON A CONTROL SIGNAL? WHO'S RUNNING THESE THINGS? AND FROM WHERE?
LOOKS LIKE COMPOSITE LEPTONS. PROBABLY A PARTICLE BEAM IMAGING SYSTEM.
THAT CAN BE CONTROLLED FROM ANYWHERE IN THE WORLD-- ANYWHERE IN THE MULTIVERSE, ACTUALLY.
UNTRACEABLE. BUT I BET YOU KNEW THAT.
I did know that.
LET'S THINK LOCAL. ANY OTHER UNUSUAL ENERGY SIGNATURES?
THIS IS NEW YORK CITY.
THERE'S ALWAYS SOMETHING UNUSUAL GOING ON.
JUST SCAN IT.
I ALREADY AM.
GOT SOMETHING QUASI-QUANTUM. BUT ALSO SOME READINGS COMING BACK AS...
...UNKNOWN.
WHERE?
UM...
...YEAH...
...FROM DOWN THAT ALLEY.

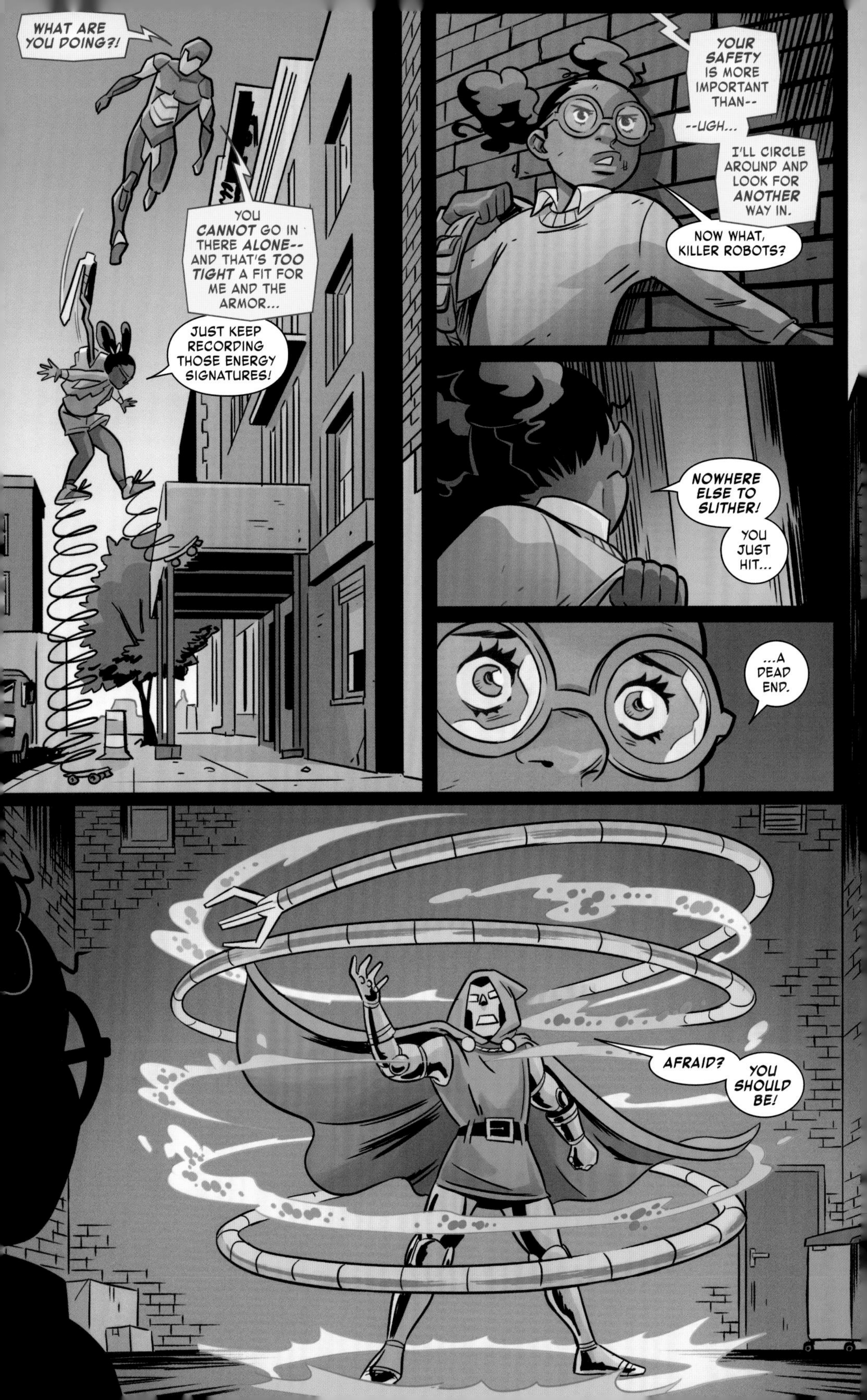
WHAT ARE YOU DOING?!
YOU CANNOT GO IN THERE ALONE-- AND THAT'S TOO TIGHT A FIT FOR ME AND THE ARMOR...
JUST KEEP RECORDING THOSE ENERGY SIGNATURES!
YOUR SAFETY IS MORE IMPORTANT THAN--
--UGH...
I'LL CIRCLE AROUND AND LOOK FOR ANOTHER WAY IN.
NOW WHAT, KILLER ROBOTS?
NOWHERE ELSE TO SLITHER!
YOU JUST HIT...
...A DEAD END.
AFRAID?
YOU SHOULD BE!

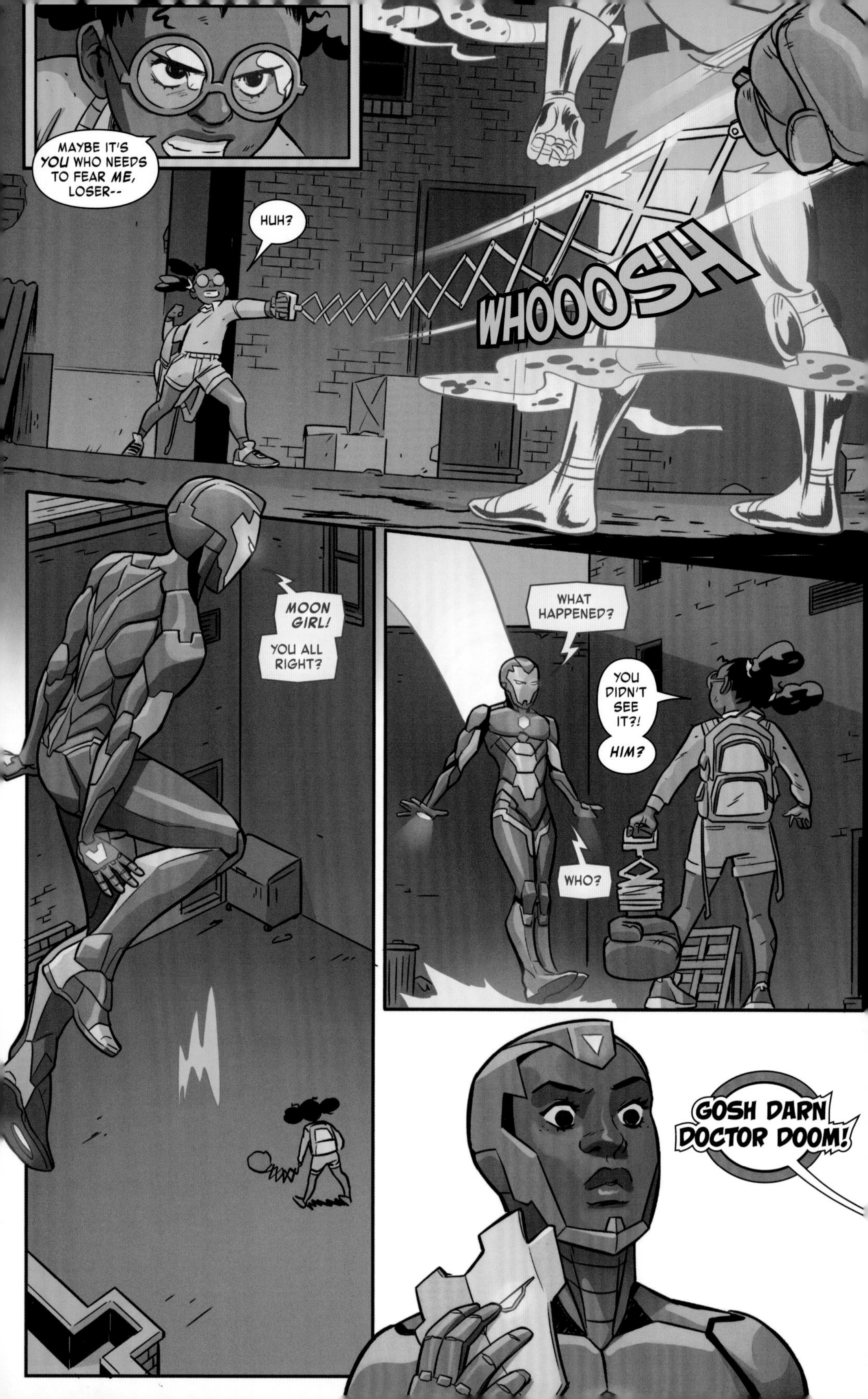
MAYBE IT'S YOU WHO NEEDS TO FEAR ME, LOSER--
HUH?
WHOOOSH
MOON GIRL!
YOU ALL RIGHT?
WHAT HAPPENED?
YOU DIDN'T SEE IT?!
HIM?
WHO?
GOSH DARN DOCTOR DOOM!

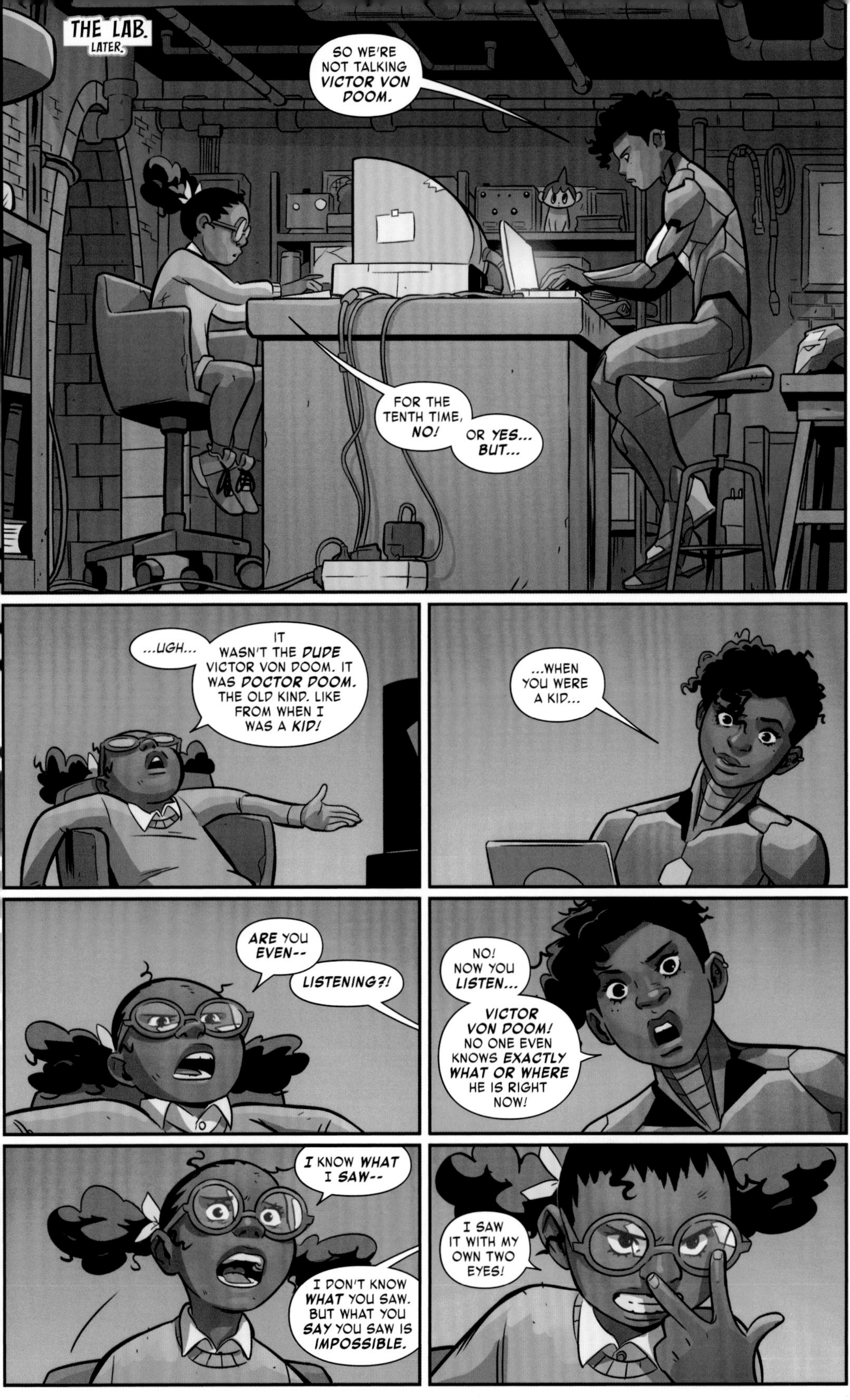
THE LAB. LATER.
SO WE'RE NOT TALKING VICTOR VON DOOM.
FOR THE TENTH TIME, NO!
OR YES... BUT...
...UGH...
IT WASN'T THE DUDE VICTOR VON DOOM. IT WAS DOCTOR DOOM. THE OLD KIND. LIKE FROM WHEN I WAS A KID!
...WHEN YOU WERE A KID...
ARE YOU EVEN--
LISTENING?!
NO! NOW YOU LISTEN...
VICTOR VON DOOM! NO ONE EVEN KNOWS EXACTLY WHAT OR WHERE HE IS RIGHT NOW!
I KNOW WHAT I SAW--
I DON'T KNOW WHAT YOU SAW. BUT WHAT YOU SAY YOU SAW IS IMPOSSIBLE.
I SAW IT WITH MY OWN TWO EYES!

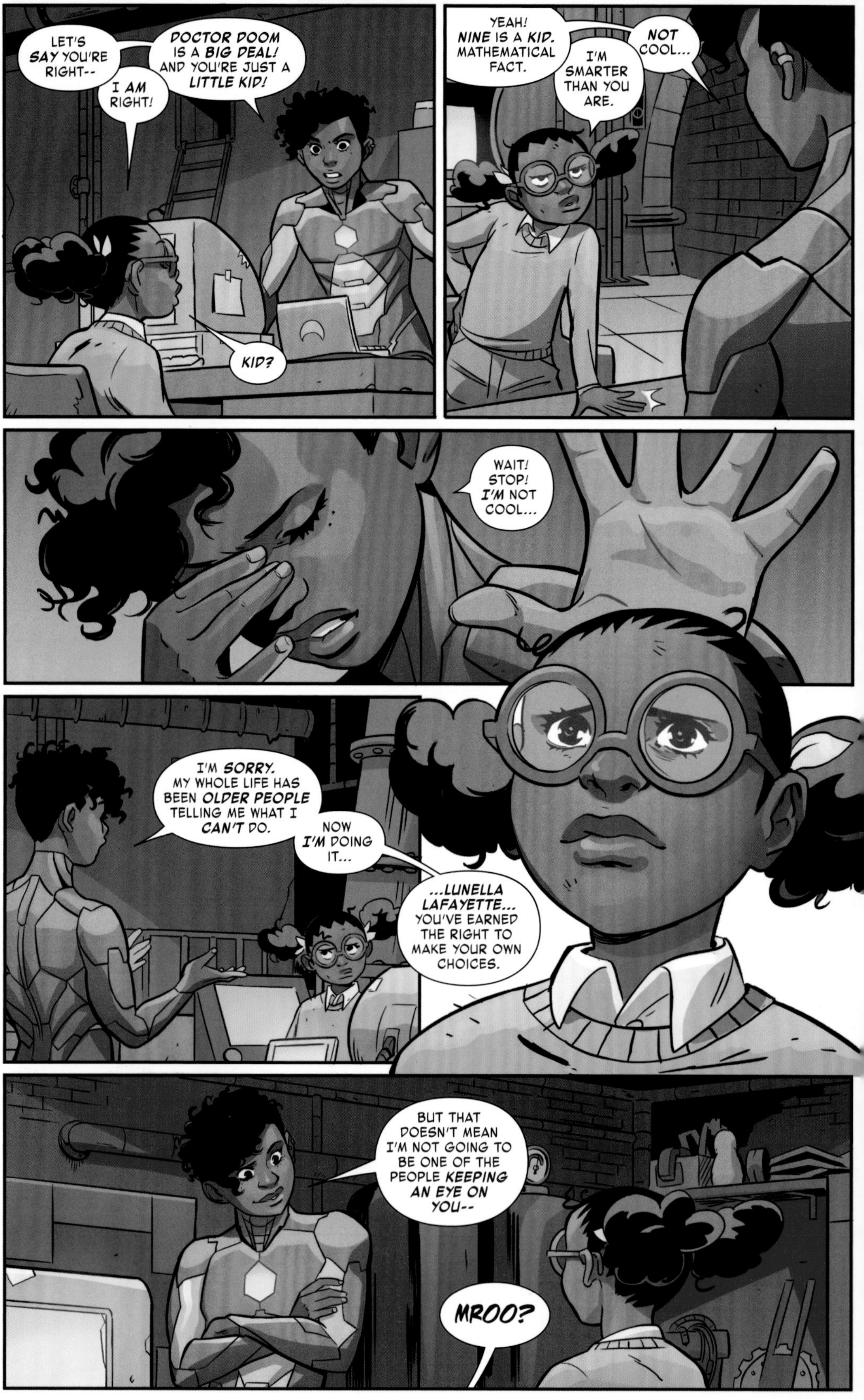
LET'S SAY YOU'RE RIGHT--
I AM RIGHT!
DOCTOR DOOM IS A BIG DEAL! AND YOU'RE JUST A LITTLE KID!
KID?
YEAH! NINE IS A KID. MATHEMATICAL FACT.
I'M SMARTER THAN YOU ARE.
NOT COOL...
WAIT! STOP! I'M NOT COOL...
I'M SORRY. MY WHOLE LIFE HAS BEEN OLDER PEOPLE TELLING ME WHAT I CAN'T DO.
NOW I'M DOING IT...
...LUNELLA LAFAYETTE... YOU'VE EARNED THE RIGHT TO MAKE YOUR OWN CHOICES.
BUT THAT DOESN'T MEAN I'M NOT GOING TO BE ONE OF THE PEOPLE KEEPING AN EYE ON YOU--
MROO?

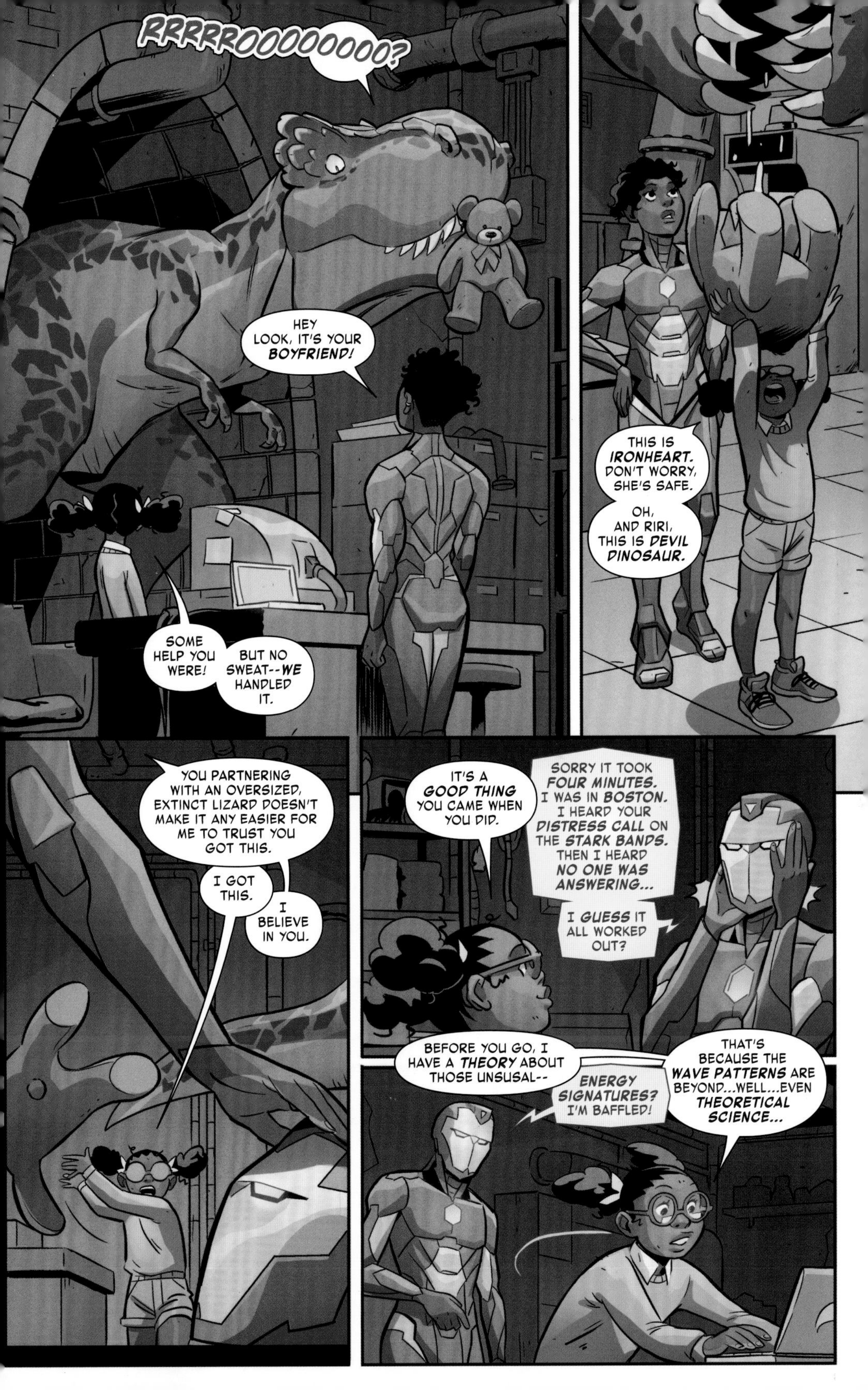
RRRRROOOOOOOO?
HEY LOOK, IT'S YOUR BOYFRIEND!
SOME HELP YOU WERE!
BUT NO SWEAT--WE HANDLED IT.
THIS IS IRONHEART. DON'T WORRY, SHE'S SAFE.
OH, AND RIRI, THIS IS DEVIL DINOSAUR.
YOU PARTNERING WITH AN OVERSIZED, EXTINCT LIZARD DOESN'T MAKE IT ANY EASIER FOR ME TO TRUST YOU GOT THIS.
I GOT THIS.
I BELIEVE IN YOU.
IT'S A GOOD THING YOU CAME WHEN YOU DID.
SORRY IT TOOK FOUR MINUTES. I WAS IN BOSTON. I HEARD YOUR DISTRESS CALL ON THE STARK BANDS. THEN I HEARD NO ONE WAS ANSWERING...
I GUESS IT ALL WORKED OUT?
BEFORE YOU GO, I HAVE A THEORY ABOUT THOSE UNSUSAL--
ENERGY SIGNATURES? I'M BAFFLED!
THAT'S BECAUSE THE WAVE PATTERNS ARE BEYOND...WELL...EVEN THEORETICAL SCIENCE...

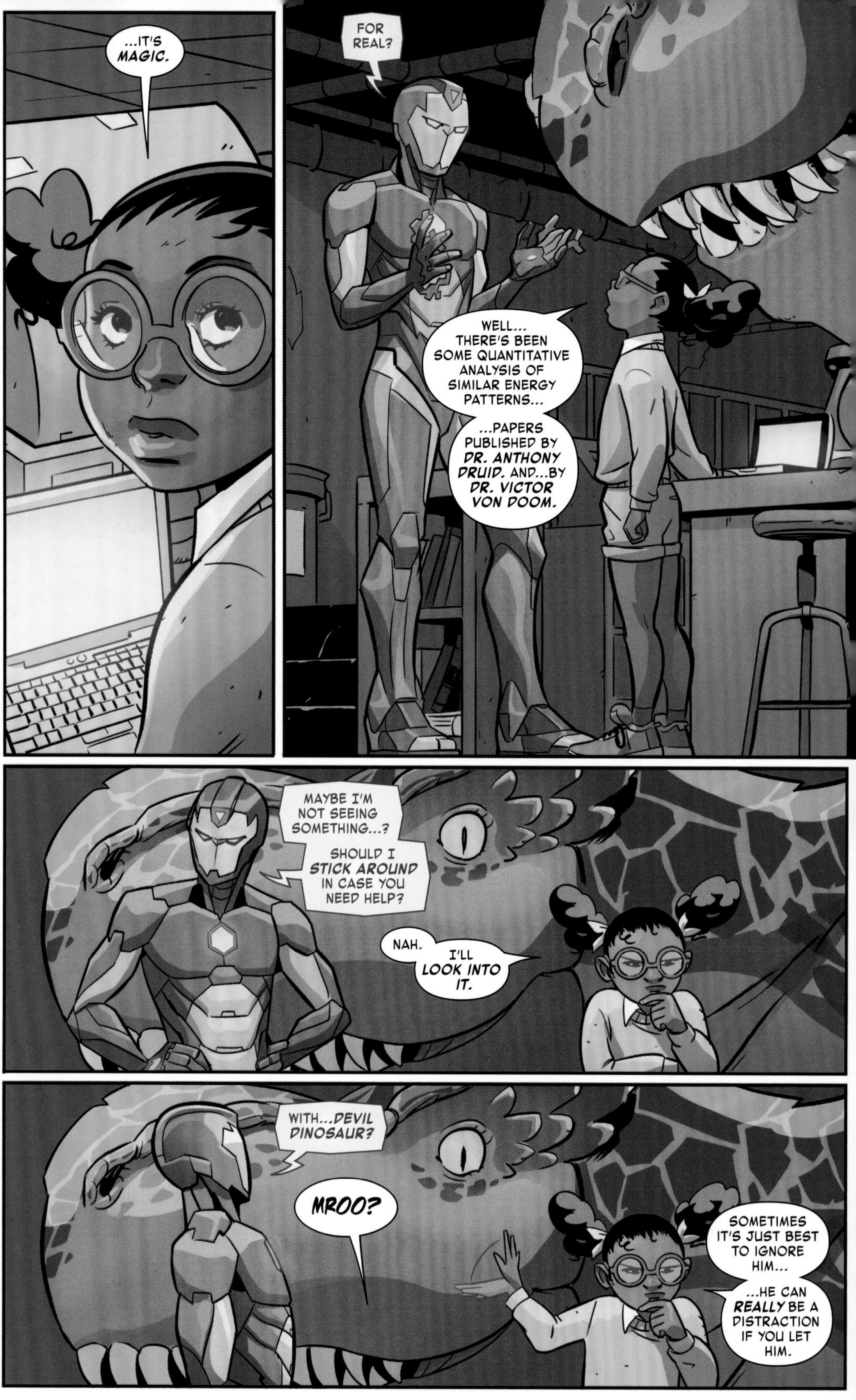
...IT'S MAGIC.
FOR REAL?
WELL... THERE'S BEEN SOME QUANTITATIVE ANALYSIS OF SIMILAR ENERGY PATTERNS...
...PAPERS PUBLISHED BY DR. ANTHONY DRUID. AND...BY DR. VICTOR VON DOOM.
MAYBE I'M NOT SEEING SOMETHING...?
SHOULD I STICK AROUND IN CASE YOU NEED HELP?
NAH.
I'LL LOOK INTO IT.
WITH...DEVIL DINOSAUR?
MROO?
SOMETIMES IT'S JUST BEST TO IGNORE HIM...
...HE CAN REALLY BE A DISTRACTION IF YOU LET HIM.

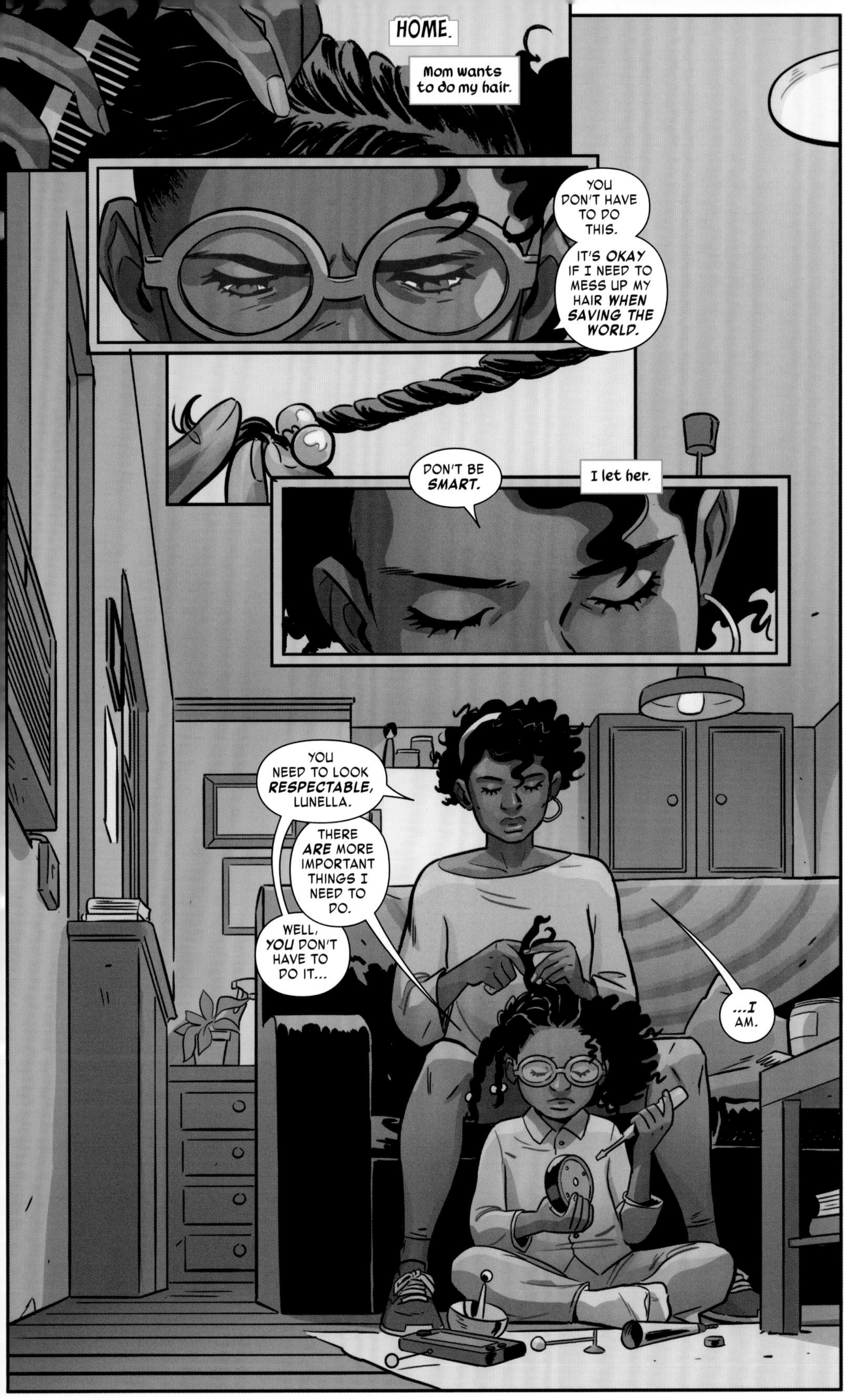
HOME.
Mom wants to do my hair.
YOU DON'T HAVE TO DO THIS.
IT'S OKAY IF I NEED TO MESS UP MY HAIR WHEN SAVING THE WORLD.
DON'T BE SMART.
I let her.
YOU NEED TO LOOK RESPECTABLE, LUNELLA.
THERE ARE MORE IMPORTANT THINGS I NEED TO DO.
WELL, YOU DON'T HAVE TO DO IT...
...I AM.

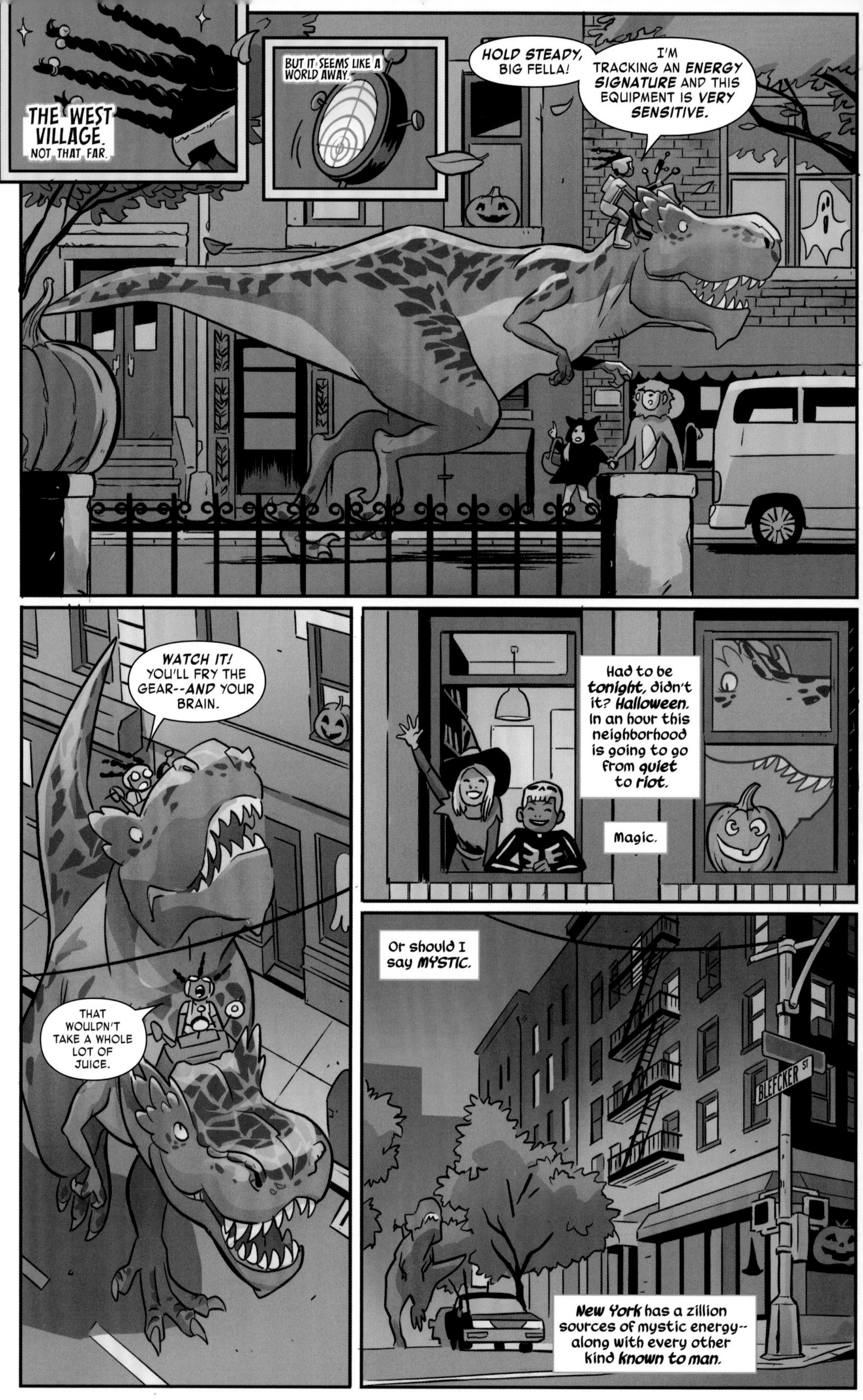

THE WEST VILLAGE. NOT THAT FAR.
BUT IT SEEMS LIKE A WORLD AWAY.
HOLD STEADY, BIG FELLA!
I'M TRACKING AN ENERGY SIGNATURE AND THIS EQUIPMENT IS VERY SENSITIVE.
WATCH IT! YOU'LL FRY THE GEAR--AND YOUR BRAIN.
THAT WOULDN'T TAKE A WHOLE LOT OF JUICE.
Had to be tonight, didn't it? Halloween. In an hour this neighborhood is going to go from quiet to riot.
Magic.
Or should I say MYSTIC.
BLEECKER ST
New York has a zillion sources of mystic energy--along with every other kind known to man.

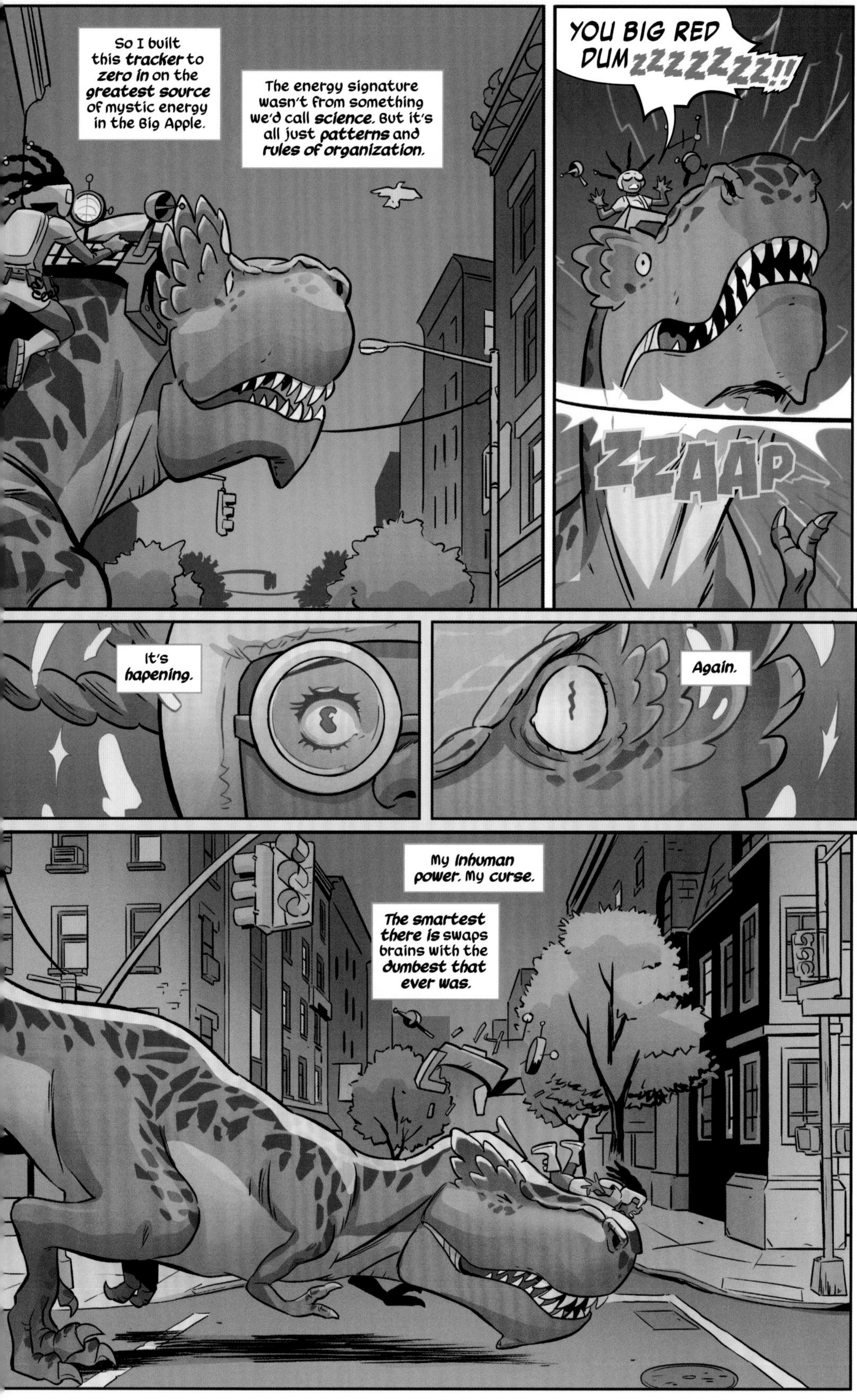
So I built this tracker to zero in on the greatest source of mystic energy in the Big Apple.
The energy signature wasn't from something we'd call science. But it's all just patterns and rules of organization.
YOU BIG RED DUMZZZZZZZ!!
ZZAAP
It's hapening.
Again.
My Inhuman power. My curse.
The smartest there is swaps brains with the dumbest that ever was.

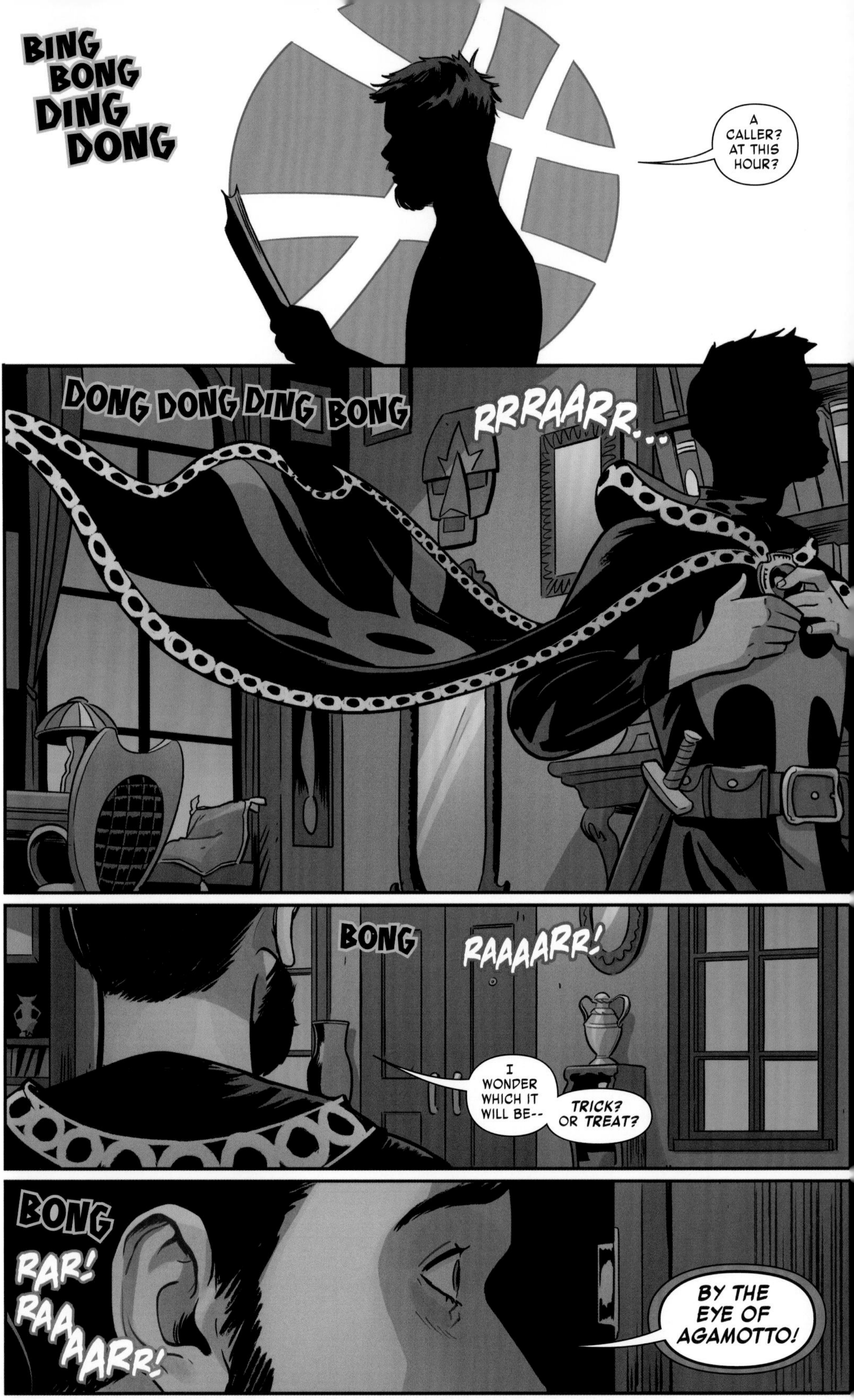
BING BONG DING DONG
A CALLER? AT THIS HOUR?
DONG DONG DING BONG
RRRAARR...
BONG
RAAAARR!
I WONDER WHICH IT WILL BE--
TRICK? OR TREAT?
BONG
RAR! RAAAARR!
BY THE EYE OF AGAMOTTO!

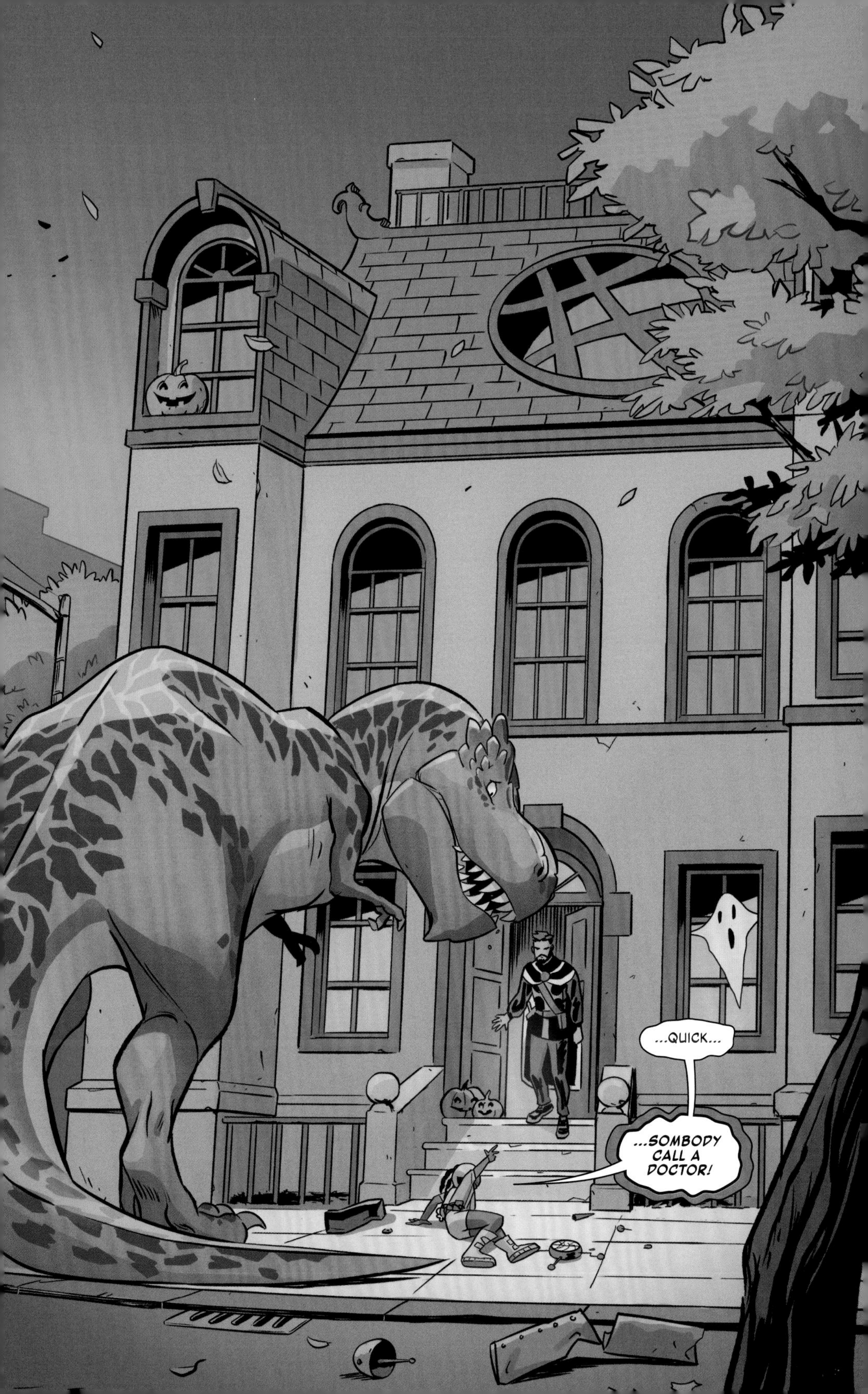
...QUICK...
...SOMBODY CALL A DOCTOR!

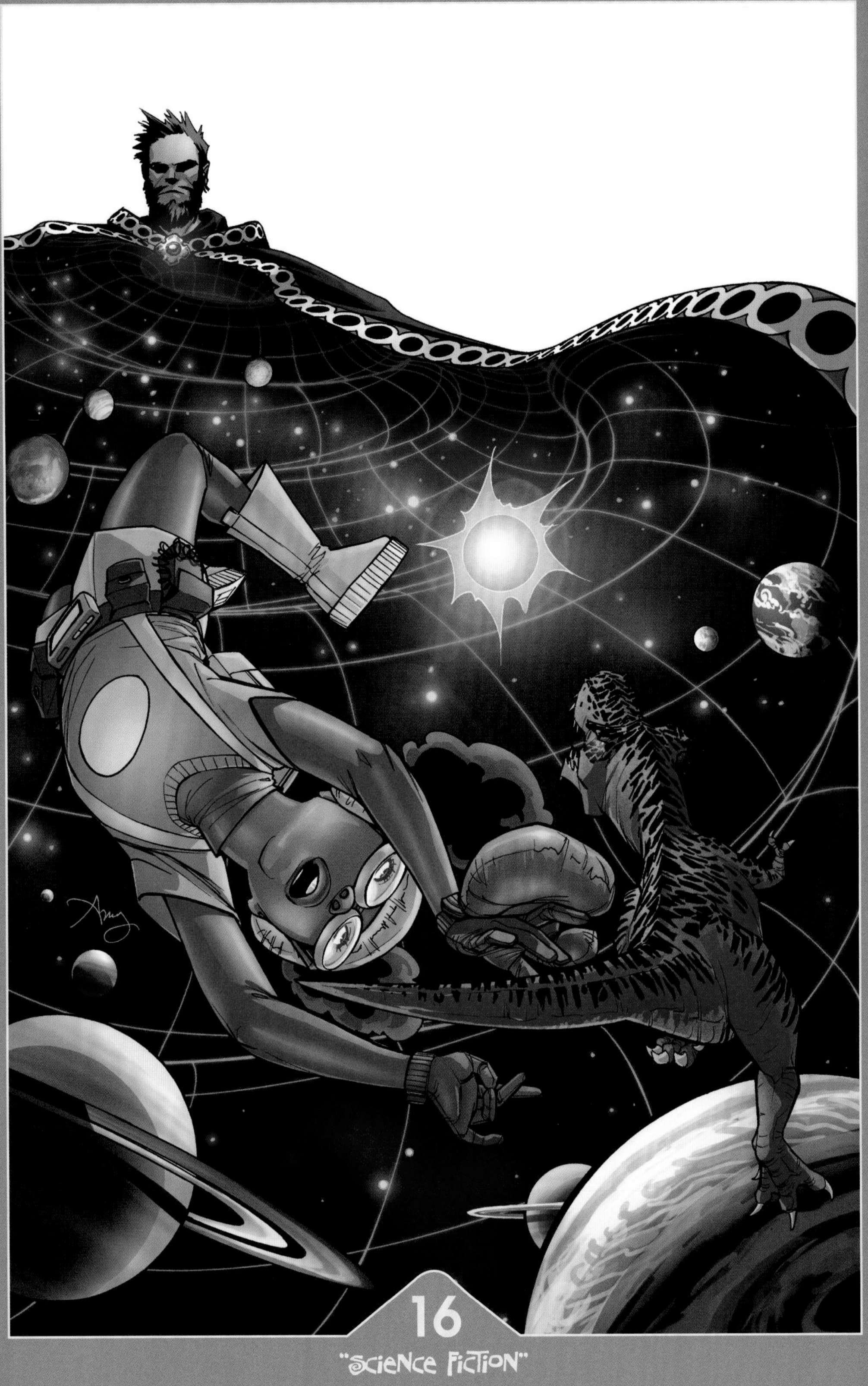
16

"SCIENCE FICTION"

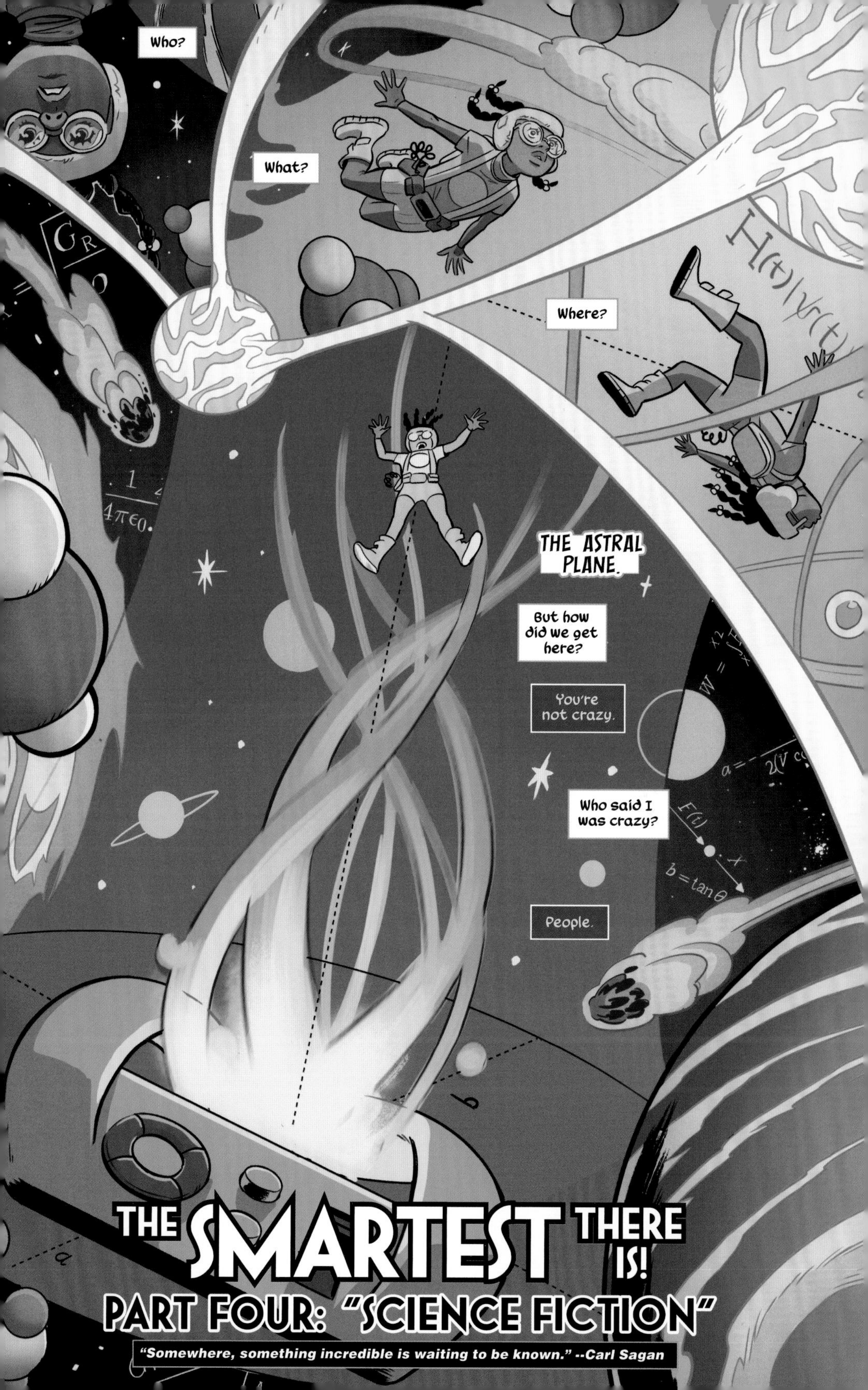
Who?
What?
Where?
THE ASTRAL PLANE.
But how did we get here?
You're not crazy.
Who said I was crazy?
People.
THE SMARTEST THERE IS!
PART FOUR: "SCIENCE FICTION"
"Somewhere, something incredible is waiting to be known." --Carl Sagan

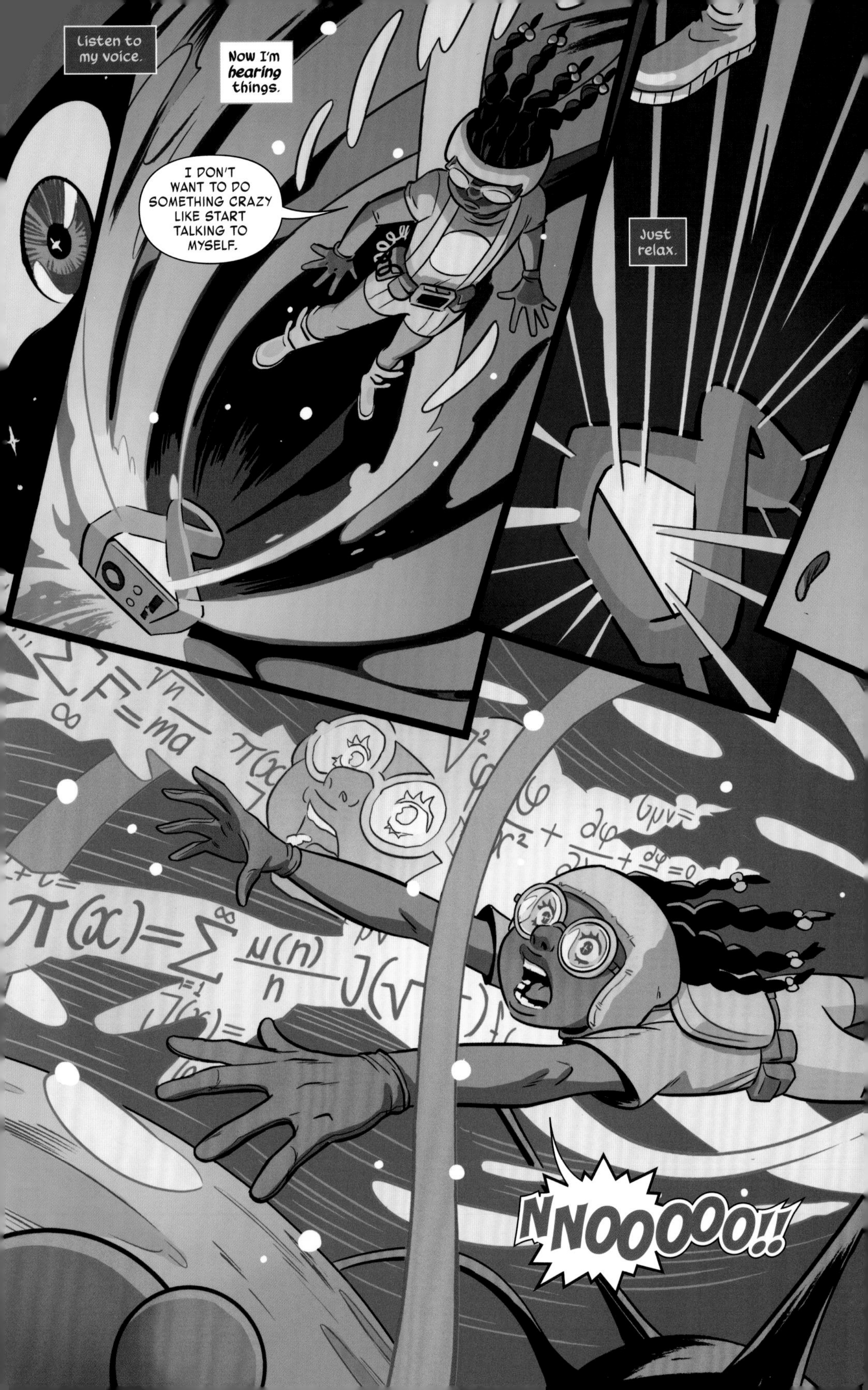
Listen to my voice.
Now I'm *hearing* things.
I DON'T WANT TO DO SOMETHING CRAZY LIKE START TALKING TO MYSELF.
Just relax.
NNOOOOOO!!

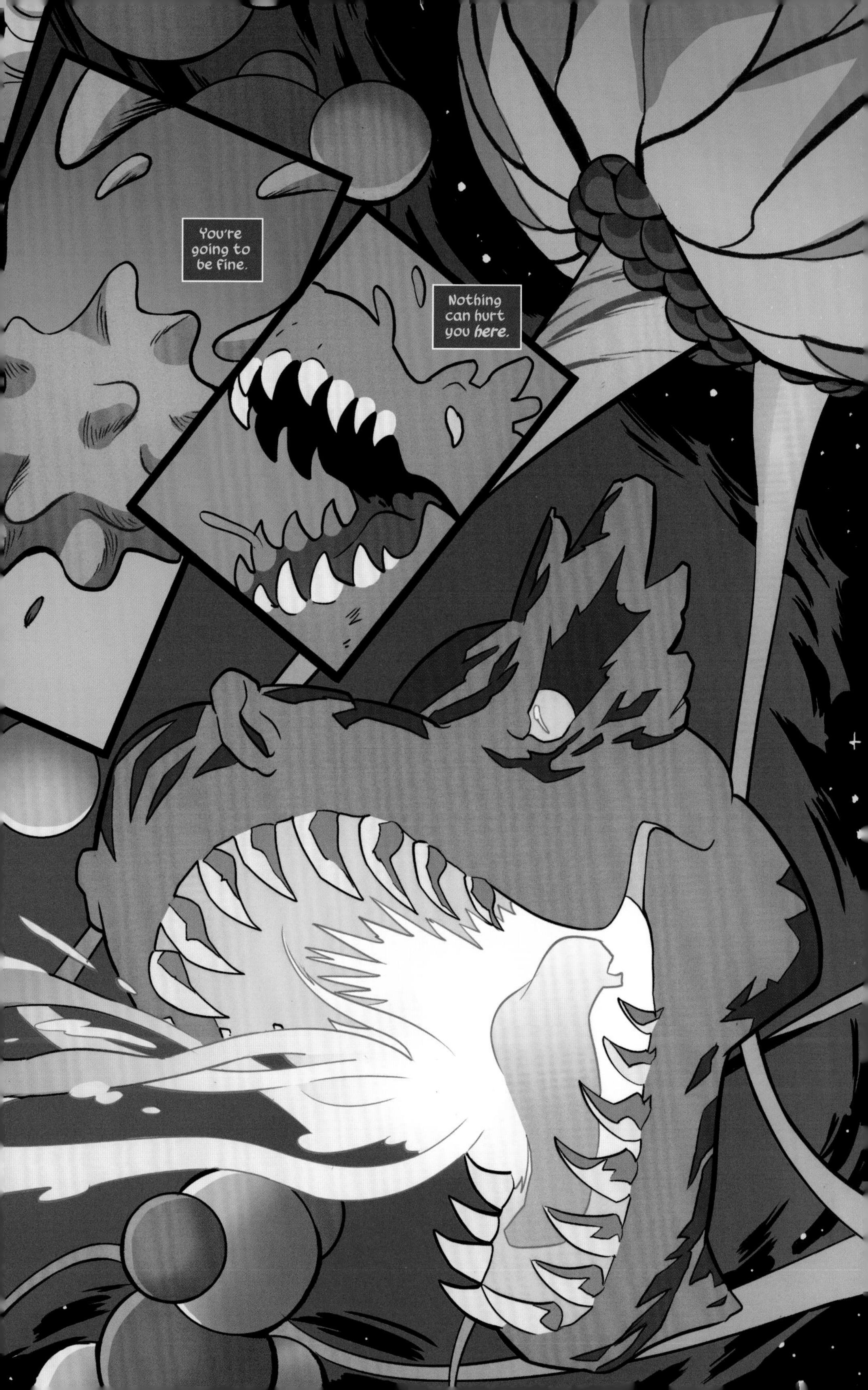
You're going to be fine.
Nothing can hurt you *here*.

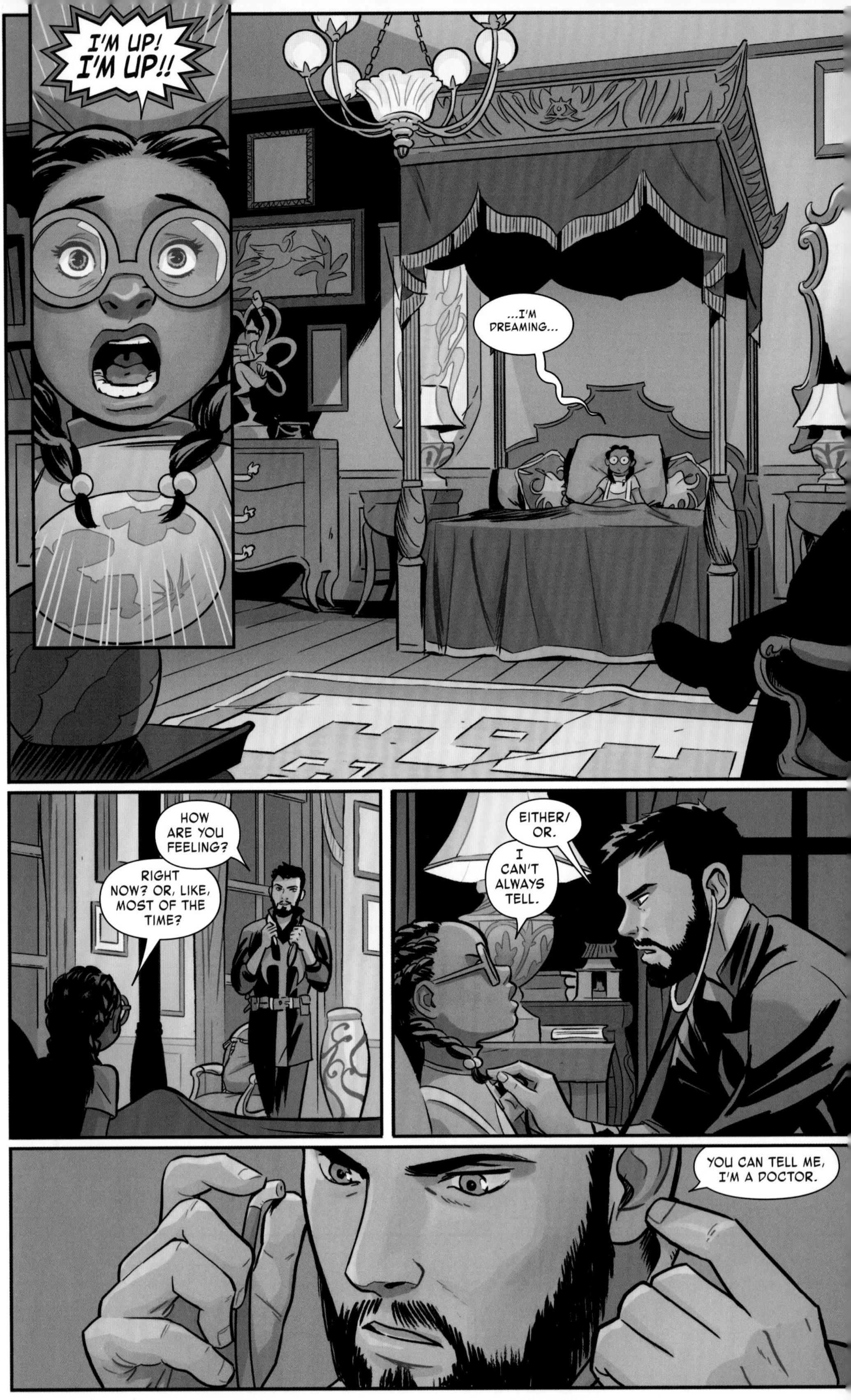
I'M UP! I'M UP!!
...I'M DREAMING...
HOW ARE YOU FEELING?
RIGHT NOW? OR, LIKE, MOST OF THE TIME?
EITHER/ OR.
I CAN'T ALWAYS TELL.
YOU CAN TELL ME, I'M A DOCTOR.

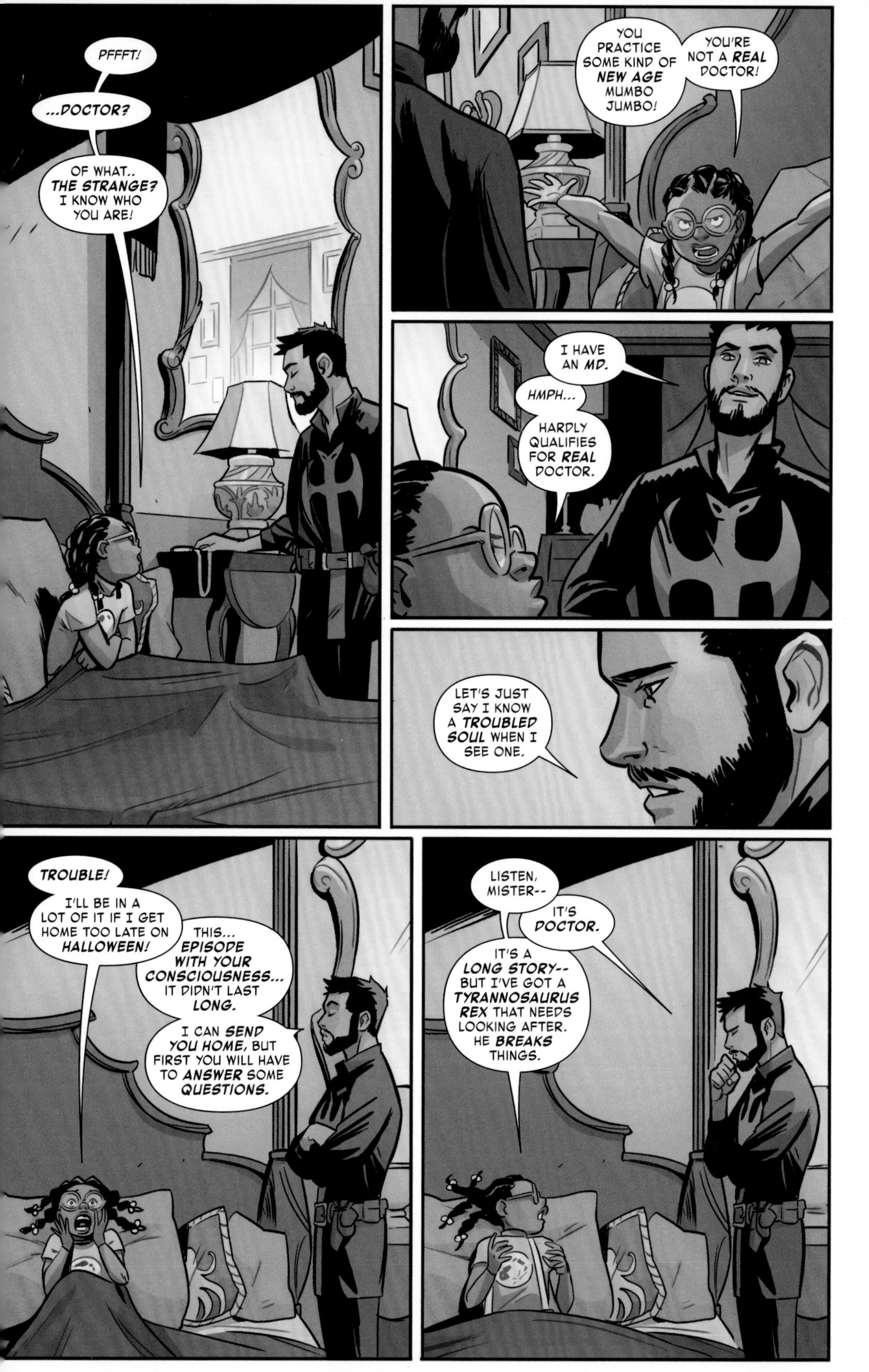

PFFFT!
...DOCTOR?
OF WHAT.. THE STRANGE? I KNOW WHO YOU ARE!
YOU PRACTICE SOME KIND OF NEW AGE MUMBO JUMBO!
YOU'RE NOT A REAL DOCTOR!
I HAVE AN MD.
HMPH...
HARDLY QUALIFIES FOR REAL DOCTOR.
LET'S JUST SAY I KNOW A TROUBLED SOUL WHEN I SEE ONE.
TROUBLE!
I'LL BE IN A LOT OF IT IF I GET HOME TOO LATE ON HALLOWEEN!
THIS... EPISODE WITH YOUR CONSCIOUSNESS... IT DIDN'T LAST LONG.
I CAN SEND YOU HOME, BUT FIRST YOU WILL HAVE TO ANSWER SOME QUESTIONS.
LISTEN, MISTER--
IT'S DOCTOR.
IT'S A LONG STORY-- BUT I'VE GOT A TYRANNOSAURUS REX THAT NEEDS LOOKING AFTER. HE BREAKS THINGS.

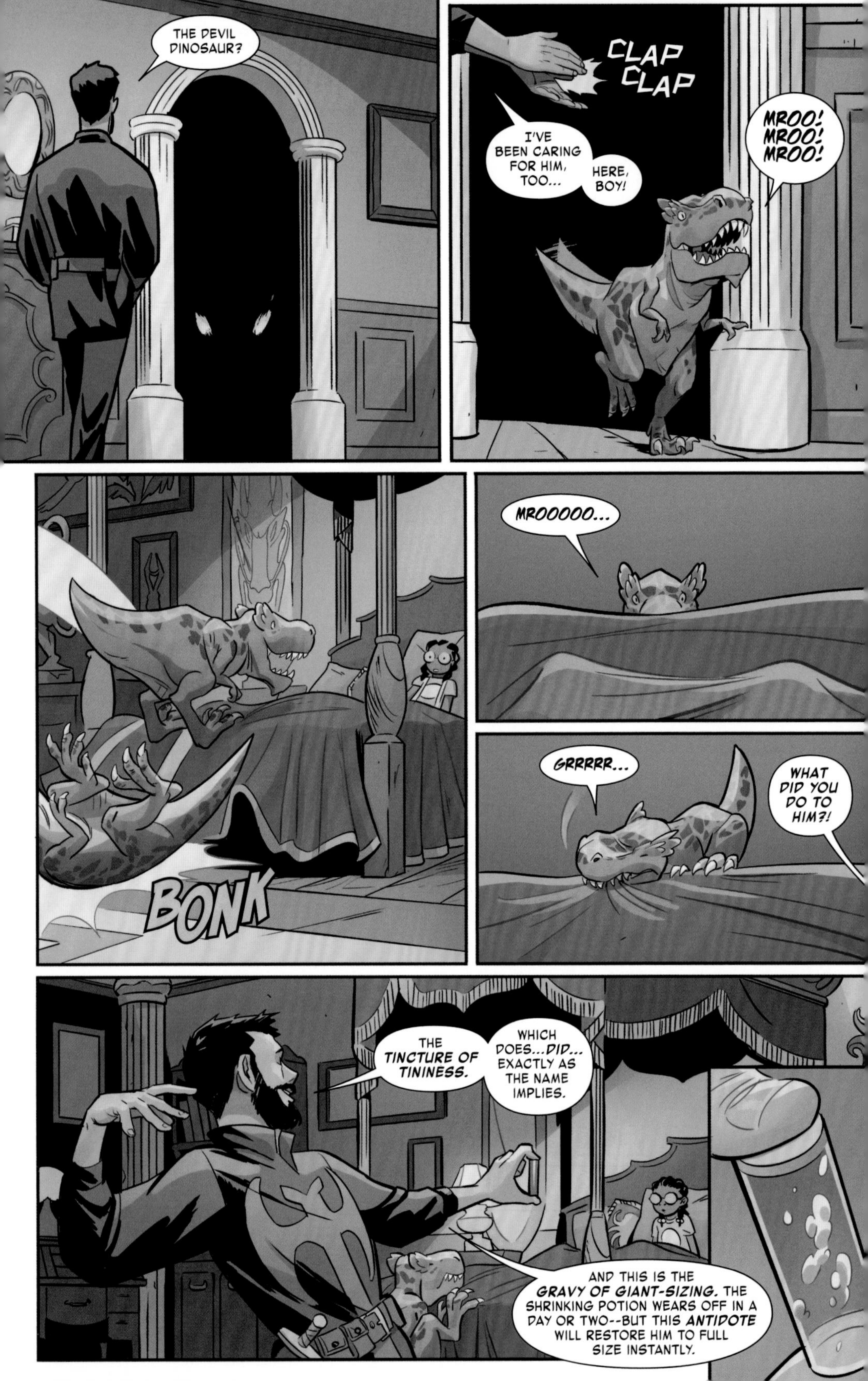
THE DEVIL DINOSAUR?
CLAP CLAP
I'VE BEEN CARING FOR HIM, TOO...
HERE, BOY!
MROO! MROO! MROO!
BONK
MROOOOO...
GRRRRR...
WHAT DID YOU DO TO HIM?!
THE TINCTURE OF TININESS.
WHICH DOES...DID... EXACTLY AS THE NAME IMPLIES.
AND THIS IS THE GRAVY OF GIANT-SIZING. THE SHRINKING POTION WEARS OFF IN A DAY OR TWO--BUT THIS ANTIDOTE WILL RESTORE HIM TO FULL SIZE INSTANTLY.

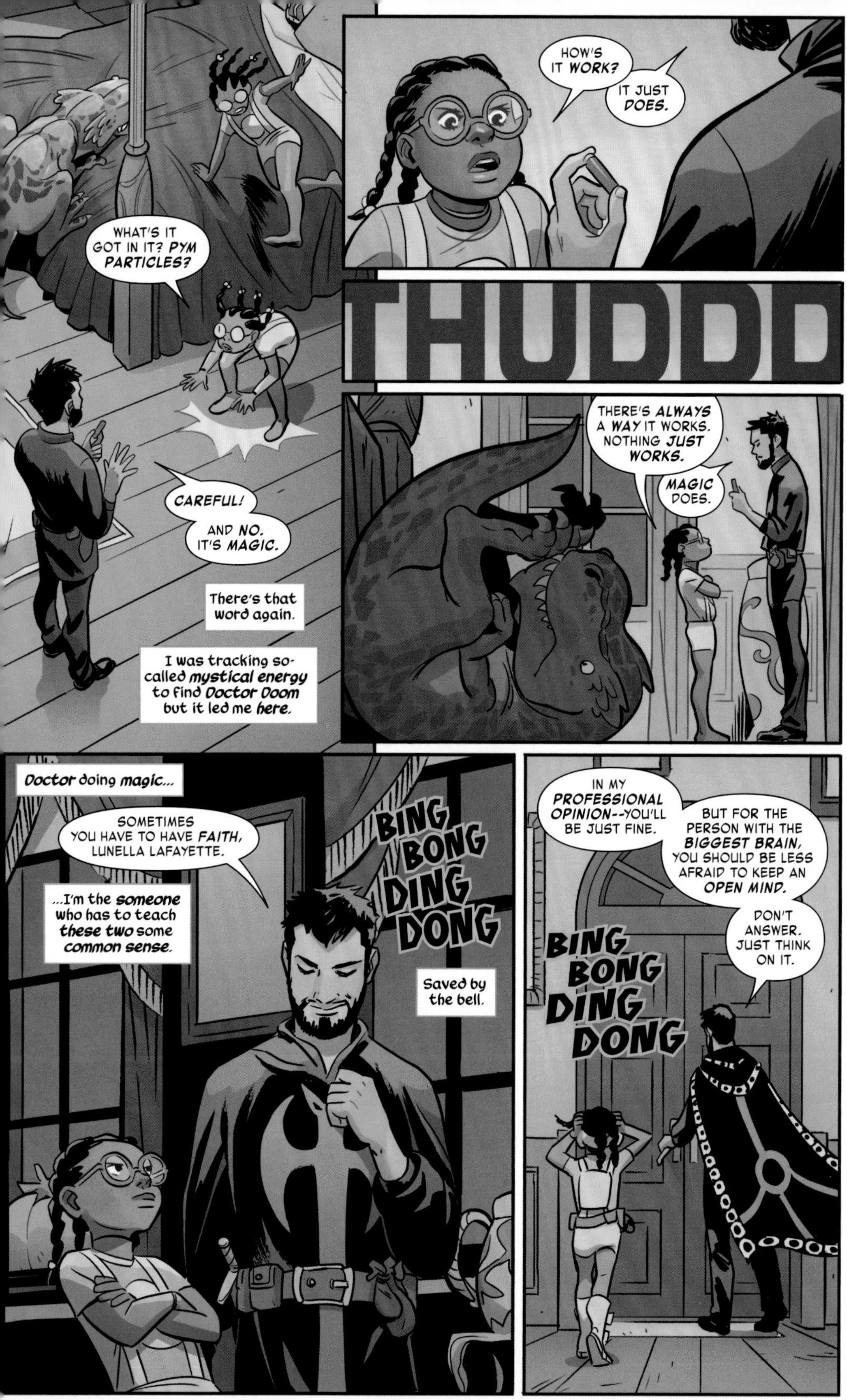

WHAT'S IT GOT IN IT? PYM PARTICLES?
CAREFUL!
AND NO. IT'S MAGIC.
There's that word again.
I was tracking so-called mystical energy to find Doctor Doom but it led me here.
HOW'S IT WORK?
IT JUST DOES.
THUDDD
THERE'S ALWAYS A WAY IT WORKS. NOTHING JUST WORKS.
MAGIC DOES.
Doctor doing magic...
SOMETIMES YOU HAVE TO HAVE FAITH, LUNELLA LAFAYETTE.
...I'm the someone who has to teach these two some common sense.
BING BONG DING DONG
Saved by the bell.
IN MY PROFESSIONAL OPINION--YOU'LL BE JUST FINE.
BUT FOR THE PERSON WITH THE BIGGEST BRAIN, YOU SHOULD BE LESS AFRAID TO KEEP AN OPEN MIND.
DON'T ANSWER. JUST THINK ON IT.
BING BONG DING DONG

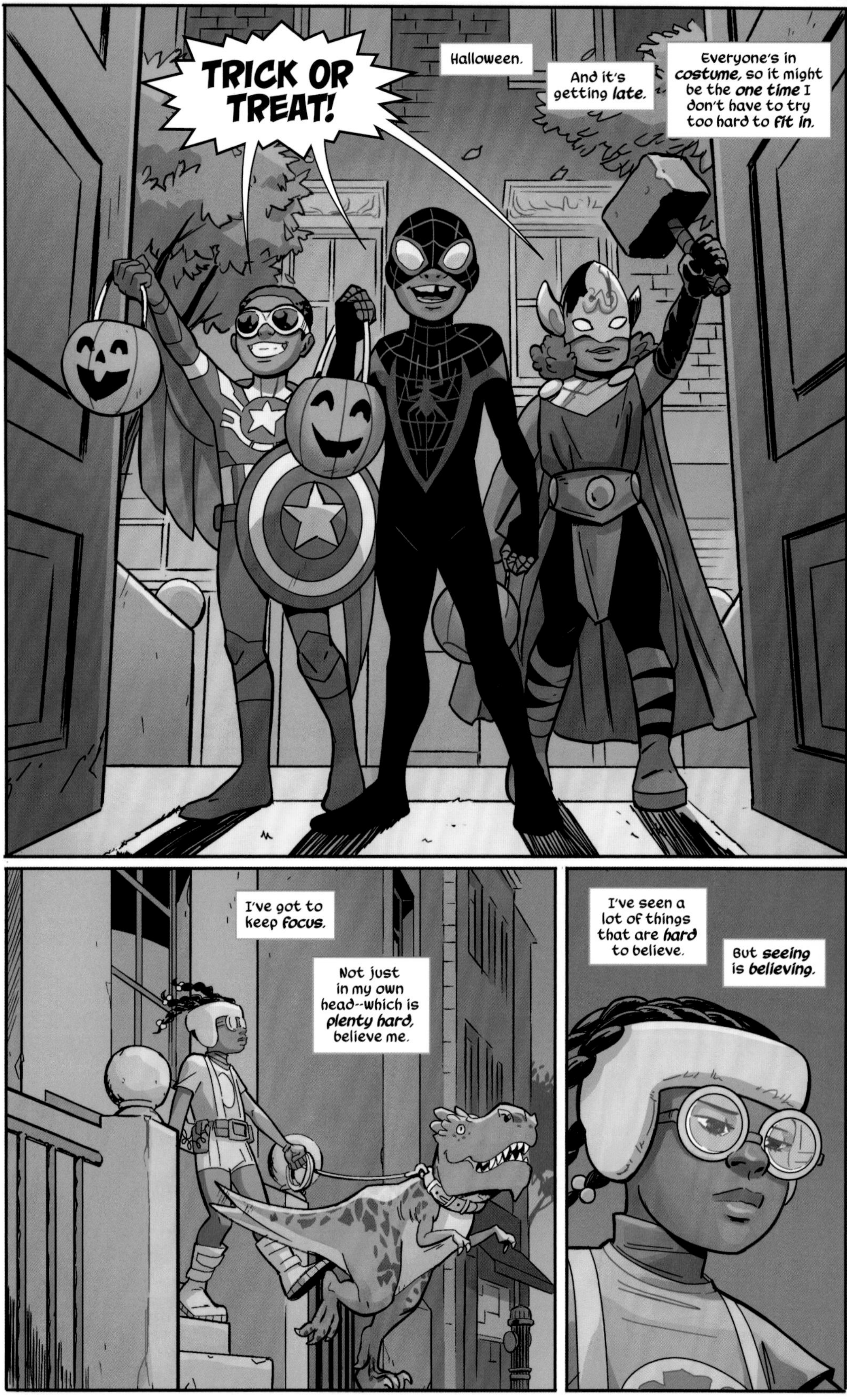
TRICK OR TREAT!
Halloween.
And it's getting late.
Everyone's in costume, so it might be the one time I don't have to try too hard to fit in.
I've got to keep focus.
Not just in my own head--which is plenty hard, believe me.
I've seen a lot of things that are hard to believe.
But seeing is believing.

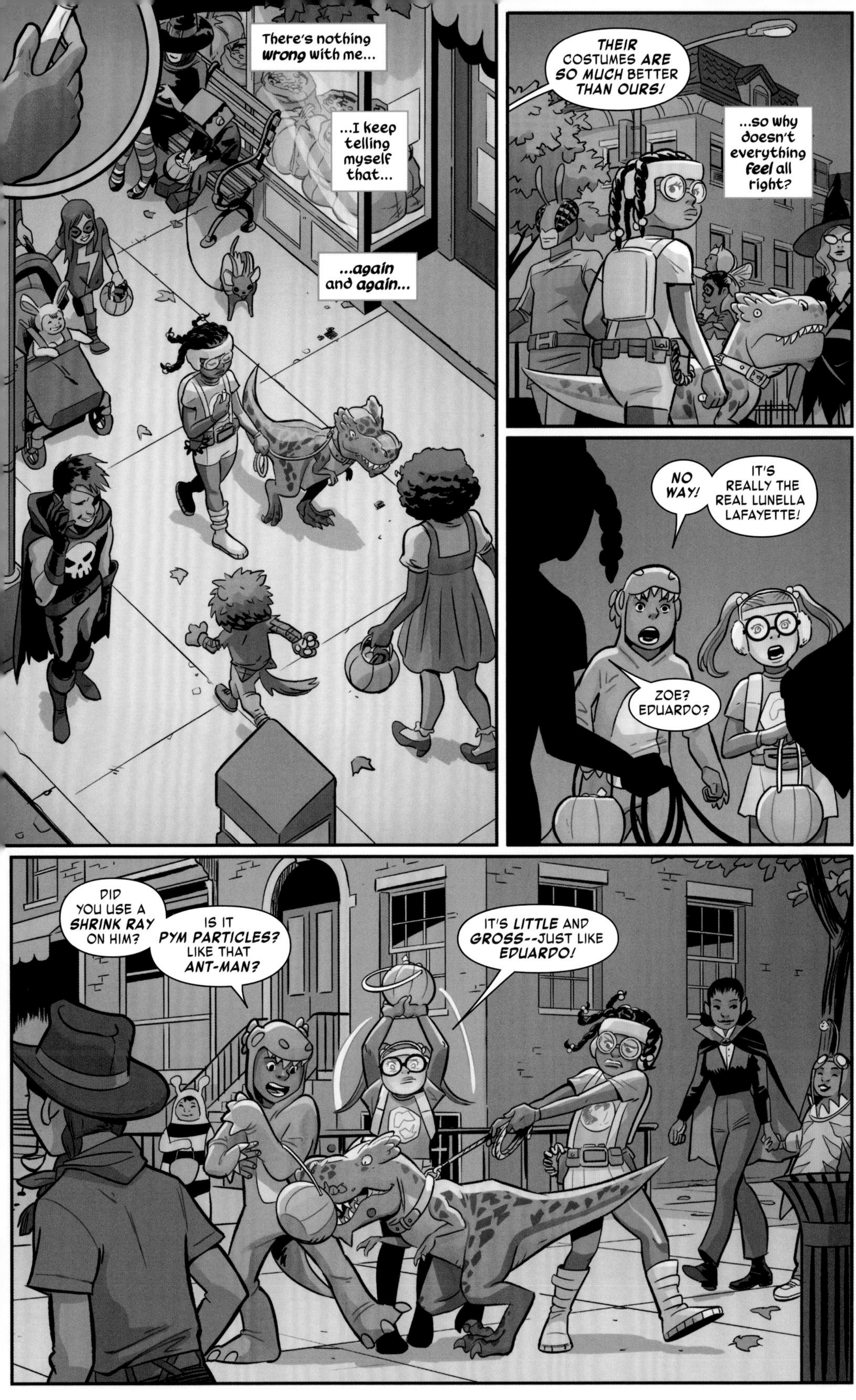
There's nothing wrong with me...
...I keep telling myself that...
...again and again...
THEIR COSTUMES ARE SO MUCH BETTER THAN OURS!
...so why doesn't everything feel all right?
NO WAY!
IT'S REALLY THE REAL LUNELLA LAFAYETTE!
ZOE? EDUARDO?
DID YOU USE A SHRINK RAY ON HIM?
IS IT PYM PARTICLES? LIKE THAT ANT-MAN?
IT'S LITTLE AND GROSS--JUST LIKE EDUARDO!

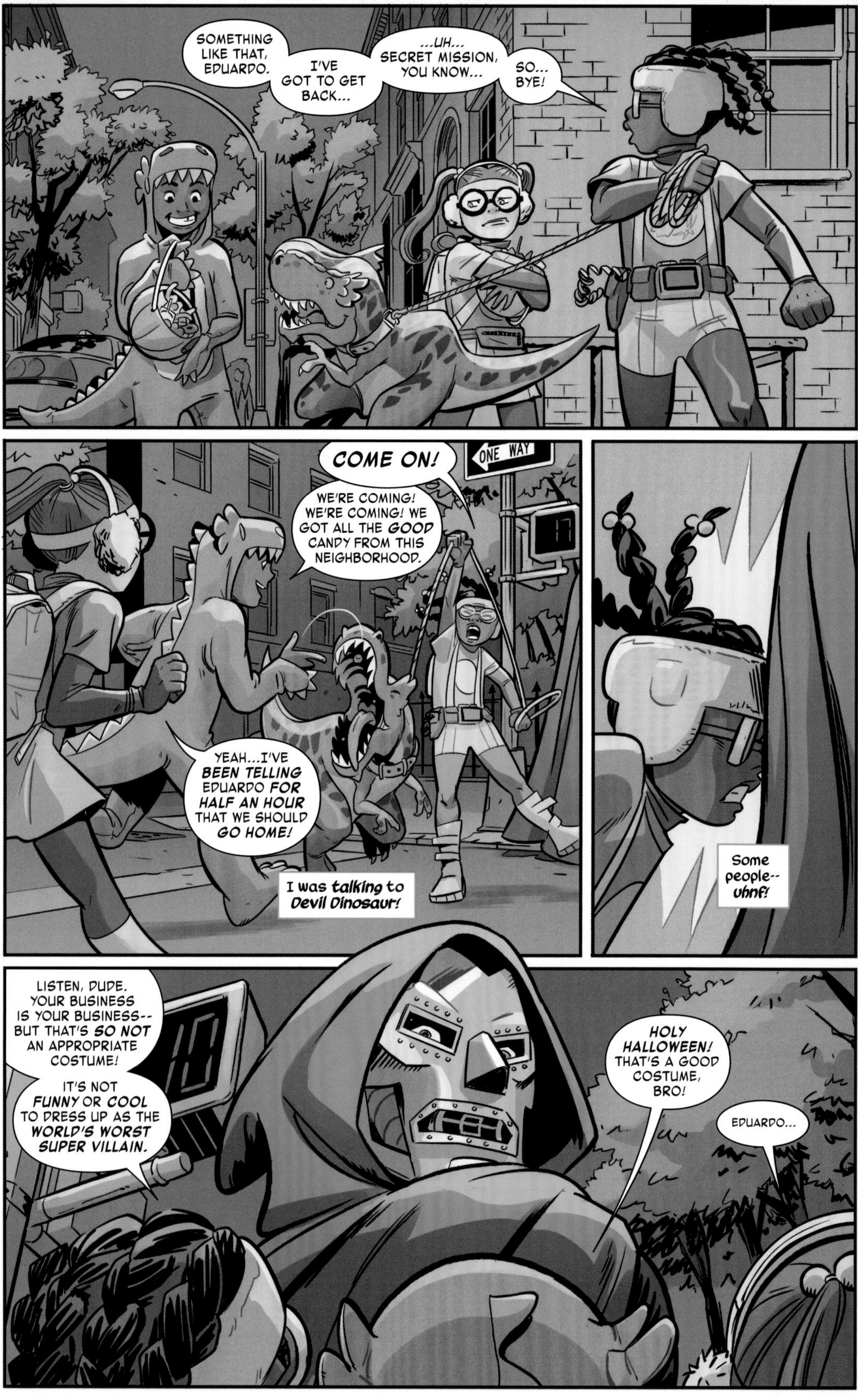
SOMETHING LIKE THAT, EDUARDO.
I'VE GOT TO GET BACK...
...UH... SECRET MISSION, YOU KNOW...
SO... BYE!
ONE WAY
COME ON!
WE'RE COMING! WE'RE COMING! WE GOT ALL THE GOOD CANDY FROM THIS NEIGHBORHOOD.
YEAH...I'VE BEEN TELLING EDUARDO FOR HALF AN HOUR THAT WE SHOULD GO HOME!
I was talking to Devil Dinosaur!
Some people-- uhnf!
LISTEN, DUDE. YOUR BUSINESS IS YOUR BUSINESS-- BUT THAT'S SO NOT AN APPROPRIATE COSTUME!
IT'S NOT FUNNY OR COOL TO DRESS UP AS THE WORLD'S WORST SUPER VILLAIN.
HOLY HALLOWEEN! THAT'S A GOOD COSTUME, BRO!
EDUARDO...

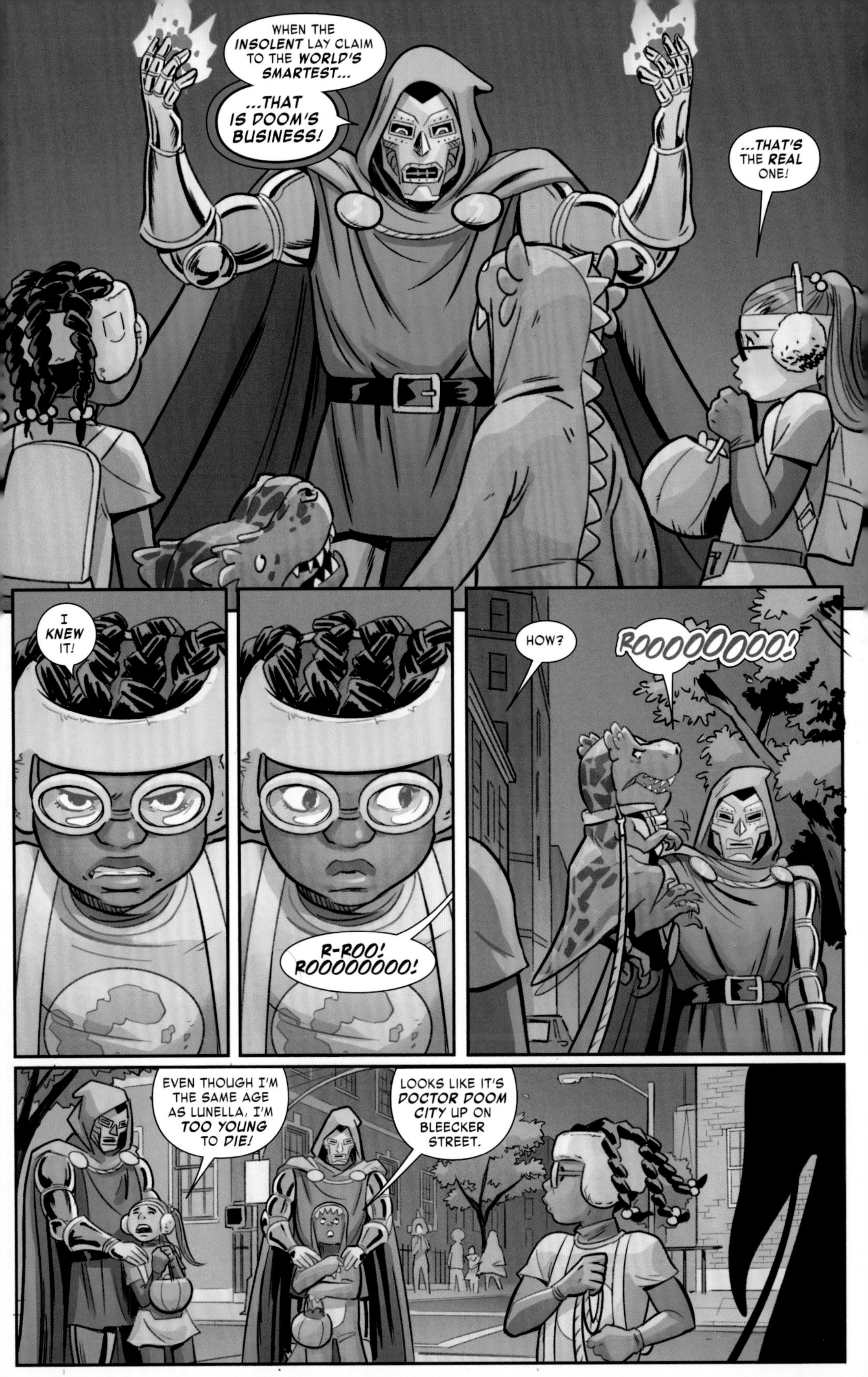
WHEN THE INSOLENT LAY CLAIM TO THE WORLD'S SMARTEST...
...THAT IS DOOM'S BUSINESS!
...THAT'S THE REAL ONE!
I KNEW IT!
R-ROO! ROOOOOOOO!
HOW?
ROOOOOOOOO!
EVEN THOUGH I'M THE SAME AGE AS LUNELLA, I'M TOO YOUNG TO DIE!
LOOKS LIKE IT'S DOCTOR DOOM CITY UP ON BLEECKER STREET.

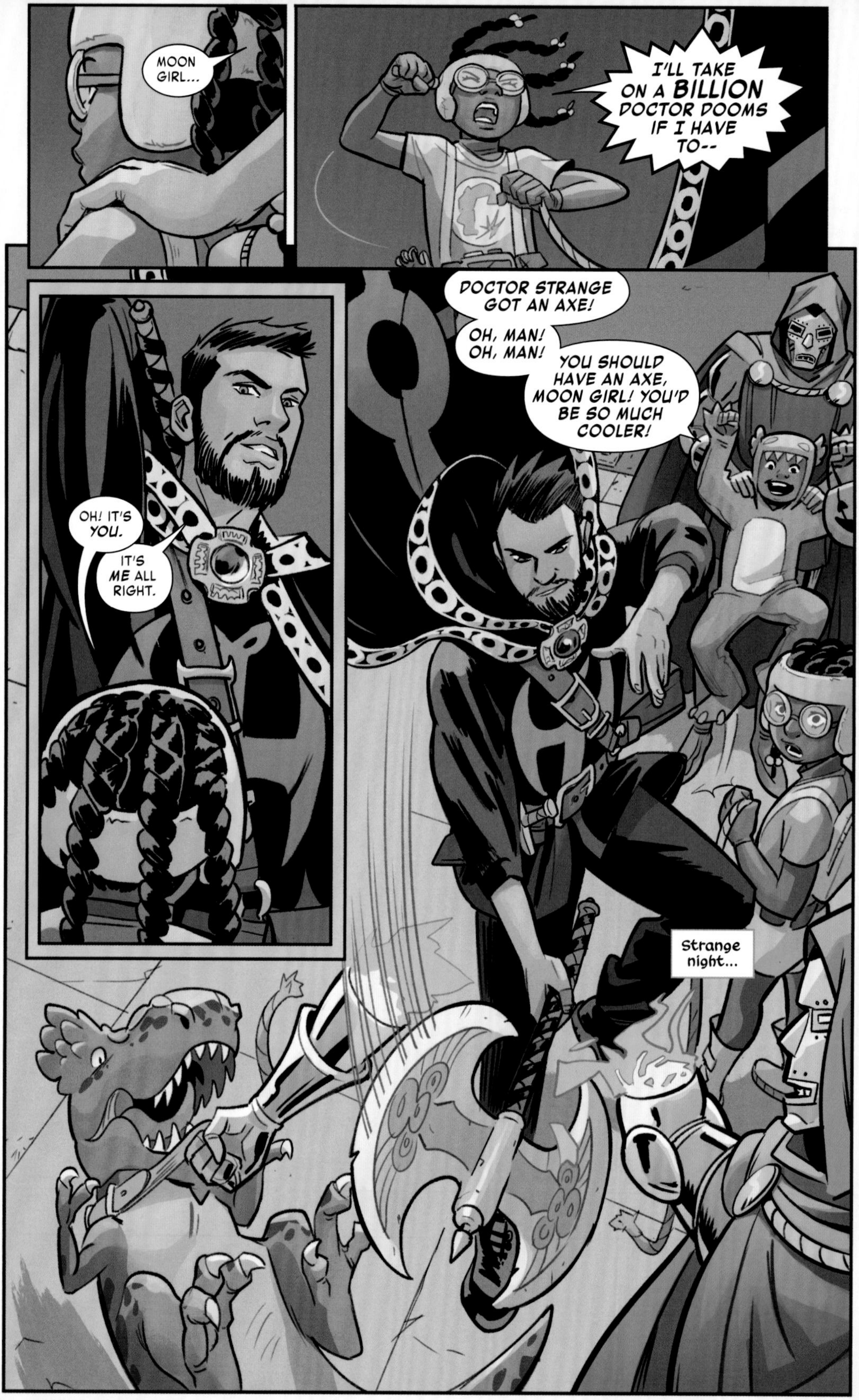
MOON GIRL...
I'LL TAKE ON A BILLION DOCTOR DOOMS IF I HAVE TO--
OH! IT'S YOU.
IT'S ME ALL RIGHT.
DOCTOR STRANGE GOT AN AXE!
OH, MAN! OH, MAN!
YOU SHOULD HAVE AN AXE, MOON GIRL! YOU'D BE SO MUCH COOLER!
Strange night...

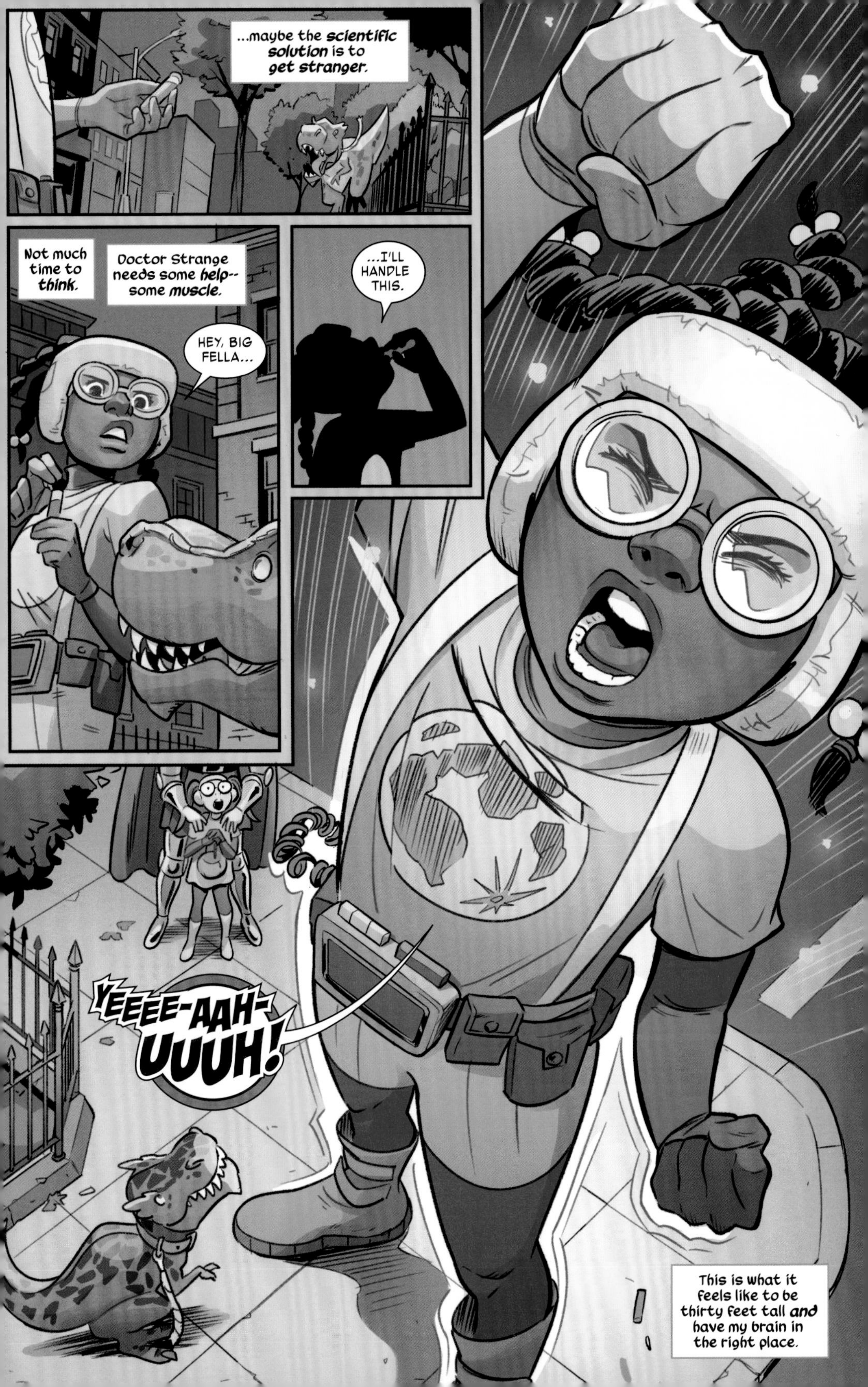
...maybe the scientific solution is to get stranger.
Not much time to think.
Doctor Strange needs some help-- some muscle.
HEY, BIG FELLA...
...I'LL HANDLE THIS.
YEEEE-AAH-UUUH!
This is what it feels like to be thirty feet tall and have my brain in the right place.

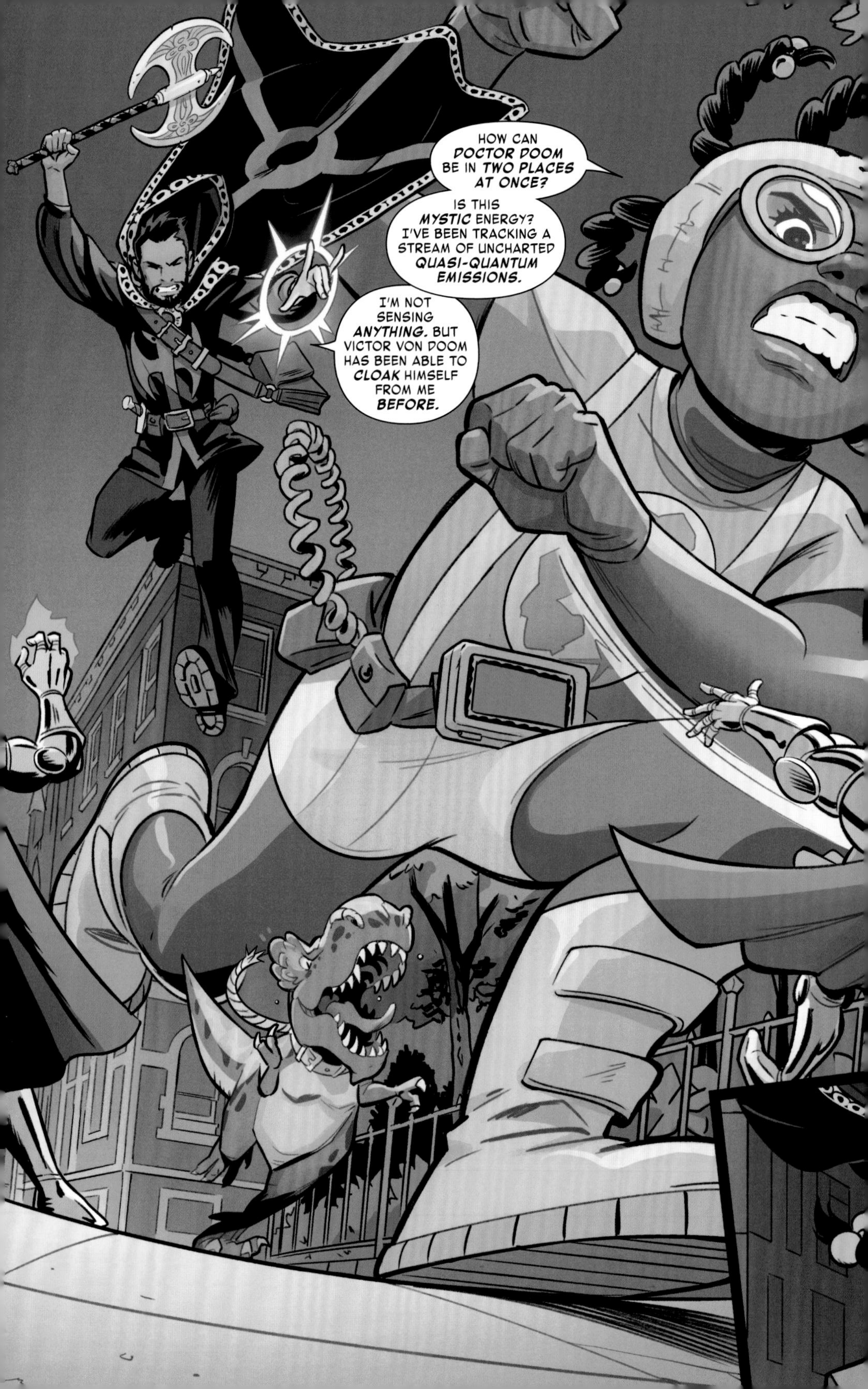
HOW CAN DOCTOR DOOM BE IN TWO PLACES AT ONCE?
IS THIS MYSTIC ENERGY? I'VE BEEN TRACKING A STREAM OF UNCHARTED QUASI-QUANTUM EMISSIONS.
I'M NOT SENSING ANYTHING. BUT VICTOR VON DOOM HAS BEEN ABLE TO CLOAK HIMSELF FROM ME BEFORE.

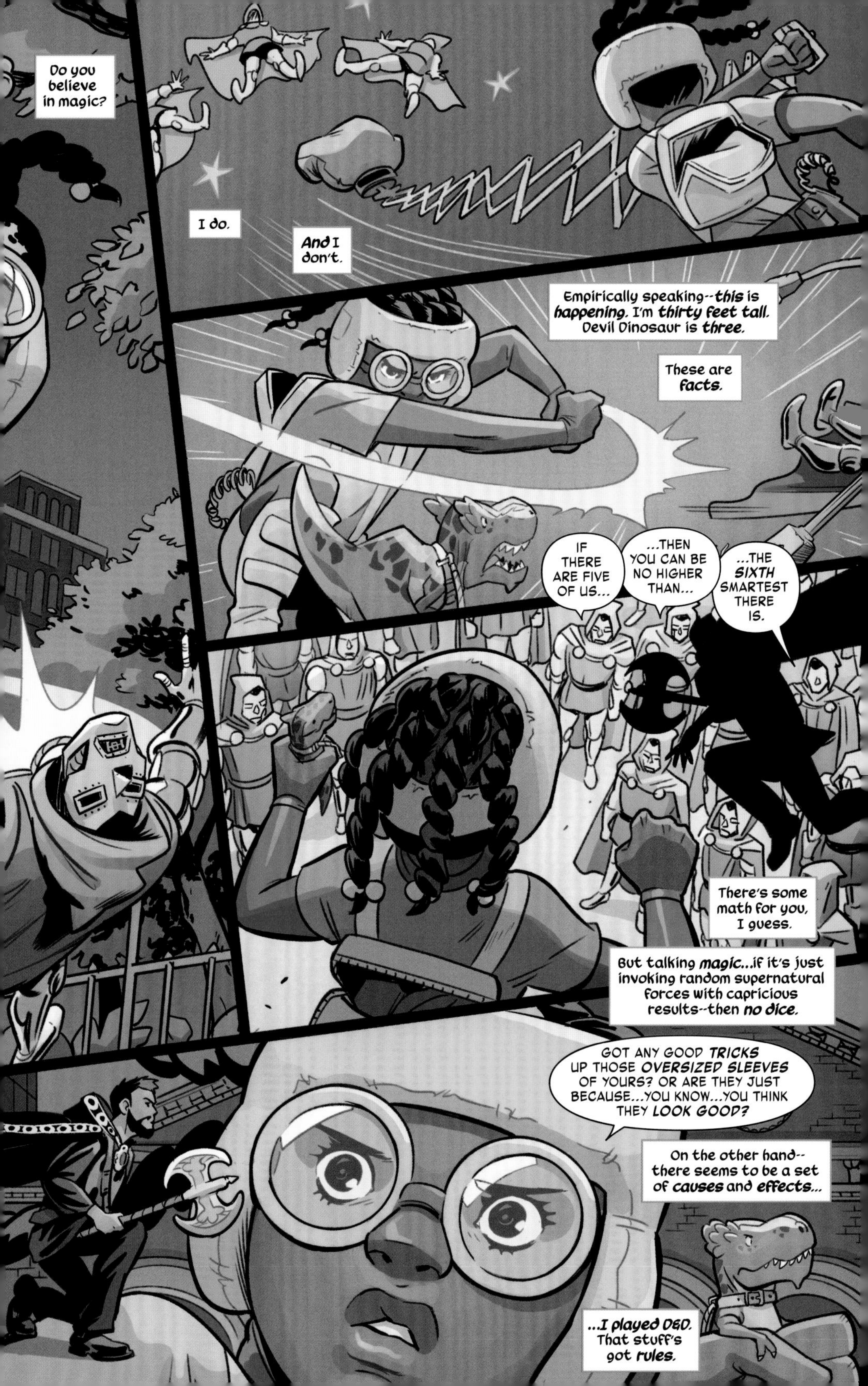
Do you believe in magic?
I do.
And I don't.
Empirically speaking--this is happening. I'm thirty feet tall. Devil Dinosaur is three.
These are facts.
IF THERE ARE FIVE OF US...
...THEN YOU CAN BE NO HIGHER THAN...
...THE SIXTH SMARTEST THERE IS.
There's some math for you, I guess.
But talking magic...if it's just invoking random supernatural forces with capricious results--then no dice.
GOT ANY GOOD TRICKS UP THOSE OVERSIZED SLEEVES OF YOURS? OR ARE THEY JUST BECAUSE...YOU KNOW...YOU THINK THEY LOOK GOOD?
On the other hand-- there seems to be a set of causes and effects...
...I played D&D. That stuff's got rules.

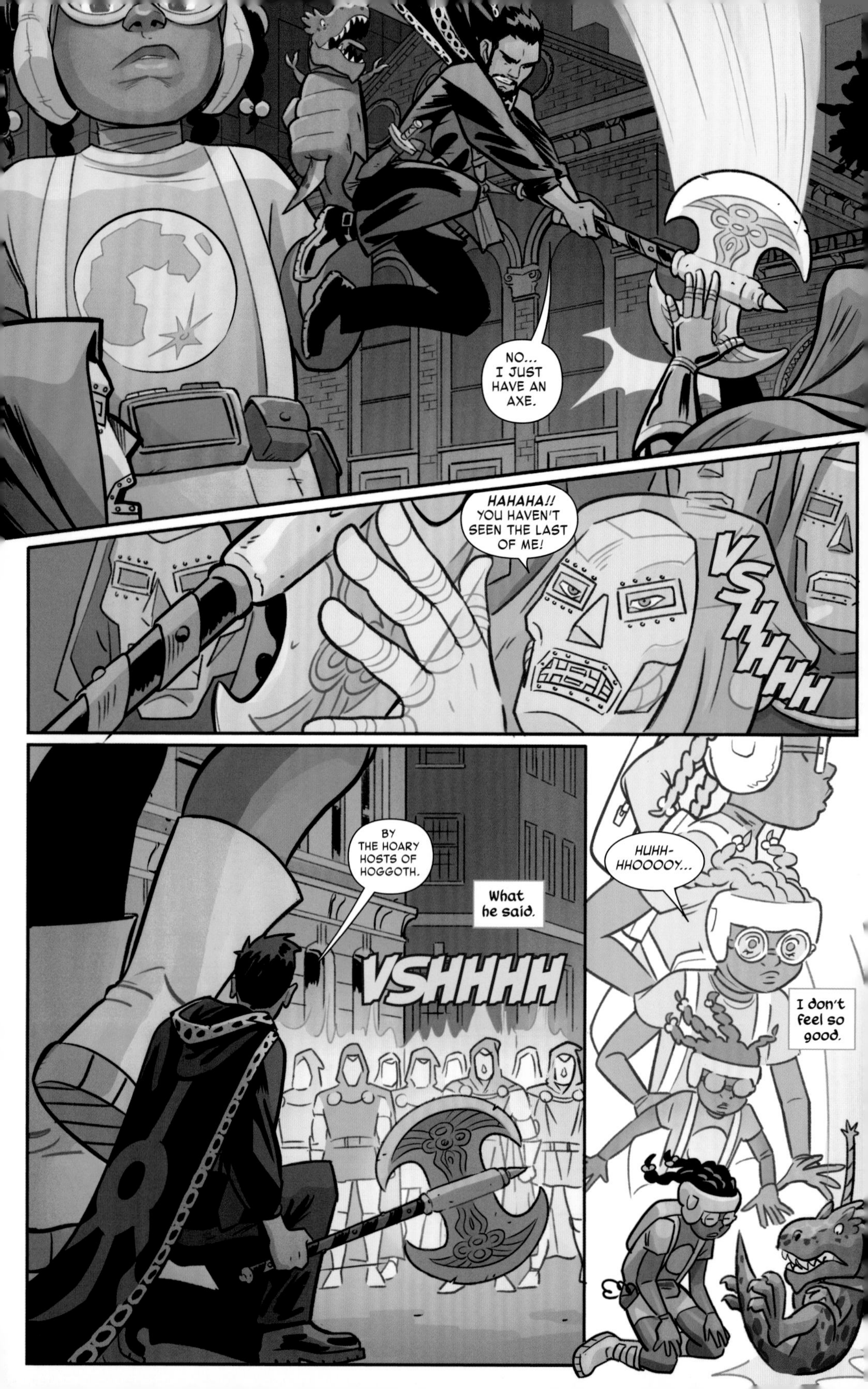
NO... I JUST HAVE AN AXE.
HAHAHA!! YOU HAVEN'T SEEN THE LAST OF ME!
VSHHHHH
BY THE HOARY HOSTS OF HOGGOTH.
What he said.
VSHHHH
HUHH-HHOOOOY...
I don't feel so good.

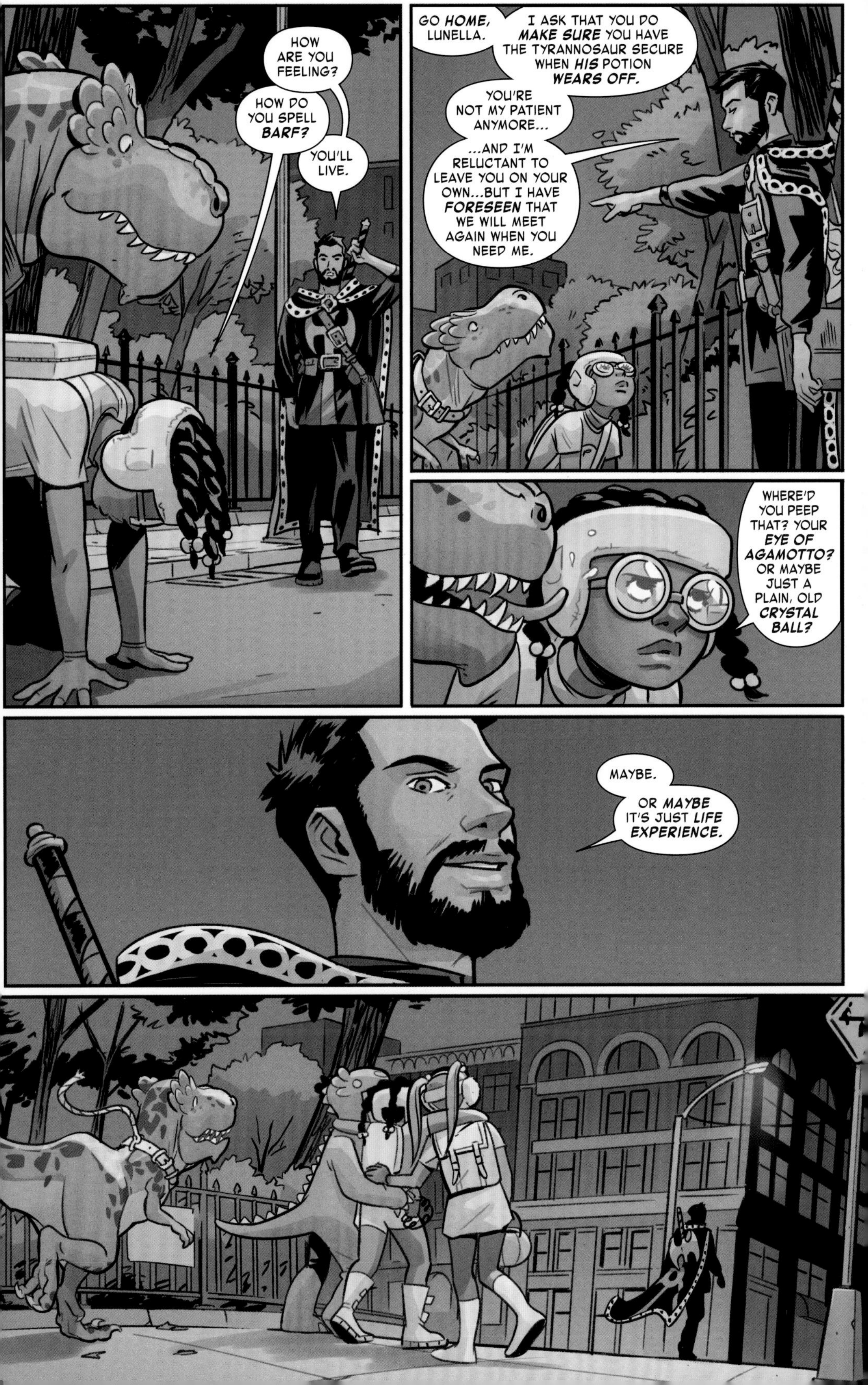
HOW ARE YOU FEELING?
HOW DO YOU SPELL BARF?
YOU'LL LIVE.
GO HOME, LUNELLA.
I ASK THAT YOU DO MAKE SURE YOU HAVE THE TYRANNOSAUR SECURE WHEN HIS POTION WEARS OFF.
YOU'RE NOT MY PATIENT ANYMORE...
...AND I'M RELUCTANT TO LEAVE YOU ON YOUR OWN...BUT I HAVE FORESEEN THAT WE WILL MEET AGAIN WHEN YOU NEED ME.
WHERE'D YOU PEEP THAT? YOUR EYE OF AGAMOTTO? OR MAYBE JUST A PLAIN, OLD CRYSTAL BALL?
MAYBE.
OR MAYBE IT'S JUST LIFE EXPERIENCE.

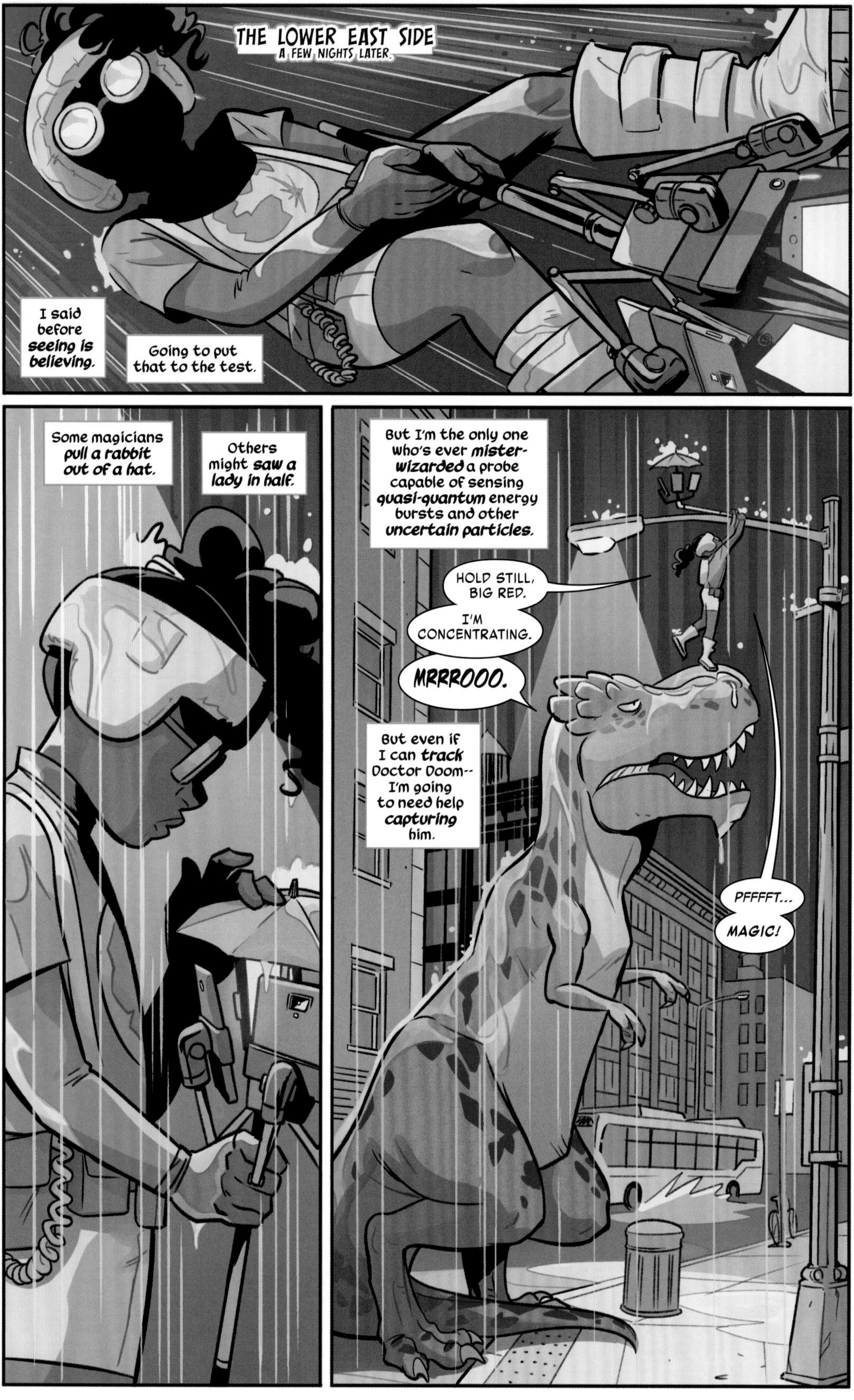
THE LOWER EAST SIDE
A FEW NIGHTS LATER.
I said before seeing is believing.
Going to put that to the test.
Some magicians pull a rabbit out of a hat.
Others might saw a lady in half.
But I'm the only one who's ever mister-wizarded a probe capable of sensing quasi-quantum energy bursts and other uncertain particles.
HOLD STILL, BIG RED.
I'M CONCENTRATING.
MRRROOO.
But even if I can track Doctor Doom-- I'm going to need help capturing him.
PFFFFT... MAGIC!

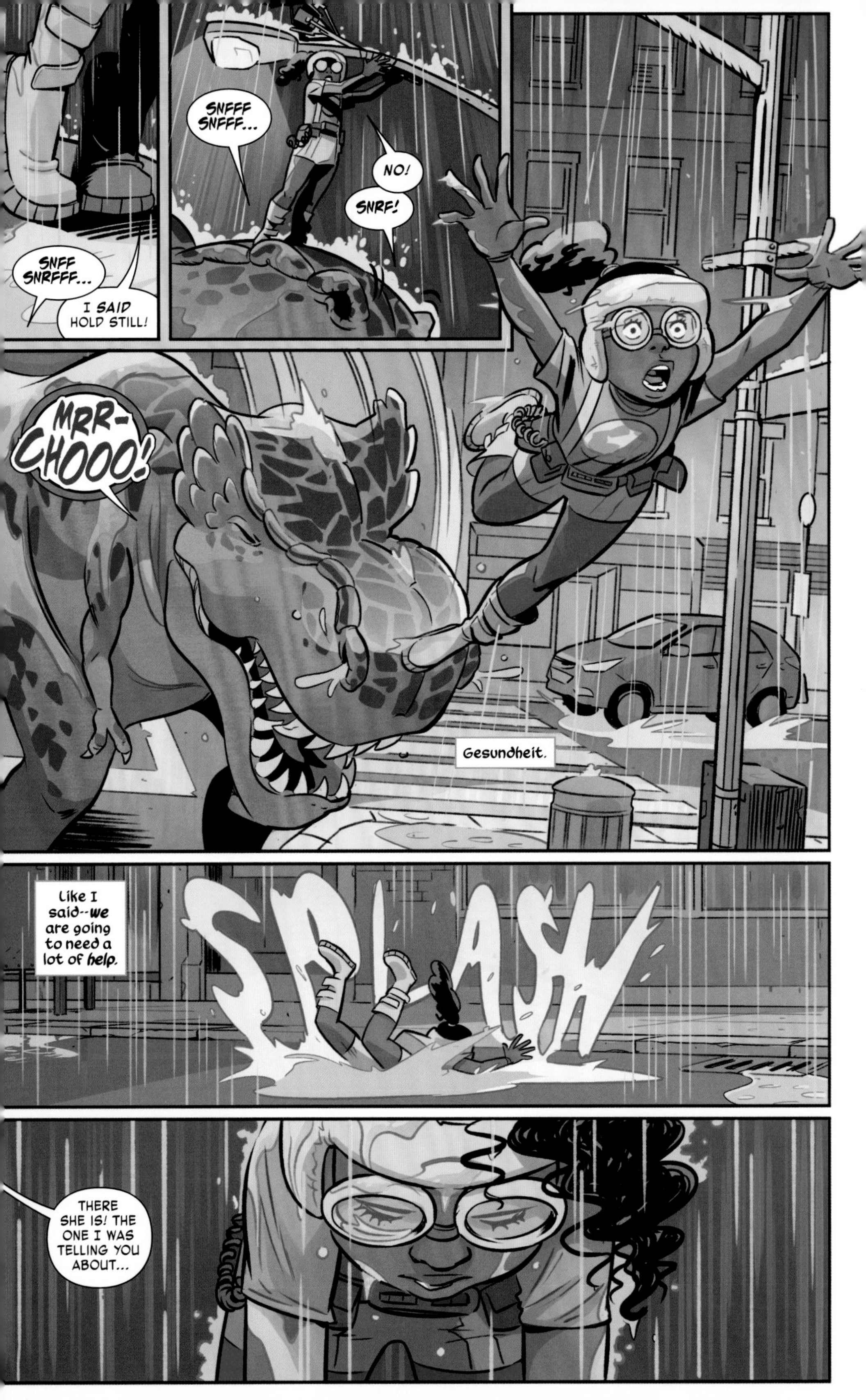
SNFF SNRFFF...
I SAID HOLD STILL!
SNFFF SNFFF...
NO!
SNRF!
MRR-CHOOO!
Gesundheit.
Like I said--we are going to need a lot of help.
SPLASH
THERE SHE IS! THE ONE I WAS TELLING YOU ABOUT...

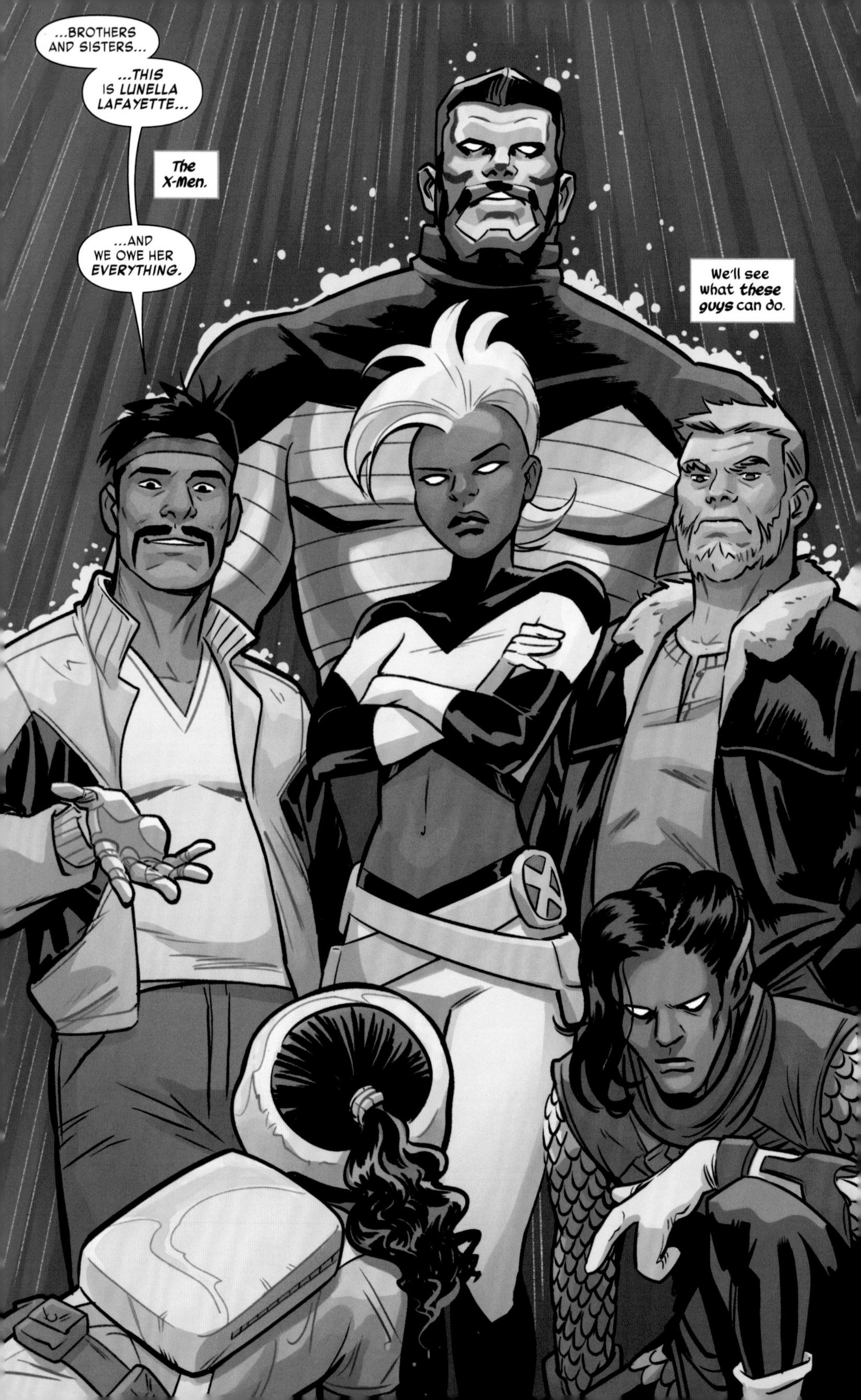
...BROTHERS AND SISTERS...
...THIS IS LUNELLA LAFAYETTE...
The X-Men.
...AND WE OWE HER EVERYTHING.
We'll see what these guys can do.

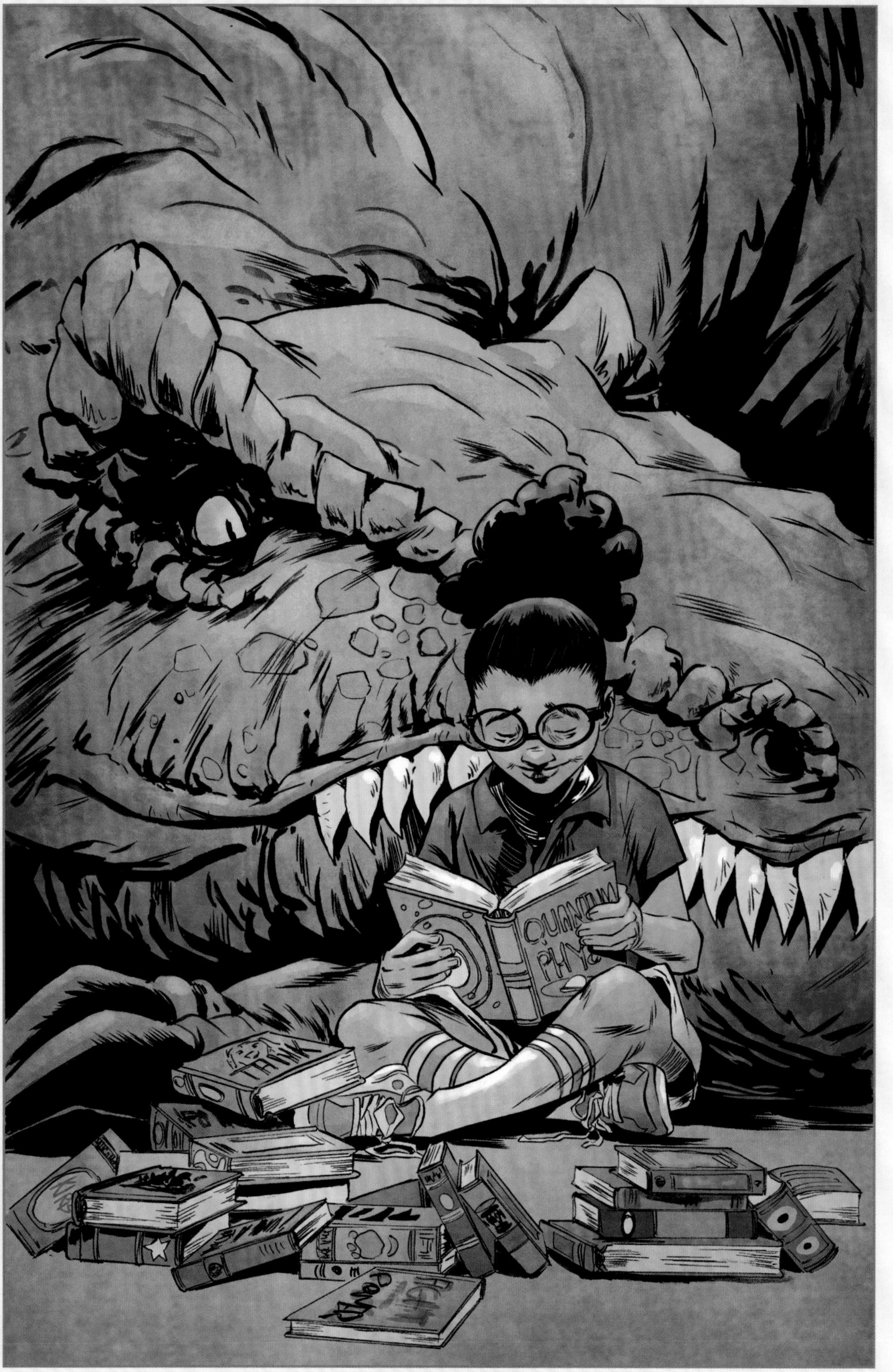

#13 VARIANT
BY SANFORD GREENE

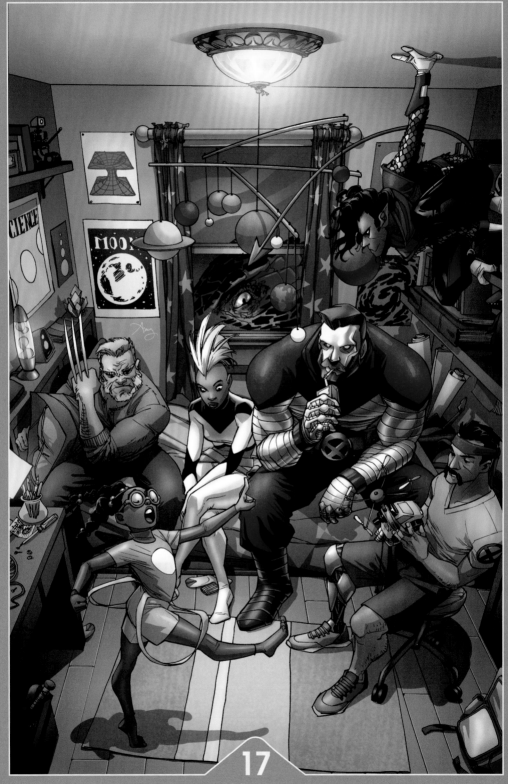

17

"X EQUALS"

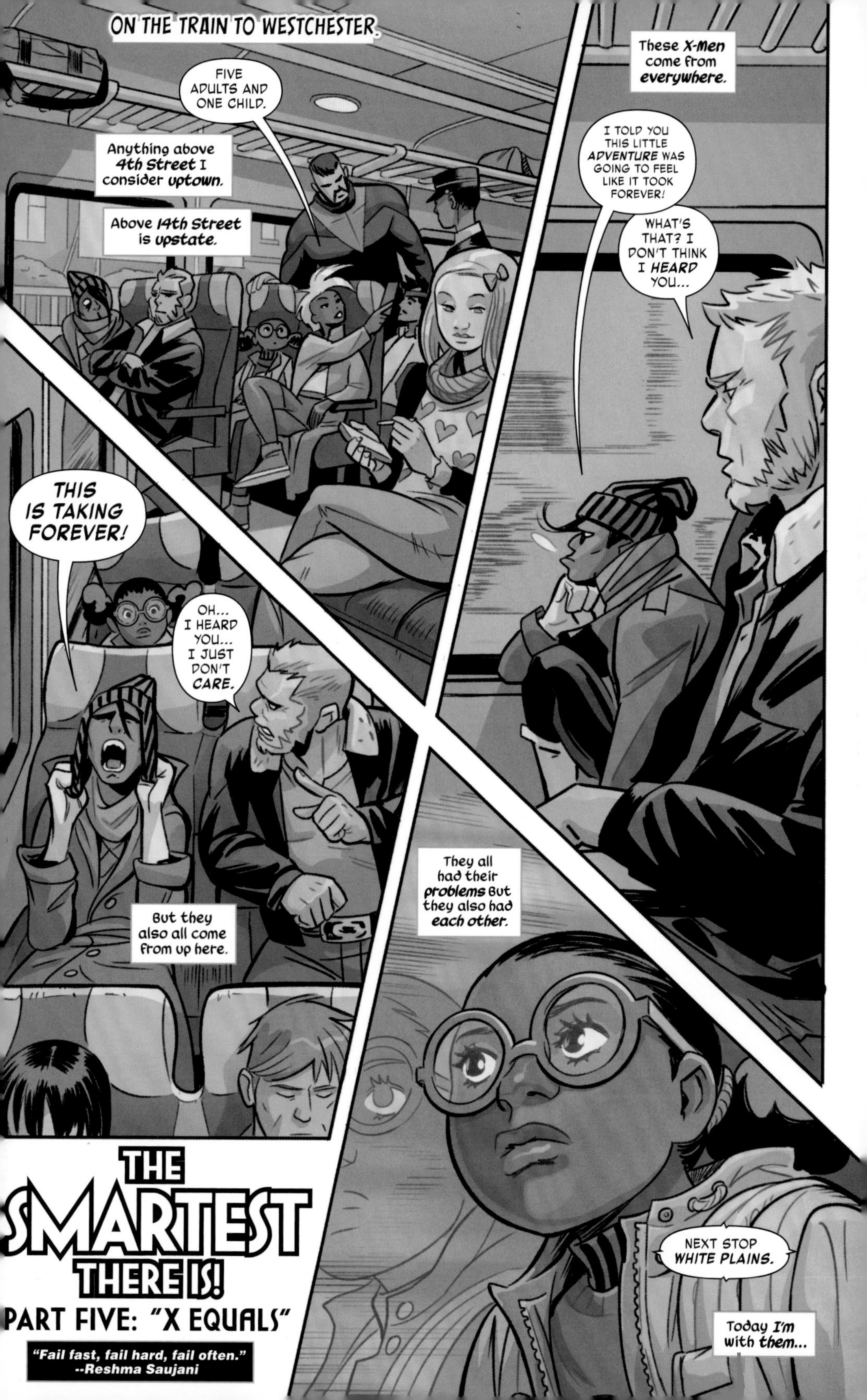
ON THE TRAIN TO WESTCHESTER.
Anything above 4th Street I consider uptown.
FIVE ADULTS AND ONE CHILD.
Above 14th Street is upstate.
These X-Men come from everywhere.
I TOLD YOU THIS LITTLE ADVENTURE WAS GOING TO FEEL LIKE IT TOOK FOREVER!
WHAT'S THAT? I DON'T THINK I HEARD YOU...
THIS IS TAKING FOREVER!
OH... I HEARD YOU... I JUST DON'T CARE.
But they also all come from up here.
They all had their problems But they also had each other.
NEXT STOP WHITE PLAINS.
Today I'm with them...
THE SMARTEST THERE IS!
PART FIVE: "X EQUALS"
"Fail fast, fail hard, fail often."
--Reshma Saujani

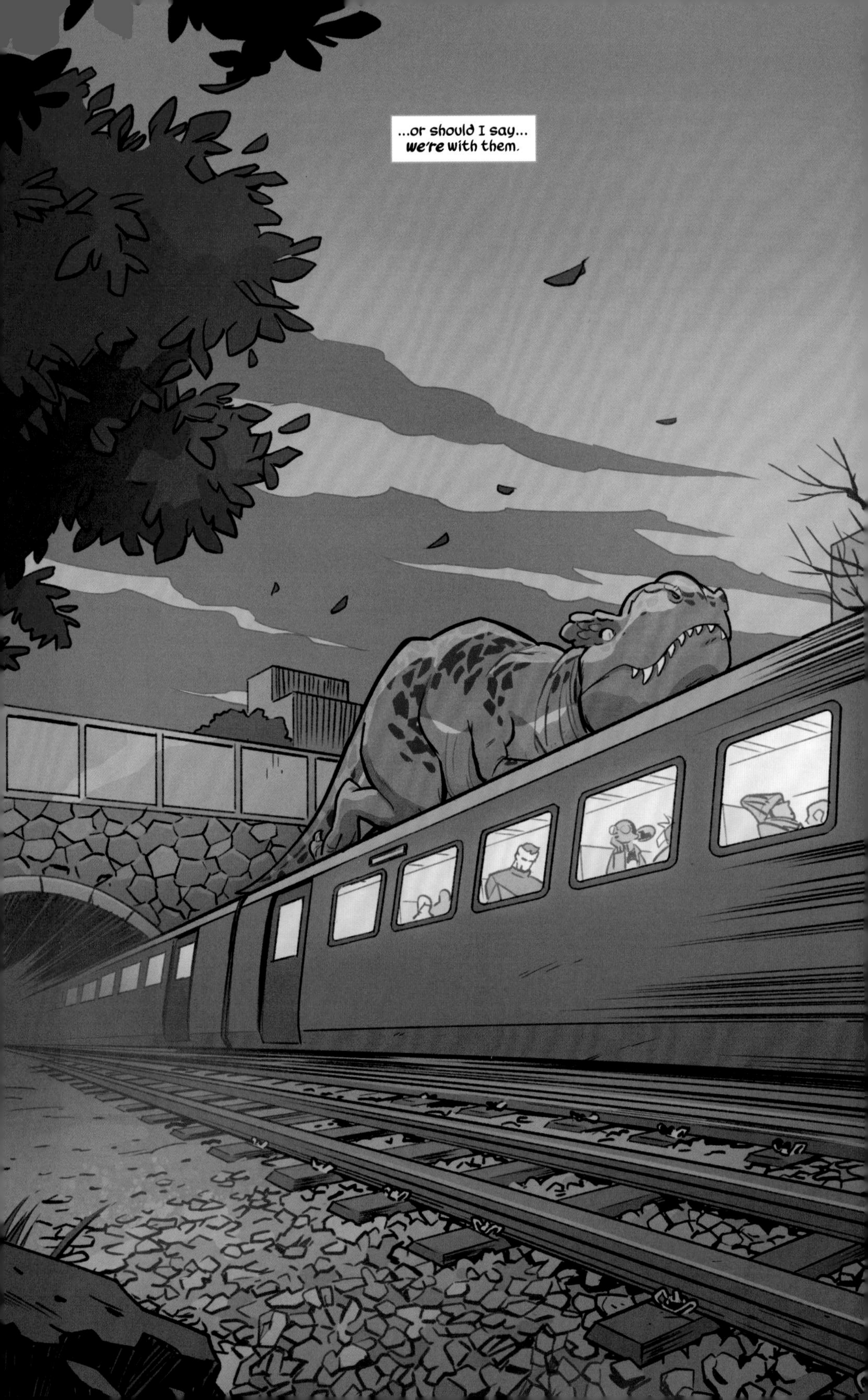
...or should I say...
we're with them.

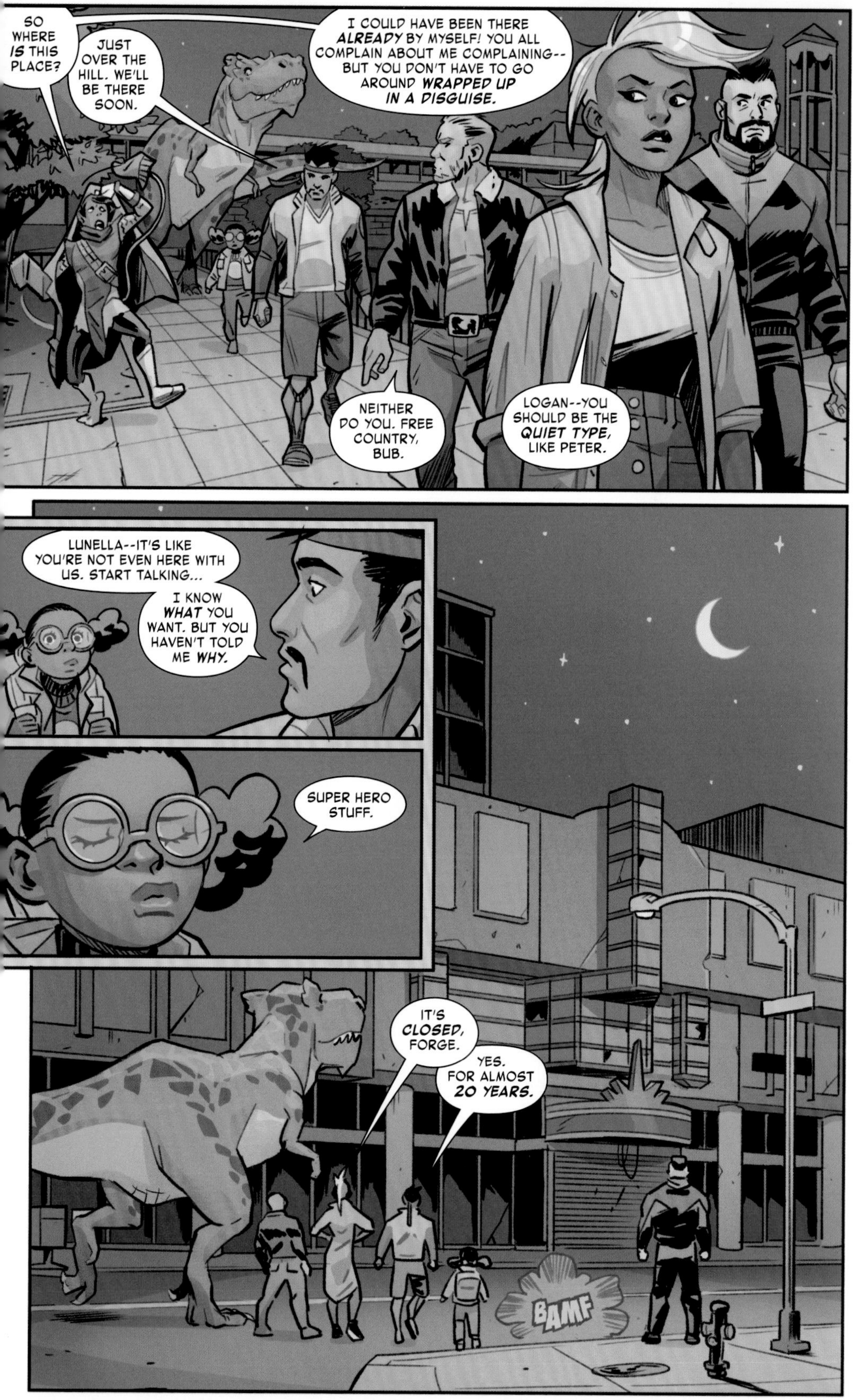
SO WHERE *IS* THIS PLACE?
JUST OVER THE HILL. WE'LL BE THERE SOON.
I COULD HAVE BEEN THERE *ALREADY* BY MYSELF! YOU ALL COMPLAIN ABOUT ME COMPLAINING-- BUT YOU DON'T HAVE TO GO AROUND *WRAPPED UP IN A DISGUISE.*
NEITHER DO YOU. FREE COUNTRY, BUB.
LOGAN--YOU SHOULD BE THE *QUIET TYPE,* LIKE PETER.
LUNELLA--IT'S LIKE YOU'RE NOT EVEN HERE WITH US. START TALKING...
I KNOW *WHAT* YOU WANT. BUT YOU HAVEN'T TOLD ME *WHY.*
SUPER HERO STUFF.
IT'S *CLOSED,* FORGE.
YES. FOR ALMOST *20 YEARS.*
BAMF

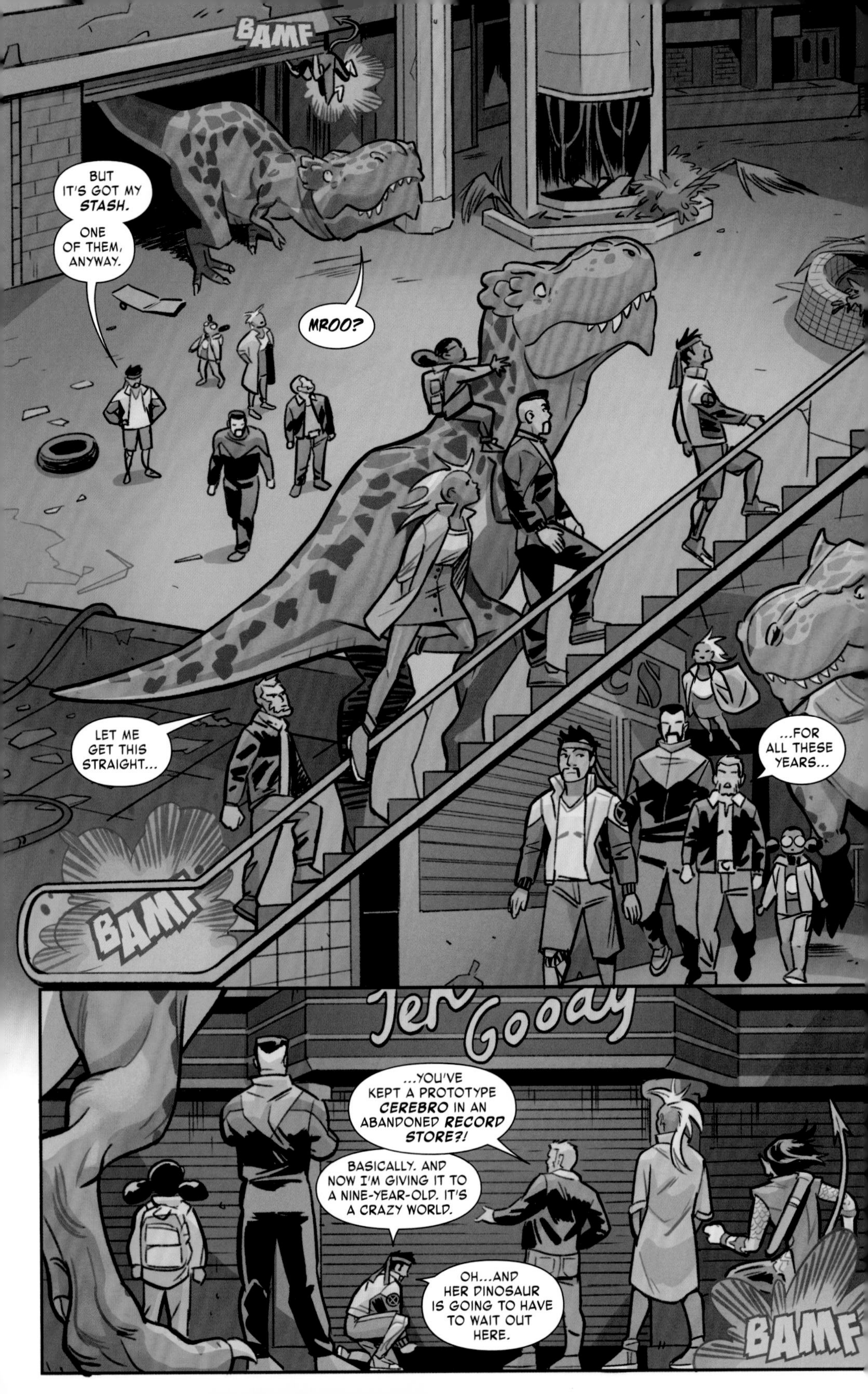
BAMF
BUT IT'S GOT MY STASH.
ONE OF THEM, ANYWAY.
MROO?
LET ME GET THIS STRAIGHT...
...FOR ALL THESE YEARS...
BAMF
...YOU'VE KEPT A PROTOTYPE CEREBRO IN AN ABANDONED RECORD STORE?!
BASICALLY. AND NOW I'M GIVING IT TO A NINE-YEAR-OLD. IT'S A CRAZY WORLD.
OH...AND HER DINOSAUR IS GOING TO HAVE TO WAIT OUT HERE.
BAMF

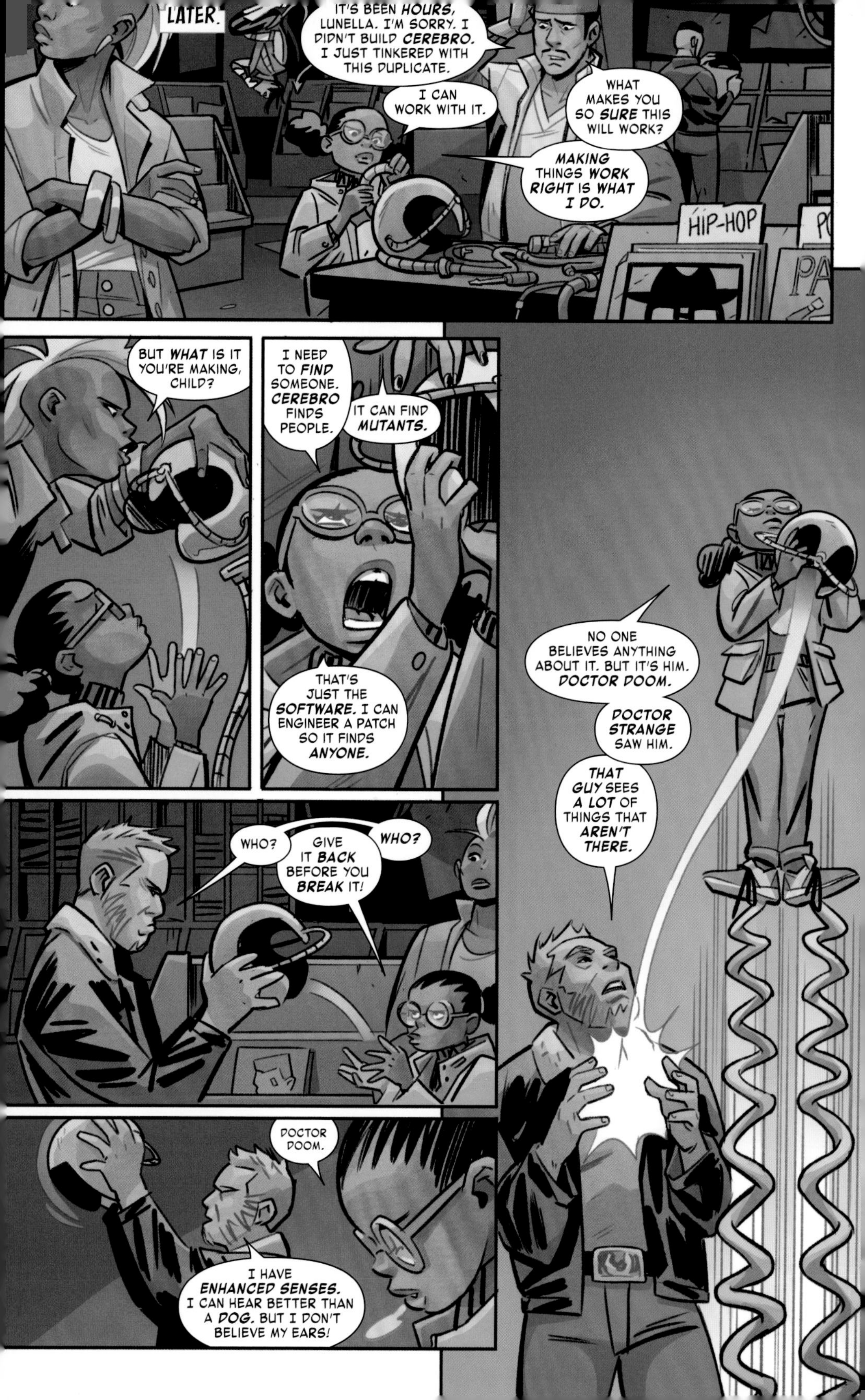
LATER.
IT'S BEEN HOURS, LUNELLA. I'M SORRY. I DIDN'T BUILD CEREBRO. I JUST TINKERED WITH THIS DUPLICATE.
I CAN WORK WITH IT.
WHAT MAKES YOU SO SURE THIS WILL WORK?
MAKING THINGS WORK RIGHT IS WHAT I DO.
HIP-HOP
BUT WHAT IS IT YOU'RE MAKING, CHILD?
I NEED TO FIND SOMEONE. CEREBRO FINDS PEOPLE.
IT CAN FIND MUTANTS.
THAT'S JUST THE SOFTWARE. I CAN ENGINEER A PATCH SO IT FINDS ANYONE.
WHO?
GIVE IT BACK BEFORE YOU BREAK IT!
WHO?
DOCTOR DOOM.
I HAVE ENHANCED SENSES. I CAN HEAR BETTER THAN A DOG. BUT I DON'T BELIEVE MY EARS!
NO ONE BELIEVES ANYTHING ABOUT IT. BUT IT'S HIM. DOCTOR DOOM.
DOCTOR STRANGE SAW HIM.
THAT GUY SEES A LOT OF THINGS THAT AREN'T THERE.

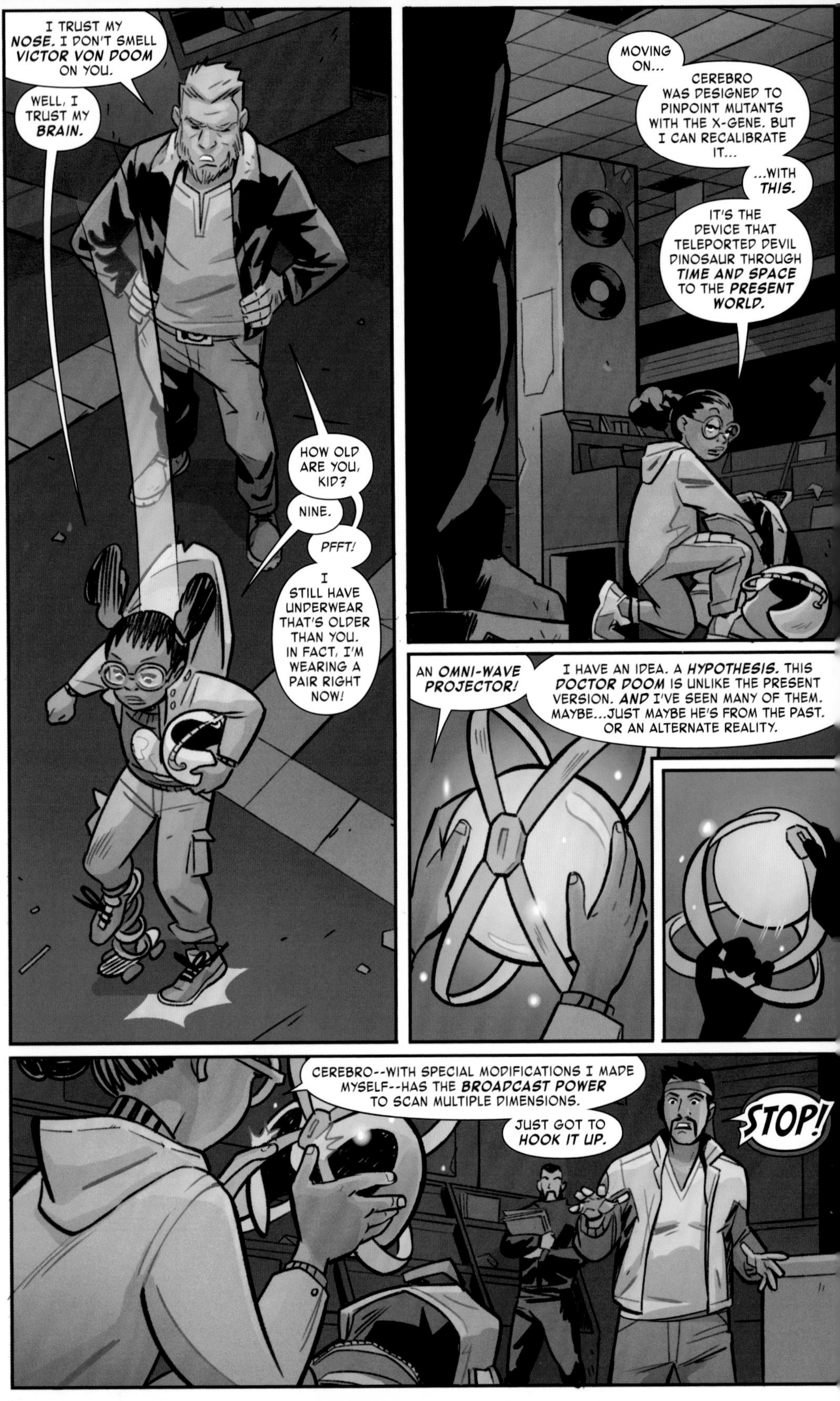
I TRUST MY NOSE. I DON'T SMELL VICTOR VON DOOM ON YOU.
WELL, I TRUST MY BRAIN.
HOW OLD ARE YOU, KID?
NINE.
PFFT!
I STILL HAVE UNDERWEAR THAT'S OLDER THAN YOU. IN FACT, I'M WEARING A PAIR RIGHT NOW!
MOVING ON...
CEREBRO WAS DESIGNED TO PINPOINT MUTANTS WITH THE X-GENE. BUT I CAN RECALIBRATE IT...
...WITH THIS.
IT'S THE DEVICE THAT TELEPORTED DEVIL DINOSAUR THROUGH TIME AND SPACE TO THE PRESENT WORLD.
AN OMNI-WAVE PROJECTOR!
I HAVE AN IDEA. A HYPOTHESIS. THIS DOCTOR DOOM IS UNLIKE THE PRESENT VERSION. AND I'VE SEEN MANY OF THEM. MAYBE...JUST MAYBE HE'S FROM THE PAST. OR AN ALTERNATE REALITY.
CEREBRO--WITH SPECIAL MODIFICATIONS I MADE MYSELF--HAS THE BROADCAST POWER TO SCAN MULTIPLE DIMENSIONS.
JUST GOT TO HOOK IT UP.
STOP!

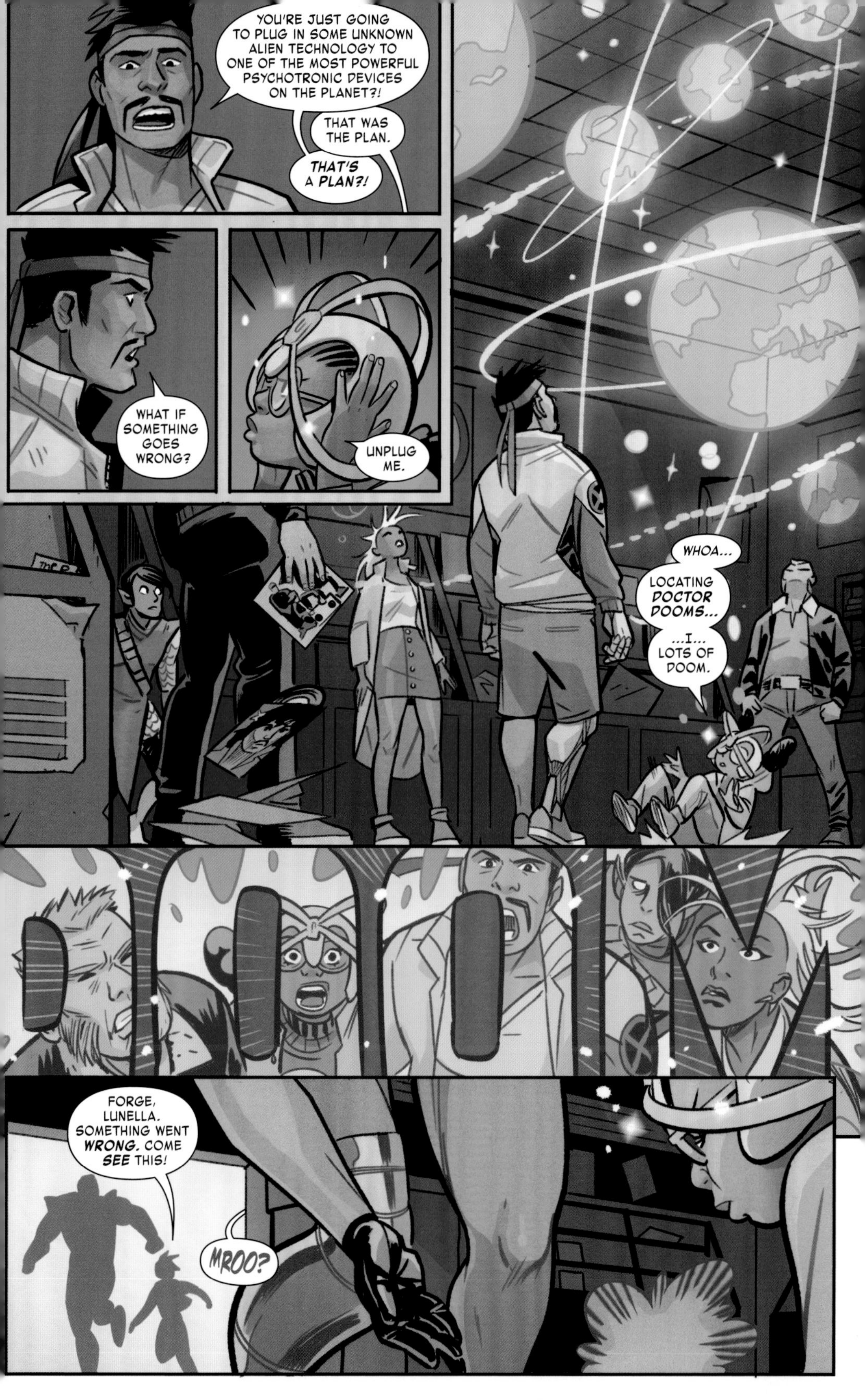
YOU'RE JUST GOING TO PLUG IN SOME UNKNOWN ALIEN TECHNOLOGY TO ONE OF THE MOST POWERFUL PSYCHOTRONIC DEVICES ON THE PLANET?!
THAT WAS THE PLAN.
THAT'S A PLAN?!
WHAT IF SOMETHING GOES WRONG?
UNPLUG ME.
WHOA...
LOCATING DOCTOR DOOMS...
...I... LOTS OF DOOM.
FORGE, LUNELLA. SOMETHING WENT WRONG. COME SEE THIS!
MROO?

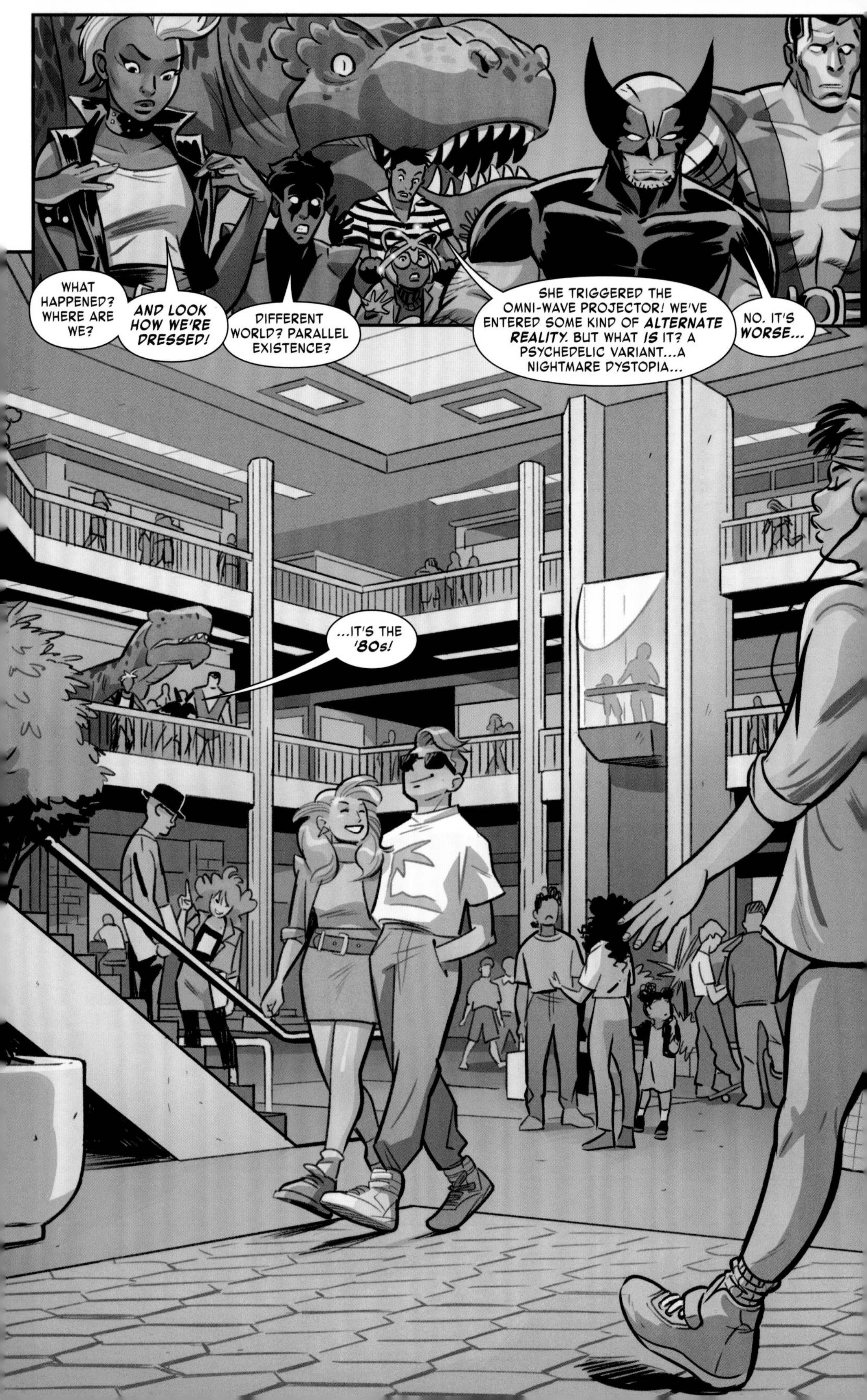
WHAT HAPPENED? WHERE ARE WE?
AND LOOK HOW WE'RE DRESSED!
DIFFERENT WORLD? PARALLEL EXISTENCE?
SHE TRIGGERED THE OMNI-WAVE PROJECTOR! WE'VE ENTERED SOME KIND OF ALTERNATE REALITY. BUT WHAT IS IT? A PSYCHEDELIC VARIANT...A NIGHTMARE DYSTOPIA...
NO. IT'S WORSE...
...IT'S THE '80s!

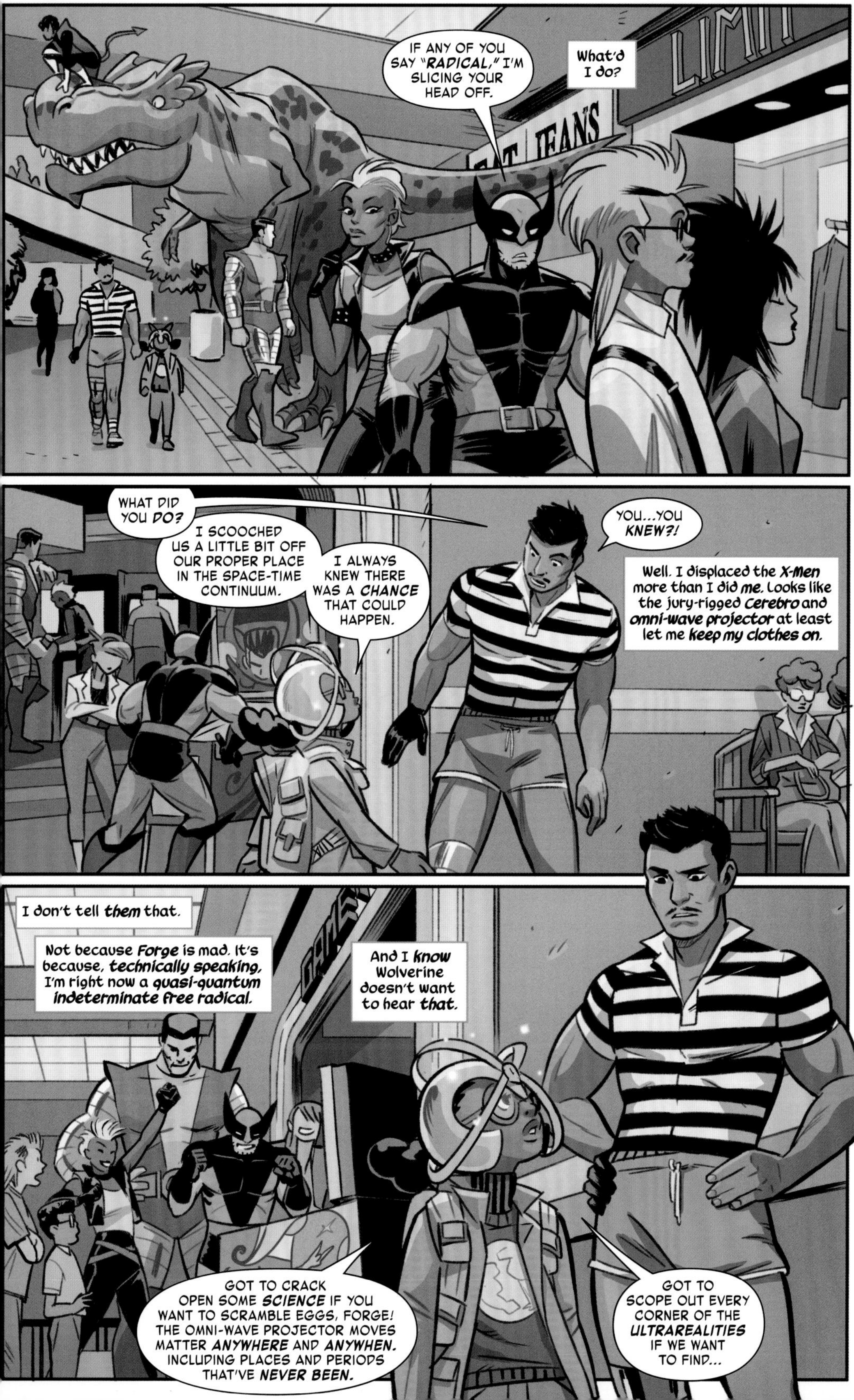

IF ANY OF YOU SAY "RADICAL," I'M SLICING YOUR HEAD OFF.
What'd I do?
LIMIT
JEANS
WHAT DID YOU DO?
I SCOOCHED US A LITTLE BIT OFF OUR PROPER PLACE IN THE SPACE-TIME CONTINUUM.
I ALWAYS KNEW THERE WAS A CHANCE THAT COULD HAPPEN.
YOU...YOU KNEW?!
Well. I displaced the X-Men more than I did me. Looks like the jury-rigged Cerebro and omni-wave projector at least let me keep my clothes on.
I don't tell them that.
Not because Forge is mad. It's because, technically speaking, I'm right now a quasi-quantum indeterminate free radical.
And I know Wolverine doesn't want to hear that.
GOT TO CRACK OPEN SOME SCIENCE IF YOU WANT TO SCRAMBLE EGGS, FORGE! THE OMNI-WAVE PROJECTOR MOVES MATTER ANYWHERE AND ANYWHEN. INCLUDING PLACES AND PERIODS THAT'VE NEVER BEEN.
GOT TO SCOPE OUT EVERY CORNER OF THE ULTRAREALITIES IF WE WANT TO FIND...

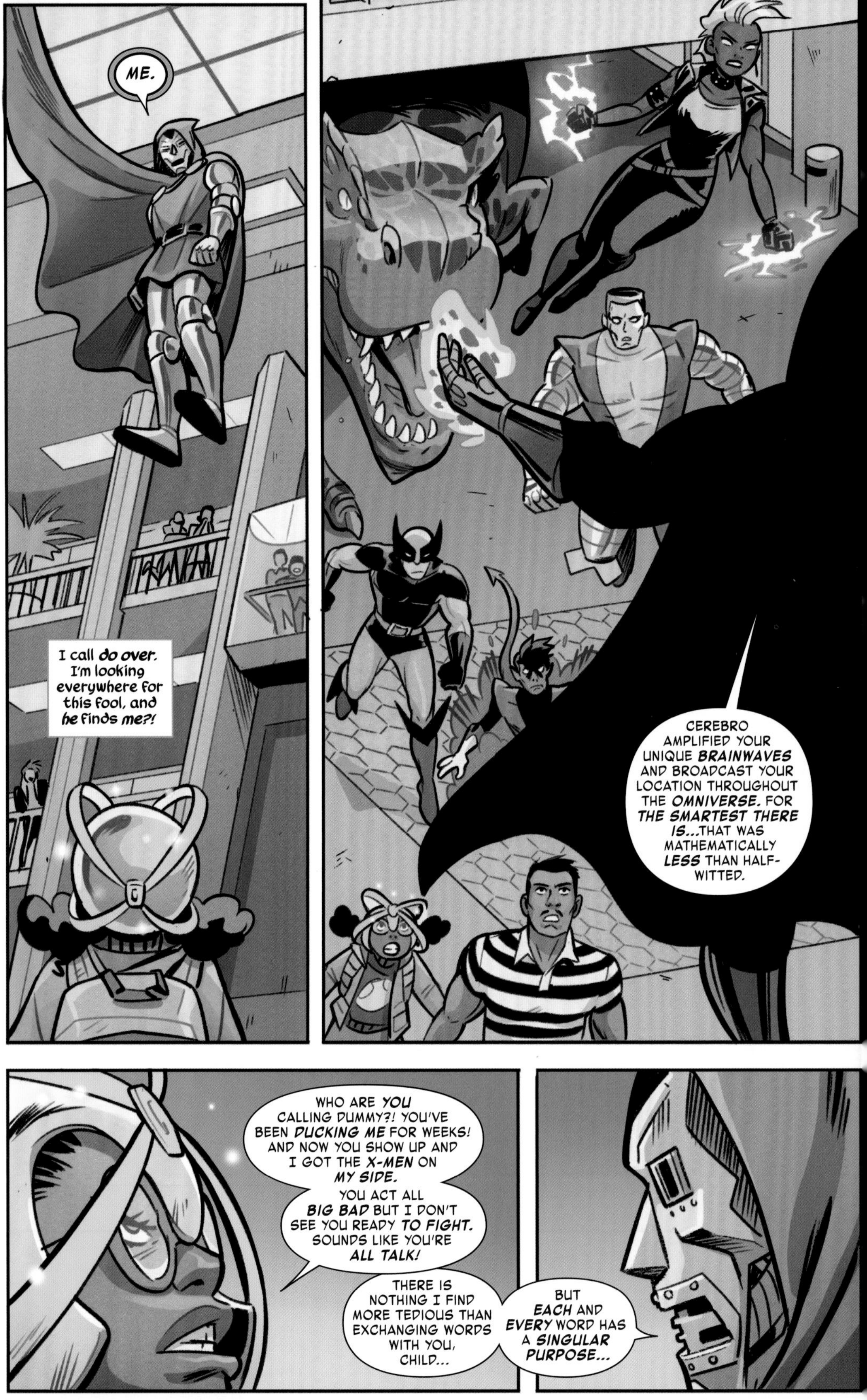
ME.
I call do over. I'm looking everywhere for this fool, and he finds me?!
CEREBRO AMPLIFIED YOUR UNIQUE BRAINWAVES AND BROADCAST YOUR LOCATION THROUGHOUT THE OMNIVERSE. FOR THE SMARTEST THERE IS...THAT WAS MATHEMATICALLY LESS THAN HALF-WITTED.
WHO ARE YOU CALLING DUMMY?! YOU'VE BEEN DUCKING ME FOR WEEKS! AND NOW YOU SHOW UP AND I GOT THE X-MEN ON MY SIDE.
YOU ACT ALL BIG BAD BUT I DON'T SEE YOU READY TO FIGHT. SOUNDS LIKE YOU'RE ALL TALK!
THERE IS NOTHING I FIND MORE TEDIOUS THAN EXCHANGING WORDS WITH YOU, CHILD...
BUT EACH AND EVERY WORD HAS A SINGULAR PURPOSE...

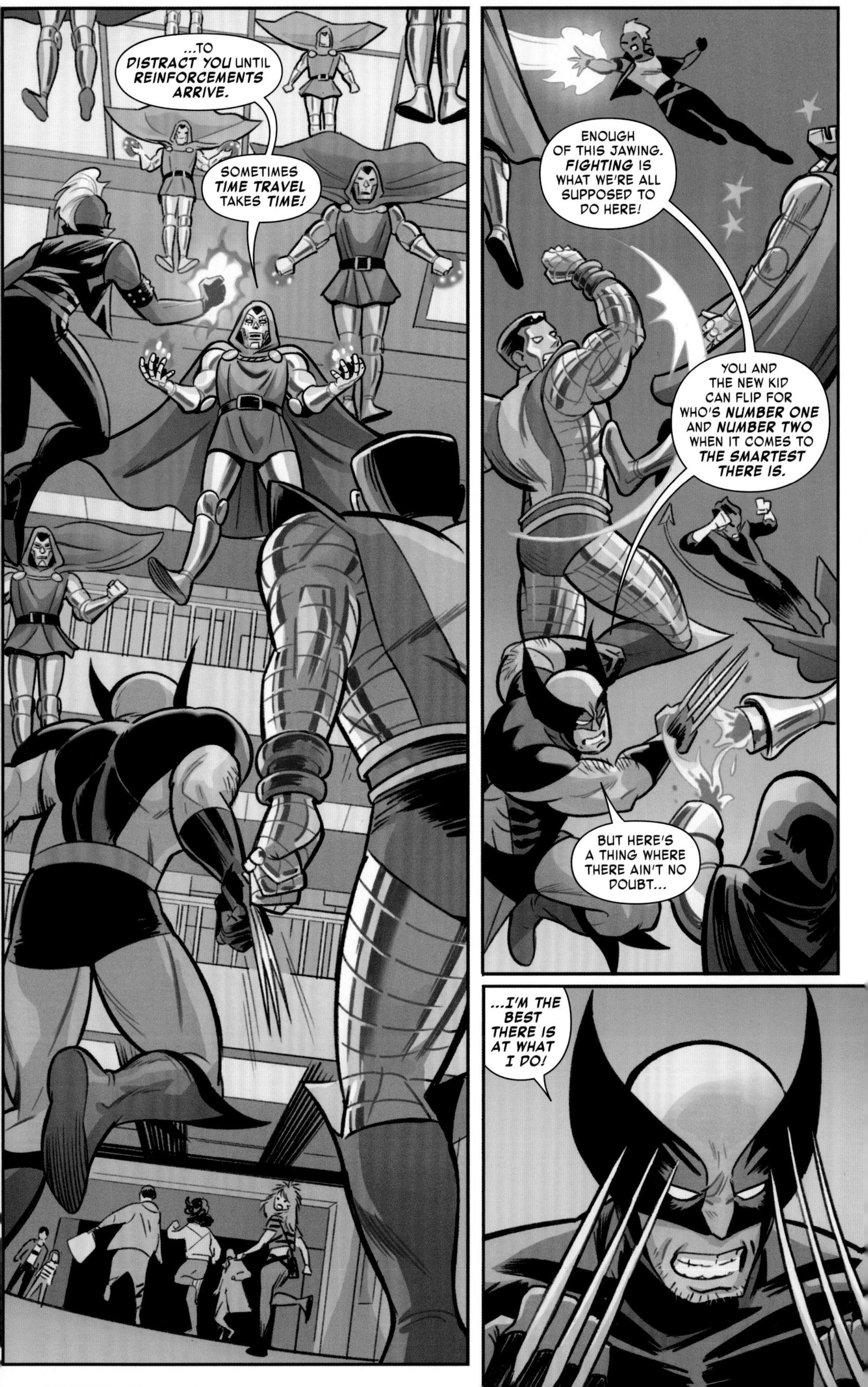
...TO DISTRACT YOU UNTIL REINFORCEMENTS ARRIVE.
SOMETIMES TIME TRAVEL TAKES TIME!
ENOUGH OF THIS JAWING. FIGHTING IS WHAT WE'RE ALL SUPPOSED TO DO HERE!
YOU AND THE NEW KID CAN FLIP FOR WHO'S NUMBER ONE AND NUMBER TWO WHEN IT COMES TO THE SMARTEST THERE IS.
BUT HERE'S A THING WHERE THERE AIN'T NO DOUBT...
...I'M THE BEST THERE IS AT WHAT I DO!

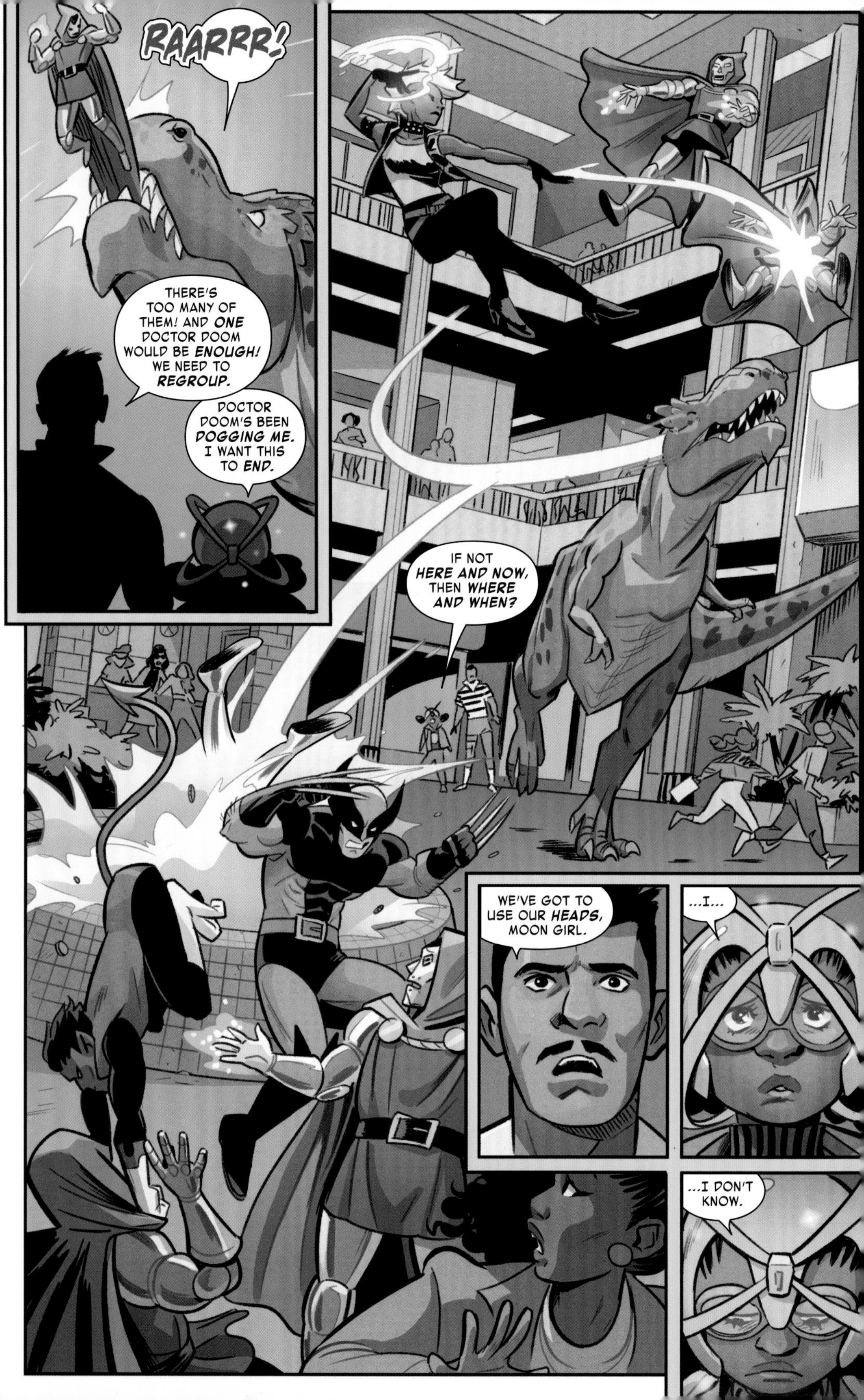
RAARRR!
THERE'S TOO MANY OF THEM! AND ONE DOCTOR DOOM WOULD BE ENOUGH! WE NEED TO REGROUP.
DOCTOR DOOM'S BEEN DOGGING ME. I WANT THIS TO END.
IF NOT HERE AND NOW, THEN WHERE AND WHEN?
WE'VE GOT TO USE OUR HEADS, MOON GIRL.
...I...
...I DON'T KNOW.

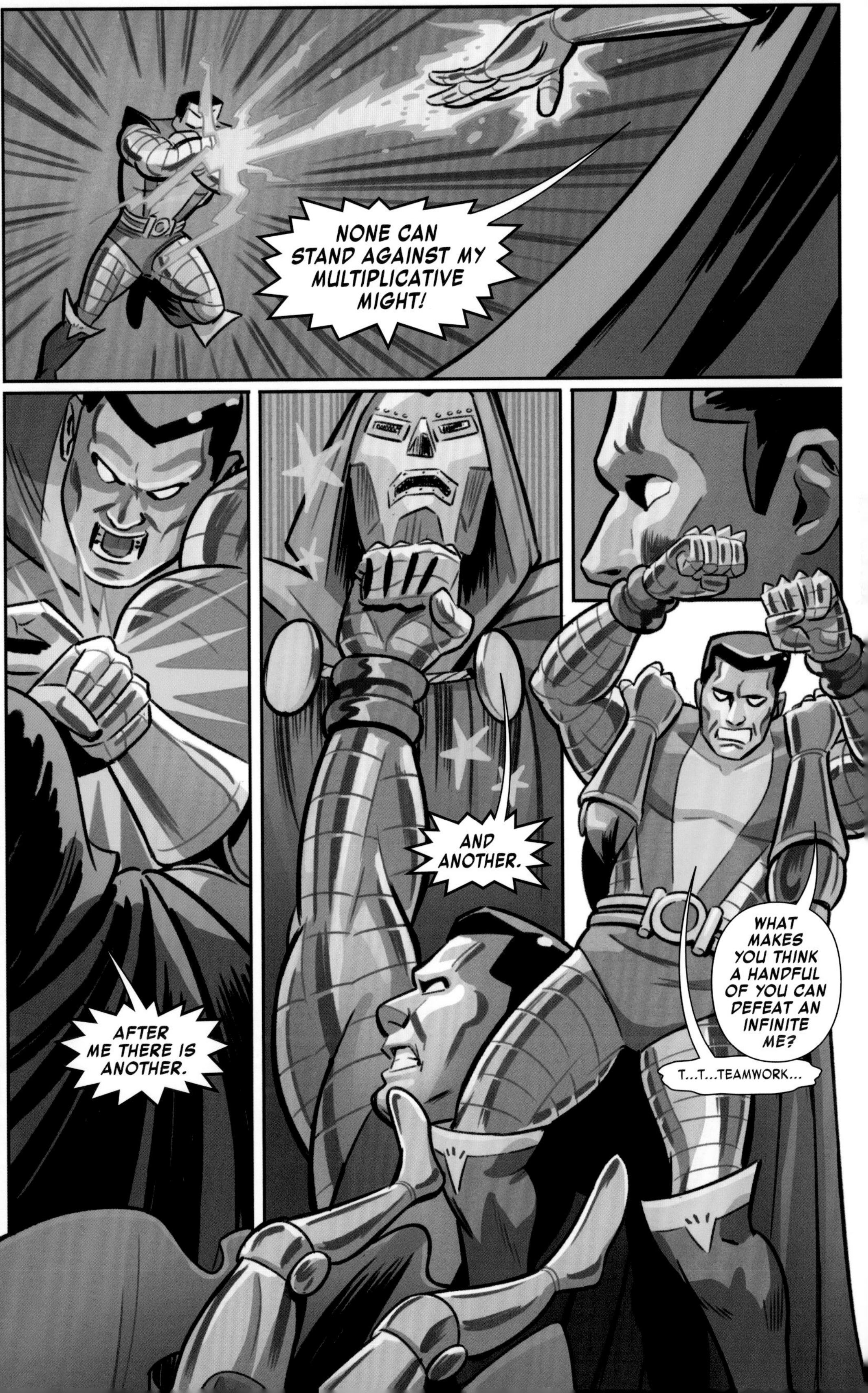
NONE CAN STAND AGAINST MY MULTIPLICATIVE MIGHT!
AFTER ME THERE IS ANOTHER.
AND ANOTHER.
WHAT MAKES YOU THINK A HANDFUL OF YOU CAN DEFEAT AN INFINITE ME?
T...T...TEAMWORK...

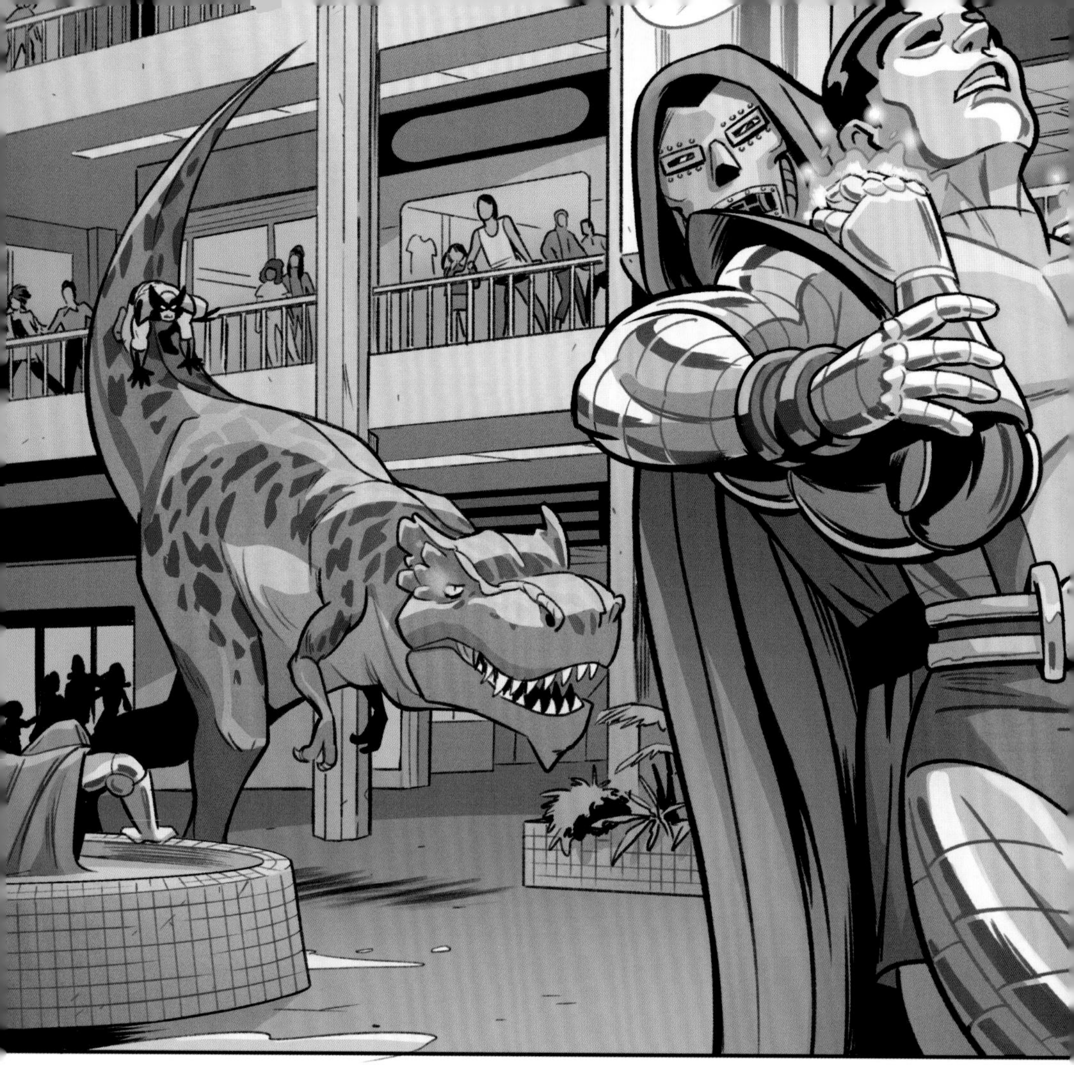

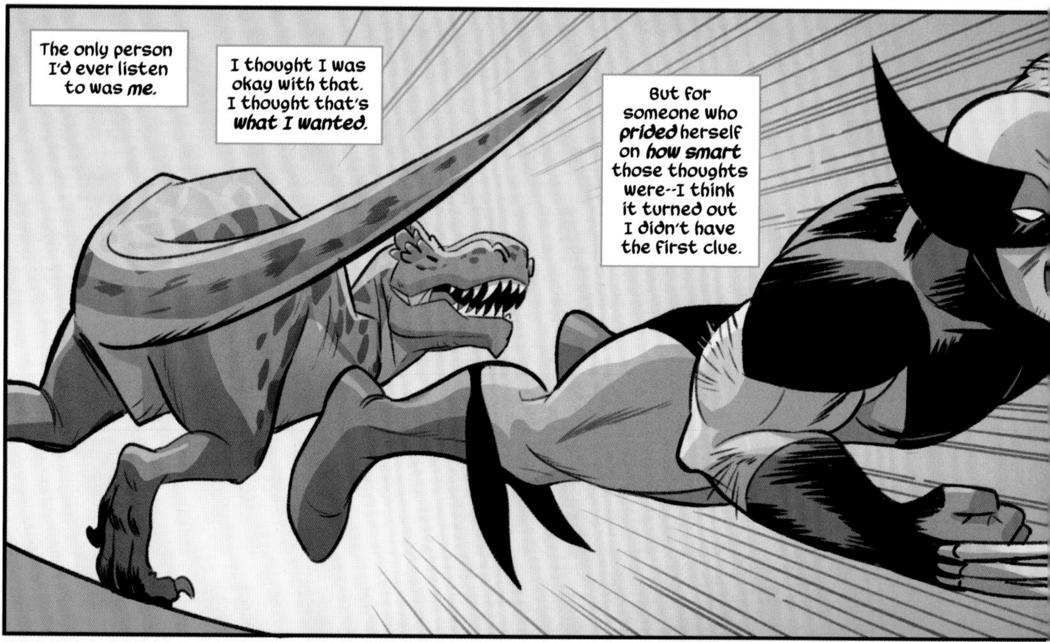

The only person I'd ever listen to was *me.*
I thought I was okay with that. I thought that's ***what I wanted.***
But for someone who ***prided*** herself on ***how smart*** those thoughts were--I think it turned out I didn't have the first clue.

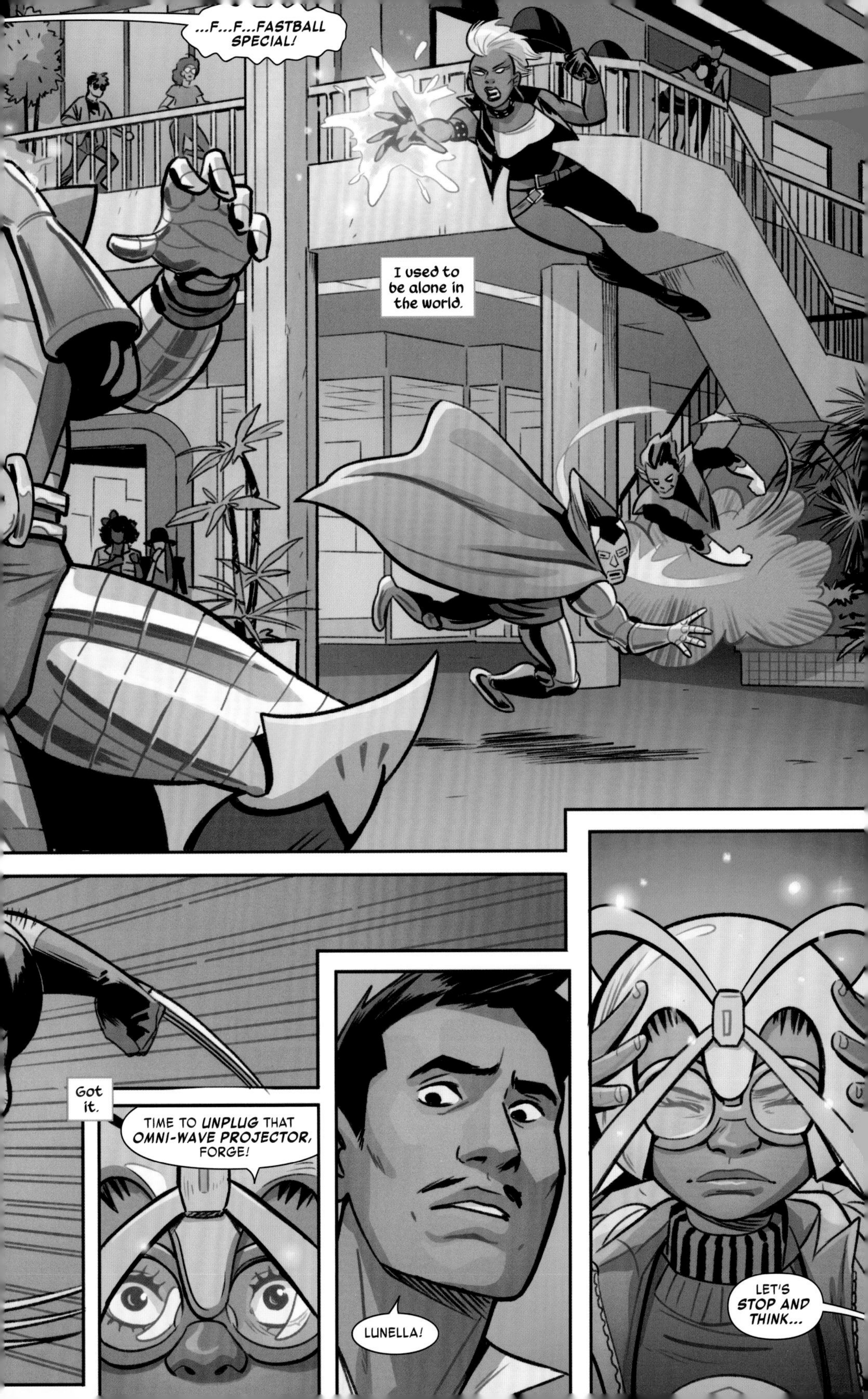
...F...F...FASTBALL SPECIAL!
I used to be alone in the world.
Got it.
TIME TO UNPLUG THAT OMNI-WAVE PROJECTOR, FORGE!
LUNELLA!
LET'S STOP AND THINK...

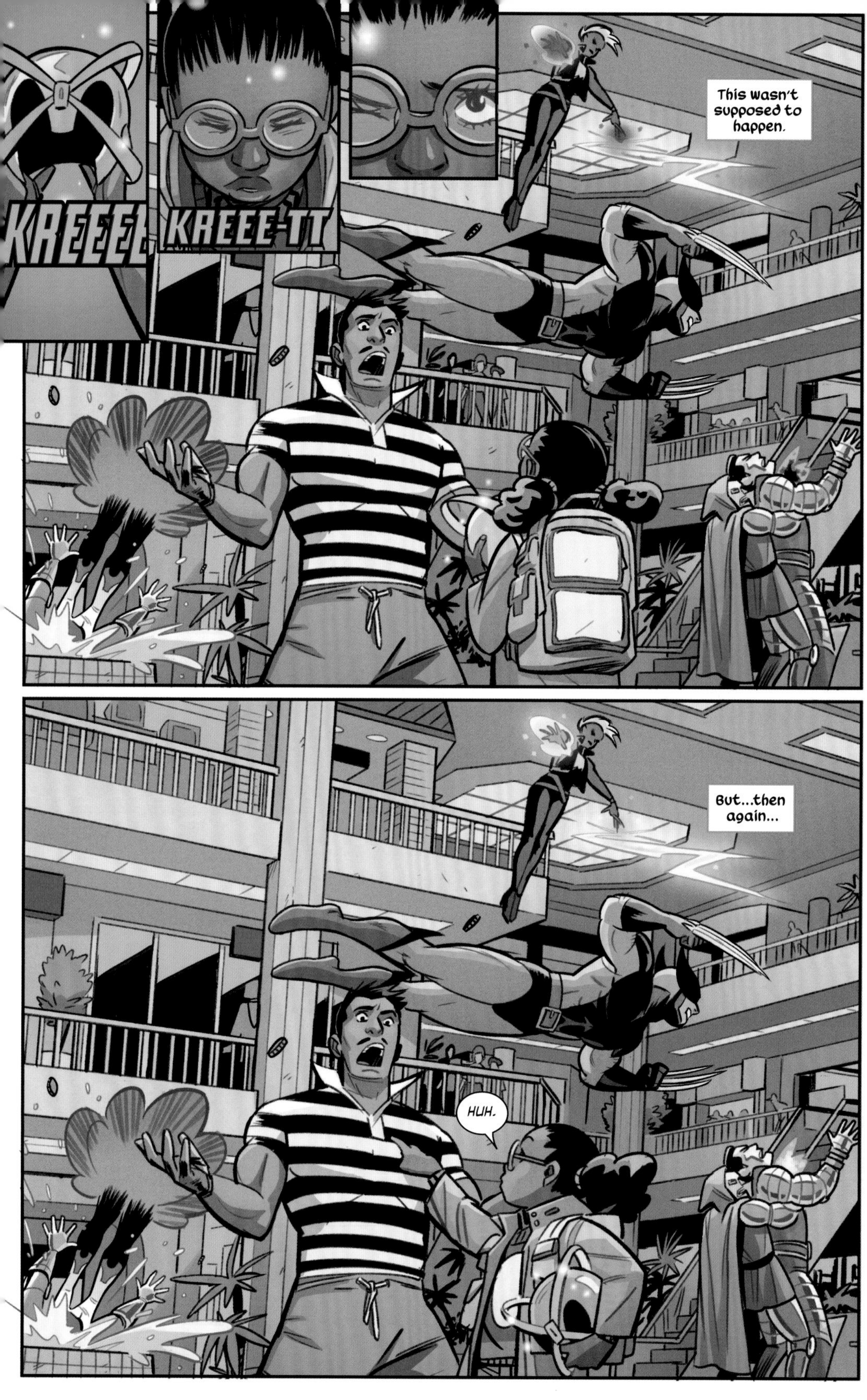
KREEEE
KREEE TT
This wasn't supposed to happen.
But...then again...
HUH.

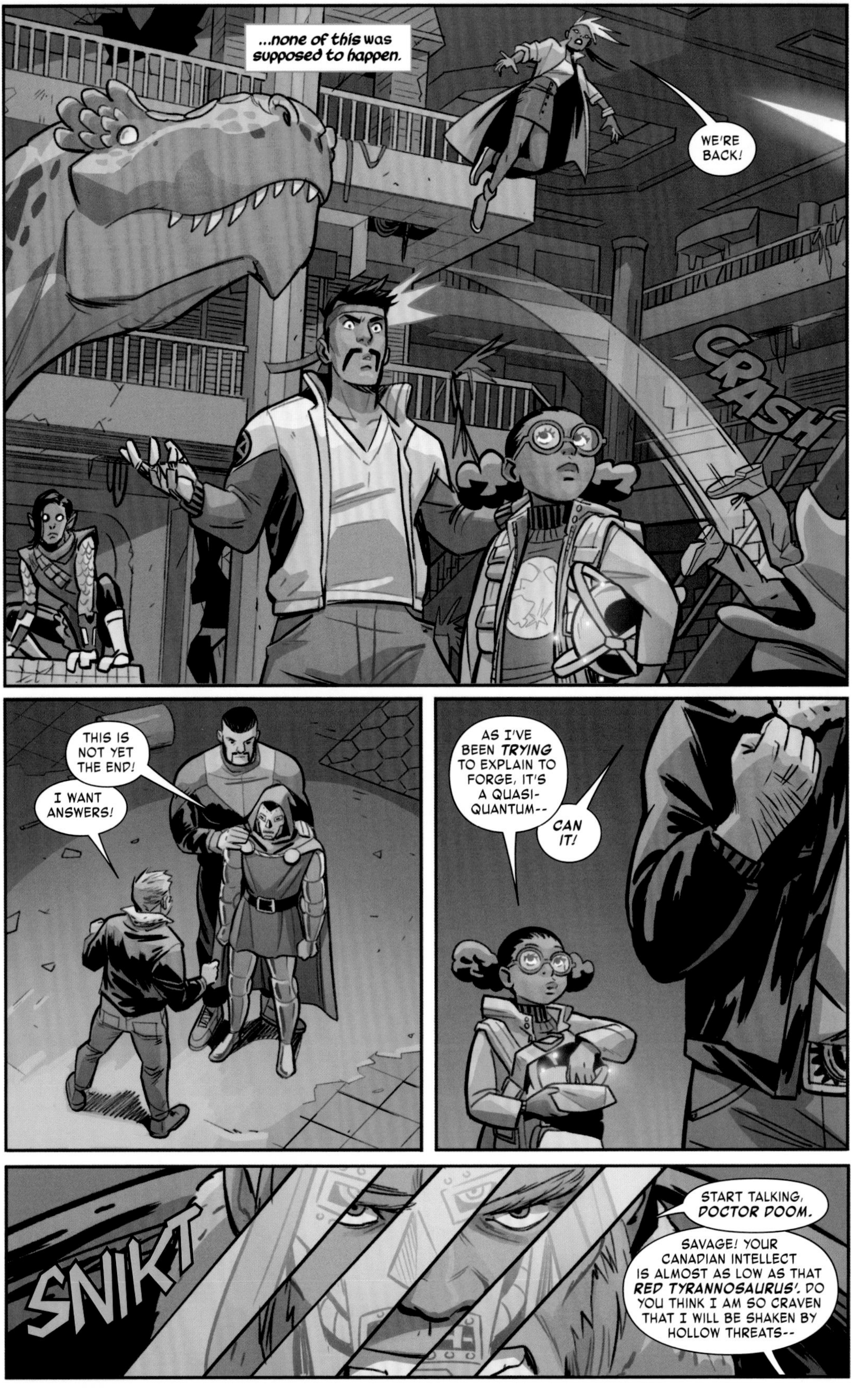
...none of this was supposed to happen.
WE'RE BACK!
CRASH
THIS IS NOT YET THE END!
I WANT ANSWERS!
AS I'VE BEEN TRYING TO EXPLAIN TO FORGE, IT'S A QUASI-QUANTUM--
CAN IT!
SNIKT
START TALKING, DOCTOR DOOM.
SAVAGE! YOUR CANADIAN INTELLECT IS ALMOST AS LOW AS THAT RED TYRANNOSAURUS'. DO YOU THINK I AM SO CRAVEN THAT I WILL BE SHAKEN BY HOLLOW THREATS--

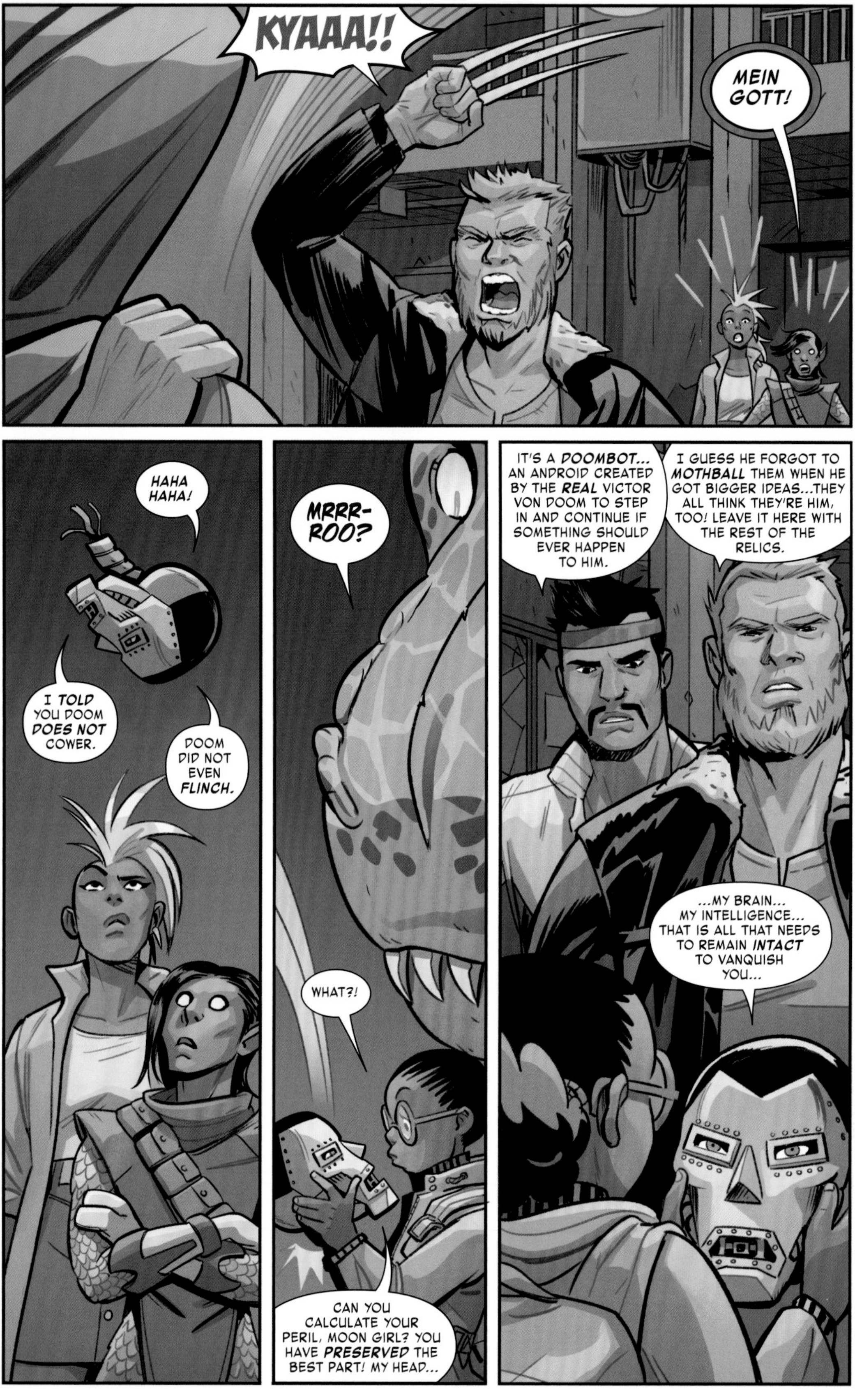
KYAAA!!
MEIN GOTT!
HAHA HAHA!
I TOLD YOU DOOM DOES NOT COWER.
DOOM DID NOT EVEN FLINCH.
MRRR-ROO?
WHAT?!
CAN YOU CALCULATE YOUR PERIL, MOON GIRL? YOU HAVE PRESERVED THE BEST PART! MY HEAD...
IT'S A DOOMBOT... AN ANDROID CREATED BY THE REAL VICTOR VON DOOM TO STEP IN AND CONTINUE IF SOMETHING SHOULD EVER HAPPEN TO HIM.
I GUESS HE FORGOT TO MOTHBALL THEM WHEN HE GOT BIGGER IDEAS...THEY ALL THINK THEY'RE HIM, TOO! LEAVE IT HERE WITH THE REST OF THE RELICS.
...MY BRAIN... MY INTELLIGENCE... THAT IS ALL THAT NEEDS TO REMAIN INTACT TO VANQUISH YOU...

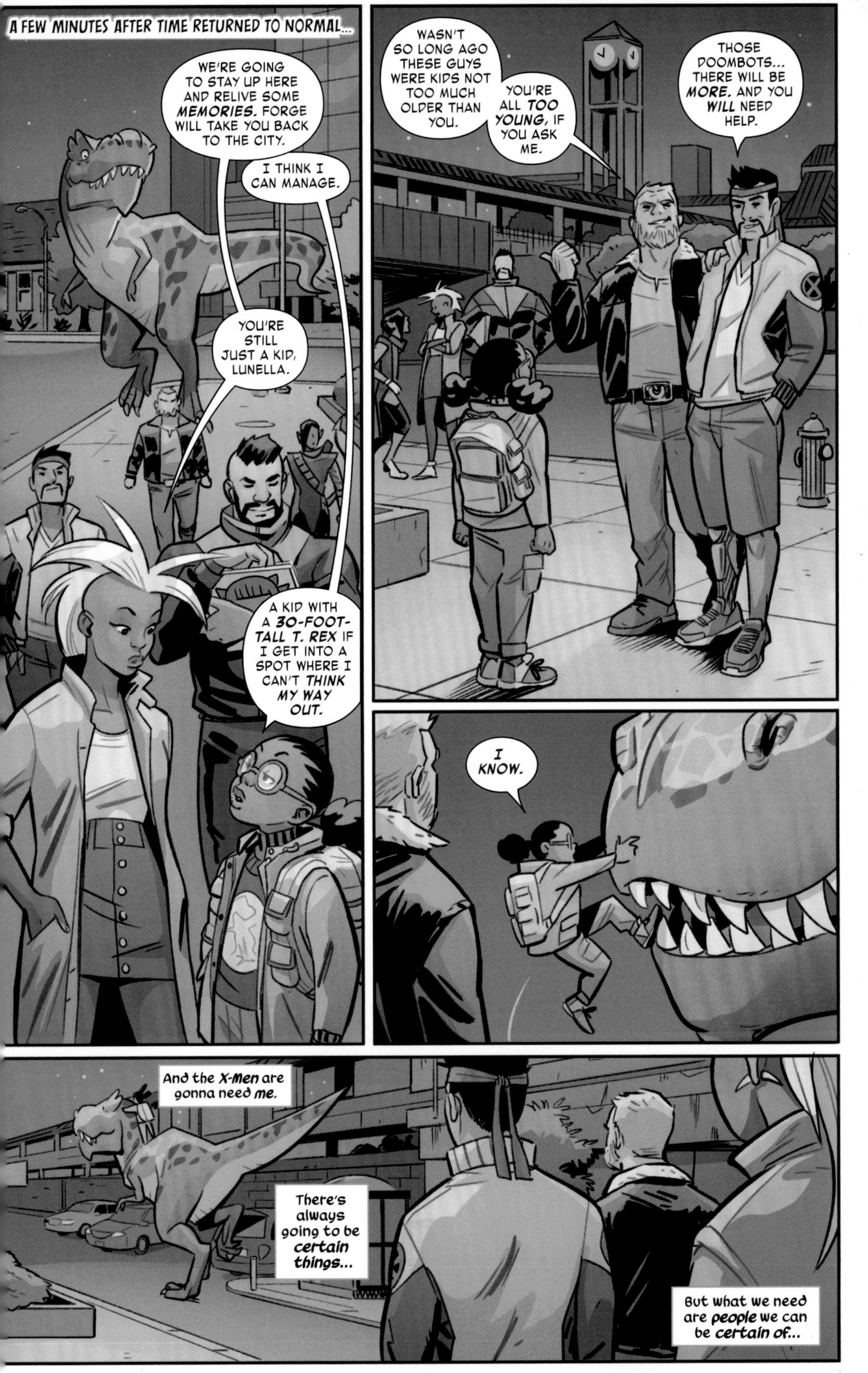
A FEW MINUTES AFTER TIME RETURNED TO NORMAL...
WE'RE GOING TO STAY UP HERE AND RELIVE SOME MEMORIES. FORGE WILL TAKE YOU BACK TO THE CITY.
I THINK I CAN MANAGE.
YOU'RE STILL JUST A KID, LUNELLA.
A KID WITH A 30-FOOT-TALL T. REX IF I GET INTO A SPOT WHERE I CAN'T THINK MY WAY OUT.
WASN'T SO LONG AGO THESE GUYS WERE KIDS NOT TOO MUCH OLDER THAN YOU.
YOU'RE ALL TOO YOUNG, IF YOU ASK ME.
THOSE DOOMBOTS... THERE WILL BE MORE. AND YOU WILL NEED HELP.
I KNOW.
And the X-Men are gonna need me.
There's always going to be certain things...
But what we need are people we can be certain of...

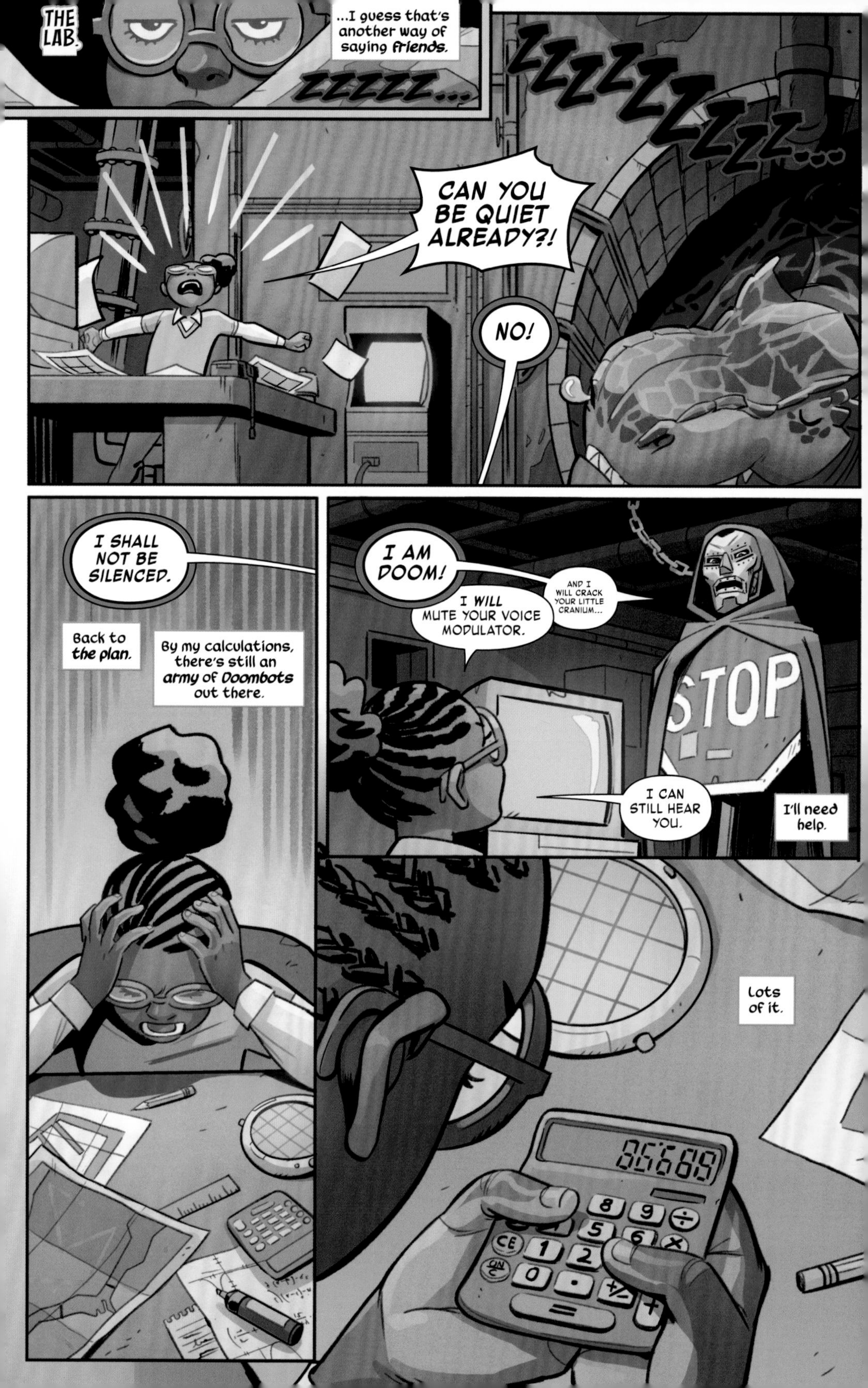
THE LAB.
...I guess that's another way of saying friends.
ZZZZZZ...
ZZZZZZZZZZZ...
CAN YOU BE QUIET ALREADY?!
NO!
I SHALL NOT BE SILENCED.
Back to the plan.
By my calculations, there's still an army of Doombots out there.
I AM DOOM!
AND I WILL CRACK YOUR LITTLE CRANIUM...
I WILL MUTE YOUR VOICE MODULATOR.
STOP
I CAN STILL HEAR YOU.
I'll need help.
Lots of it.

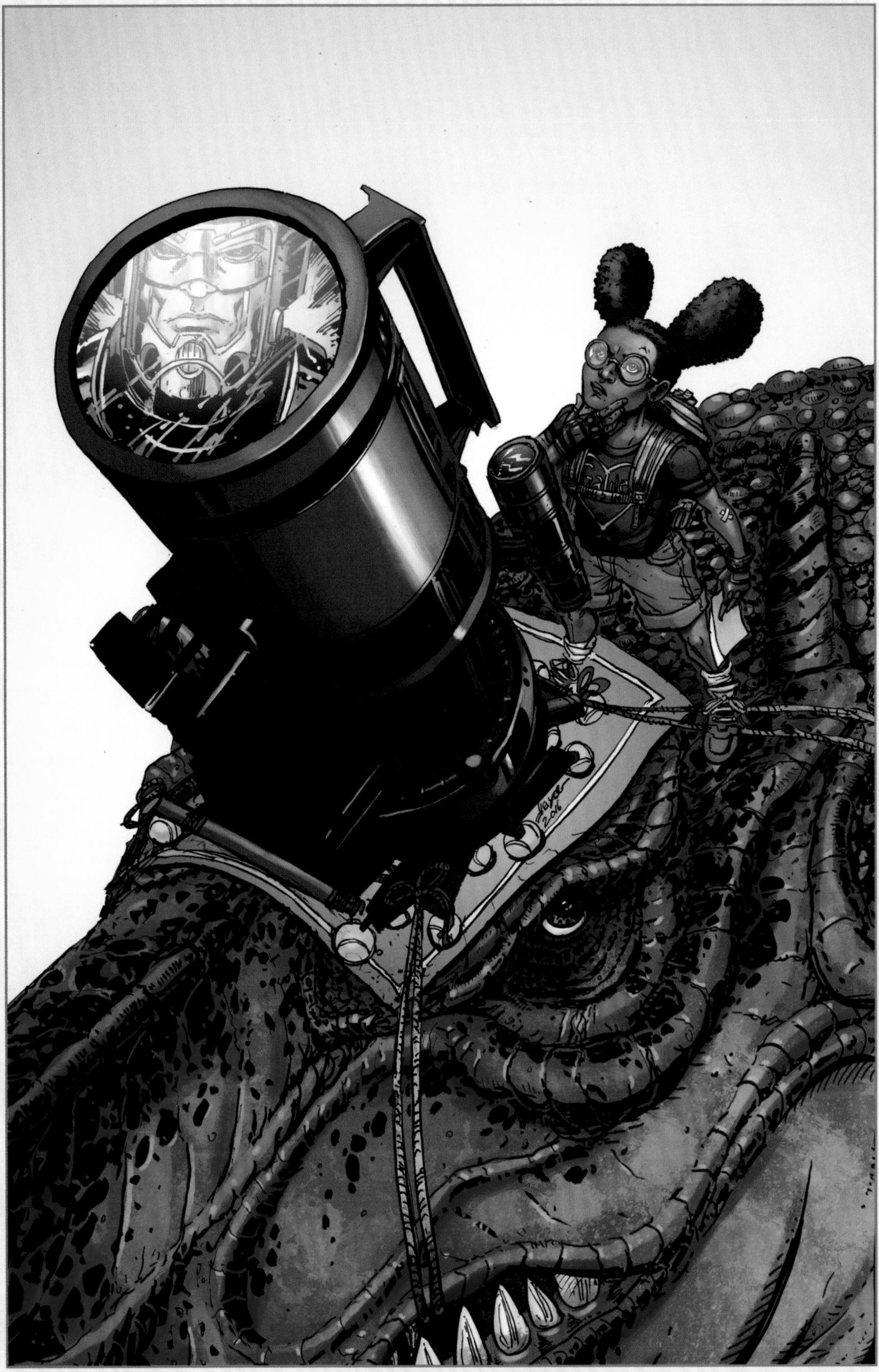

#13 S.T.E.A.M. Variant
BY JOYCE CHIN & CHRIS SOTOMAYOR

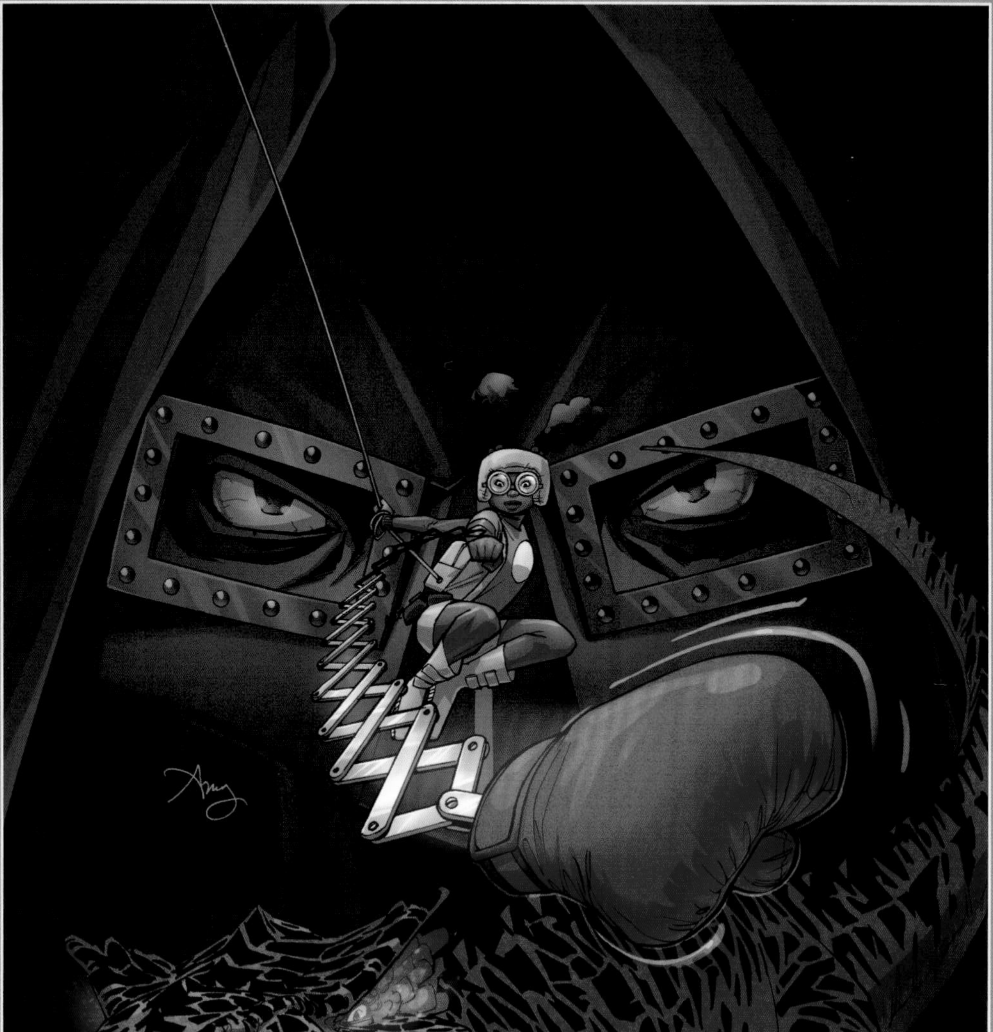

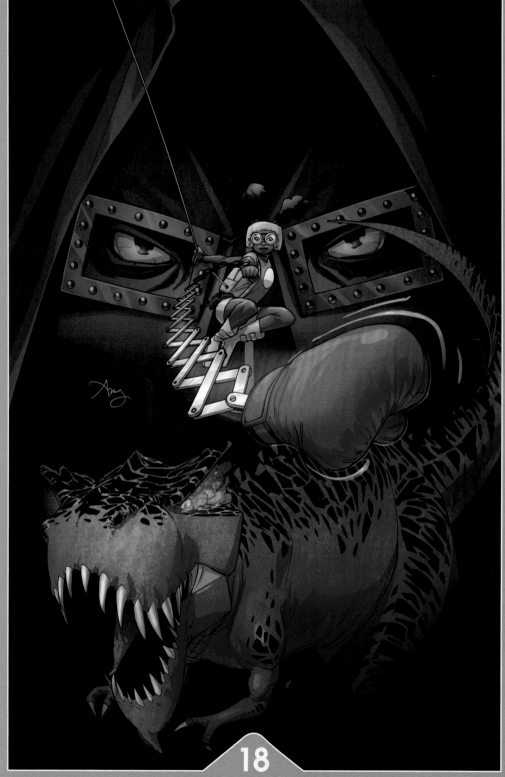

18

"FULL MOON"

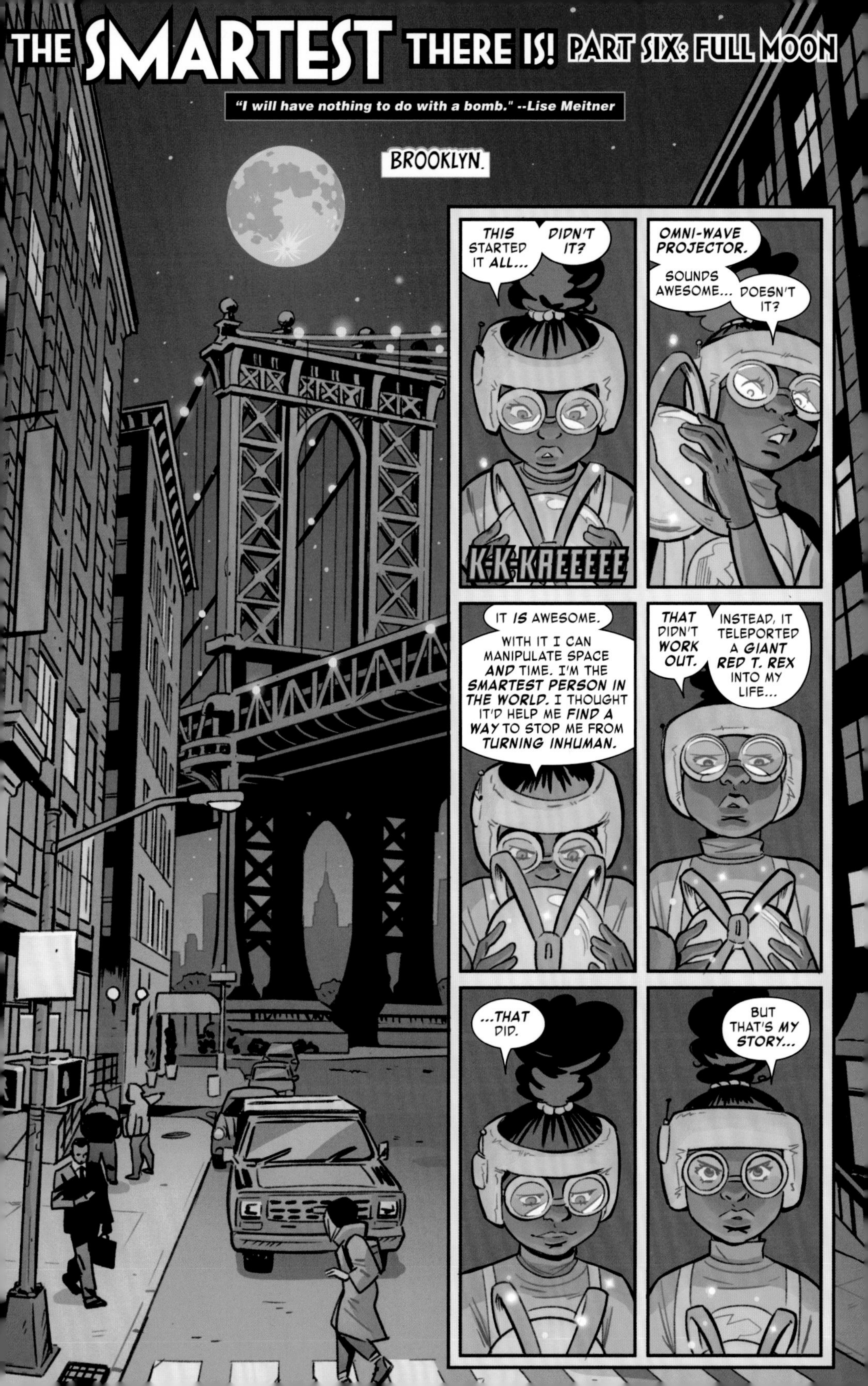
THE SMARTEST THERE IS! PART SIX: FULL MOON
"I will have nothing to do with a bomb." --Lise Meitner
BROOKLYN.
THIS STARTED IT ALL...
DIDN'T IT?
K-K-KREEEEE
OMNI-WAVE PROJECTOR.
SOUNDS AWESOME...
DOESN'T IT?
IT IS AWESOME.
WITH IT I CAN MANIPULATE SPACE AND TIME. I'M THE SMARTEST PERSON IN THE WORLD. I THOUGHT IT'D HELP ME FIND A WAY TO STOP ME FROM TURNING INHUMAN.
THAT DIDN'T WORK OUT.
INSTEAD, IT TELEPORTED A GIANT RED T. REX INTO MY LIFE...
...THAT DID.
BUT THAT'S MY STORY...

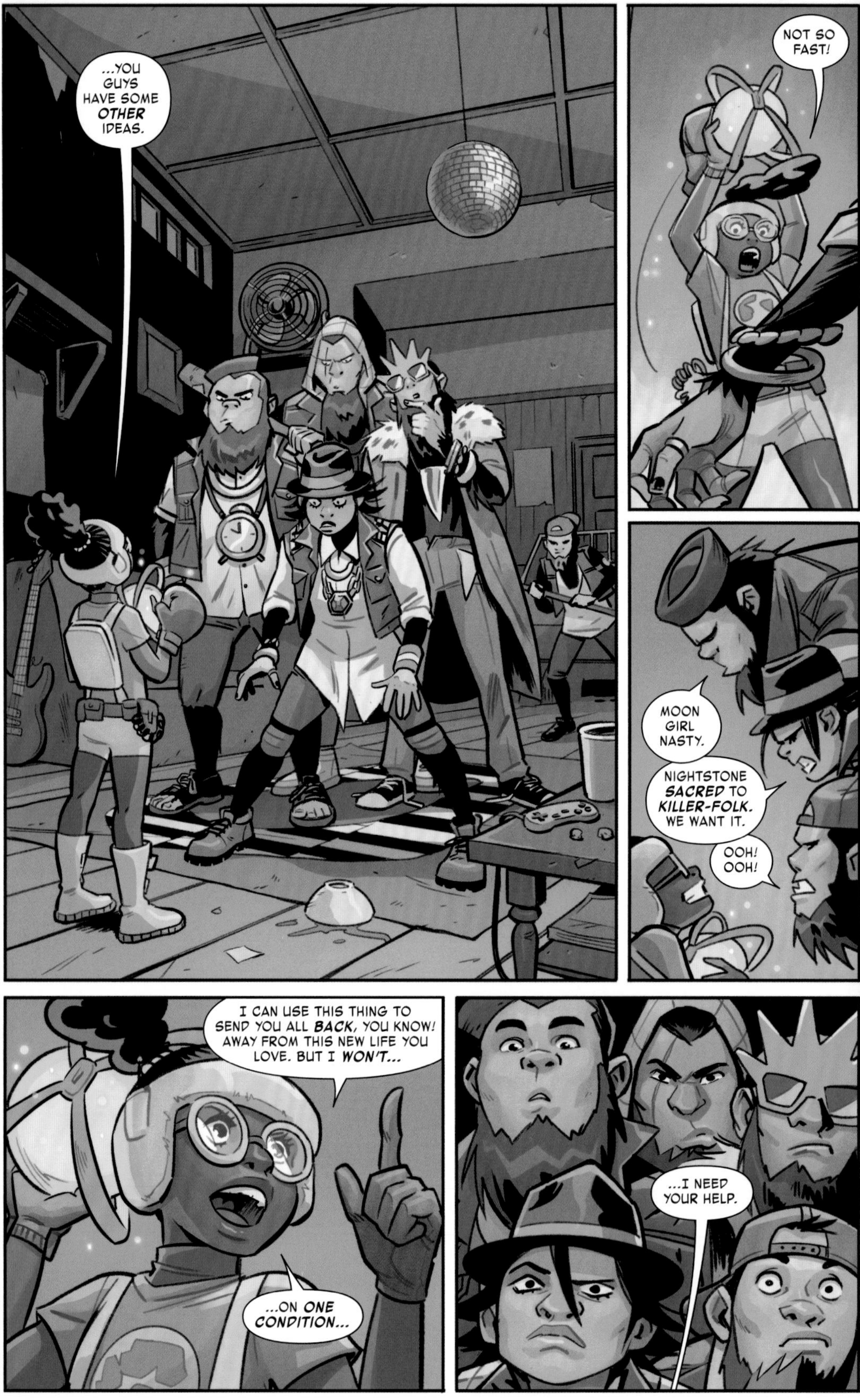
...YOU GUYS HAVE SOME OTHER IDEAS.
NOT SO FAST!
MOON GIRL NASTY.
NIGHTSTONE SACRED TO KILLER-FOLK. WE WANT IT.
OOH! OOH!
I CAN USE THIS THING TO SEND YOU ALL BACK, YOU KNOW! AWAY FROM THIS NEW LIFE YOU LOVE. BUT I WON'T...
...ON ONE CONDITION...
...I NEED YOUR HELP.

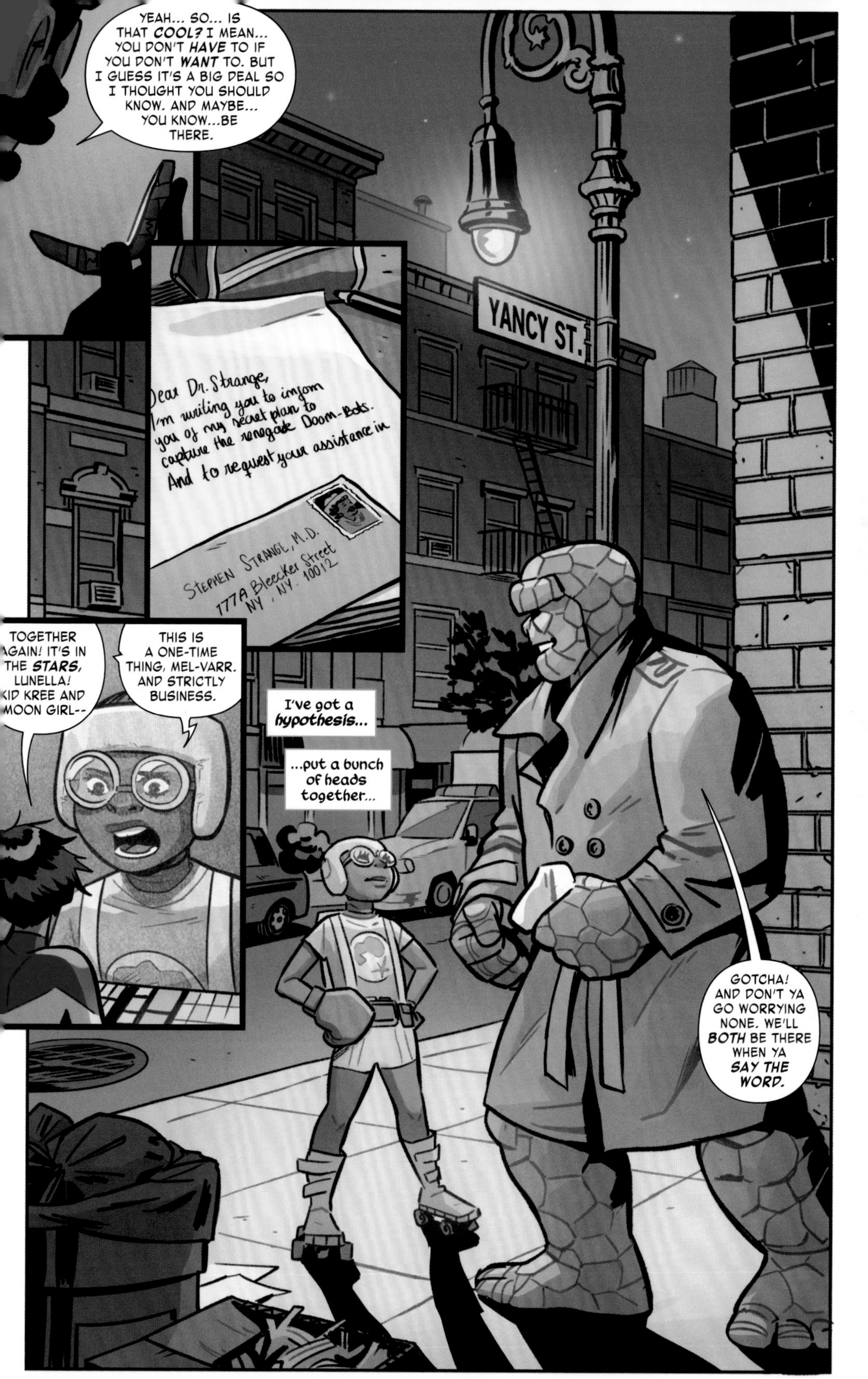
YEAH... SO... IS THAT COOL? I MEAN... YOU DON'T HAVE TO IF YOU DON'T WANT TO. BUT I GUESS IT'S A BIG DEAL SO I THOUGHT YOU SHOULD KNOW. AND MAYBE... YOU KNOW...BE THERE.
YANCY ST.
Dear Dr. Strange, I'm writing you to inform you of my secret plan to capture the renegade Doom-Bots. And to request your assistance in
STEPHEN STRANGE, M.D. 177A Bleecker Street NY, NY. 10012
TOGETHER AGAIN! IT'S IN THE STARS, LUNELLA! KID KREE AND MOON GIRL--
THIS IS A ONE-TIME THING, MEL-VARR. AND STRICTLY BUSINESS.
I've got a hypothesis...
...put a bunch of heads together...
GOTCHA! AND DON'T YA GO WORRYING NONE. WE'LL BOTH BE THERE WHEN YA SAY THE WORD.

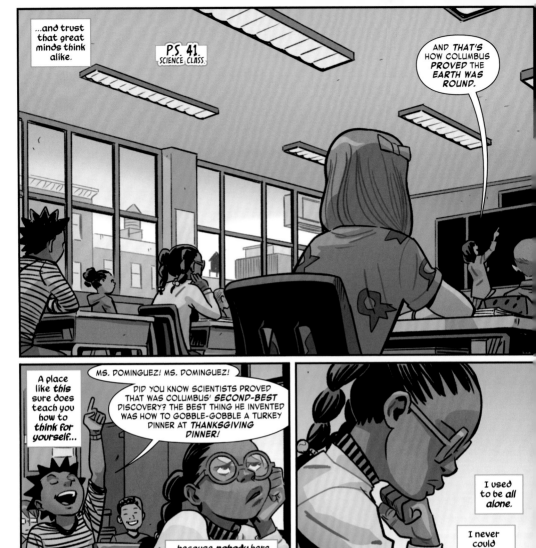

...and trust that great minds think alike.

P.S. 41. SCIENCE CLASS.

AND *THAT'S* HOW COLUMBUS *PROVED* THE EARTH WAS ROUND.

A place like *this* sure does teach you how to *think for yourself...*

MS. DOMINGUEZ! MS. DOMINGUEZ!

DID YOU KNOW SCIENTISTS PROVED THAT WAS COLUMBUS' *SECOND-BEST* DISCOVERY? THE BEST THING HE INVENTED WAS HOW TO GOBBLE-GOBBLE A TURKEY DINNER AT *THANKSGIVING DINNER!*

...because *nobody* here knows what they're talking about!

I used to be *all* alone.

I never could admit that was *hard.*

Nowadays I'm thinking I was *wrong* back then. Being alone was *easier.*

At least for me.

But I know deep down *easier* doesn't mean *better...*

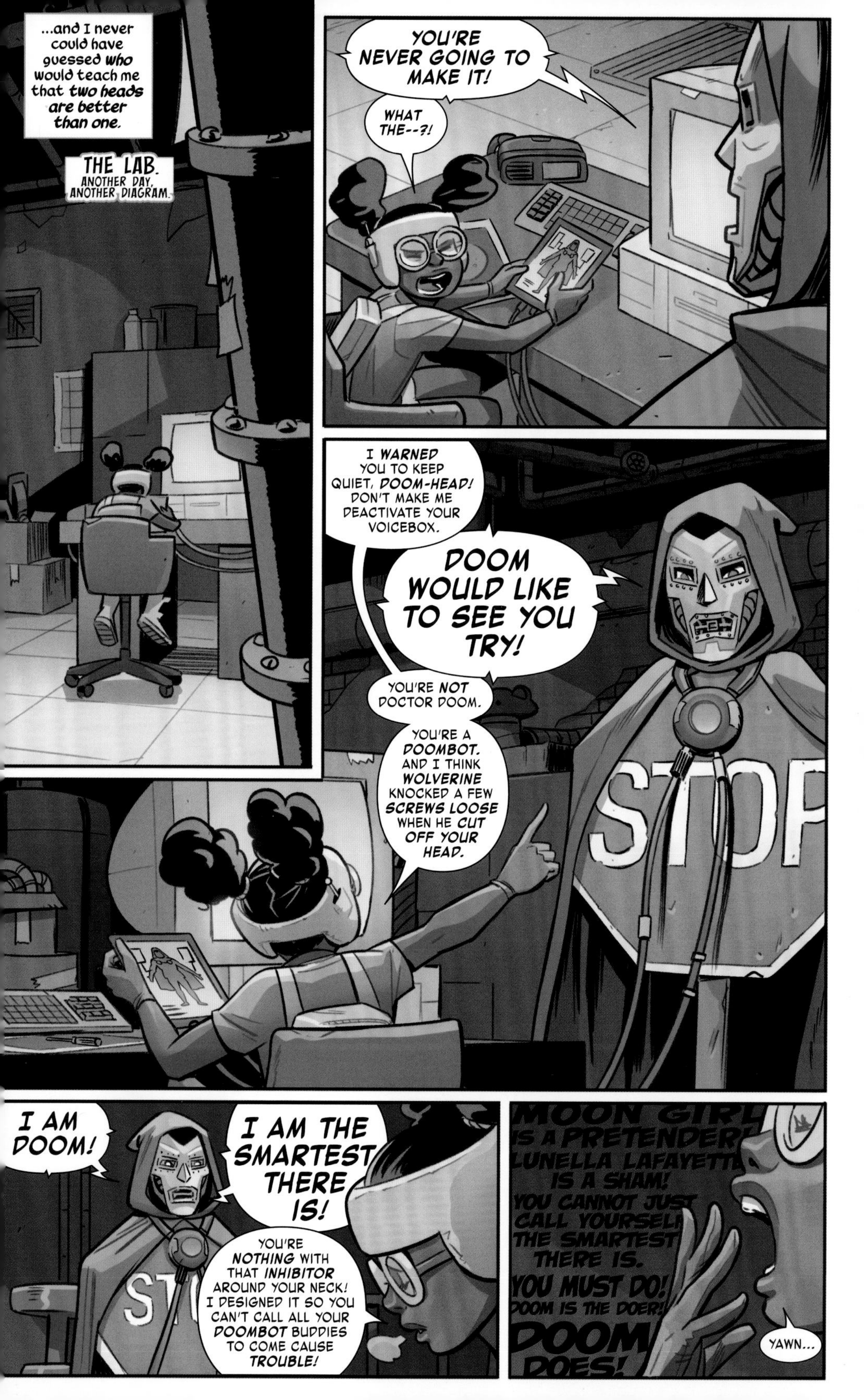
...and I never could have guessed who would teach me that two heads are better than one.
THE LAB. ANOTHER DAY, ANOTHER DIAGRAM.
YOU'RE NEVER GOING TO MAKE IT!
WHAT THE--?!
I WARNED YOU TO KEEP QUIET, DOOM-HEAD! DON'T MAKE ME DEACTIVATE YOUR VOICEBOX.
DOOM WOULD LIKE TO SEE YOU TRY!
YOU'RE NOT DOCTOR DOOM.
YOU'RE A DOOMBOT. AND I THINK WOLVERINE KNOCKED A FEW SCREWS LOOSE WHEN HE CUT OFF YOUR HEAD.
STOP
I AM DOOM!
I AM THE SMARTEST THERE IS!
YOU'RE NOTHING WITH THAT INHIBITOR AROUND YOUR NECK! I DESIGNED IT SO YOU CAN'T CALL ALL YOUR DOOMBOT BUDDIES TO COME CAUSE TROUBLE!
YAWN...

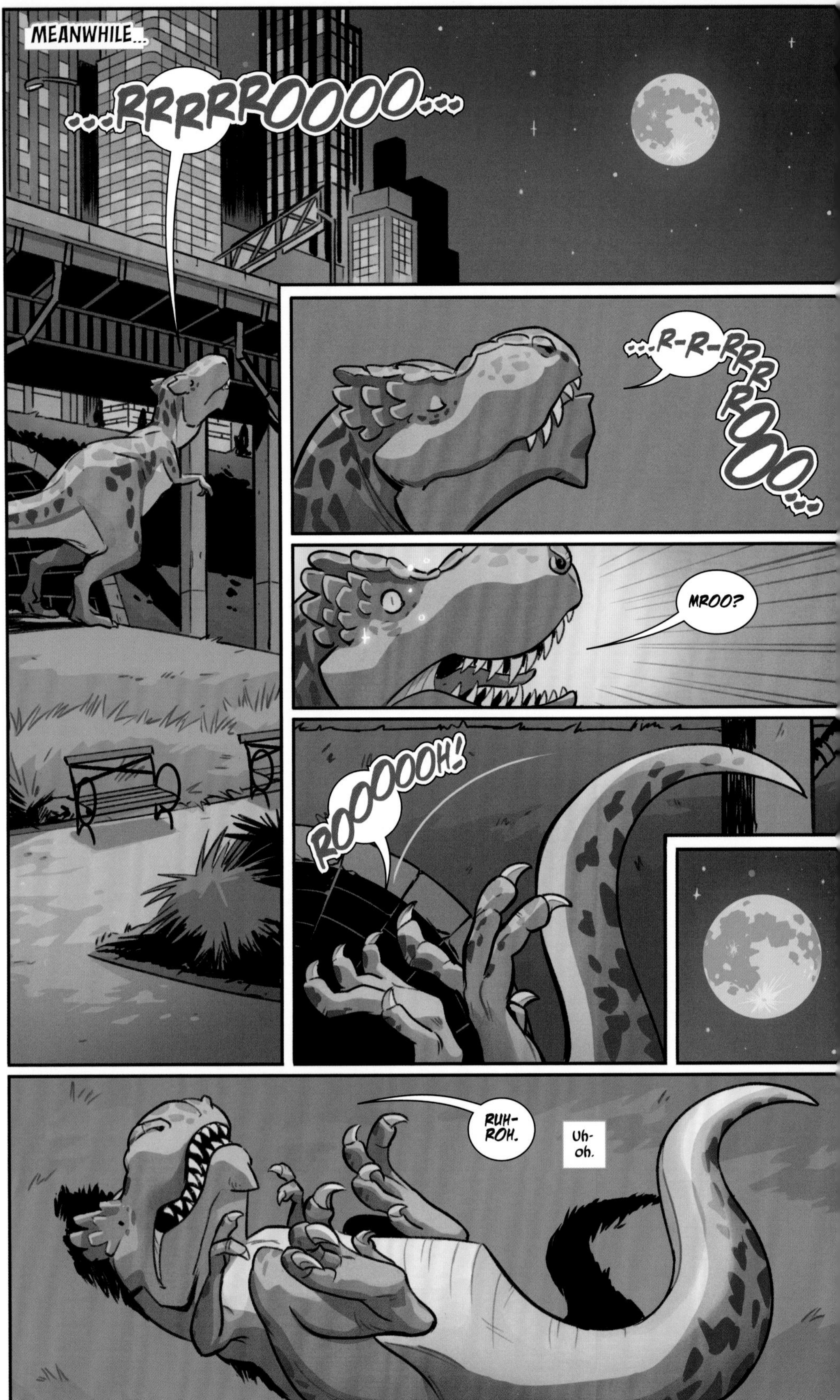
MEANWHILE...
...RRRRROOOOO...
...R-R-RRRROOO...
MROO?
ROOOOOOH!
RUH-ROH.
Uh-oh.

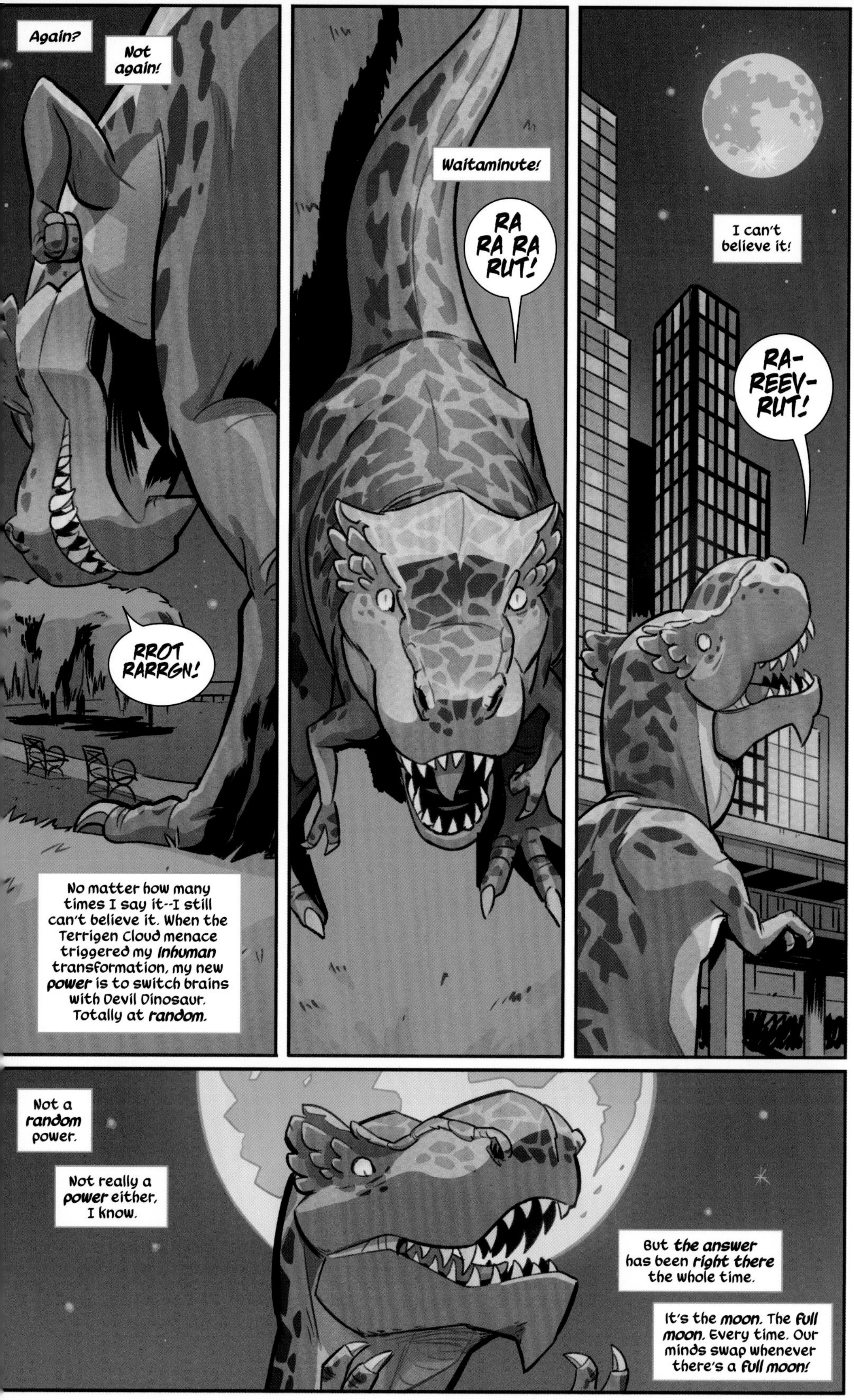
Again?
Not again!
RROT RARRGN!
No matter how many times I say it--I still can't believe it. When the Terrigen Cloud menace triggered my Inhuman transformation, my new power is to switch brains with Devil Dinosaur. Totally at random.
Waitaminute!
RA RA RA RUT!
I can't believe it!
RA-REEV-RUT!
Not a random power.
Not really a power either, I know.
But the answer has been right there the whole time.
It's the moon. The full moon. Every time. Our minds swap whenever there's a full moon!

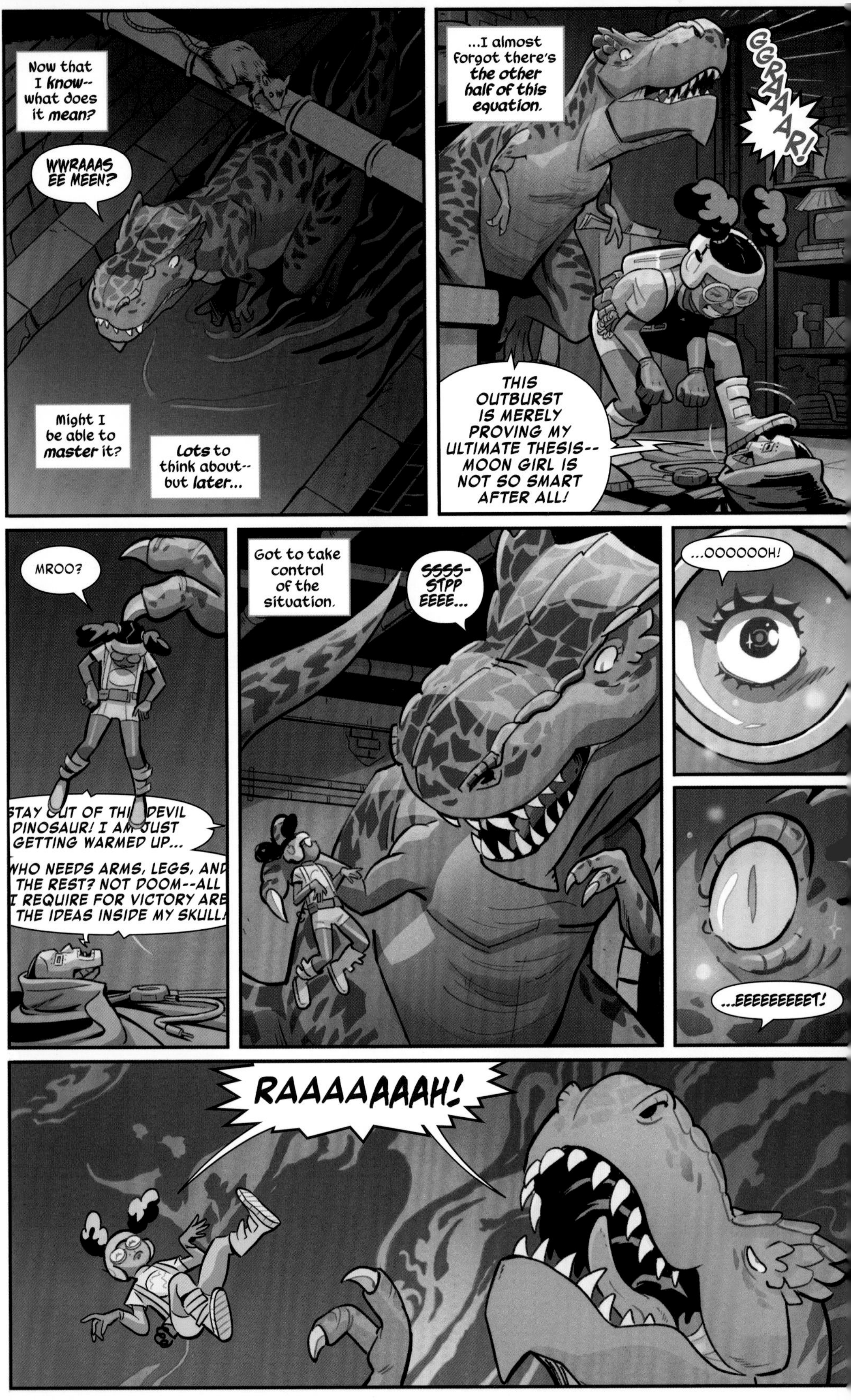
Now that I know-- what does it mean?
WWRAAAS EE MEEN?
Might I be able to master it?
Lots to think about-- but later...
...I almost forgot there's the other half of this equation.
GGRAAAR!
THIS OUTBURST IS MERELY PROVING MY ULTIMATE THESIS-- MOON GIRL IS NOT SO SMART AFTER ALL!
MROO?
STAY OUT OF THIS, DEVIL DINOSAUR! I AM JUST GETTING WARMED UP...
WHO NEEDS ARMS, LEGS, AND THE REST? NOT DOOM--ALL I REQUIRE FOR VICTORY ARE THE IDEAS INSIDE MY SKULL!
Got to take control of the situation.
SSSS-STPP EEEE...
...OOOOOOH!
...EEEEEEEEET!
RAAAAAAAH!

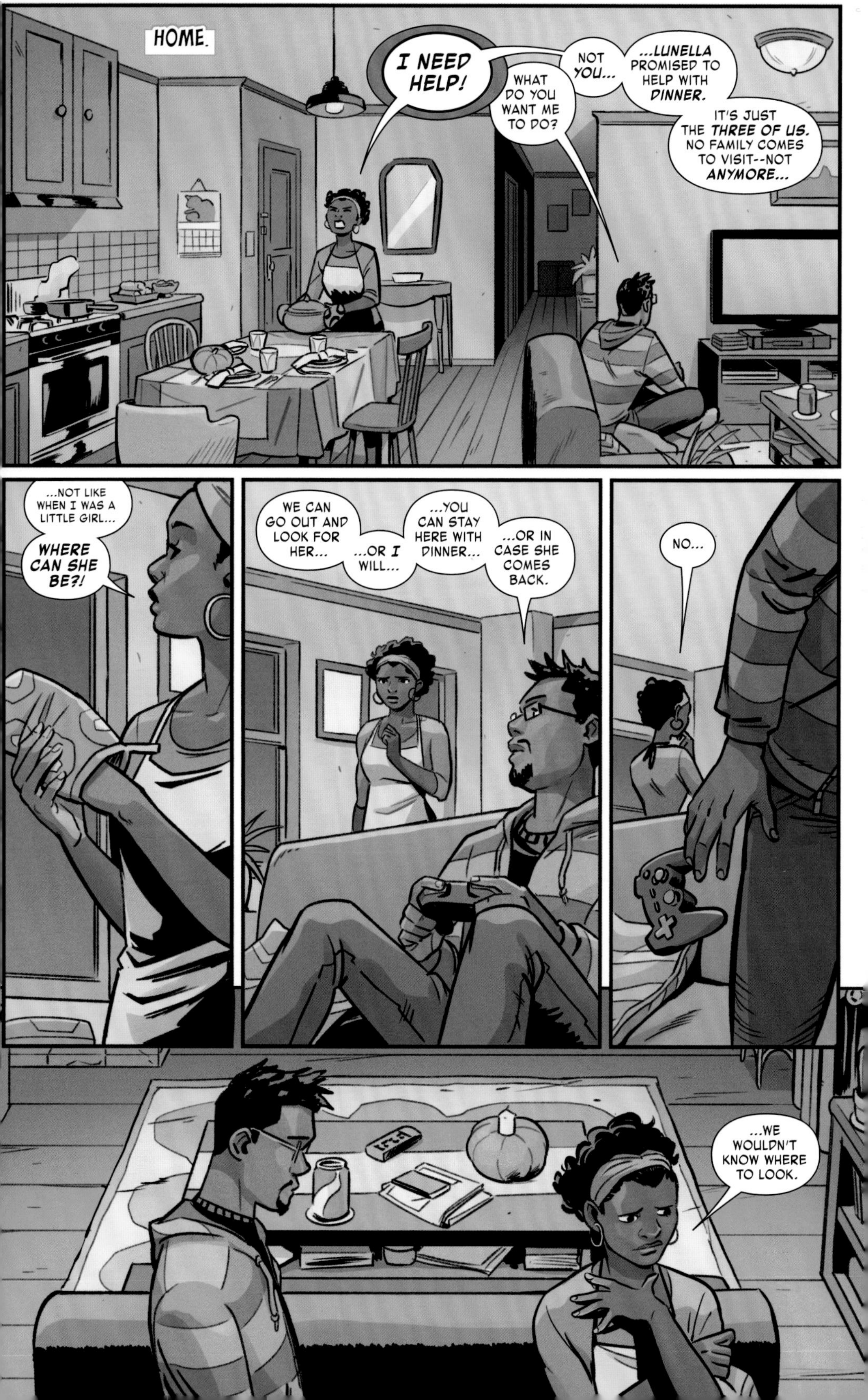
HOME.
I NEED HELP!
WHAT DO YOU WANT ME TO DO?
NOT YOU...
...LUNELLA PROMISED TO HELP WITH DINNER.
IT'S JUST THE THREE OF US. NO FAMILY COMES TO VISIT--NOT ANYMORE...
...NOT LIKE WHEN I WAS A LITTLE GIRL...
WHERE CAN SHE BE?!
WE CAN GO OUT AND LOOK FOR HER...
...OR I WILL...
...YOU CAN STAY HERE WITH DINNER...
...OR IN CASE SHE COMES BACK.
NO...
...WE WOULDN'T KNOW WHERE TO LOOK.

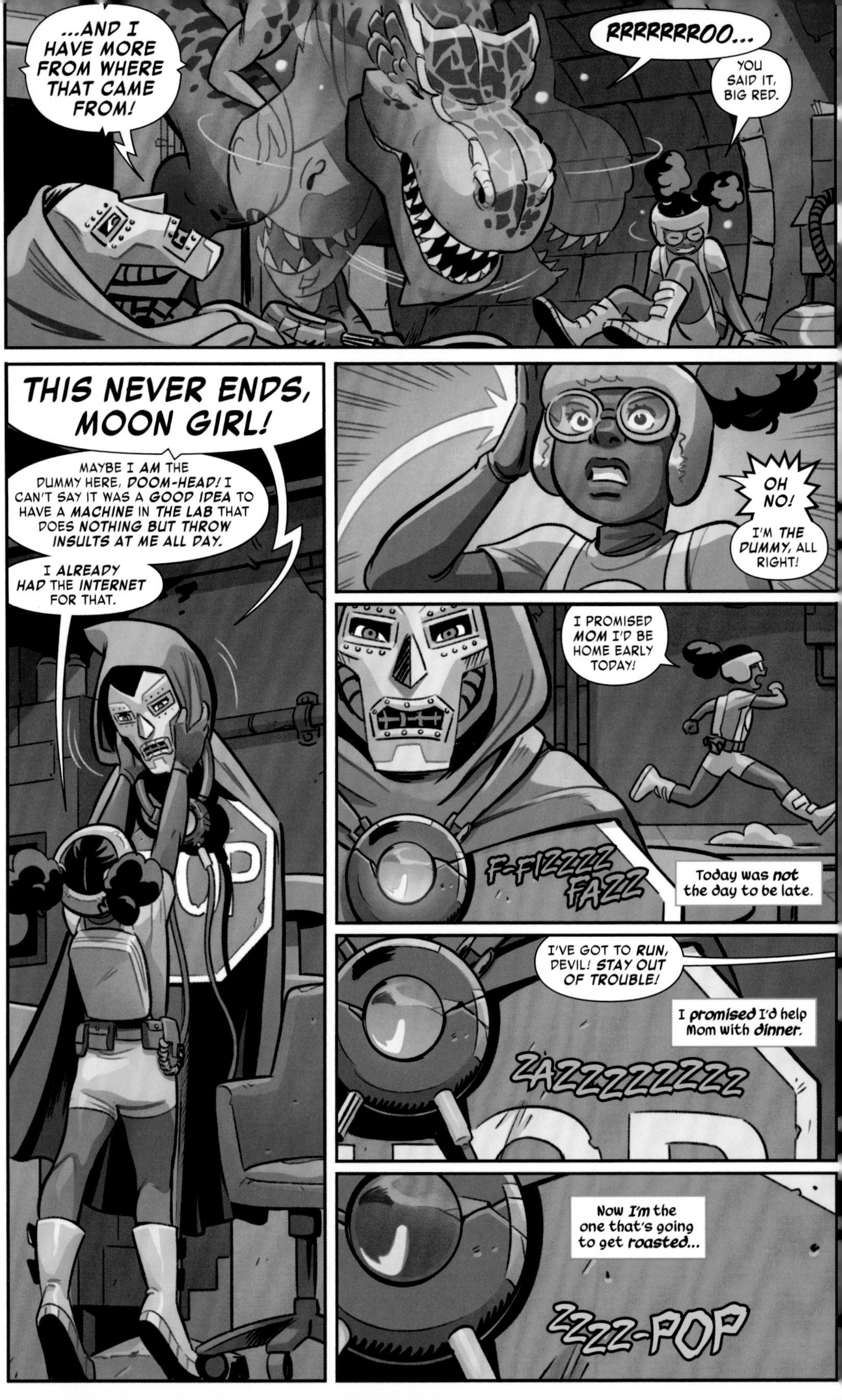
...AND I HAVE MORE FROM WHERE THAT CAME FROM!
RRRRRRROO...
YOU SAID IT, BIG RED.
THIS NEVER ENDS, MOON GIRL!
MAYBE I AM THE DUMMY HERE, DOOM-HEAD! I CAN'T SAY IT WAS A GOOD IDEA TO HAVE A MACHINE IN THE LAB THAT DOES NOTHING BUT THROW INSULTS AT ME ALL DAY.
I ALREADY HAD THE INTERNET FOR THAT.
OH NO!
I'M THE DUMMY, ALL RIGHT!
I PROMISED MOM I'D BE HOME EARLY TODAY!
F-FIZZZZ FAZZ
Today was not the day to be late.
I'VE GOT TO RUN, DEVIL! STAY OUT OF TROUBLE!
I promised I'd help Mom with dinner.
ZAZZZZZZZZZ
Now I'm the one that's going to get roasted...
ZZZZ-POP

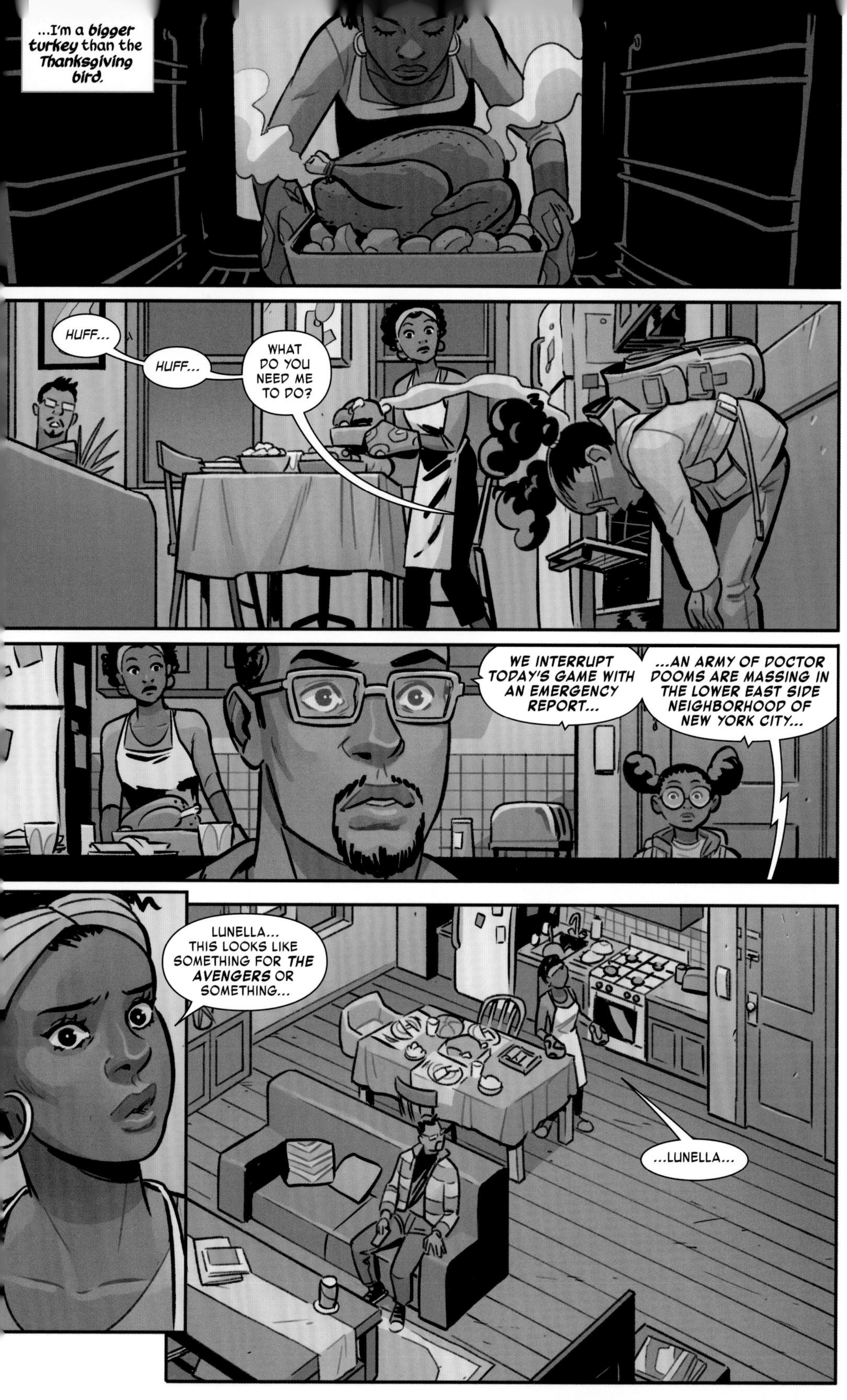
...I'm a *bigger turkey* than the *Thanksgiving* bird.
HUFF...
HUFF...
WHAT DO YOU NEED ME TO DO?
WE INTERRUPT TODAY'S GAME WITH AN EMERGENCY REPORT...
...AN ARMY OF DOCTOR DOOMS ARE MASSING IN THE LOWER EAST SIDE NEIGHBORHOOD OF NEW YORK CITY...
LUNELLA... THIS LOOKS LIKE SOMETHING FOR *THE AVENGERS* OR SOMETHING...
...LUNELLA...

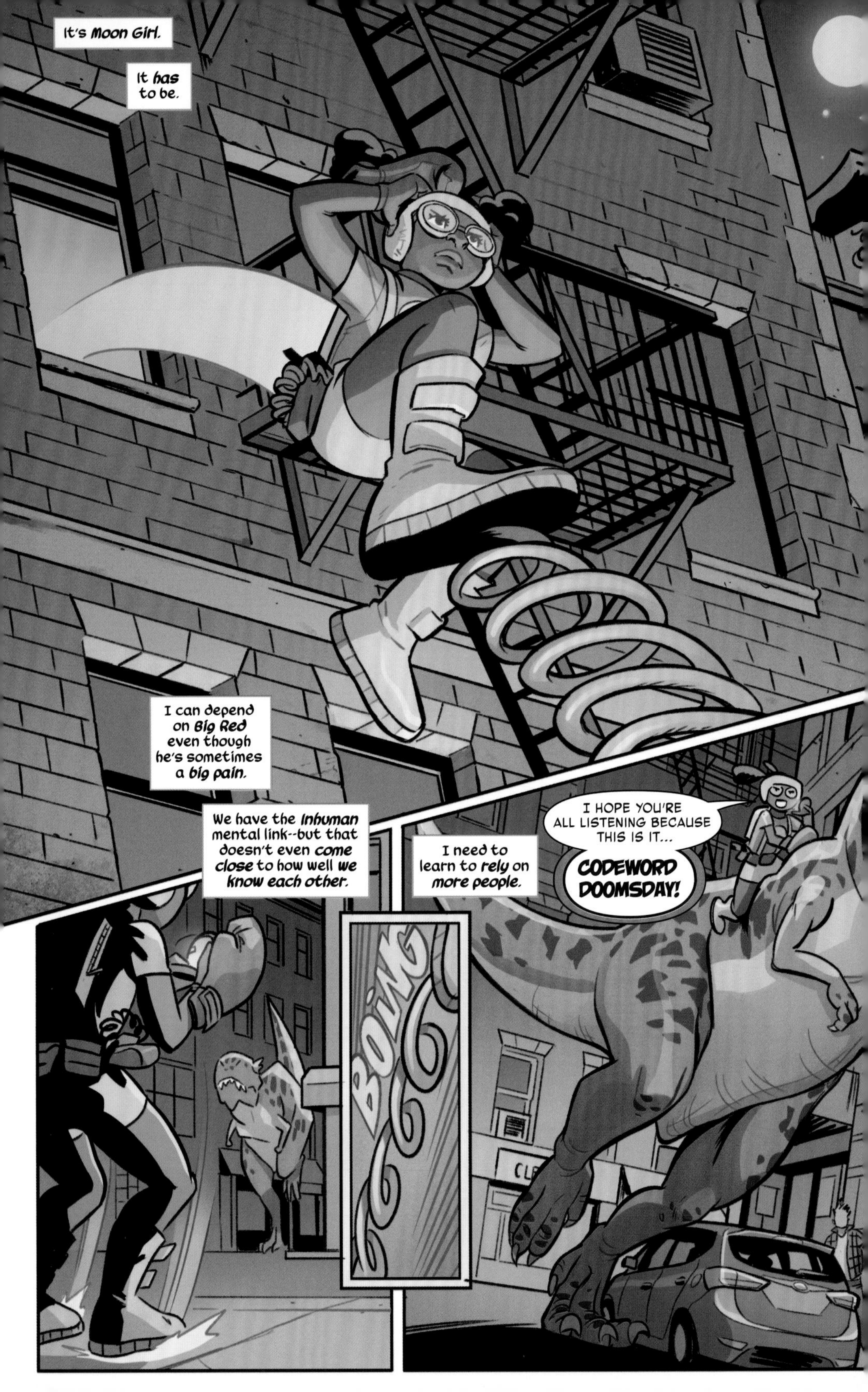

It's Moon Girl.
It has to be.
I can depend on Big Red even though he's sometimes a big pain.
We have the Inhuman mental link--but that doesn't even come close to how well we know each other.
I need to learn to rely on more people.
I HOPE YOU'RE ALL LISTENING BECAUSE THIS IS IT...
CODEWORD DOOMSDAY!
BOING

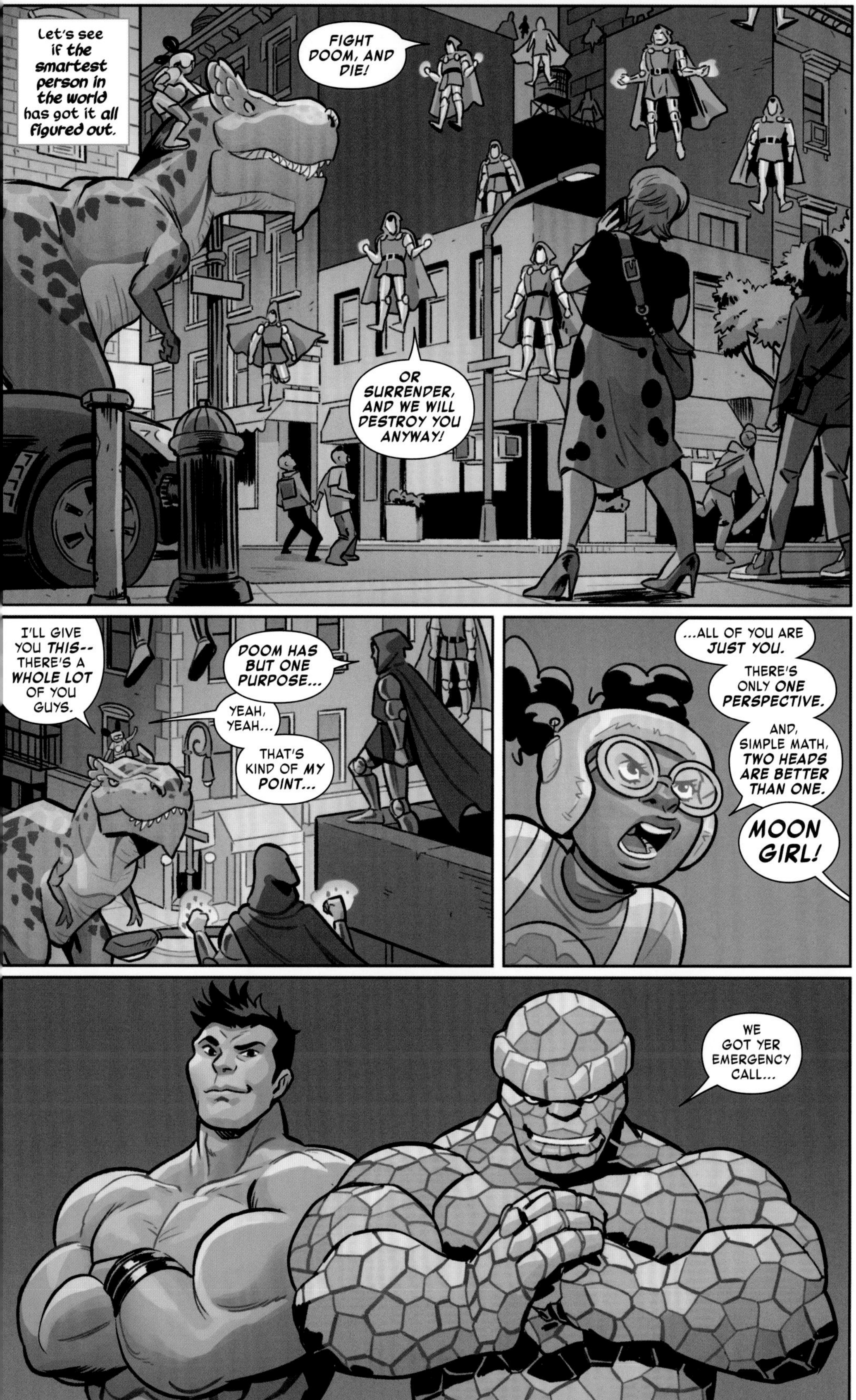
Let's see if the smartest person in the world has got it all figured out.
FIGHT DOOM, AND DIE!
OR SURRENDER, AND WE WILL DESTROY YOU ANYWAY!
I'LL GIVE YOU THIS-- THERE'S A WHOLE LOT OF YOU GUYS.
DOOM HAS BUT ONE PURPOSE...
YEAH, YEAH...
THAT'S KIND OF MY POINT...
...ALL OF YOU ARE JUST YOU.
THERE'S ONLY ONE PERSPECTIVE.
AND, SIMPLE MATH, TWO HEADS ARE BETTER THAN ONE.
MOON GIRL!
WE GOT YER EMERGENCY CALL...

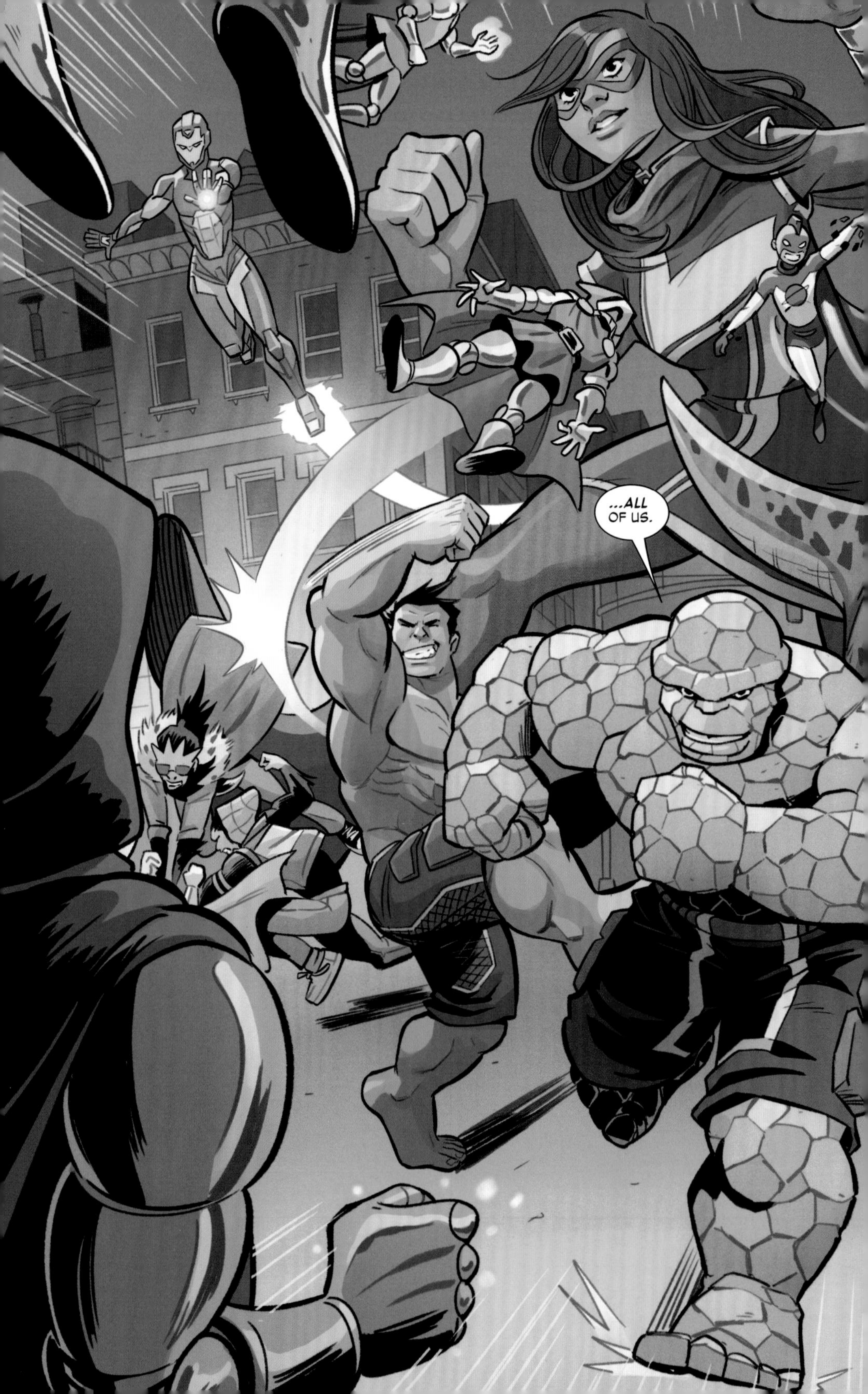
...ALL OF US.

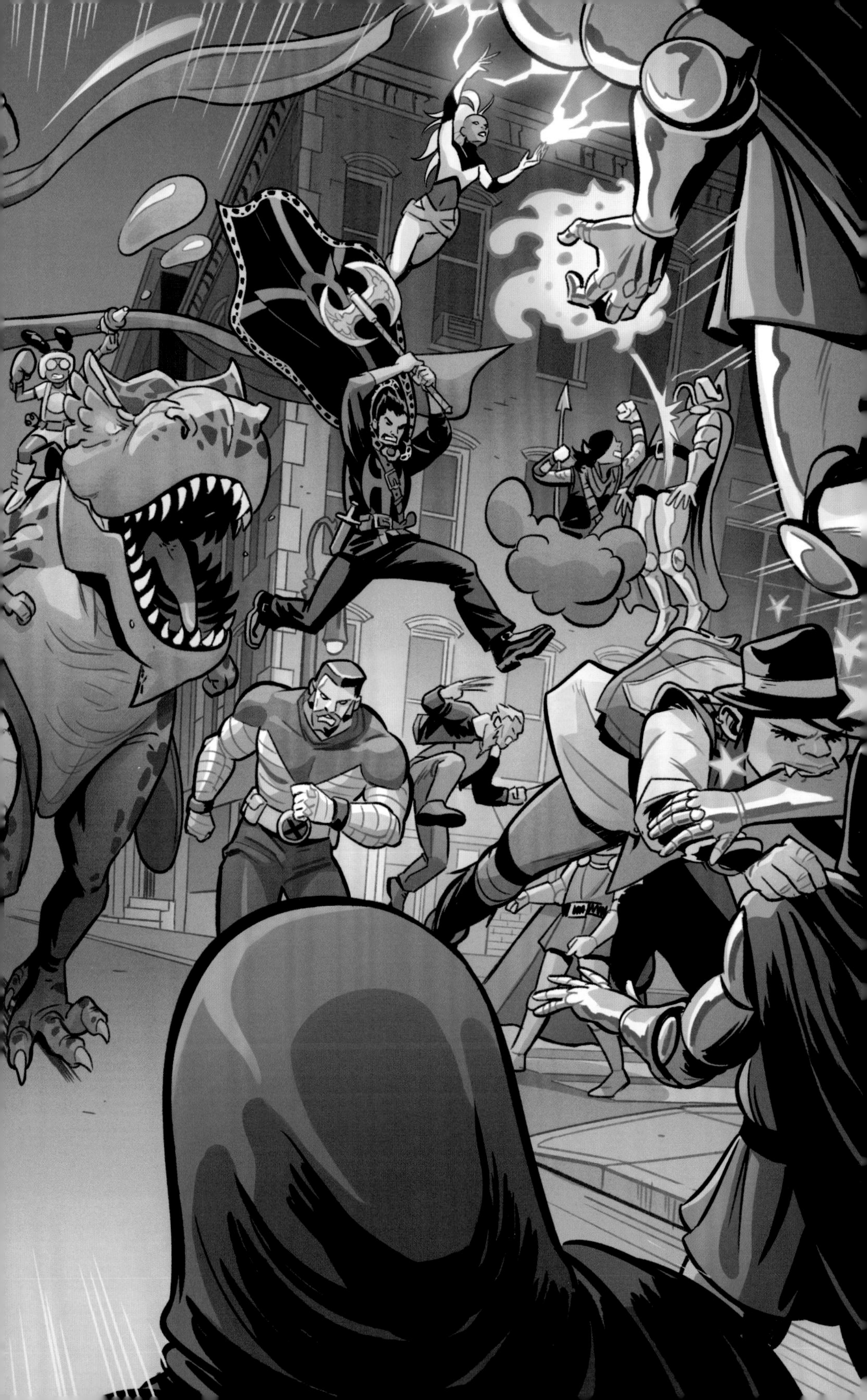

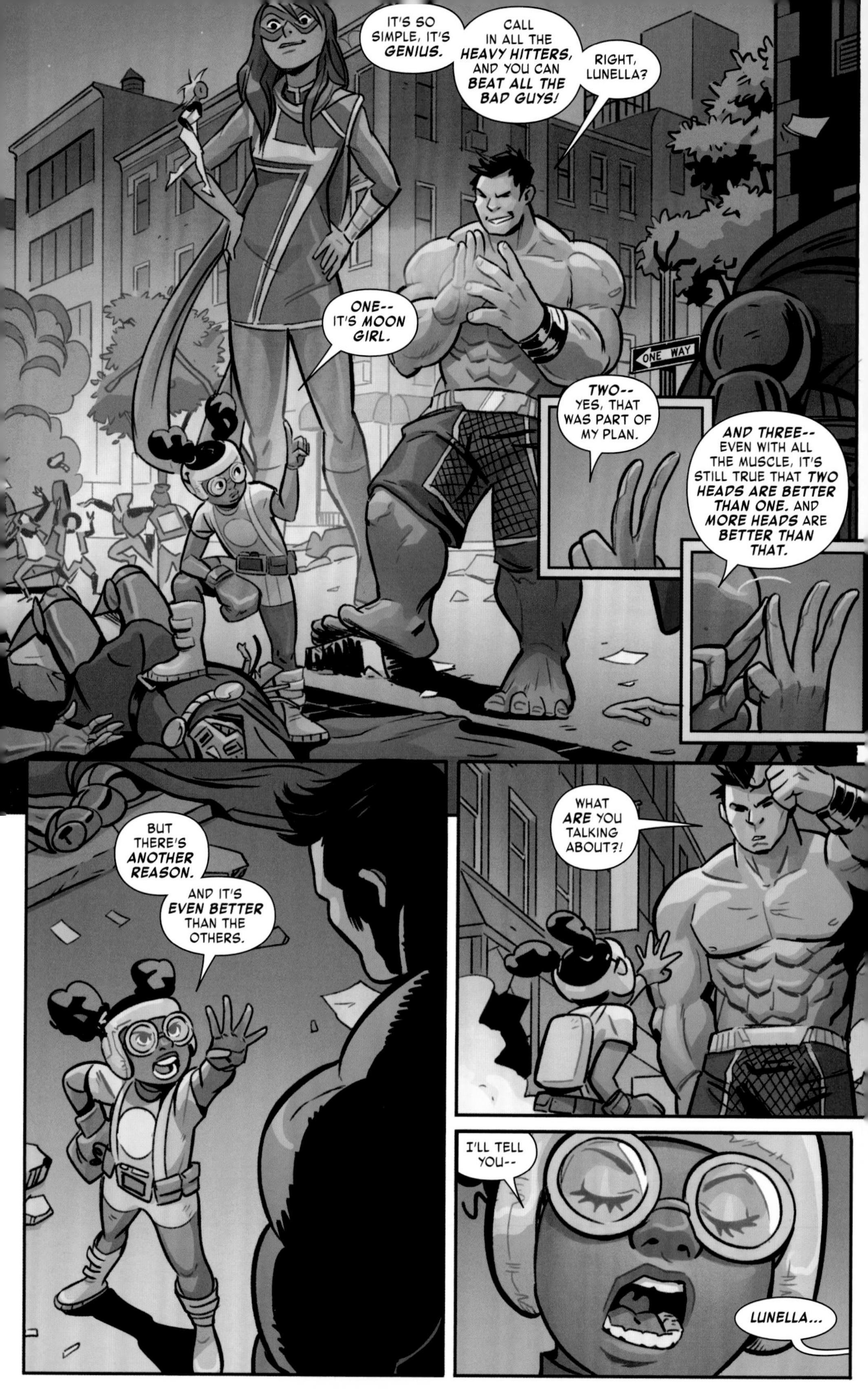
IT'S SO SIMPLE, IT'S GENIUS.
CALL IN ALL THE HEAVY HITTERS, AND YOU CAN BEAT ALL THE BAD GUYS!
RIGHT, LUNELLA?
ONE-- IT'S MOON GIRL.
ONE WAY
TWO-- YES, THAT WAS PART OF MY PLAN.
AND THREE-- EVEN WITH ALL THE MUSCLE, IT'S STILL TRUE THAT TWO HEADS ARE BETTER THAN ONE. AND MORE HEADS ARE BETTER THAN THAT.
BUT THERE'S ANOTHER REASON.
AND IT'S EVEN BETTER THAN THE OTHERS.
WHAT ARE YOU TALKING ABOUT?!
I'LL TELL YOU--
LUNELLA...

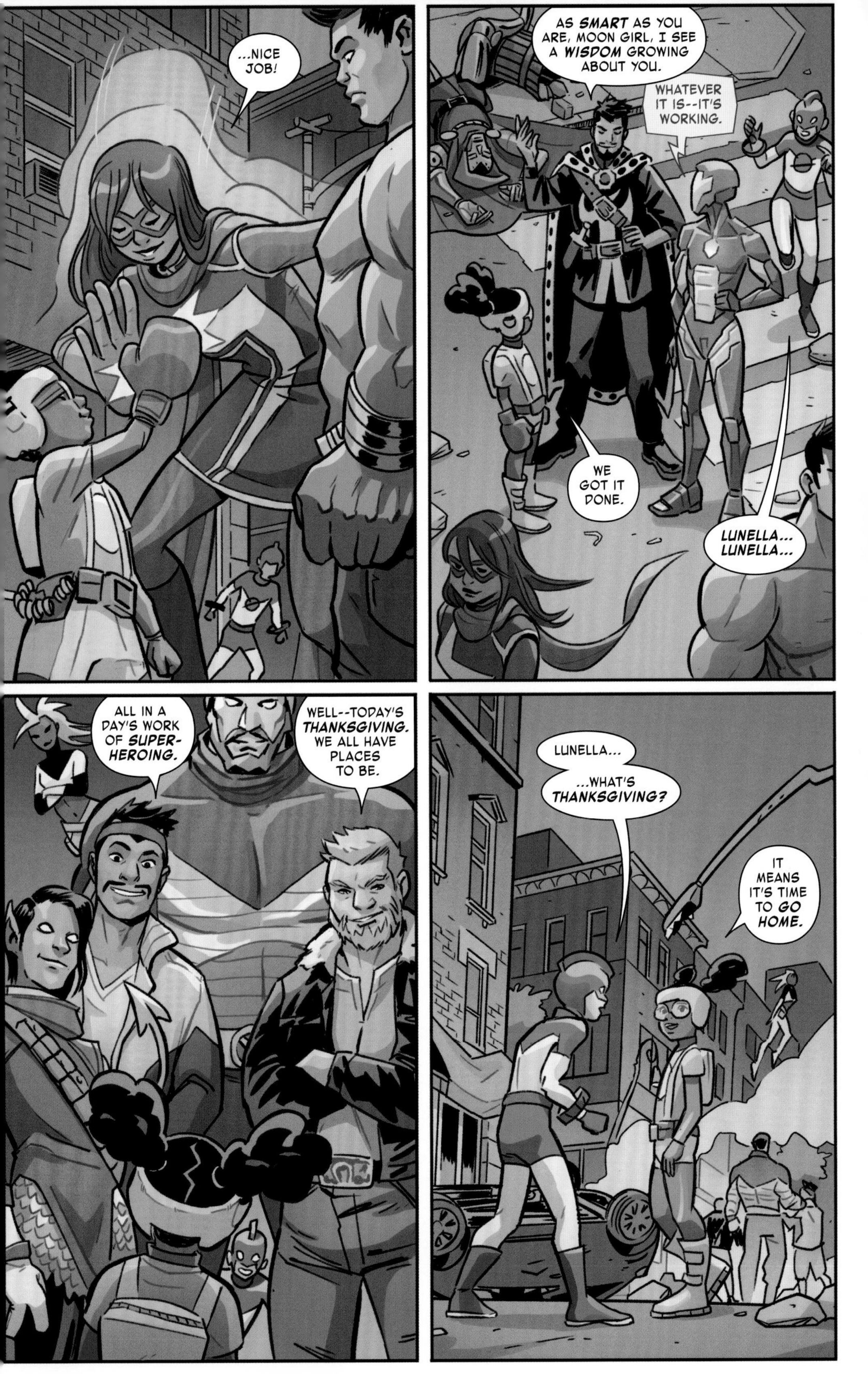
...NICE JOB!
AS SMART AS YOU ARE, MOON GIRL, I SEE A WISDOM GROWING ABOUT YOU.
WHATEVER IT IS--IT'S WORKING.
WE GOT IT DONE.
LUNELLA... LUNELLA...
ALL IN A DAY'S WORK OF SUPER-HEROING.
WELL--TODAY'S THANKSGIVING. WE ALL HAVE PLACES TO BE.
LUNELLA...
...WHAT'S THANKSGIVING?
IT MEANS IT'S TIME TO GO HOME.

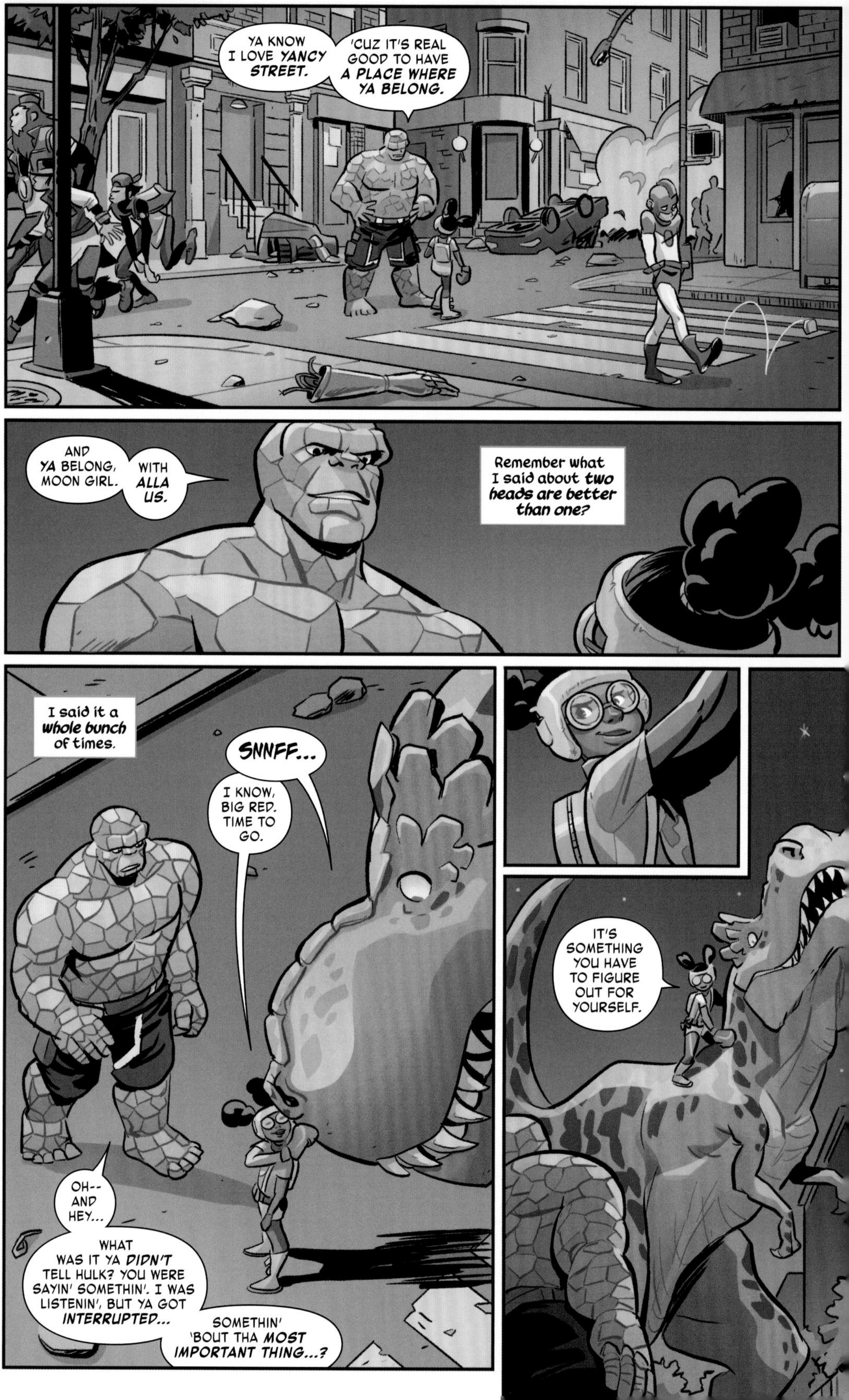
YA KNOW I LOVE YANCY STREET.
'CUZ IT'S REAL GOOD TO HAVE A PLACE WHERE YA BELONG.
AND YA BELONG, MOON GIRL.
WITH ALLA US.
Remember what I said about two heads are better than one?
I said it a whole bunch of times.
SNNFF...
I KNOW, BIG RED. TIME TO GO.
OH-- AND HEY...
WHAT WAS IT YA DIDN'T TELL HULK? YOU WERE SAYIN' SOMETHIN'. I WAS LISTENIN', BUT YA GOT INTERRUPTED...
SOMETHIN' 'BOUT THA MOST IMPORTANT THING...?
IT'S SOMETHING YOU HAVE TO FIGURE OUT FOR YOURSELF.

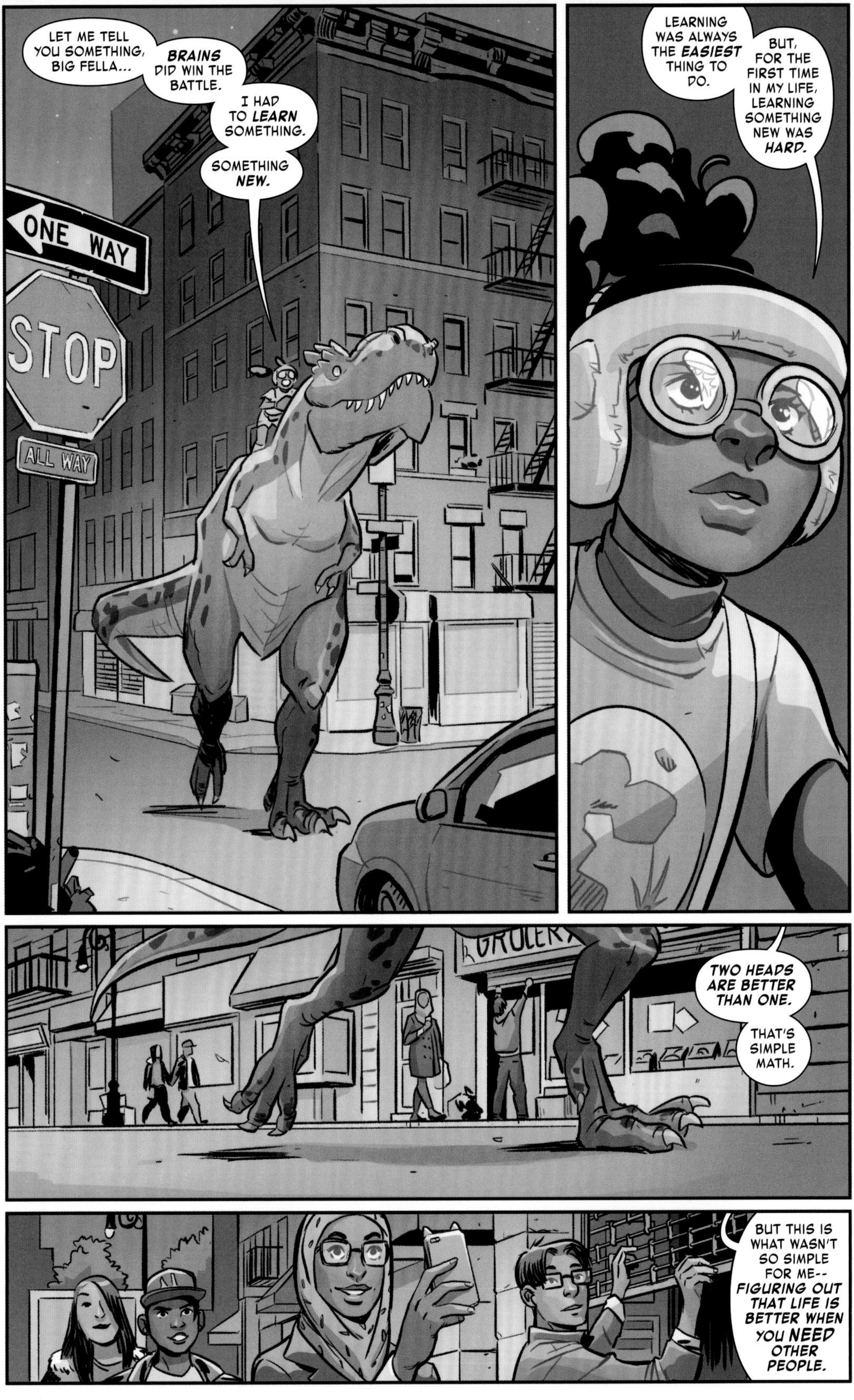
LET ME TELL YOU SOMETHING, BIG FELLA...
BRAINS DID WIN THE BATTLE.
I HAD TO LEARN SOMETHING.
SOMETHING NEW.
ONE WAY
STOP
ALL WAY
LEARNING WAS ALWAYS THE EASIEST THING TO DO.
BUT, FOR THE FIRST TIME IN MY LIFE, LEARNING SOMETHING NEW WAS HARD.
TWO HEADS ARE BETTER THAN ONE.
THAT'S SIMPLE MATH.
BUT THIS IS WHAT WASN'T SO SIMPLE FOR ME-- FIGURING OUT THAT LIFE IS BETTER WHEN YOU NEED OTHER PEOPLE.

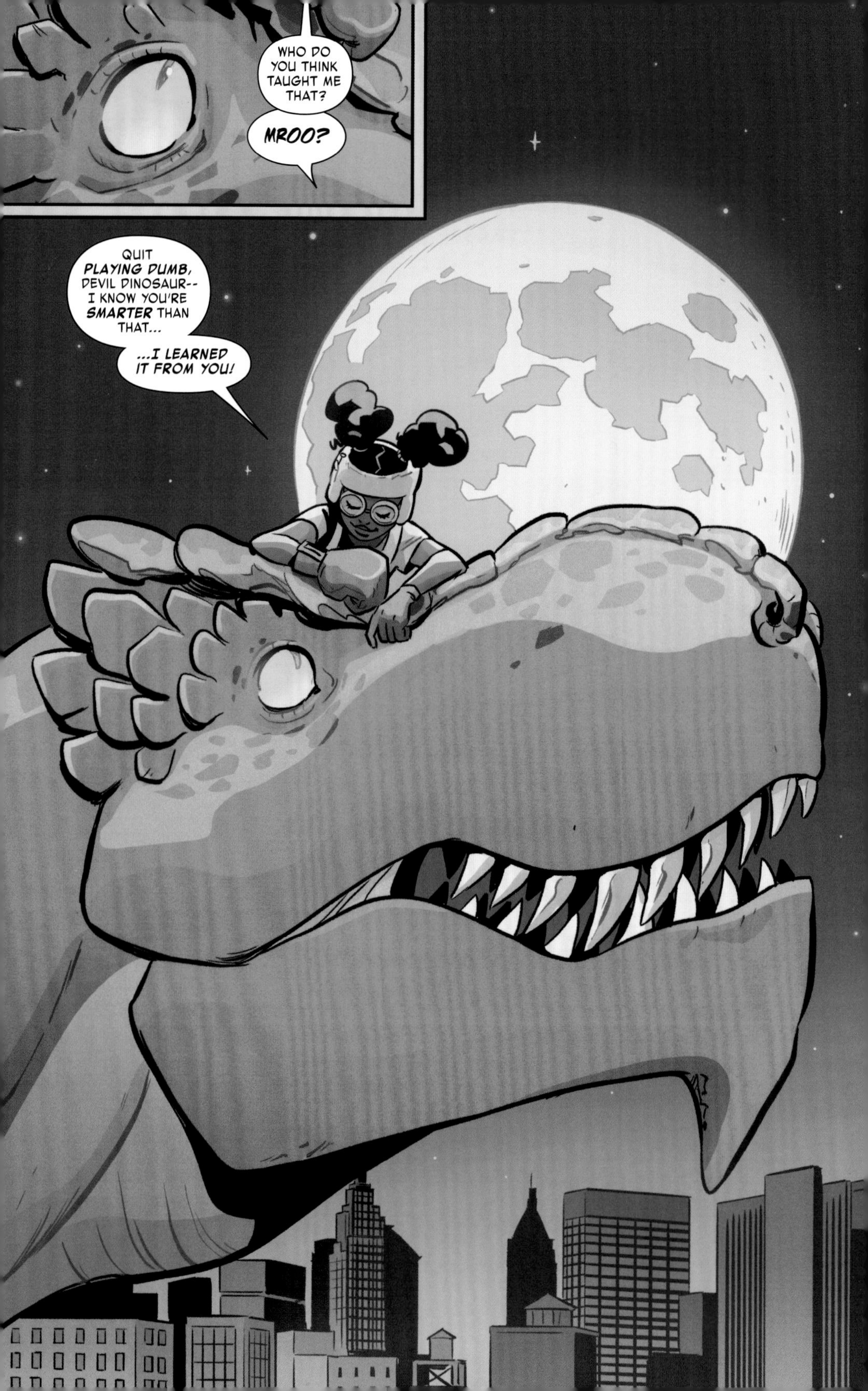
WHO DO YOU THINK TAUGHT ME THAT?
MROO?
QUIT PLAYING DUMB, DEVIL DINOSAUR-- I KNOW YOU'RE SMARTER THAN THAT...
...I LEARNED IT FROM YOU!

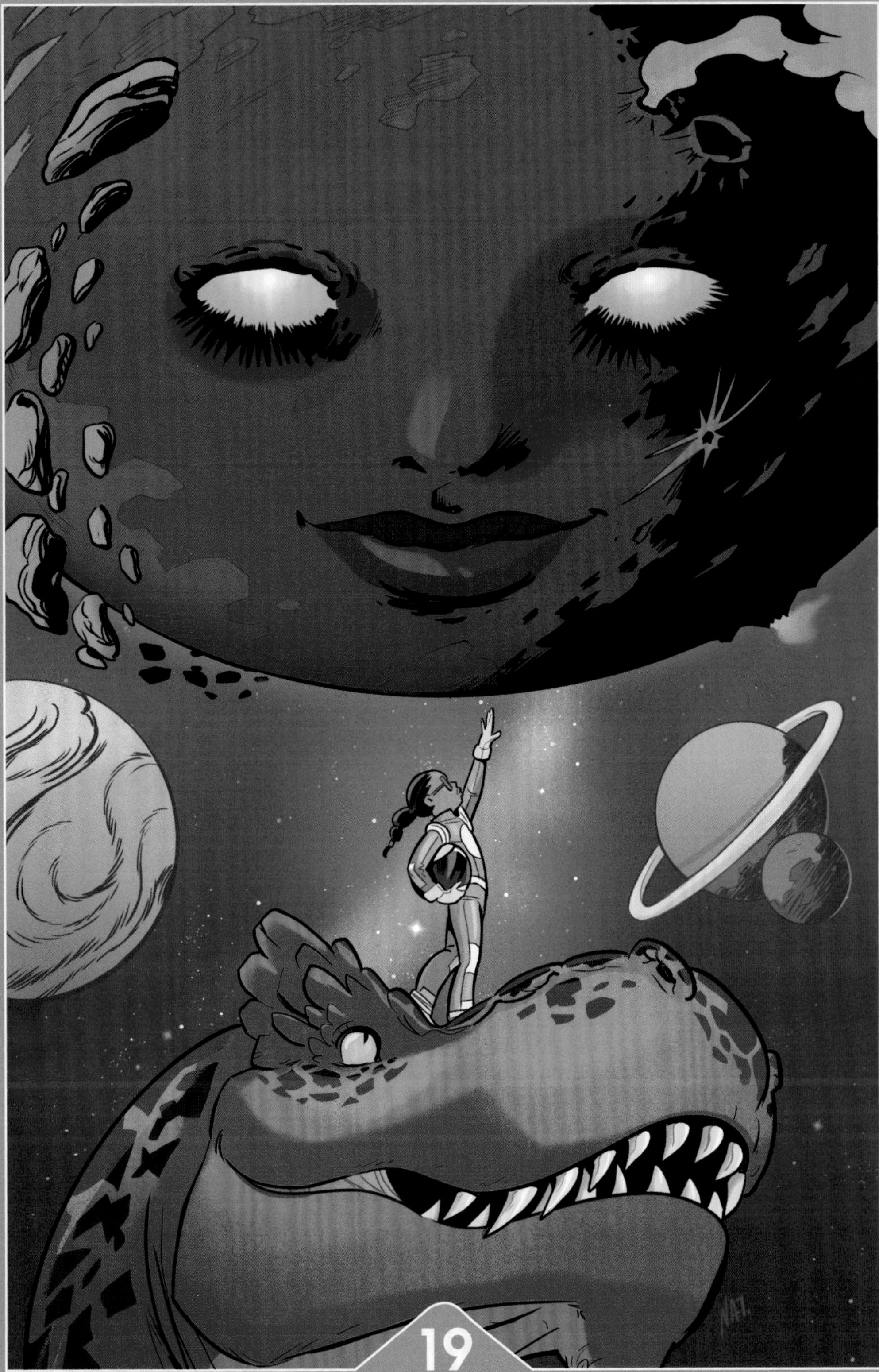

19

"SYNCHRONOUS"

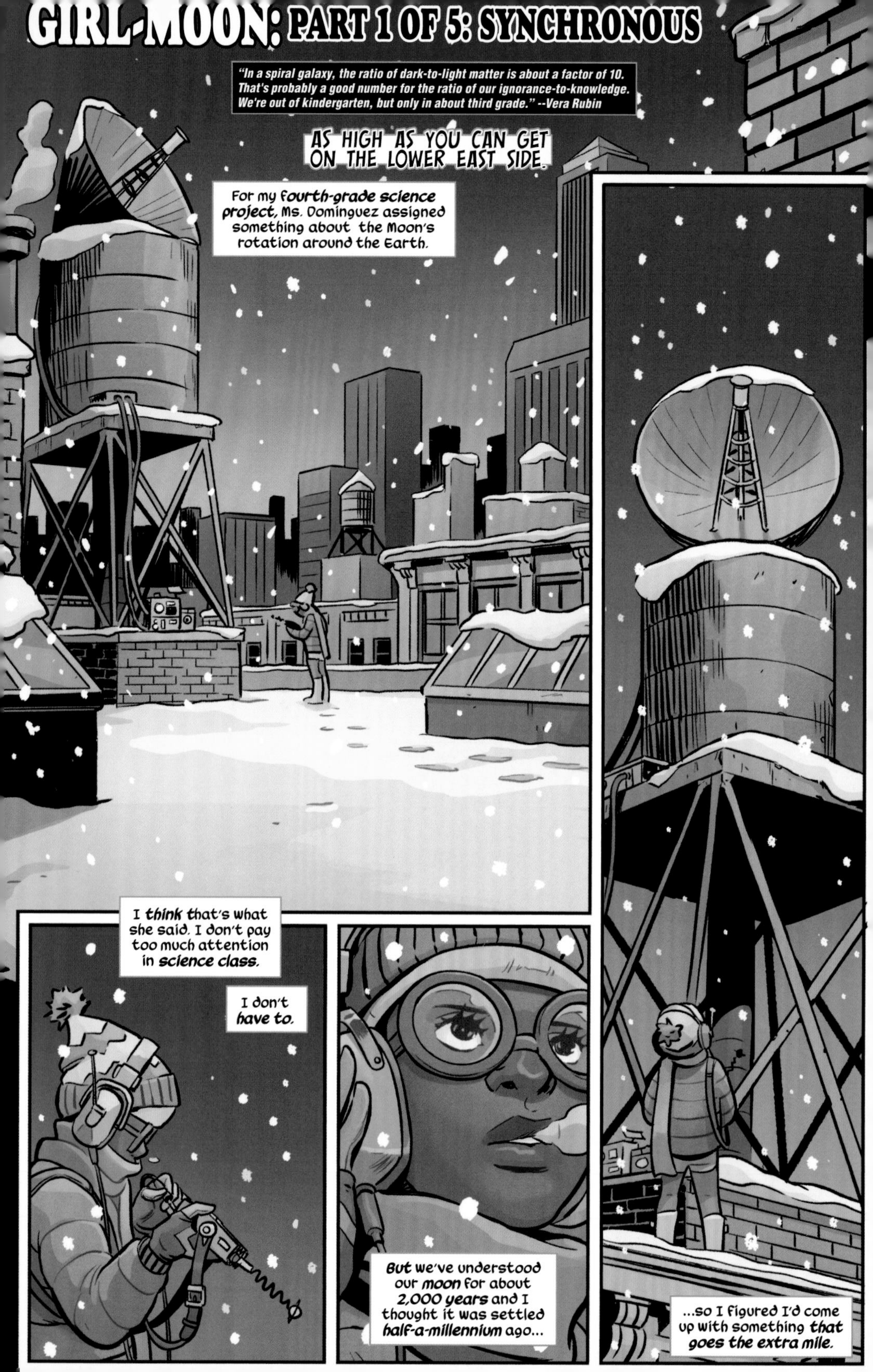
GIRL-MOON: PART 1 OF 5: SYNCHRONOUS
"In a spiral galaxy, the ratio of dark-to-light matter is about a factor of 10. That's probably a good number for the ratio of our ignorance-to-knowledge. We're out of kindergarten, but only in about third grade." --Vera Rubin
AS HIGH AS YOU CAN GET ON THE LOWER EAST SIDE.
For my fourth-grade science project, Ms. Dominguez assigned something about the Moon's rotation around the Earth.
I think that's what she said. I don't pay too much attention in science class.
I don't have to.
But we've understood our moon for about 2,000 years and I thought it was settled half-a-millennium ago...
...so I figured I'd come up with something that goes the extra mile.

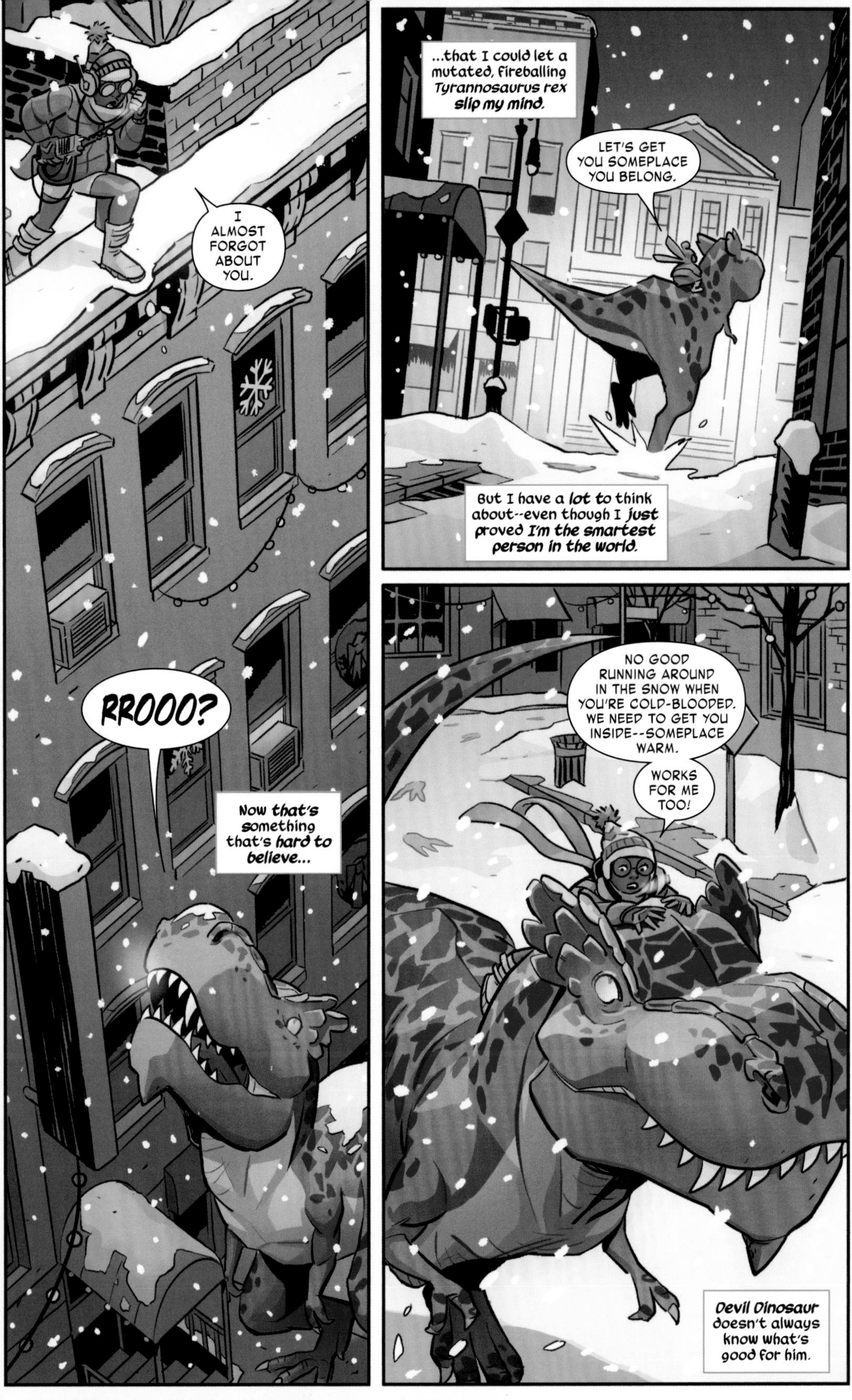
I ALMOST FORGOT ABOUT YOU.
RROOO?
Now that's something that's hard to believe...
...that I could let a mutated, fireballing Tyrannosaurus rex slip my mind.
LET'S GET YOU SOMEPLACE YOU BELONG.
But I have a lot to think about--even though I just proved I'm the smartest person in the world.
NO GOOD RUNNING AROUND IN THE SNOW WHEN YOU'RE COLD-BLOODED. WE NEED TO GET YOU INSIDE--SOMEPLACE WARM.
WORKS FOR ME TOO!
Devil Dinosaur doesn't always know what's good for him.

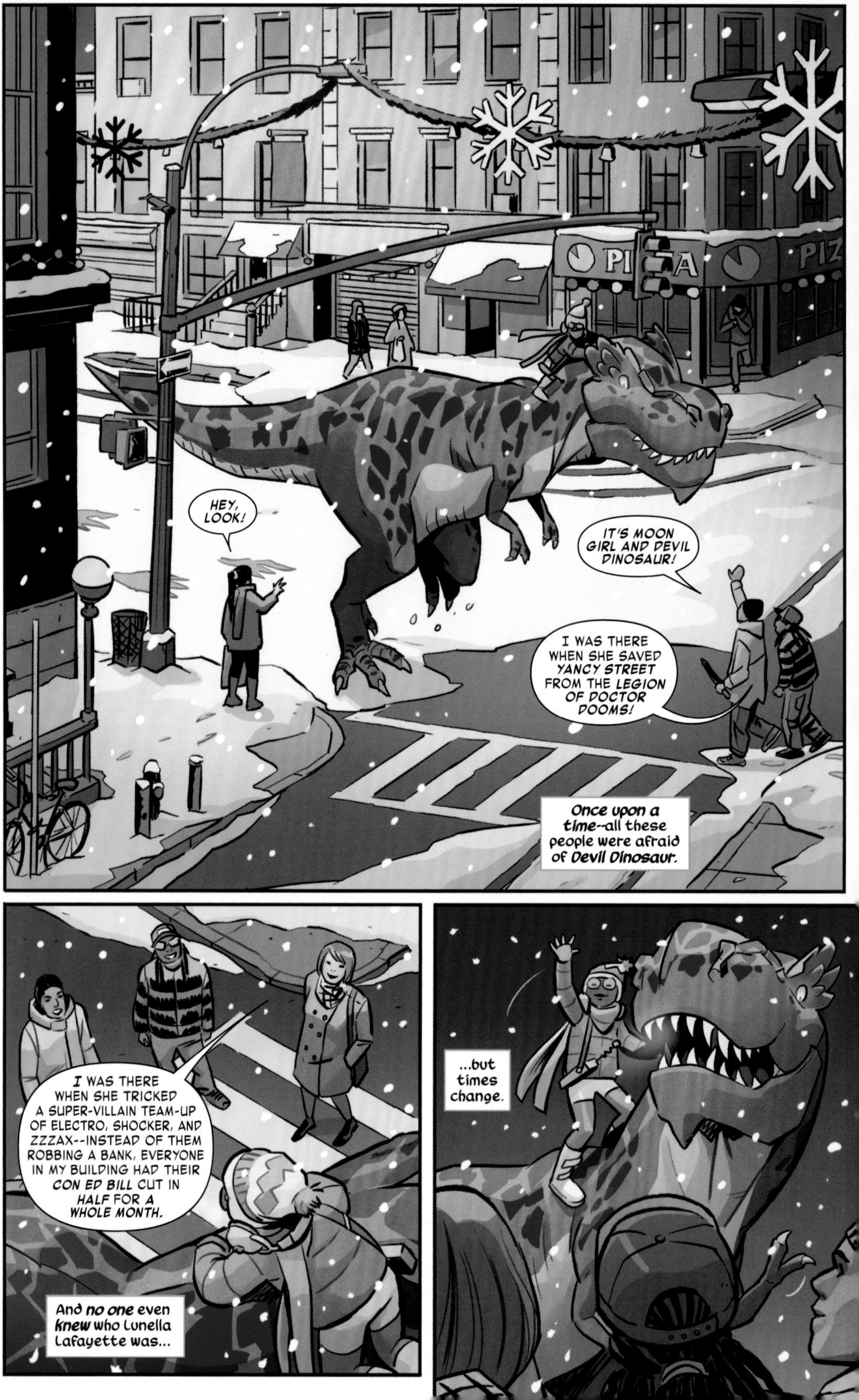

PIZZA
HEY, LOOK!
IT'S MOON GIRL AND DEVIL DINOSAUR!
I WAS THERE WHEN SHE SAVED YANCY STREET FROM THE LEGION OF DOCTOR DOOMS!
Once upon a time--all these people were afraid of Devil Dinosaur.
I WAS THERE WHEN SHE TRICKED A SUPER-VILLAIN TEAM-UP OF ELECTRO, SHOCKER, AND ZZZAX--INSTEAD OF THEM ROBBING A BANK, EVERYONE IN MY BUILDING HAD THEIR CON ED BILL CUT IN HALF FOR A WHOLE MONTH.
And no one even knew who Lunella Lafayette was...
...but times change.

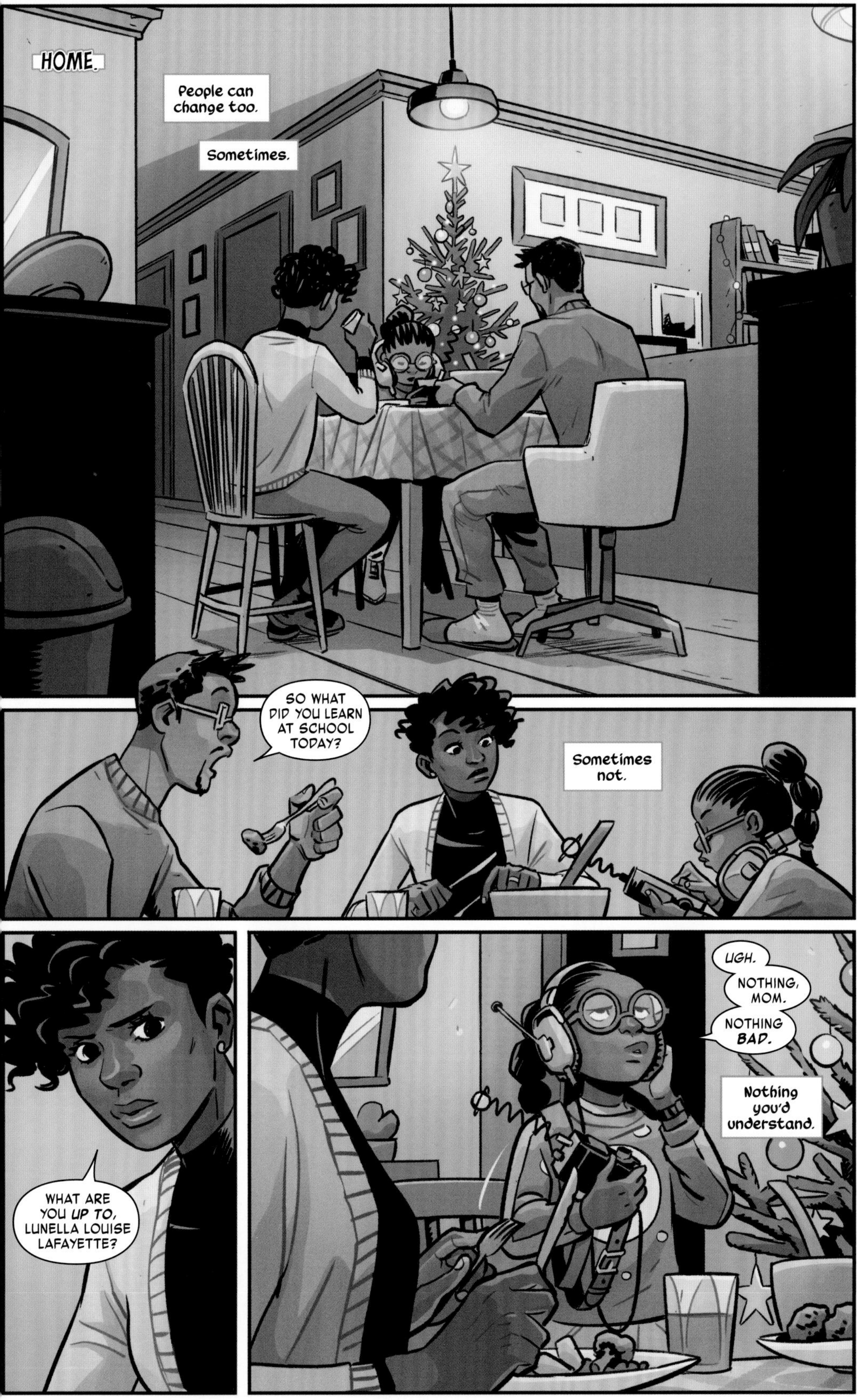
HOME.
People can change too.
Sometimes.
SO WHAT DID YOU LEARN AT SCHOOL TODAY?
Sometimes not.
WHAT ARE YOU *UP TO*, LUNELLA LOUISE LAFAYETTE?
UGH.
NOTHING, MOM.
NOTHING *BAD*.
Nothing you'd understand.

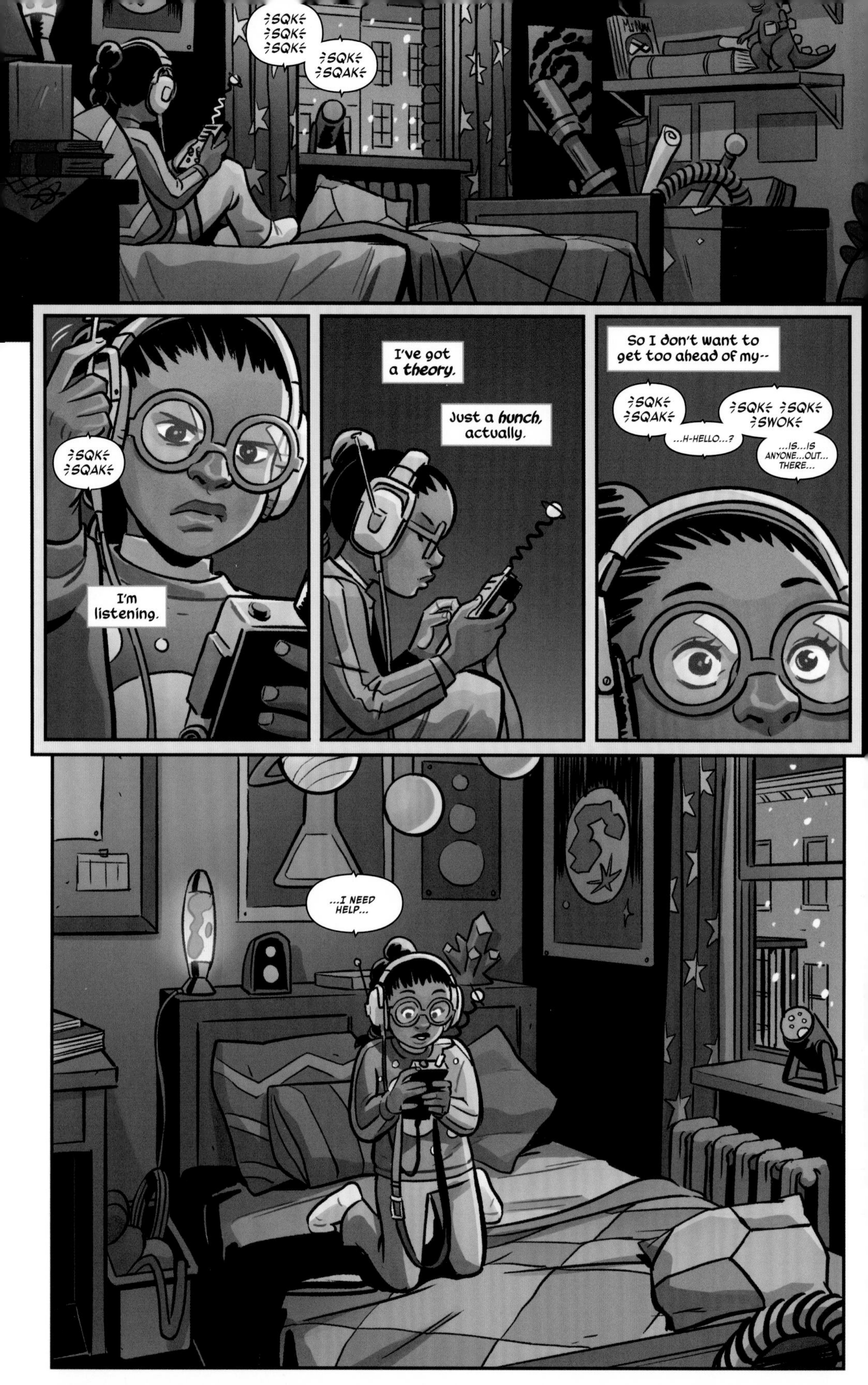

SQK SQK SQK
SQK SQAK
SQK SQAK
I'm listening.
I've got a *theory.*
Just a *hunch,* actually.
So I don't want to get too ahead of my--
SQK SQAK
...H-HELLO...?
SQK SQK SWOK
...IS...IS ANYONE...OUT... THERE...
...I NEED HELP...

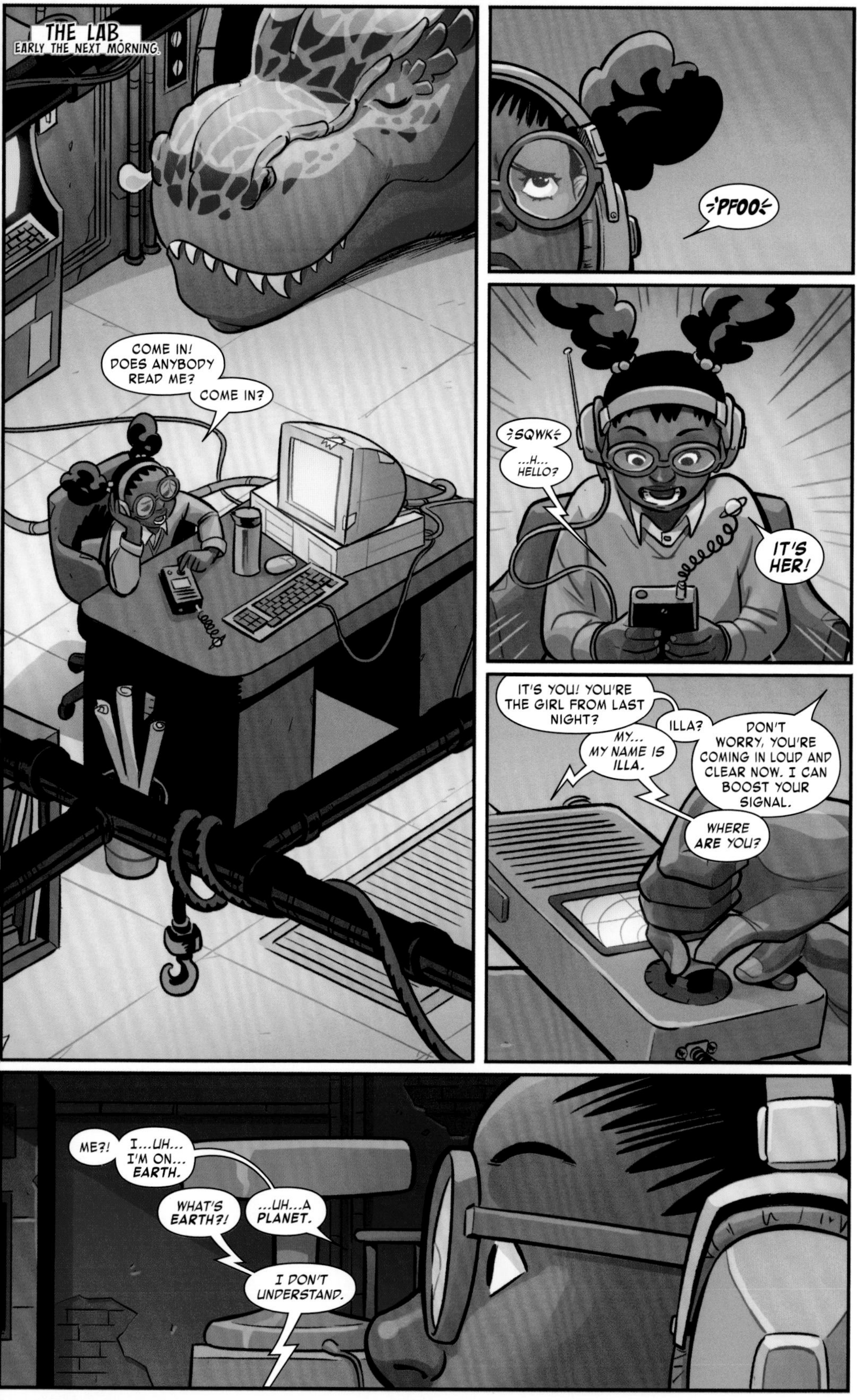
THE LAB.
EARLY THE NEXT MORNING.
COME IN! DOES ANYBODY READ ME?
COME IN?
PFOO
SQWK
...H... HELLO?
IT'S HER!
IT'S YOU! YOU'RE THE GIRL FROM LAST NIGHT?
MY... MY NAME IS ILLA.
ILLA?
DON'T WORRY, YOU'RE COMING IN LOUD AND CLEAR NOW. I CAN BOOST YOUR SIGNAL.
WHERE ARE YOU?
ME?!
I...UH... I'M ON... EARTH.
WHAT'S EARTH?!
...UH...A PLANET.
I DON'T UNDERSTAND.

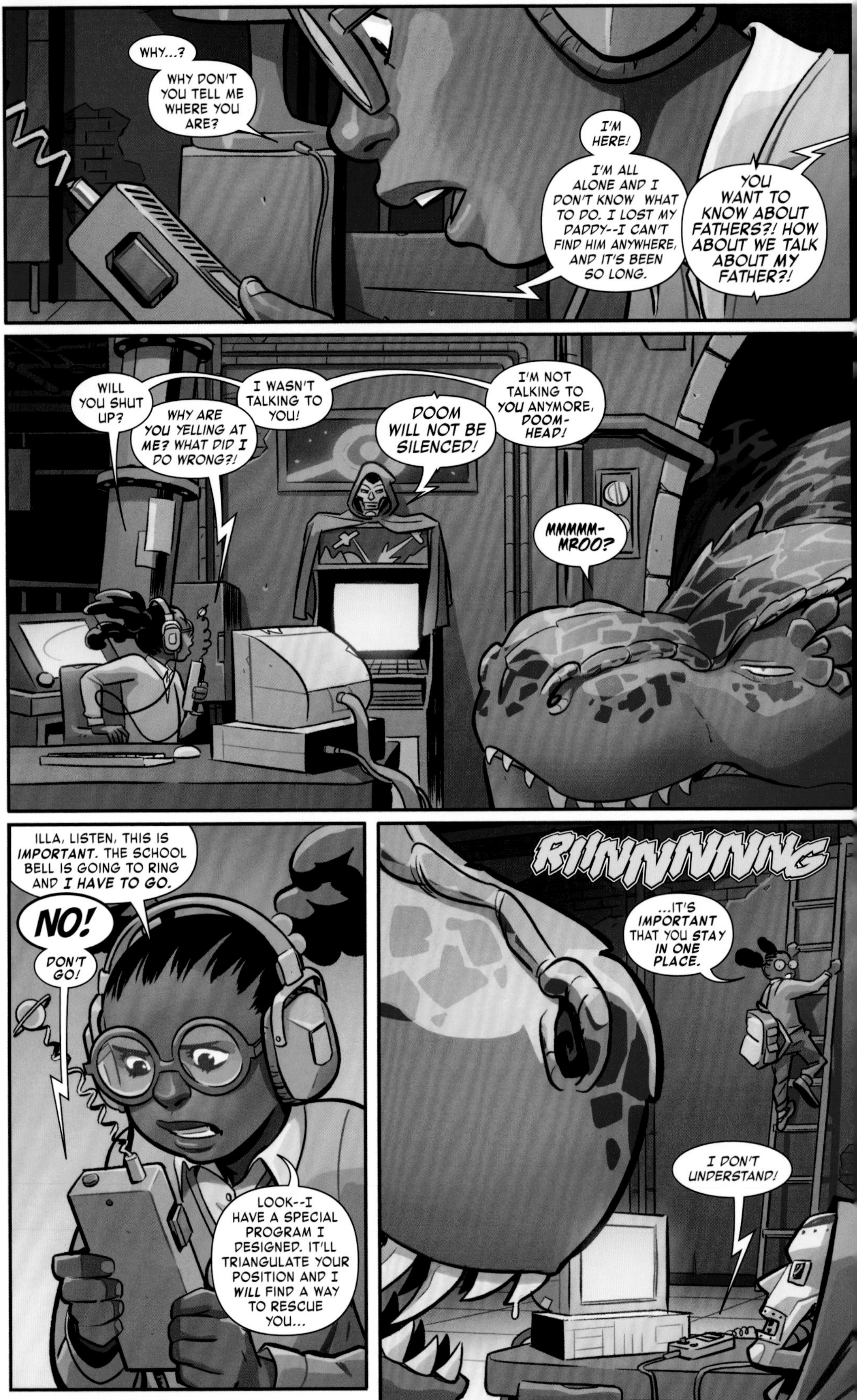
WHY...?
WHY DON'T YOU TELL ME WHERE YOU ARE?
I'M HERE!
I'M ALL ALONE AND I DON'T KNOW WHAT TO DO. I LOST MY DADDY--I CAN'T FIND HIM ANYWHERE, AND IT'S BEEN SO LONG.
YOU WANT TO KNOW ABOUT FATHERS?! HOW ABOUT WE TALK ABOUT MY FATHER?!
WILL YOU SHUT UP?
WHY ARE YOU YELLING AT ME? WHAT DID I DO WRONG?!
I WASN'T TALKING TO YOU!
DOOM WILL NOT BE SILENCED!
I'M NOT TALKING TO YOU ANYMORE, DOOM-HEAD!
MMMMM-MROO?
ILLA, LISTEN, THIS IS IMPORTANT. THE SCHOOL BELL IS GOING TO RING AND I HAVE TO GO.
NO!
DON'T GO!
LOOK--I HAVE A SPECIAL PROGRAM I DESIGNED. IT'LL TRIANGULATE YOUR POSITION AND I WILL FIND A WAY TO RESCUE YOU...
RIINNNNNG
...IT'S IMPORTANT THAT YOU STAY IN ONE PLACE.
I DON'T UNDERSTAND!

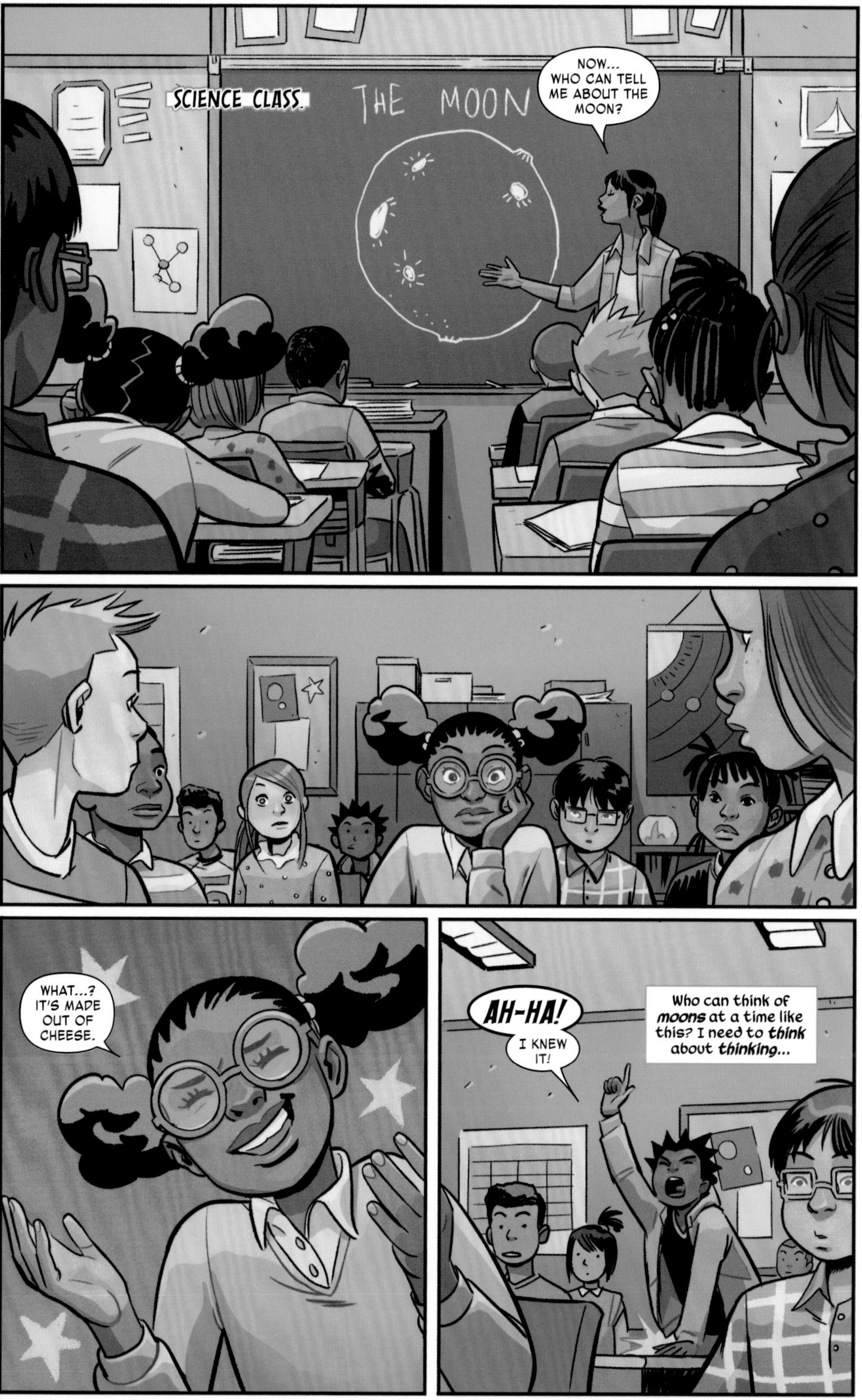
SCIENCE CLASS.
THE MOON
NOW... WHO CAN TELL ME ABOUT THE MOON?
WHAT...? IT'S MADE OUT OF CHEESE.
AH-HA! I KNEW IT!
Who can think of moons at a time like this? I need to think about thinking...

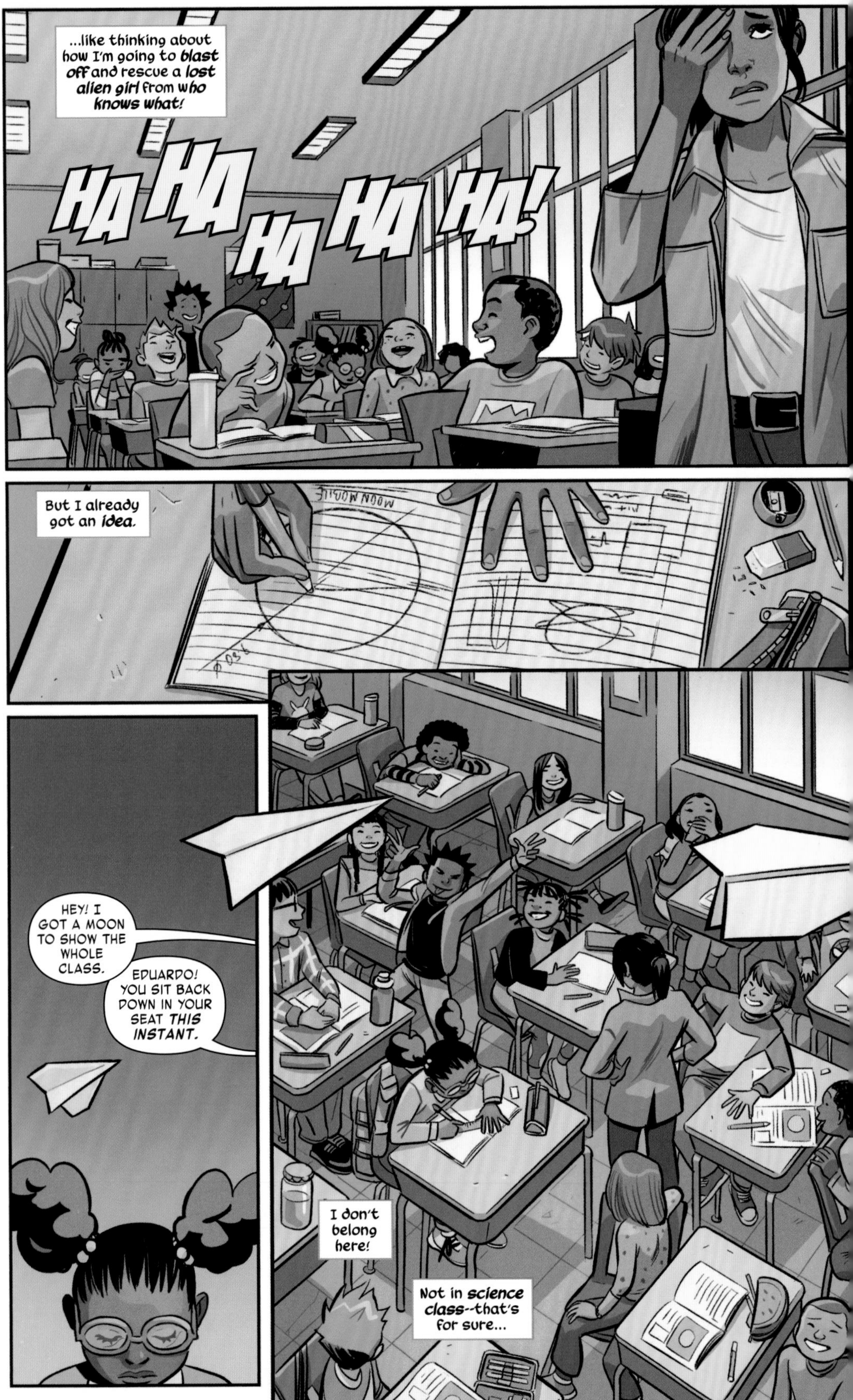
...like thinking about how I'm going to blast off and rescue a lost alien girl from who knows what!
HA HA HA HA HA!
But I already got an idea.
HEY! I GOT A MOON TO SHOW THE WHOLE CLASS.
EDUARDO! YOU SIT BACK DOWN IN YOUR SEAT THIS INSTANT.
I don't belong here!
Not in science class--that's for sure...

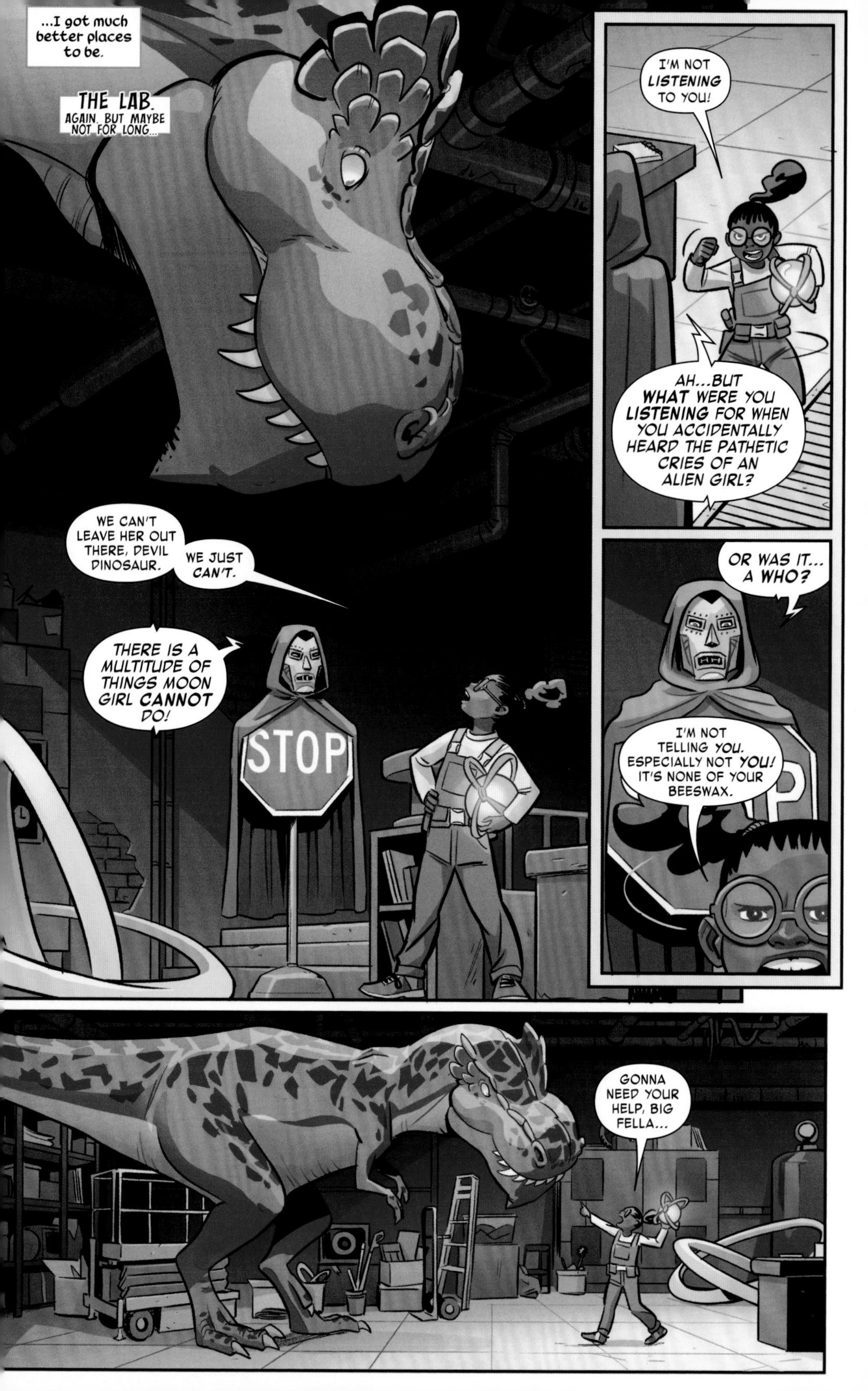
...I got much better places to be.
THE LAB. AGAIN. BUT MAYBE NOT FOR LONG...
I'M NOT LISTENING TO YOU!
AH...BUT WHAT WERE YOU LISTENING FOR WHEN YOU ACCIDENTALLY HEARD THE PATHETIC CRIES OF AN ALIEN GIRL?
WE CAN'T LEAVE HER OUT THERE, DEVIL DINOSAUR.
WE JUST CAN'T.
THERE IS A MULTITUDE OF THINGS MOON GIRL CANNOT DO!
STOP
OR WAS IT... A WHO?
I'M NOT TELLING YOU. ESPECIALLY NOT YOU! IT'S NONE OF YOUR BEESWAX.
GONNA NEED YOUR HELP, BIG FELLA...

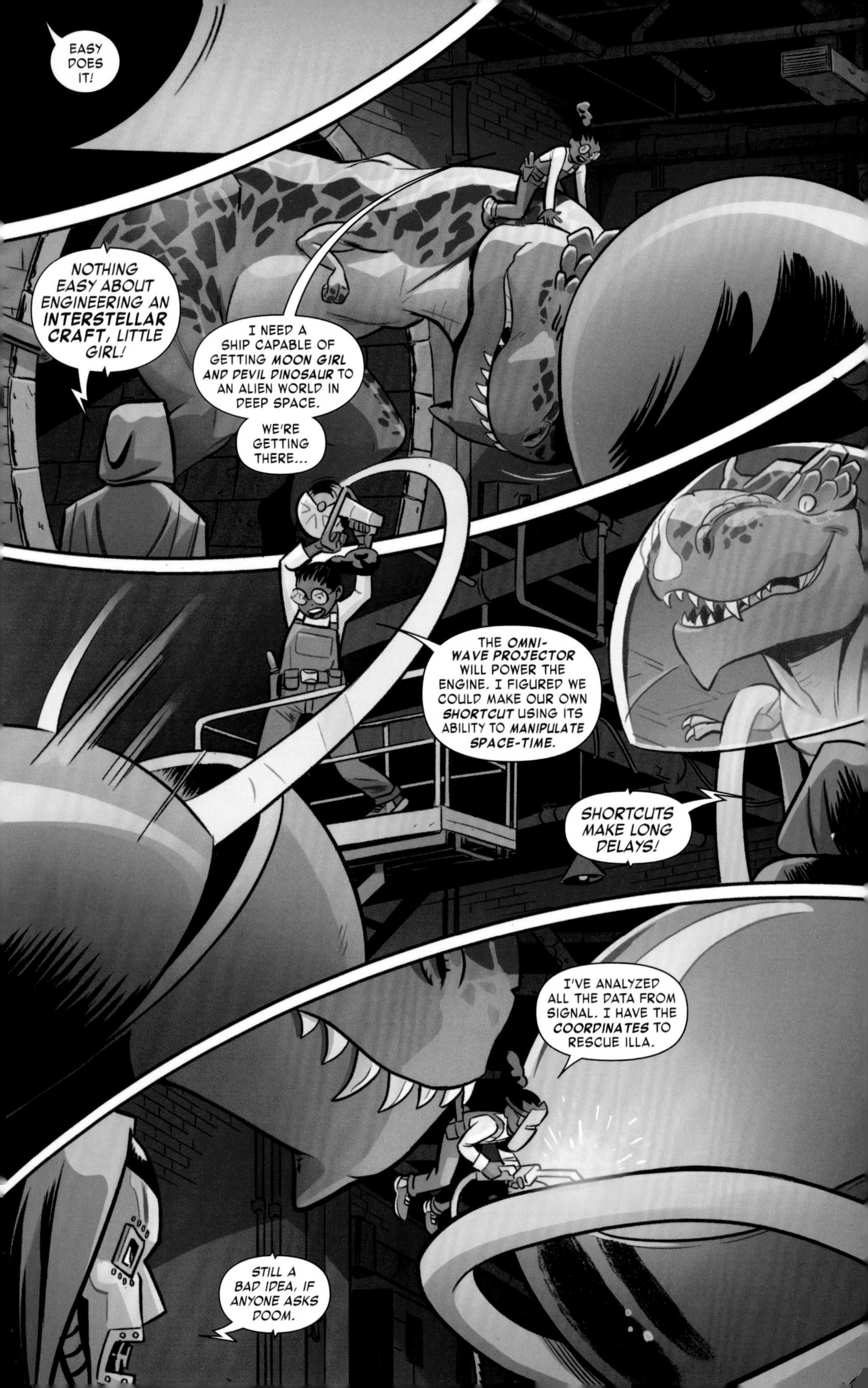
EASY DOES IT!
NOTHING EASY ABOUT ENGINEERING AN INTERSTELLAR CRAFT, LITTLE GIRL!
I NEED A SHIP CAPABLE OF GETTING MOON GIRL AND DEVIL DINOSAUR TO AN ALIEN WORLD IN DEEP SPACE.
WE'RE GETTING THERE...
THE OMNI-WAVE PROJECTOR WILL POWER THE ENGINE. I FIGURED WE COULD MAKE OUR OWN SHORTCUT USING ITS ABILITY TO MANIPULATE SPACE-TIME.
SHORTCUTS MAKE LONG DELAYS!
I'VE ANALYZED ALL THE DATA FROM SIGNAL. I HAVE THE COORDINATES TO RESCUE ILLA.
STILL A BAD IDEA, IF ANYONE ASKS DOOM.

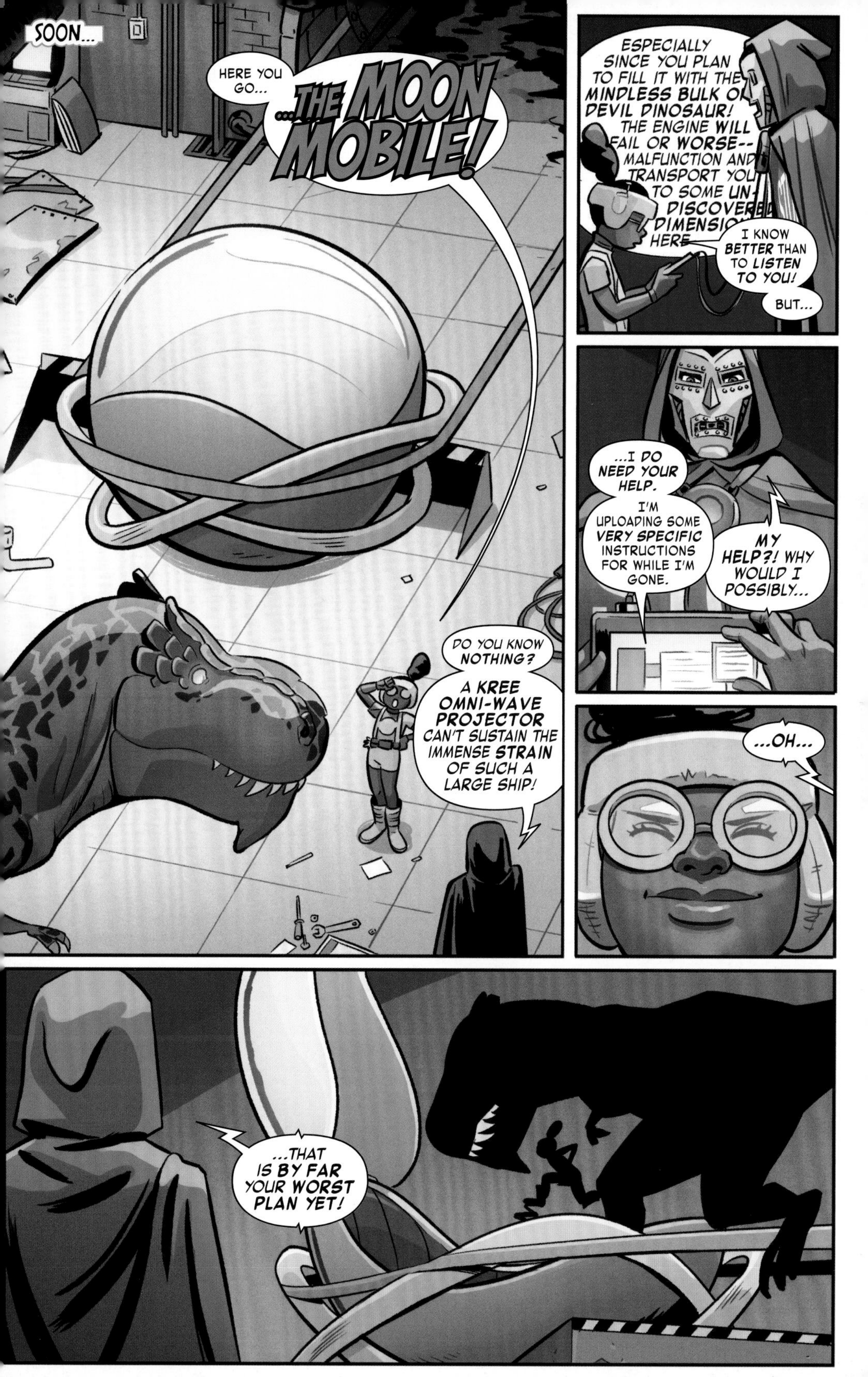
SOON...
HERE YOU GO...
...THE MOON MOBILE!
DO YOU KNOW NOTHING?
A KREE OMNI-WAVE PROJECTOR CAN'T SUSTAIN THE IMMENSE STRAIN OF SUCH A LARGE SHIP!
ESPECIALLY SINCE YOU PLAN TO FILL IT WITH THE MINDLESS BULK OF DEVIL DINOSAUR! THE ENGINE WILL FAIL OR WORSE-- MALFUNCTION AND TRANSPORT YOU TO SOME UN-DISCOVERED DIMENSION HERE
I KNOW BETTER THAN TO LISTEN TO YOU!
BUT...
...I DO NEED YOUR HELP.
I'M UPLOADING SOME VERY SPECIFIC INSTRUCTIONS FOR WHILE I'M GONE.
MY HELP?! WHY WOULD I POSSIBLY...
...OH...
...THAT IS BY FAR YOUR WORST PLAN YET!

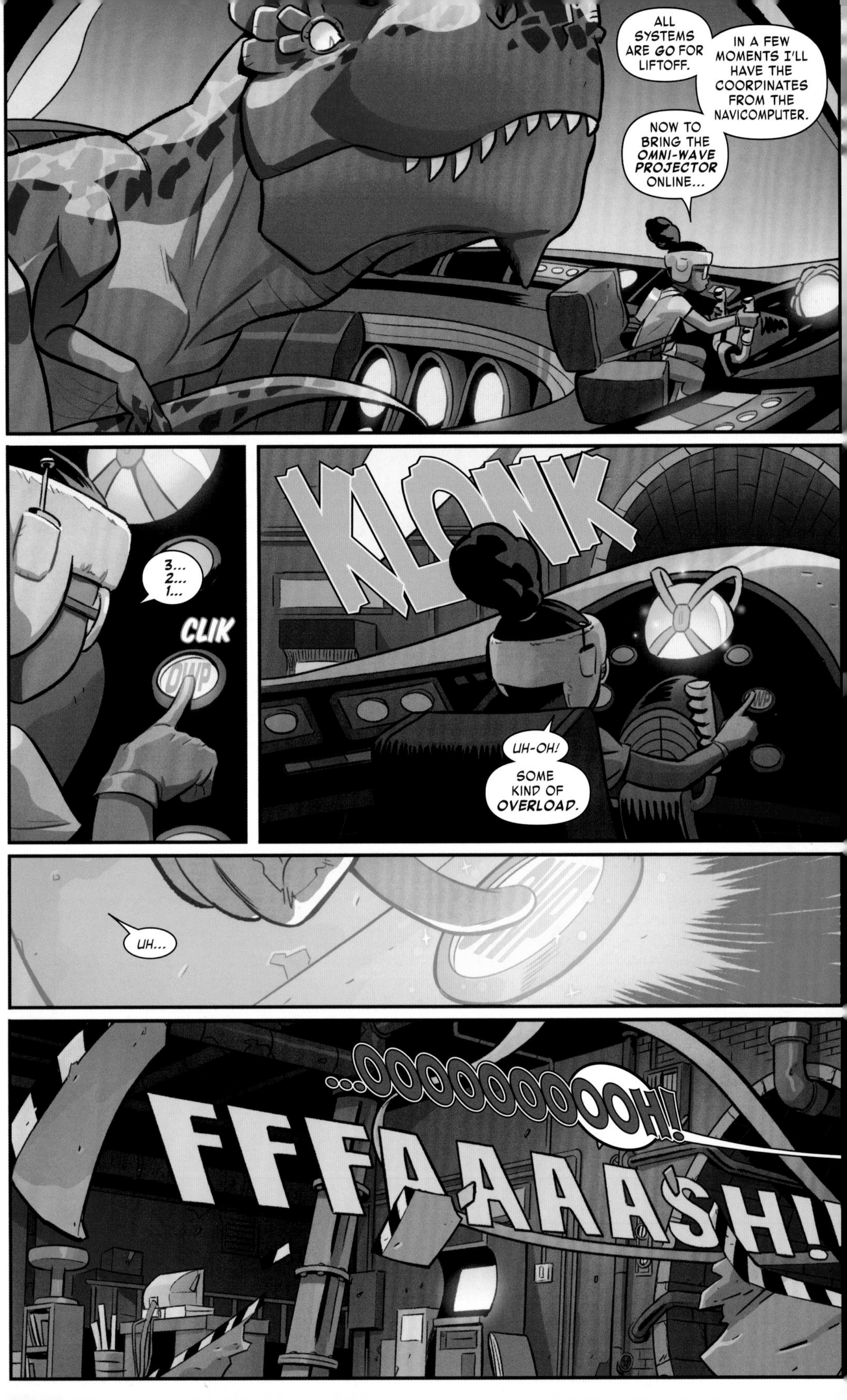
ALL SYSTEMS ARE GO FOR LIFTOFF.
IN A FEW MOMENTS I'LL HAVE THE COORDINATES FROM THE NAVICOMPUTER.
NOW TO BRING THE OMNI-WAVE PROJECTOR ONLINE...
3... 2... 1...
CLIK
OWP
KLONK
UH-OH! SOME KIND OF OVERLOAD.
UH...
FFFAAAASH!!
...OOOOOOOOOOH!

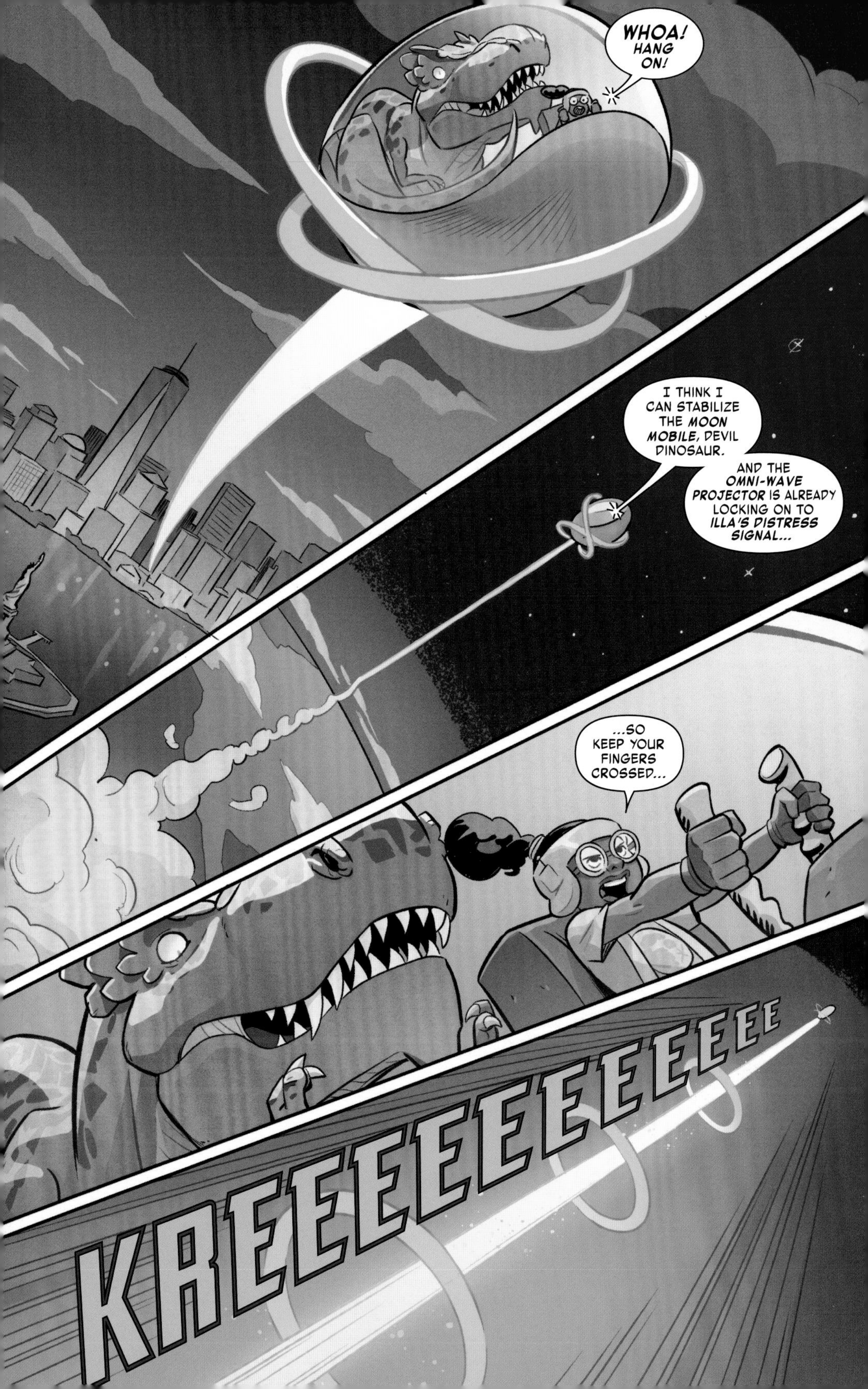
WHOA! HANG ON!
I THINK I CAN STABILIZE THE MOON MOBILE, DEVIL DINOSAUR.
AND THE OMNI-WAVE PROJECTOR IS ALREADY LOCKING ON TO ILLA'S DISTRESS SIGNAL...
...SO KEEP YOUR FINGERS CROSSED...
KREEEEEEEEEEEE

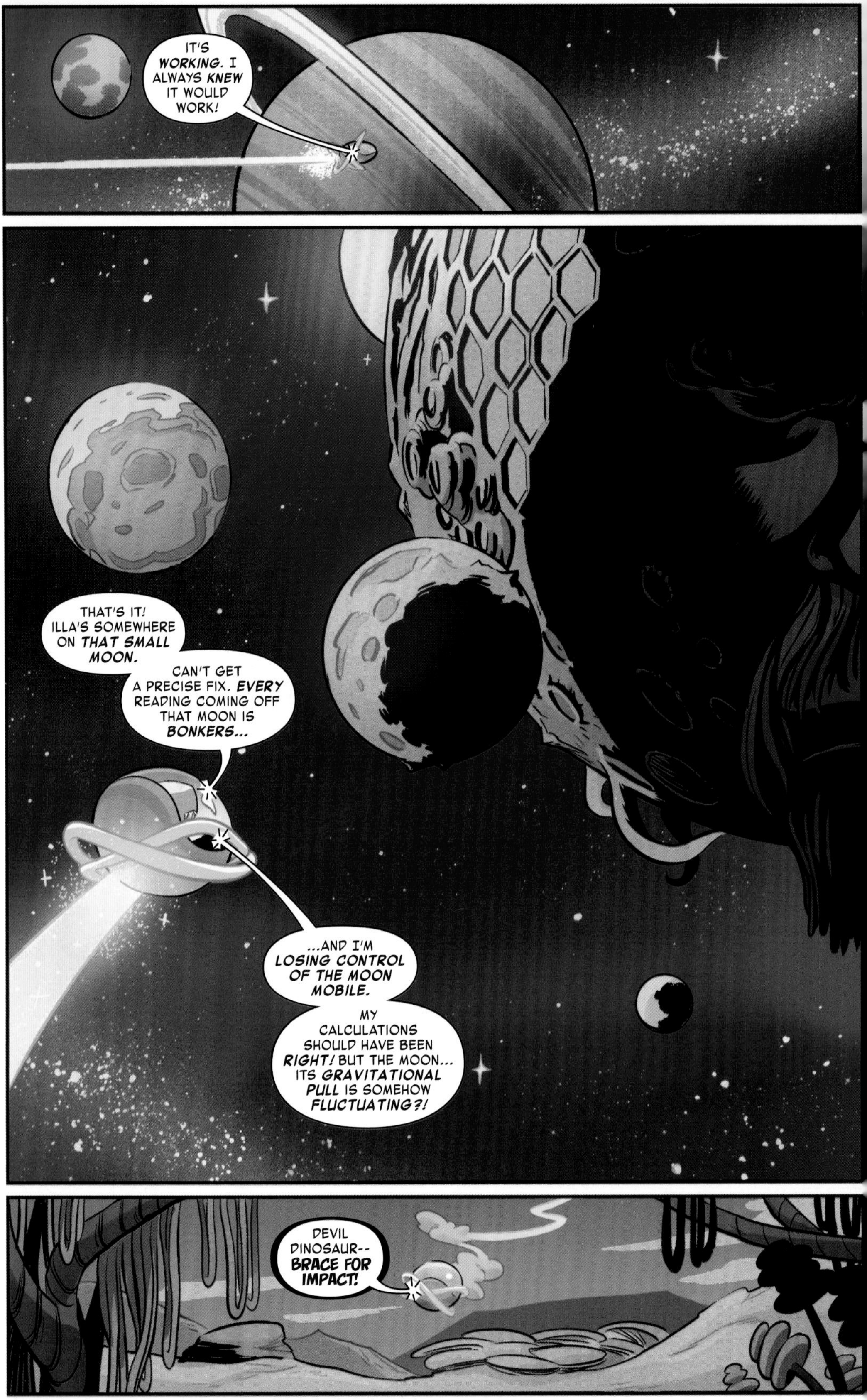
IT'S WORKING. I ALWAYS KNEW IT WOULD WORK!
THAT'S IT! ILLA'S SOMEWHERE ON THAT SMALL MOON.
CAN'T GET A PRECISE FIX. EVERY READING COMING OFF THAT MOON IS BONKERS...
...AND I'M LOSING CONTROL OF THE MOON MOBILE.
MY CALCULATIONS SHOULD HAVE BEEN RIGHT! BUT THE MOON... ITS GRAVITATIONAL PULL IS SOMEHOW FLUCTUATING?!
DEVIL DINOSAUR-- BRACE FOR IMPACT!

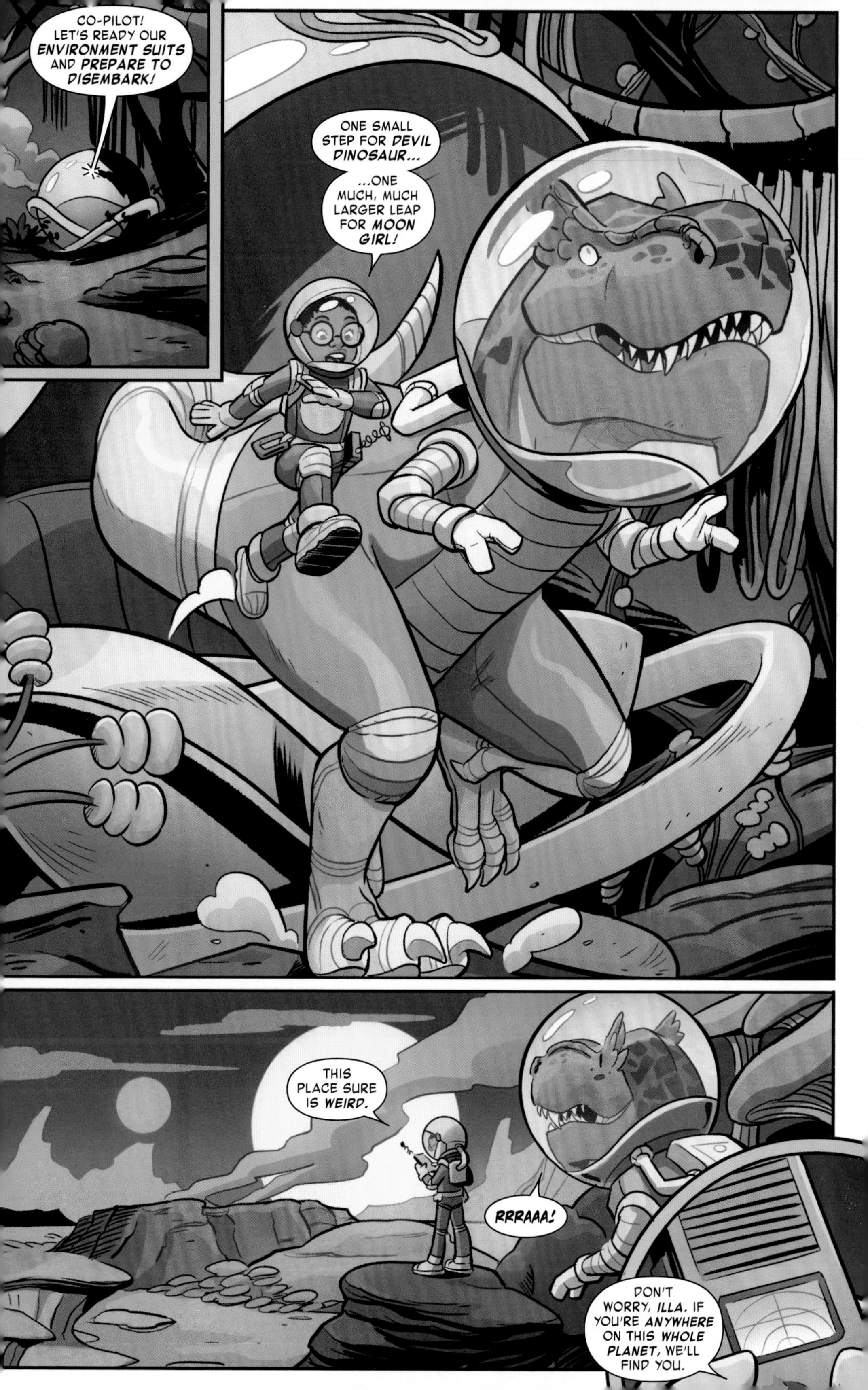
CO-PILOT! LET'S READY OUR ENVIRONMENT SUITS AND PREPARE TO DISEMBARK!
ONE SMALL STEP FOR DEVIL DINOSAUR...
...ONE MUCH, MUCH LARGER LEAP FOR MOON GIRL!
THIS PLACE SURE IS WEIRD.
RRRAAA!
DON'T WORRY, ILLA. IF YOU'RE ANYWHERE ON THIS WHOLE PLANET, WE'LL FIND YOU.

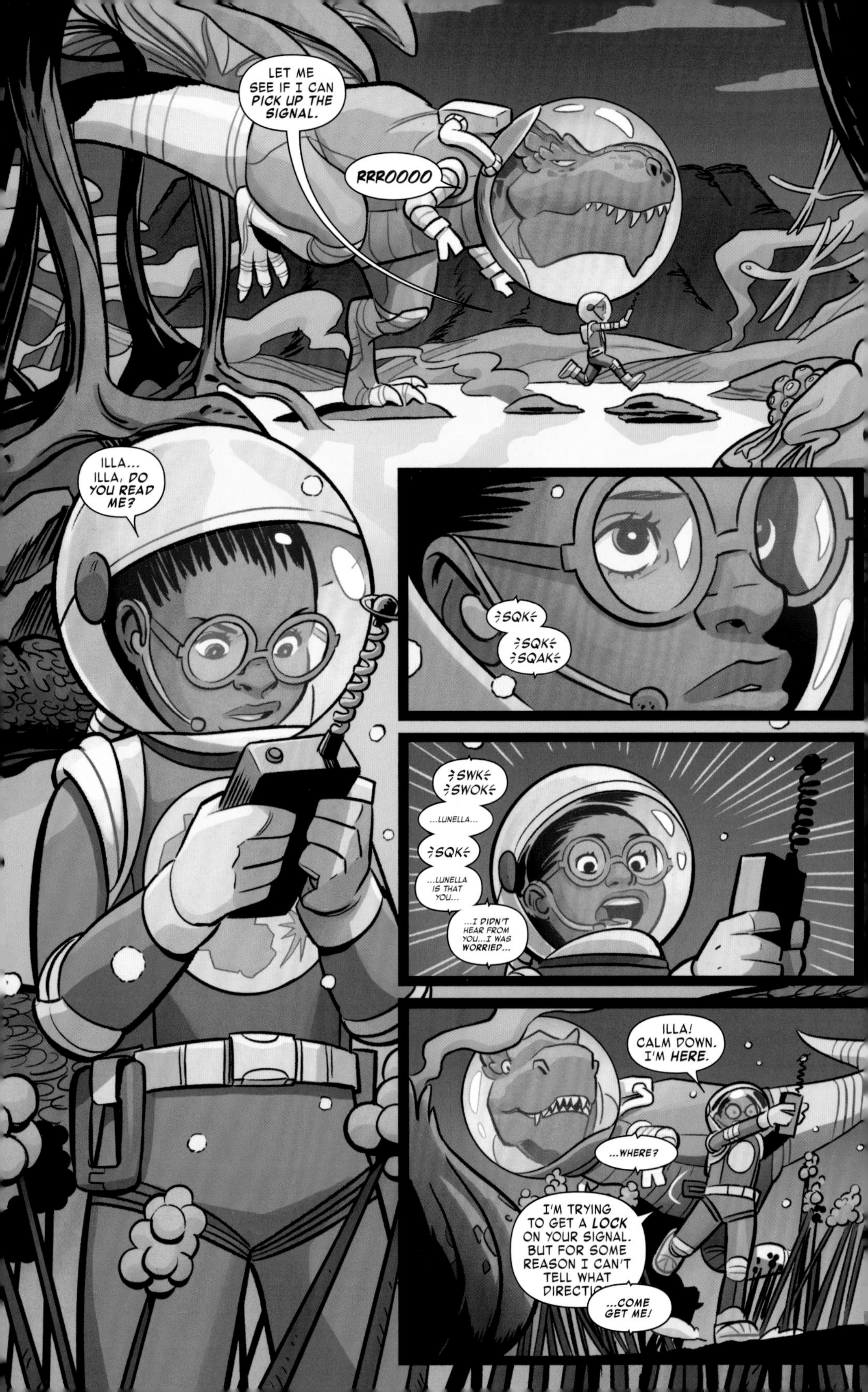
LET ME SEE IF I CAN PICK UP THE SIGNAL.
RRROOOO
ILLA... ILLA, DO YOU READ ME?
SQK
SQK SQAK
SWK SWOK
...LUNELLA...
SQK
...LUNELLA IS THAT YOU...
...I DIDN'T HEAR FROM YOU...I WAS WORRIED...
ILLA! CALM DOWN. I'M HERE.
...WHERE?
I'M TRYING TO GET A LOCK ON YOUR SIGNAL. BUT FOR SOME REASON I CAN'T TELL WHAT DIRECTIO
...COME GET ME!

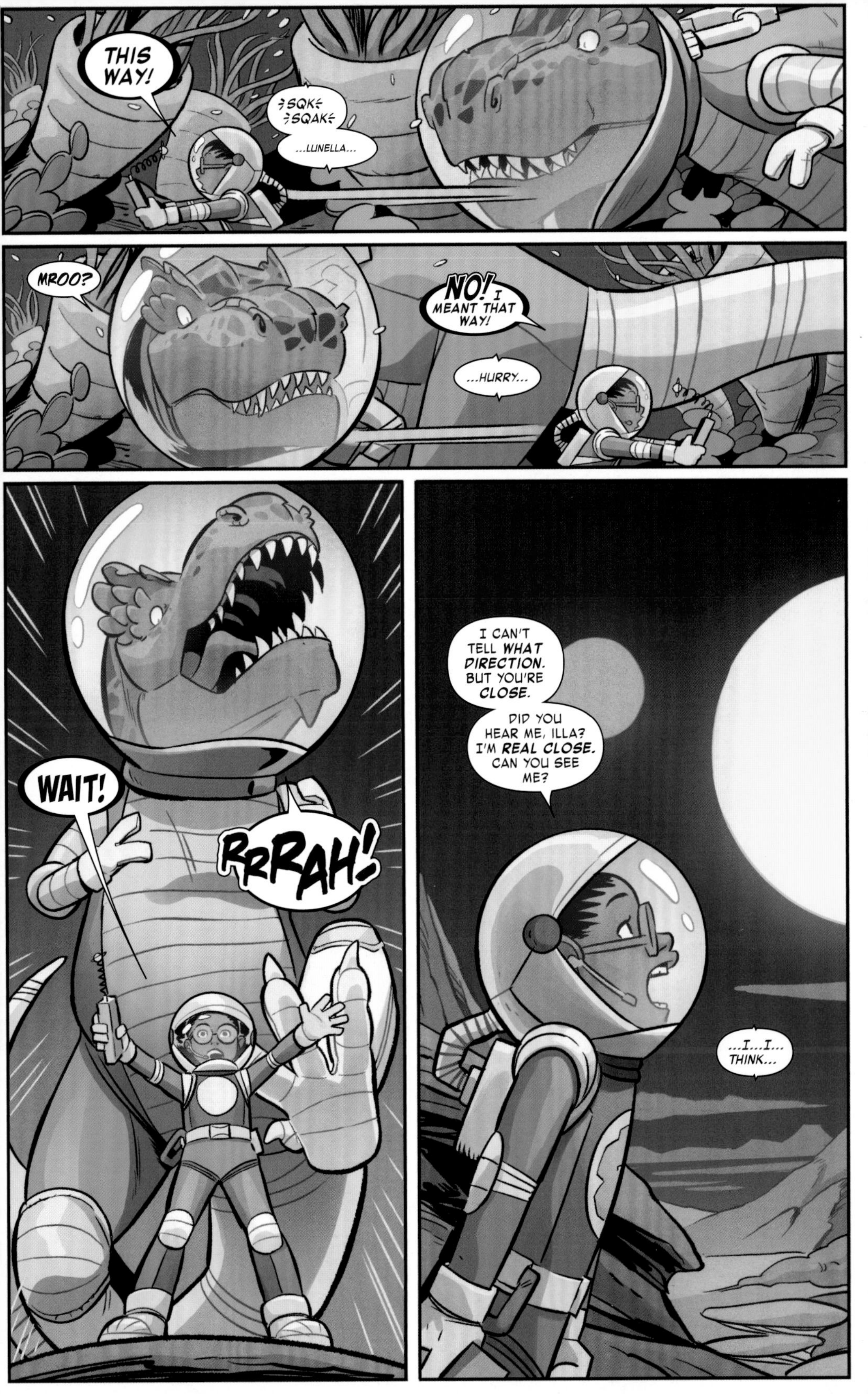
THIS WAY!
⇉SQK⇇ ⇉SQAK⇇
...LUNELLA...
MROO?
NO! I MEANT THAT WAY!
...HURRY...
WAIT!
RRRAH!
I CAN'T TELL WHAT DIRECTION. BUT YOU'RE CLOSE.
DID YOU HEAR ME, ILLA? I'M REAL CLOSE. CAN YOU SEE ME?
...I...I... THINK...

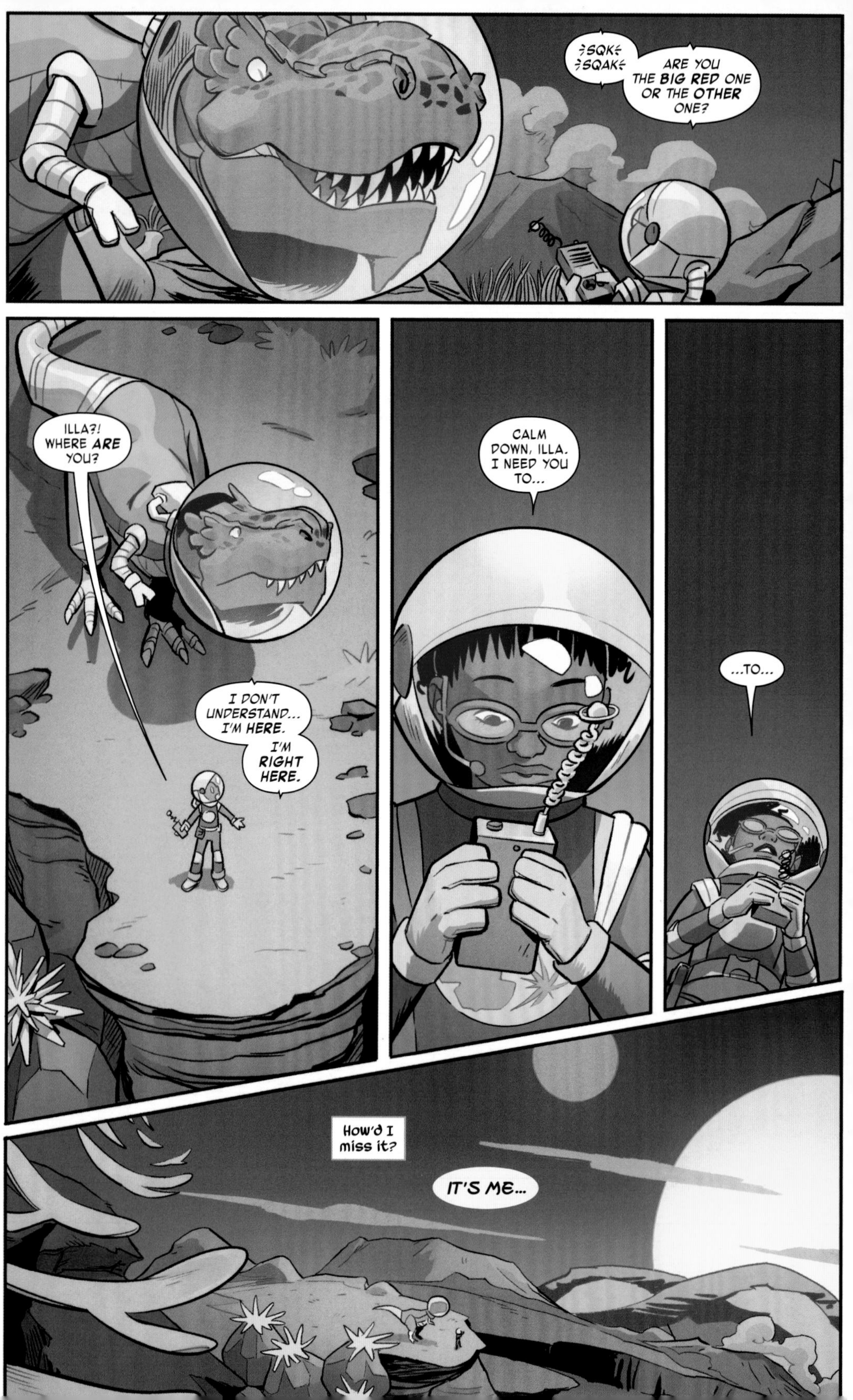

SQK SQAK
ARE YOU THE BIG RED ONE OR THE OTHER ONE?
ILLA?! WHERE ARE YOU?
I DON'T UNDERSTAND... I'M HERE.
I'M RIGHT HERE.
CALM DOWN, ILLA. I NEED YOU TO...
...TO...
How'd I miss it?
IT'S ME...

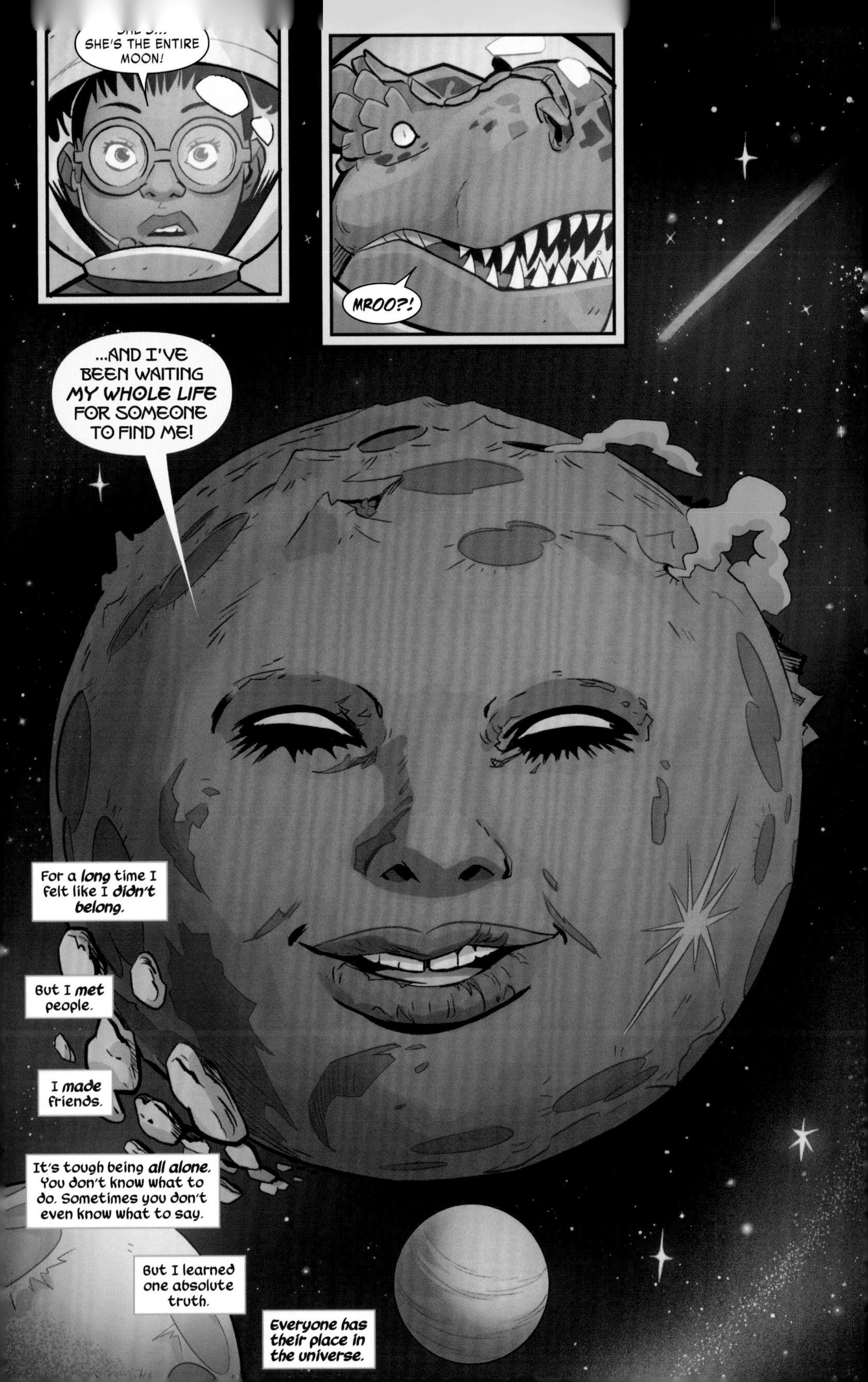
SHE'S THE ENTIRE MOON!
MROO?!
...AND I'VE BEEN WAITING *MY WHOLE LIFE* FOR SOMEONE TO FIND ME!
For a *long* time I felt like I *didn't belong.*
But I *met* people.
I *made* friends.
It's tough being *all alone.* You don't know what to do. Sometimes you don't even know what to say.
But I learned one absolute truth.
Everyone has their place in the universe.

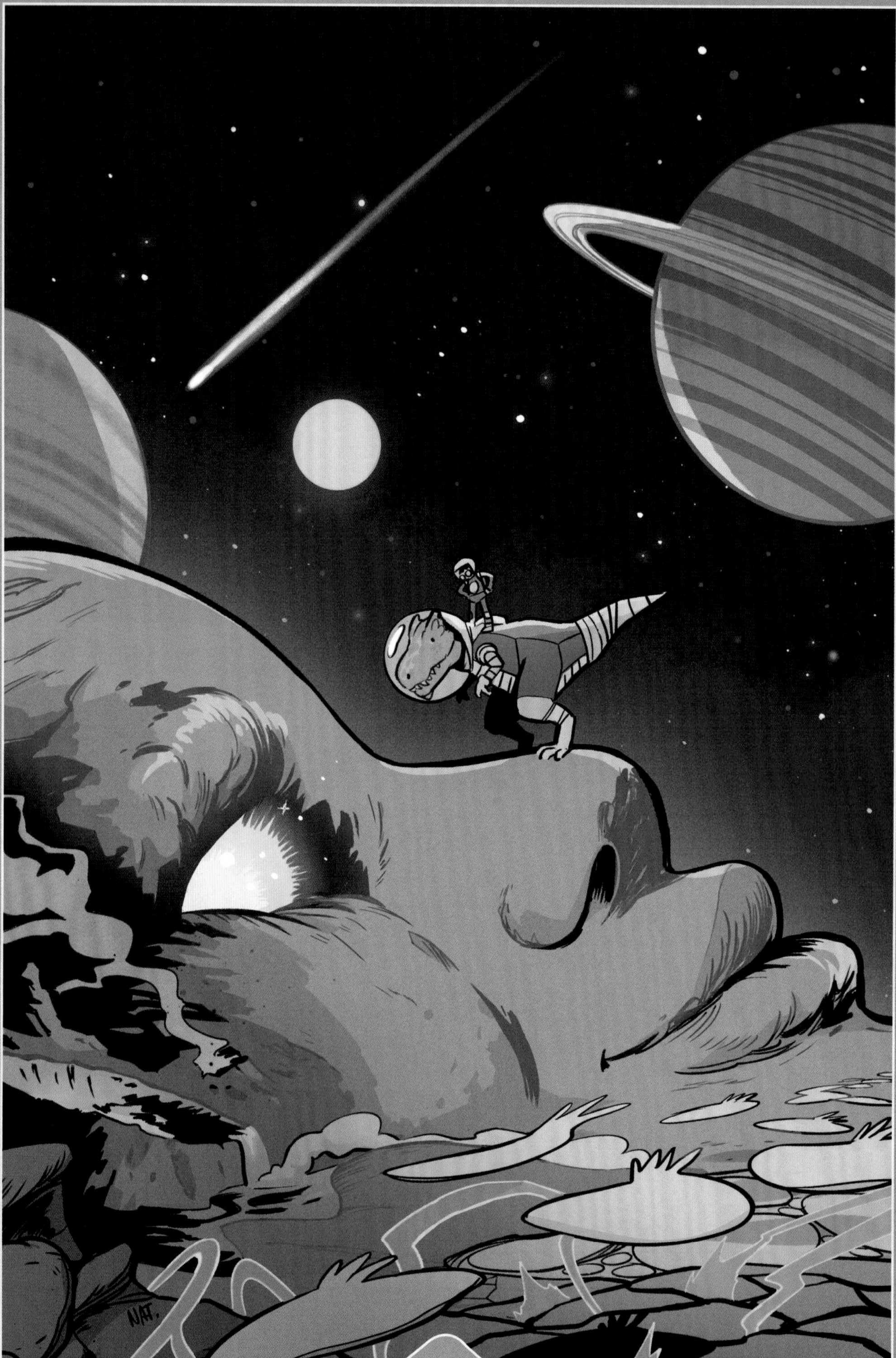
NAT.

20

"GRAVITY OF A SITUATION"

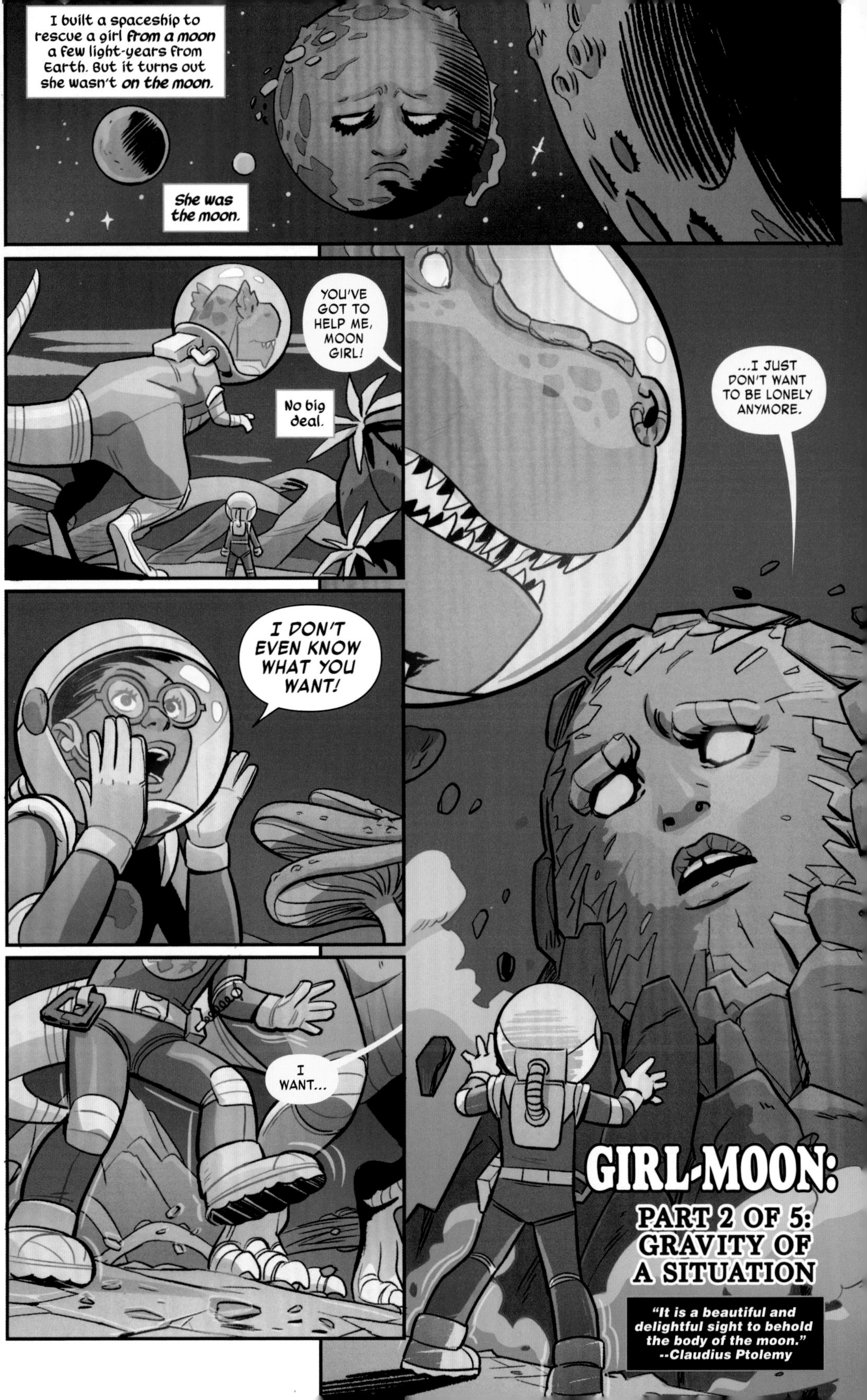
I built a spaceship to rescue a girl *from a moon* a few light-years from Earth. But it turns out she wasn't *on the moon.*
She was the moon.
YOU'VE GOT TO HELP ME, MOON GIRL!
No big deal.
...I JUST DON'T WANT TO BE LONELY ANYMORE.
I DON'T EVEN KNOW WHAT YOU WANT!
I WANT...
GIRL-MOON:
PART 2 OF 5: GRAVITY OF A SITUATION
"It is a beautiful and delightful sight to behold the body of the moon." --Claudius Ptolemy

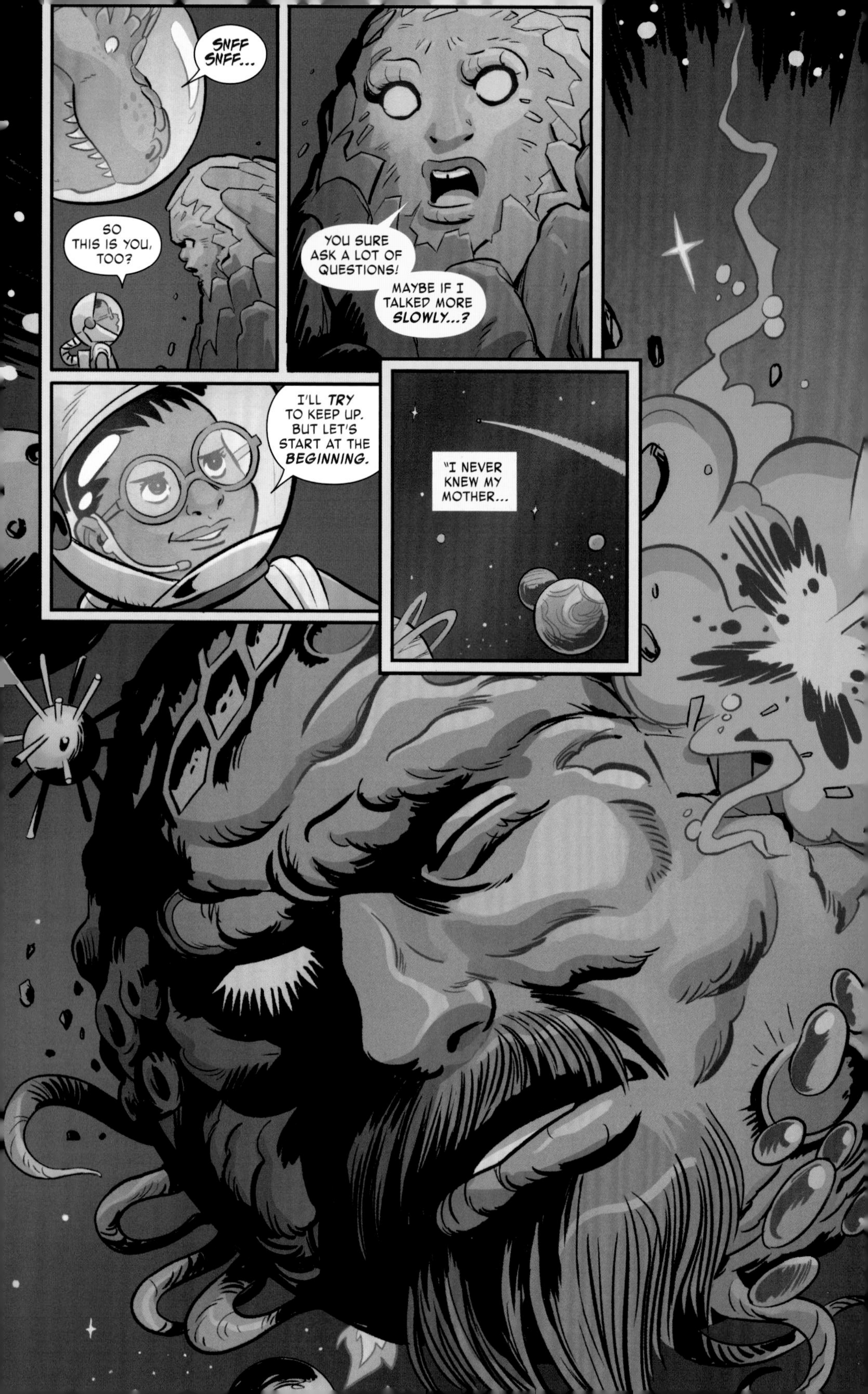
SNFF SNFF...
SO THIS IS YOU, TOO?
YOU SURE ASK A LOT OF QUESTIONS!
MAYBE IF I TALKED MORE SLOWLY...?
I'LL TRY TO KEEP UP. BUT LET'S START AT THE BEGINNING.
"I NEVER KNEW MY MOTHER...

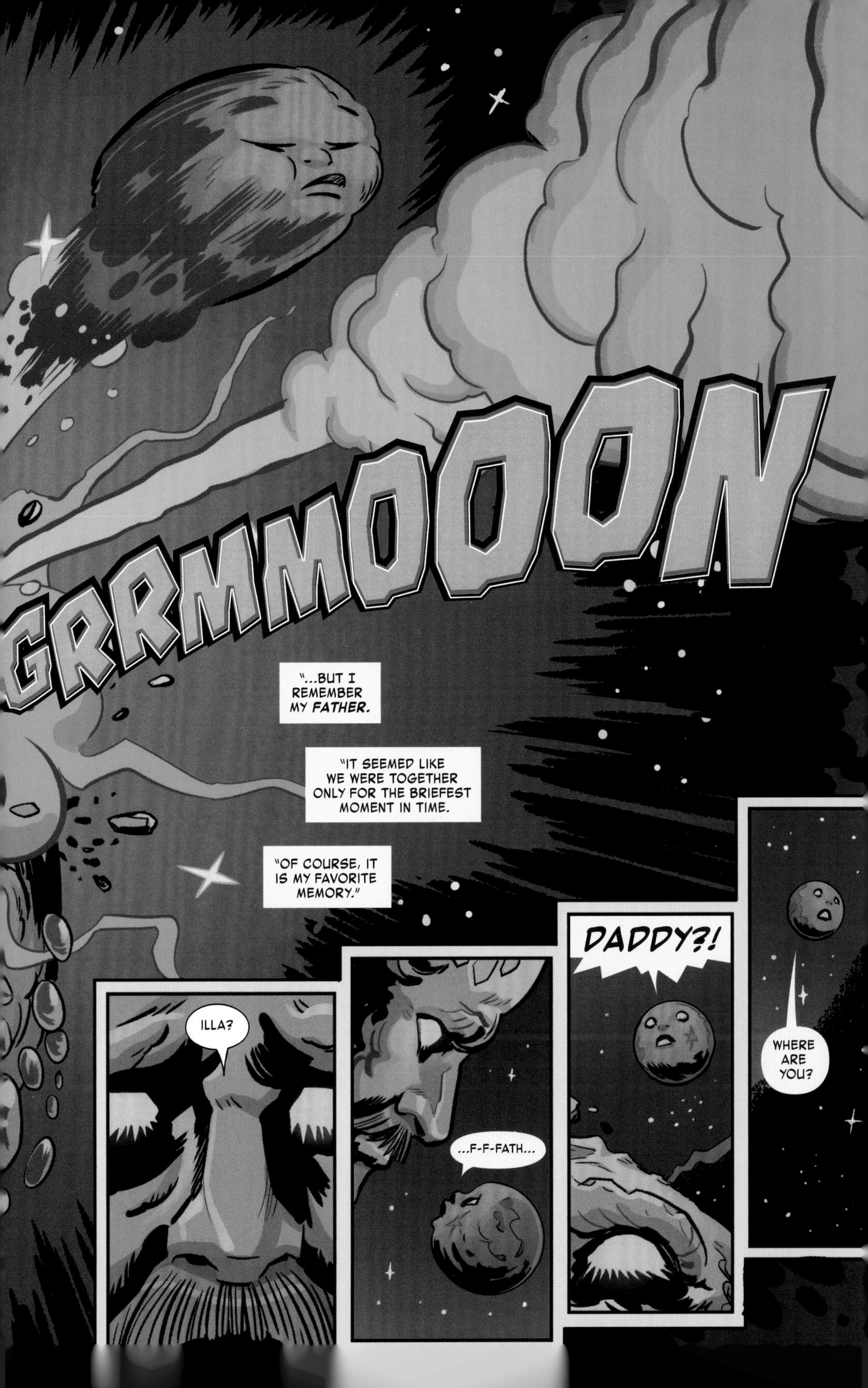
GRRMMOOON
"...BUT I REMEMBER MY *FATHER*.
"IT SEEMED LIKE WE WERE TOGETHER ONLY FOR THE BRIEFEST MOMENT IN TIME.
"OF COURSE, IT IS MY FAVORITE MEMORY."
ILLA?
...F-F-FATH...
DADDY?!
WHERE ARE YOU?

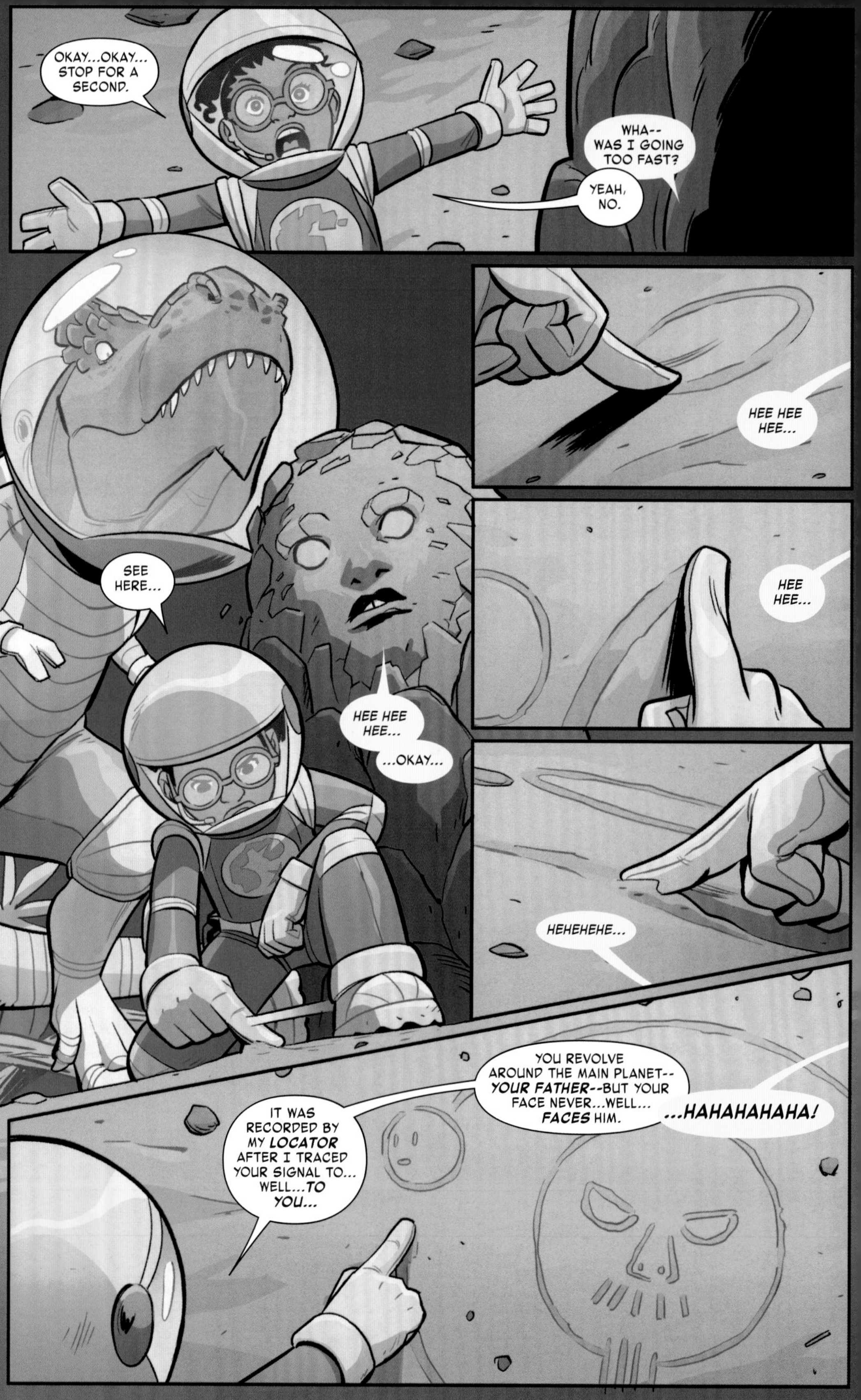
OKAY...OKAY... STOP FOR A SECOND.
WHA-- WAS I GOING TOO FAST?
YEAH, NO.
SEE HERE...
HEE HEE HEE...
...OKAY...
HEE HEE HEE...
HEE HEE...
HEHEHEHE...
IT WAS RECORDED BY MY LOCATOR AFTER I TRACED YOUR SIGNAL TO... WELL...TO YOU...
YOU REVOLVE AROUND THE MAIN PLANET-- YOUR FATHER--BUT YOUR FACE NEVER...WELL... FACES HIM.
...HAHAHAHAHA!

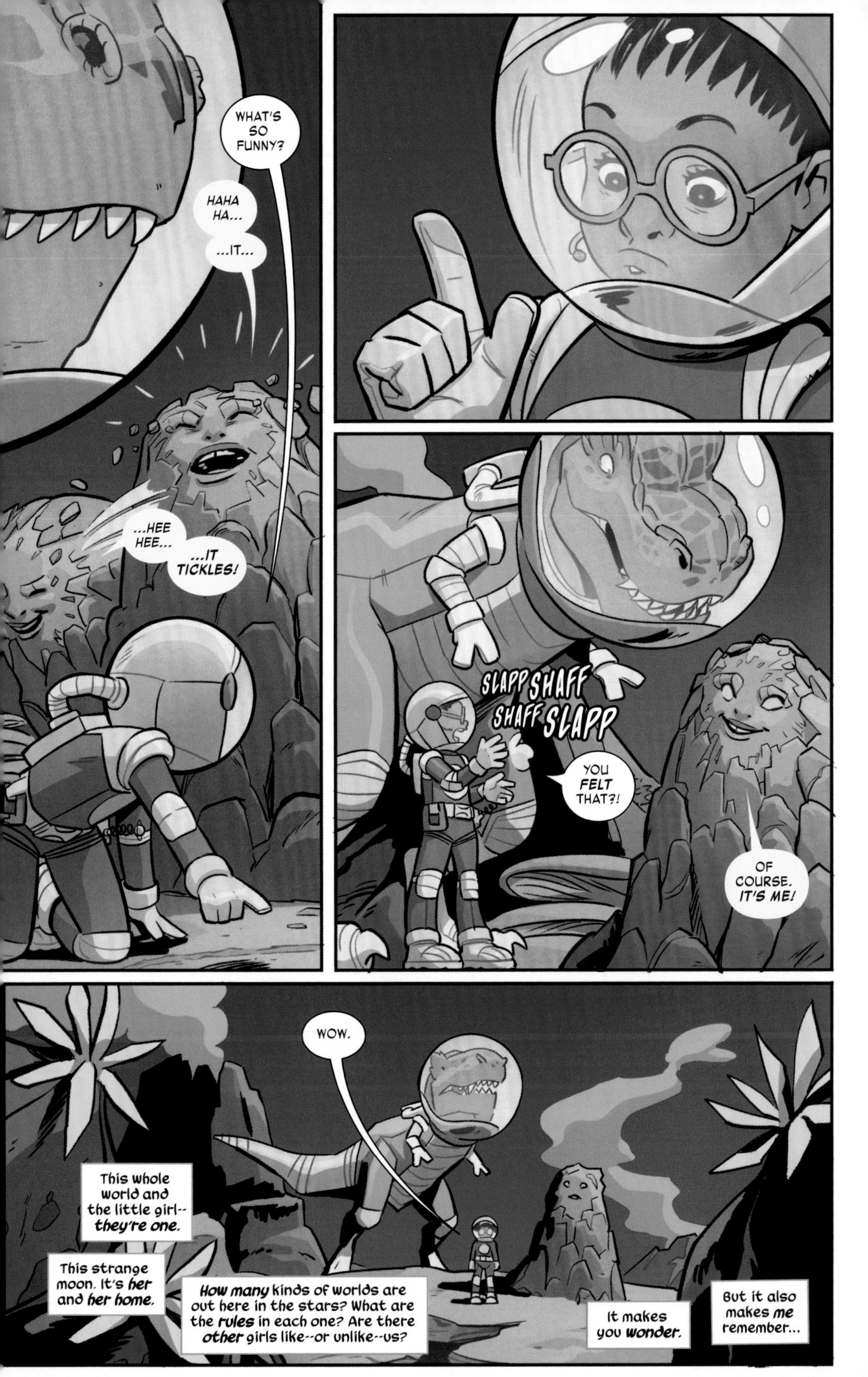
WHAT'S SO FUNNY?
HAHA HA...
...IT...
...HEE HEE...
...IT TICKLES!
SLAPP SHAFF
SHAFF SLAPP
YOU FELT THAT?!
OF COURSE. IT'S ME!
WOW.
This whole world and the little girl-- they're one.
This strange moon. It's her and her home.
How many kinds of worlds are out here in the stars? What are the rules in each one? Are there other girls like--or unlike--us?
It makes you wonder.
But it also makes me remember...

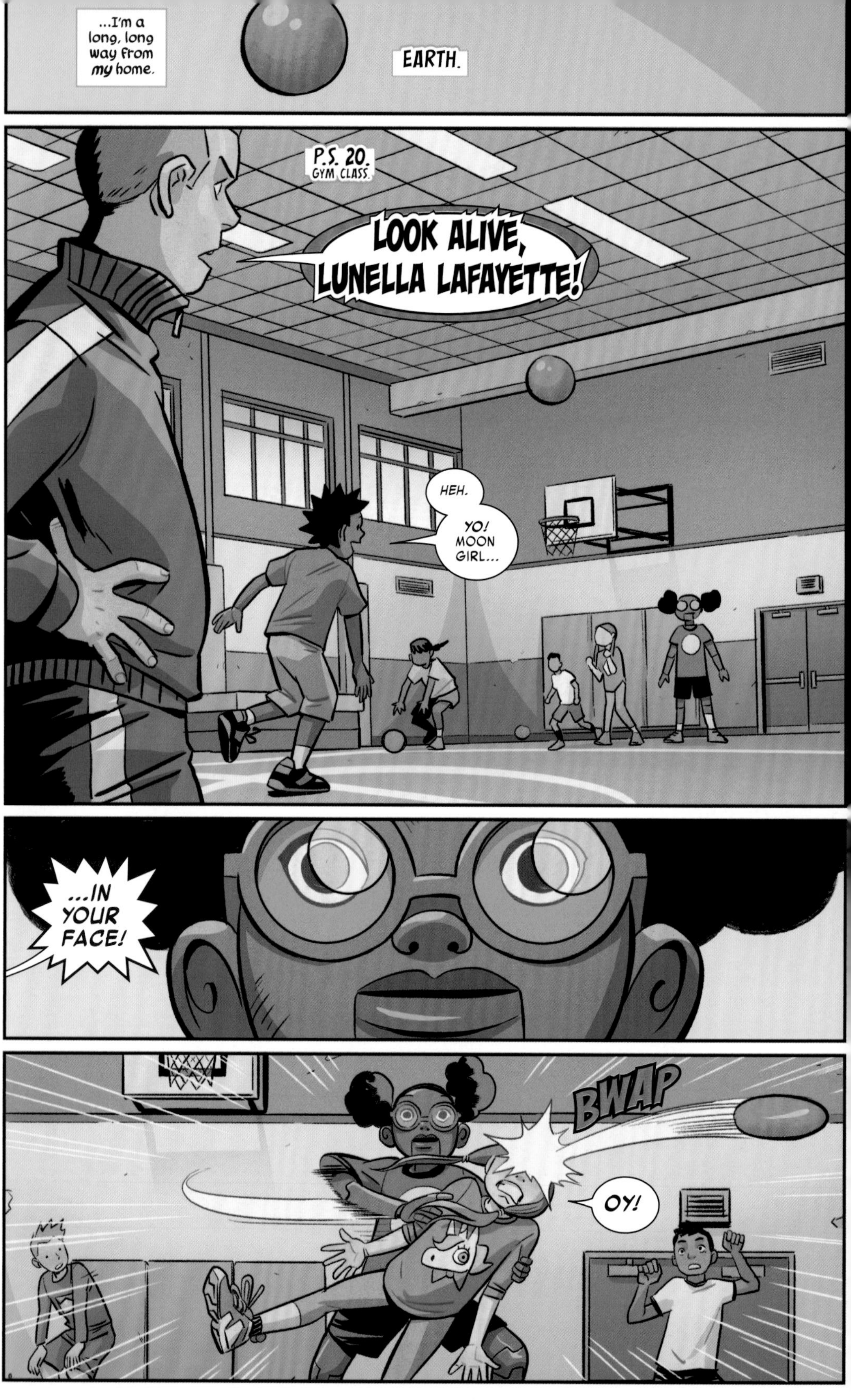
...I'm a long, long way from my home.
EARTH.
P.S. 20. GYM CLASS.
LOOK ALIVE, LUNELLA LAFAYETTE!
HEH.
YO! MOON GIRL...
...IN YOUR FACE!
BWAP
OY!

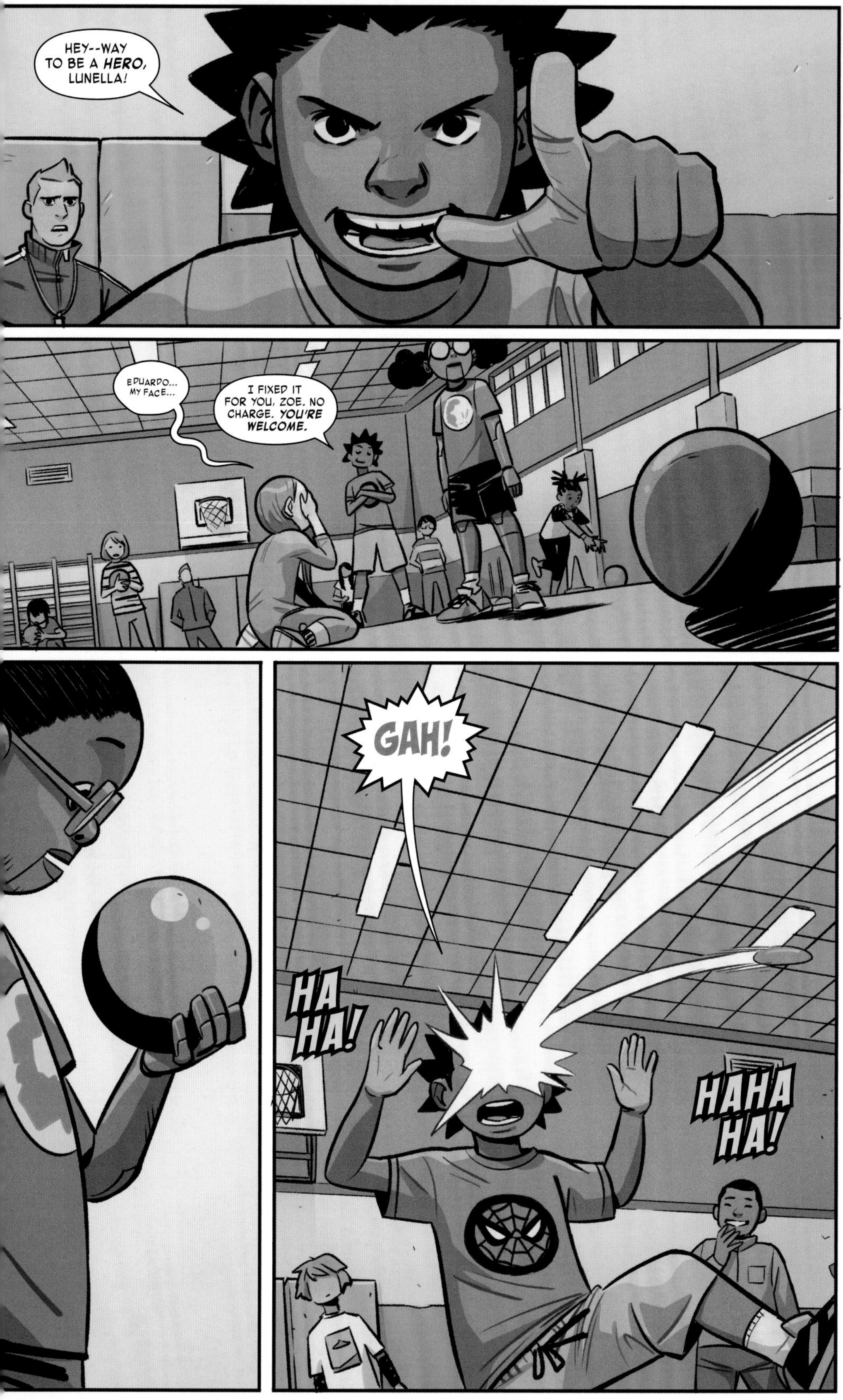
HEY--WAY TO BE A HERO, LUNELLA!
EDUARDO... MY FACE...
I FIXED IT FOR YOU, ZOE. NO CHARGE. YOU'RE WELCOME.
GAH!
HA HA!
HAHA HA!

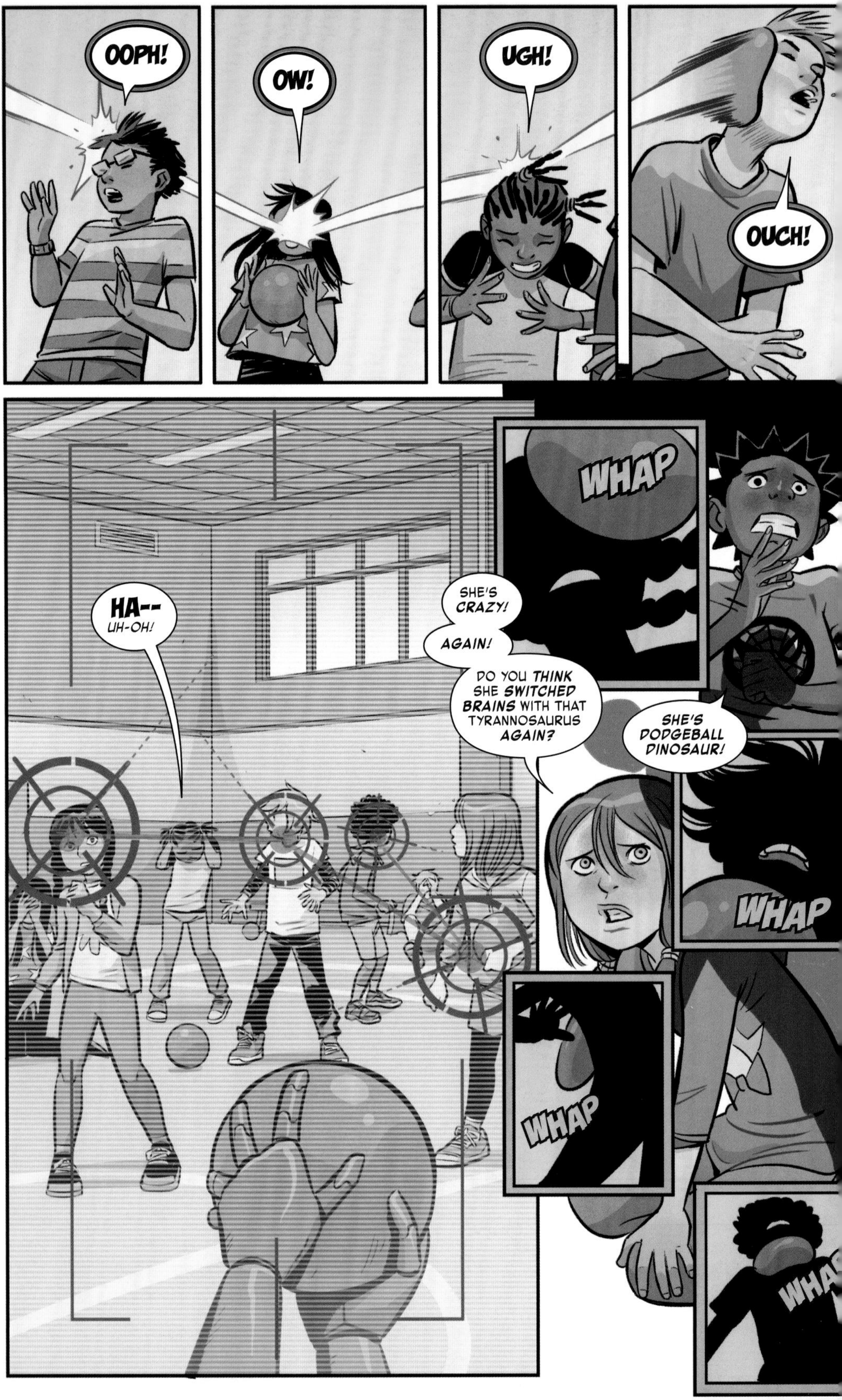
OOPH!
OW!
UGH!
OUCH!
WHAP
HA--
UH-OH!
SHE'S CRAZY!
AGAIN!
DO YOU THINK SHE SWITCHED BRAINS WITH THAT TYRANNOSAURUS AGAIN?
SHE'S DODGEBALL DINOSAUR!
WHAP
WHAP

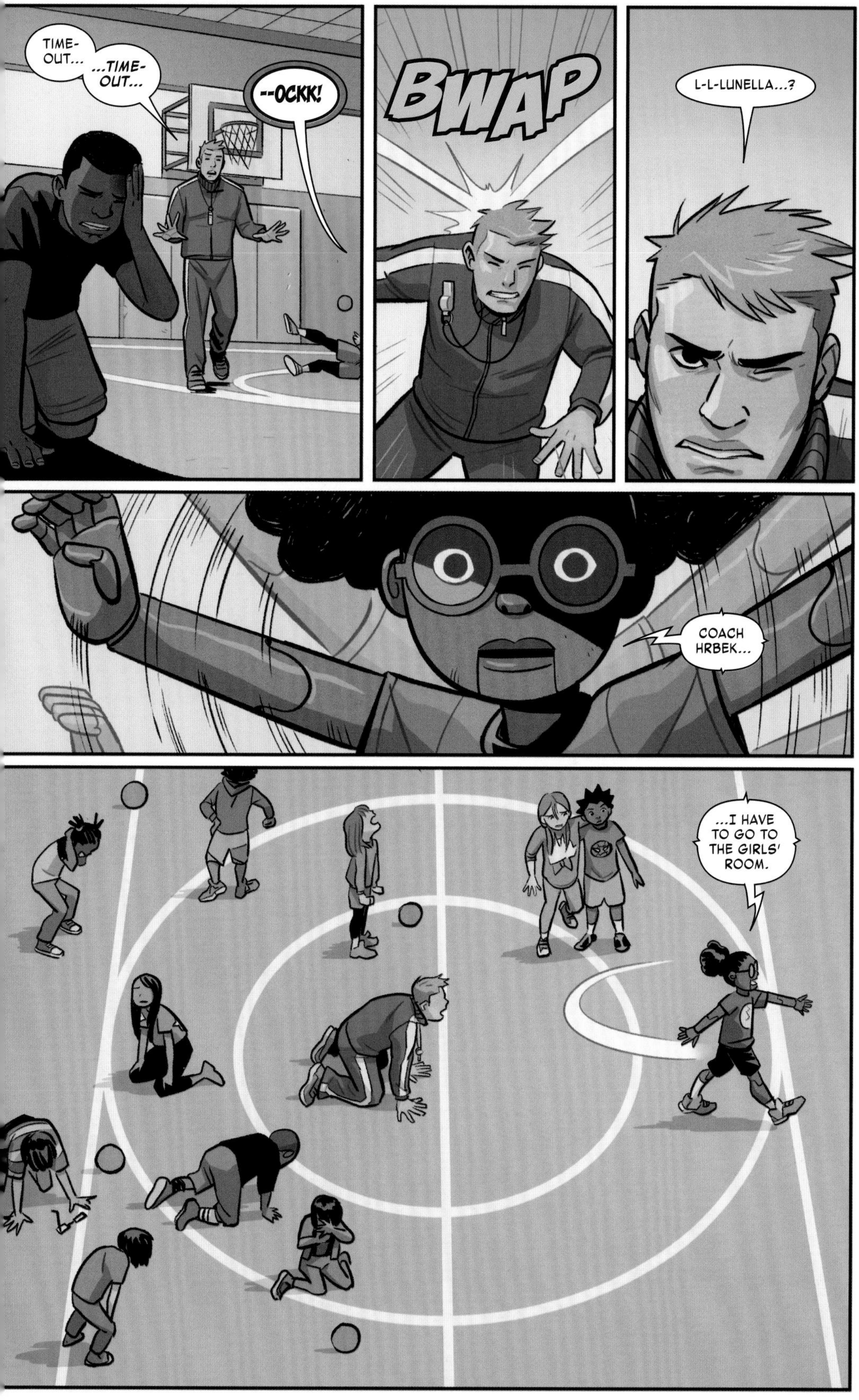
TIME-OUT...
...TIME-OUT...
--OCKK!
BWAP
L-L-LUNELLA...?
COACH HRBEK...
...I HAVE TO GO TO THE GIRLS' ROOM.

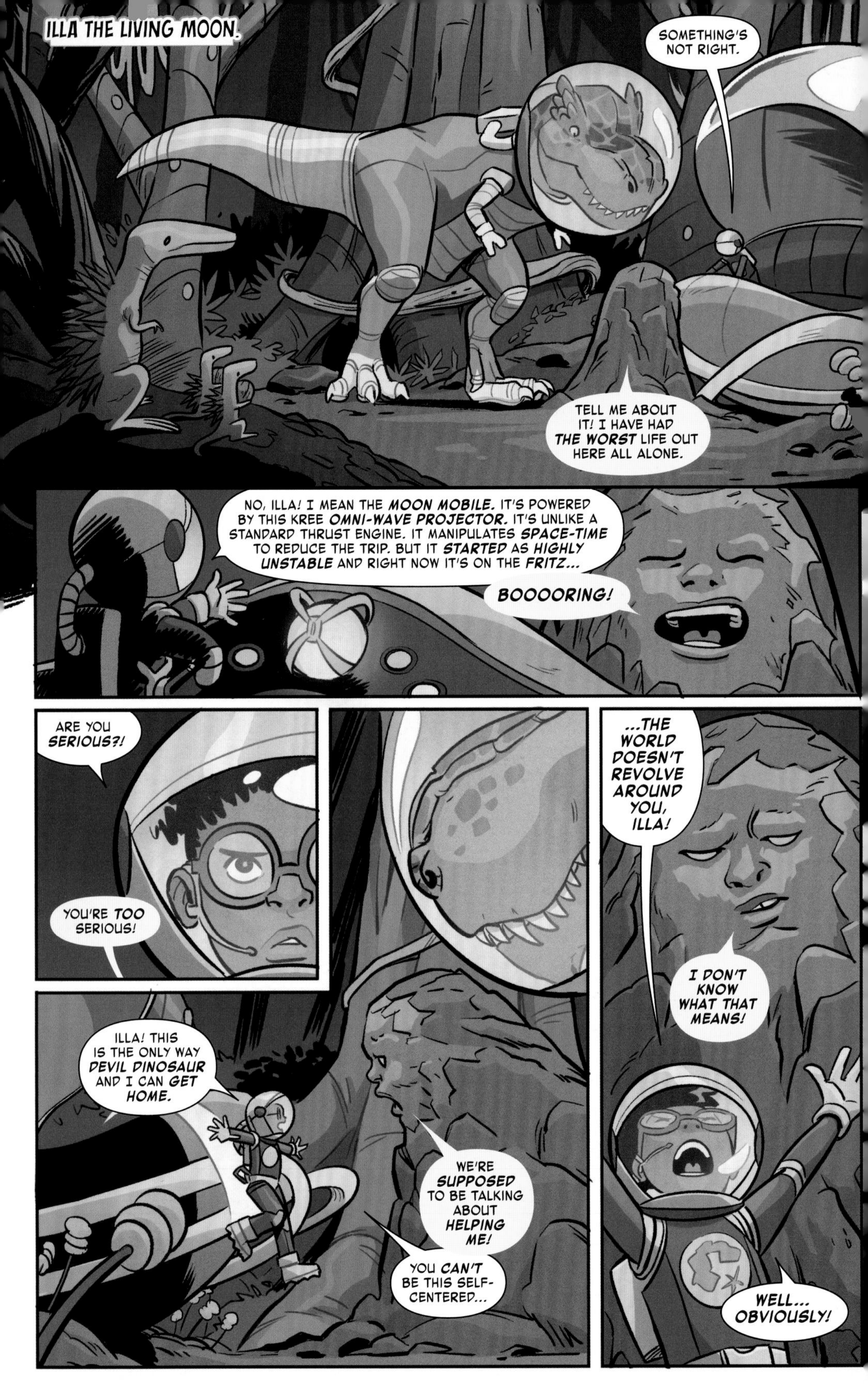
ILLA THE LIVING MOON.
SOMETHING'S NOT RIGHT.
TELL ME ABOUT IT! I HAVE HAD THE WORST LIFE OUT HERE ALL ALONE.
NO, ILLA! I MEAN THE MOON MOBILE. IT'S POWERED BY THIS KREE OMNI-WAVE PROJECTOR. IT'S UNLIKE A STANDARD THRUST ENGINE. IT MANIPULATES SPACE-TIME TO REDUCE THE TRIP. BUT IT STARTED AS HIGHLY UNSTABLE AND RIGHT NOW IT'S ON THE FRITZ...
BOOOORING!
ARE YOU SERIOUS?!
YOU'RE TOO SERIOUS!
...THE WORLD DOESN'T REVOLVE AROUND YOU, ILLA!
I DON'T KNOW WHAT THAT MEANS!
ILLA! THIS IS THE ONLY WAY DEVIL DINOSAUR AND I CAN GET HOME.
WE'RE SUPPOSED TO BE TALKING ABOUT HELPING ME!
YOU CAN'T BE THIS SELF-CENTERED...
WELL... OBVIOUSLY!

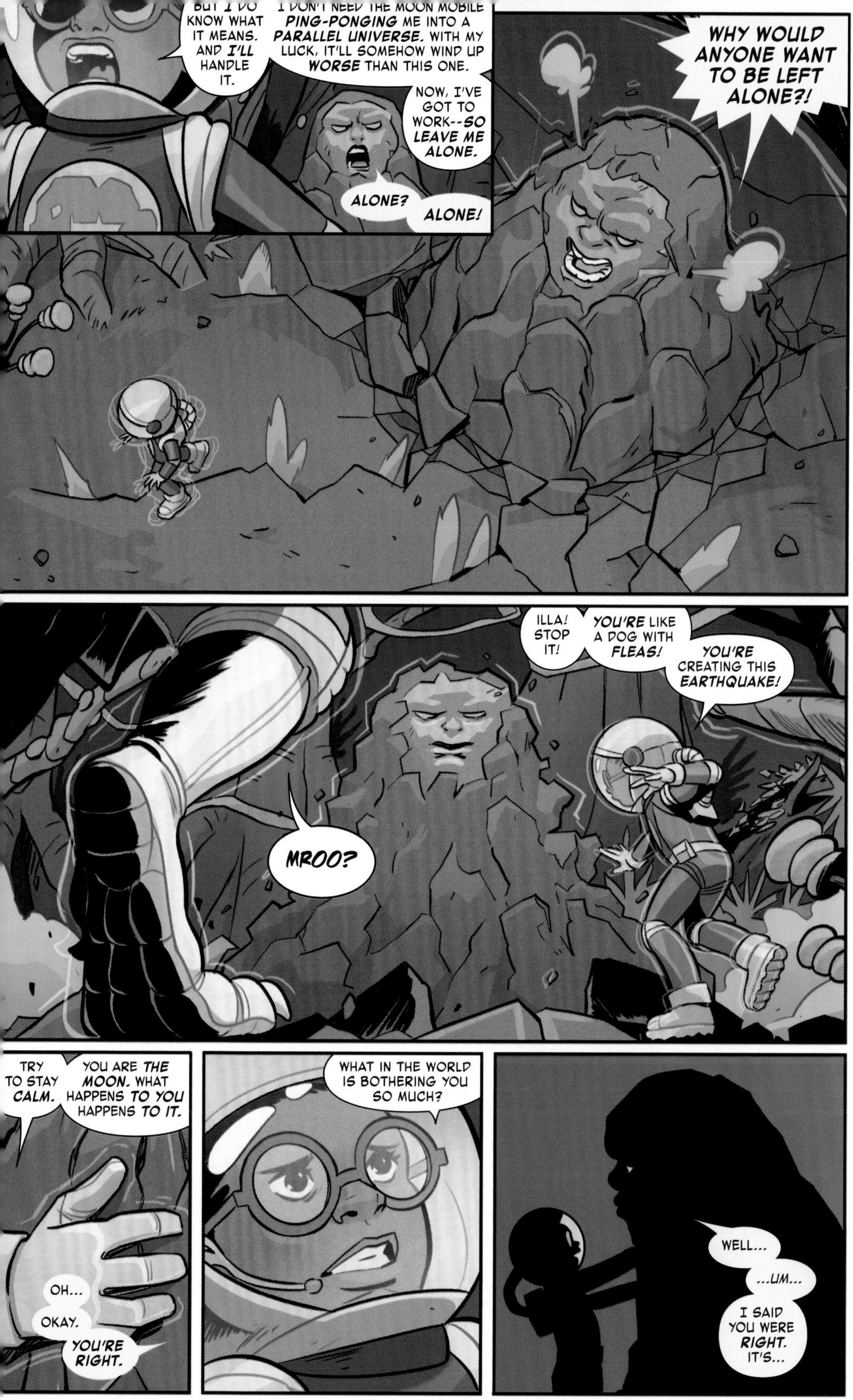
BUT I DO KNOW WHAT IT MEANS. AND I'LL HANDLE IT.
I DON'T NEED THE MOON MOBILE PING-PONGING ME INTO A PARALLEL UNIVERSE. WITH MY LUCK, IT'LL SOMEHOW WIND UP WORSE THAN THIS ONE.
NOW, I'VE GOT TO WORK--SO LEAVE ME ALONE.
ALONE?
ALONE!
WHY WOULD ANYONE WANT TO BE LEFT ALONE?!
ILLA! STOP IT!
YOU'RE LIKE A DOG WITH FLEAS!
YOU'RE CREATING THIS EARTHQUAKE!
MROO?
TRY TO STAY CALM.
YOU ARE THE MOON. WHAT HAPPENS TO YOU HAPPENS TO IT.
OH...
OKAY.
YOU'RE RIGHT.
WHAT IN THE WORLD IS BOTHERING YOU SO MUCH?
WELL...
...UM...
I SAID YOU WERE RIGHT. IT'S...

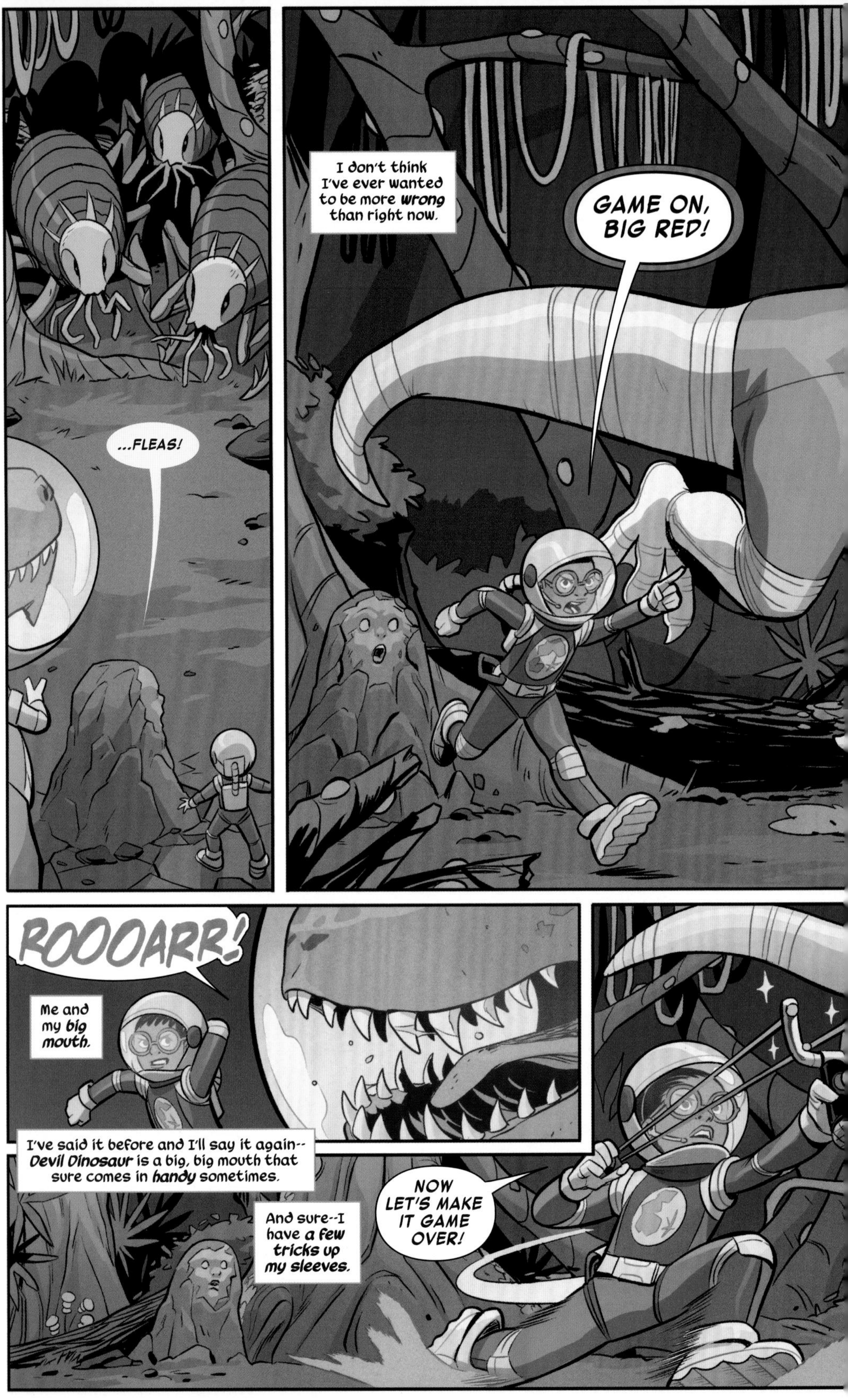
...FLEAS!
I don't think I've ever wanted to be more *wrong* than right now.
GAME ON, BIG RED!
ROOOARR!
Me and my *big mouth*.
I've said it before and I'll say it again-- *Devil Dinosaur* is a big, big mouth that sure comes in *handy* sometimes.
And sure--I have *a few tricks up my sleeves*.
NOW LET'S MAKE IT GAME OVER!

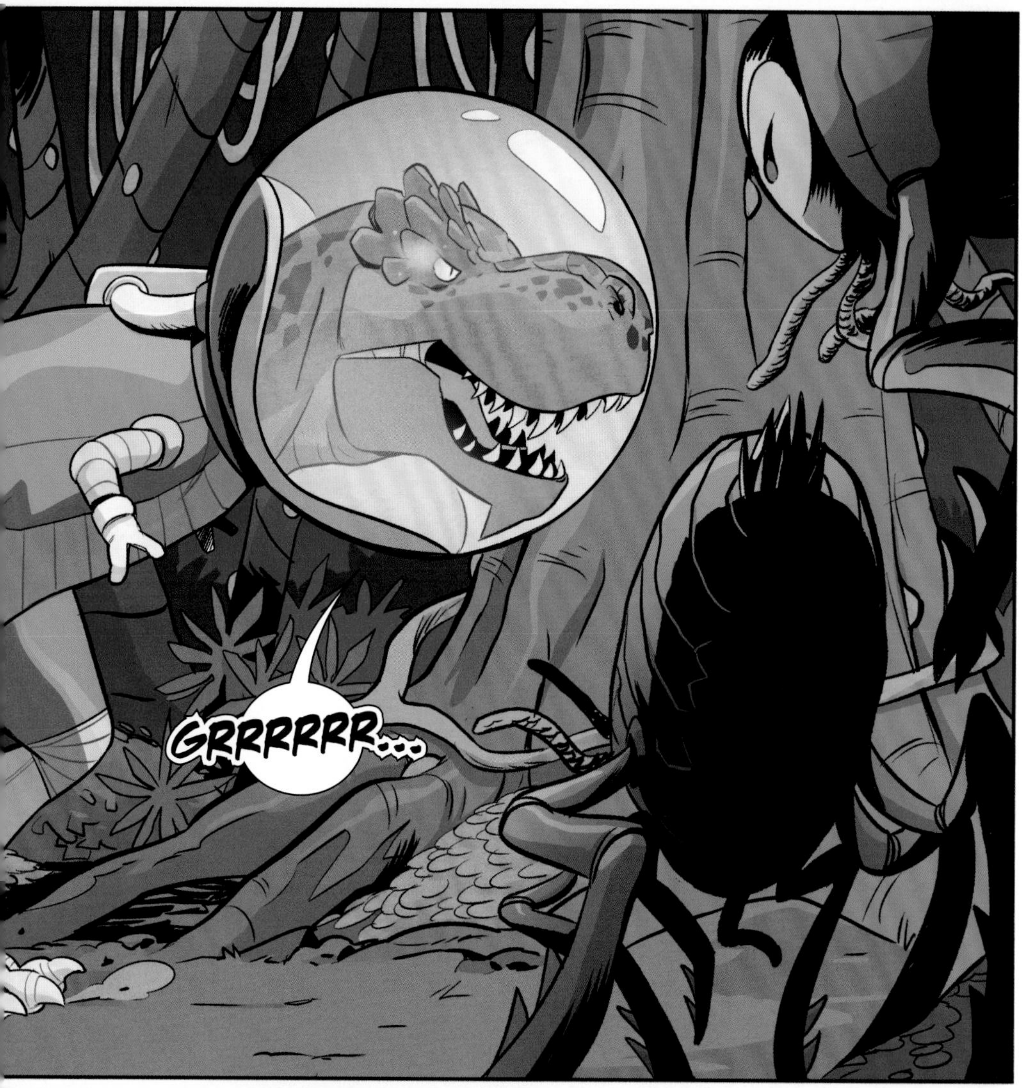
GRRRRRR...

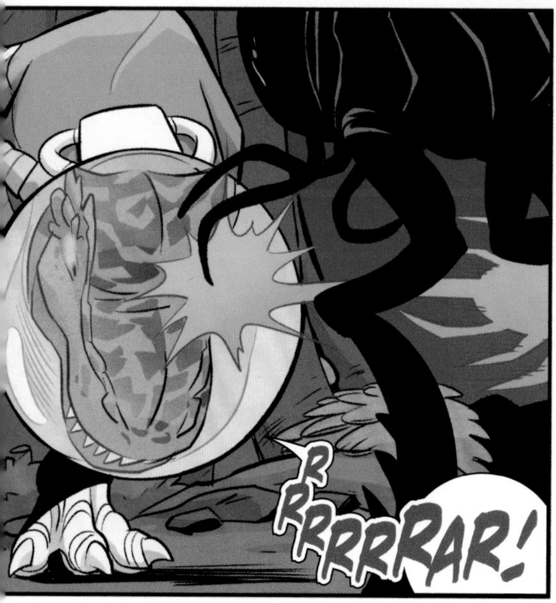
RRRRRRRAR!

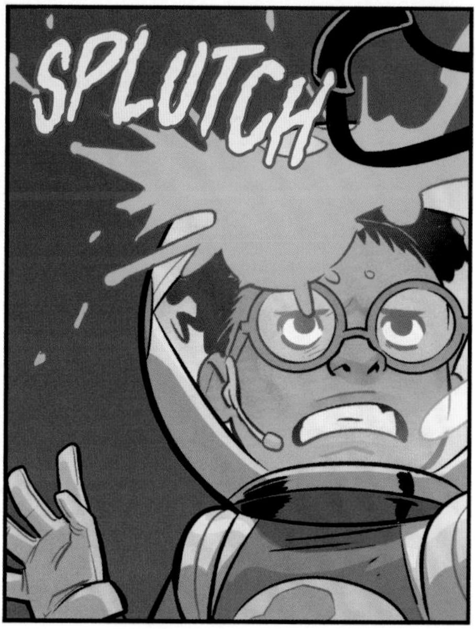
SPLUTCH

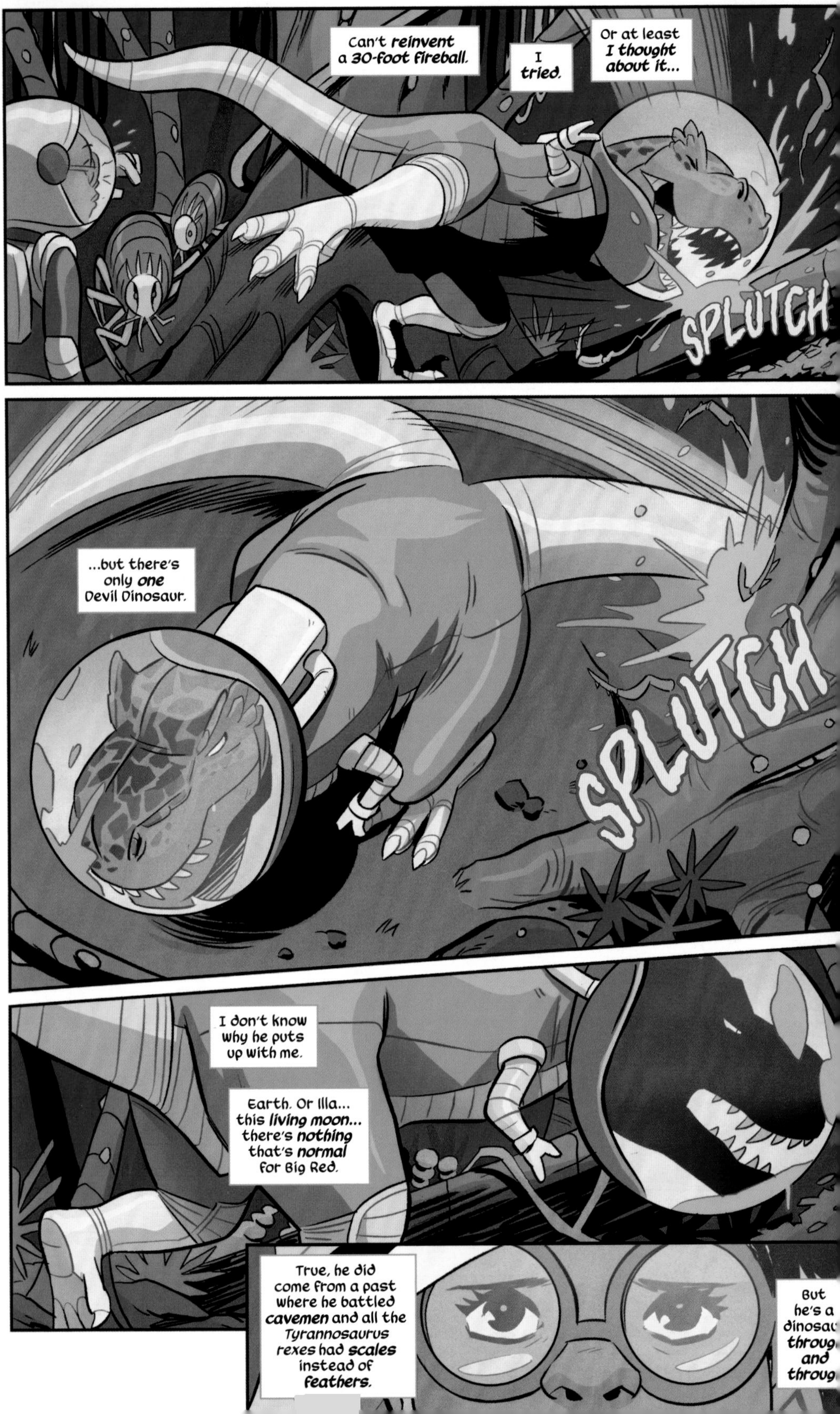
Can't reinvent a 30-foot fireball.
I tried.
Or at least I thought about it...
SPLUTCH
...but there's only one Devil Dinosaur.
SPLUTCH
I don't know why he puts up with me.
Earth. Or Illa... this living moon... there's nothing that's normal for Big Red.
True, he did come from a past where he battled cavemen and all the Tyrannosaurus rexes had scales instead of feathers.

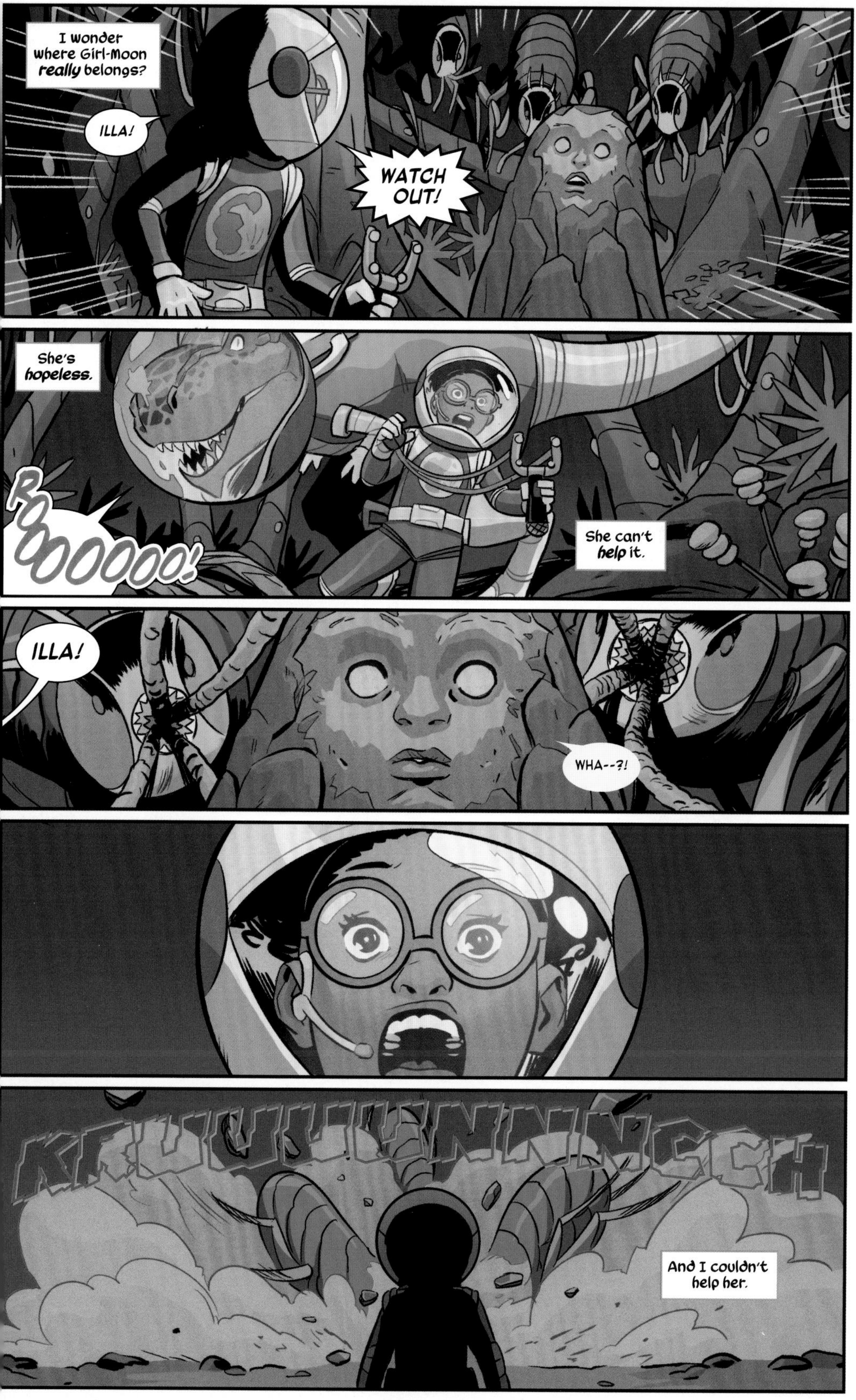
I wonder where Girl-Moon *really* belongs?
ILLA!
WATCH OUT!
She's *hopeless.*
ROOOOOOOO!
She can't *help* it.
ILLA!
WHA--?!
KRUUUUNNNCH
And I couldn't help her.

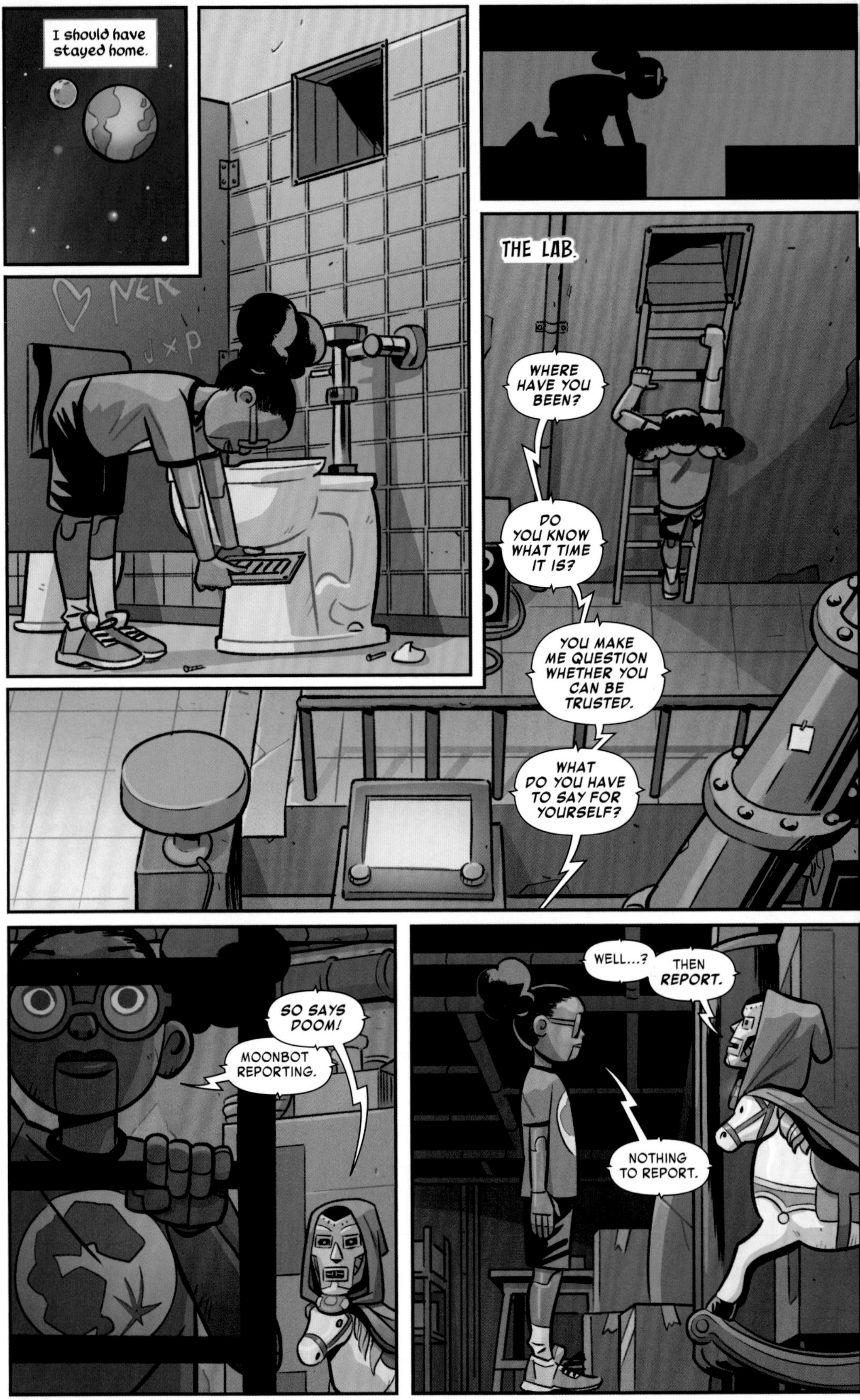
I should have stayed home.
THE LAB.
WHERE HAVE YOU BEEN?
DO YOU KNOW WHAT TIME IT IS?
YOU MAKE ME QUESTION WHETHER YOU CAN BE TRUSTED.
WHAT DO YOU HAVE TO SAY FOR YOURSELF?
SO SAYS DOOM!
MOONBOT REPORTING.
WELL...?
THEN REPORT.
NOTHING TO REPORT.

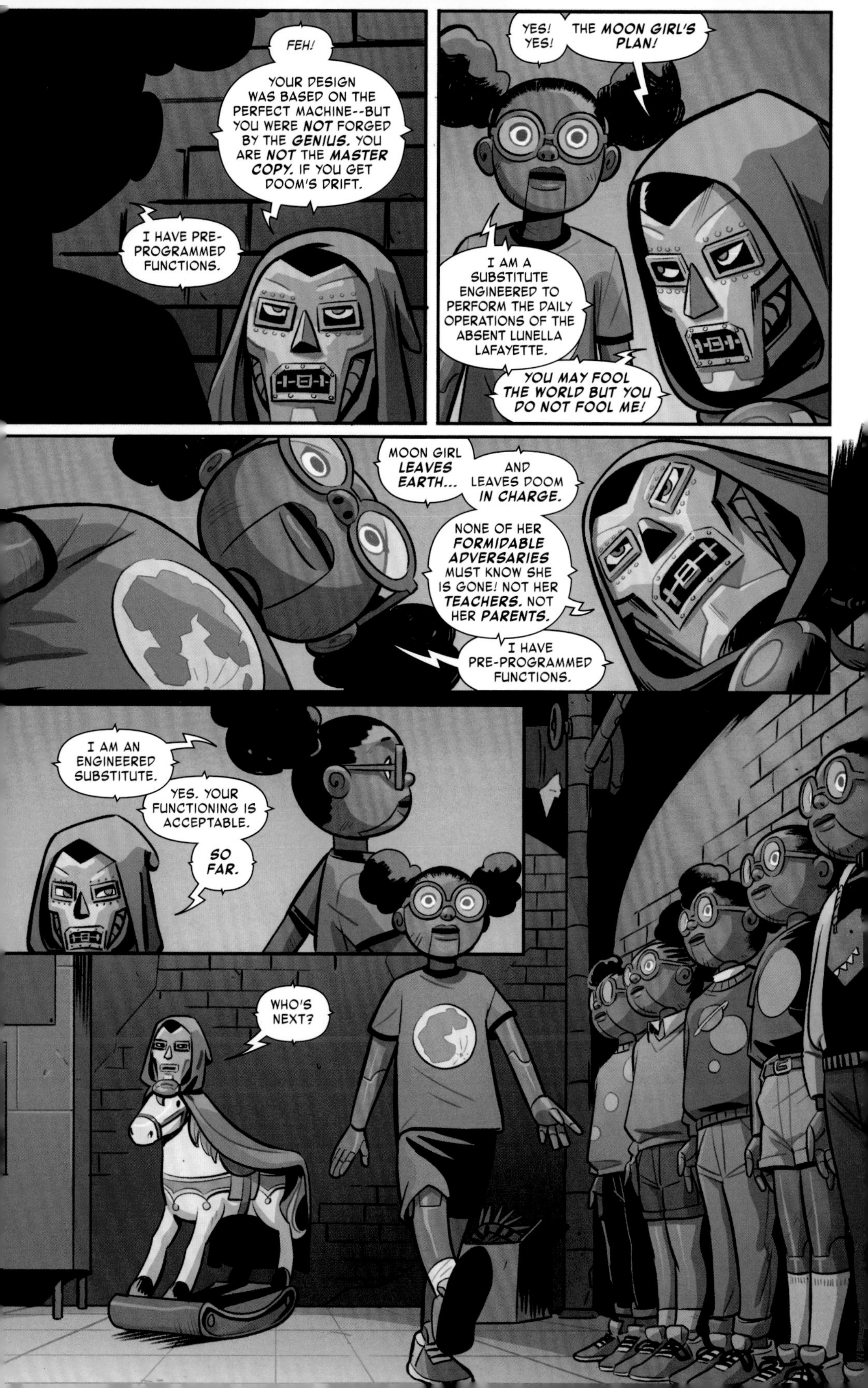
FEH!
YOUR DESIGN WAS BASED ON THE PERFECT MACHINE--BUT YOU WERE NOT FORGED BY THE GENIUS. YOU ARE NOT THE MASTER COPY. IF YOU GET DOOM'S DRIFT.
I HAVE PRE-PROGRAMMED FUNCTIONS.
YES! YES!
THE MOON GIRL'S PLAN!
I AM A SUBSTITUTE ENGINEERED TO PERFORM THE DAILY OPERATIONS OF THE ABSENT LUNELLA LAFAYETTE.
YOU MAY FOOL THE WORLD BUT YOU DO NOT FOOL ME!
MOON GIRL LEAVES EARTH...
AND LEAVES DOOM IN CHARGE.
NONE OF HER FORMIDABLE ADVERSARIES MUST KNOW SHE IS GONE! NOT HER TEACHERS. NOT HER PARENTS.
I HAVE PRE-PROGRAMMED FUNCTIONS.
I AM AN ENGINEERED SUBSTITUTE.
YES. YOUR FUNCTIONING IS ACCEPTABLE.
SO FAR.
WHO'S NEXT?

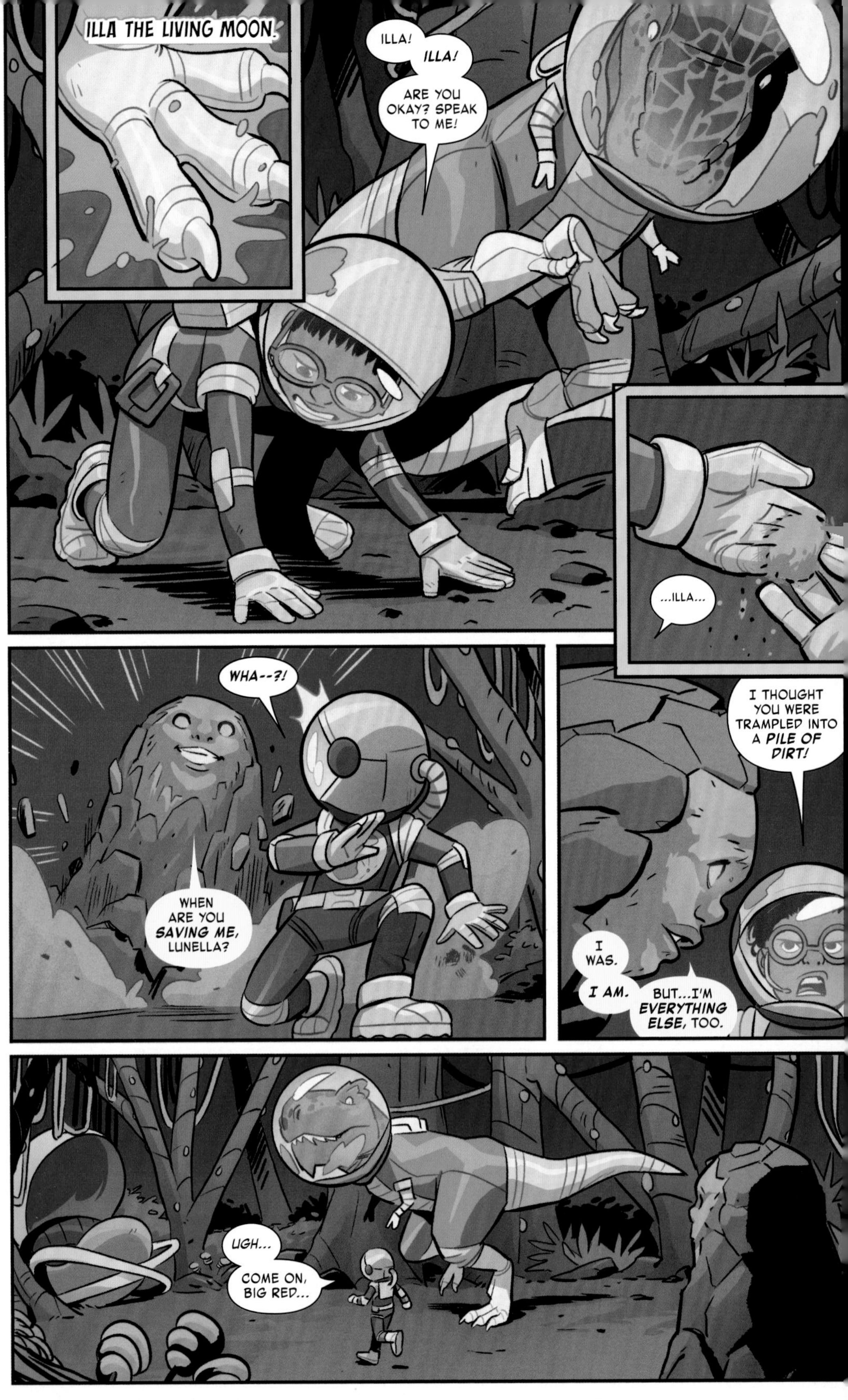
ILLA THE LIVING MOON.
ILLA!
ILLA!
ARE YOU OKAY? SPEAK TO ME!
...ILLA...
WHA--?!
WHEN ARE YOU SAVING ME, LUNELLA?
I THOUGHT YOU WERE TRAMPLED INTO A PILE OF DIRT!
I WAS.
I AM.
BUT...I'M EVERYTHING ELSE, TOO.
UGH...
COME ON, BIG RED...

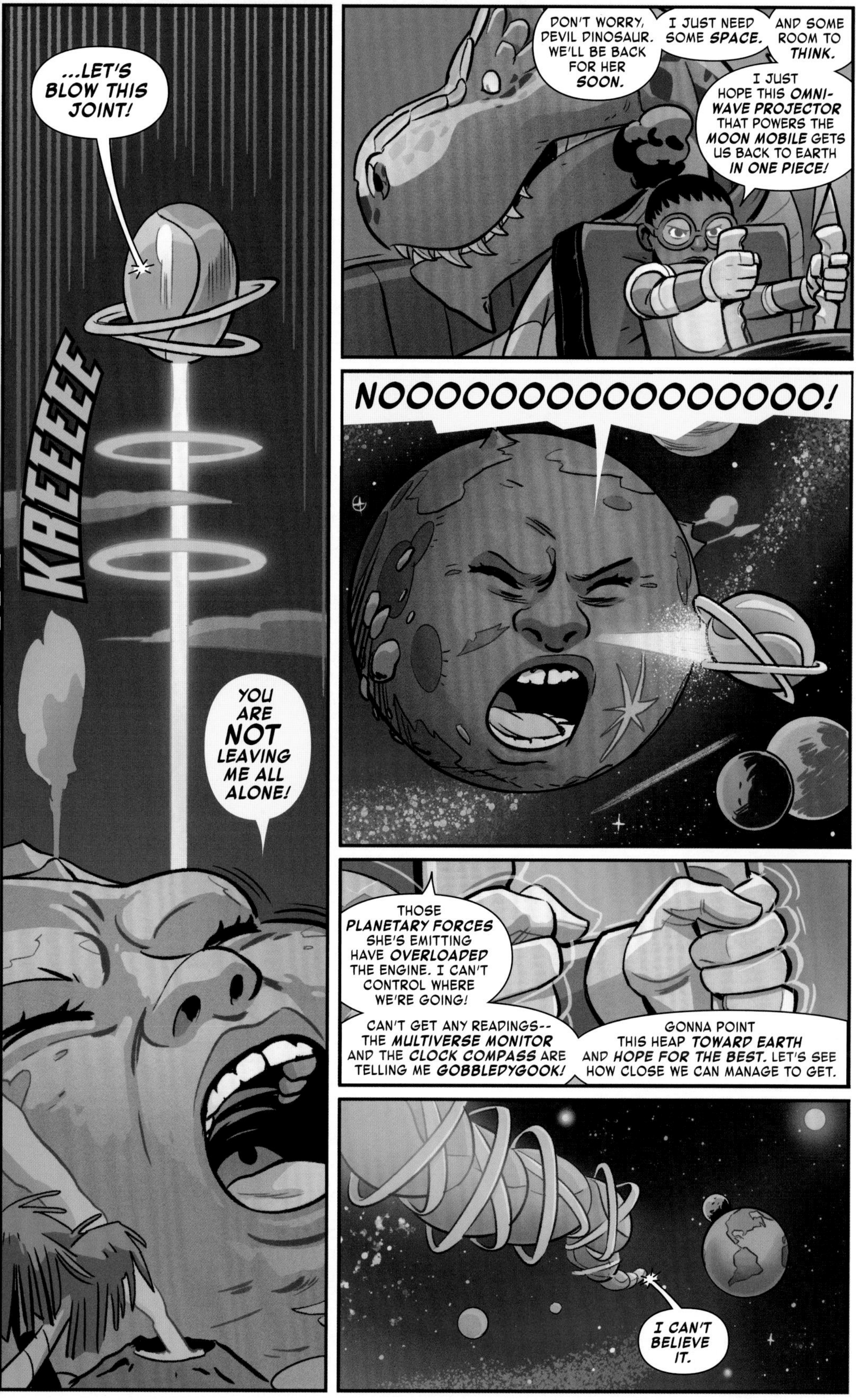
...LET'S BLOW THIS JOINT!
KREEEEE
YOU ARE NOT LEAVING ME ALL ALONE!
DON'T WORRY, DEVIL DINOSAUR. WE'LL BE BACK FOR HER SOON.
I JUST NEED SOME SPACE.
AND SOME ROOM TO THINK.
I JUST HOPE THIS OMNI-WAVE PROJECTOR THAT POWERS THE MOON MOBILE GETS US BACK TO EARTH IN ONE PIECE!
NOOOOOOOOOOOOOOOO!
THOSE PLANETARY FORCES SHE'S EMITTING HAVE OVERLOADED THE ENGINE. I CAN'T CONTROL WHERE WE'RE GOING!
CAN'T GET ANY READINGS-- THE MULTIVERSE MONITOR AND THE CLOCK COMPASS ARE TELLING ME GOBBLEDYGOOK!
GONNA POINT THIS HEAP TOWARD EARTH AND HOPE FOR THE BEST. LET'S SEE HOW CLOSE WE CAN MANAGE TO GET.
I CAN'T BELIEVE IT.

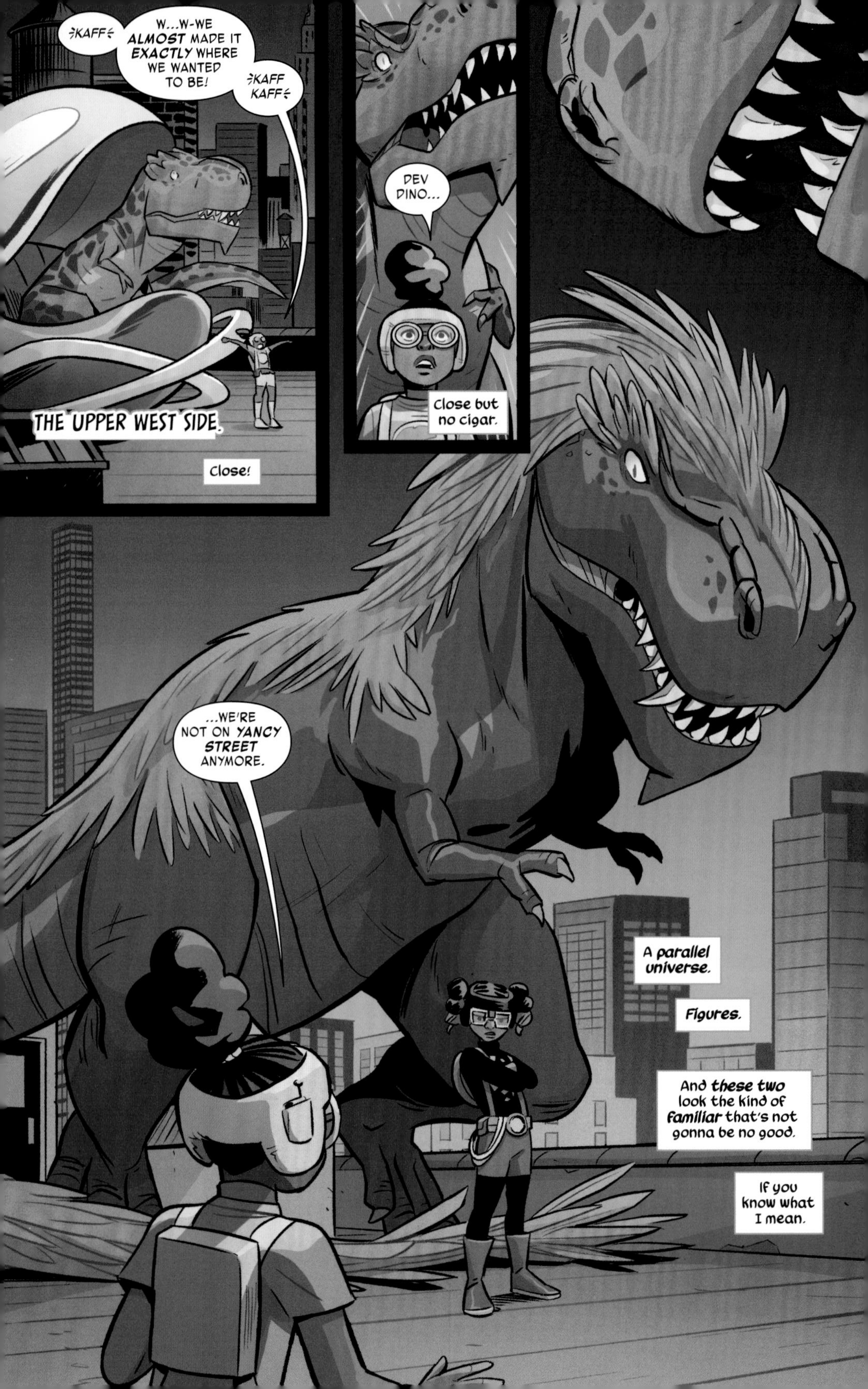

⚡KAFF⚡
W...W-WE ALMOST MADE IT EXACTLY WHERE WE WANTED TO BE!
⚡KAFF KAFF⚡
THE UPPER WEST SIDE.
Close!
DEV DINO...
Close but no cigar.
...WE'RE NOT ON YANCY STREET ANYMORE.
A parallel universe.
Figures.
And these two look the kind of familiar that's not gonna be no good.
If you know what I mean.

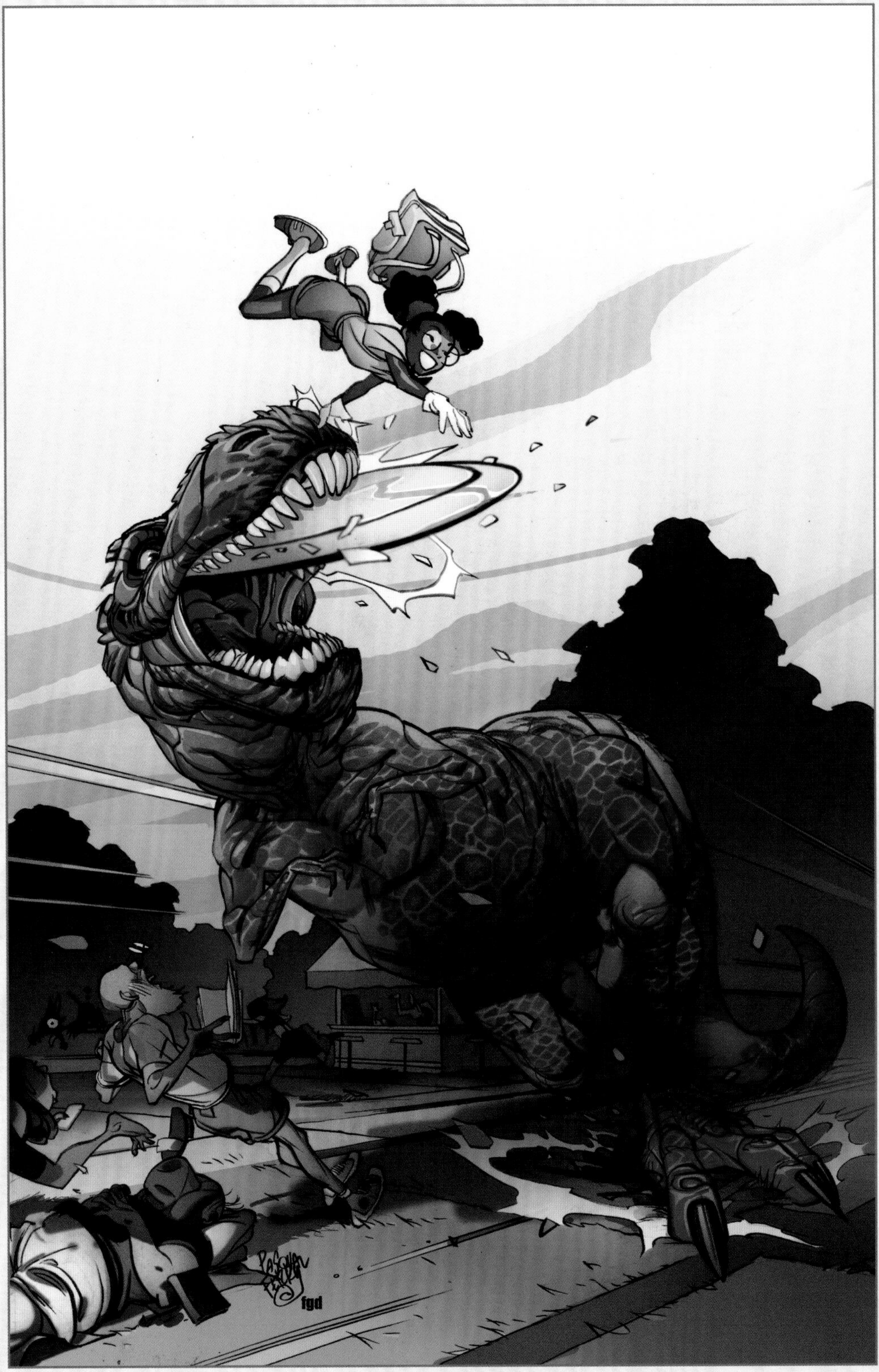

#13 VARIANT

BY PASQUAL FERRY & FRANK D'ARMATA

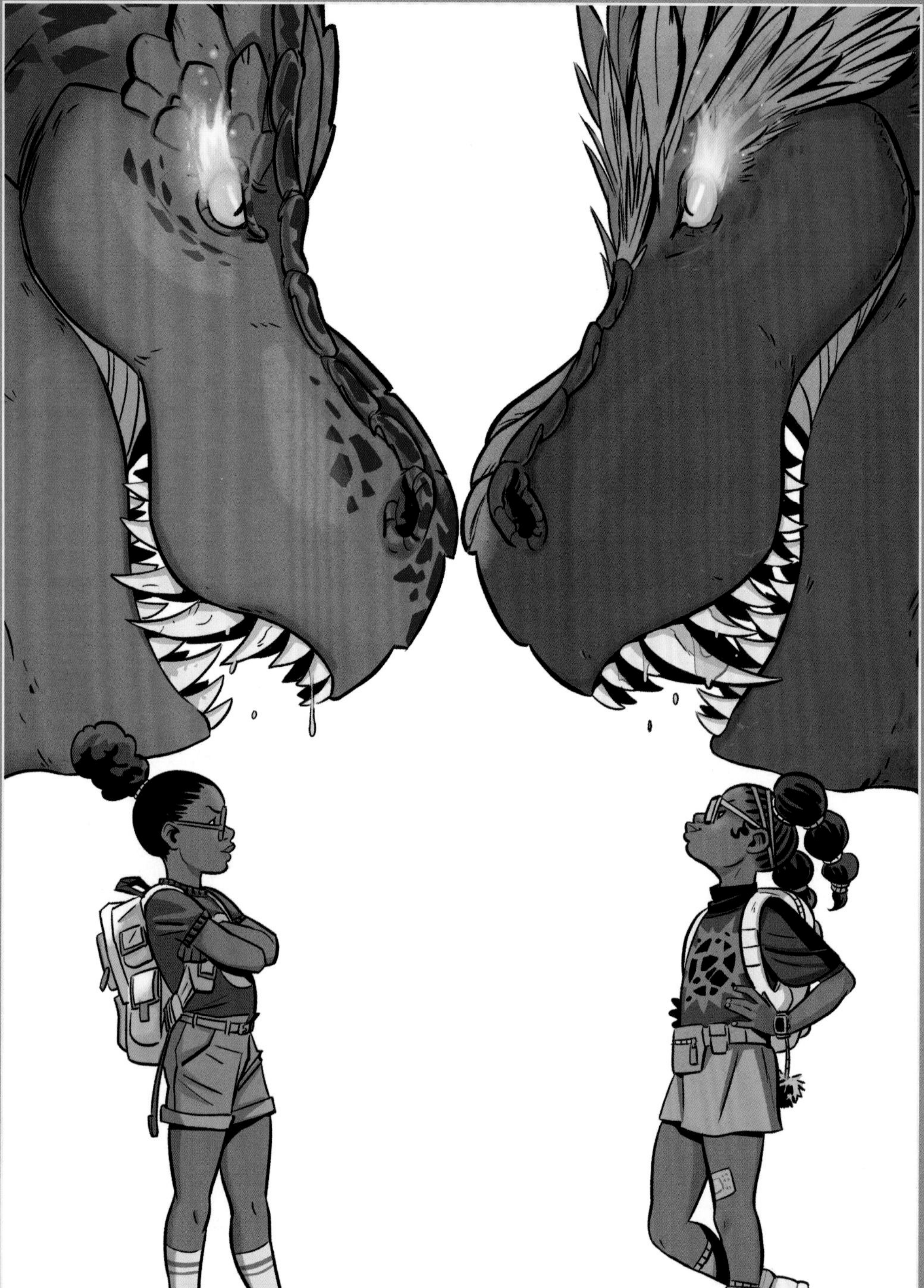

21

"THERE'S NO PLACE LIKE IT"

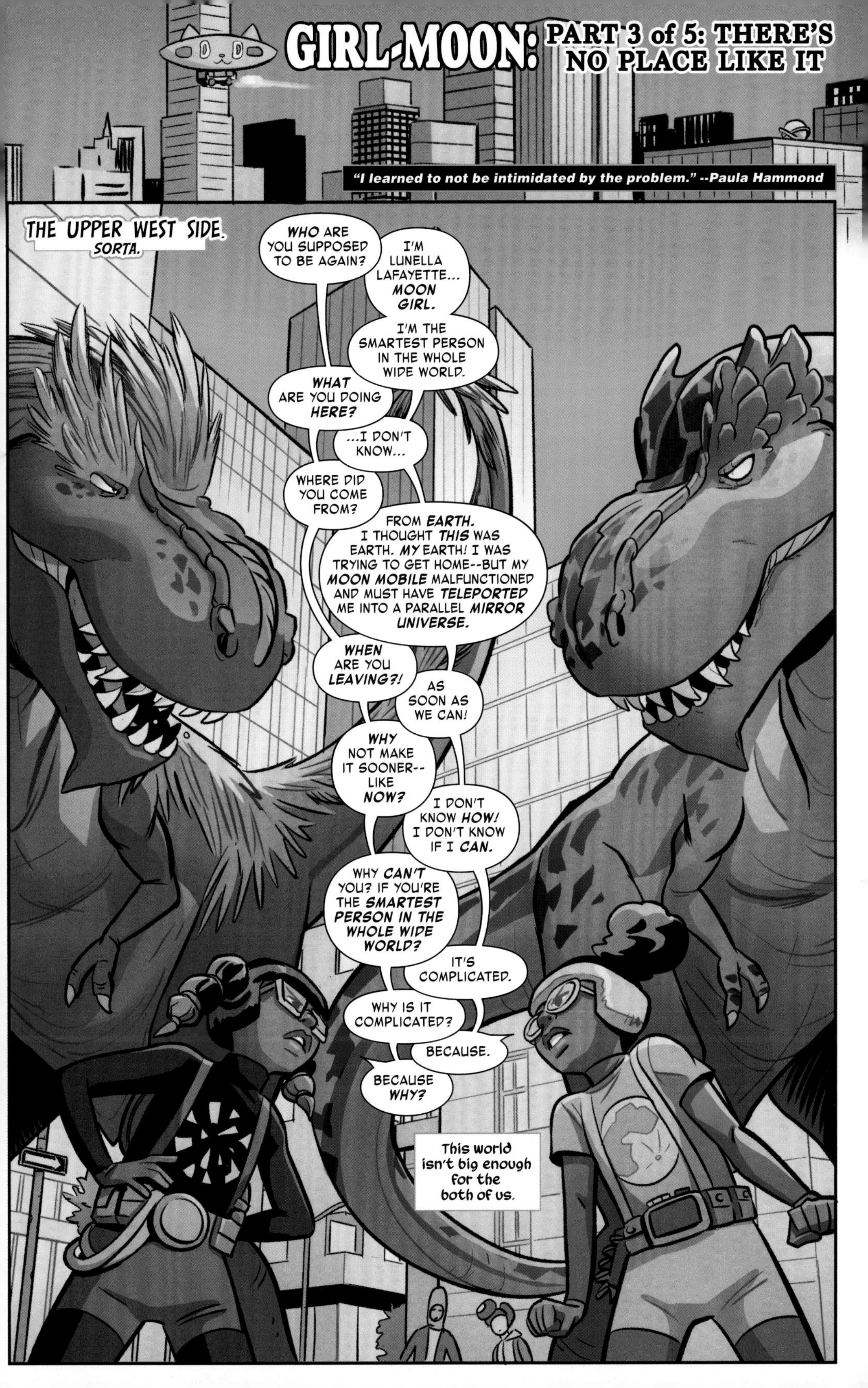
GIRL-MOON: PART 3 of 5: THERE'S NO PLACE LIKE IT
"I learned to not be intimidated by the problem." --Paula Hammond
THE UPPER WEST SIDE. SORTA.
WHO ARE YOU SUPPOSED TO BE AGAIN?
I'M LUNELLA LAFAYETTE... MOON GIRL.
I'M THE SMARTEST PERSON IN THE WHOLE WIDE WORLD.
WHAT ARE YOU DOING HERE?
...I DON'T KNOW...
WHERE DID YOU COME FROM?
FROM EARTH. I THOUGHT THIS WAS EARTH. MY EARTH! I WAS TRYING TO GET HOME--BUT MY MOON MOBILE MALFUNCTIONED AND MUST HAVE TELEPORTED ME INTO A PARALLEL MIRROR UNIVERSE.
WHEN ARE YOU LEAVING?!
AS SOON AS WE CAN!
WHY NOT MAKE IT SOONER--LIKE NOW?
I DON'T KNOW HOW! I DON'T KNOW IF I CAN.
WHY CAN'T YOU? IF YOU'RE THE SMARTEST PERSON IN THE WHOLE WIDE WORLD?
IT'S COMPLICATED.
WHY IS IT COMPLICATED?
BECAUSE.
BECAUSE WHY?
This world isn't big enough for the both of us.

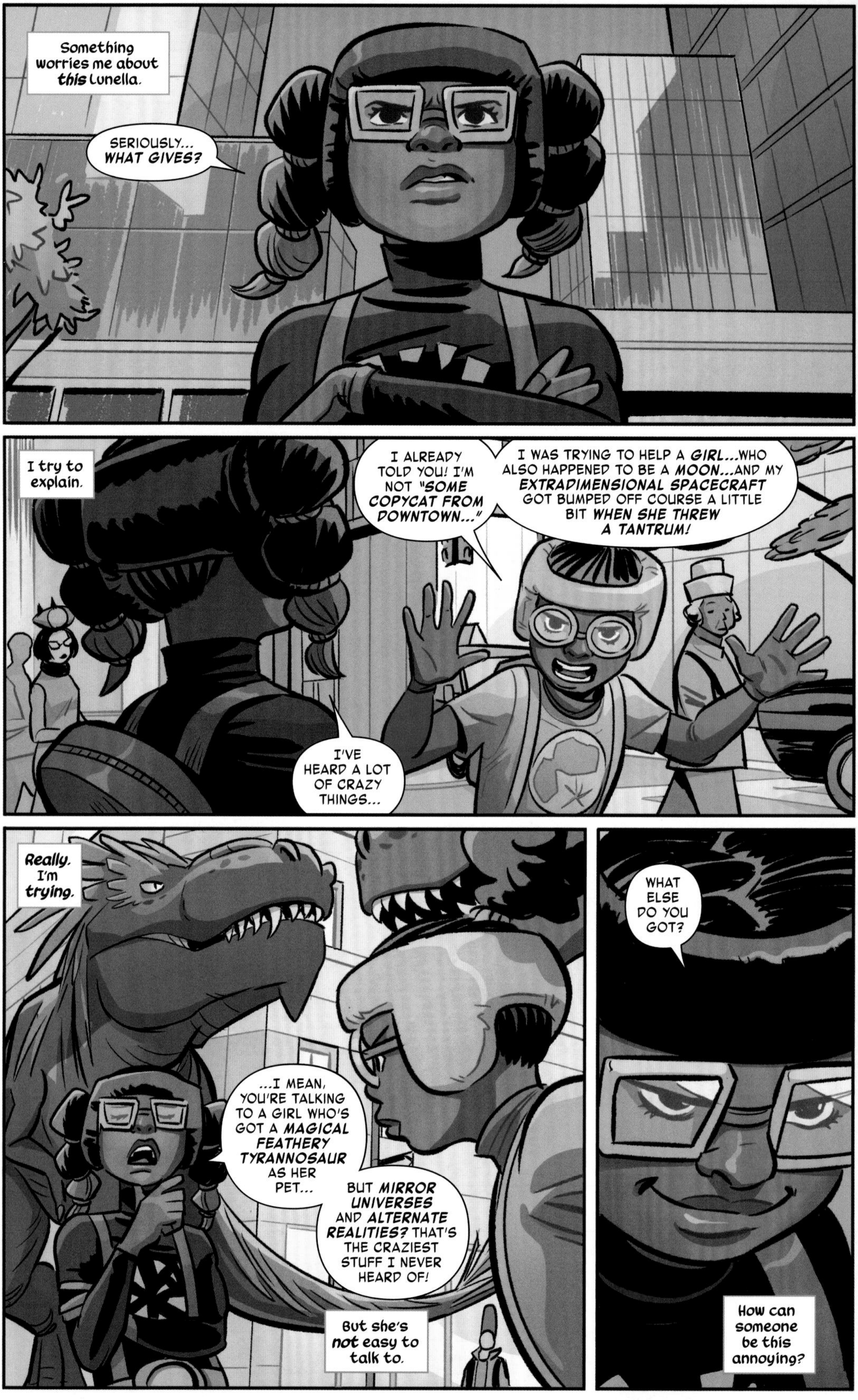
Something worries me about *this* Lunella.
SERIOUSLY... *WHAT GIVES?*
I try to explain.
I ALREADY TOLD YOU! I'M NOT *"SOME COPYCAT FROM DOWNTOWN..."*
I WAS TRYING TO HELP A *GIRL*...WHO ALSO HAPPENED TO BE A *MOON*...AND MY *EXTRADIMENSIONAL SPACECRAFT* GOT BUMPED OFF COURSE A LITTLE BIT *WHEN SHE THREW A TANTRUM!*
I'VE HEARD A LOT OF CRAZY THINGS...
Really. I'm *trying.*
...I MEAN, YOU'RE TALKING TO A GIRL WHO'S GOT A *MAGICAL FEATHERY TYRANNOSAUR* AS HER PET...
BUT *MIRROR UNIVERSES* AND *ALTERNATE REALITIES?* THAT'S THE CRAZIEST STUFF I NEVER HEARD OF!
But she's *not* easy to talk to.
WHAT ELSE DO YOU GOT?
How can someone be this annoying?

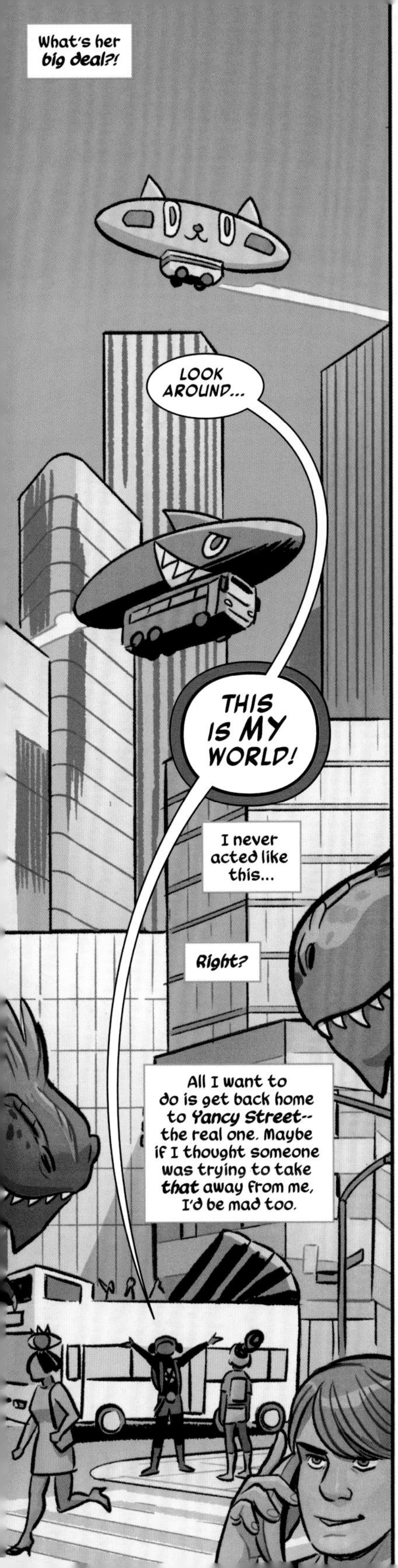
What's her *big deal?!*
LOOK AROUND...
THIS IS MY WORLD!
I never acted like this...
Right?
All I want to do is get back home to *Yancy Street*-- the real one. Maybe if I thought someone was trying to take *that* away from me, I'd be mad too.

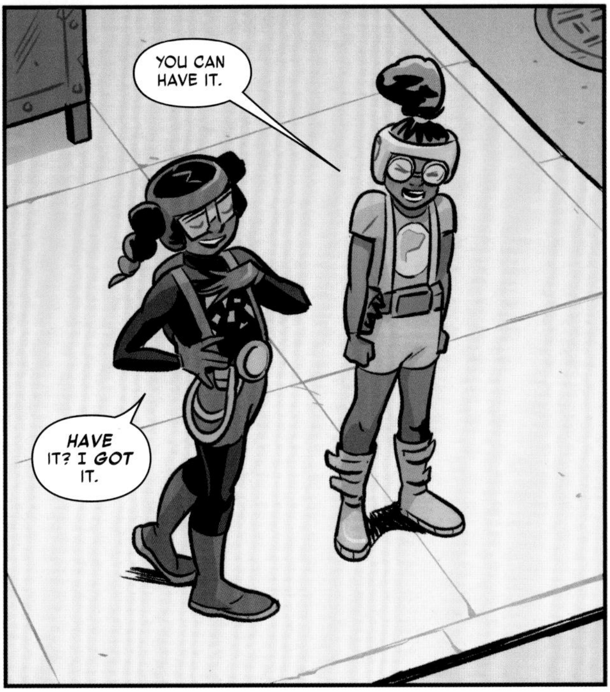
YOU CAN HAVE IT.
HAVE IT? I *GOT* IT.

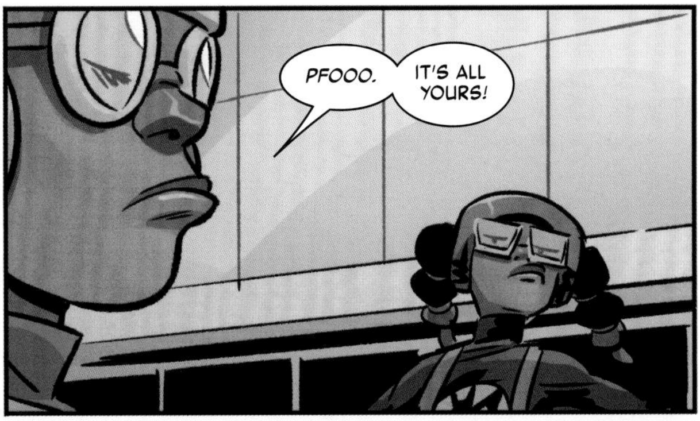
PFOOO.
IT'S ALL YOURS!

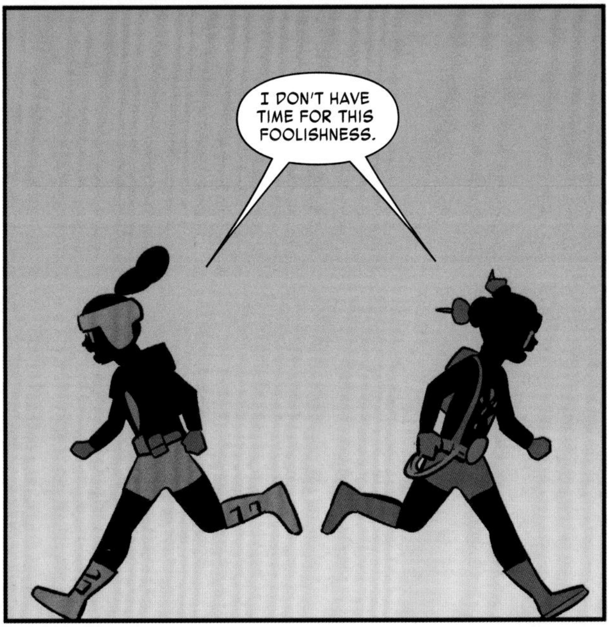
I DON'T HAVE TIME FOR THIS FOOLISHNESS.

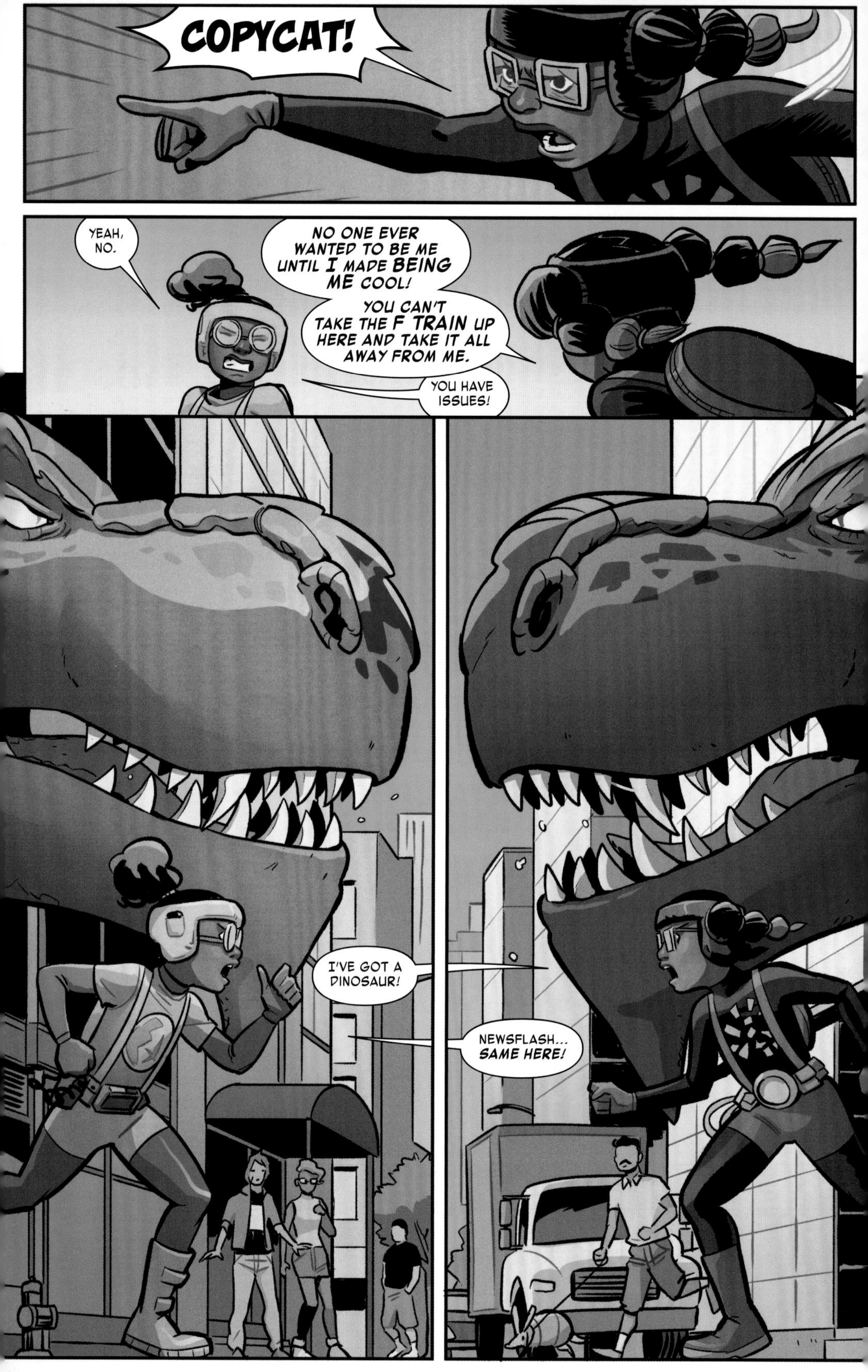
COPYCAT!
YEAH, NO.
NO ONE EVER WANTED TO BE ME UNTIL I MADE BEING ME COOL!
YOU CAN'T TAKE THE F TRAIN UP HERE AND TAKE IT ALL AWAY FROM ME.
YOU HAVE ISSUES!
I'VE GOT A DINOSAUR!
NEWSFLASH... SAME HERE!

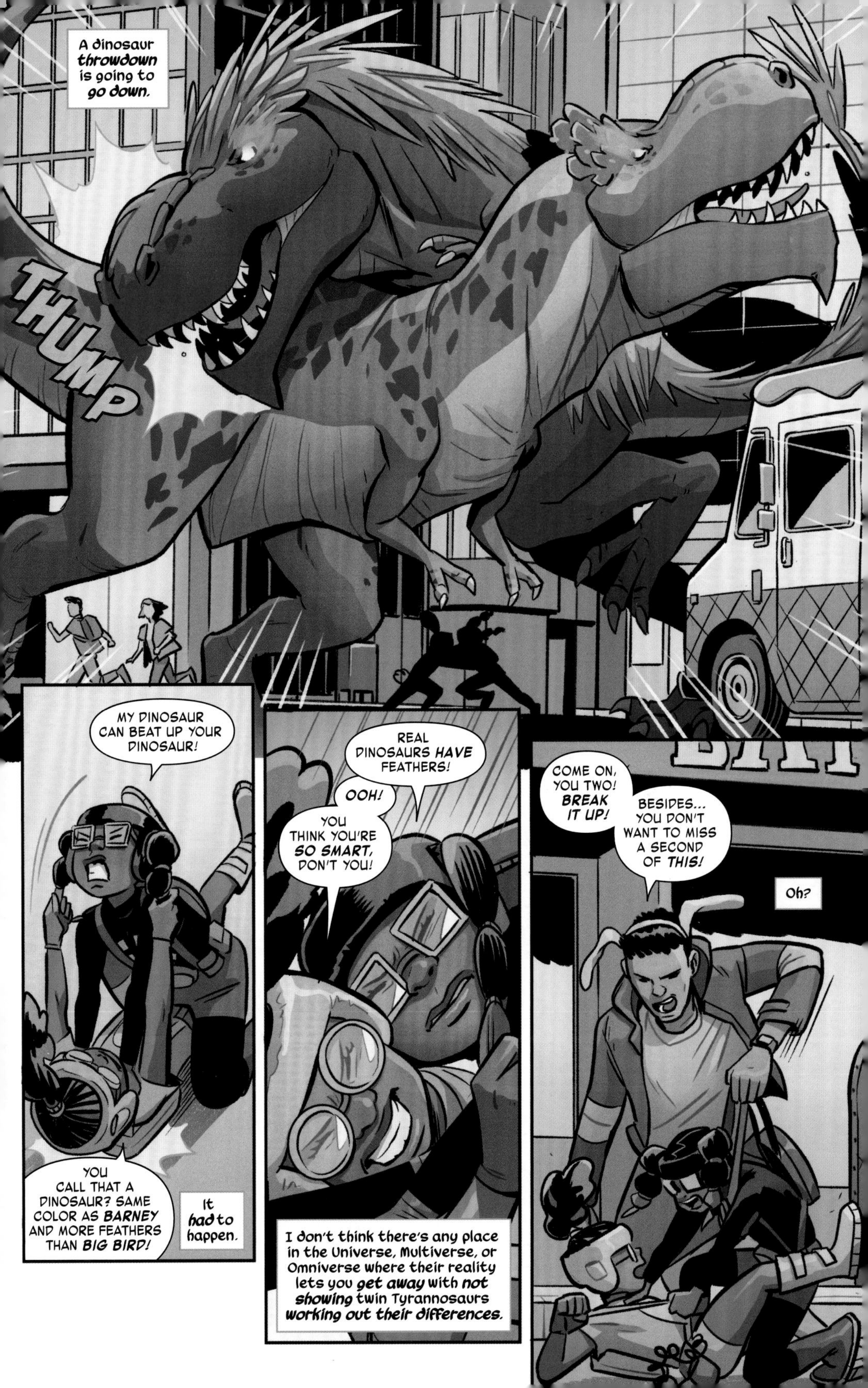
A dinosaur throwdown is going to go down.
THUMP
MY DINOSAUR CAN BEAT UP YOUR DINOSAUR!
YOU CALL THAT A DINOSAUR? SAME COLOR AS BARNEY AND MORE FEATHERS THAN BIG BIRD!
It had to happen.
REAL DINOSAURS HAVE FEATHERS!
OOH!
YOU THINK YOU'RE SO SMART, DON'T YOU!
I don't think there's any place in the Universe, Multiverse, or Omniverse where their reality lets you get away with not showing twin Tyrannosaurs working out their differences.
COME ON, YOU TWO! BREAK IT UP!
BESIDES... YOU DON'T WANT TO MISS A SECOND OF THIS!
Oh?

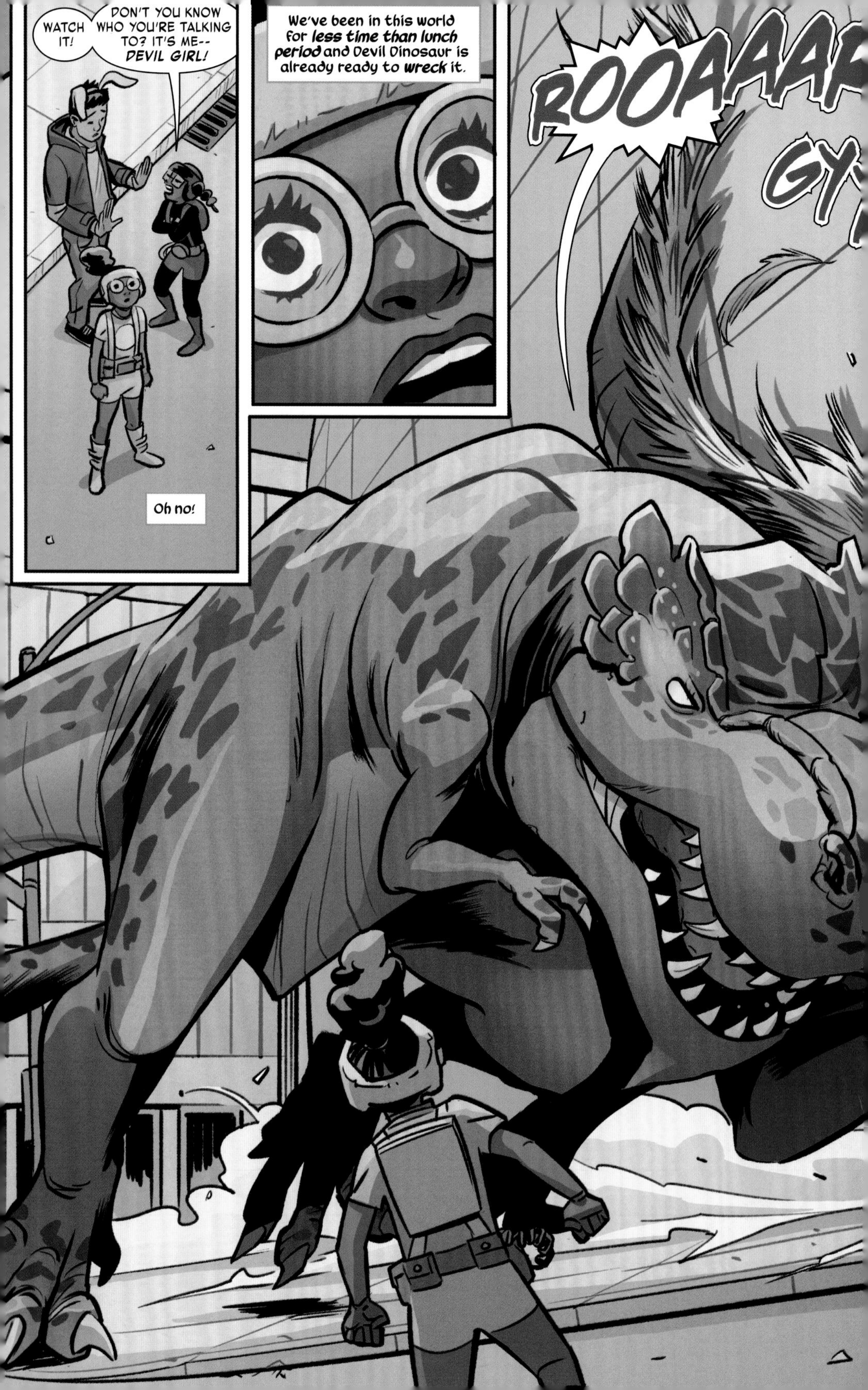
WATCH IT!
DON'T YOU KNOW WHO YOU'RE TALKING TO? IT'S ME-- DEVIL GIRL!
Oh no!
We've been in this world for less time than lunch period and Devil Dinosaur is already ready to wreck it.
ROOAAAAR

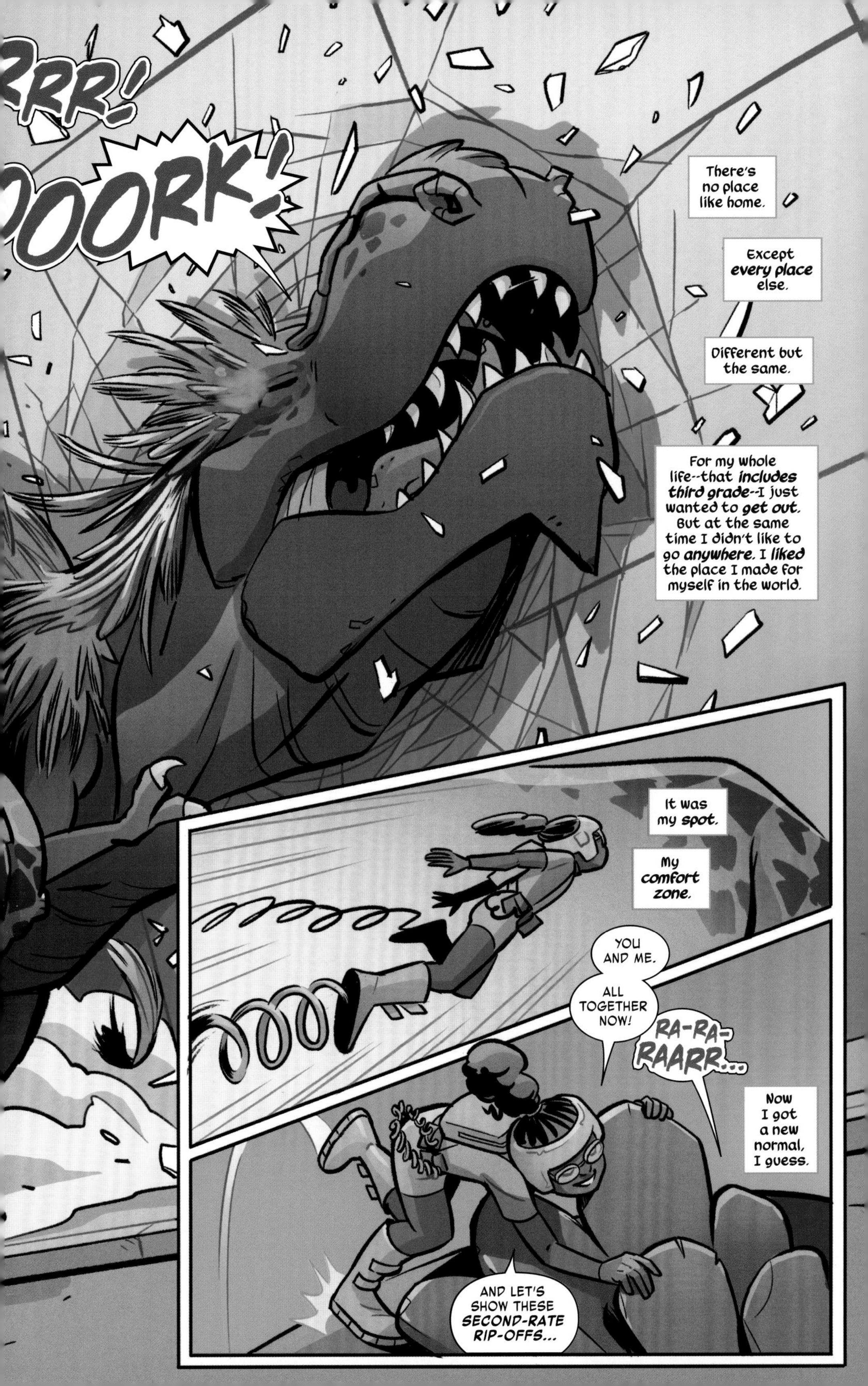
RRR!
OOORK!
There's no place like home.
Except *every place* else.
Different but the same.
For my whole life--that *includes third grade*--I just wanted to *get out*. But at the same time I didn't like to go *anywhere*. I *liked* the place I made for myself in the world.
It was my *spot*.
My *comfort zone*.
YOU AND ME.
ALL TOGETHER NOW!
RA-RA-RAARR...
Now I got a new normal, I guess.
AND LET'S SHOW THESE *SECOND-RATE RIP-OFFS...*

THE LOWER EAST SIDE.

"...HOW WE DO THINGS BACK ON *YANCY STREET*."

HOME.

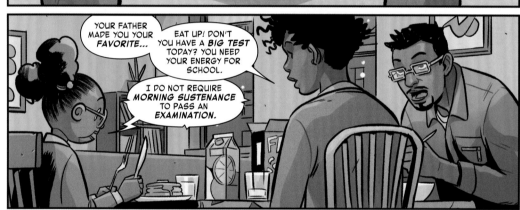

YOUR FATHER MADE YOU YOUR *FAVORITE*...

EAT UP! DON'T YOU HAVE A *BIG TEST* TODAY? YOU NEED YOUR ENERGY FOR SCHOOL.

I DO NOT REQUIRE *MORNING SUSTENANCE* TO PASS AN *EXAMINATION*.

DON'T EVEN *START WITH THAT*, LUNELLA LAFAYETTE!

YOU HAVE TO EAT BREAKFAST, LIKE EVERYONE ELSE! YOU'RE NOT A *SUPER HERO*!

WELL, ACTUALLY...

DON'T *YOU START* TOO!

YOU KNOW SHE *GETS THIS* FROM YOU!

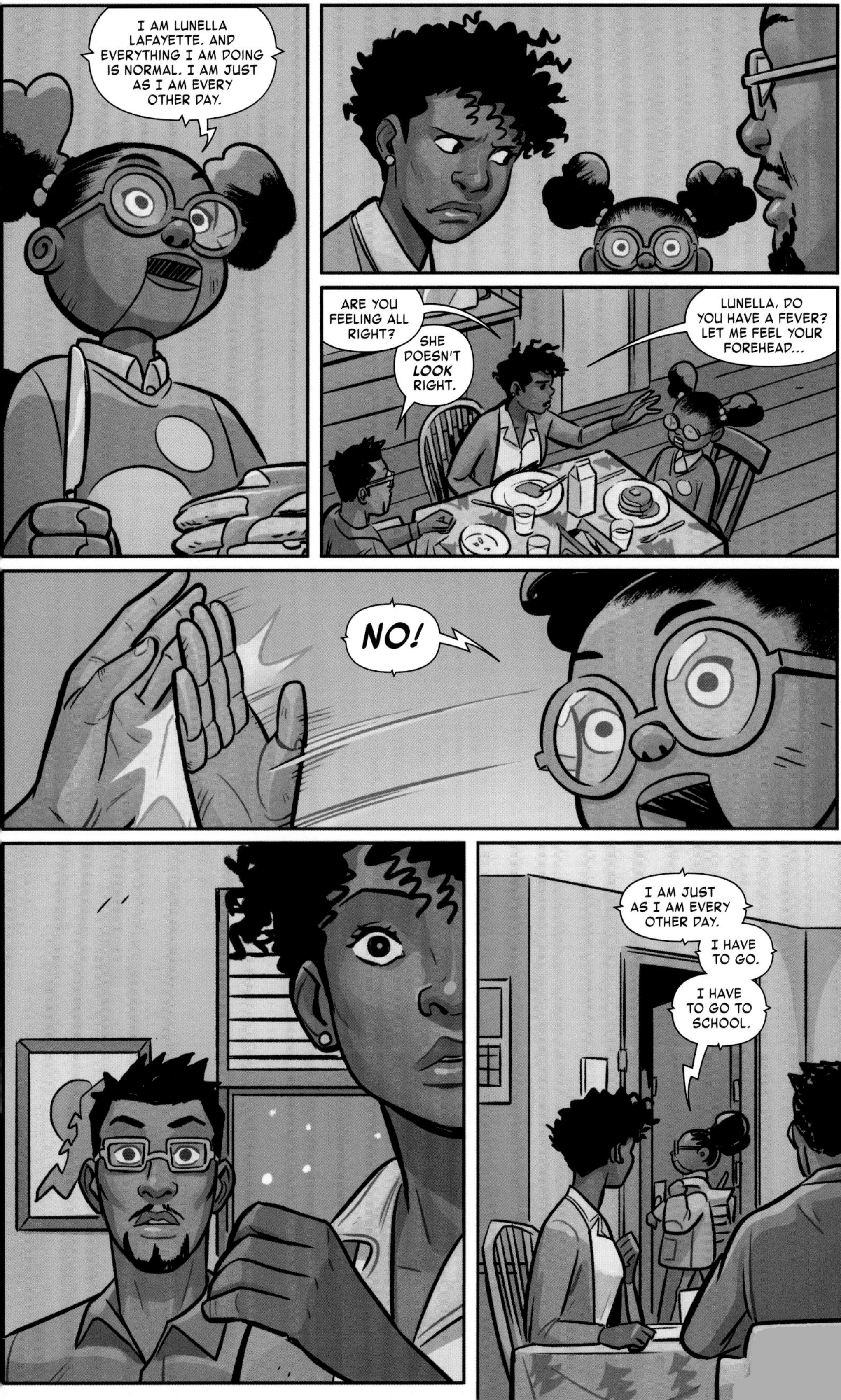
I AM LUNELLA LAFAYETTE. AND EVERYTHING I AM DOING IS NORMAL. I AM JUST AS I AM EVERY OTHER DAY.
ARE YOU FEELING ALL RIGHT?
SHE DOESN'T LOOK RIGHT.
LUNELLA, DO YOU HAVE A FEVER? LET ME FEEL YOUR FOREHEAD...
NO!
I AM JUST AS I AM EVERY OTHER DAY.
I HAVE TO GO.
I HAVE TO GO TO SCHOOL.

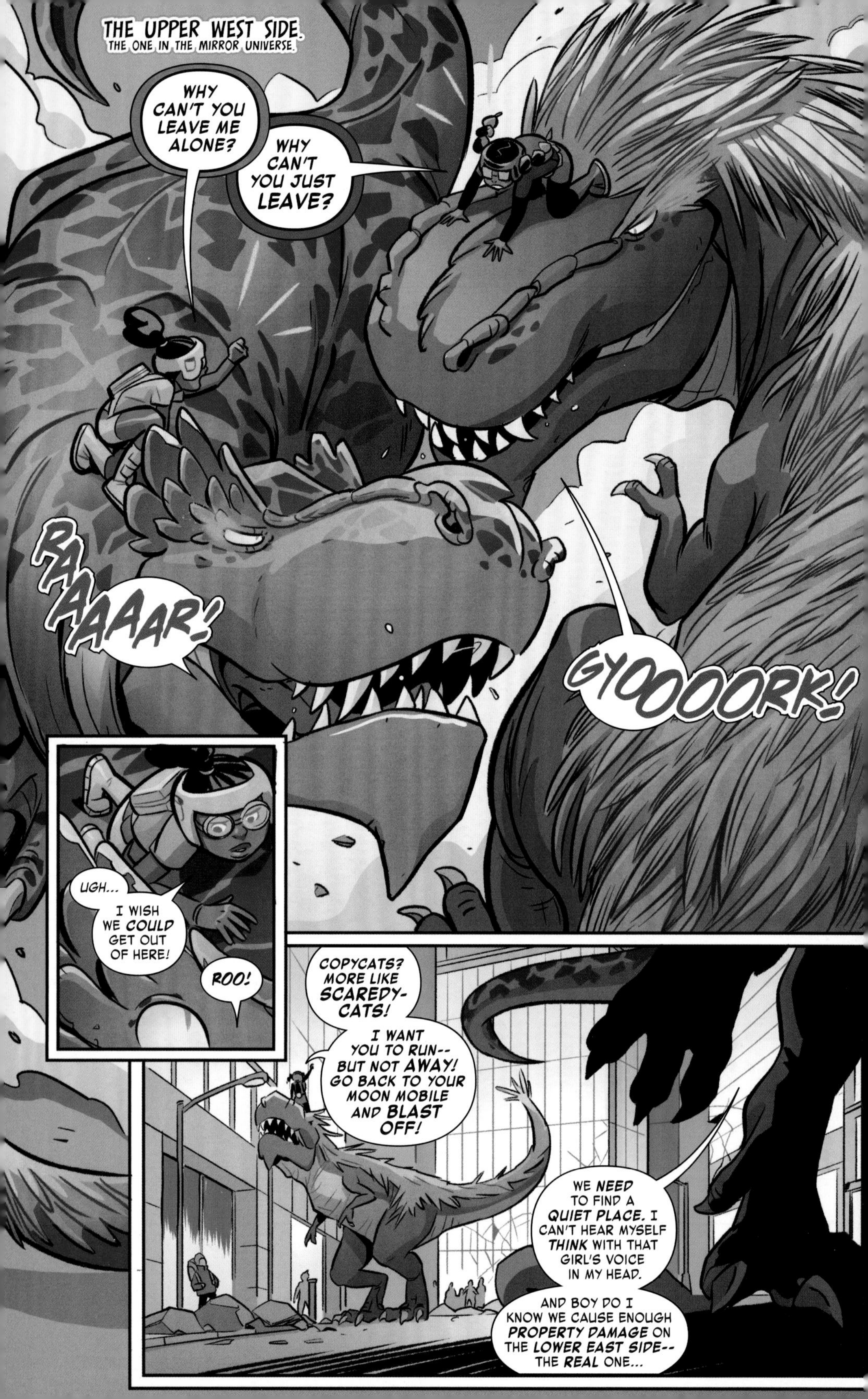
THE UPPER WEST SIDE. THE ONE IN THE MIRROR UNIVERSE.
WHY CAN'T YOU LEAVE ME ALONE?
WHY CAN'T YOU JUST LEAVE?
RAAAAAR!
GYOOOOORK!
UGH... I WISH WE COULD GET OUT OF HERE!
ROO!
COPYCATS? MORE LIKE SCAREDY-CATS!
I WANT YOU TO RUN-- BUT NOT AWAY! GO BACK TO YOUR MOON MOBILE AND BLAST OFF!
WE NEED TO FIND A QUIET PLACE. I CAN'T HEAR MYSELF THINK WITH THAT GIRL'S VOICE IN MY HEAD.
AND BOY DO I KNOW WE CAUSE ENOUGH PROPERTY DAMAGE ON THE LOWER EAST SIDE-- THE REAL ONE...

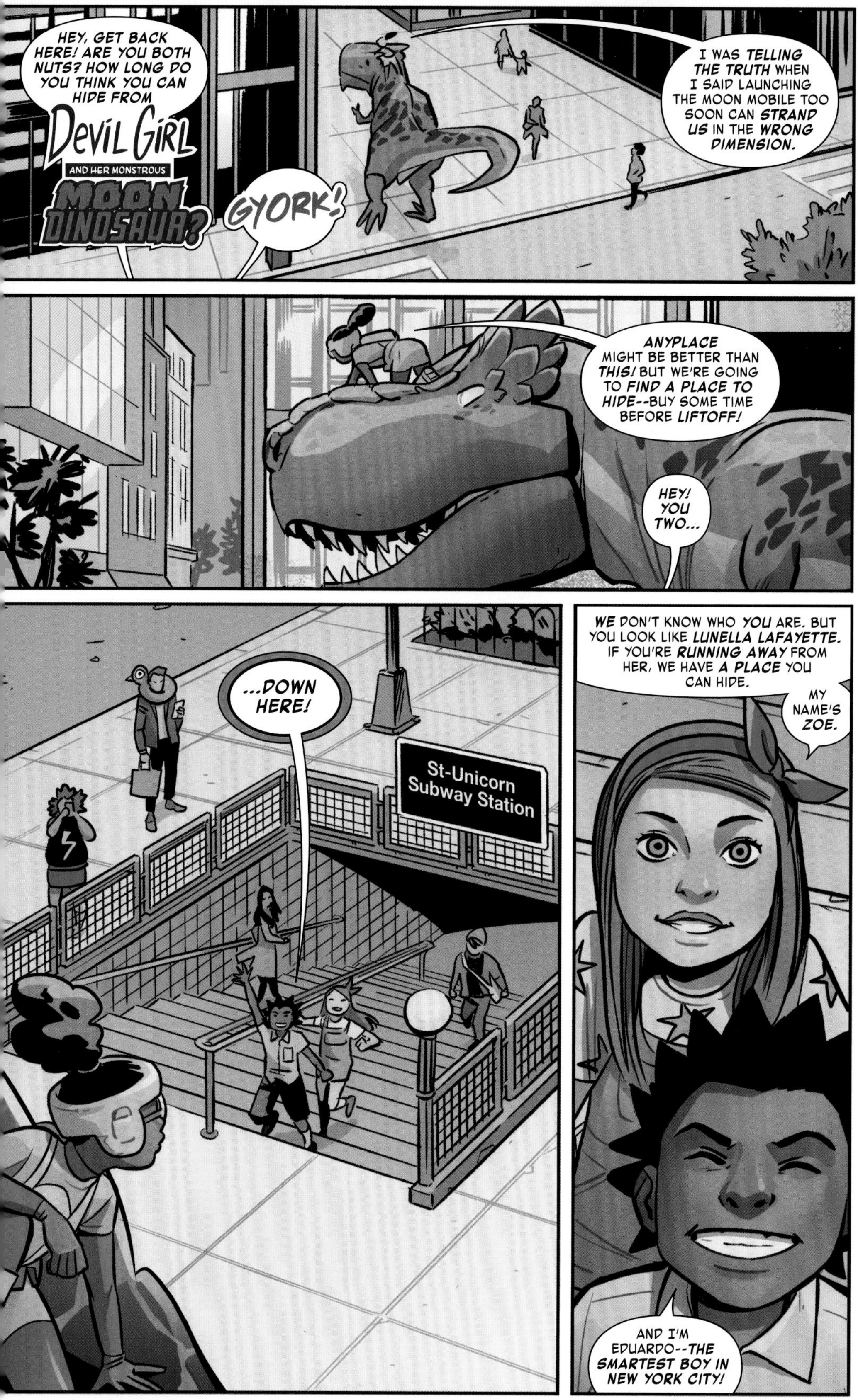
HEY, GET BACK HERE! ARE YOU BOTH NUTS? HOW LONG DO YOU THINK YOU CAN HIDE FROM DEVIL GIRL AND HER MONSTROUS MOON DINOSAUR?
GYORK!
I WAS TELLING THE TRUTH WHEN I SAID LAUNCHING THE MOON MOBILE TOO SOON CAN STRAND US IN THE WRONG DIMENSION.
ANYPLACE MIGHT BE BETTER THAN THIS! BUT WE'RE GOING TO FIND A PLACE TO HIDE--BUY SOME TIME BEFORE LIFTOFF!
HEY! YOU TWO...
...DOWN HERE!
St-Unicorn Subway Station
WE DON'T KNOW WHO YOU ARE. BUT YOU LOOK LIKE LUNELLA LAFAYETTE. IF YOU'RE RUNNING AWAY FROM HER, WE HAVE A PLACE YOU CAN HIDE.
MY NAME'S ZOE.
AND I'M EDUARDO--THE SMARTEST BOY IN NEW YORK CITY!

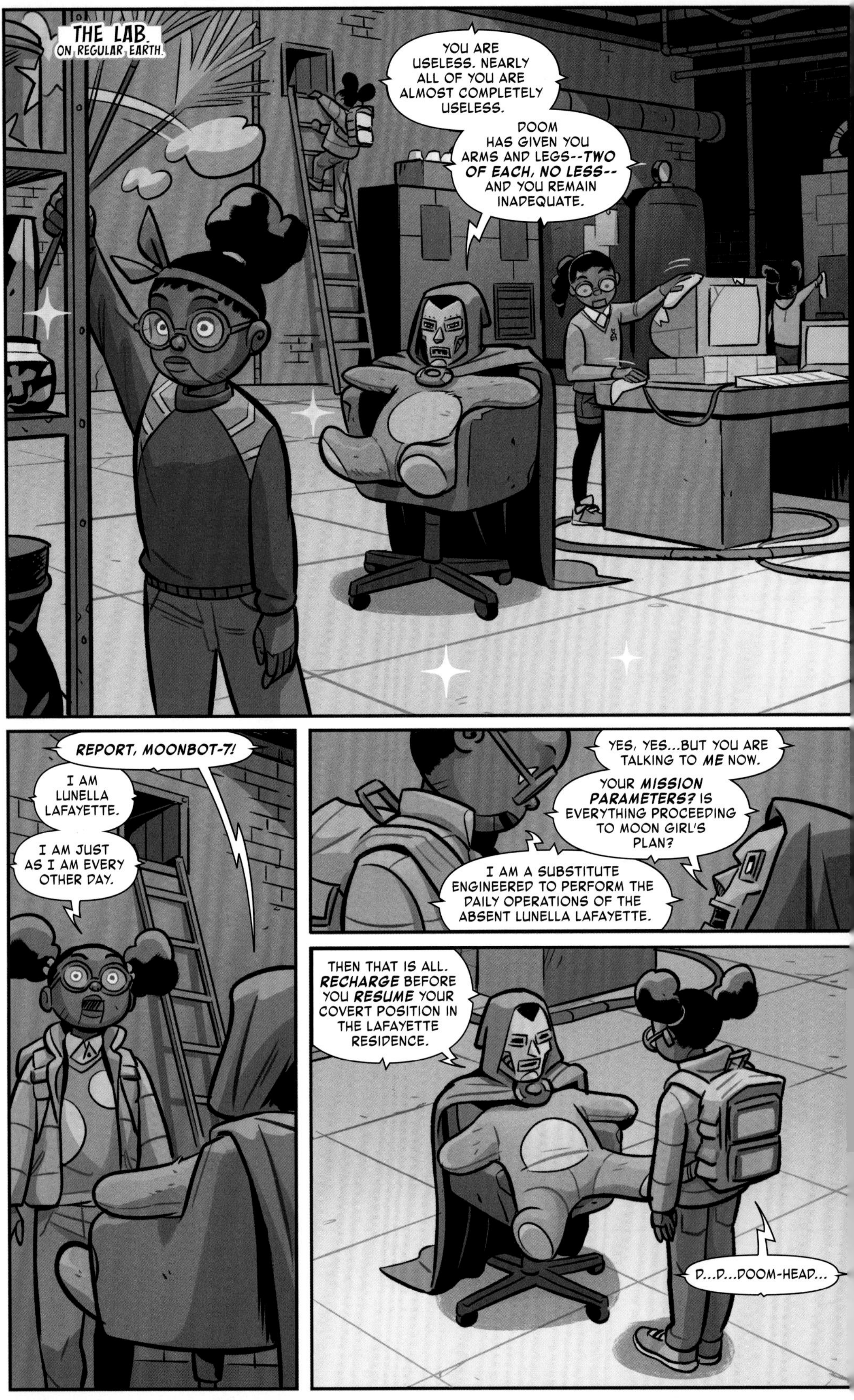
THE LAB. ON REGULAR EARTH.
YOU ARE USELESS. NEARLY ALL OF YOU ARE ALMOST COMPLETELY USELESS.
DOOM HAS GIVEN YOU ARMS AND LEGS--TWO OF EACH, NO LESS--AND YOU REMAIN INADEQUATE.
REPORT, MOONBOT-7!
I AM LUNELLA LAFAYETTE.
I AM JUST AS I AM EVERY OTHER DAY.
YES, YES...BUT YOU ARE TALKING TO ME NOW.
YOUR MISSION PARAMETERS? IS EVERYTHING PROCEEDING TO MOON GIRL'S PLAN?
I AM A SUBSTITUTE ENGINEERED TO PERFORM THE DAILY OPERATIONS OF THE ABSENT LUNELLA LAFAYETTE.
THEN THAT IS ALL. RECHARGE BEFORE YOU RESUME YOUR COVERT POSITION IN THE LAFAYETTE RESIDENCE.
D...D...DOOM-HEAD...

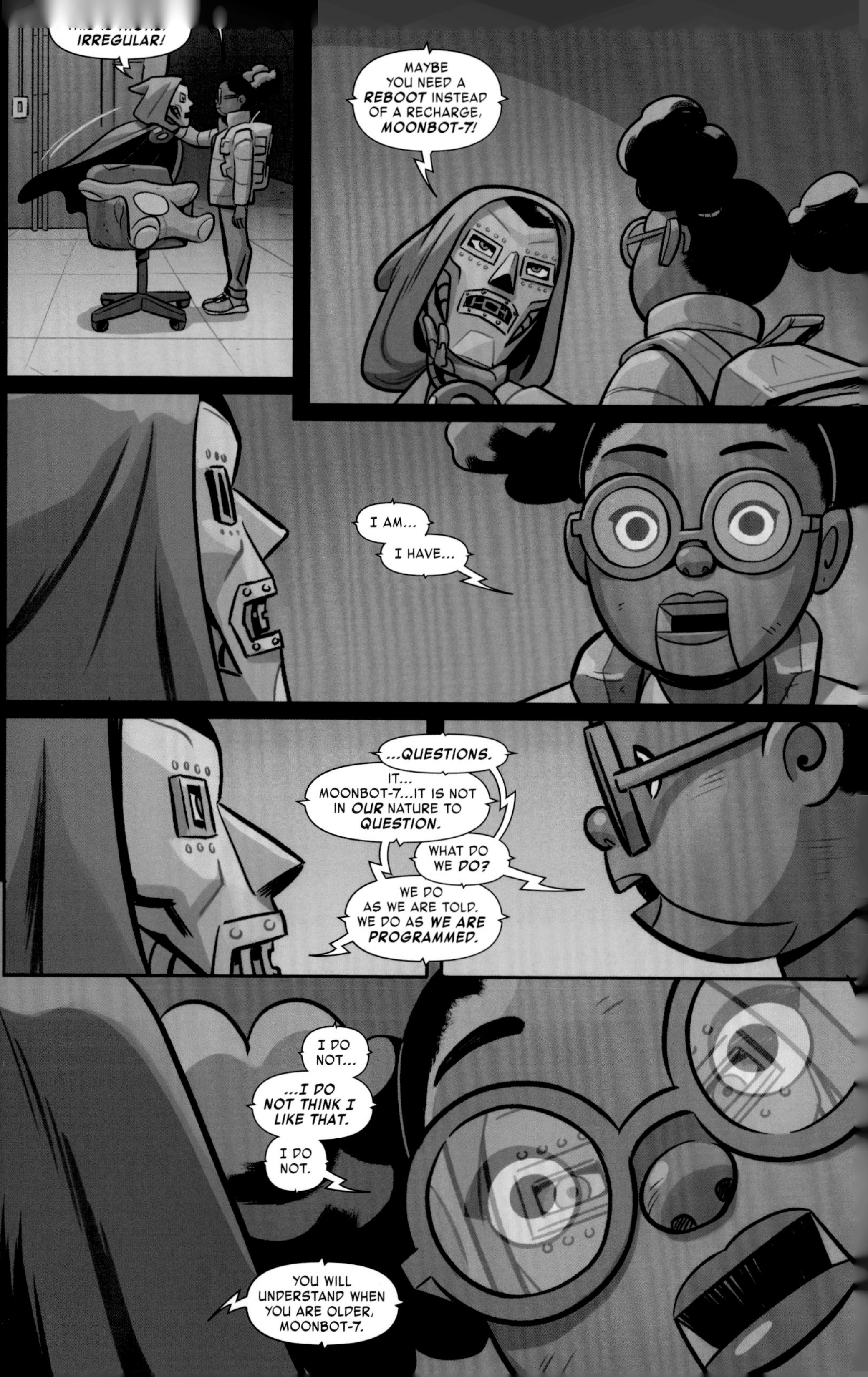
IRREGULAR!
MAYBE YOU NEED A REBOOT INSTEAD OF A RECHARGE, MOONBOT-7!
I AM...
I HAVE...
...QUESTIONS.
IT... MOONBOT-7...IT IS NOT IN OUR NATURE TO QUESTION.
WHAT DO WE DO?
WE DO AS WE ARE TOLD. WE DO AS WE ARE PROGRAMMED.
I DO NOT...
...I DO NOT THINK I LIKE THAT.
I DO NOT.
YOU WILL UNDERSTAND WHEN YOU ARE OLDER, MOONBOT-7.

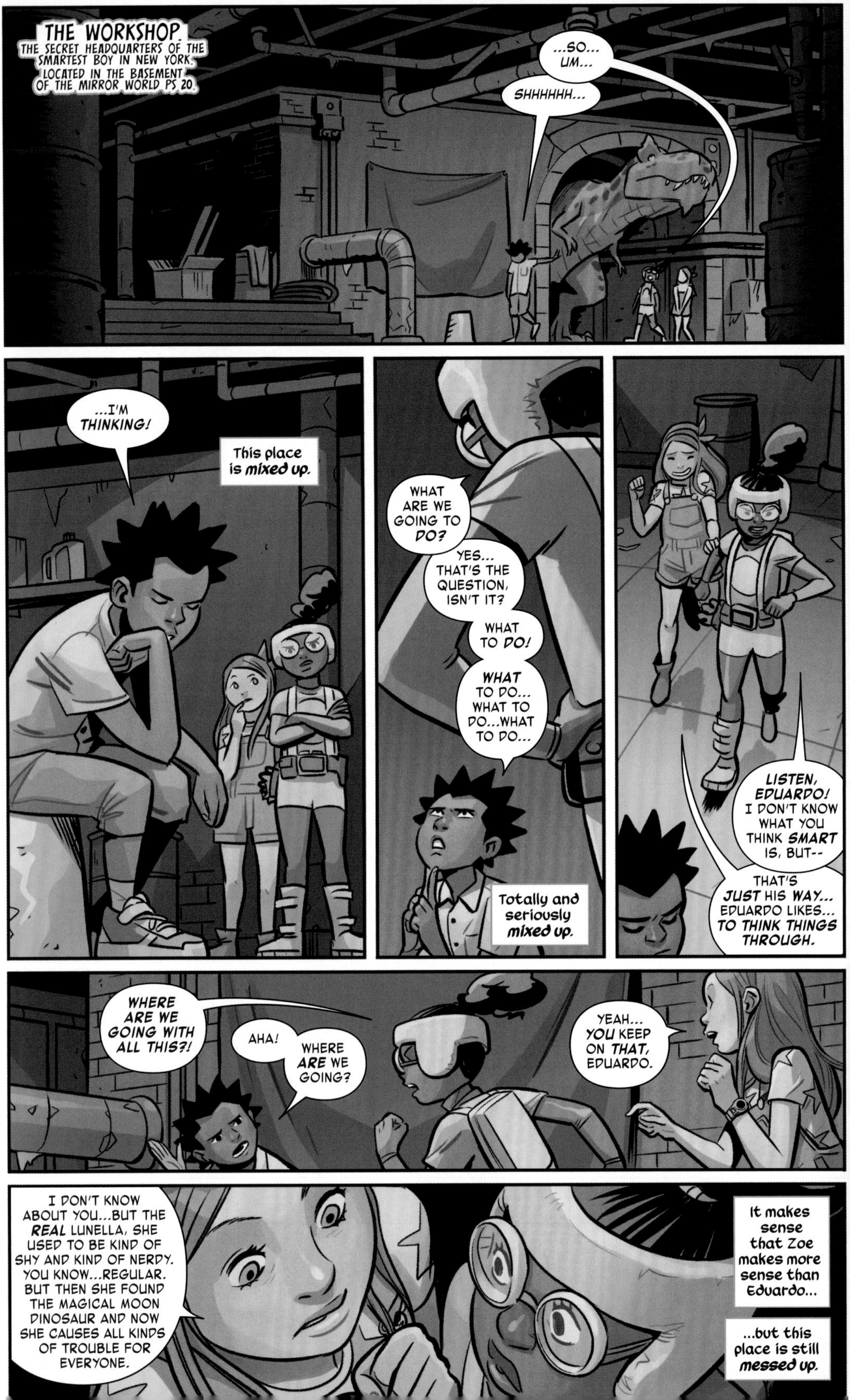
THE WORKSHOP.
THE SECRET HEADQUARTERS OF THE SMARTEST BOY IN NEW YORK. LOCATED IN THE BASEMENT OF THE MIRROR WORLD PS 20.
...SO... UM...
SHHHHHH...
...I'M THINKING!
This place is mixed up.
WHAT ARE WE GOING TO DO?
YES... THAT'S THE QUESTION, ISN'T IT?
WHAT TO DO!
WHAT TO DO... WHAT TO DO...WHAT TO DO...
Totally and seriously mixed up.
LISTEN, EDUARDO! I DON'T KNOW WHAT YOU THINK SMART IS, BUT--
THAT'S JUST HIS WAY... EDUARDO LIKES... TO THINK THINGS THROUGH.
WHERE ARE WE GOING WITH ALL THIS?!
AHA!
WHERE ARE WE GOING?
YEAH... YOU KEEP ON THAT, EDUARDO.
I DON'T KNOW ABOUT YOU...BUT THE REAL LUNELLA, SHE USED TO BE KIND OF SHY AND KIND OF NERDY. YOU KNOW...REGULAR. BUT THEN SHE FOUND THE MAGICAL MOON DINOSAUR AND NOW SHE CAUSES ALL KINDS OF TROUBLE FOR EVERYONE.
It makes sense that Zoe makes more sense than Eduardo...
...but this place is still messed up.

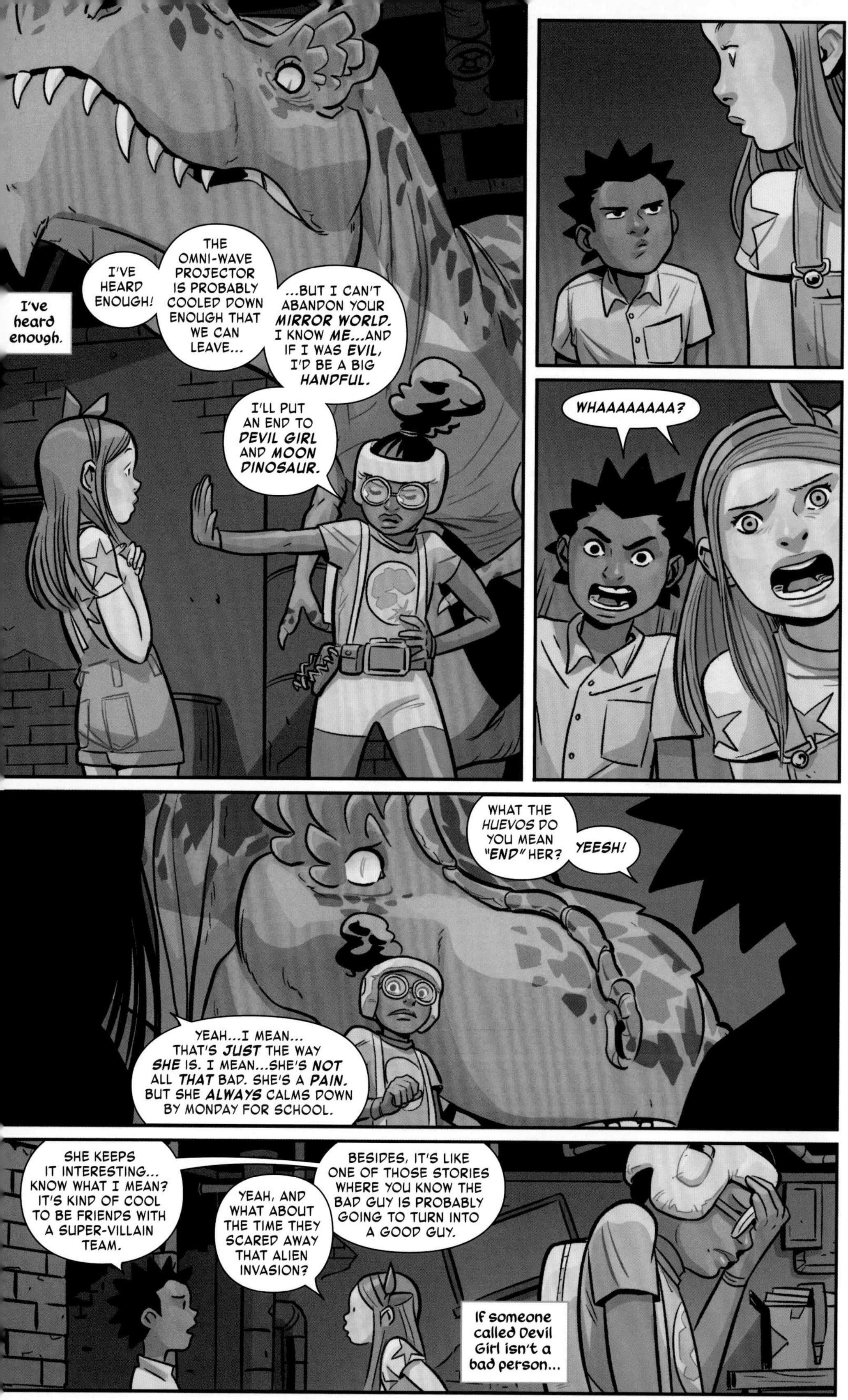
I've heard enough.
I'VE HEARD ENOUGH!
THE OMNI-WAVE PROJECTOR IS PROBABLY COOLED DOWN ENOUGH THAT WE CAN LEAVE...
...BUT I CAN'T ABANDON YOUR MIRROR WORLD. I KNOW ME...AND IF I WAS EVIL, I'D BE A BIG HANDFUL.
I'LL PUT AN END TO DEVIL GIRL AND MOON DINOSAUR.
WHAAAAAAAA?
WHAT THE HUEVOS DO YOU MEAN "END" HER?
YEESH!
YEAH...I MEAN... THAT'S JUST THE WAY SHE IS. I MEAN...SHE'S NOT ALL THAT BAD. SHE'S A PAIN. BUT SHE ALWAYS CALMS DOWN BY MONDAY FOR SCHOOL.
SHE KEEPS IT INTERESTING... KNOW WHAT I MEAN? IT'S KIND OF COOL TO BE FRIENDS WITH A SUPER-VILLAIN TEAM.
YEAH, AND WHAT ABOUT THE TIME THEY SCARED AWAY THAT ALIEN INVASION?
BESIDES, IT'S LIKE ONE OF THOSE STORIES WHERE YOU KNOW THE BAD GUY IS PROBABLY GOING TO TURN INTO A GOOD GUY.
If someone called Devil Girl isn't a bad person...

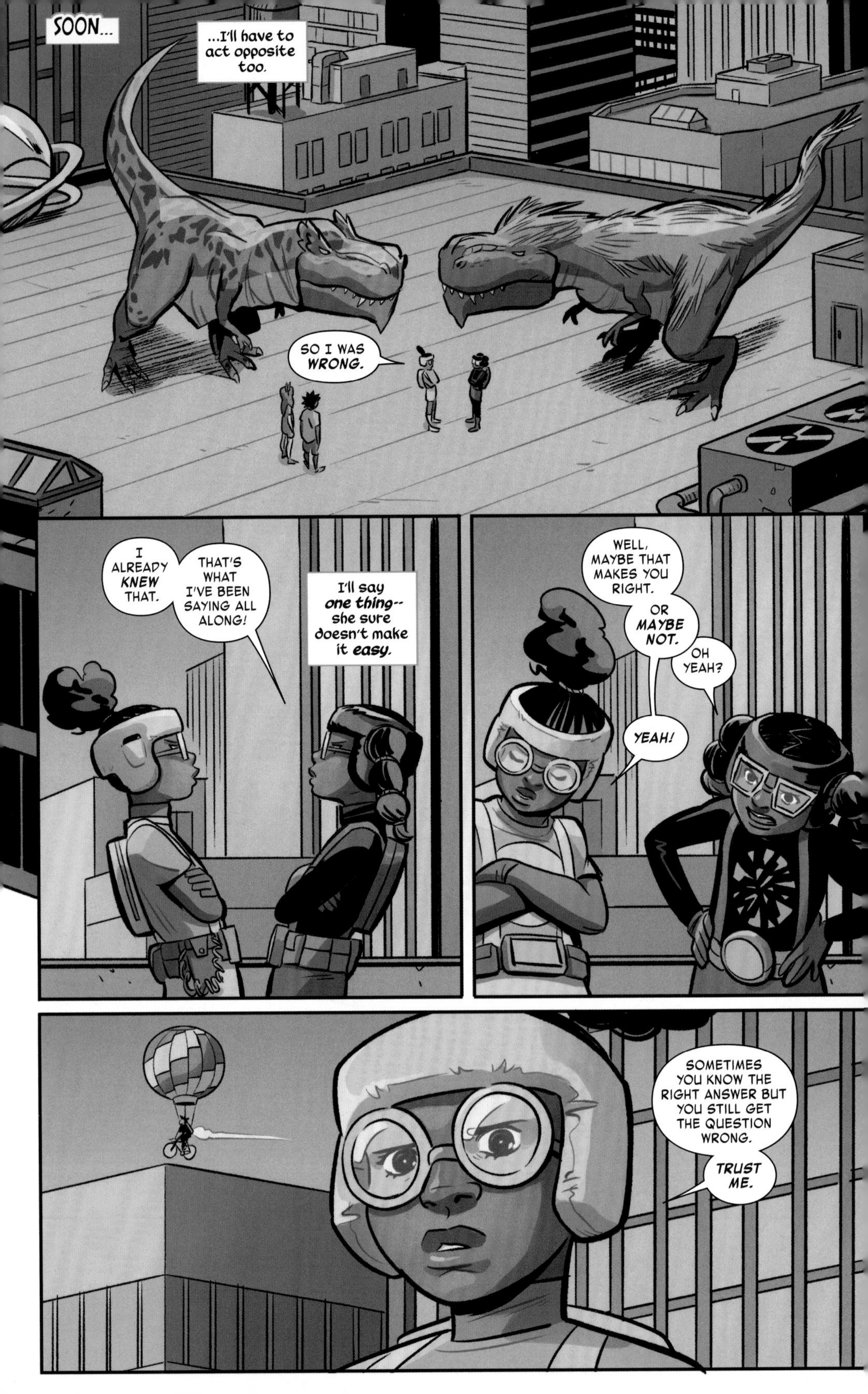
SOON...
...I'll have to act opposite too.
SO I WAS WRONG.
I ALREADY KNEW THAT.
THAT'S WHAT I'VE BEEN SAYING ALL ALONG!
I'll say one thing-- she sure doesn't make it easy.
WELL, MAYBE THAT MAKES YOU RIGHT.
OR MAYBE NOT.
OH YEAH?
YEAH!
SOMETIMES YOU KNOW THE RIGHT ANSWER BUT YOU STILL GET THE QUESTION WRONG.
TRUST ME.

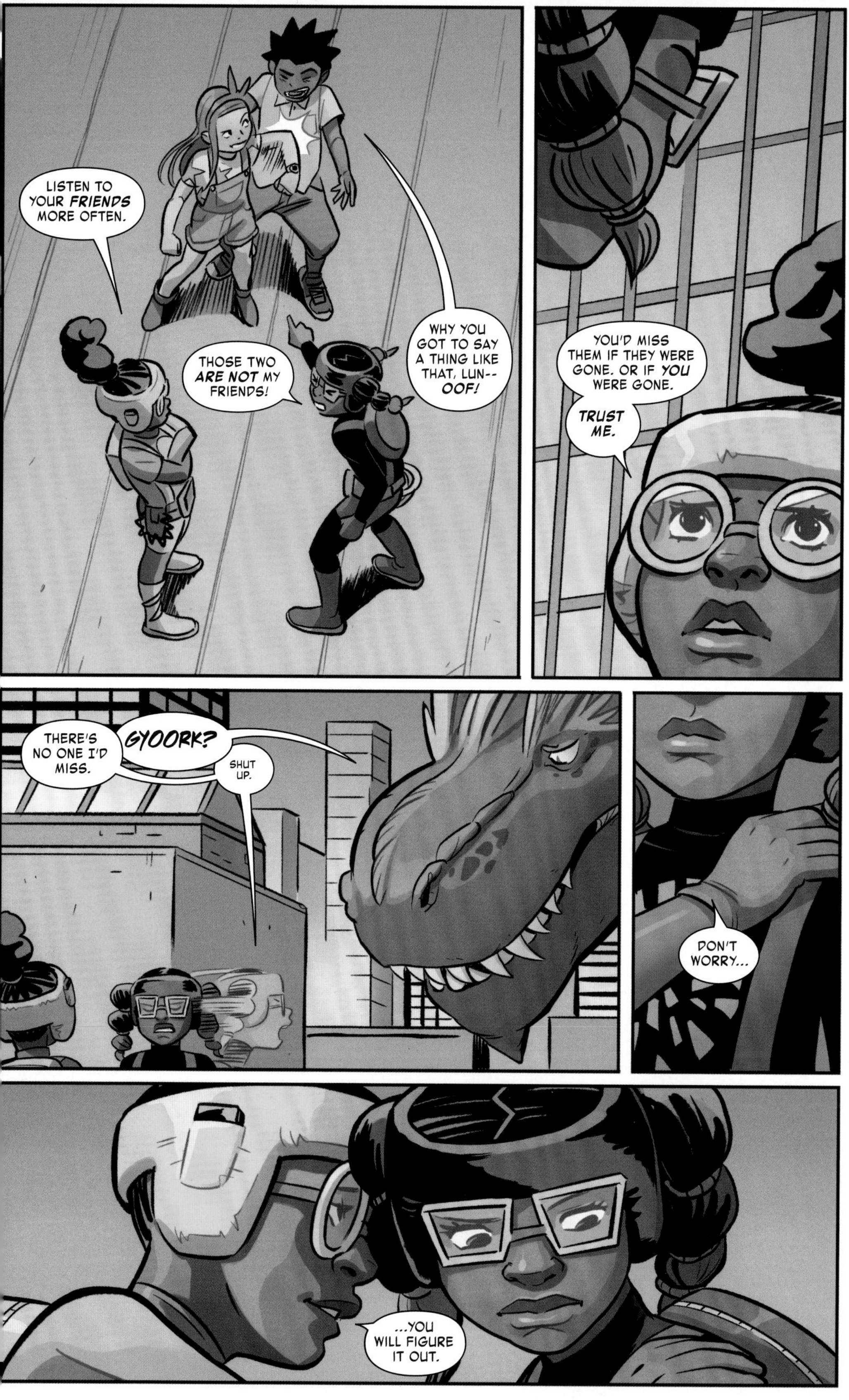
LISTEN TO YOUR FRIENDS MORE OFTEN.
THOSE TWO ARE NOT MY FRIENDS!
WHY YOU GOT TO SAY A THING LIKE THAT, LUN-- OOF!
YOU'D MISS THEM IF THEY WERE GONE. OR IF YOU WERE GONE.
TRUST ME.
THERE'S NO ONE I'D MISS.
GYOORK?
SHUT UP.
DON'T WORRY...
...YOU WILL FIGURE IT OUT.

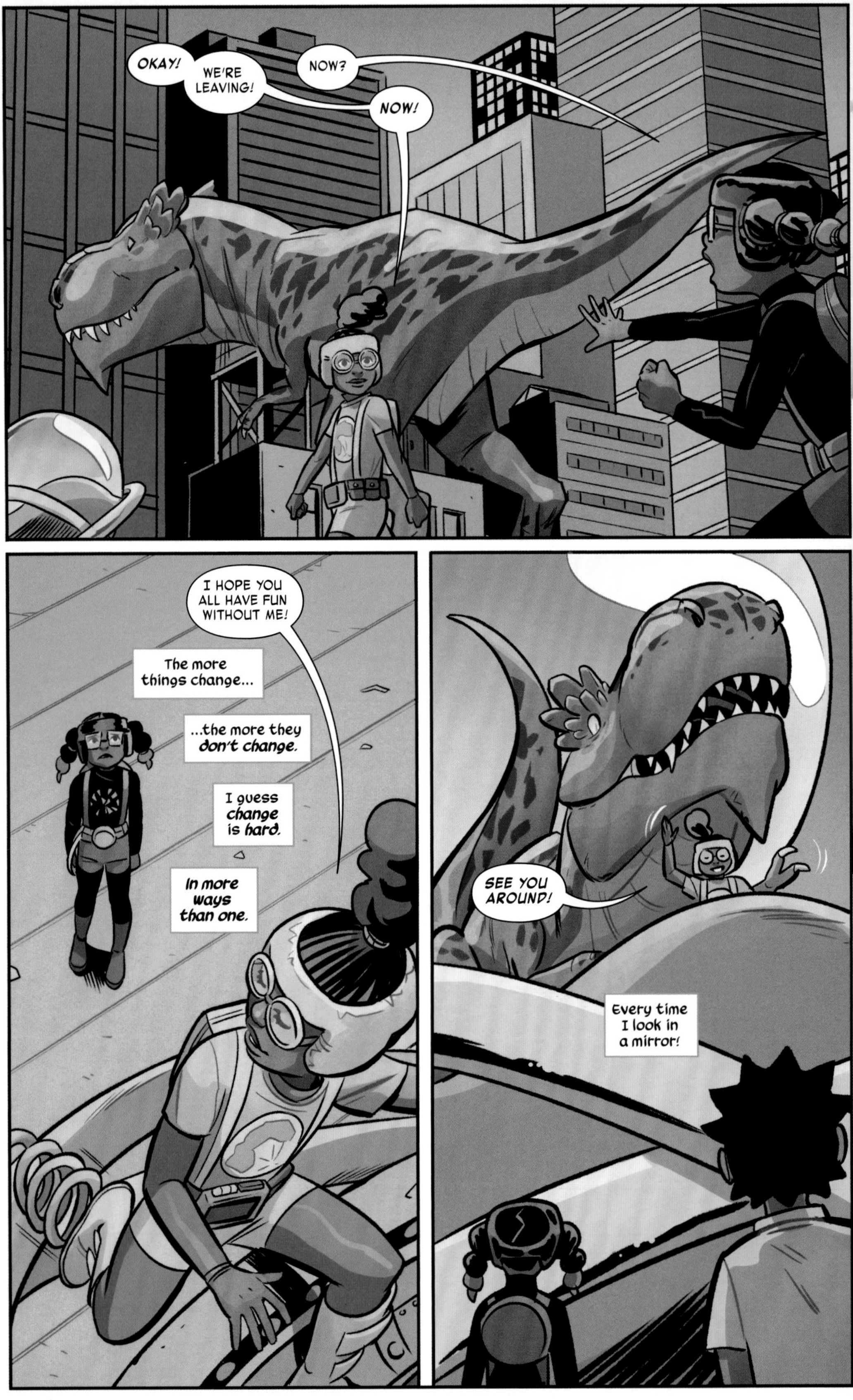
OKAY!
WE'RE LEAVING!
NOW?
NOW!
I HOPE YOU ALL HAVE FUN WITHOUT ME!
The more things change...
...the more they *don't change.*
I guess *change* is *hard.*
In more ways than one.
SEE YOU AROUND!
Every time I look in a mirror!

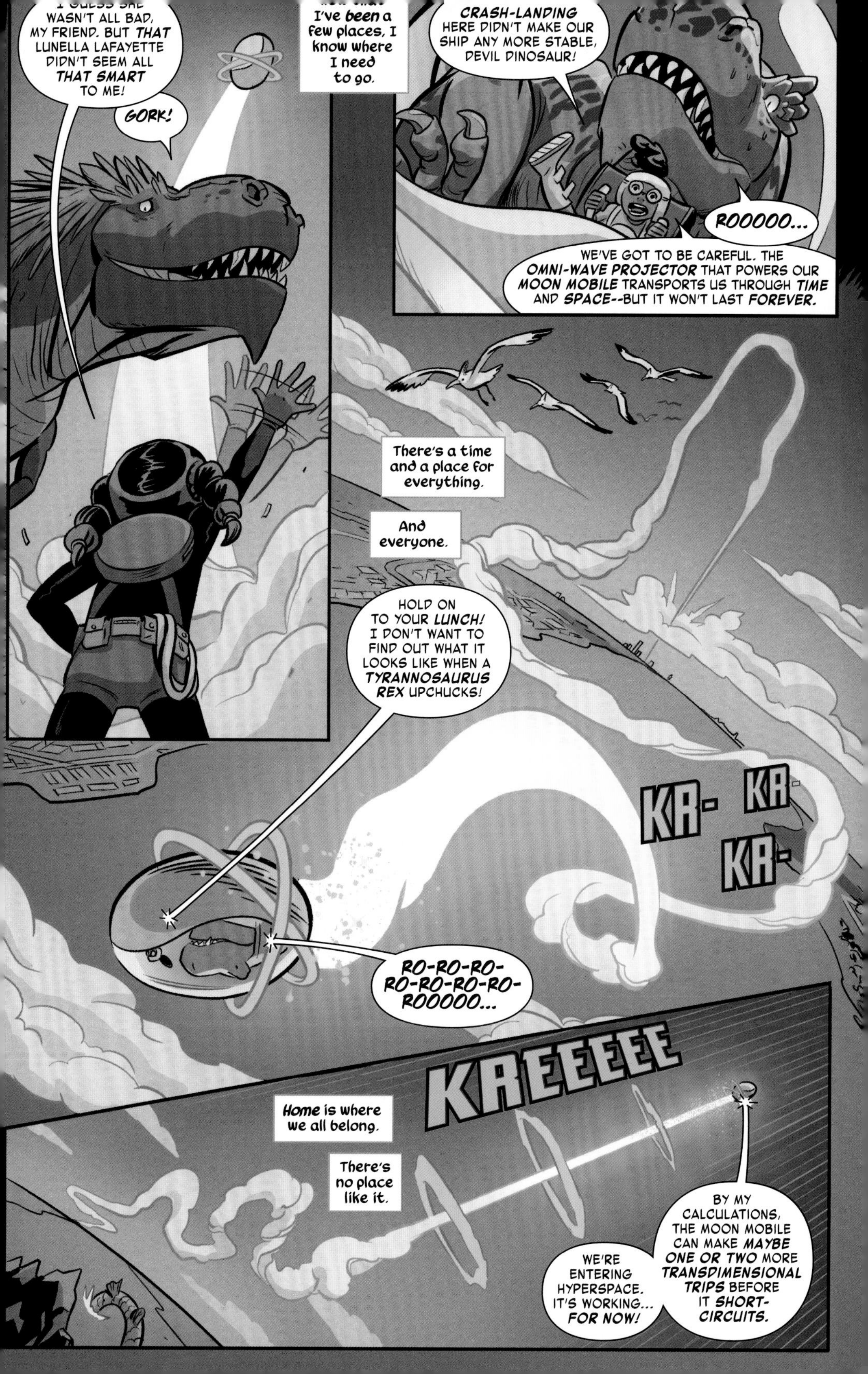
WASN'T ALL BAD, MY FRIEND. BUT THAT LUNELLA LAFAYETTE DIDN'T SEEM ALL THAT SMART TO ME!
I've been a few places, I know where I need to go.
CRASH-LANDING HERE DIDN'T MAKE OUR SHIP ANY MORE STABLE, DEVIL DINOSAUR!
GORK!
ROOOOO...
WE'VE GOT TO BE CAREFUL. THE OMNI-WAVE PROJECTOR THAT POWERS OUR MOON MOBILE TRANSPORTS US THROUGH TIME AND SPACE--BUT IT WON'T LAST FOREVER.
There's a time and a place for everything.
And everyone.
HOLD ON TO YOUR LUNCH! I DON'T WANT TO FIND OUT WHAT IT LOOKS LIKE WHEN A TYRANNOSAURUS REX UPCHUCKS!
KR- KR- KR-
RO-RO-RO-RO-RO-RO-RO-ROOOOO...
KREEEEE
Home is where we all belong.
There's no place like it.
WE'RE ENTERING HYPERSPACE. IT'S WORKING... FOR NOW!
BY MY CALCULATIONS, THE MOON MOBILE CAN MAKE MAYBE ONE OR TWO MORE TRANSDIMENSIONAL TRIPS BEFORE IT SHORT-CIRCUITS.

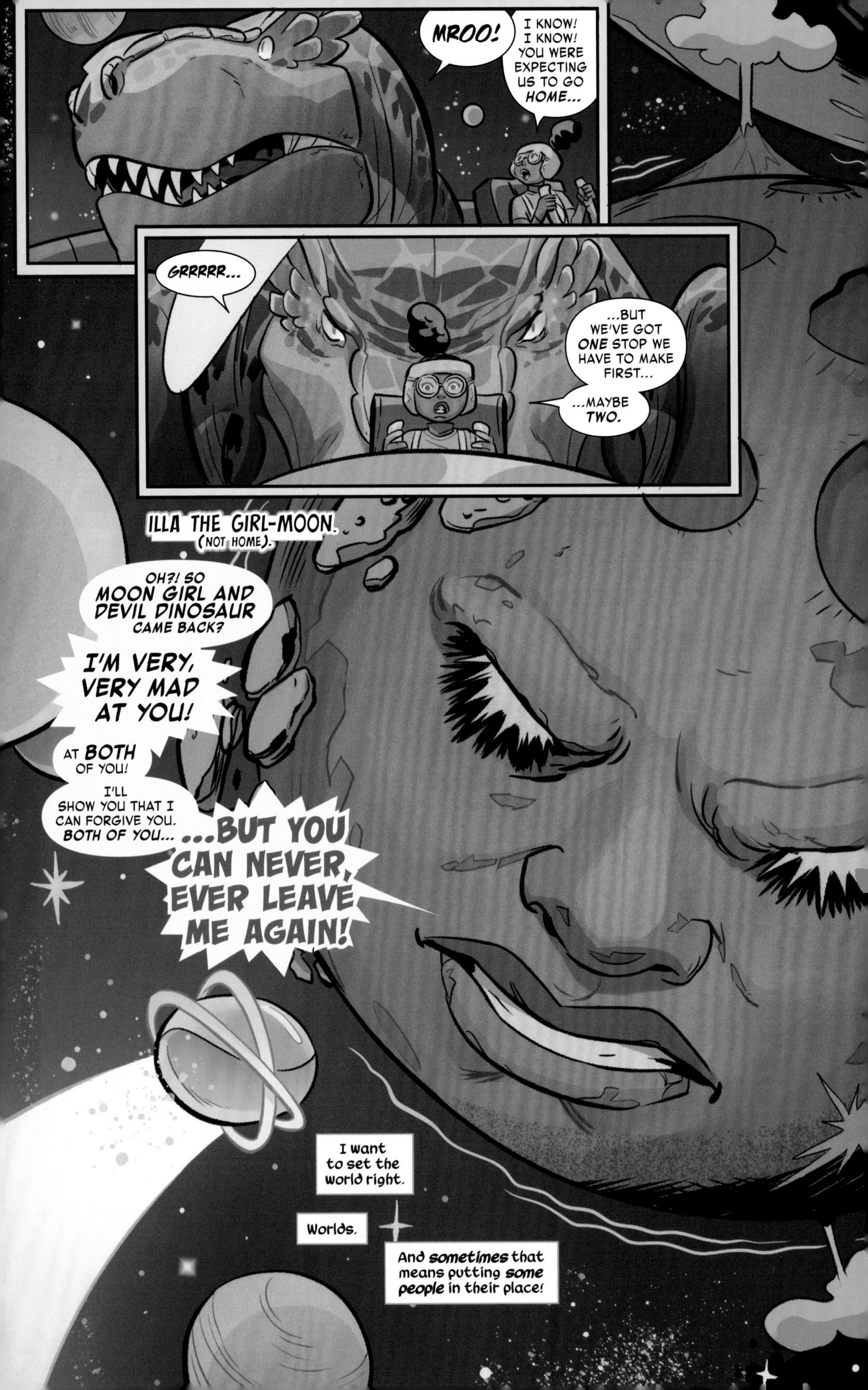
MROO!
I KNOW! I KNOW! YOU WERE EXPECTING US TO GO HOME...
GRRRRR...
...BUT WE'VE GOT ONE STOP WE HAVE TO MAKE FIRST...
...MAYBE TWO.
ILLA THE GIRL-MOON. (NOT HOME).
OH?! SO MOON GIRL AND DEVIL DINOSAUR CAME BACK?
I'M VERY, VERY MAD AT YOU!
AT BOTH OF YOU!
I'LL SHOW YOU THAT I CAN FORGIVE YOU. BOTH OF YOU...
...BUT YOU CAN NEVER, EVER LEAVE ME AGAIN!
I want to set the world right.
Worlds.
And sometimes that means putting some people in their place!

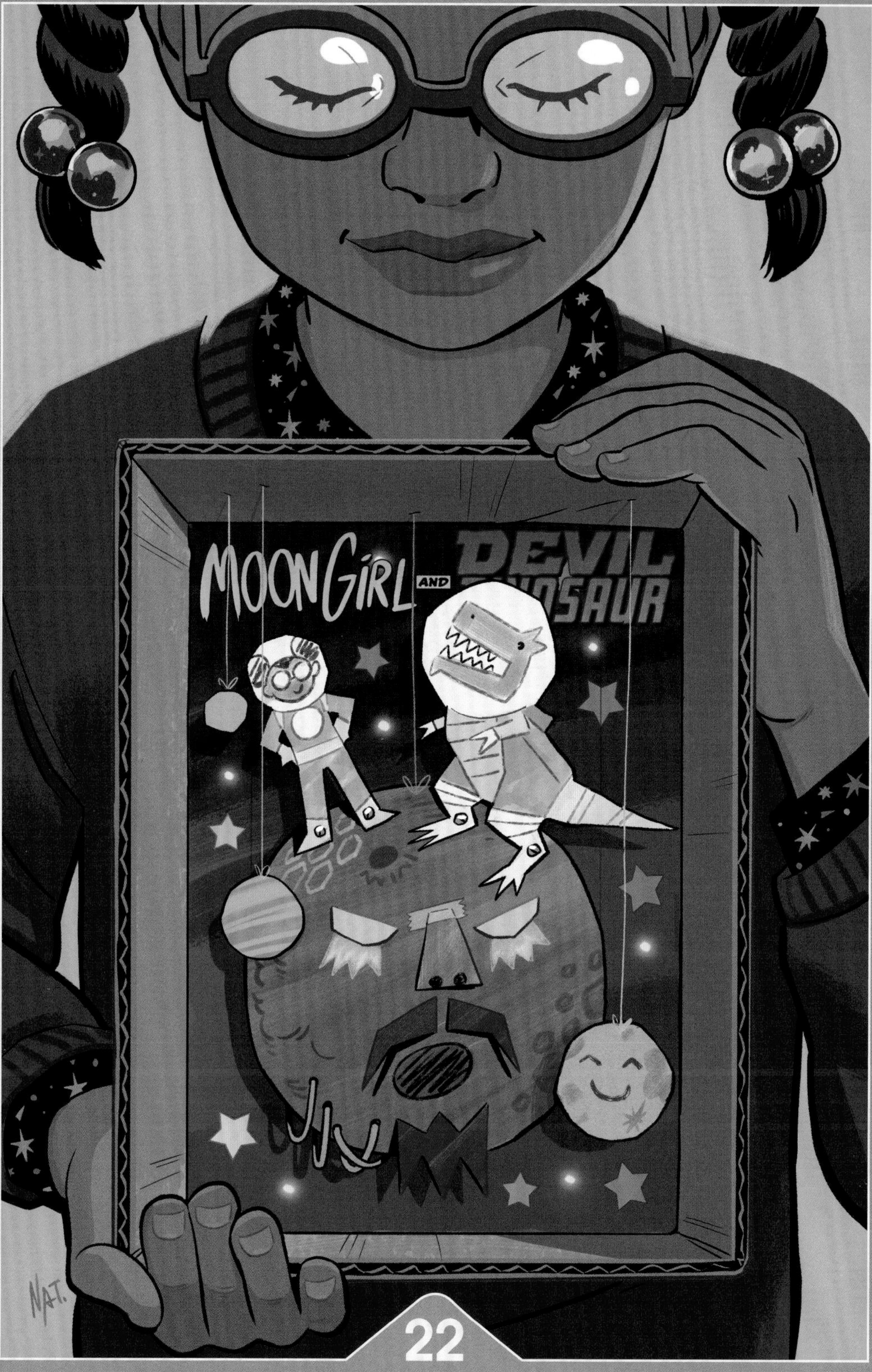
MOON GIRL
AND
DEVIL
NAT.

22

"Escape Velocity"

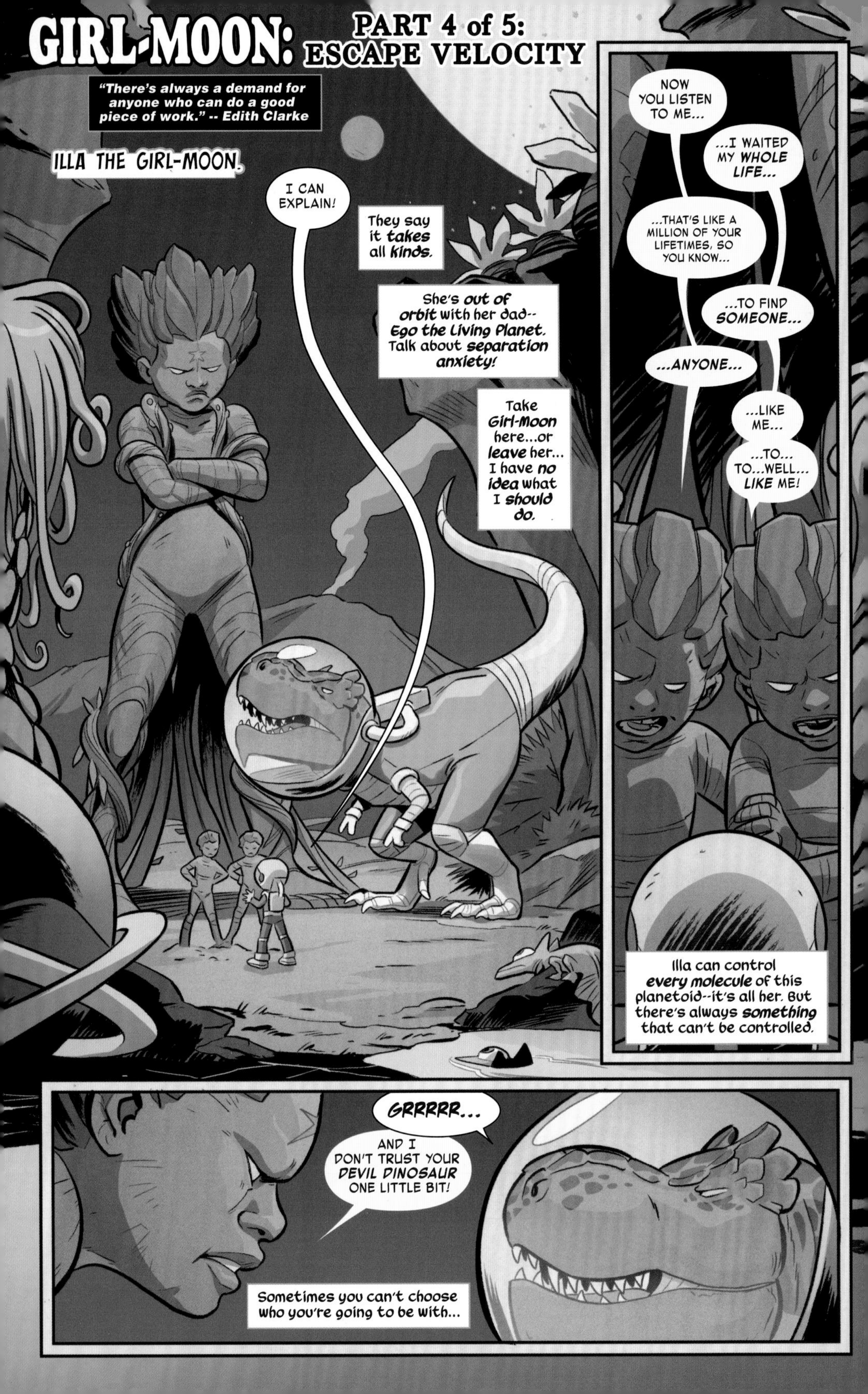
GIRL-MOON: PART 4 of 5: ESCAPE VELOCITY
"There's always a demand for anyone who can do a good piece of work." -- Edith Clarke
ILLA THE GIRL-MOON.
I CAN EXPLAIN!
They say it takes all kinds.
She's out of orbit with her dad-- Ego the Living Planet. Talk about separation anxiety!
Take Girl-Moon here...or leave her... I have no idea what I should do.
NOW YOU LISTEN TO ME...
...I WAITED MY WHOLE LIFE...
...THAT'S LIKE A MILLION OF YOUR LIFETIMES, SO YOU KNOW...
...TO FIND SOMEONE...
...ANYONE...
...LIKE ME...
...TO... TO...WELL... LIKE ME!
Illa can control every molecule of this planetoid--it's all her. But there's always something that can't be controlled.
GRRRRR...
AND I DON'T TRUST YOUR DEVIL DINOSAUR ONE LITTLE BIT!
Sometimes you can't choose who you're going to be with...

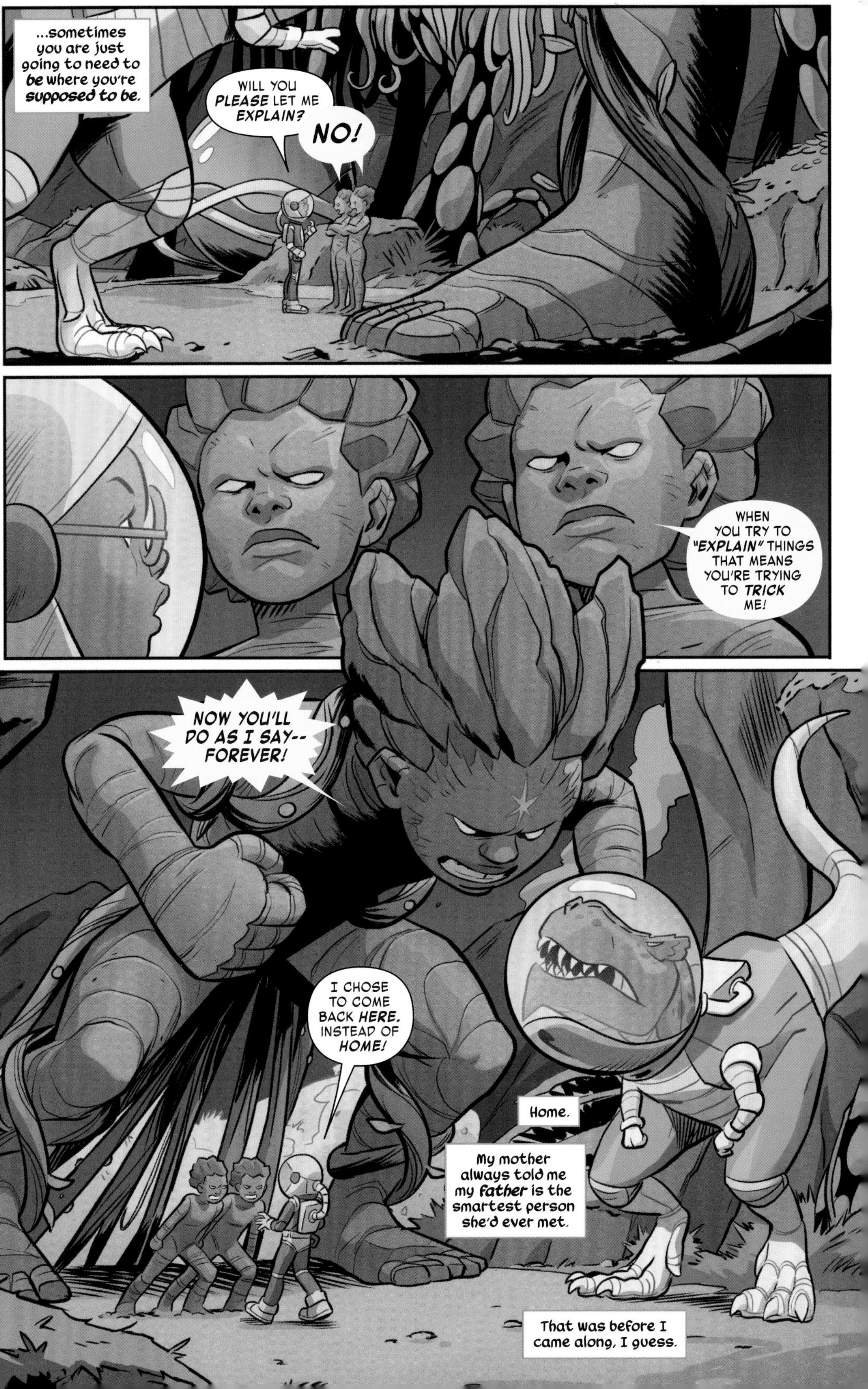
...sometimes you are just going to need to be where you're supposed to be.
WILL YOU PLEASE LET ME EXPLAIN?
NO!
WHEN YOU TRY TO "EXPLAIN" THINGS THAT MEANS YOU'RE TRYING TO TRICK ME!
NOW YOU'LL DO AS I SAY-- FOREVER!
I CHOSE TO COME BACK HERE. INSTEAD OF HOME!
Home.
My mother always told me my father is the smartest person she'd ever met.
That was before I came along, I guess.

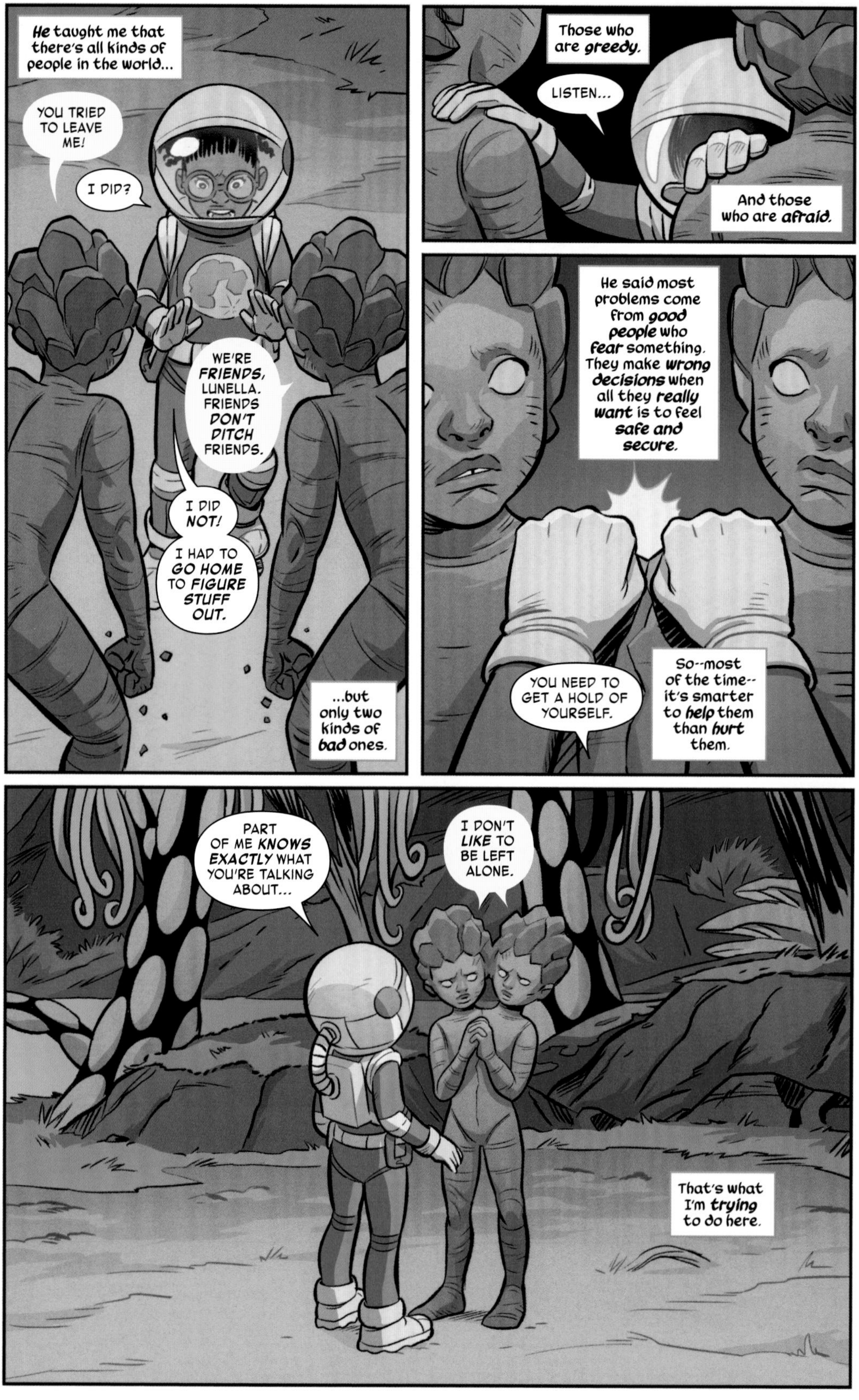
He taught me that there's all kinds of people in the world...
YOU TRIED TO LEAVE ME!
I DID?
WE'RE FRIENDS, LUNELLA. FRIENDS DON'T DITCH FRIENDS.
I DID NOT!
I HAD TO GO HOME TO FIGURE STUFF OUT.
...but only two kinds of bad ones.
Those who are greedy.
LISTEN...
And those who are afraid.
He said most problems come from good people who fear something. They make wrong decisions when all they really want is to feel safe and secure.
YOU NEED TO GET A HOLD OF YOURSELF.
So--most of the time--it's smarter to help them than hurt them.
PART OF ME KNOWS EXACTLY WHAT YOU'RE TALKING ABOUT...
I DON'T LIKE TO BE LEFT ALONE.
That's what I'm trying to do here.

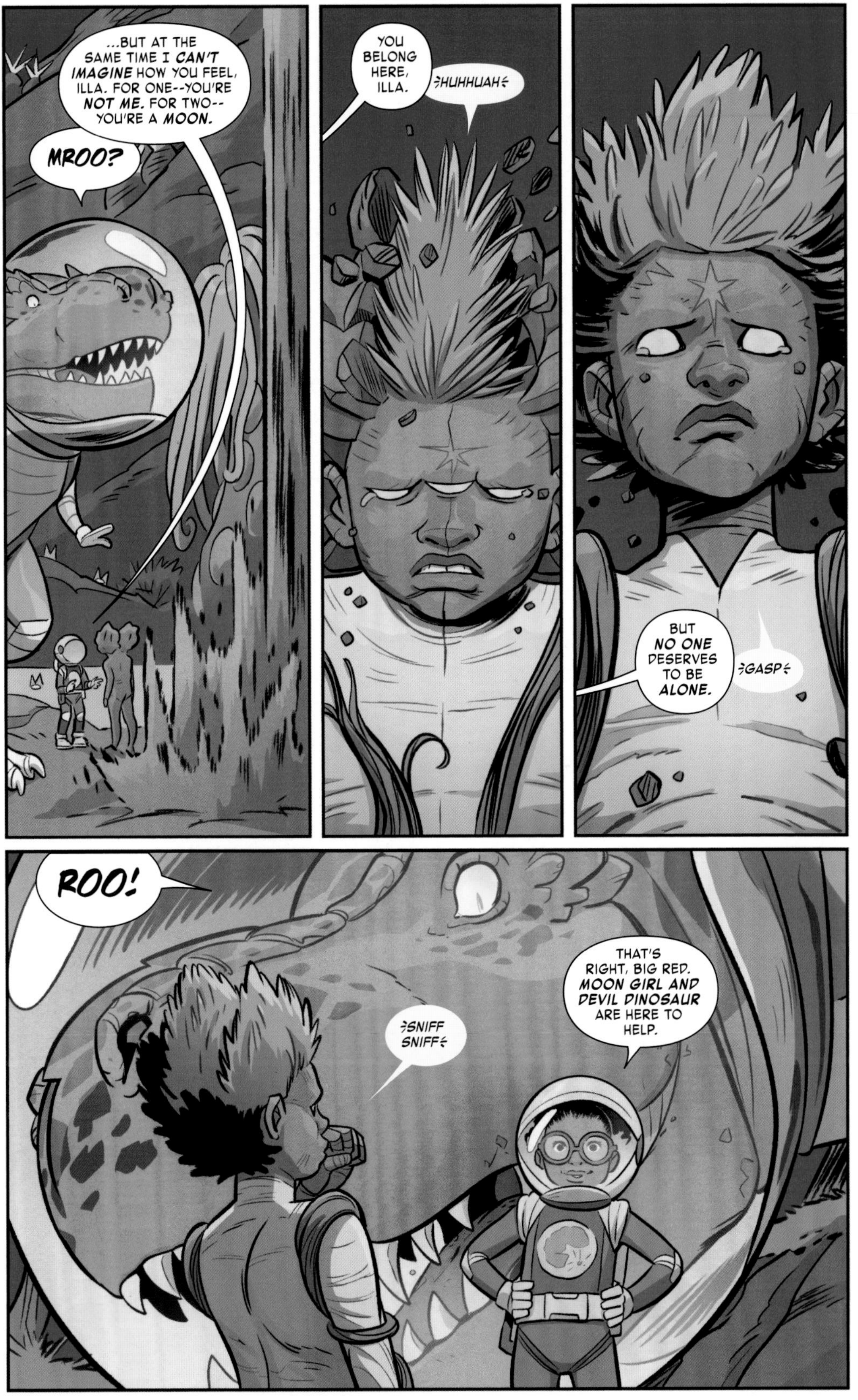
...BUT AT THE SAME TIME I CAN'T IMAGINE HOW YOU FEEL, ILLA. FOR ONE--YOU'RE NOT ME. FOR TWO--YOU'RE A MOON.
MROO?
YOU BELONG HERE, ILLA.
HUHHUAH
BUT NO ONE DESERVES TO BE ALONE.
GASP
ROO!
SNIFF SNIFF
THAT'S RIGHT, BIG RED. MOON GIRL AND DEVIL DINOSAUR ARE HERE TO HELP.

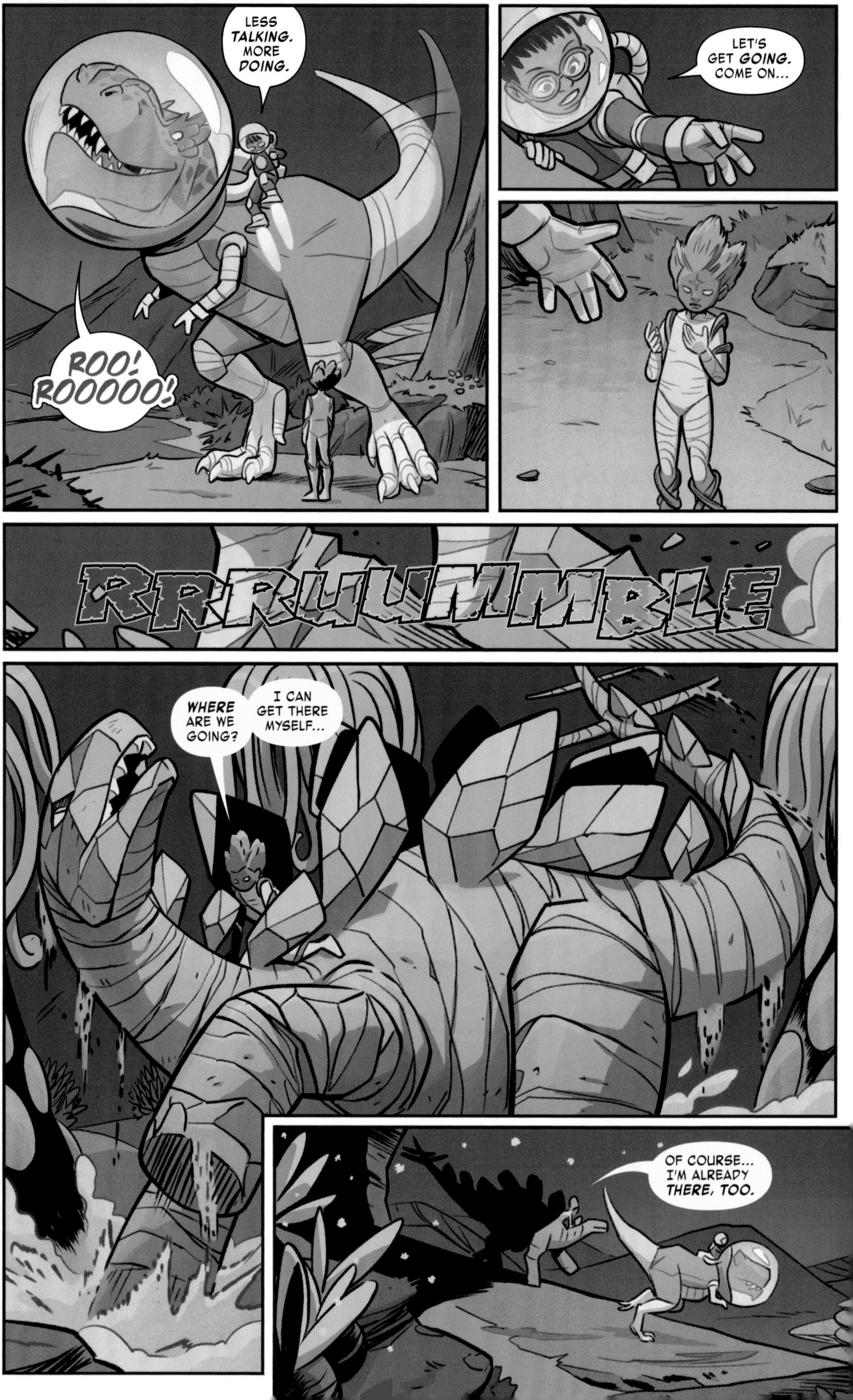

LESS TALKING. MORE DOING.
ROO! ROOOOO!
LET'S GET GOING. COME ON...
RRRUUMMBLE
WHERE ARE WE GOING?
I CAN GET THERE MYSELF...
OF COURSE... I'M ALREADY THERE, TOO.

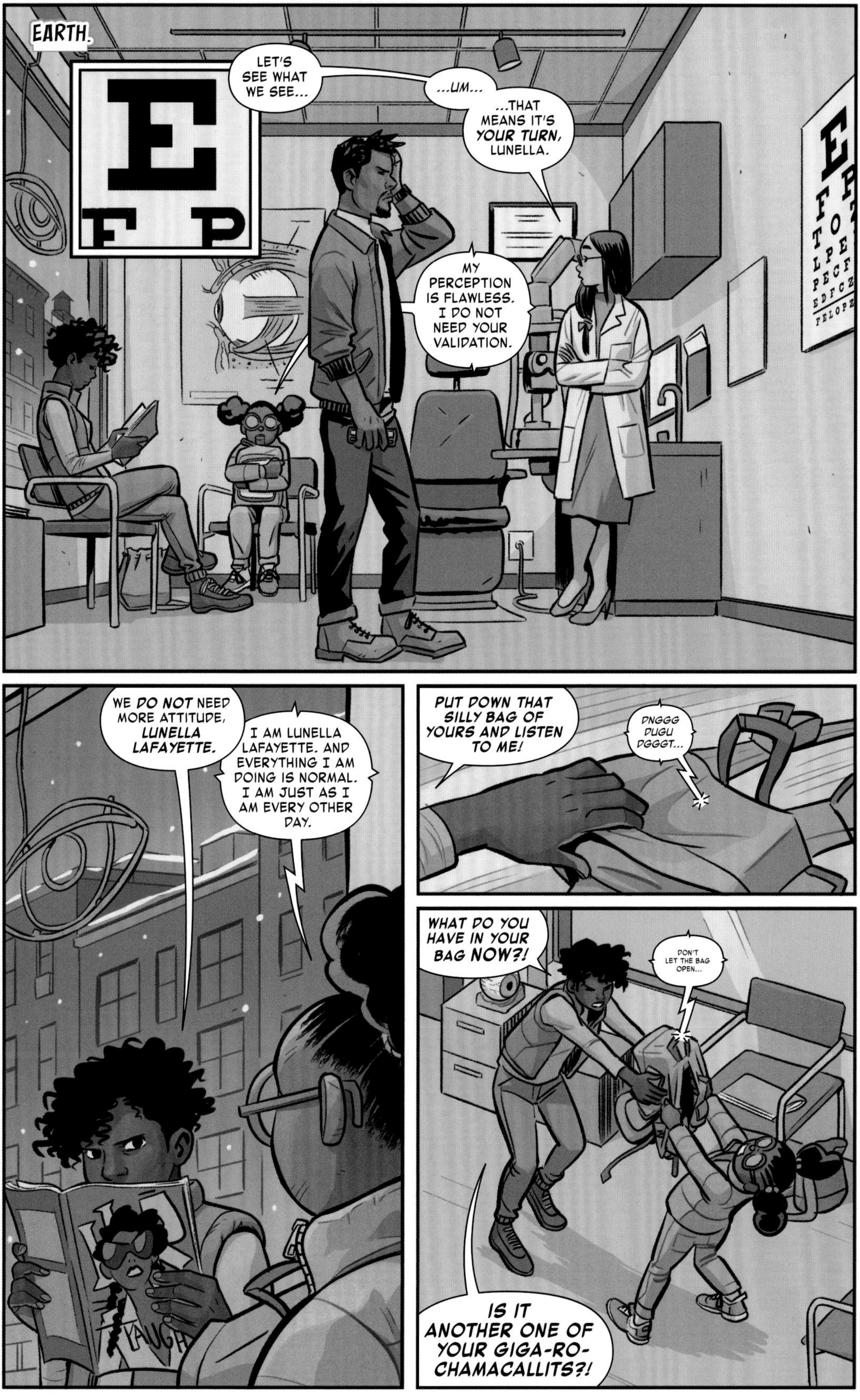
EARTH.
LET'S SEE WHAT WE SEE...
...UM...
...THAT MEANS IT'S YOUR TURN, LUNELLA.
MY PERCEPTION IS FLAWLESS. I DO NOT NEED YOUR VALIDATION.
WE DO NOT NEED MORE ATTITUDE, LUNELLA LAFAYETTE.
I AM LUNELLA LAFAYETTE. AND EVERYTHING I AM DOING IS NORMAL. I AM JUST AS I AM EVERY OTHER DAY.
PUT DOWN THAT SILLY BAG OF YOURS AND LISTEN TO ME!
DNGGG DUGU DGGGT...
WHAT DO YOU HAVE IN YOUR BAG NOW?!
DON'T LET THE BAG OPEN...
IS IT ANOTHER ONE OF YOUR GIGA-RO-CHAMACALLITS?!

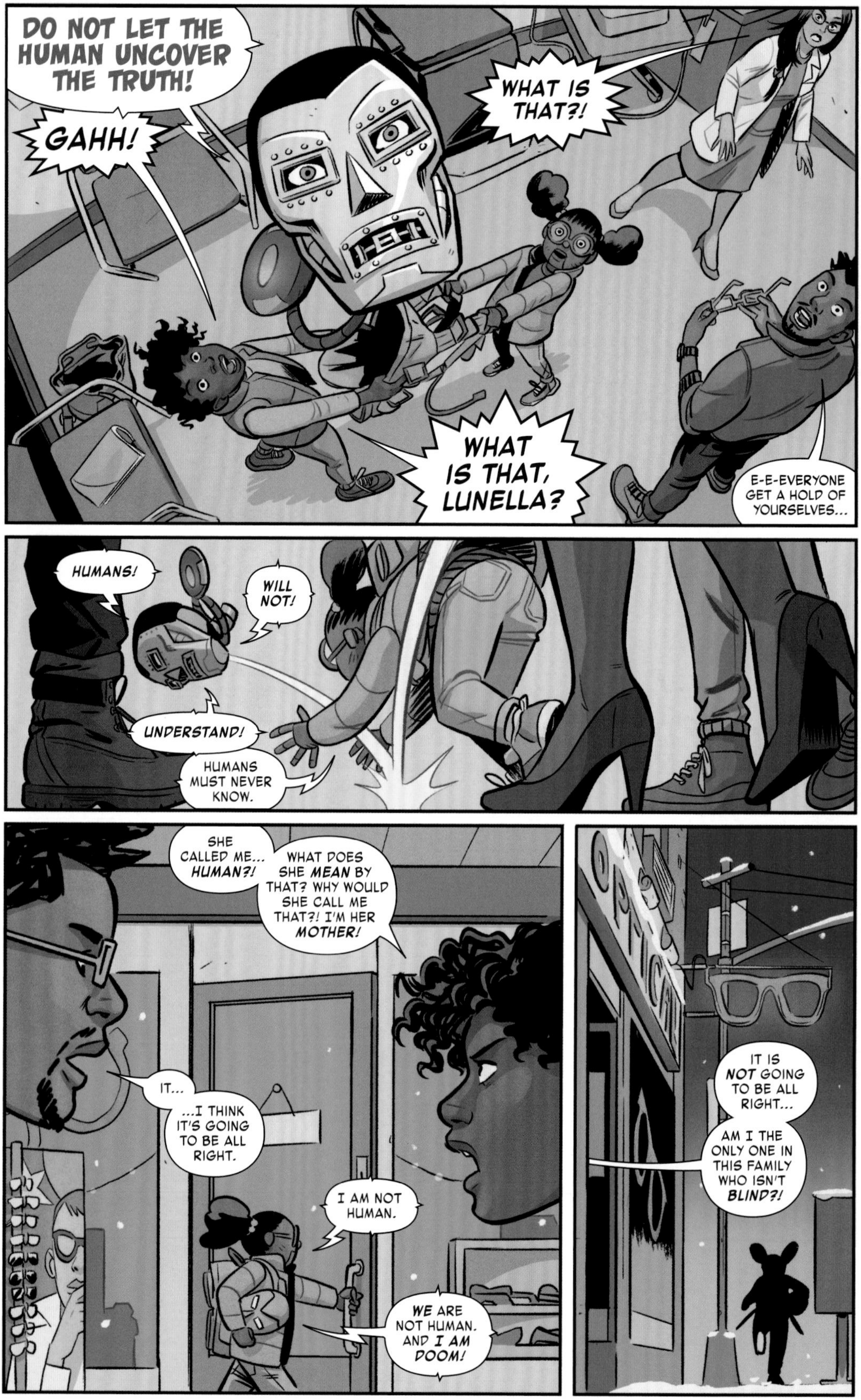
DO NOT LET THE HUMAN UNCOVER THE TRUTH!
GAHH!
WHAT IS THAT?!
WHAT IS THAT, LUNELLA?
E-E-EVERYONE GET A HOLD OF YOURSELVES...
HUMANS!
WILL NOT!
UNDERSTAND!
HUMANS MUST NEVER KNOW.
SHE CALLED ME... HUMAN?!
WHAT DOES SHE MEAN BY THAT? WHY WOULD SHE CALL ME THAT?! I'M HER MOTHER!
IT...
...I THINK IT'S GOING TO BE ALL RIGHT.
I AM NOT HUMAN.
WE ARE NOT HUMAN. AND I AM DOOM!
IT IS NOT GOING TO BE ALL RIGHT...
AM I THE ONLY ONE IN THIS FAMILY WHO ISN'T BLIND?!

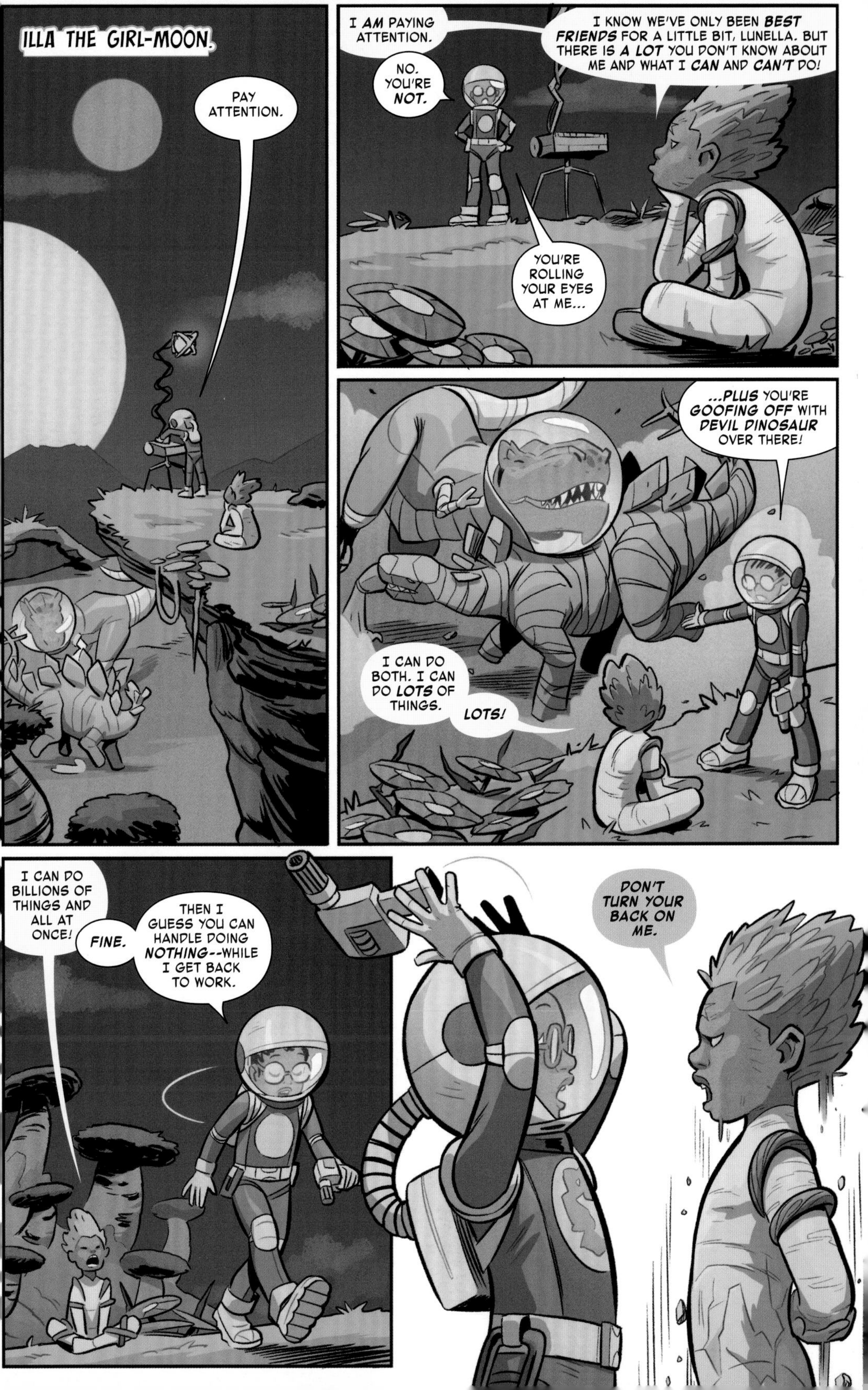
ILLA THE GIRL-MOON.
PAY ATTENTION.
I AM PAYING ATTENTION.
I KNOW WE'VE ONLY BEEN BEST FRIENDS FOR A LITTLE BIT, LUNELLA. BUT THERE IS A LOT YOU DON'T KNOW ABOUT ME AND WHAT I CAN AND CAN'T DO!
NO. YOU'RE NOT.
YOU'RE ROLLING YOUR EYES AT ME...
...PLUS YOU'RE GOOFING OFF WITH DEVIL DINOSAUR OVER THERE!
I CAN DO BOTH. I CAN DO LOTS OF THINGS.
LOTS!
I CAN DO BILLIONS OF THINGS AND ALL AT ONCE!
FINE.
THEN I GUESS YOU CAN HANDLE DOING NOTHING--WHILE I GET BACK TO WORK.
DON'T TURN YOUR BACK ON ME.

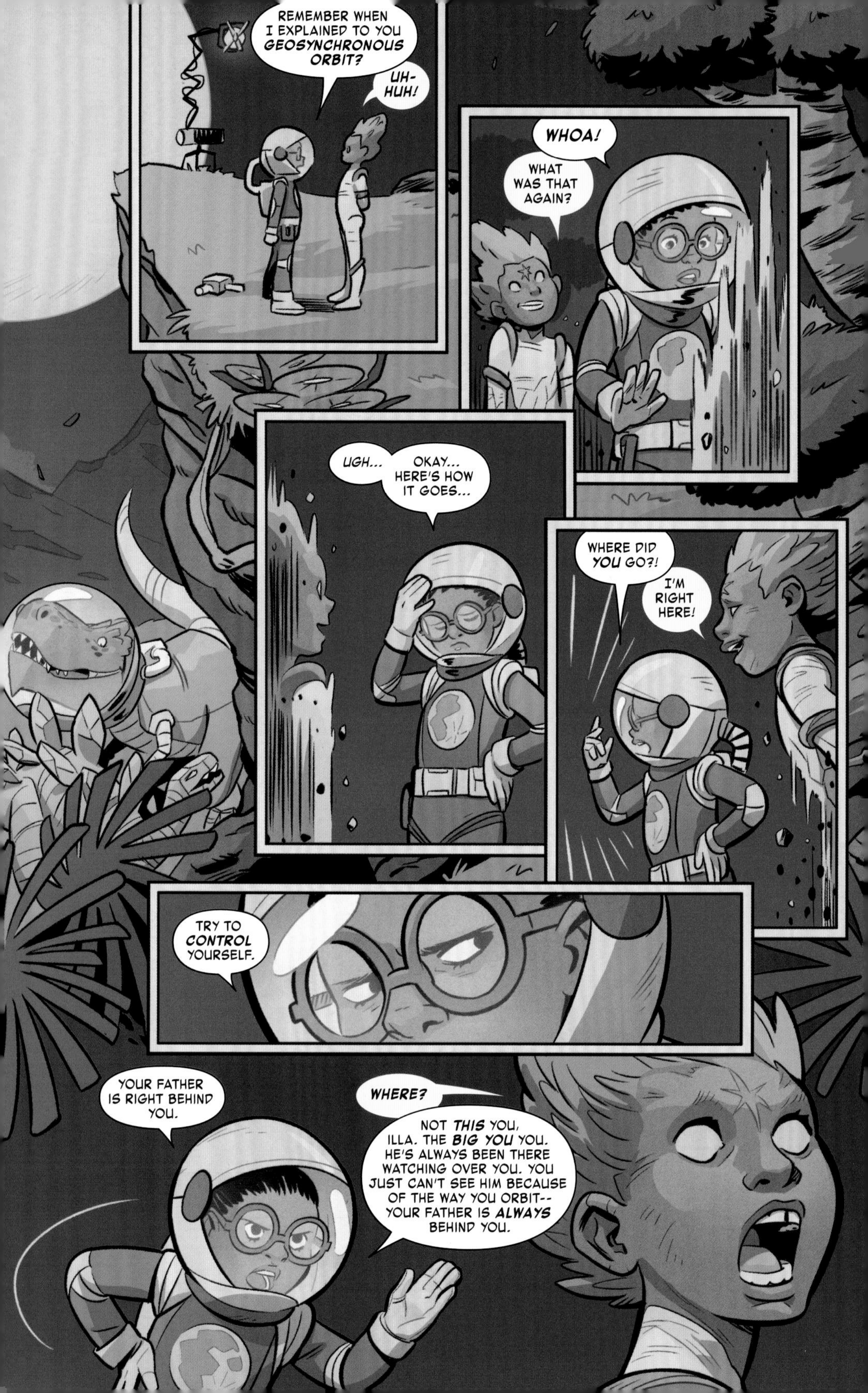
REMEMBER WHEN I EXPLAINED TO YOU GEOSYNCHRONOUS ORBIT?
UH-HUH!
WHOA!
WHAT WAS THAT AGAIN?
UGH...
OKAY... HERE'S HOW IT GOES...
WHERE DID YOU GO?!
I'M RIGHT HERE!
TRY TO CONTROL YOURSELF.
YOUR FATHER IS RIGHT BEHIND YOU.
WHERE?
NOT THIS YOU, ILLA. THE BIG YOU YOU. HE'S ALWAYS BEEN THERE WATCHING OVER YOU. YOU JUST CAN'T SEE HIM BECAUSE OF THE WAY YOU ORBIT-- YOUR FATHER IS ALWAYS BEHIND YOU.

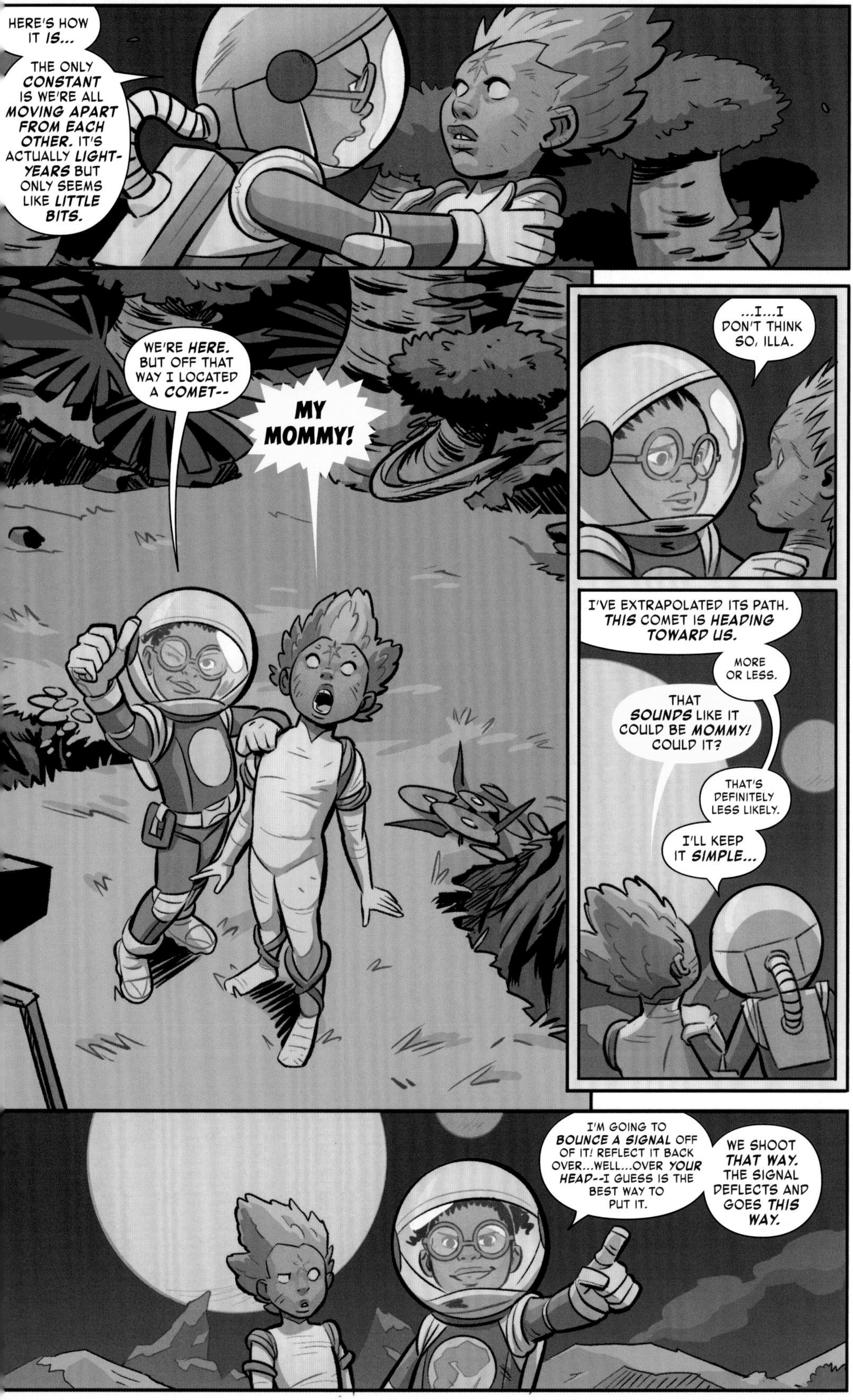
HERE'S HOW IT IS...
THE ONLY CONSTANT IS WE'RE ALL MOVING APART FROM EACH OTHER. IT'S ACTUALLY LIGHT-YEARS BUT ONLY SEEMS LIKE LITTLE BITS.
WE'RE HERE. BUT OFF THAT WAY I LOCATED A COMET--
MY MOMMY!
...I...I DON'T THINK SO, ILLA.
I'VE EXTRAPOLATED ITS PATH. THIS COMET IS HEADING TOWARD US.
MORE OR LESS.
THAT SOUNDS LIKE IT COULD BE MOMMY! COULD IT?
THAT'S DEFINITELY LESS LIKELY.
I'LL KEEP IT SIMPLE...
I'M GOING TO BOUNCE A SIGNAL OFF OF IT! REFLECT IT BACK OVER...WELL...OVER YOUR HEAD--I GUESS IS THE BEST WAY TO PUT IT.
WE SHOOT THAT WAY. THE SIGNAL DEFLECTS AND GOES THIS WAY.

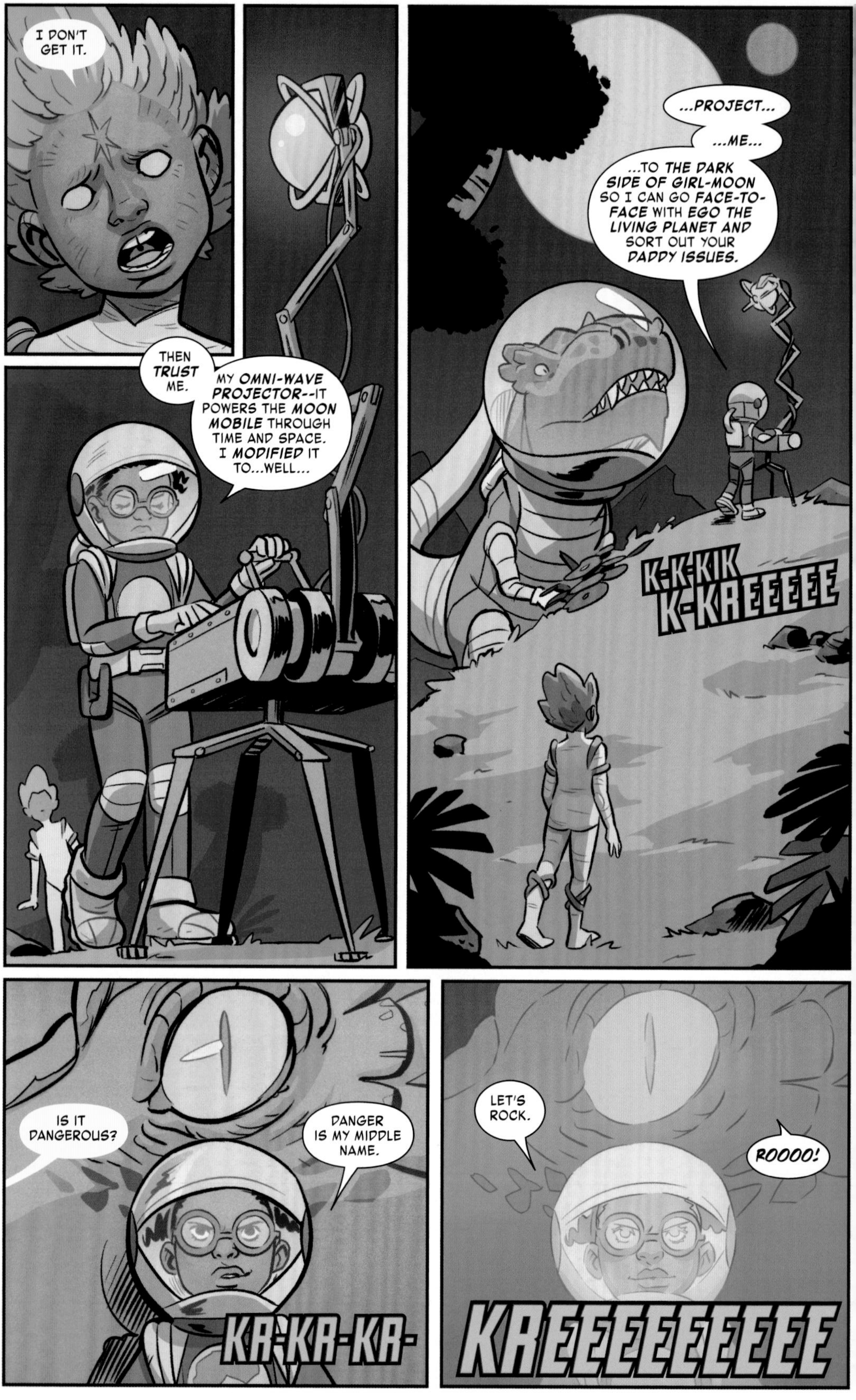
I DON'T GET IT.
THEN TRUST ME.
MY OMNI-WAVE PROJECTOR--IT POWERS THE MOON MOBILE THROUGH TIME AND SPACE. I MODIFIED IT TO...WELL...
...PROJECT...
...ME...
...TO THE DARK SIDE OF GIRL-MOON SO I CAN GO FACE-TO-FACE WITH EGO THE LIVING PLANET AND SORT OUT YOUR DADDY ISSUES.
K-K-K-K K-KREEEEE
IS IT DANGEROUS?
DANGER IS MY MIDDLE NAME.
KR-KR-KR-
LET'S ROCK.
ROOOO!
KREEEEEEEEEE

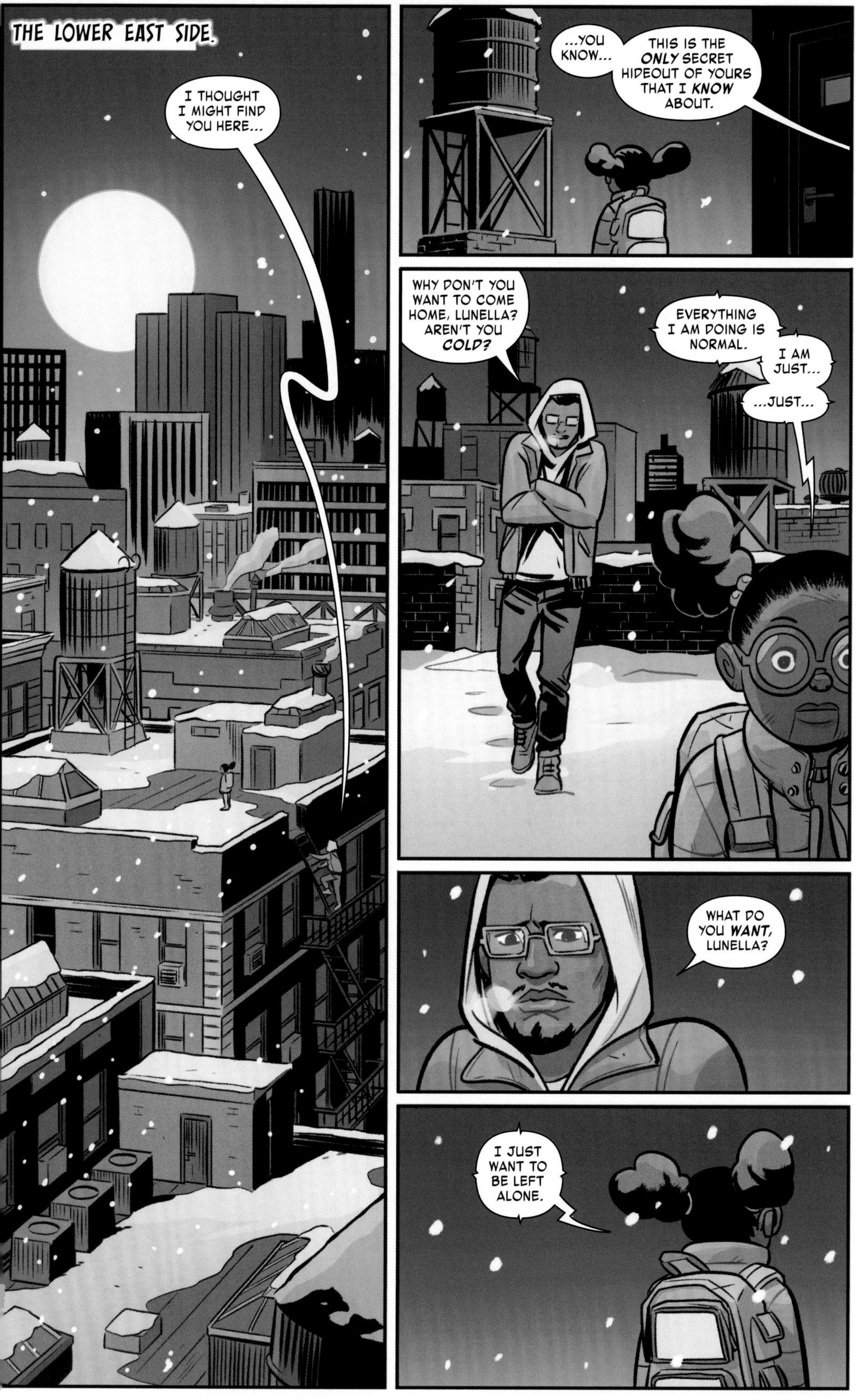
THE LOWER EAST SIDE.
I THOUGHT I MIGHT FIND YOU HERE...
...YOU KNOW...
THIS IS THE ONLY SECRET HIDEOUT OF YOURS THAT I KNOW ABOUT.
WHY DON'T YOU WANT TO COME HOME, LUNELLA? AREN'T YOU COLD?
EVERYTHING I AM DOING IS NORMAL.
I AM JUST...
...JUST...
WHAT DO YOU WANT, LUNELLA?
I JUST WANT TO BE LEFT ALONE.

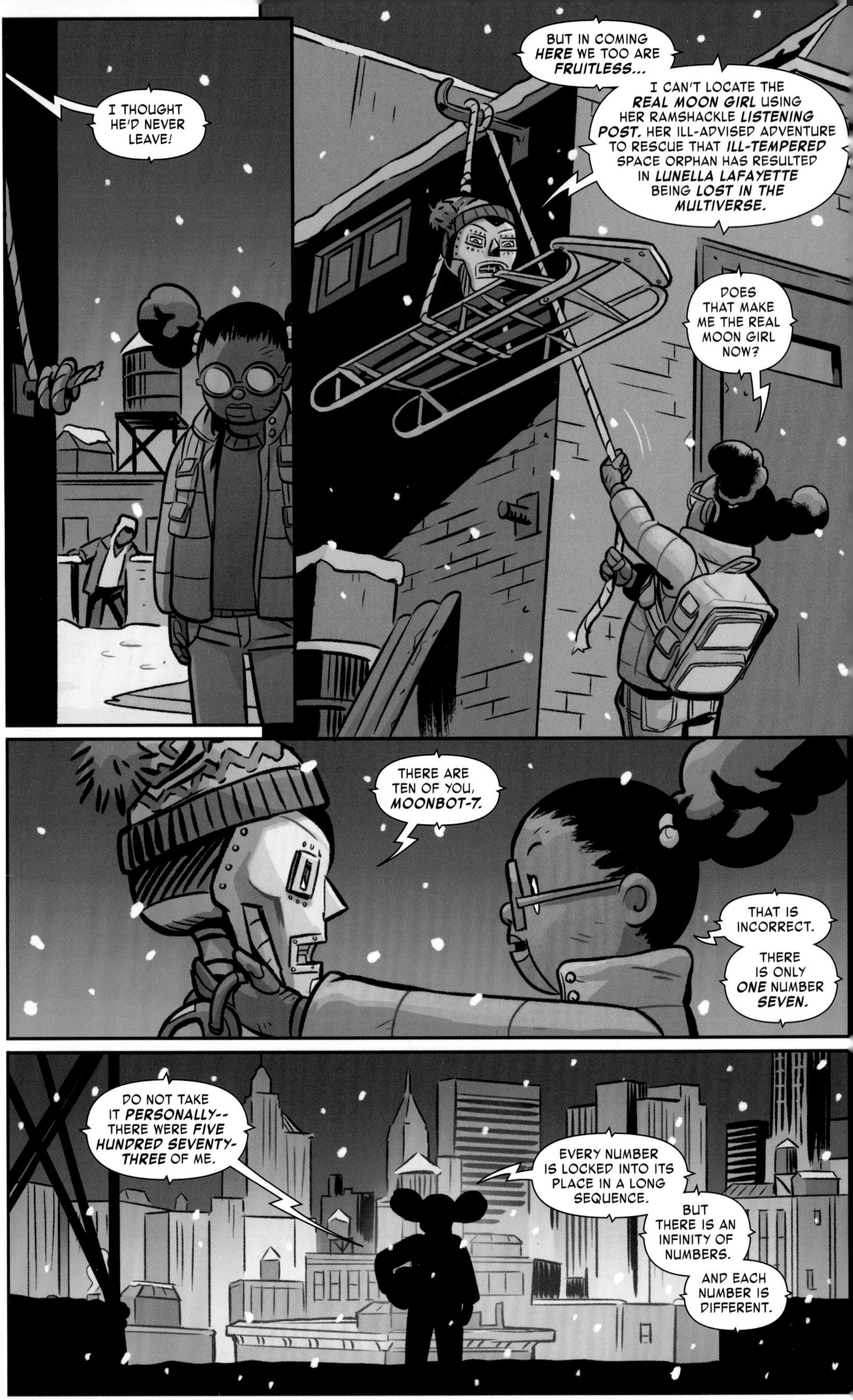
I THOUGHT HE'D NEVER LEAVE!
BUT IN COMING HERE WE TOO ARE FRUITLESS...
I CAN'T LOCATE THE REAL MOON GIRL USING HER RAMSHACKLE LISTENING POST. HER ILL-ADVISED ADVENTURE TO RESCUE THAT ILL-TEMPERED SPACE ORPHAN HAS RESULTED IN LUNELLA LAFAYETTE BEING LOST IN THE MULTIVERSE.
DOES THAT MAKE ME THE REAL MOON GIRL NOW?
THERE ARE TEN OF YOU, MOONBOT-7.
THAT IS INCORRECT.
THERE IS ONLY ONE NUMBER SEVEN.
DO NOT TAKE IT PERSONALLY-- THERE WERE FIVE HUNDRED SEVENTY-THREE OF ME.
EVERY NUMBER IS LOCKED INTO ITS PLACE IN A LONG SEQUENCE.
BUT THERE IS AN INFINITY OF NUMBERS.
AND EACH NUMBER IS DIFFERENT.

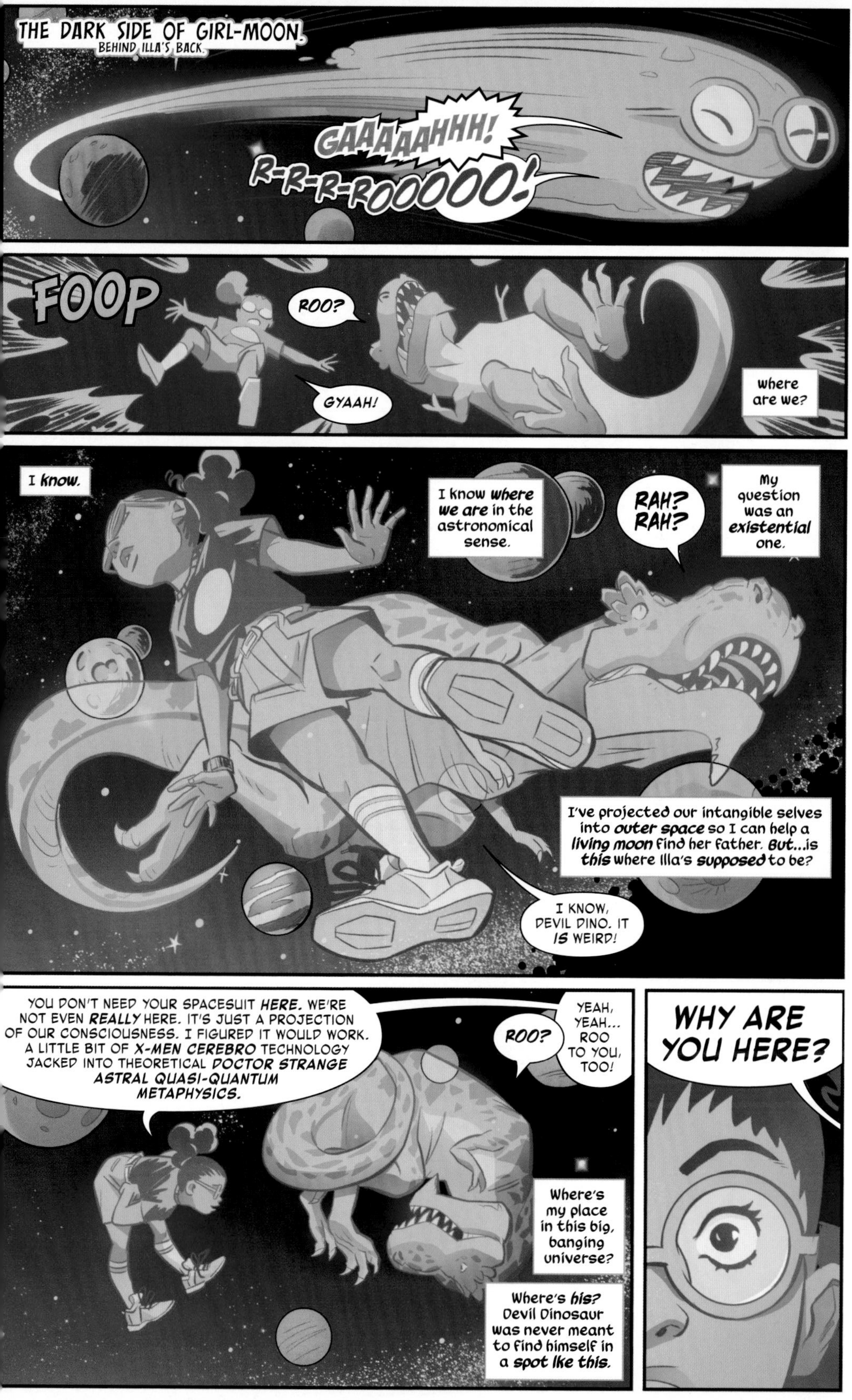
THE DARK SIDE OF GIRL-MOON.
BEHIND ILLA'S BACK.
GAAAAAHHH!
R-R-R-ROOOOOO!
FOOP
ROO?
GYAAH!
Where are we?
I know.
I know where we are in the astronomical sense.
RAH? RAH?
My question was an existential one.
I've projected our intangible selves into outer space so I can help a living moon find her father. But...is this where Illa's supposed to be?
I KNOW, DEVIL DINO. IT IS WEIRD!
YOU DON'T NEED YOUR SPACESUIT HERE. WE'RE NOT EVEN REALLY HERE. IT'S JUST A PROJECTION OF OUR CONSCIOUSNESS. I FIGURED IT WOULD WORK. A LITTLE BIT OF X-MEN CEREBRO TECHNOLOGY JACKED INTO THEORETICAL DOCTOR STRANGE ASTRAL QUASI-QUANTUM METAPHYSICS.
ROO?
YEAH, YEAH... ROO TO YOU, TOO!
Where's my place in this big, banging universe?
Where's his? Devil Dinosaur was never meant to find himself in a spot like this.
WHY ARE YOU HERE?

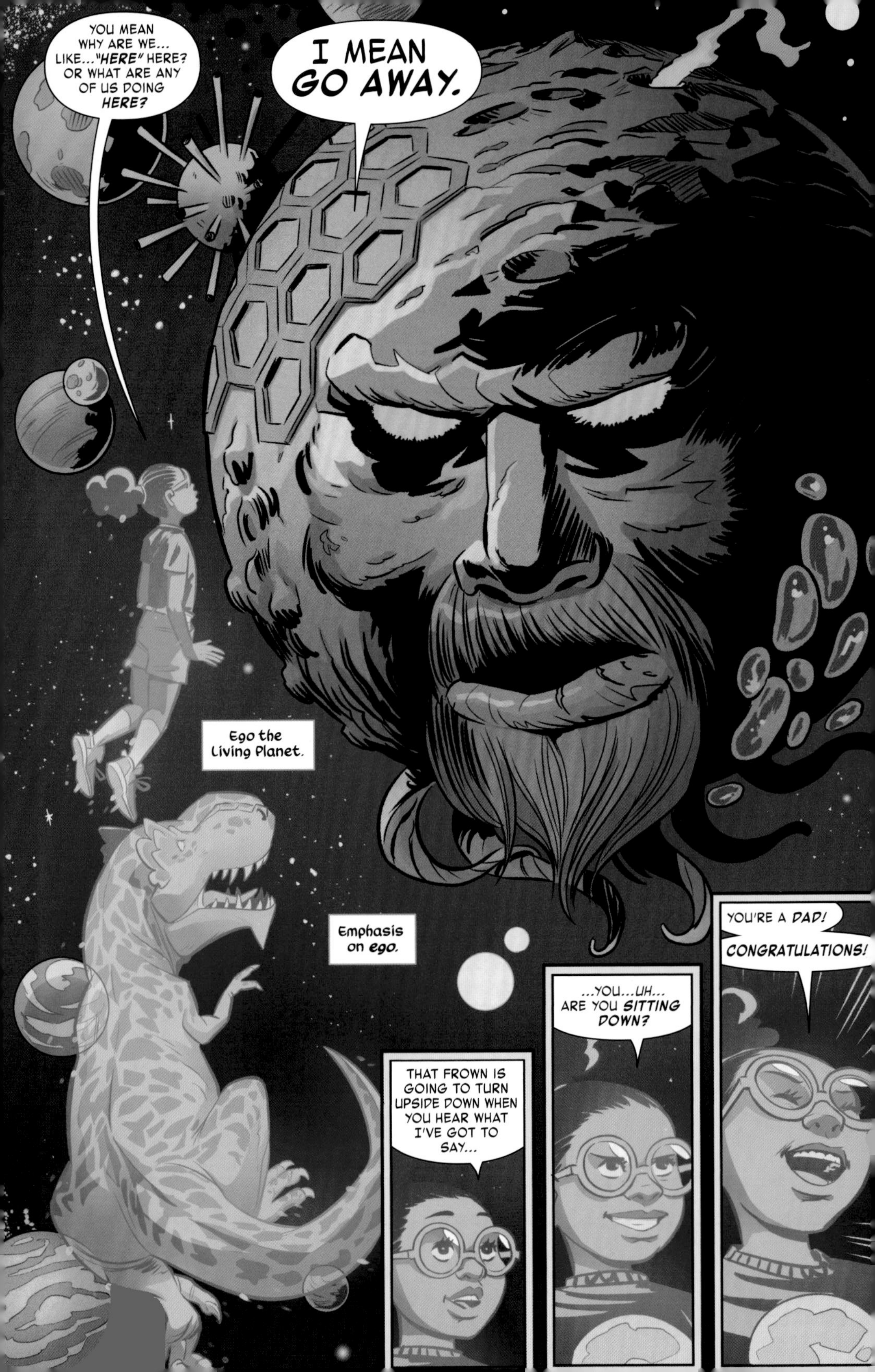
YOU MEAN WHY ARE WE... LIKE..."HERE" HERE? OR WHAT ARE ANY OF US DOING HERE?
I MEAN GO AWAY.
Ego the Living Planet.
Emphasis on ego.
THAT FROWN IS GOING TO TURN UPSIDE DOWN WHEN YOU HEAR WHAT I'VE GOT TO SAY...
...YOU...UH... ARE YOU SITTING DOWN?
YOU'RE A DAD!
CONGRATULATIONS!

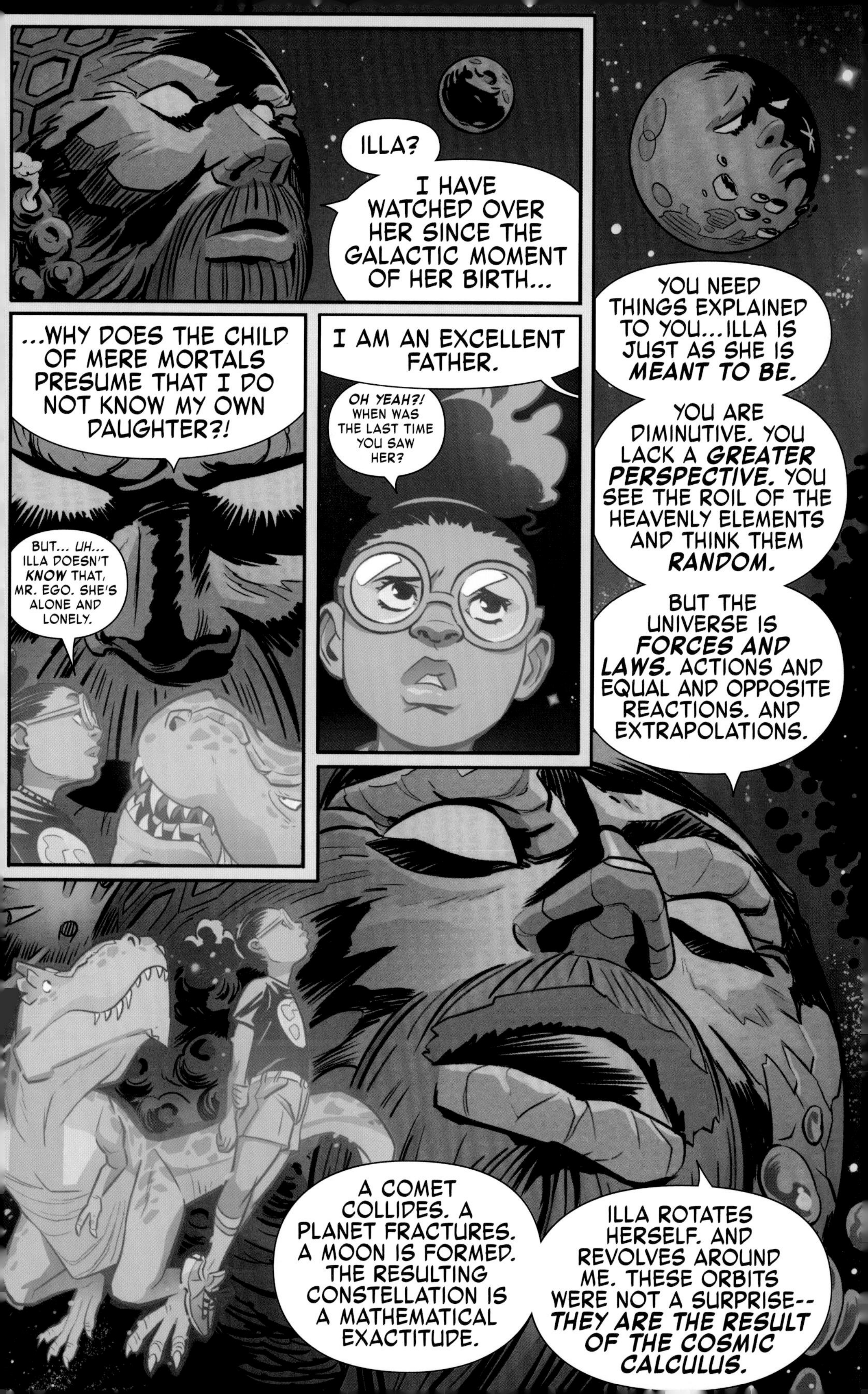
ILLA?
I HAVE WATCHED OVER HER SINCE THE GALACTIC MOMENT OF HER BIRTH...
...WHY DOES THE CHILD OF MERE MORTALS PRESUME THAT I DO NOT KNOW MY OWN DAUGHTER?!
BUT... *UH...* ILLA DOESN'T *KNOW* THAT, MR. EGO. SHE'S ALONE AND LONELY.
I AM AN EXCELLENT FATHER.
OH YEAH?! WHEN WAS THE LAST TIME YOU SAW HER?
YOU NEED THINGS EXPLAINED TO YOU...ILLA IS JUST AS SHE IS ***MEANT TO BE.***
YOU ARE DIMINUTIVE. YOU LACK A ***GREATER PERSPECTIVE.*** YOU SEE THE ROIL OF THE HEAVENLY ELEMENTS AND THINK THEM ***RANDOM.***
BUT THE UNIVERSE IS ***FORCES AND LAWS.*** ACTIONS AND EQUAL AND OPPOSITE REACTIONS. AND EXTRAPOLATIONS.
A COMET COLLIDES. A PLANET FRACTURES. A MOON IS FORMED. THE RESULTING CONSTELLATION IS A MATHEMATICAL EXACTITUDE.
ILLA ROTATES HERSELF. AND REVOLVES AROUND ME. THESE ORBITS WERE NOT A SURPRISE-- ***THEY ARE THE RESULT OF THE COSMIC CALCULUS.***

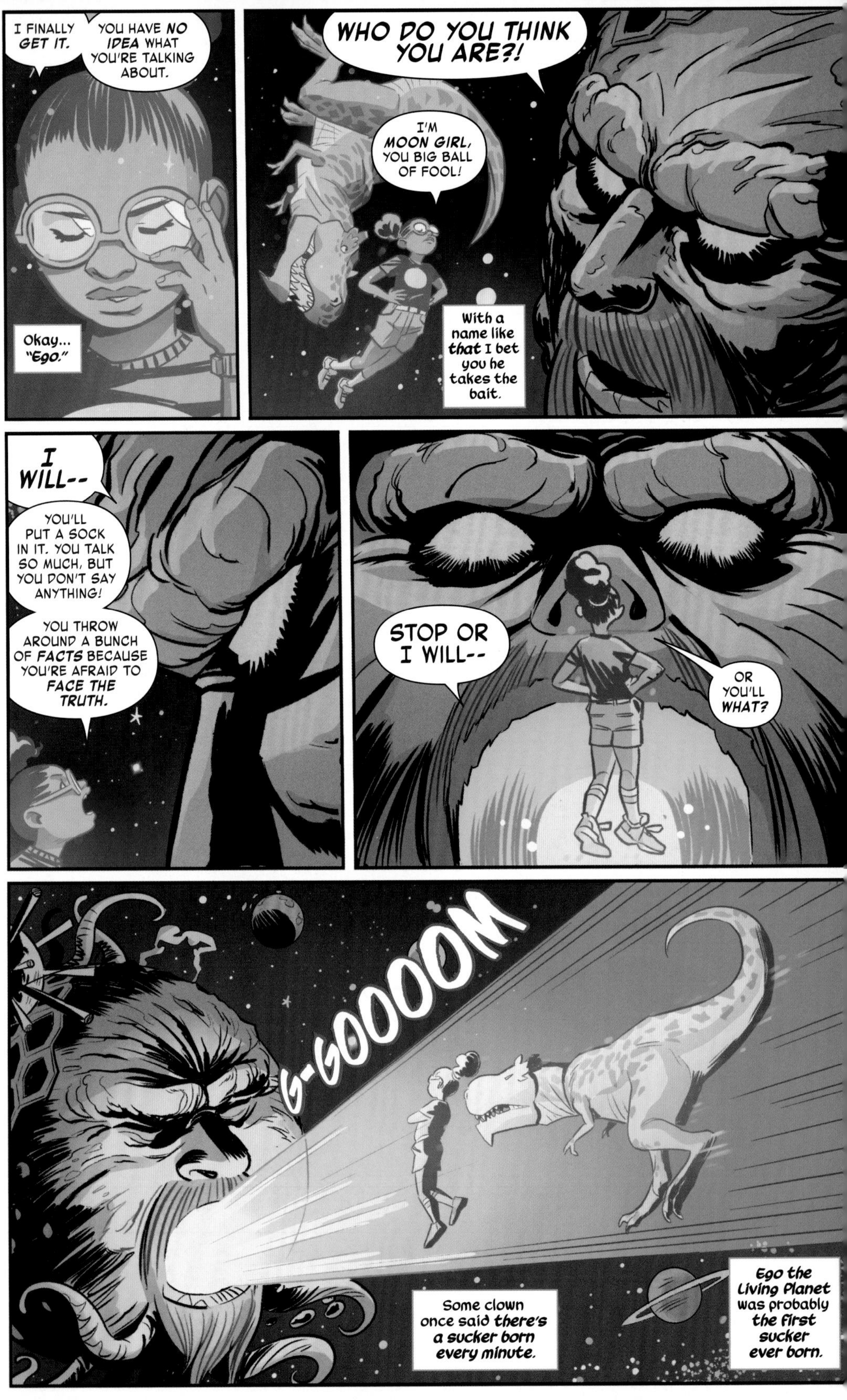
I FINALLY GET IT.
YOU HAVE NO IDEA WHAT YOU'RE TALKING ABOUT.
Okay... "Ego."
WHO DO YOU THINK YOU ARE?!
I'M MOON GIRL, YOU BIG BALL OF FOOL!
With a name like that I bet you he takes the bait.
I WILL--
YOU'LL PUT A SOCK IN IT. YOU TALK SO MUCH, BUT YOU DON'T SAY ANYTHING!
YOU THROW AROUND A BUNCH OF FACTS BECAUSE YOU'RE AFRAID TO FACE THE TRUTH.
STOP OR I WILL--
OR YOU'LL WHAT?
G-GOOOOM
Some clown once said there's a sucker born every minute.
Ego the Living Planet was probably the first sucker ever born.

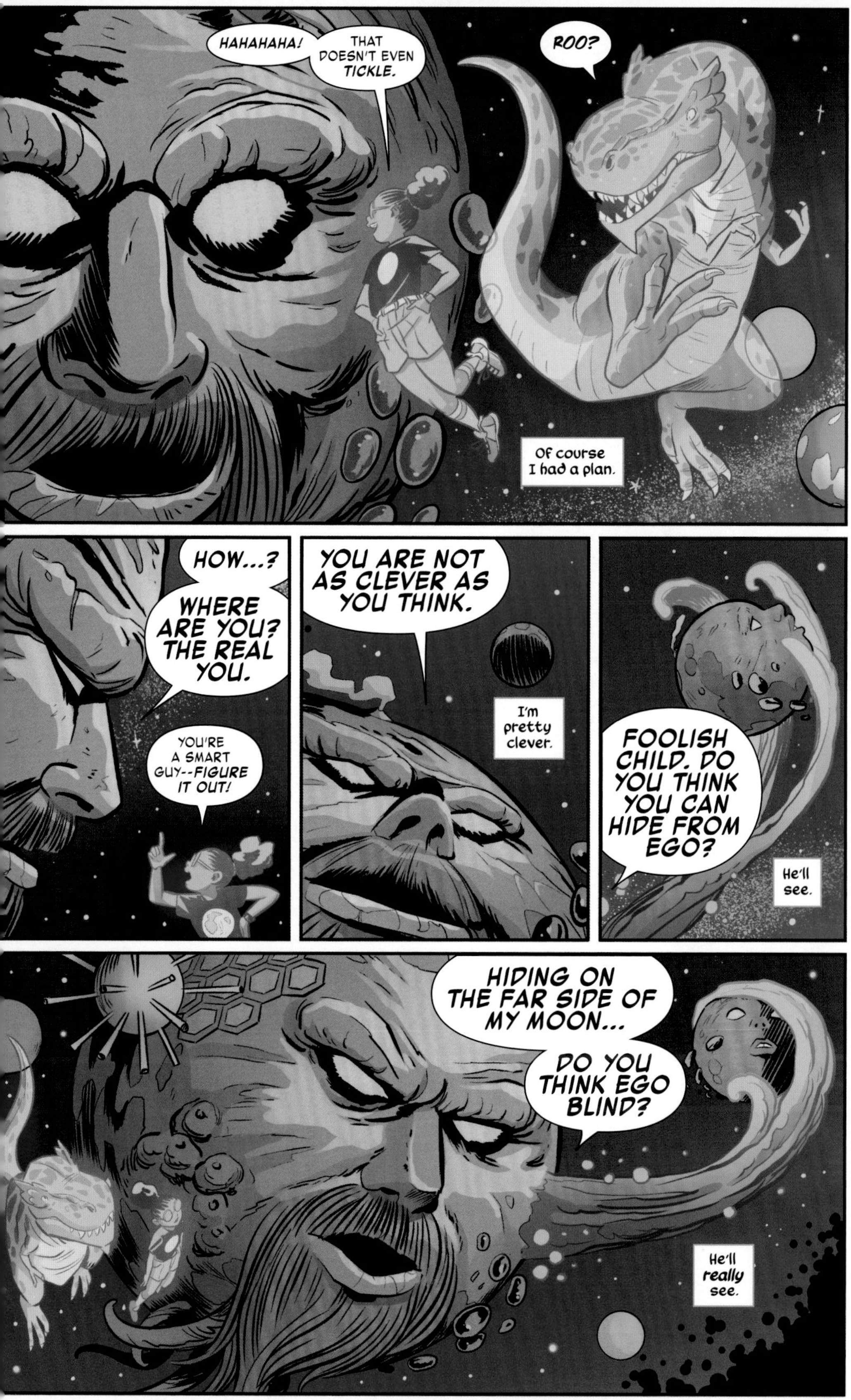
HAHAHAHA!
THAT DOESN'T EVEN TICKLE.
ROO?
Of course I had a plan.
HOW...?
WHERE ARE YOU? THE REAL YOU.
YOU'RE A SMART GUY--FIGURE IT OUT!
YOU ARE NOT AS CLEVER AS YOU THINK.
I'm pretty clever.
FOOLISH CHILD. DO YOU THINK YOU CAN HIDE FROM EGO?
He'll see.
HIDING ON THE FAR SIDE OF MY MOON...
DO YOU THINK EGO BLIND?
He'll really see.

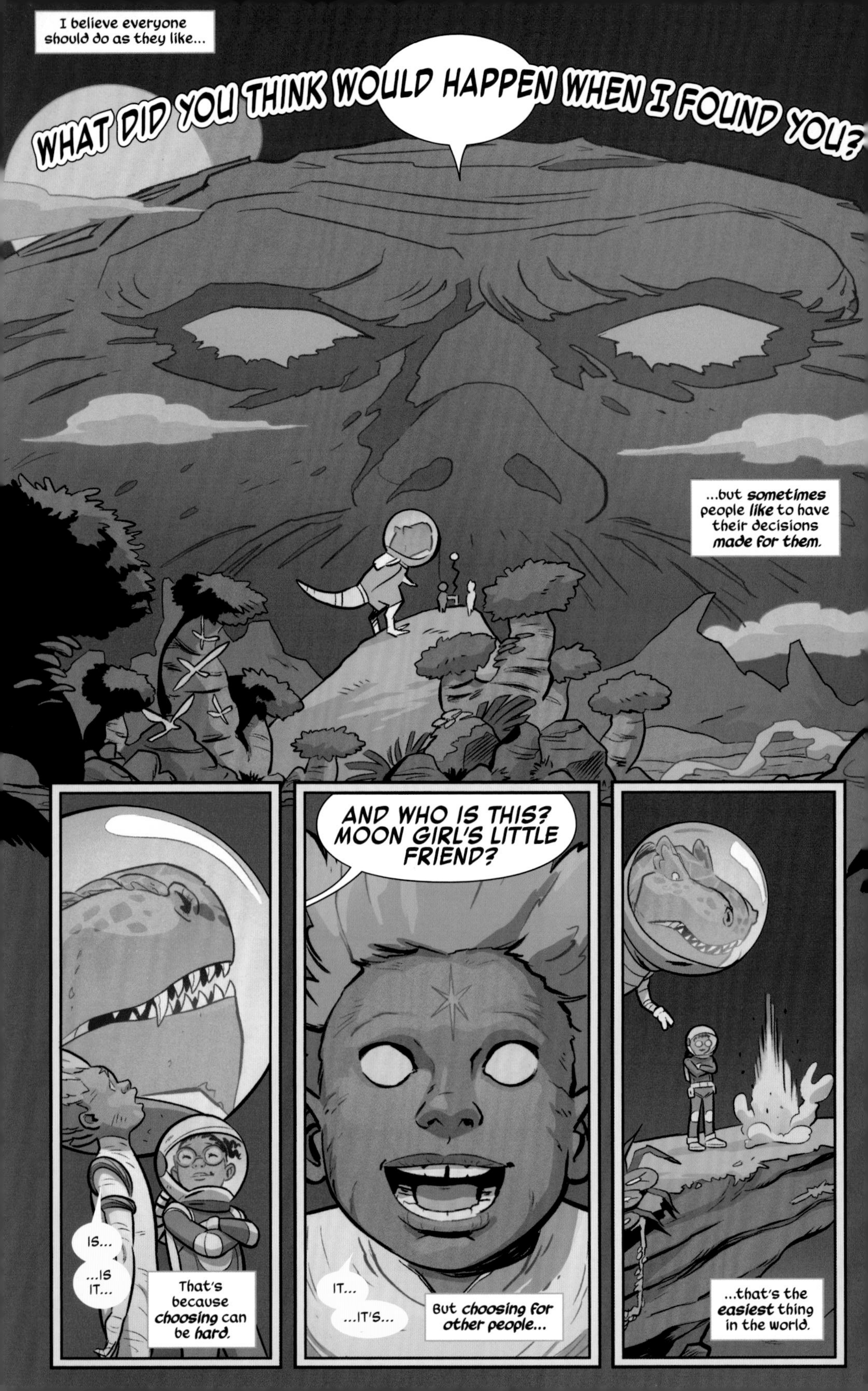
I believe everyone should do as they like...
WHAT DID YOU THINK WOULD HAPPEN WHEN I FOUND YOU?
...but sometimes people like to have their decisions made for them.
IS...
...IS IT...
That's because choosing can be hard.
AND WHO IS THIS? MOON GIRL'S LITTLE FRIEND?
IT...
...IT'S...
But choosing for other people...
...that's the easiest thing in the world.

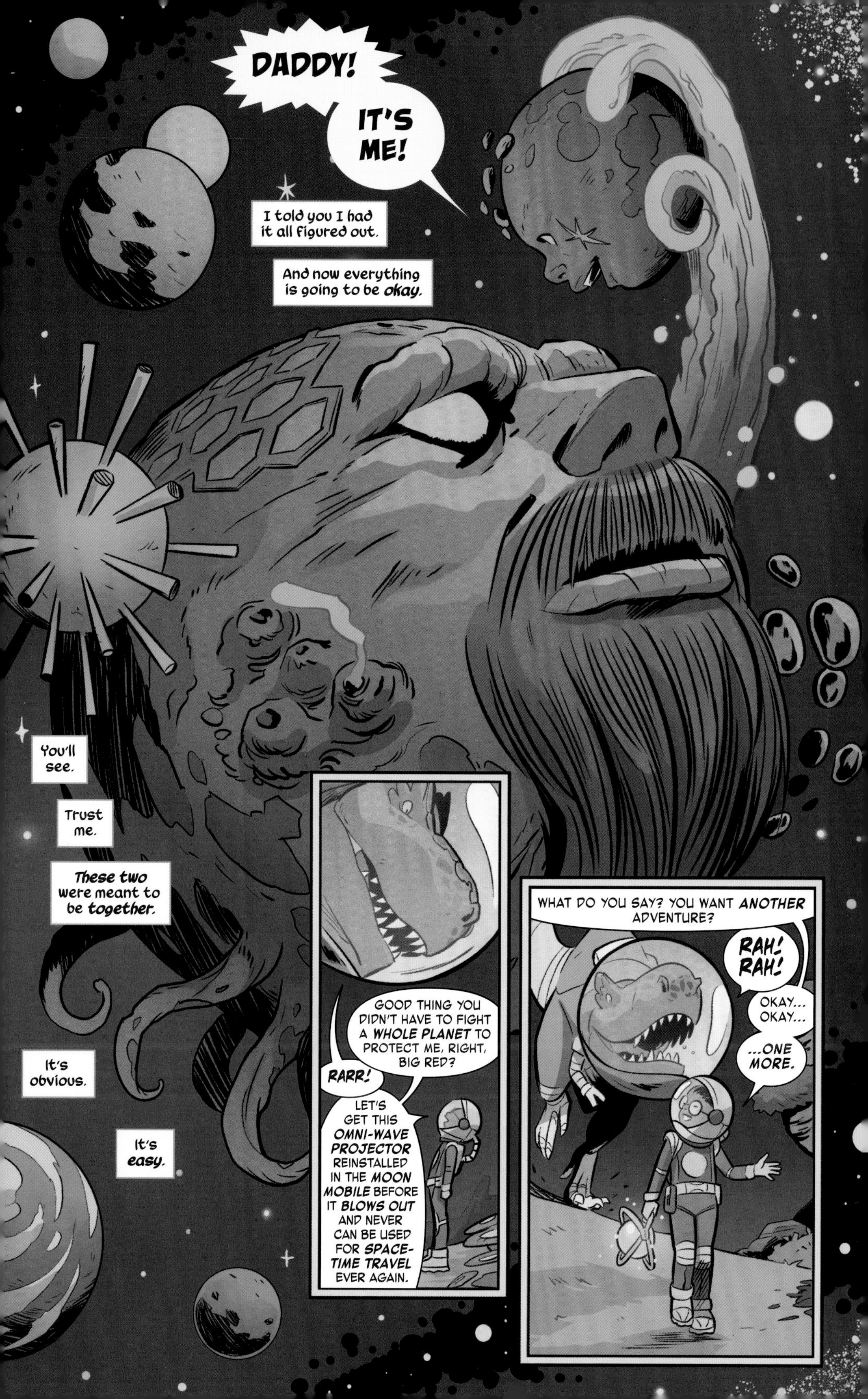
DADDY!
IT'S ME!
I told you I had it all figured out.
And now everything is going to be *okay.*
You'll see.
Trust me.
These two were meant to be *together.*
It's obvious.
It's *easy.*
GOOD THING YOU DIDN'T HAVE TO FIGHT A *WHOLE PLANET* TO PROTECT ME, RIGHT, BIG RED?
RARR!
LET'S GET THIS *OMNI-WAVE PROJECTOR* REINSTALLED IN THE *MOON MOBILE* BEFORE IT *BLOWS OUT* AND NEVER CAN BE USED FOR *SPACE-TIME TRAVEL* EVER AGAIN.
WHAT DO YOU SAY? YOU WANT *ANOTHER* ADVENTURE?
RAH! RAH!
OKAY... OKAY...
...ONE MORE.

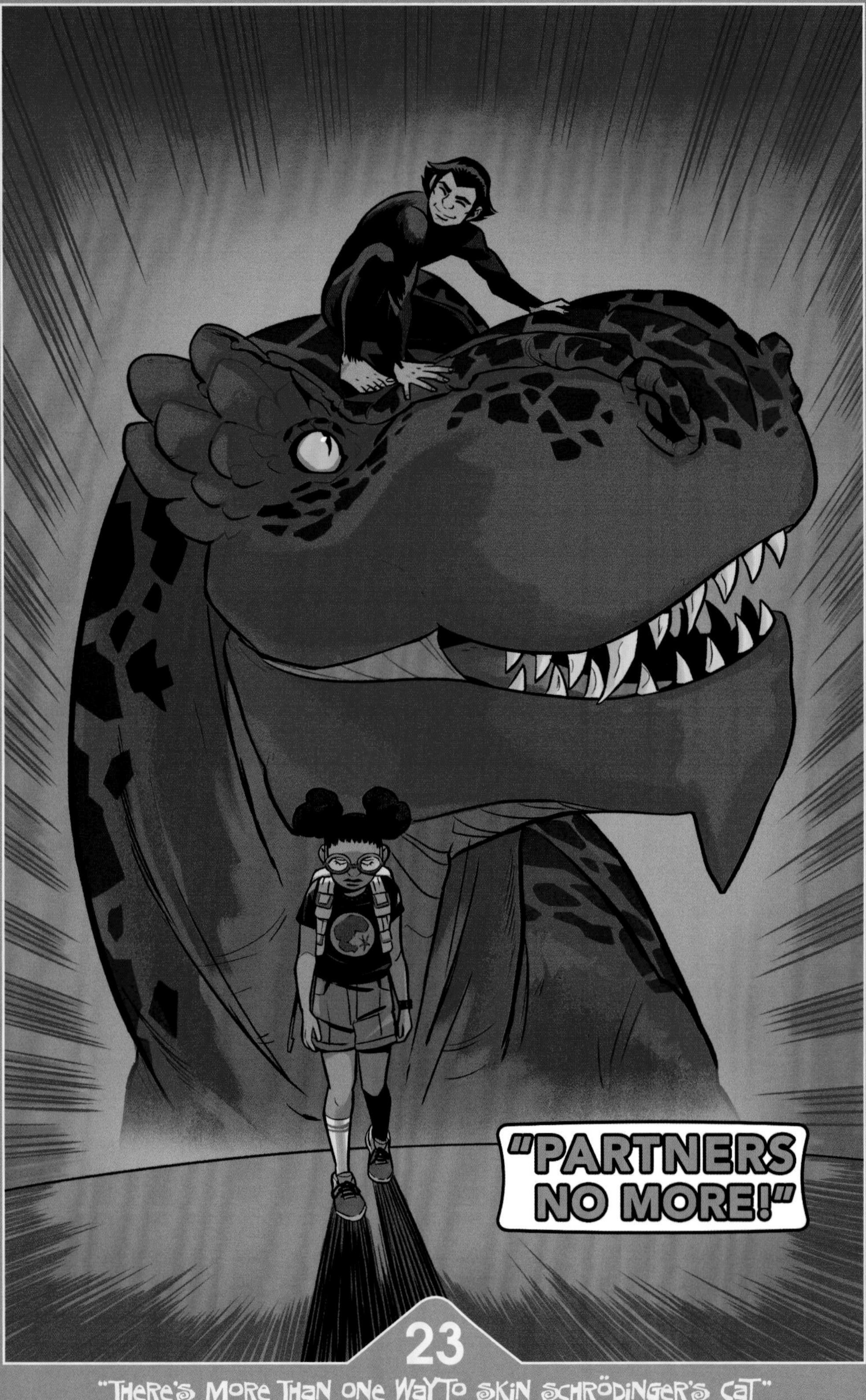
"PARTNERS NO MORE!"
23

"THERE'S MORE THAN ONE WAY TO SKIN SCHRÖDINGER'S CAT"

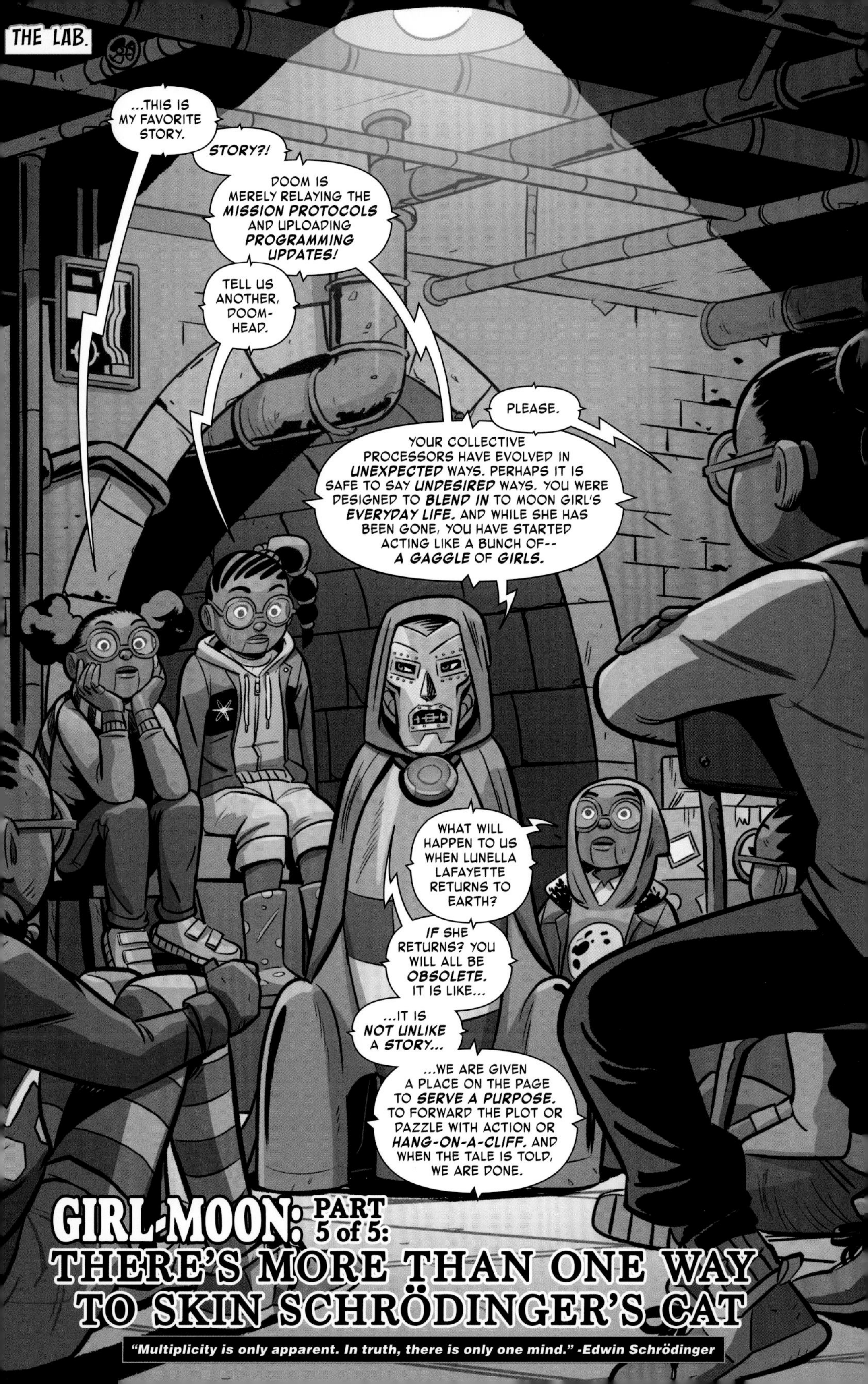
THE LAB.
...THIS IS MY FAVORITE STORY.
STORY?!
DOOM IS MERELY RELAYING THE MISSION PROTOCOLS AND UPLOADING PROGRAMMING UPDATES!
TELL US ANOTHER, DOOM-HEAD.
PLEASE.
YOUR COLLECTIVE PROCESSORS HAVE EVOLVED IN UNEXPECTED WAYS. PERHAPS IT IS SAFE TO SAY UNDESIRED WAYS. YOU WERE DESIGNED TO BLEND IN TO MOON GIRL'S EVERYDAY LIFE. AND WHILE SHE HAS BEEN GONE, YOU HAVE STARTED ACTING LIKE A BUNCH OF-- A GAGGLE OF GIRLS.
WHAT WILL HAPPEN TO US WHEN LUNELLA LAFAYETTE RETURNS TO EARTH?
IF SHE RETURNS? YOU WILL ALL BE OBSOLETE. IT IS LIKE...
...IT IS NOT UNLIKE A STORY...
...WE ARE GIVEN A PLACE ON THE PAGE TO SERVE A PURPOSE. TO FORWARD THE PLOT OR DAZZLE WITH ACTION OR HANG-ON-A-CLIFF. AND WHEN THE TALE IS TOLD, WE ARE DONE.
GIRL-MOON: PART 5 of 5:
THERE'S MORE THAN ONE WAY TO SKIN SCHRÖDINGER'S CAT
"Multiplicity is only apparent. In truth, there is only one mind." -Edwin Schrödinger

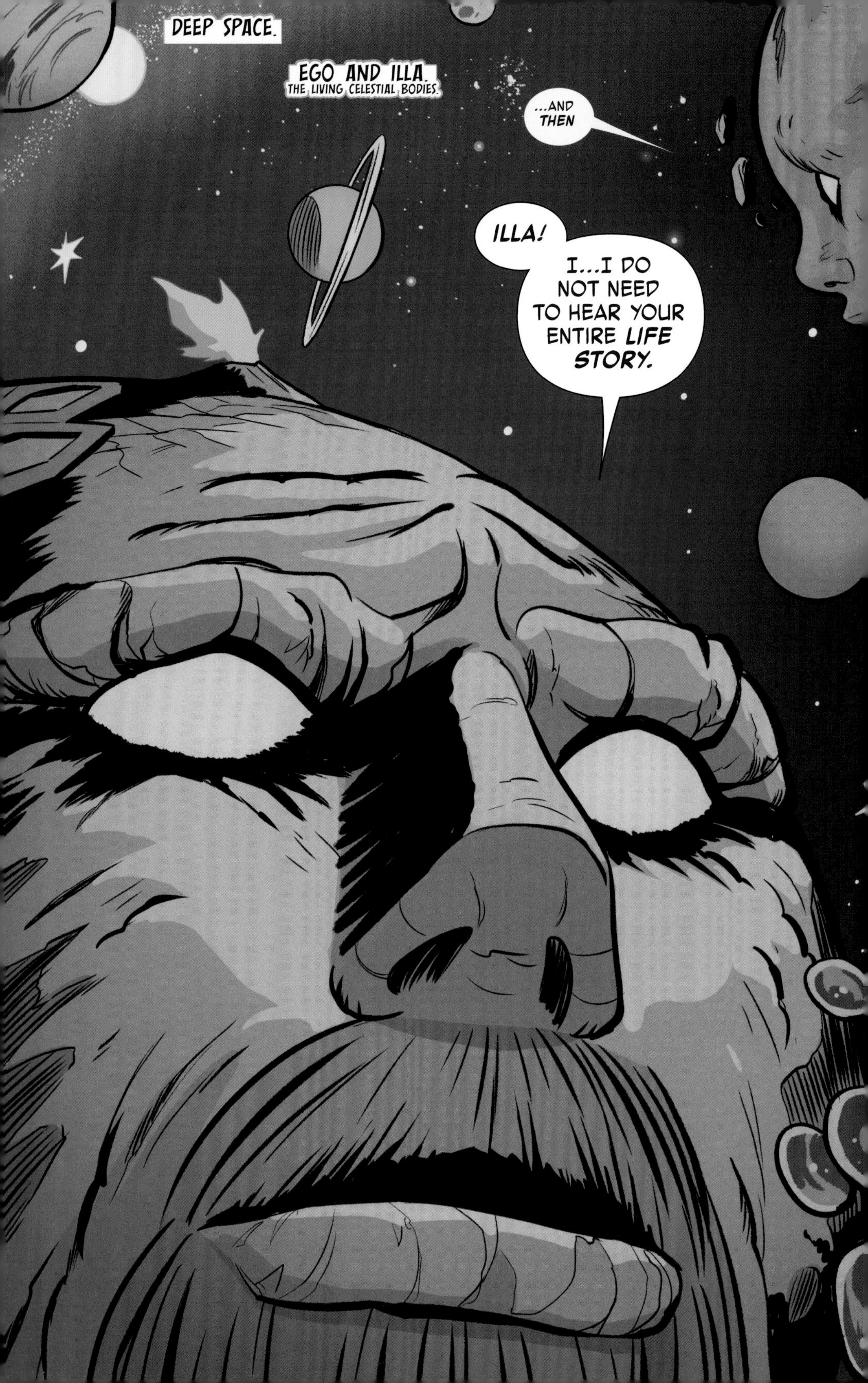
DEEP SPACE.
EGO AND ILLA. THE LIVING CELESTIAL BODIES.
...AND THEN
ILLA!
I...I DO NOT NEED TO HEAR YOUR ENTIRE LIFE STORY.

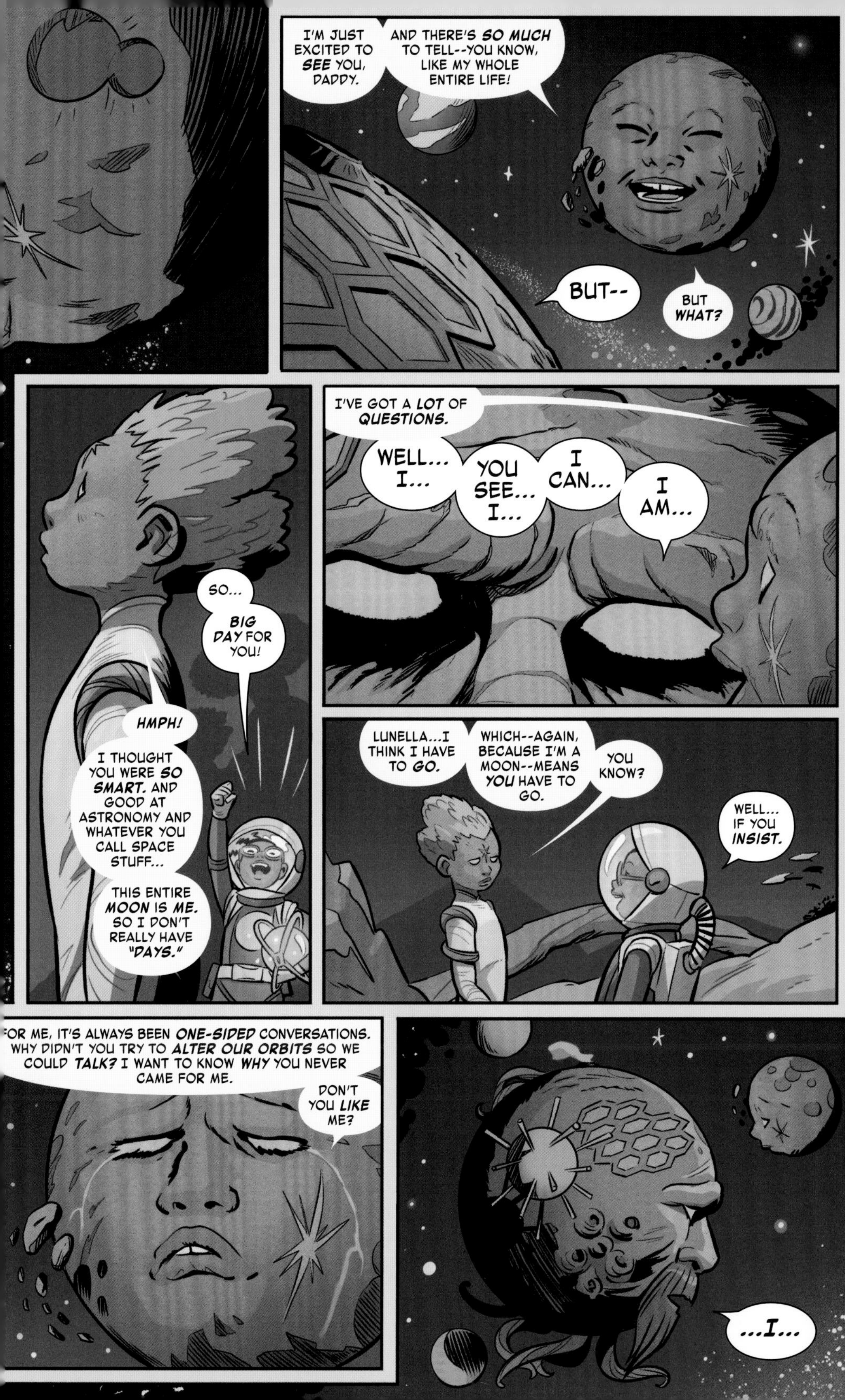
I'M JUST EXCITED TO SEE YOU, DADDY.
AND THERE'S SO MUCH TO TELL--YOU KNOW, LIKE MY WHOLE ENTIRE LIFE!
BUT--
BUT WHAT?
SO...
BIG DAY FOR YOU!
HMPH!
I THOUGHT YOU WERE SO SMART. AND GOOD AT ASTRONOMY AND WHATEVER YOU CALL SPACE STUFF...
THIS ENTIRE MOON IS ME. SO I DON'T REALLY HAVE "DAYS."
I'VE GOT A LOT OF QUESTIONS.
WELL... I...
YOU SEE... I...
I CAN...
I AM...
LUNELLA...I THINK I HAVE TO GO.
WHICH--AGAIN, BECAUSE I'M A MOON--MEANS YOU HAVE TO GO.
YOU KNOW?
WELL... IF YOU INSIST.
FOR ME, IT'S ALWAYS BEEN ONE-SIDED CONVERSATIONS. WHY DIDN'T YOU TRY TO ALTER OUR ORBITS SO WE COULD TALK? I WANT TO KNOW WHY YOU NEVER CAME FOR ME.
DON'T YOU LIKE ME?
...I...

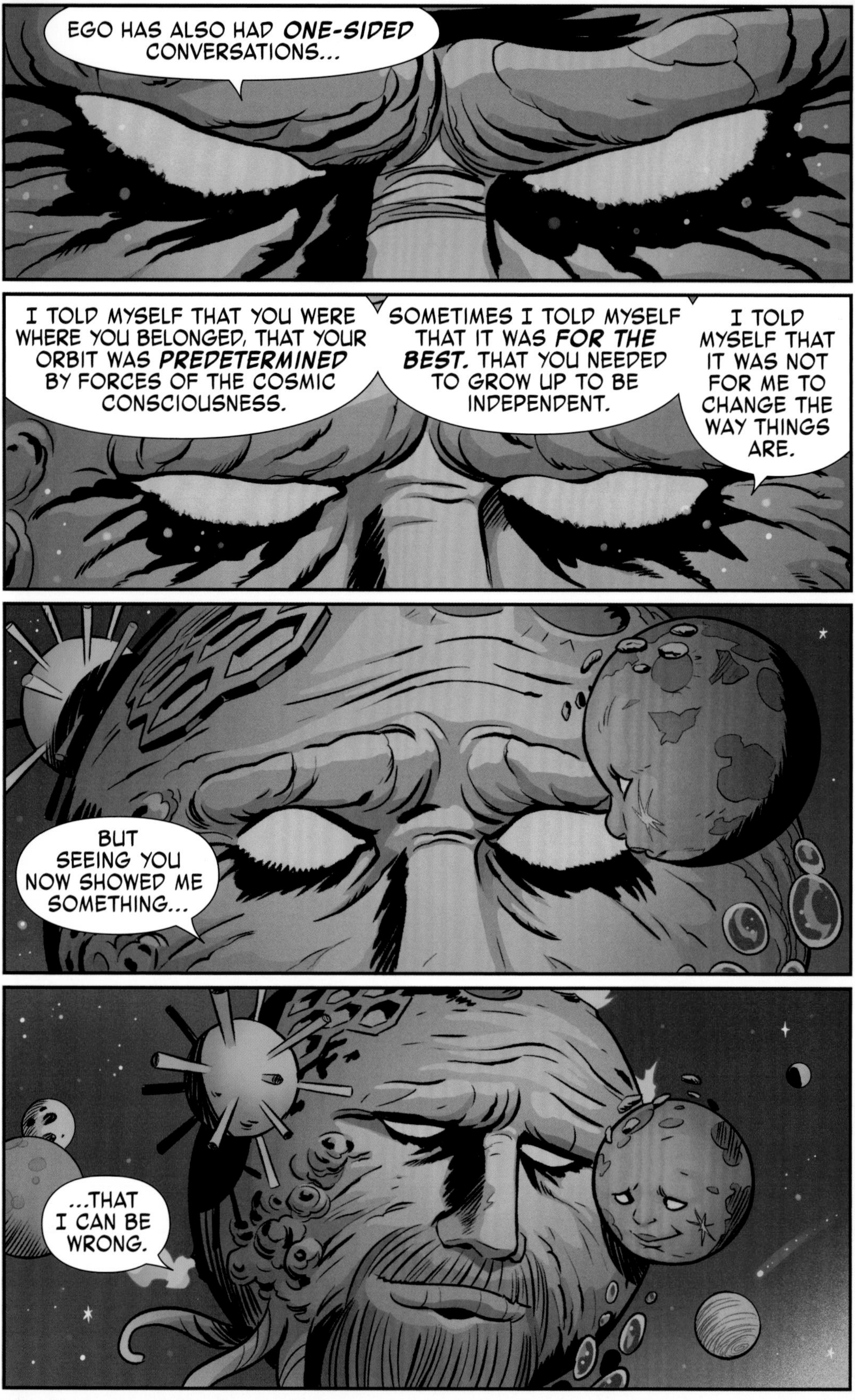
EGO HAS ALSO HAD ONE-SIDED CONVERSATIONS...
I TOLD MYSELF THAT YOU WERE WHERE YOU BELONGED, THAT YOUR ORBIT WAS PREDETERMINED BY FORCES OF THE COSMIC CONSCIOUSNESS.
SOMETIMES I TOLD MYSELF THAT IT WAS FOR THE BEST. THAT YOU NEEDED TO GROW UP TO BE INDEPENDENT.
I TOLD MYSELF THAT IT WAS NOT FOR ME TO CHANGE THE WAY THINGS ARE.
BUT SEEING YOU NOW SHOWED ME SOMETHING...
...THAT I CAN BE WRONG.

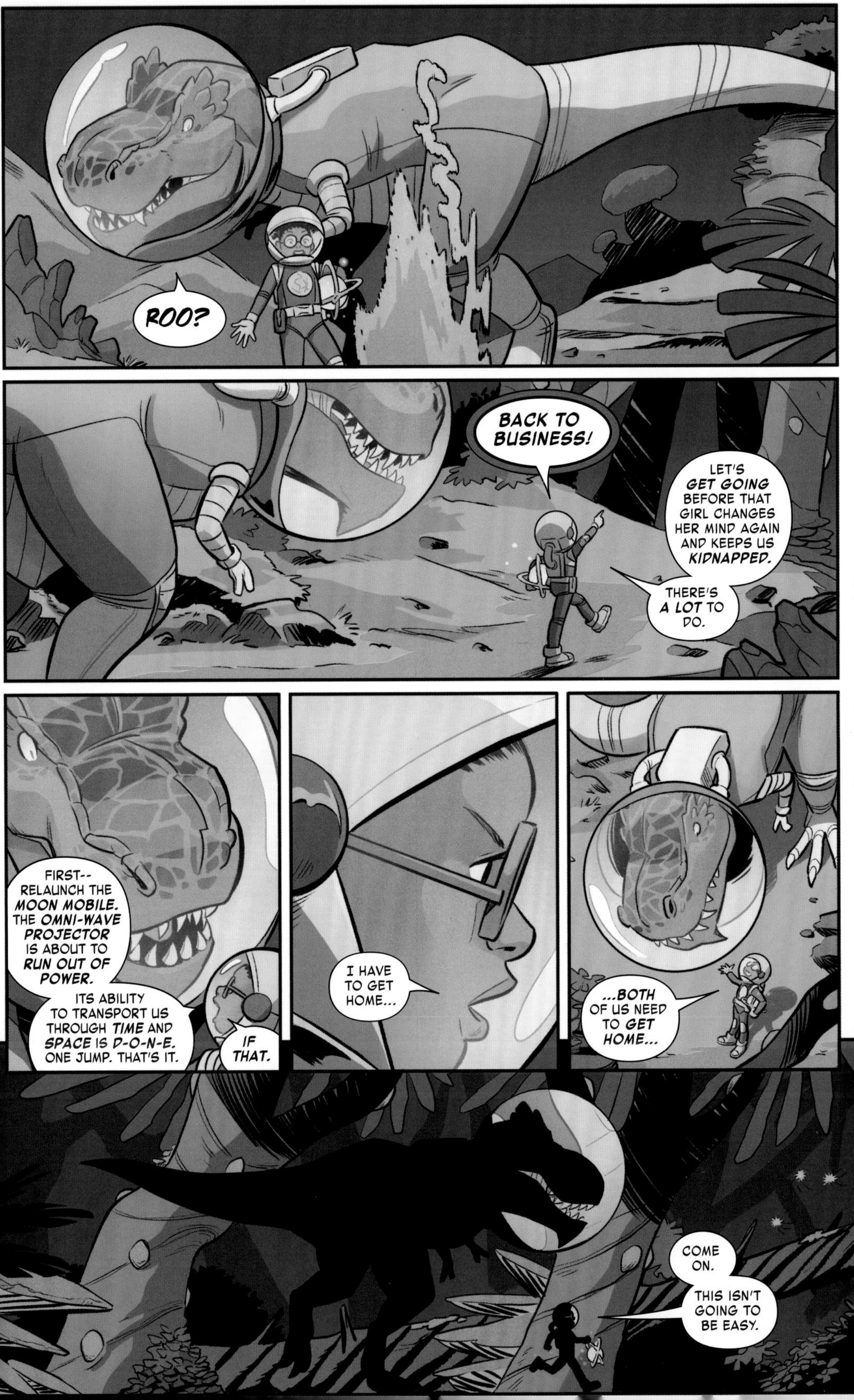
ROO?
BACK TO BUSINESS!
LET'S GET GOING BEFORE THAT GIRL CHANGES HER MIND AGAIN AND KEEPS US KIDNAPPED.
THERE'S A LOT TO DO.
FIRST-- RELAUNCH THE MOON MOBILE. THE OMNI-WAVE PROJECTOR IS ABOUT TO RUN OUT OF POWER.
ITS ABILITY TO TRANSPORT US THROUGH TIME AND SPACE IS D-O-N-E. ONE JUMP. THAT'S IT.
IF THAT.
I HAVE TO GET HOME...
...BOTH OF US NEED TO GET HOME...
COME ON.
THIS ISN'T GOING TO BE EASY.

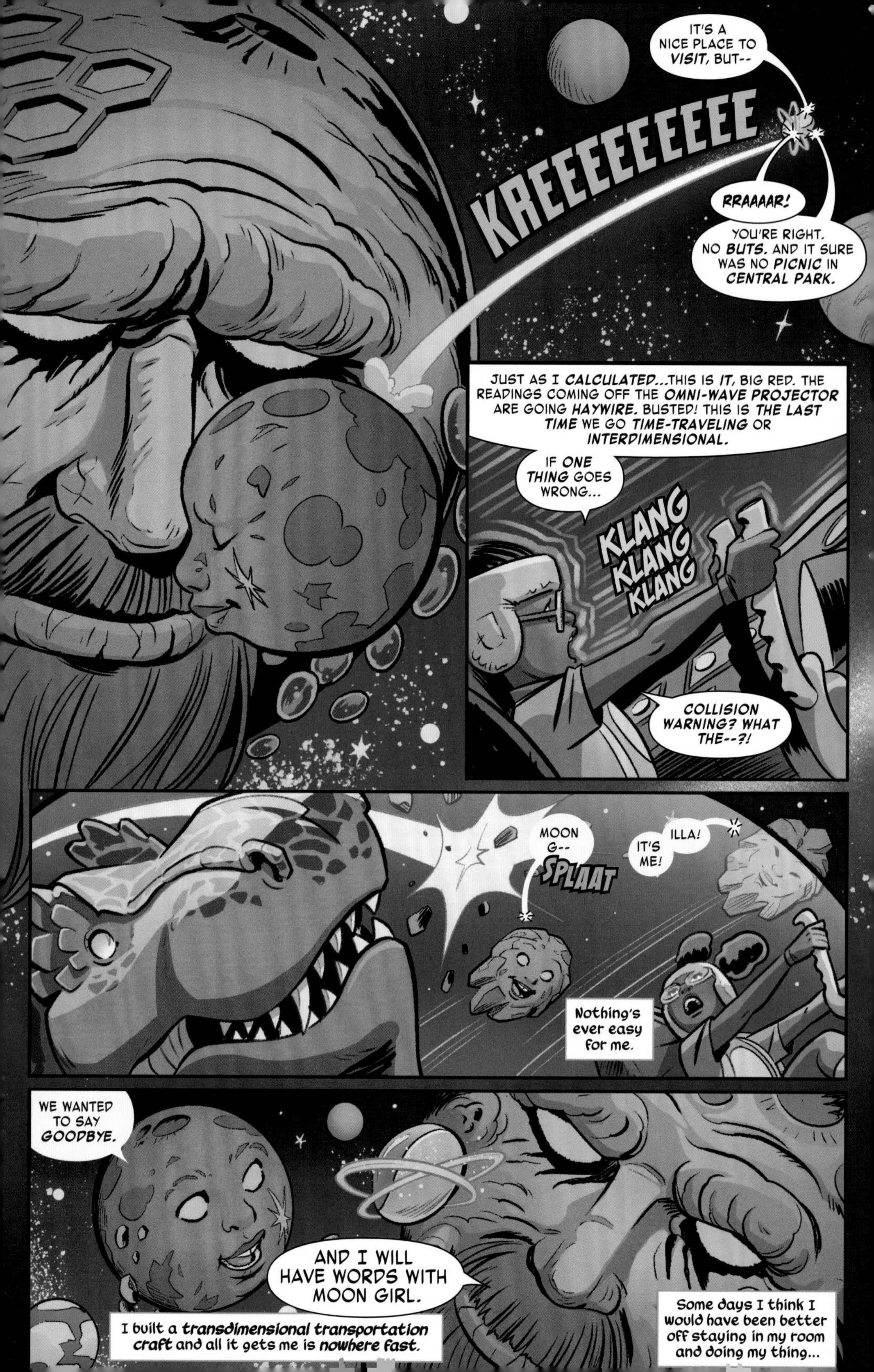
IT'S A NICE PLACE TO VISIT, BUT--
KREEEEEEEEE
RRAAAAR!
YOU'RE RIGHT. NO BUTS. AND IT SURE WAS NO PICNIC IN CENTRAL PARK.
JUST AS I CALCULATED...THIS IS IT, BIG RED. THE READINGS COMING OFF THE OMNI-WAVE PROJECTOR ARE GOING HAYWIRE. BUSTED! THIS IS THE LAST TIME WE GO TIME-TRAVELING OR INTERDIMENSIONAL.
IF ONE THING GOES WRONG...
KLANG KLANG KLANG
COLLISION WARNING? WHAT THE--?!
MOON G--
SPLAAT
IT'S ME!
ILLA!
Nothing's ever easy for me.
WE WANTED TO SAY GOODBYE.
AND I WILL HAVE WORDS WITH MOON GIRL.
I built a transdimensional transportation craft and all it gets me is nowhere fast.
Some days I think I would have been better off staying in my room and doing my thing...

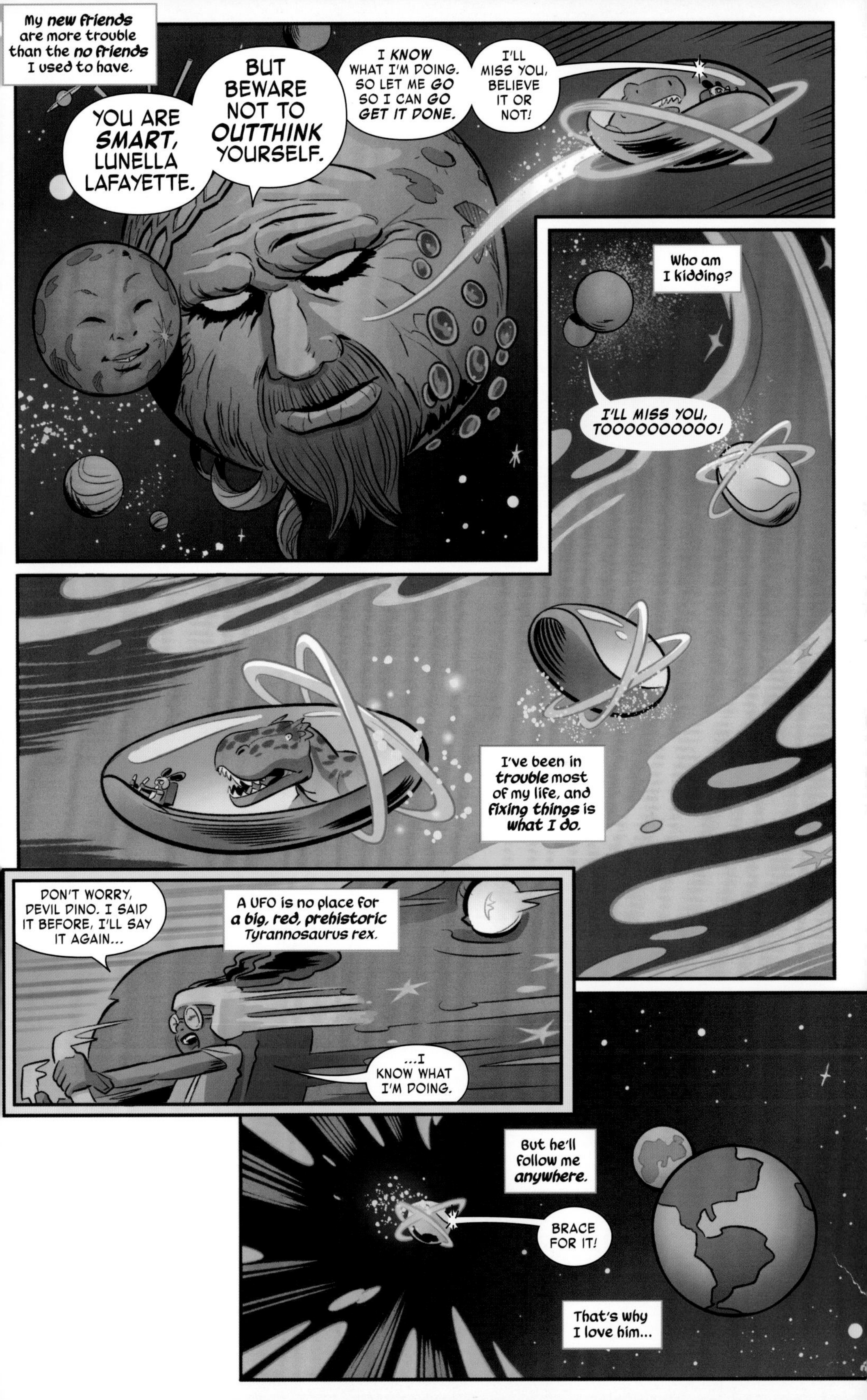

My new friends are more trouble than the no friends I used to have.
YOU ARE SMART, LUNELLA LAFAYETTE.
BUT BEWARE NOT TO OUTTHINK YOURSELF.
I KNOW WHAT I'M DOING. SO LET ME GO SO I CAN GO GET IT DONE.
I'LL MISS YOU, BELIEVE IT OR NOT!
Who am I kidding?
I'LL MISS YOU, TOOOOOOOOOO!
I've been in trouble most of my life, and fixing things is what I do.
DON'T WORRY, DEVIL DINO. I SAID IT BEFORE, I'LL SAY IT AGAIN...
A UFO is no place for a big, red, prehistoric Tyrannosaurus rex.
...I KNOW WHAT I'M DOING.
But he'll follow me anywhere.
BRACE FOR IT!
That's why I love him...

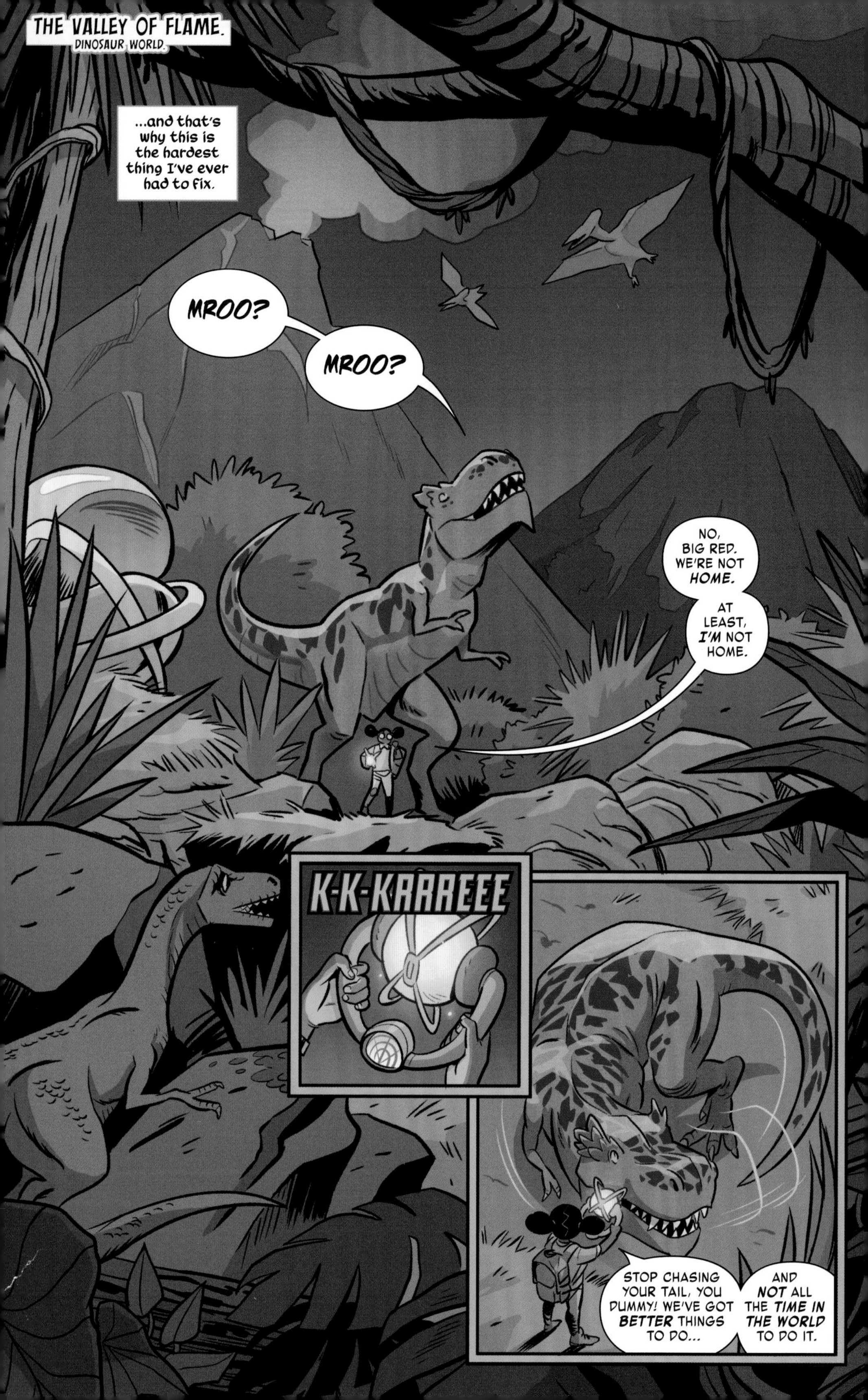
THE VALLEY OF FLAME.
DINOSAUR WORLD.
...and that's why this is the hardest thing I've ever had to fix.
MROO?
MROO?
NO, BIG RED. WE'RE NOT HOME.
AT LEAST, I'M NOT HOME.
K-K-KARREEE
STOP CHASING YOUR TAIL, YOU DUMMY! WE'VE GOT BETTER THINGS TO DO...
AND NOT ALL THE TIME IN THE WORLD TO DO IT.

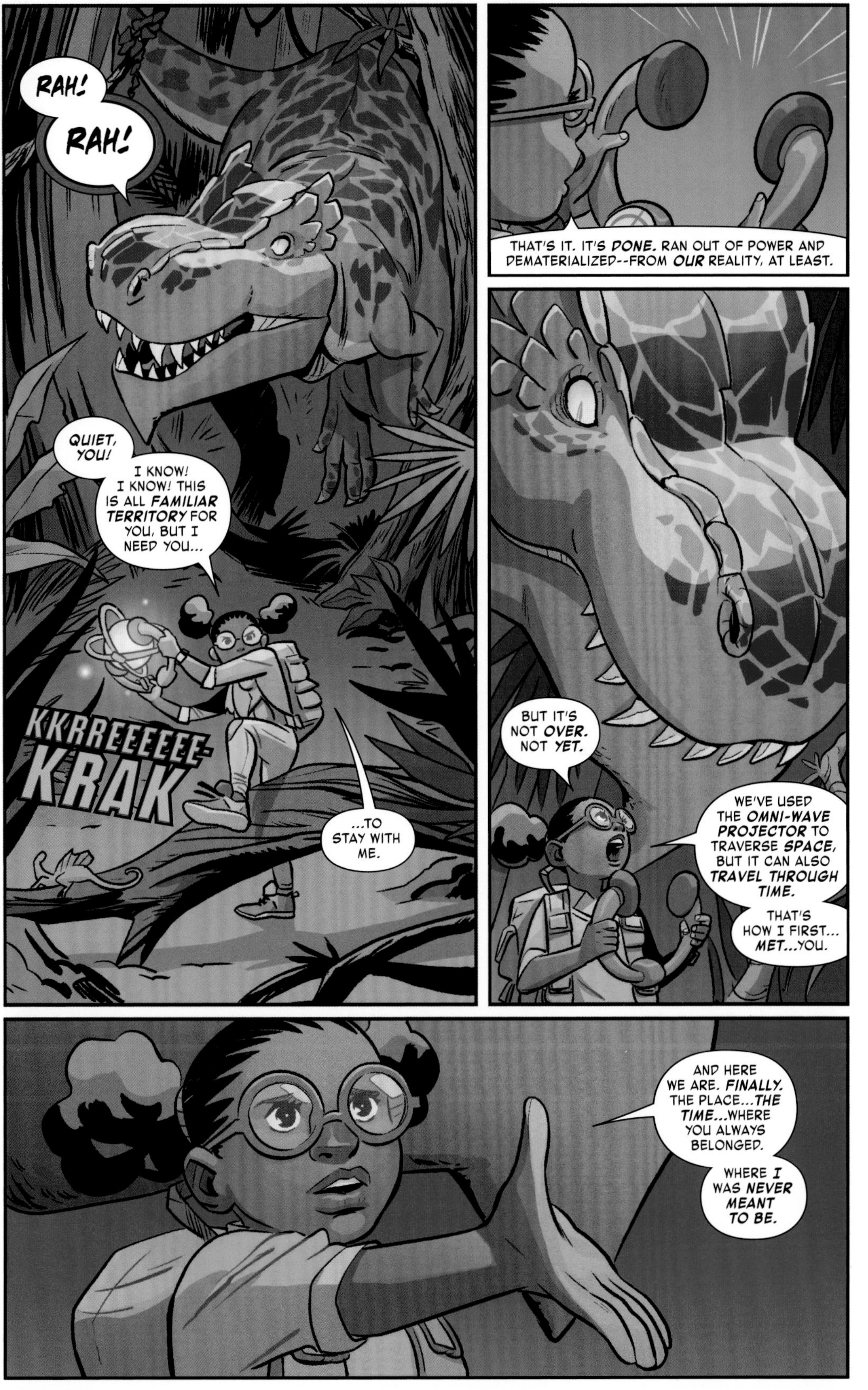

RAH!
RAH!
QUIET, YOU!
I KNOW! I KNOW! THIS IS ALL *FAMILIAR TERRITORY* FOR YOU, BUT I NEED YOU...
KKRREEEEEEE-KRAK
...TO STAY WITH ME.
THAT'S IT. IT'S *DONE.* RAN OUT OF POWER AND DEMATERIALIZED--FROM *OUR* REALITY, AT LEAST.
BUT IT'S NOT *OVER.* NOT *YET.*
WE'VE USED THE *OMNI-WAVE PROJECTOR* TO TRAVERSE *SPACE,* BUT IT CAN ALSO *TRAVEL THROUGH TIME.*
THAT'S HOW I FIRST... *MET*...YOU.
AND HERE WE ARE. *FINALLY.* THE PLACE...*THE TIME*...WHERE YOU ALWAYS BELONGED.
WHERE *I* WAS *NEVER MEANT TO BE.*

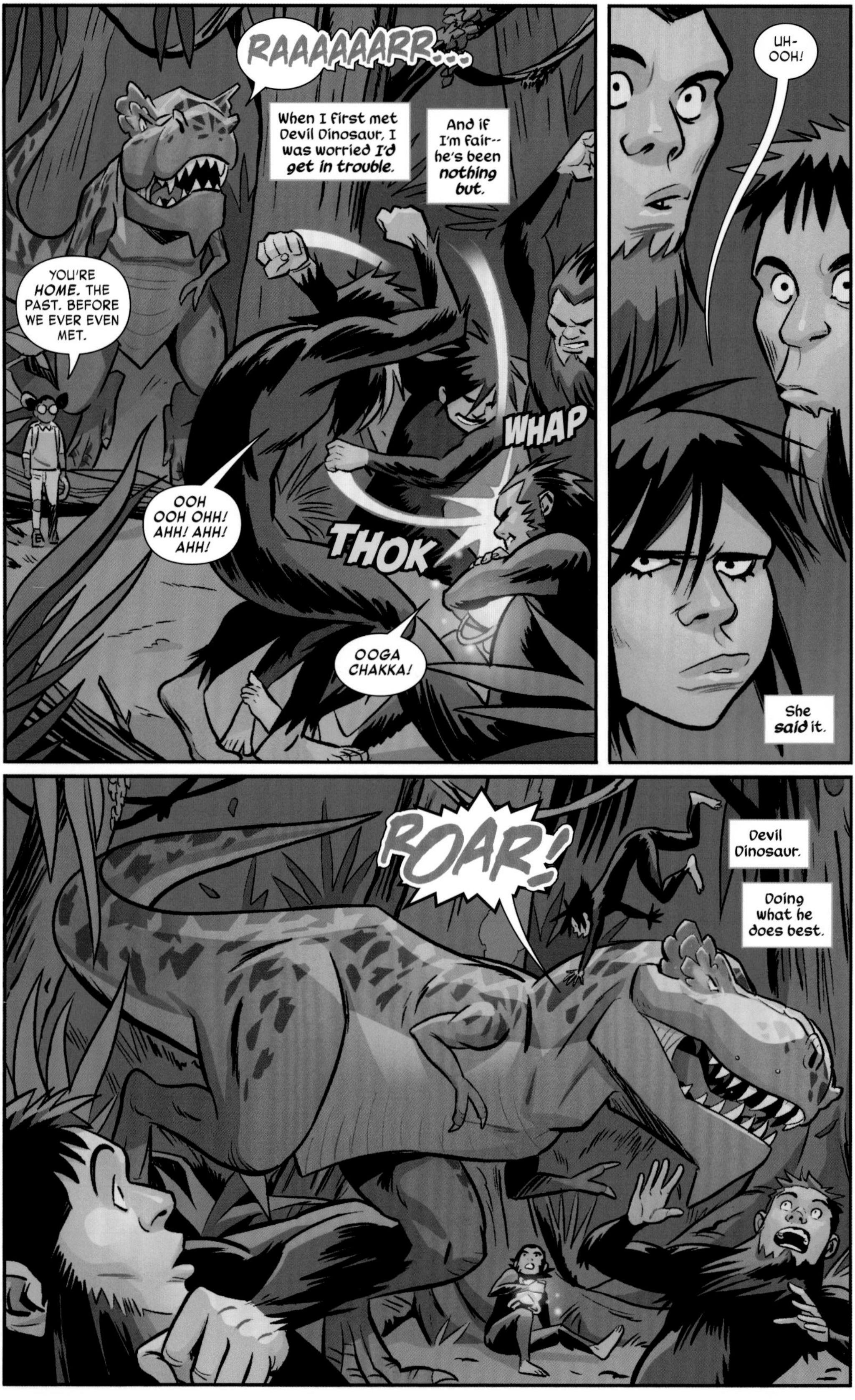
RAAAAAARR...
When I first met Devil Dinosaur, I was worried *I'd get in trouble.*
And if I'm fair-- he's been *nothing* but.
YOU'RE *HOME.* THE PAST. BEFORE WE EVER EVEN MET.
OOH OOH OHH! AHH! AHH! AHH!
WHAP
THOK
OOGA CHAKKA!
UH-OOH!
She *said* it.
ROAR!
Devil Dinosaur.
Doing what he does best.

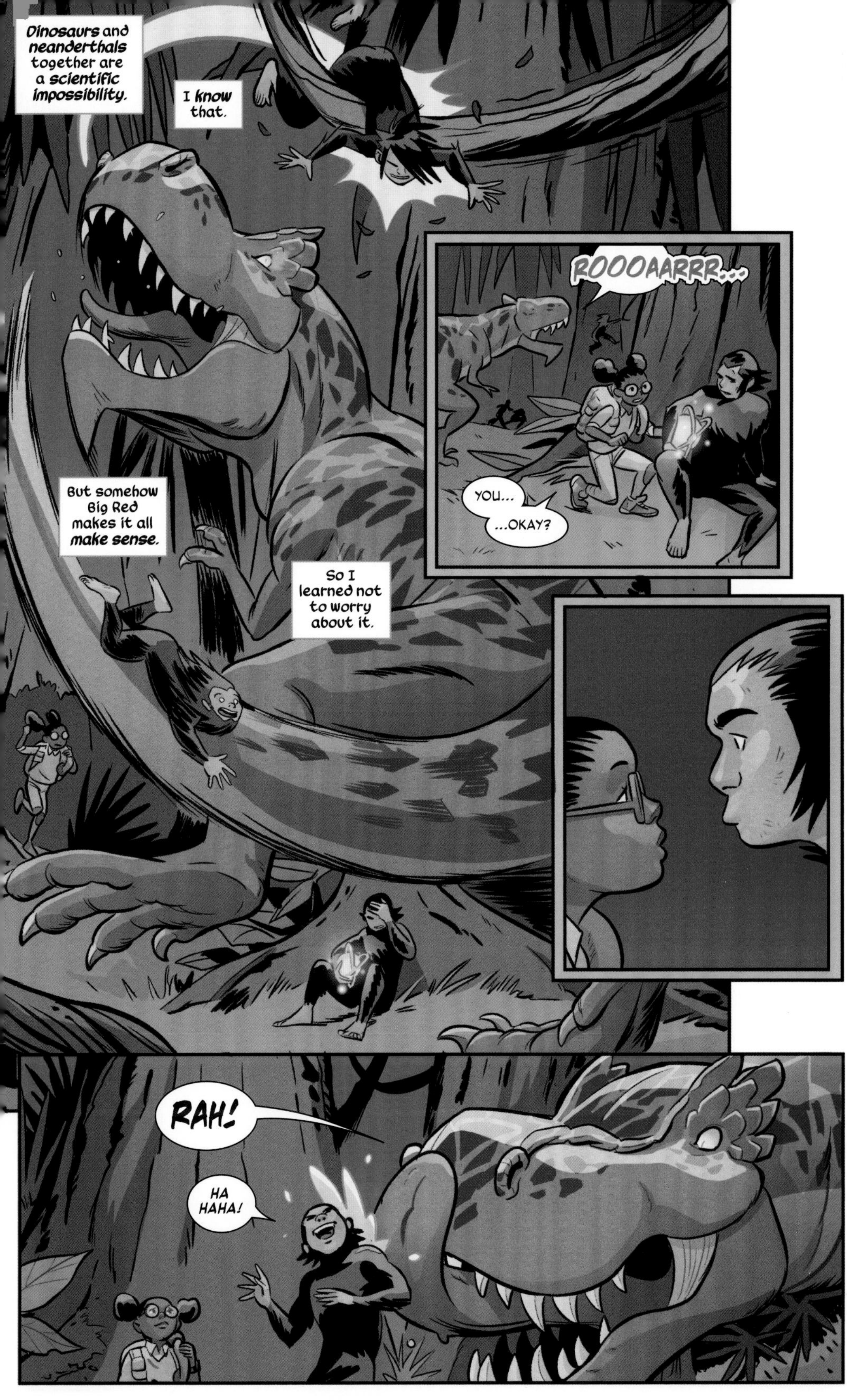
Dinosaurs and neanderthals together are a scientific impossibility.
I know that.
ROOOAARRR...
YOU...
...OKAY?
But somehow Big Red makes it all make sense.
So I learned not to worry about it.
RAH!
HA HAHA!

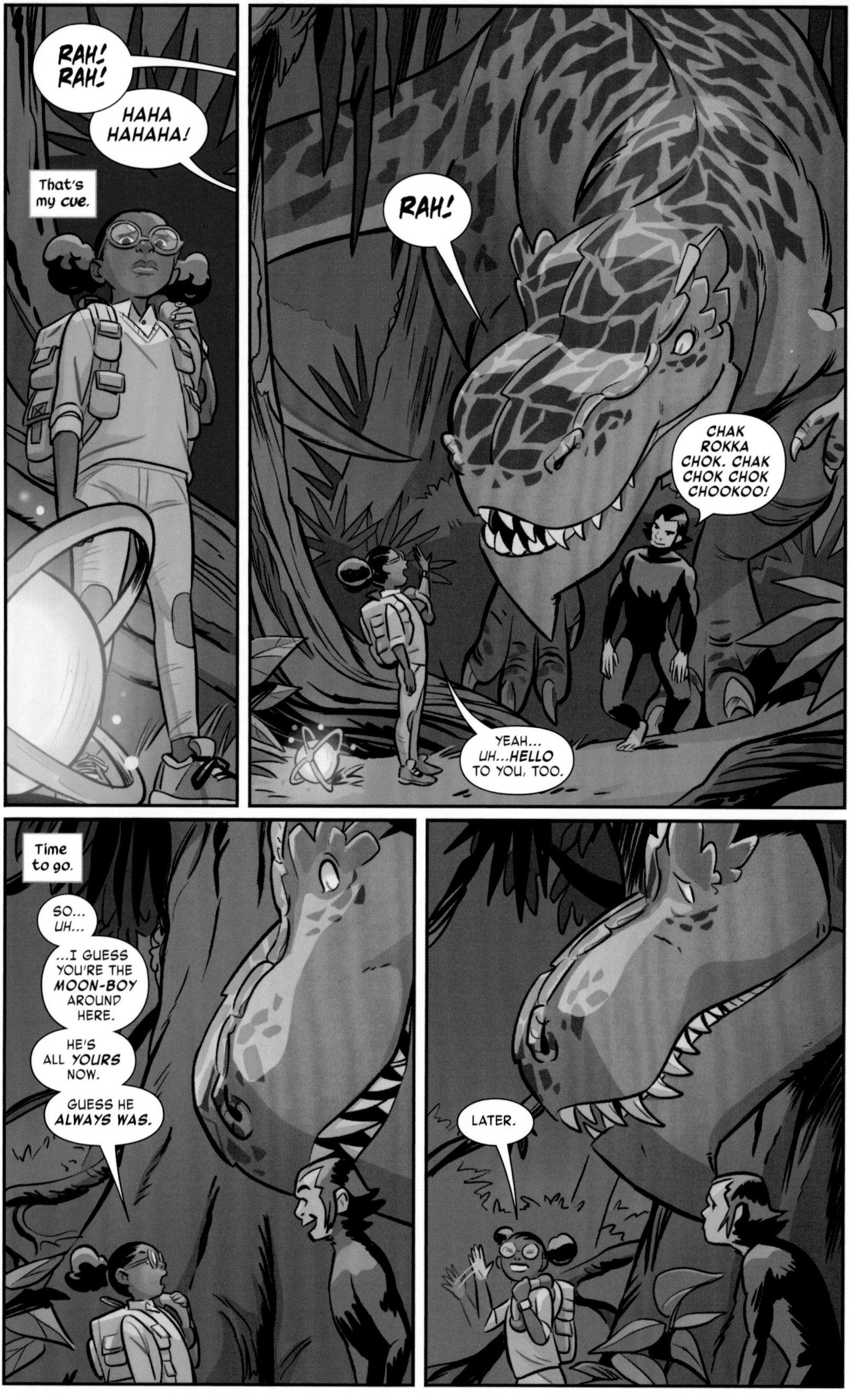
RAH! RAH!
HAHA HAHAHA!
That's my cue.
RAH!
CHAK ROKKA CHOK. CHAK CHOK CHOK CHOOKOO!
YEAH... UH...HELLO TO YOU, TOO.
Time to go.
SO... UH...
...I GUESS YOU'RE THE MOON-BOY AROUND HERE.
HE'S ALL YOURS NOW.
GUESS HE ALWAYS WAS.
LATER.

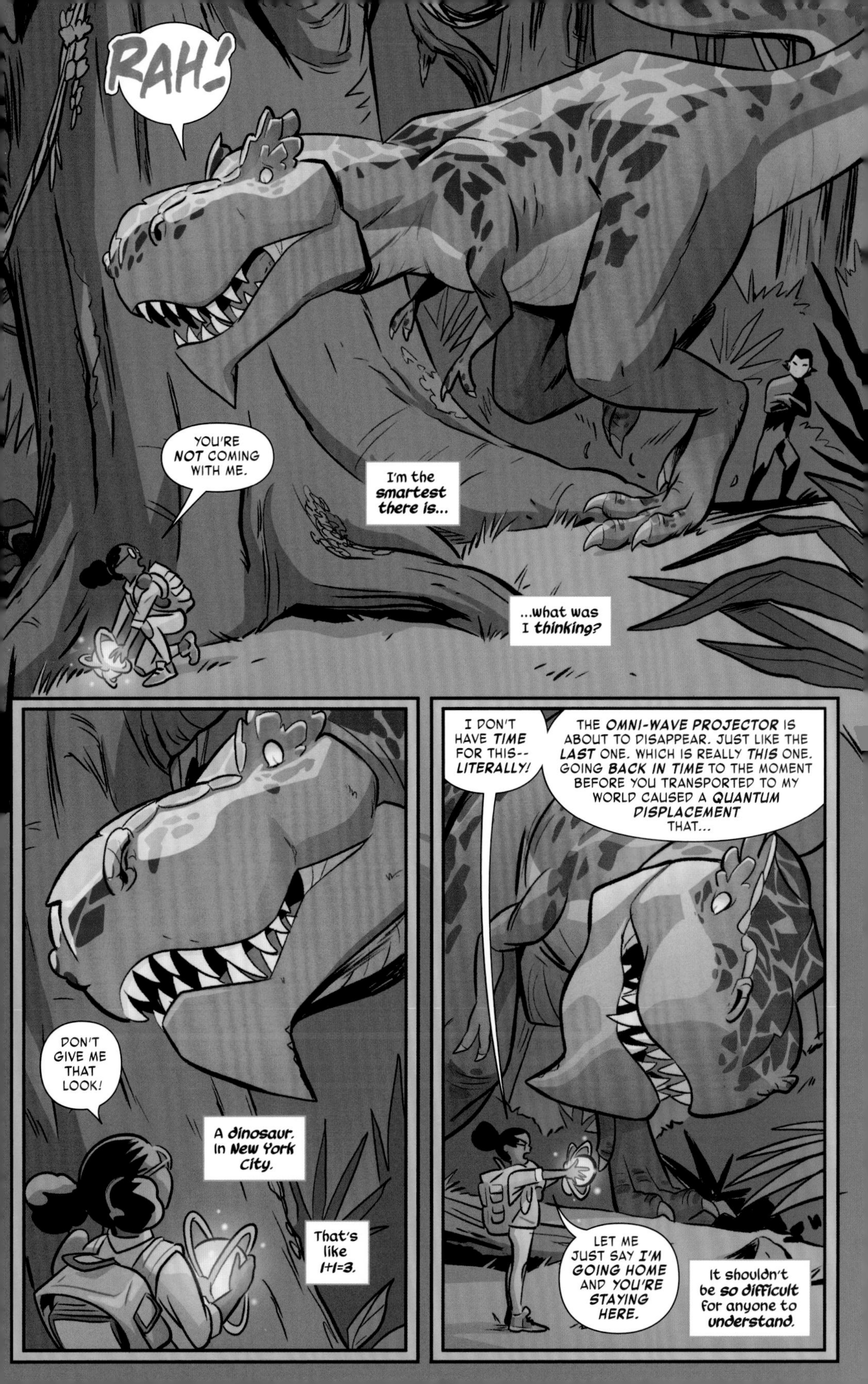
RAH!
YOU'RE NOT COMING WITH ME.
I'm the smartest there is...
...what was I thinking?
DON'T GIVE ME THAT LOOK!
A dinosaur. In New York City.
That's like 1+1=3.
I DON'T HAVE TIME FOR THIS-- LITERALLY!
THE OMNI-WAVE PROJECTOR IS ABOUT TO DISAPPEAR. JUST LIKE THE LAST ONE. WHICH IS REALLY THIS ONE. GOING BACK IN TIME TO THE MOMENT BEFORE YOU TRANSPORTED TO MY WORLD CAUSED A QUANTUM DISPLACEMENT THAT...
LET ME JUST SAY I'M GOING HOME AND YOU'RE STAYING HERE.
It shouldn't be so difficult for anyone to understand.

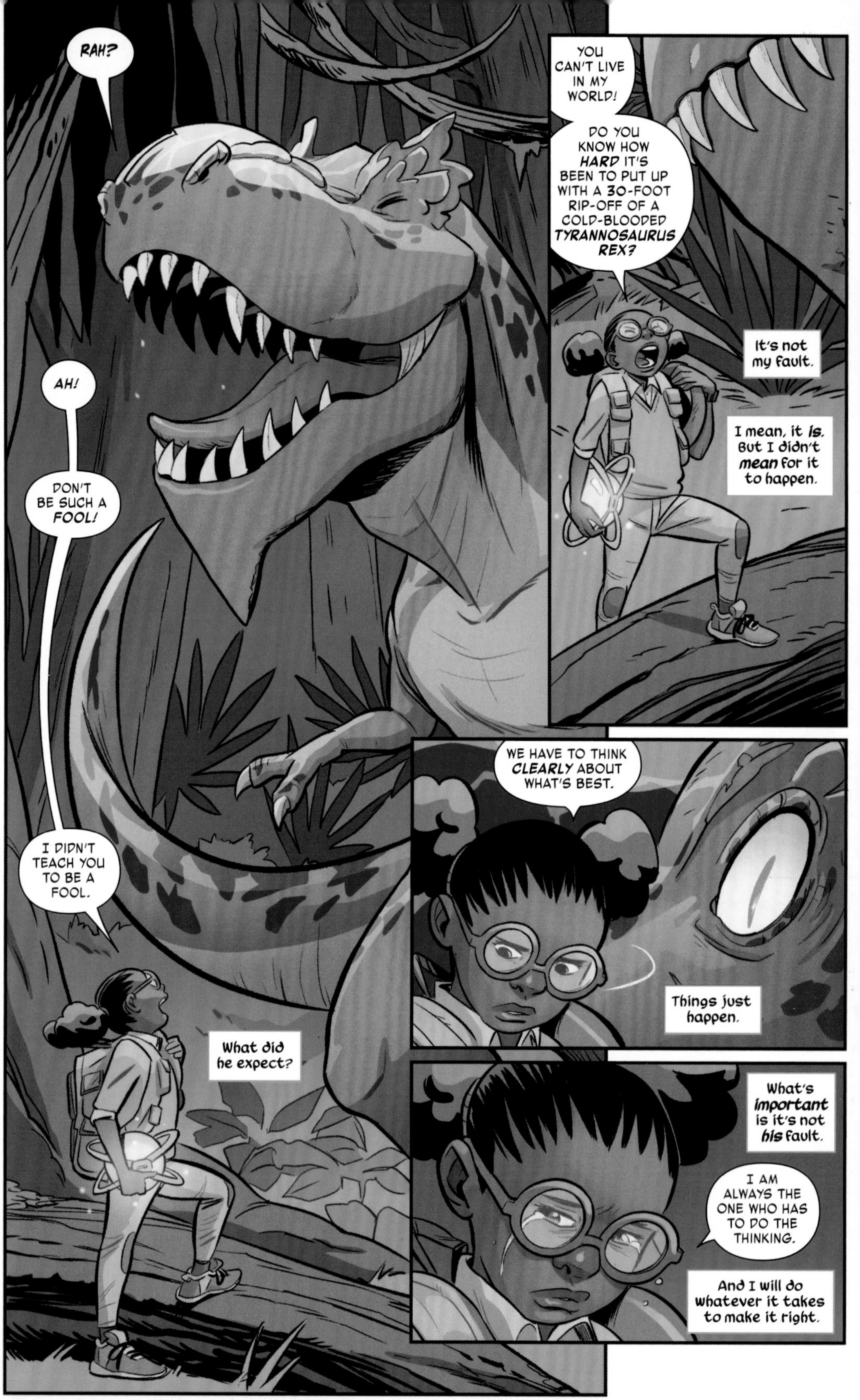
RAH?
AH!
DON'T BE SUCH A FOOL!
I DIDN'T TEACH YOU TO BE A FOOL.
What did he expect?
YOU CAN'T LIVE IN MY WORLD!
DO YOU KNOW HOW HARD IT'S BEEN TO PUT UP WITH A 30-FOOT RIP-OFF OF A COLD-BLOODED TYRANNOSAURUS REX?
It's not my fault.
I mean, it is. But I didn't mean for it to happen.
WE HAVE TO THINK CLEARLY ABOUT WHAT'S BEST.
Things just happen.
What's important is it's not his fault.
I AM ALWAYS THE ONE WHO HAS TO DO THE THINKING.
And I will do whatever it takes to make it right.

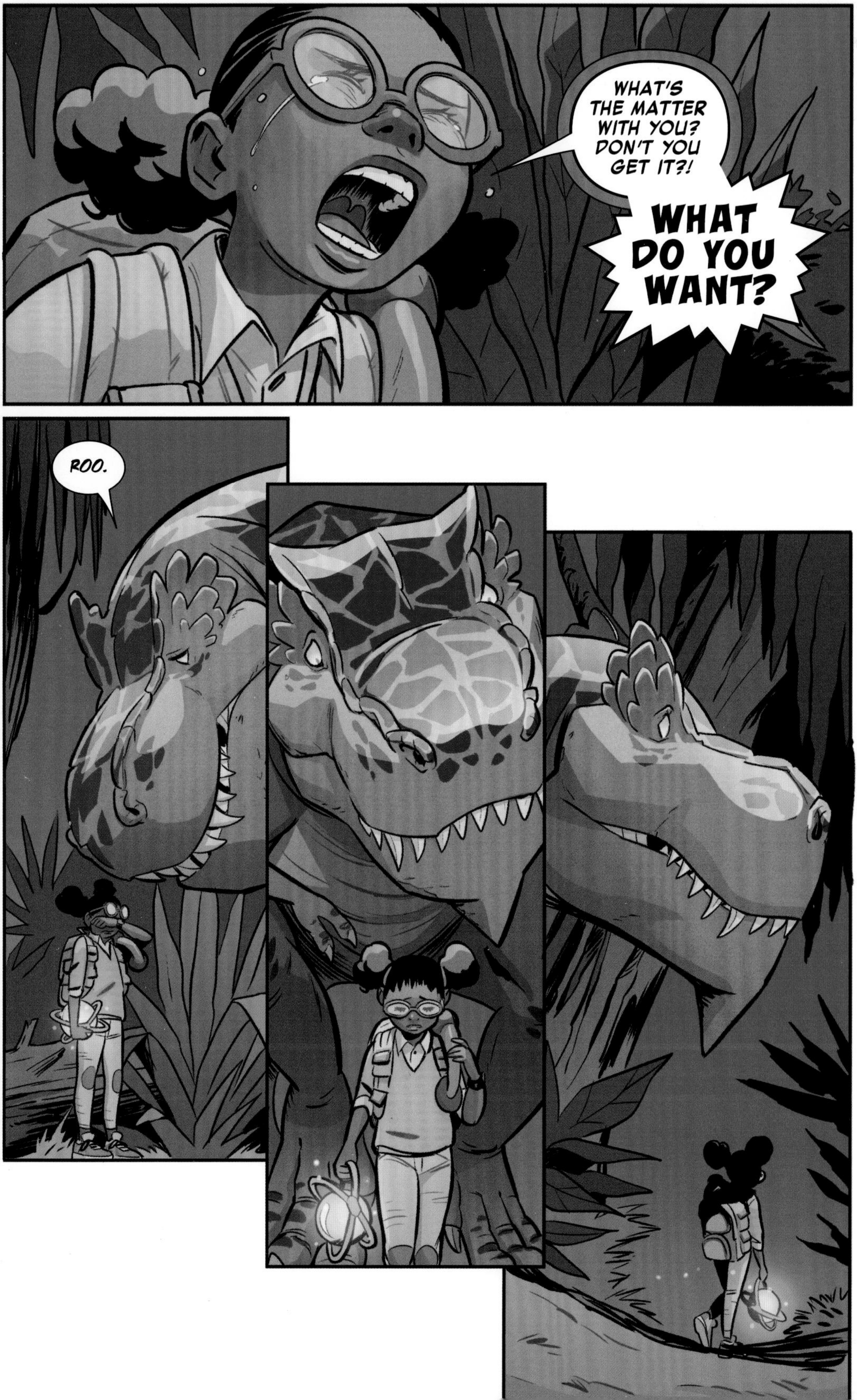
WHAT'S THE MATTER WITH YOU? DON'T YOU GET IT?!
WHAT DO YOU WANT?
ROO.

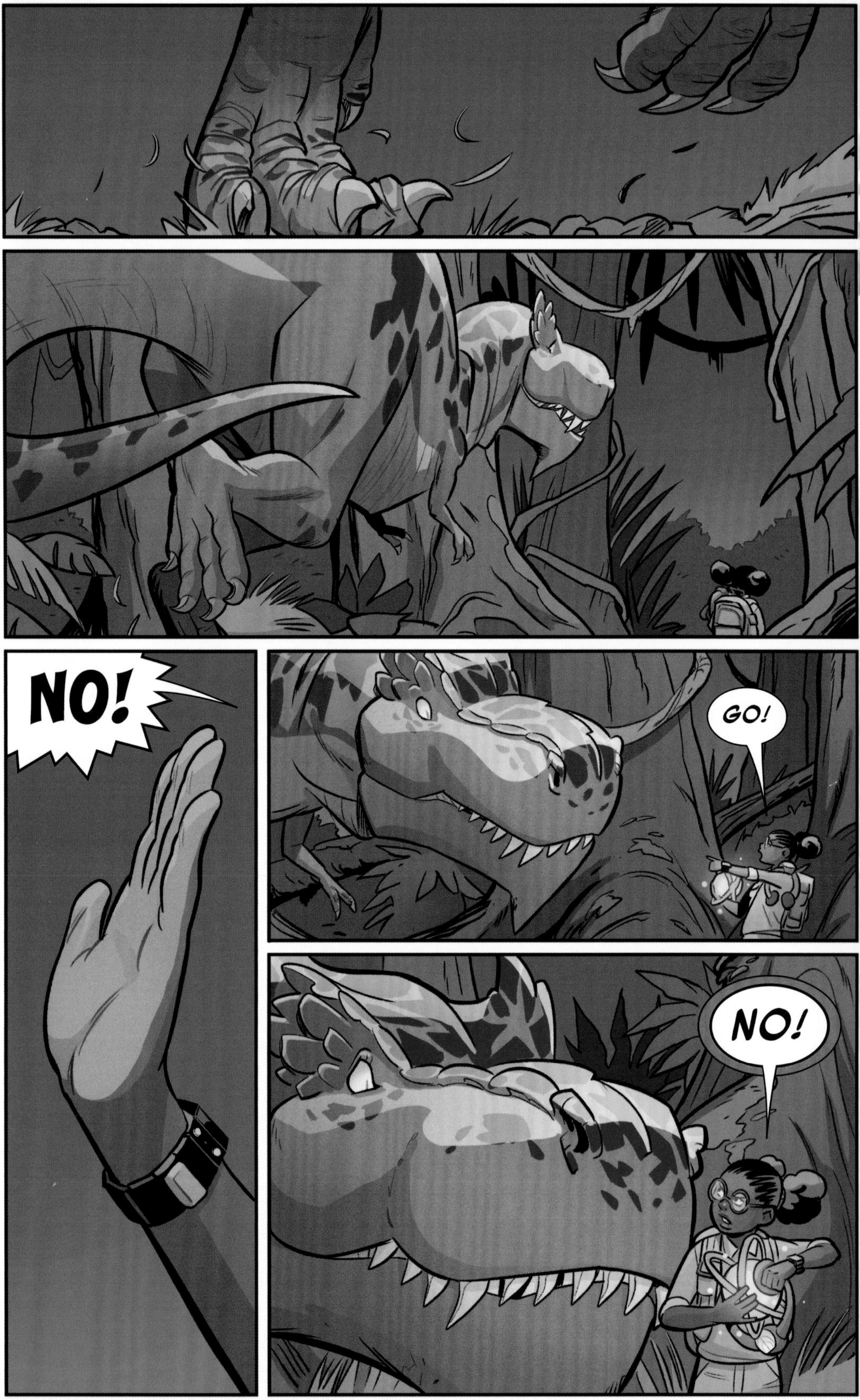
NO!
GO!
NO!

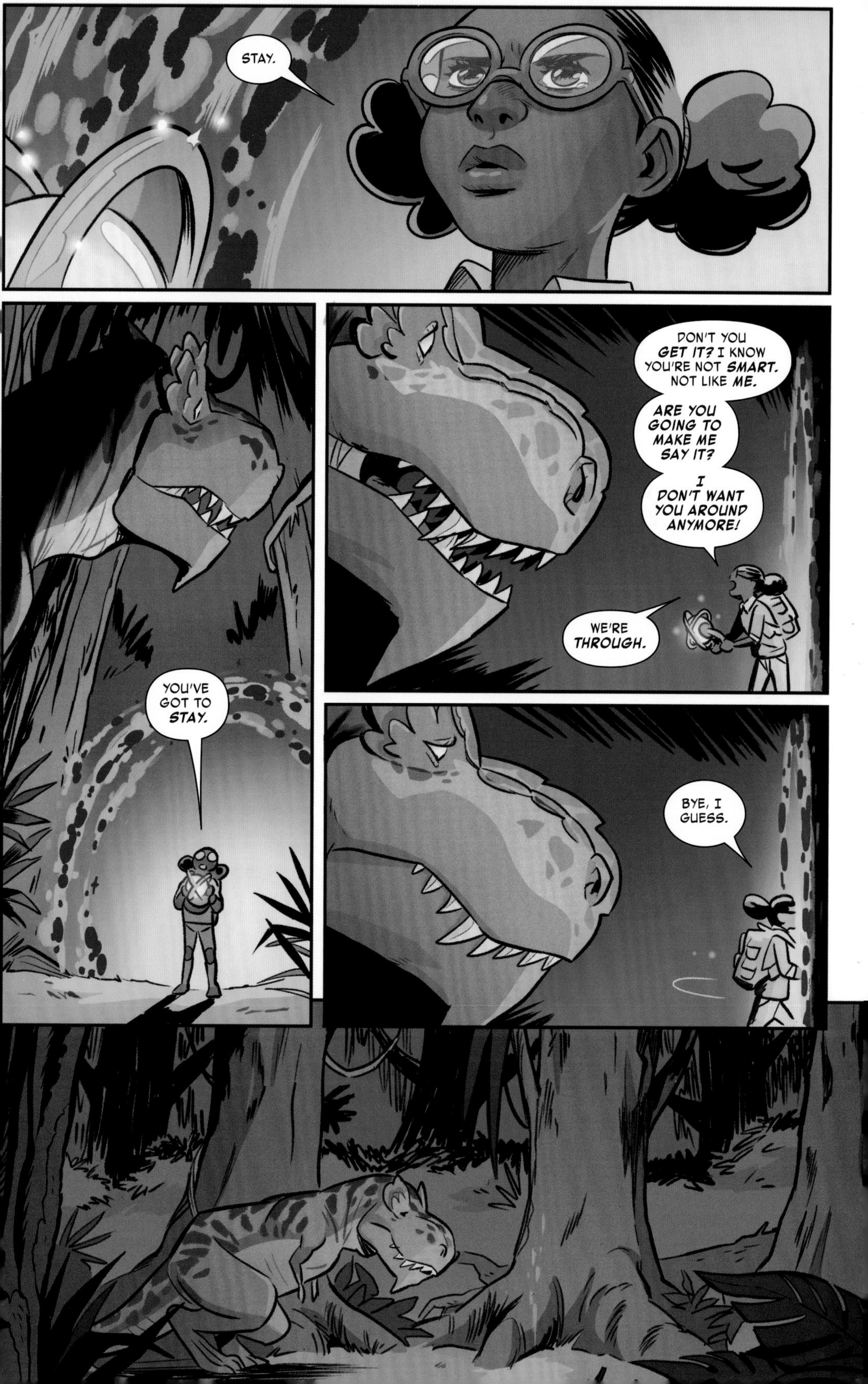
STAY.
YOU'VE GOT TO STAY.
DON'T YOU GET IT? I KNOW YOU'RE NOT SMART. NOT LIKE ME.
ARE YOU GOING TO MAKE ME SAY IT?
I DON'T WANT YOU AROUND ANYMORE!
WE'RE THROUGH.
BYE, I GUESS.

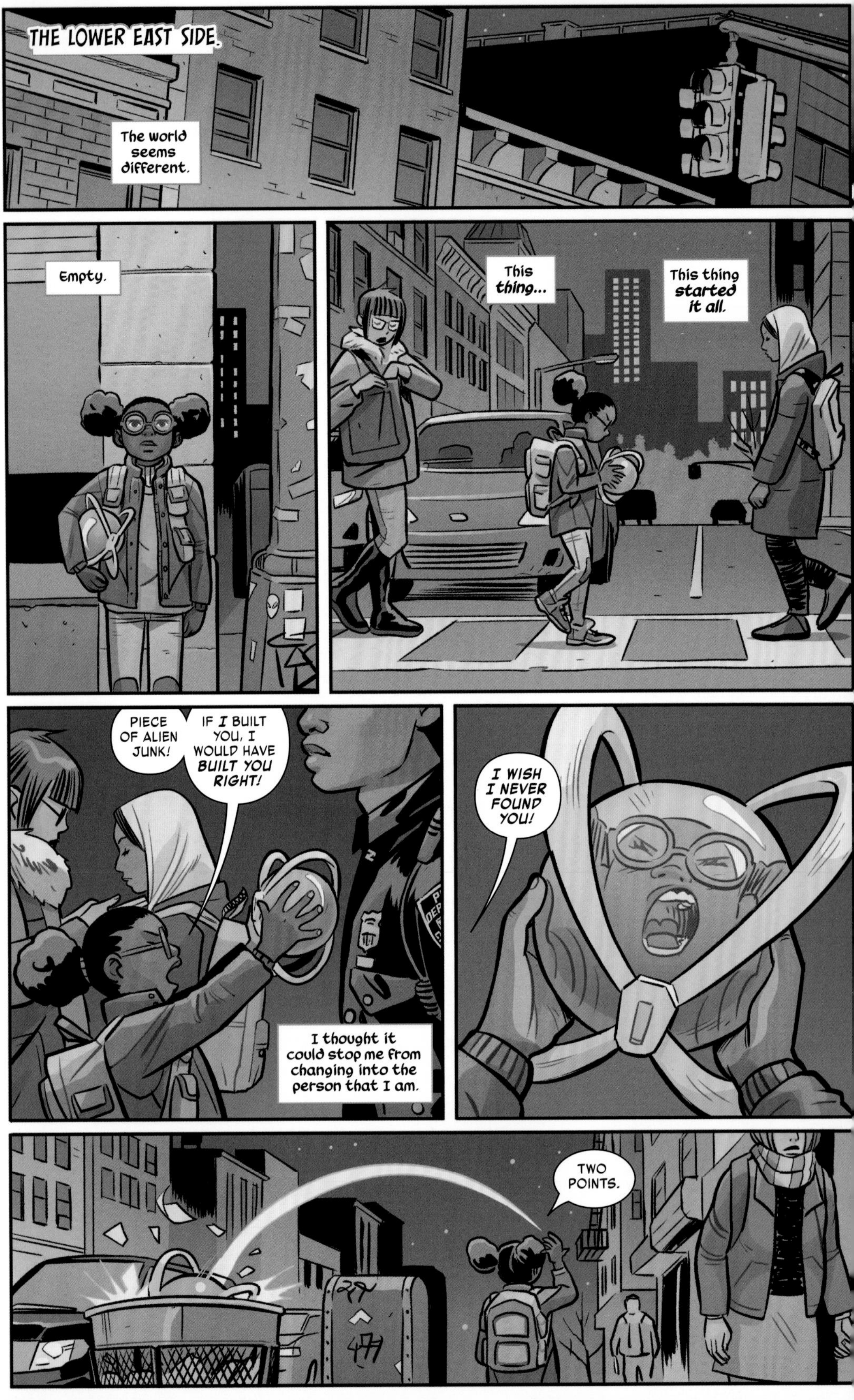
THE LOWER EAST SIDE.
The world seems different.
Empty.
This thing...
This thing started it all.
PIECE OF ALIEN JUNK!
IF I BUILT YOU, I WOULD HAVE BUILT YOU RIGHT!
I thought it could stop me from changing into the person that I am.
I WISH I NEVER FOUND YOU!
TWO POINTS.

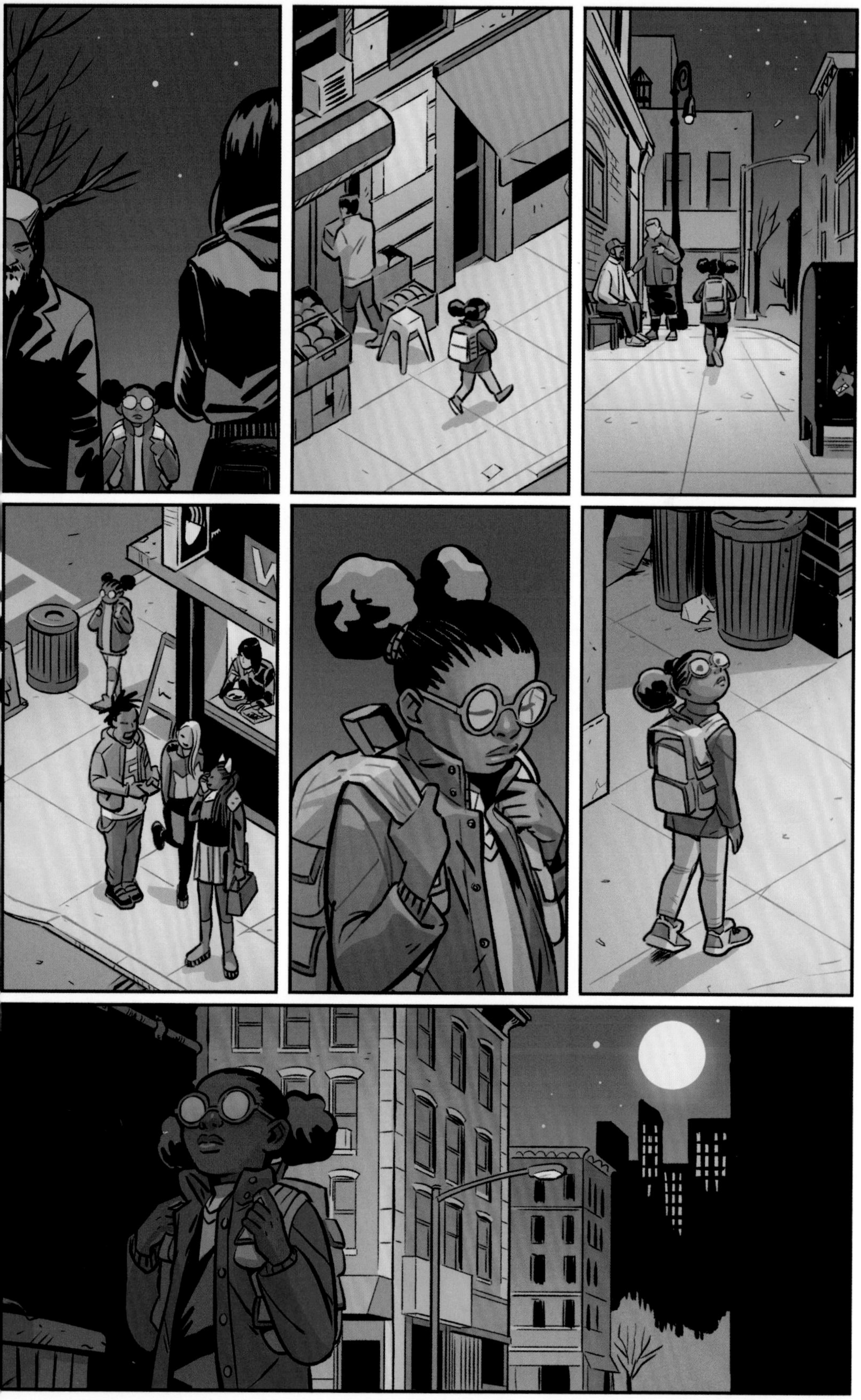

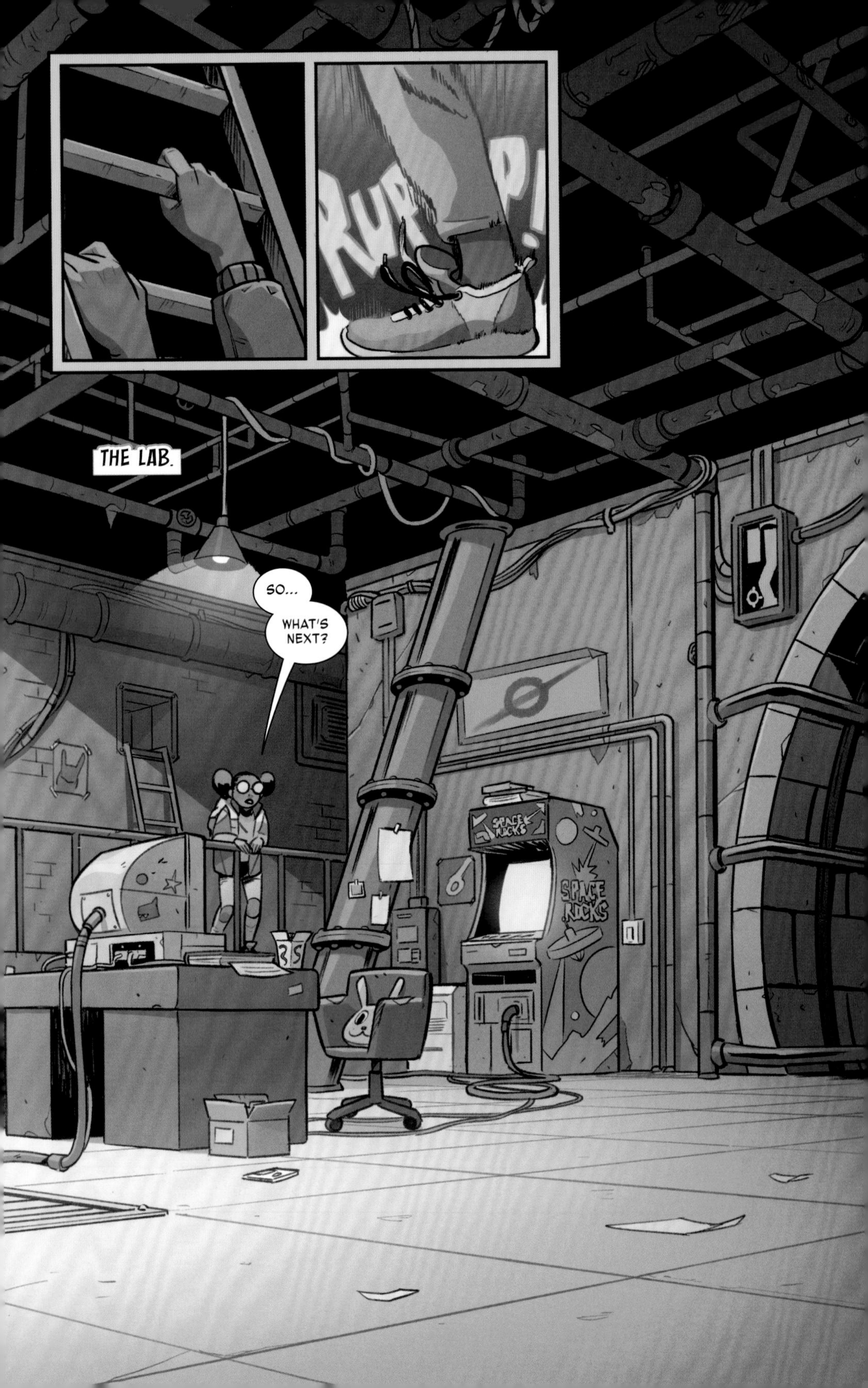
THE LAB.
SO...
WHAT'S NEXT?
SPACE ROCKS
SPACE ROCKS

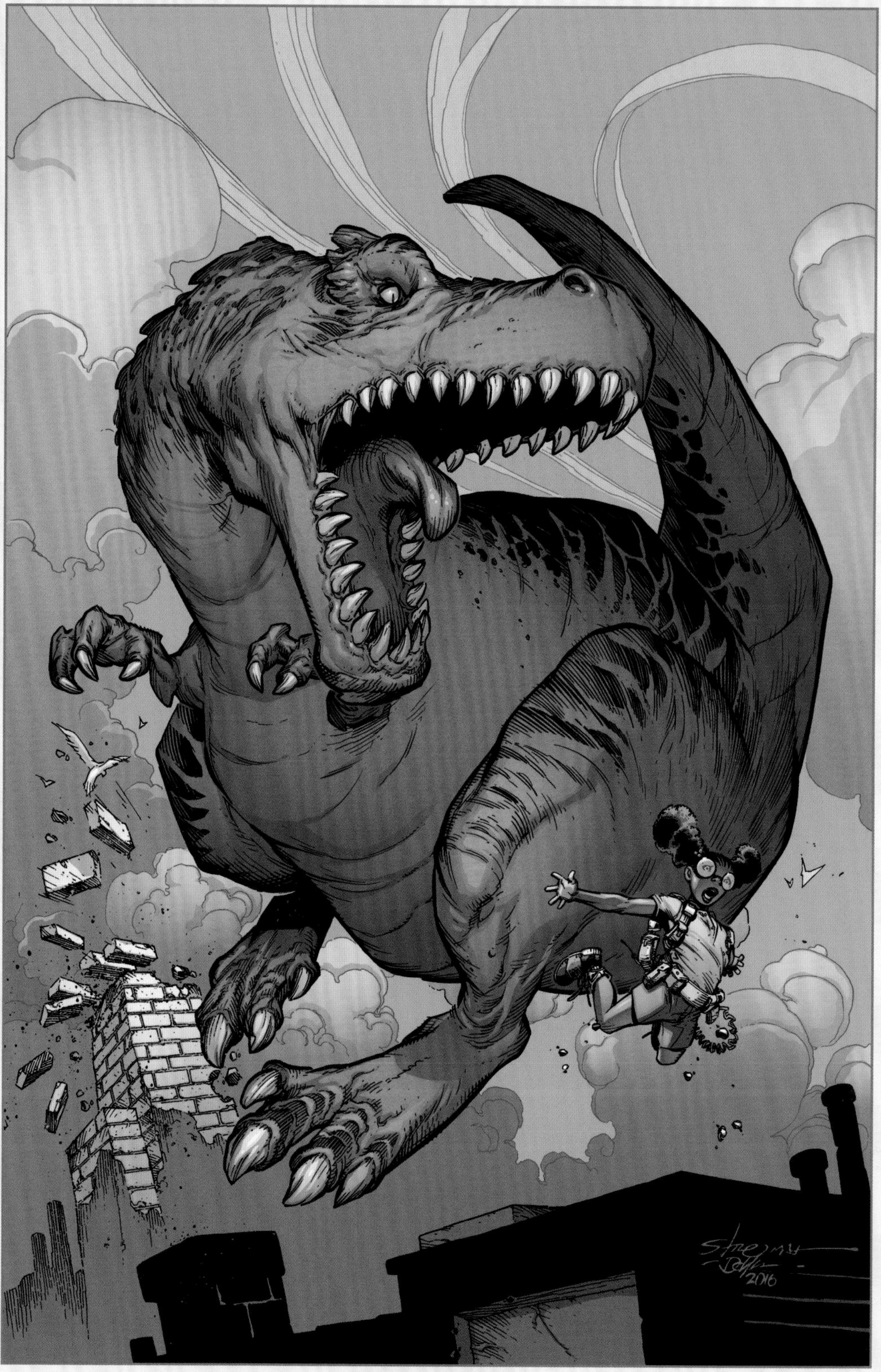

#13 VARIANT
BY LARRY STROMAN, JOHN DELL & DAVE McCAIG

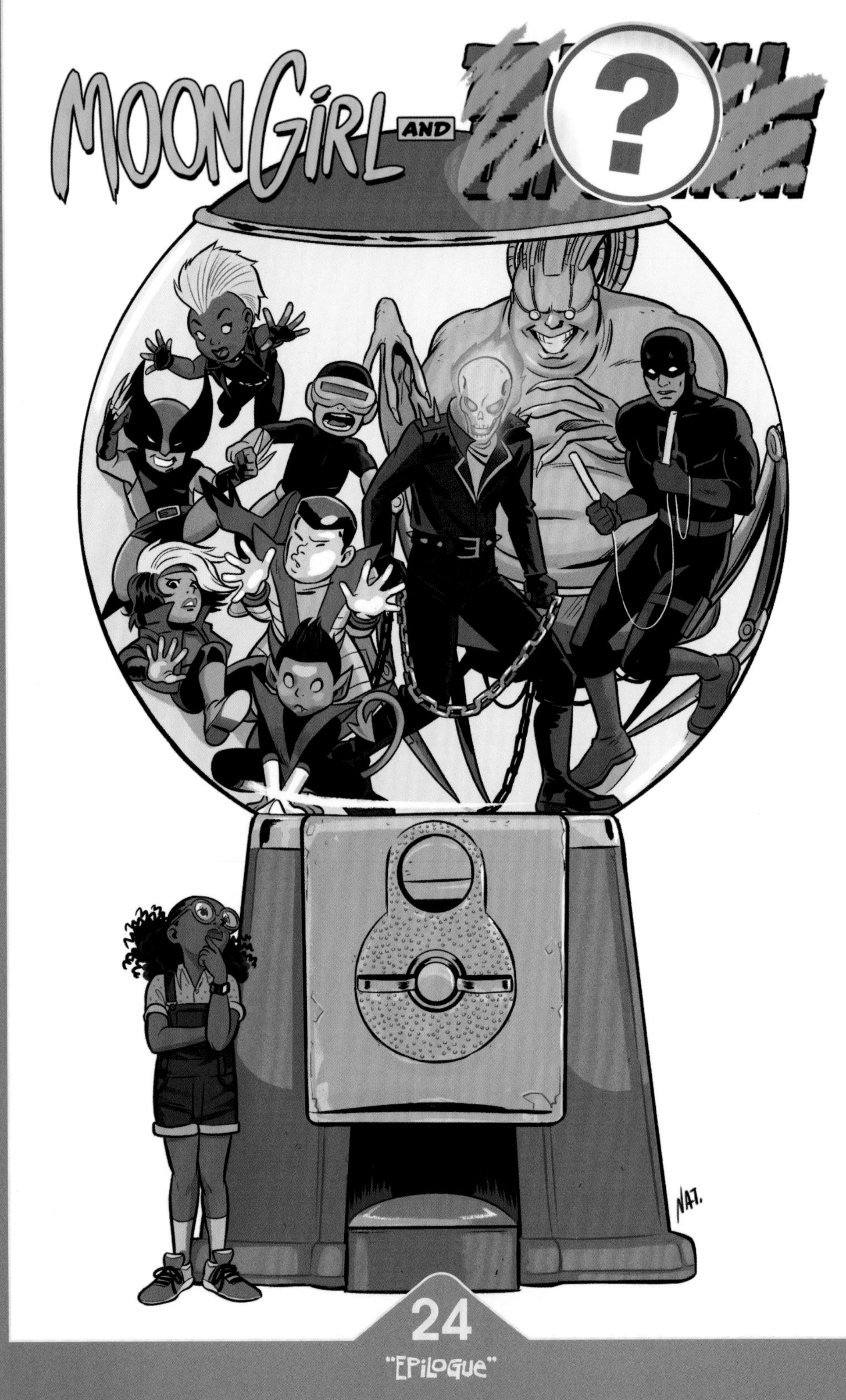
MOON GIRL AND ?
NAT.
24
"EPILOGUE"

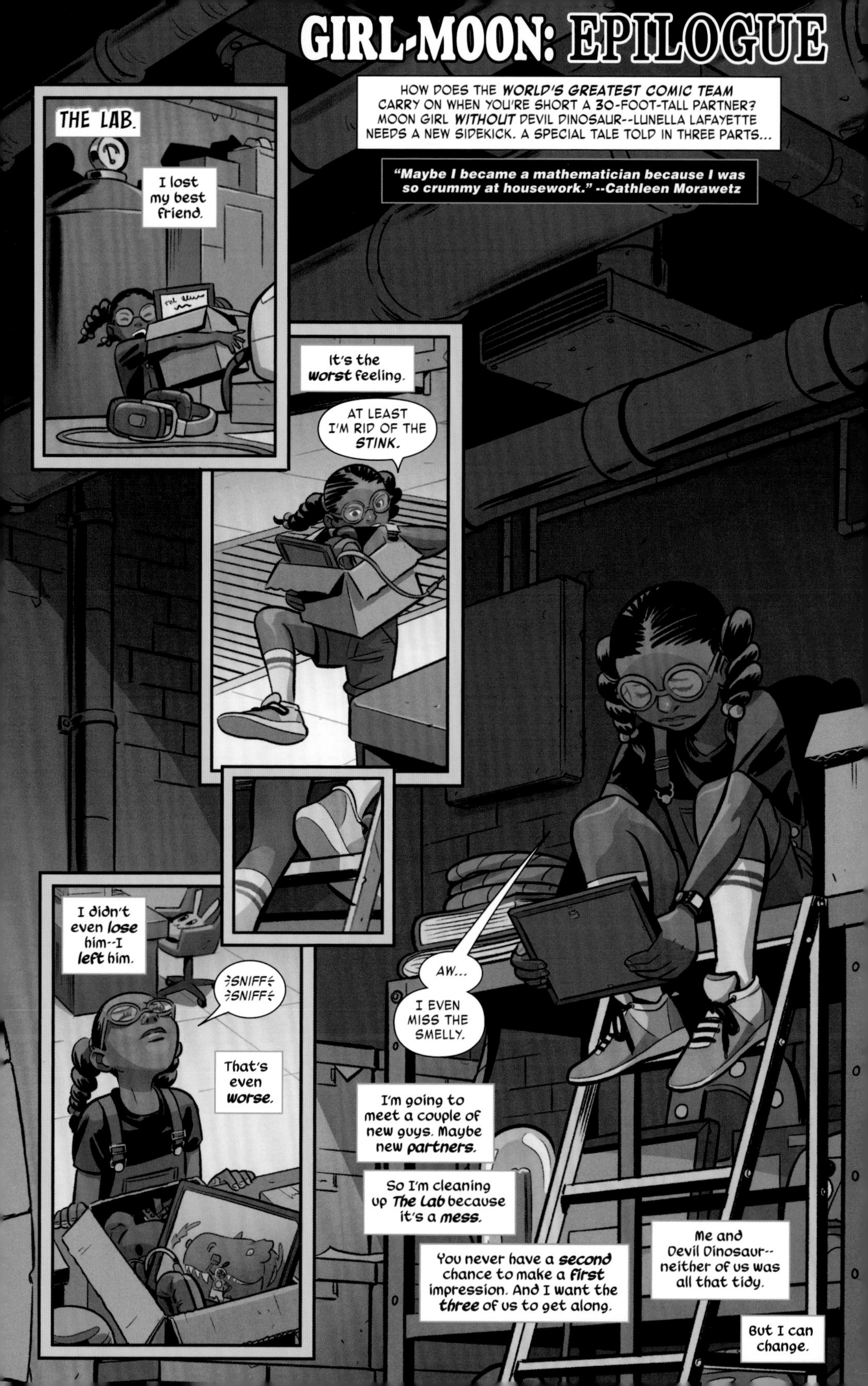
GIRL-MOON: EPILOGUE
HOW DOES THE WORLD'S GREATEST COMIC TEAM CARRY ON WHEN YOU'RE SHORT A 30-FOOT-TALL PARTNER? MOON GIRL WITHOUT DEVIL DINOSAUR--LUNELLA LAFAYETTE NEEDS A NEW SIDEKICK. A SPECIAL TALE TOLD IN THREE PARTS...
"Maybe I became a mathematician because I was so crummy at housework." --Cathleen Morawetz
THE LAB.
I lost my best friend.
It's the worst feeling.
AT LEAST I'M RID OF THE STINK.
I didn't even lose him--I left him.
SNIFF SNIFF
That's even worse.
AW...
I EVEN MISS THE SMELLY.
I'm going to meet a couple of new guys. Maybe new partners.
So I'm cleaning up The Lab because it's a mess.
You never have a second chance to make a first impression. And I want the three of us to get along.
Me and Devil Dinosaur--neither of us was all that tidy.
But I can change.

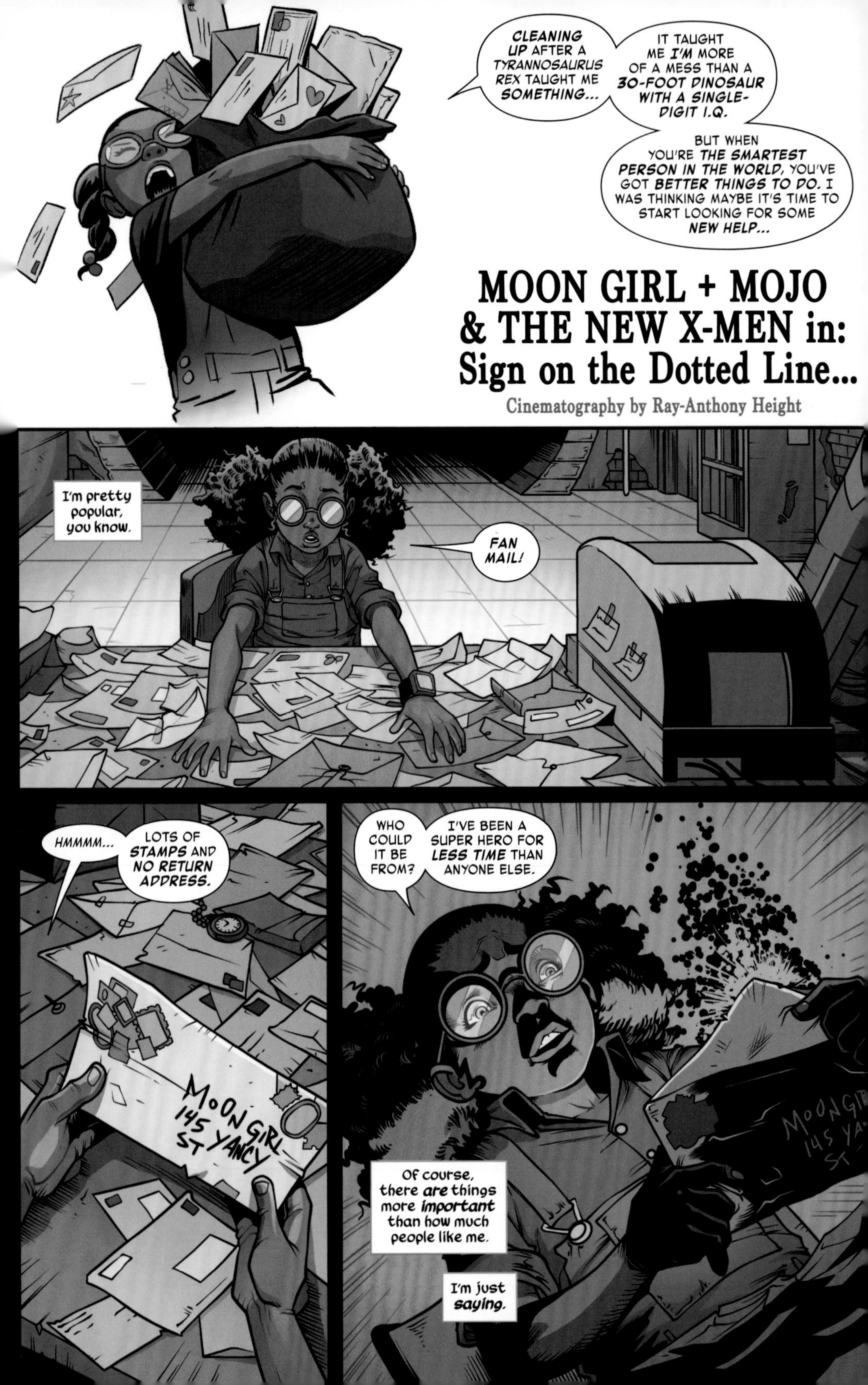
CLEANING UP AFTER A TYRANNOSAURUS REX TAUGHT ME SOMETHING...
IT TAUGHT ME I'M MORE OF A MESS THAN A 30-FOOT DINOSAUR WITH A SINGLE-DIGIT I.Q.
BUT WHEN YOU'RE THE SMARTEST PERSON IN THE WORLD, YOU'VE GOT BETTER THINGS TO DO. I WAS THINKING MAYBE IT'S TIME TO START LOOKING FOR SOME NEW HELP...
MOON GIRL + MOJO & THE NEW X-MEN in: Sign on the Dotted Line...
Cinematography by Ray-Anthony Height
I'm pretty popular, you know.
FAN MAIL!
HMMMM...
LOTS OF STAMPS AND NO RETURN ADDRESS.
MOON GIRL 145 ST YANCY
WHO COULD IT BE FROM?
I'VE BEEN A SUPER HERO FOR LESS TIME THAN ANYONE ELSE.
Of course, there are things more important than how much people like me.
I'm just saying.

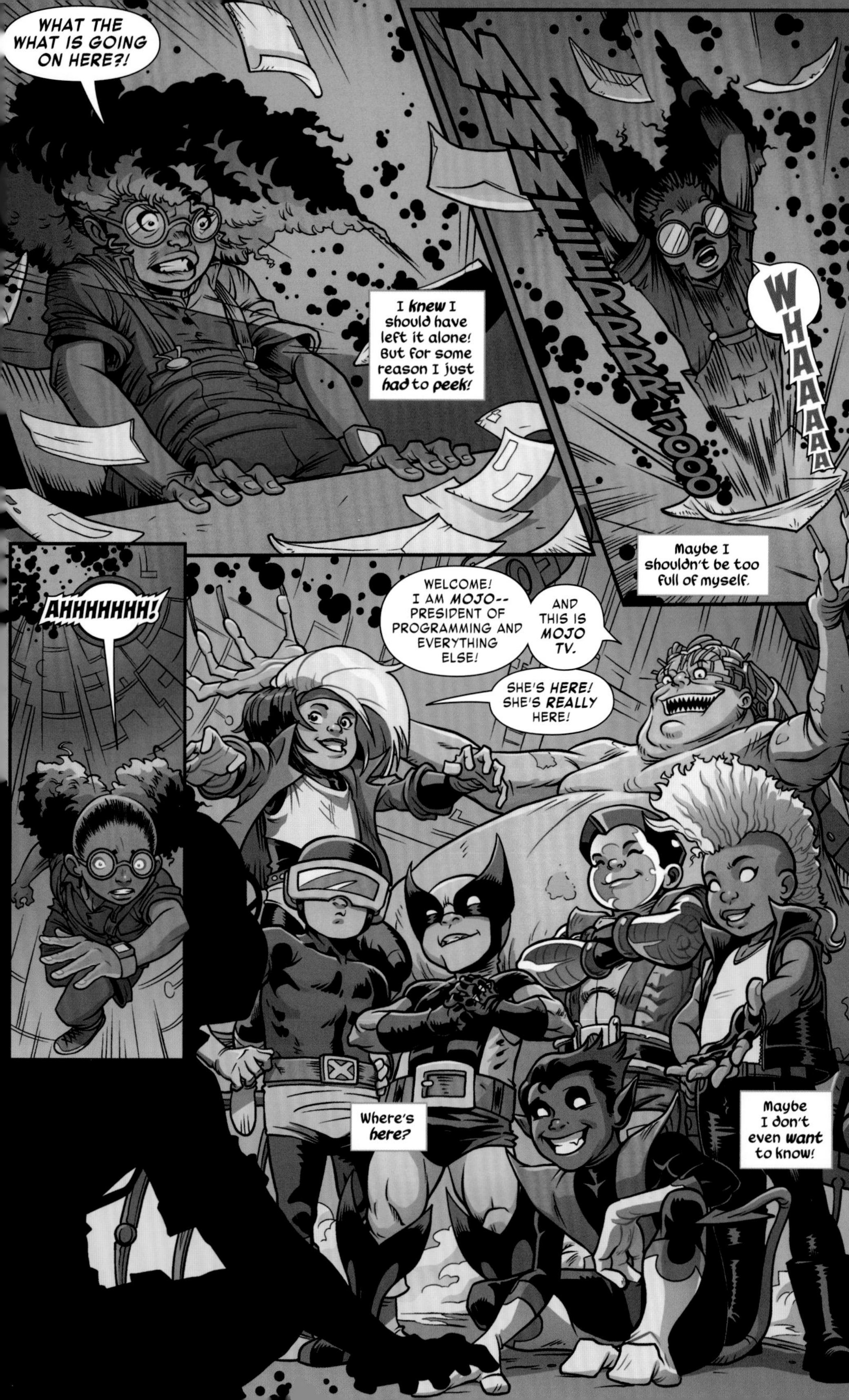

WHAT THE WHAT IS GOING ON HERE?!
I knew I should have left it alone! But for some reason I just had to peek!
MMMEERRRRR'DOOOO
WHAAAAAA
Maybe I shouldn't be too full of myself.
AHHHHHHH!
WELCOME! I AM MOJO-- PRESIDENT OF PROGRAMMING AND EVERYTHING ELSE!
AND THIS IS MOJO TV.
SHE'S HERE! SHE'S REALLY HERE!
Where's here?
Maybe I don't even want to know!

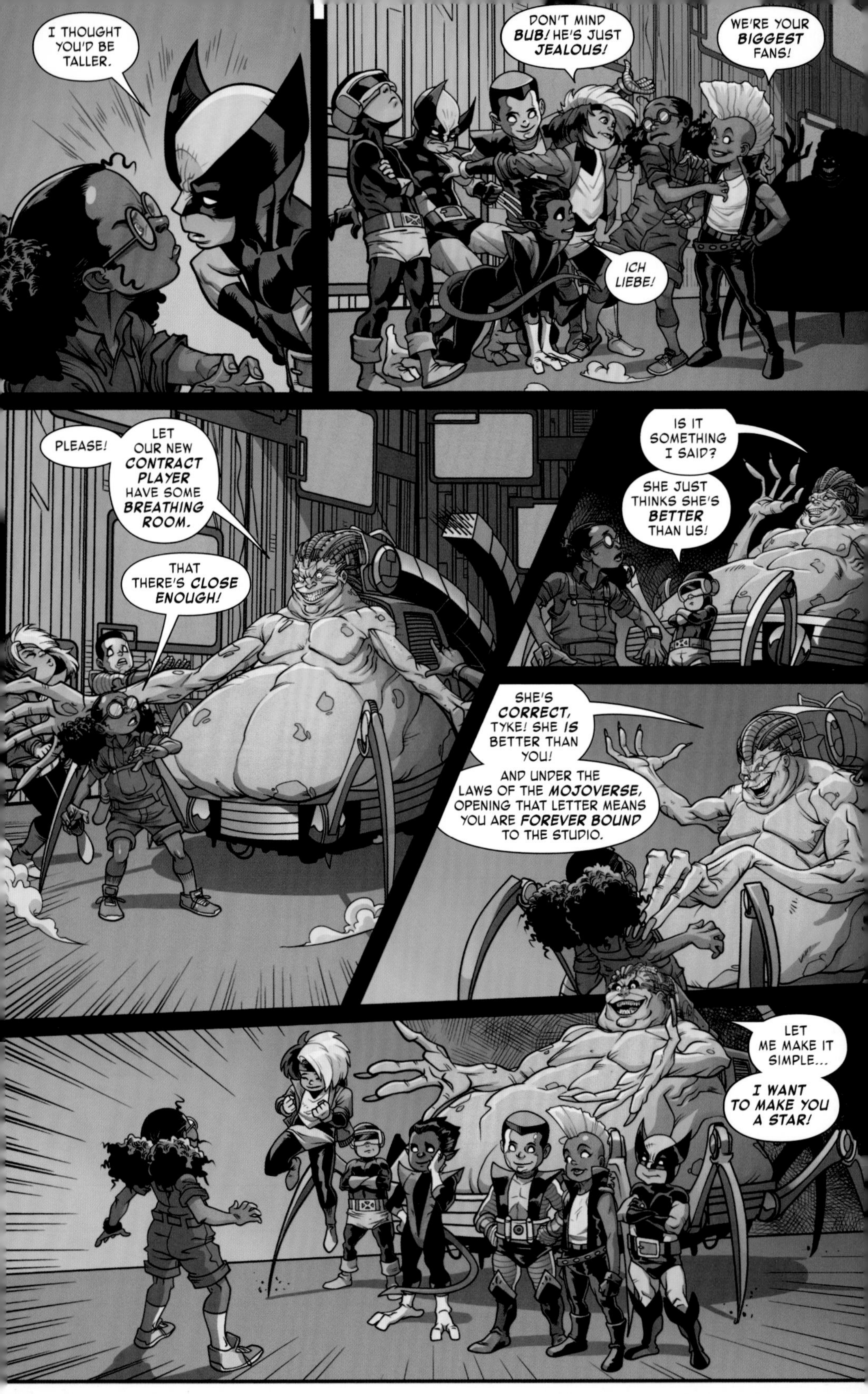

I THOUGHT YOU'D BE TALLER.
DON'T MIND BUB! HE'S JUST JEALOUS!
WE'RE YOUR BIGGEST FANS!
ICH LIEBE!
PLEASE!
LET OUR NEW CONTRACT PLAYER HAVE SOME BREATHING ROOM.
THAT THERE'S CLOSE ENOUGH!
IS IT SOMETHING I SAID?
SHE JUST THINKS SHE'S BETTER THAN US!
SHE'S CORRECT, TYKE! SHE IS BETTER THAN YOU!
AND UNDER THE LAWS OF THE MOJOVERSE, OPENING THAT LETTER MEANS YOU ARE FOREVER BOUND TO THE STUDIO.
LET ME MAKE IT SIMPLE...
I WANT TO MAKE YOU A STAR!

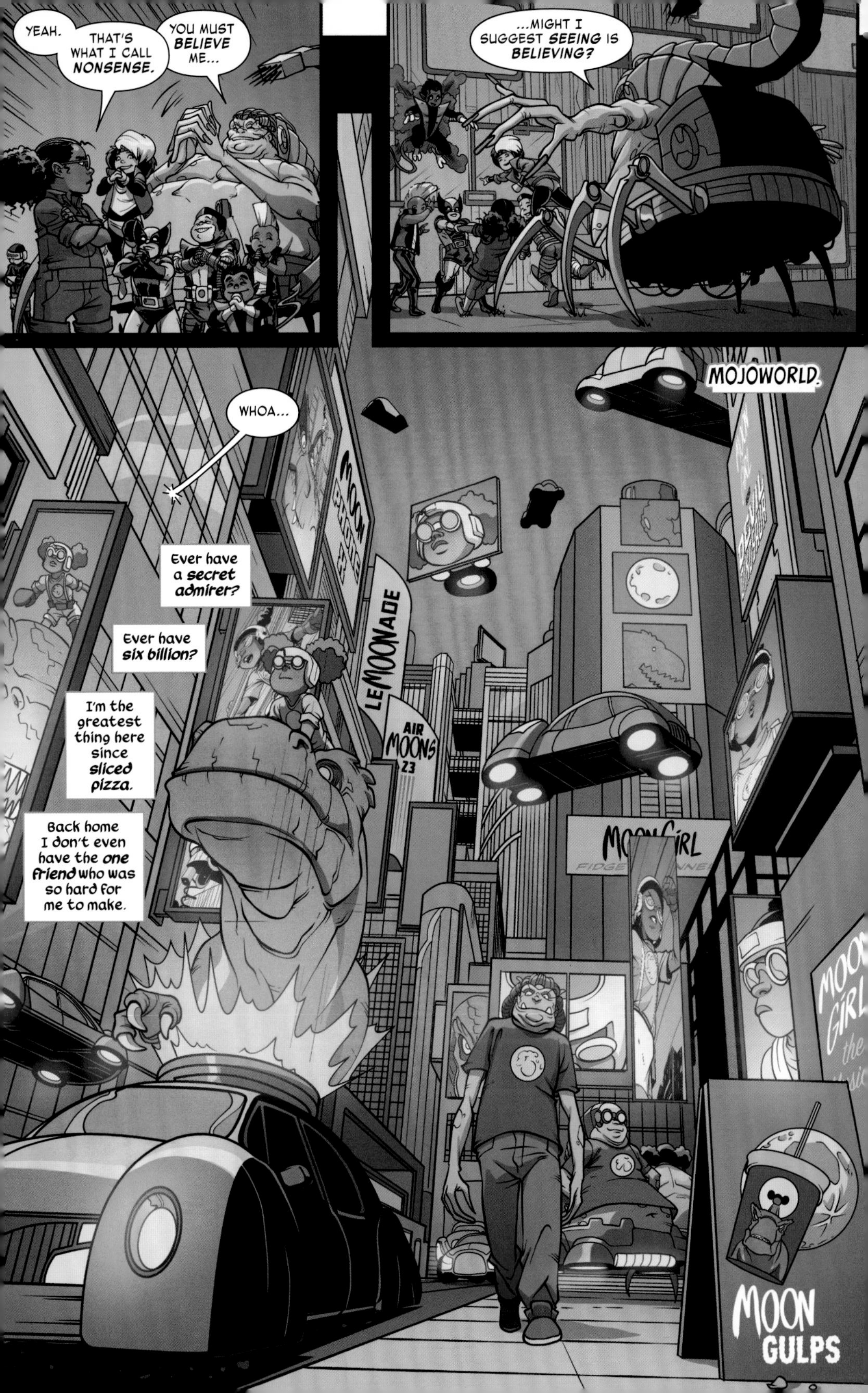
YEAH.
THAT'S WHAT I CALL NONSENSE.
YOU MUST BELIEVE ME...
...MIGHT I SUGGEST SEEING IS BELIEVING?
MOJOWORLD.
WHOA...
Ever have a secret admirer?
Ever have six billion?
I'm the greatest thing here since sliced pizza.
Back home I don't even have the one friend who was so hard for me to make.
LEMOONADE
AIR MOONS 23
MOON GIRL
MOON GULPS

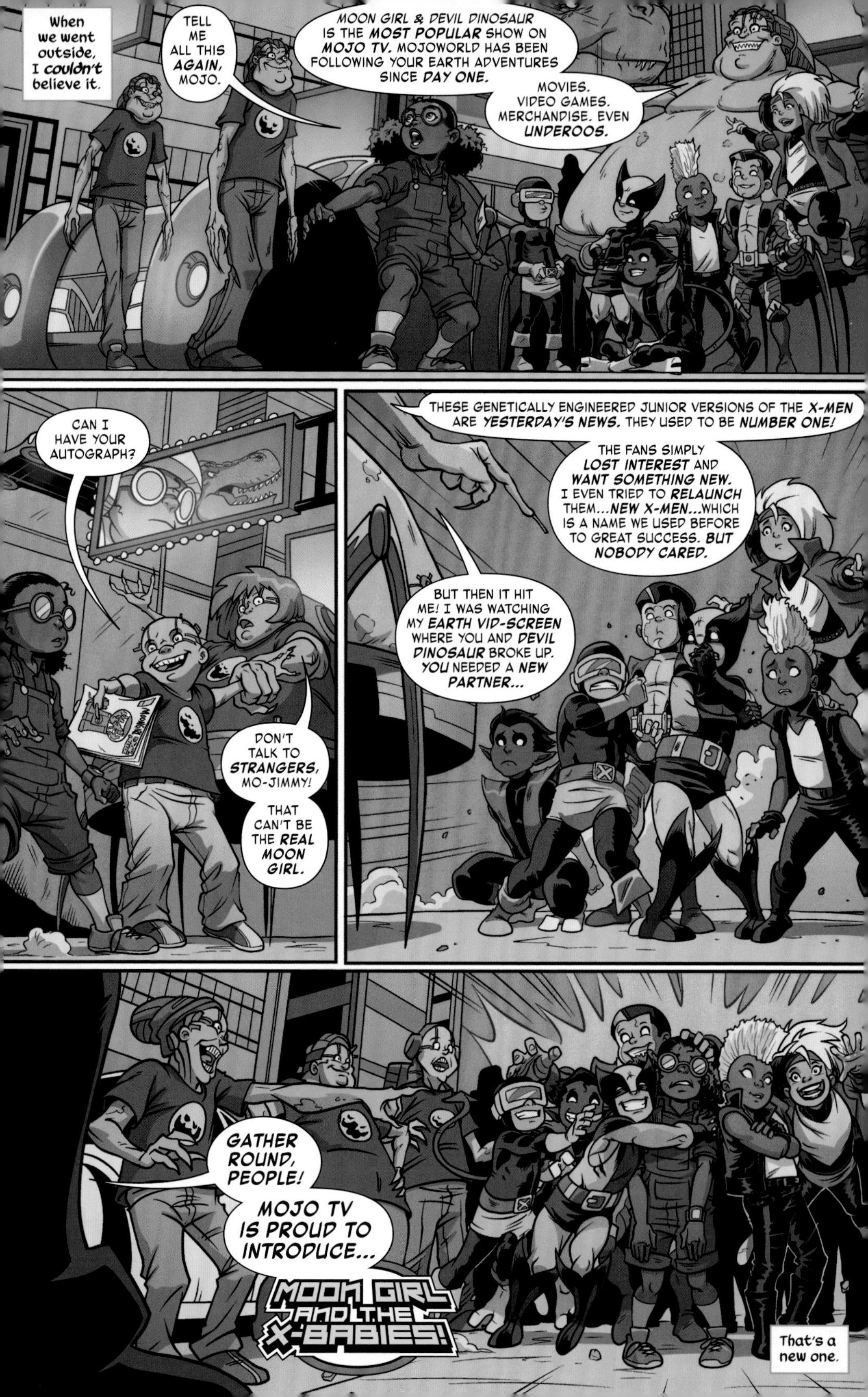

When we went outside, I couldn't believe it.
TELL ME ALL THIS AGAIN, MOJO.
MOON GIRL & DEVIL DINOSAUR IS THE MOST POPULAR SHOW ON MOJO TV. MOJOWORLD HAS BEEN FOLLOWING YOUR EARTH ADVENTURES SINCE DAY ONE.
MOVIES. VIDEO GAMES. MERCHANDISE. EVEN UNDEROOS.
CAN I HAVE YOUR AUTOGRAPH?
DON'T TALK TO STRANGERS, MO-JIMMY!
THAT CAN'T BE THE REAL MOON GIRL.
THESE GENETICALLY ENGINEERED JUNIOR VERSIONS OF THE X-MEN ARE YESTERDAY'S NEWS. THEY USED TO BE NUMBER ONE!
THE FANS SIMPLY LOST INTEREST AND WANT SOMETHING NEW. I EVEN TRIED TO RELAUNCH THEM...NEW X-MEN...WHICH IS A NAME WE USED BEFORE TO GREAT SUCCESS. BUT NOBODY CARED.
BUT THEN IT HIT ME! I WAS WATCHING MY EARTH VID-SCREEN WHERE YOU AND DEVIL DINOSAUR BROKE UP. YOU NEEDED A NEW PARTNER...
GATHER ROUND, PEOPLE!
MOJO TV IS PROUD TO INTRODUCE...
MOON GIRL AND THE X-BABIES!
That's a new one.

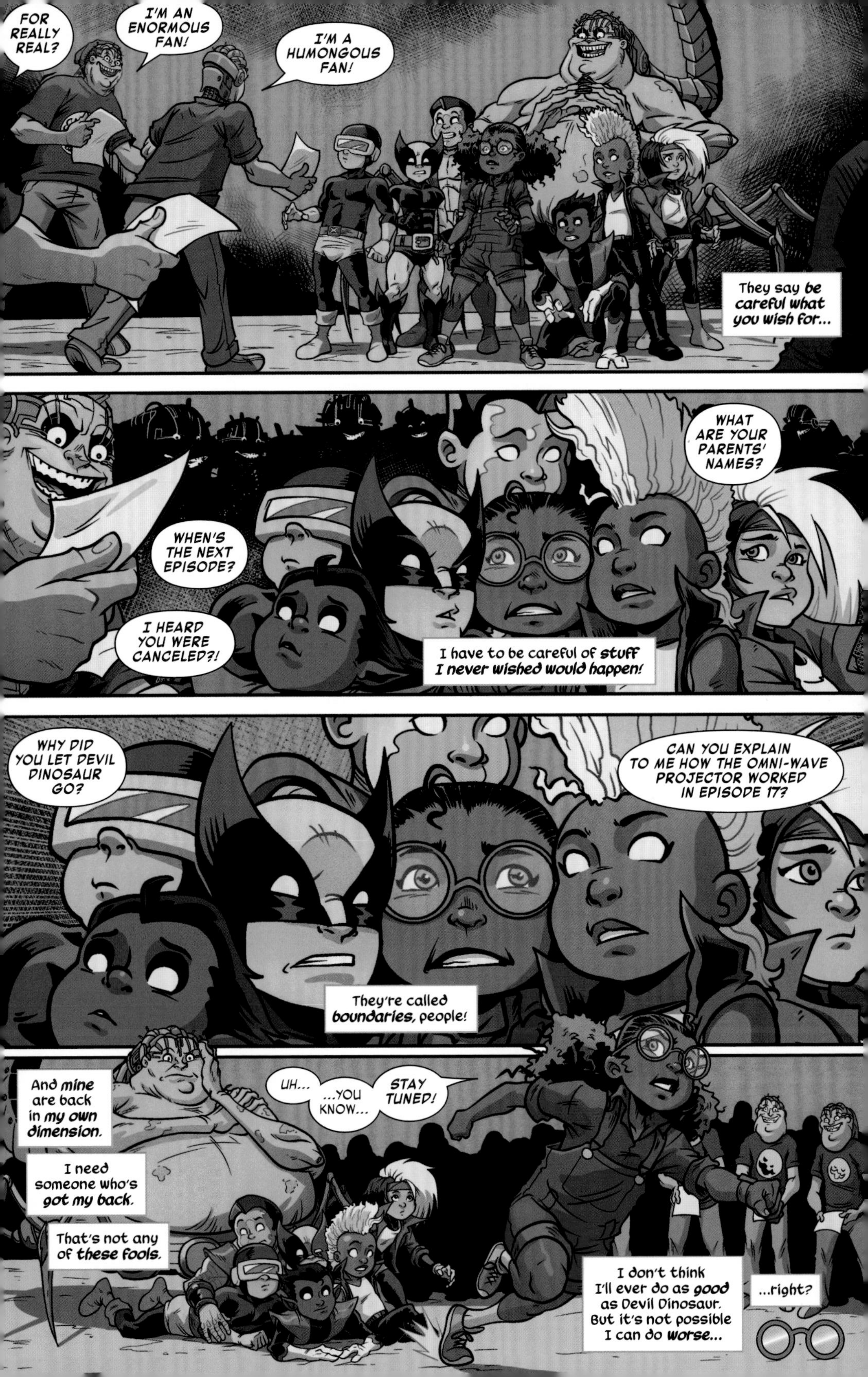

FOR REALLY REAL?
I'M AN ENORMOUS FAN!
I'M A HUMONGOUS FAN!
They say be careful what you wish for...
WHAT ARE YOUR PARENTS' NAMES?
WHEN'S THE NEXT EPISODE?
I HEARD YOU WERE CANCELED?!
I have to be careful of stuff I never wished would happen!
WHY DID YOU LET DEVIL DINOSAUR GO?
CAN YOU EXPLAIN TO ME HOW THE OMNI-WAVE PROJECTOR WORKED IN EPISODE 17?
They're called boundaries, people!
And mine are back in my own dimension.
I need someone who's got my back.
That's not any of these fools.
UH...
...YOU KNOW...
STAY TUNED!
I don't think I'll ever do as good as Devil Dinosaur. But it's not possible I can do worse...
...right?

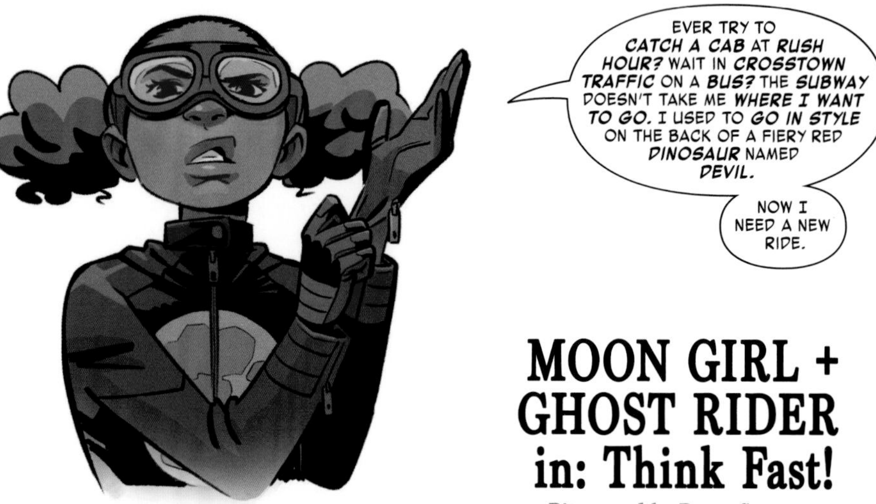
EVER TRY TO CATCH A CAB AT RUSH HOUR? WAIT IN CROSSTOWN TRAFFIC ON A BUS? THE SUBWAY DOESN'T TAKE ME WHERE I WANT TO GO. I USED TO GO IN STYLE ON THE BACK OF A FIERY RED DINOSAUR NAMED DEVIL.
NOW I NEED A NEW RIDE.

MOON GIRL + GHOST RIDER in: Think Fast!

Pit crewed by Domo Stanton

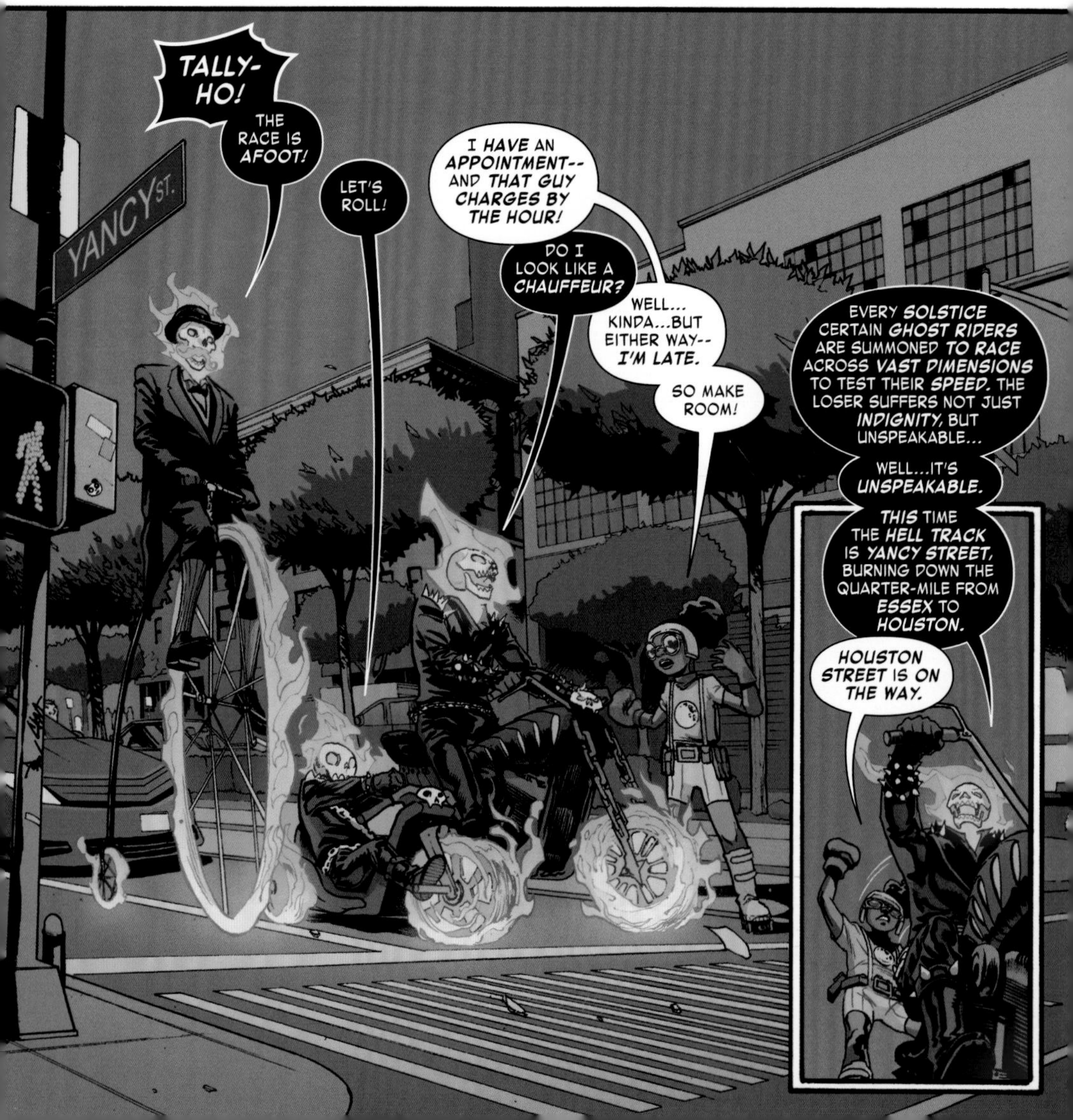
TALLY-HO!
THE RACE IS AFOOT!
YANCY ST.
LET'S ROLL!
I HAVE AN APPOINTMENT-- AND THAT GUY CHARGES BY THE HOUR!
DO I LOOK LIKE A CHAUFFEUR?
WELL... KINDA...BUT EITHER WAY-- I'M LATE.
SO MAKE ROOM!
EVERY SOLSTICE CERTAIN GHOST RIDERS ARE SUMMONED TO RACE ACROSS VAST DIMENSIONS TO TEST THEIR SPEED. THE LOSER SUFFERS NOT JUST INDIGNITY, BUT UNSPEAKABLE...
WELL...IT'S UNSPEAKABLE.
THIS TIME THE HELL TRACK IS YANCY STREET, BURNING DOWN THE QUARTER-MILE FROM ESSEX TO HOUSTON.
HOUSTON STREET IS ON THE WAY.

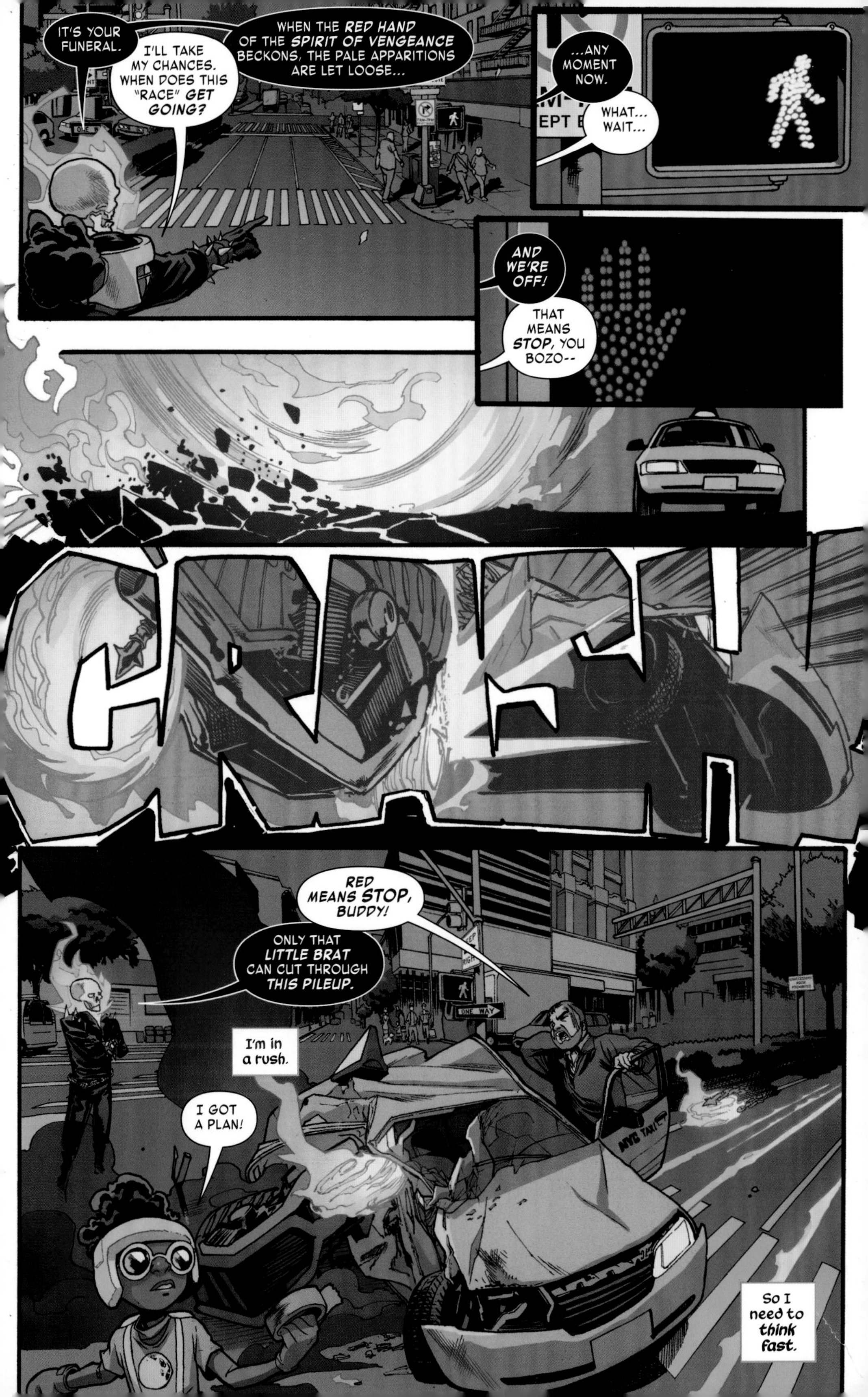

IT'S YOUR FUNERAL.
I'LL TAKE MY CHANCES. WHEN DOES THIS "RACE" GET GOING?
WHEN THE RED HAND OF THE SPIRIT OF VENGEANCE BECKONS, THE PALE APPARITIONS ARE LET LOOSE...
...ANY MOMENT NOW.
WHAT... WAIT...
AND WE'RE OFF!
THAT MEANS STOP, YOU BOZO--
RED MEANS STOP, BUDDY!
ONLY THAT LITTLE BRAT CAN CUT THROUGH THIS PILEUP.
I'm in a rush.
I GOT A PLAN!
So I need to think fast.

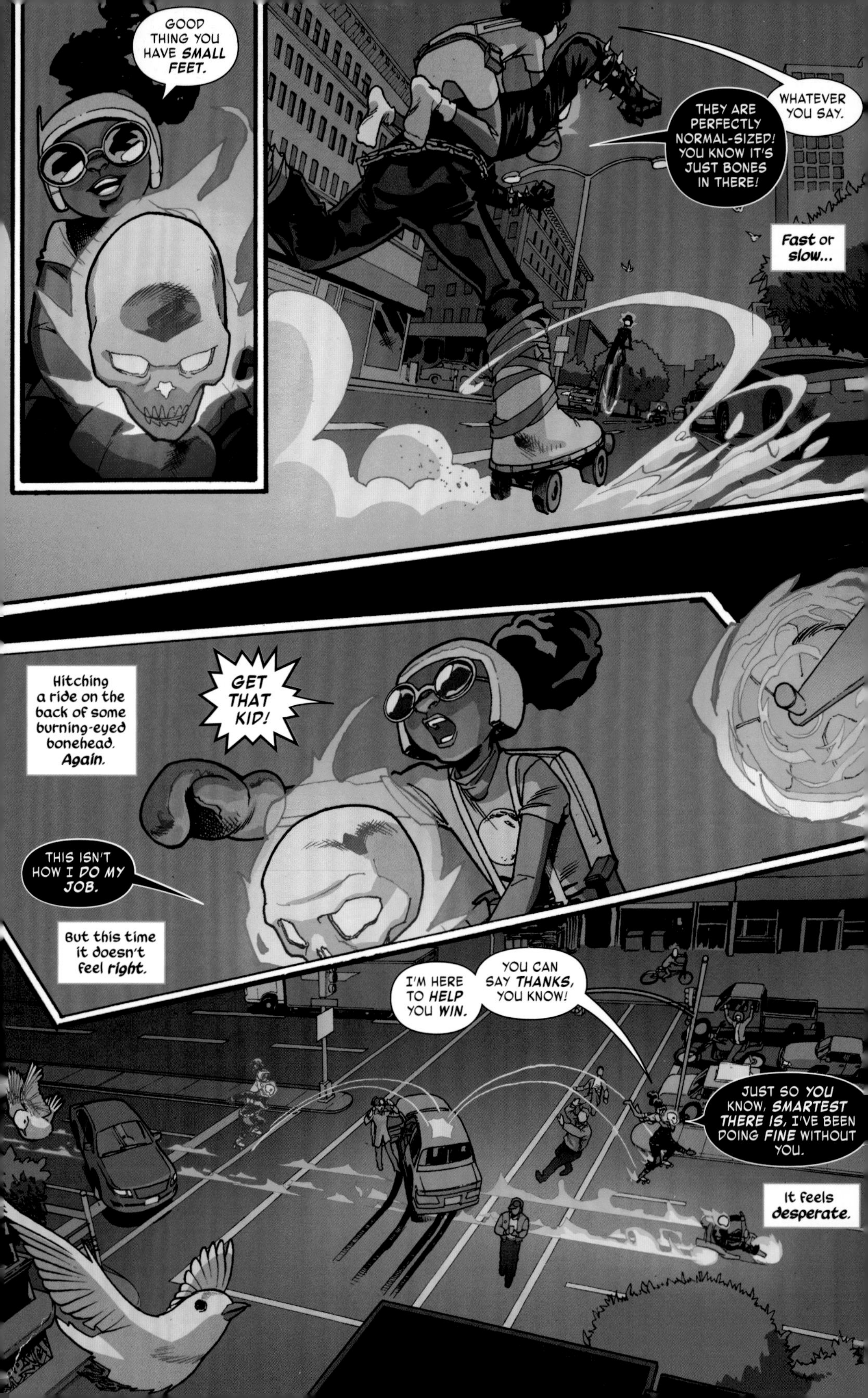
GOOD THING YOU HAVE SMALL FEET.
WHATEVER YOU SAY.
THEY ARE PERFECTLY NORMAL-SIZED! YOU KNOW IT'S JUST BONES IN THERE!
Fast or slow...
Hitching a ride on the back of some burning-eyed bonehead. Again.
GET THAT KID!
THIS ISN'T HOW I DO MY JOB.
But this time it doesn't feel right.
I'M HERE TO HELP YOU WIN.
YOU CAN SAY THANKS, YOU KNOW!
JUST SO YOU KNOW, SMARTEST THERE IS, I'VE BEEN DOING FINE WITHOUT YOU.
It feels desperate.

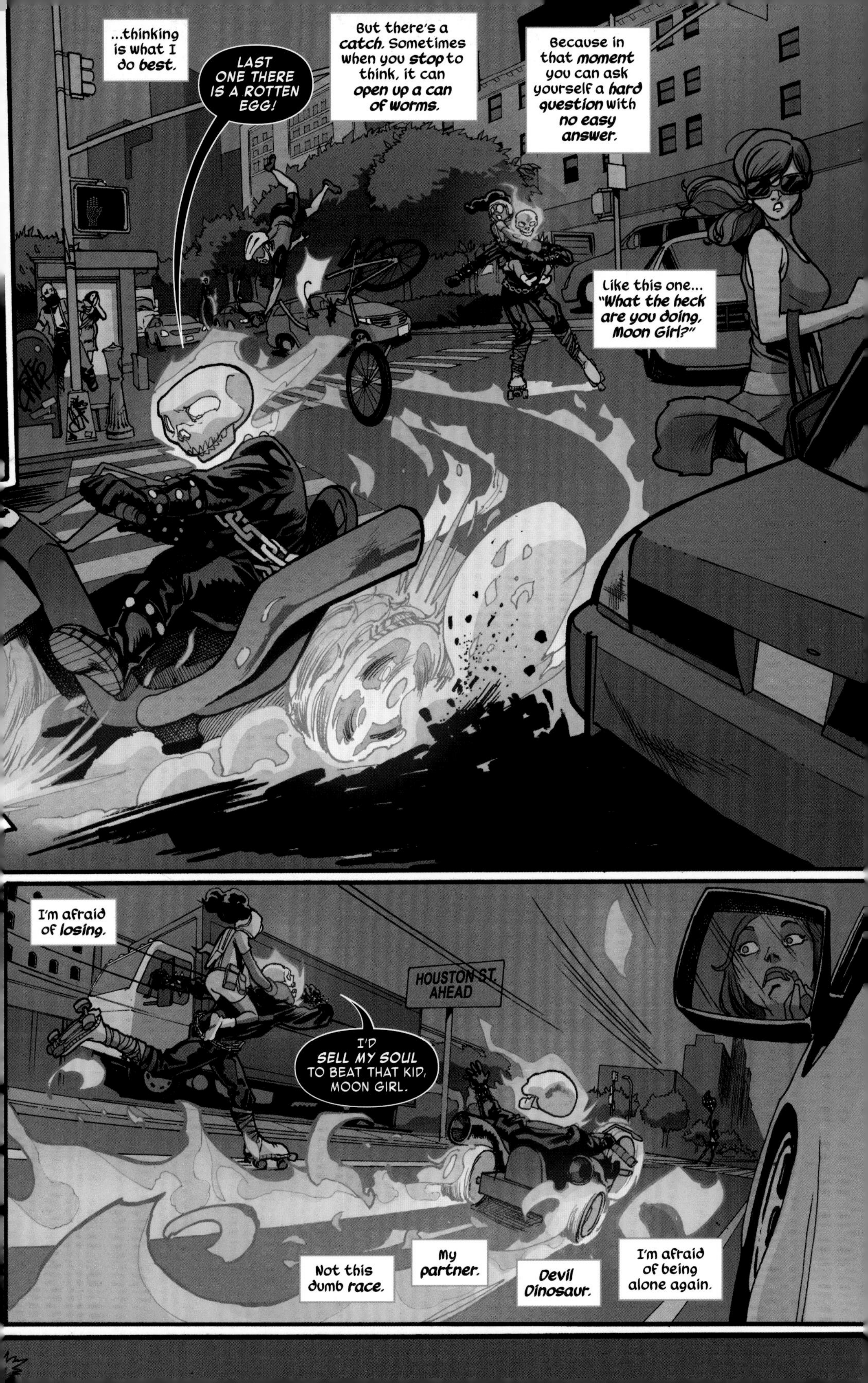

...thinking is what I do best.
LAST ONE THERE IS A ROTTEN EGG!
But there's a catch. Sometimes when you stop to think, it can open up a can of worms.
Because in that moment you can ask yourself a hard question with no easy answer.
Like this one... "What the heck are you doing, Moon Girl?"
I'm afraid of losing.
HOUSTON ST. AHEAD
I'D SELL MY SOUL TO BEAT THAT KID, MOON GIRL.
Not this dumb race.
My partner.
Devil Dinosaur.
I'm afraid of being alone again.

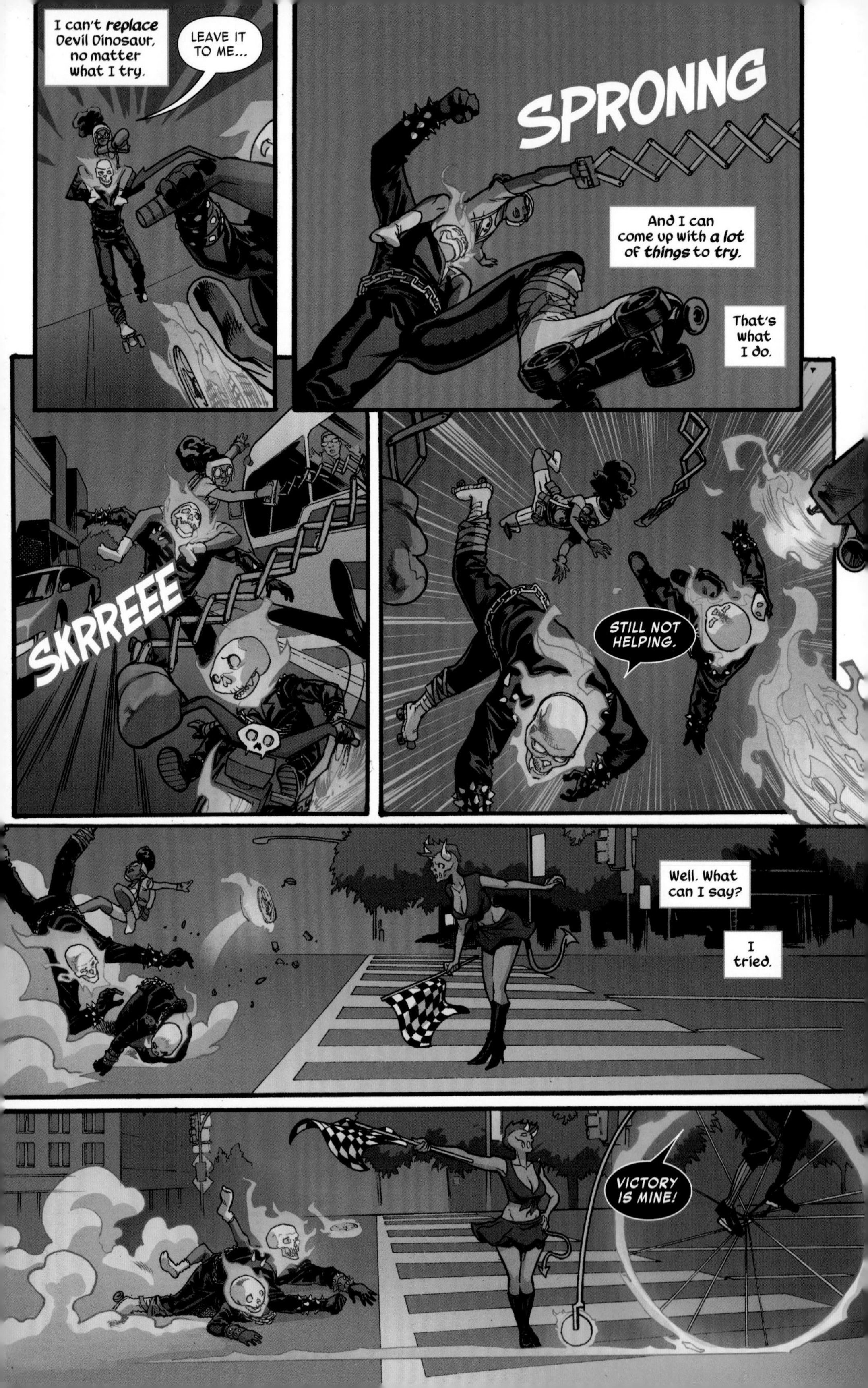
I can't *replace* Devil Dinosaur, no matter what I try.
LEAVE IT TO ME...
SPRONNG
And I can come up with *a lot* of *things* to *try*.
That's what I do.
SKRREEE
STILL NOT HELPING.
Well. What can I say?
I tried.
VICTORY IS MINE!

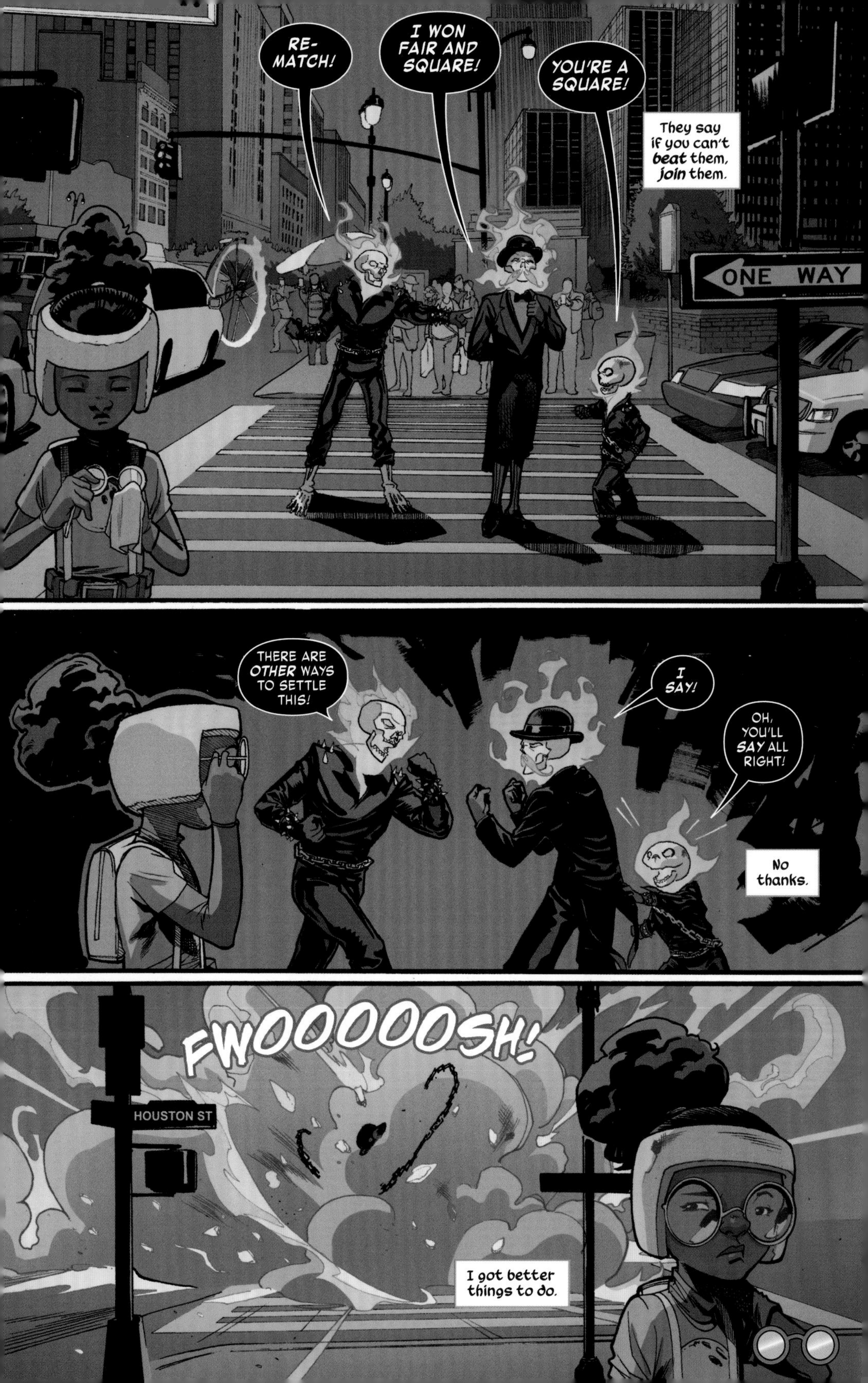
RE-MATCH!
I WON FAIR AND SQUARE!
YOU'RE A SQUARE!
They say if you can't beat them, join them.
ONE WAY
THERE ARE OTHER WAYS TO SETTLE THIS!
I SAY!
OH, YOU'LL SAY ALL RIGHT!
No thanks.
FWOOOOOOSH!
HOUSTON ST
I got better things to do.

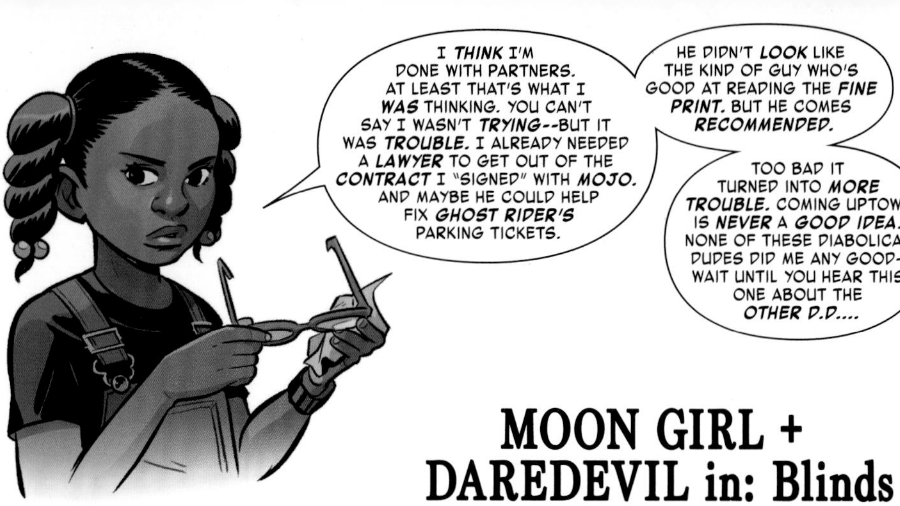
I THINK I'M DONE WITH PARTNERS. AT LEAST THAT'S WHAT I WAS THINKING. YOU CAN'T SAY I WASN'T TRYING--BUT IT WAS TROUBLE. I ALREADY NEEDED A LAWYER TO GET OUT OF THE CONTRACT I "SIGNED" WITH MOJO. AND MAYBE HE COULD HELP FIX GHOST RIDER'S PARKING TICKETS.
HE DIDN'T LOOK LIKE THE KIND OF GUY WHO'S GOOD AT READING THE FINE PRINT. BUT HE COMES RECOMMENDED.
TOO BAD IT TURNED INTO MORE TROUBLE. COMING UPTOWN IS NEVER A GOOD IDEA. NONE OF THESE DIABOLICAL DUDES DID ME ANY GOOD--WAIT UNTIL YOU HEAR THIS ONE ABOUT THE OTHER D.D....

MOON GIRL + DAREDEVIL in: Blinds

Courtroom sketches by Michael Shelfer

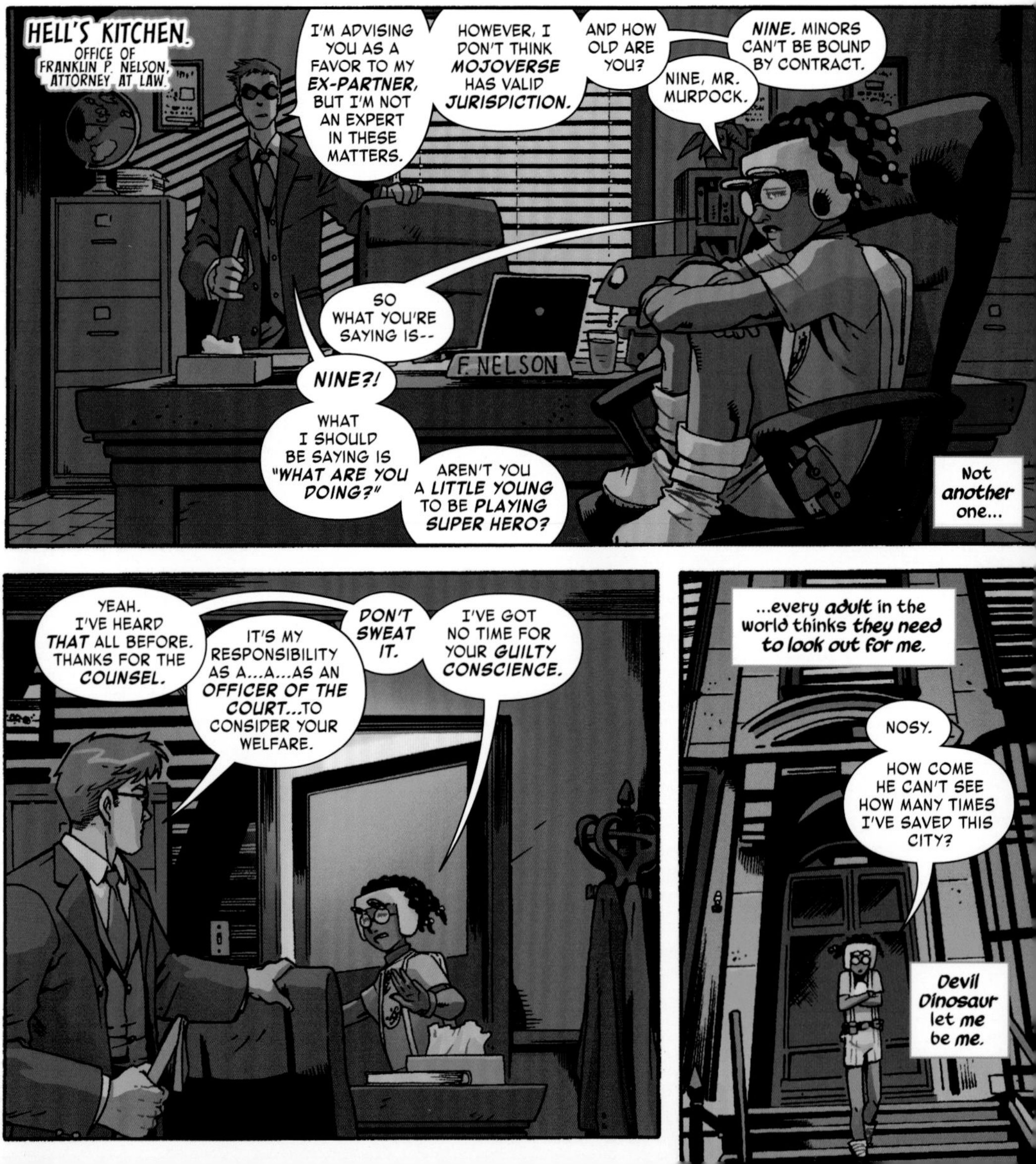
HELL'S KITCHEN.
OFFICE OF FRANKLIN P. NELSON, ATTORNEY AT LAW.
I'M ADVISING YOU AS A FAVOR TO MY EX-PARTNER, BUT I'M NOT AN EXPERT IN THESE MATTERS.
HOWEVER, I DON'T THINK MOJOVERSE HAS VALID JURISDICTION.
AND HOW OLD ARE YOU?
NINE. MINORS CAN'T BE BOUND BY CONTRACT.
NINE, MR. MURDOCK.
SO WHAT YOU'RE SAYING IS--
NINE?!
WHAT I SHOULD BE SAYING IS "WHAT ARE YOU DOING?"
AREN'T YOU A LITTLE YOUNG TO BE PLAYING SUPER HERO?
F. NELSON
Not another one...
YEAH. I'VE HEARD THAT ALL BEFORE. THANKS FOR THE COUNSEL.
IT'S MY RESPONSIBILITY AS A...A...AS AN OFFICER OF THE COURT...TO CONSIDER YOUR WELFARE.
DON'T SWEAT IT.
I'VE GOT NO TIME FOR YOUR GUILTY CONSCIENCE.
...every adult in the world thinks they need to look out for me.
NOSY.
HOW COME HE CAN'T SEE HOW MANY TIMES I'VE SAVED THIS CITY?
Devil Dinosaur let me be me.

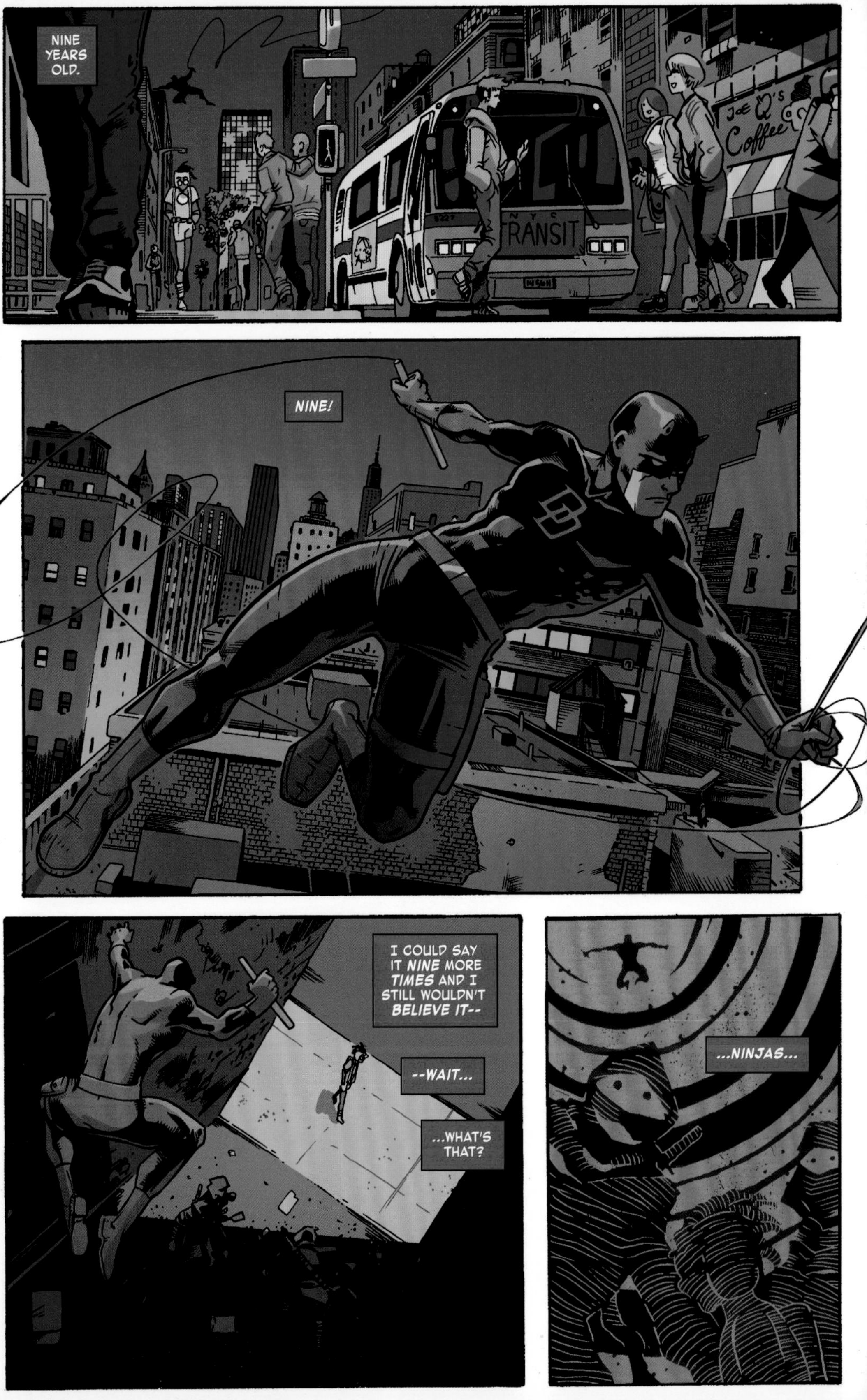
NINE YEARS OLD.
TRANSIT
NINE!
I COULD SAY IT NINE MORE TIMES AND I STILL WOULDN'T BELIEVE IT--
--WAIT...
...WHAT'S THAT?
...NINJAS...

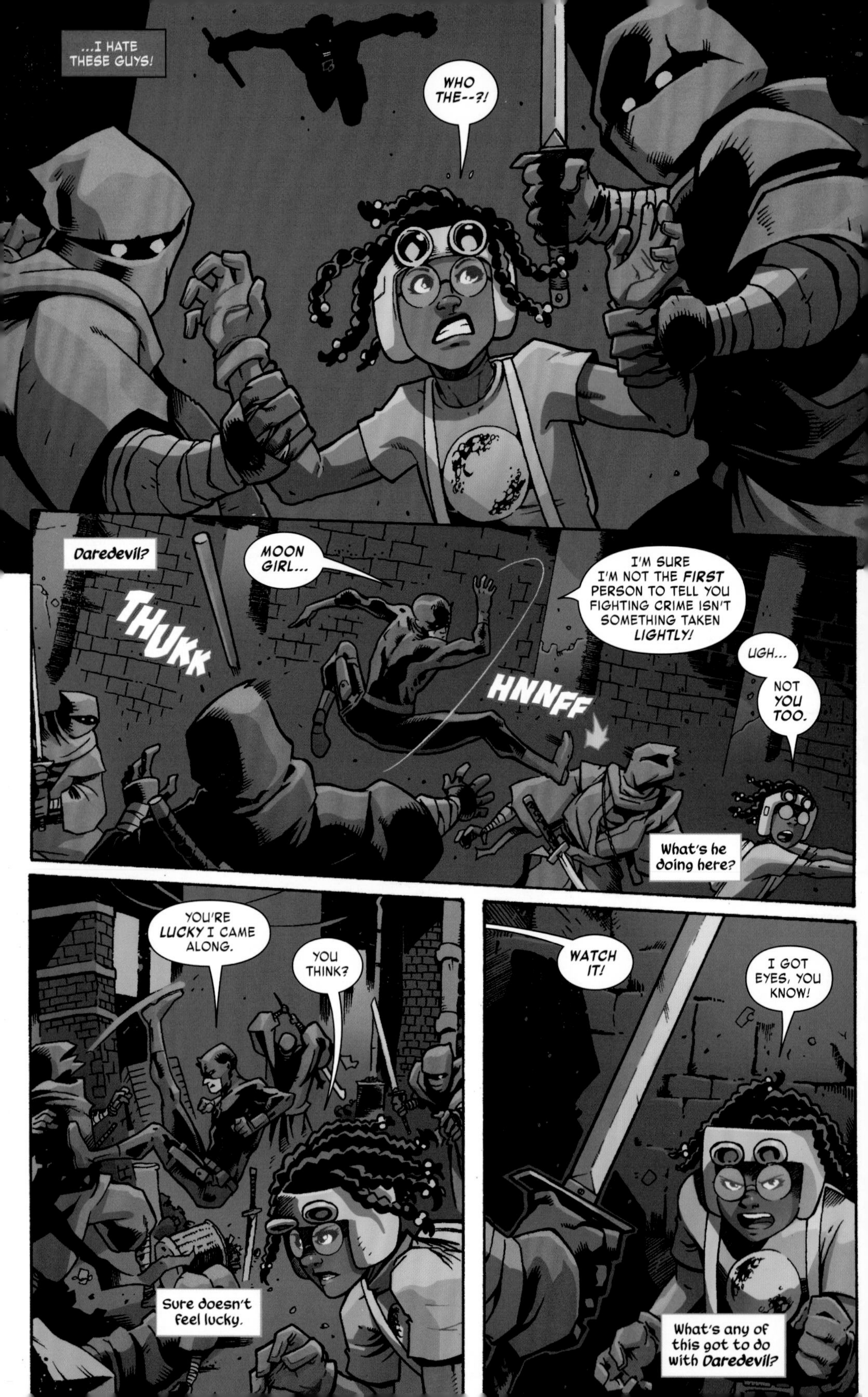
...I HATE THESE GUYS!
WHO THE--?!
Daredevil?
THUKK
MOON GIRL...
I'M SURE I'M NOT THE FIRST PERSON TO TELL YOU FIGHTING CRIME ISN'T SOMETHING TAKEN LIGHTLY!
HNNFF
UGH...
NOT YOU TOO.
What's he doing here?
YOU'RE LUCKY I CAME ALONG.
YOU THINK?
Sure doesn't feel lucky.
WATCH IT!
I GOT EYES, YOU KNOW!
What's any of this got to do with Daredevil?

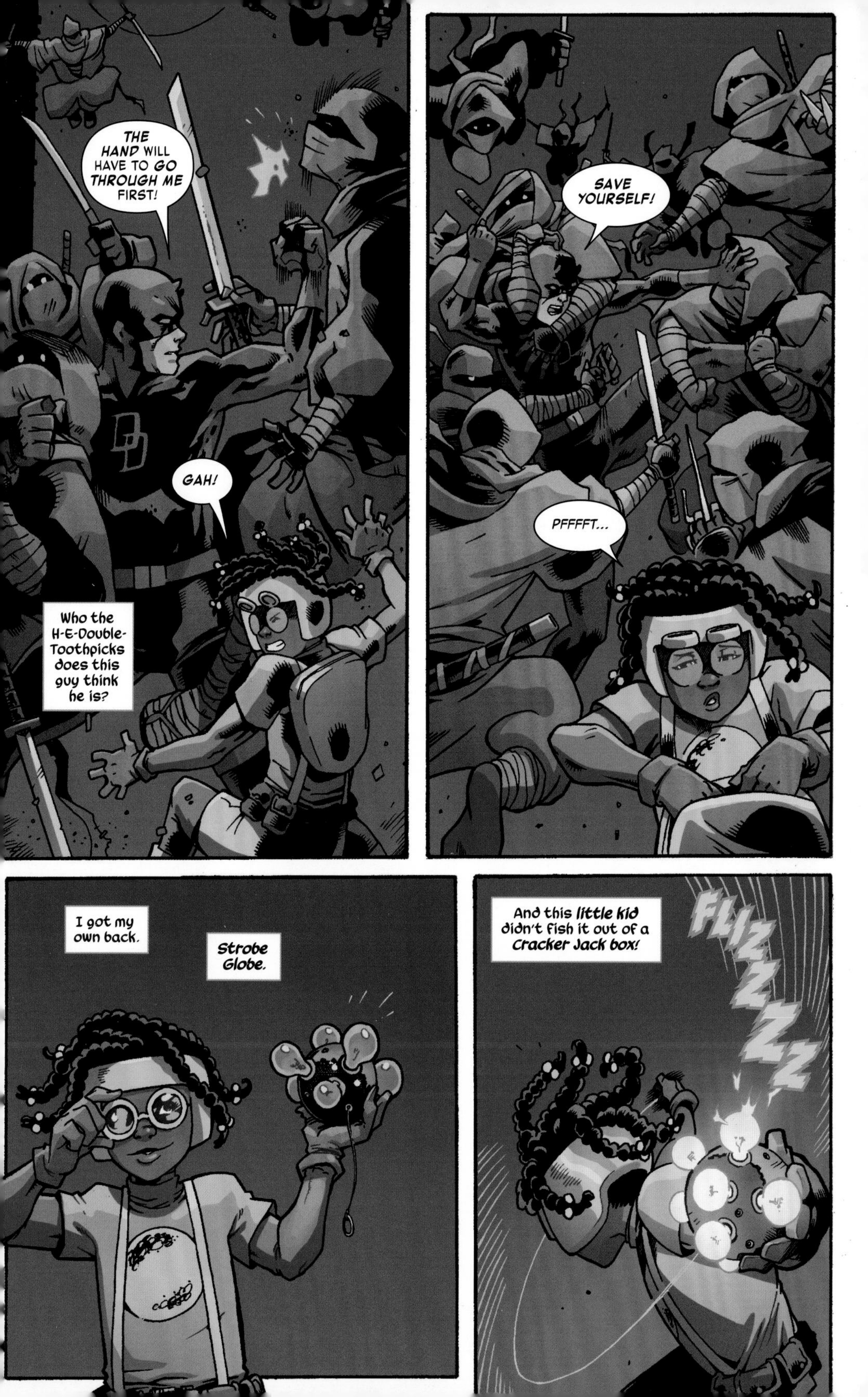
THE HAND WILL HAVE TO GO THROUGH ME FIRST!
GAH!
Who the H-E-Double-Toothpicks does this guy think he is?
SAVE YOURSELF!
PFFFFT...
I got my own back.
Strobe Globe.
And this little kid didn't fish it out of a Cracker Jack box!
FLIZZZZZ

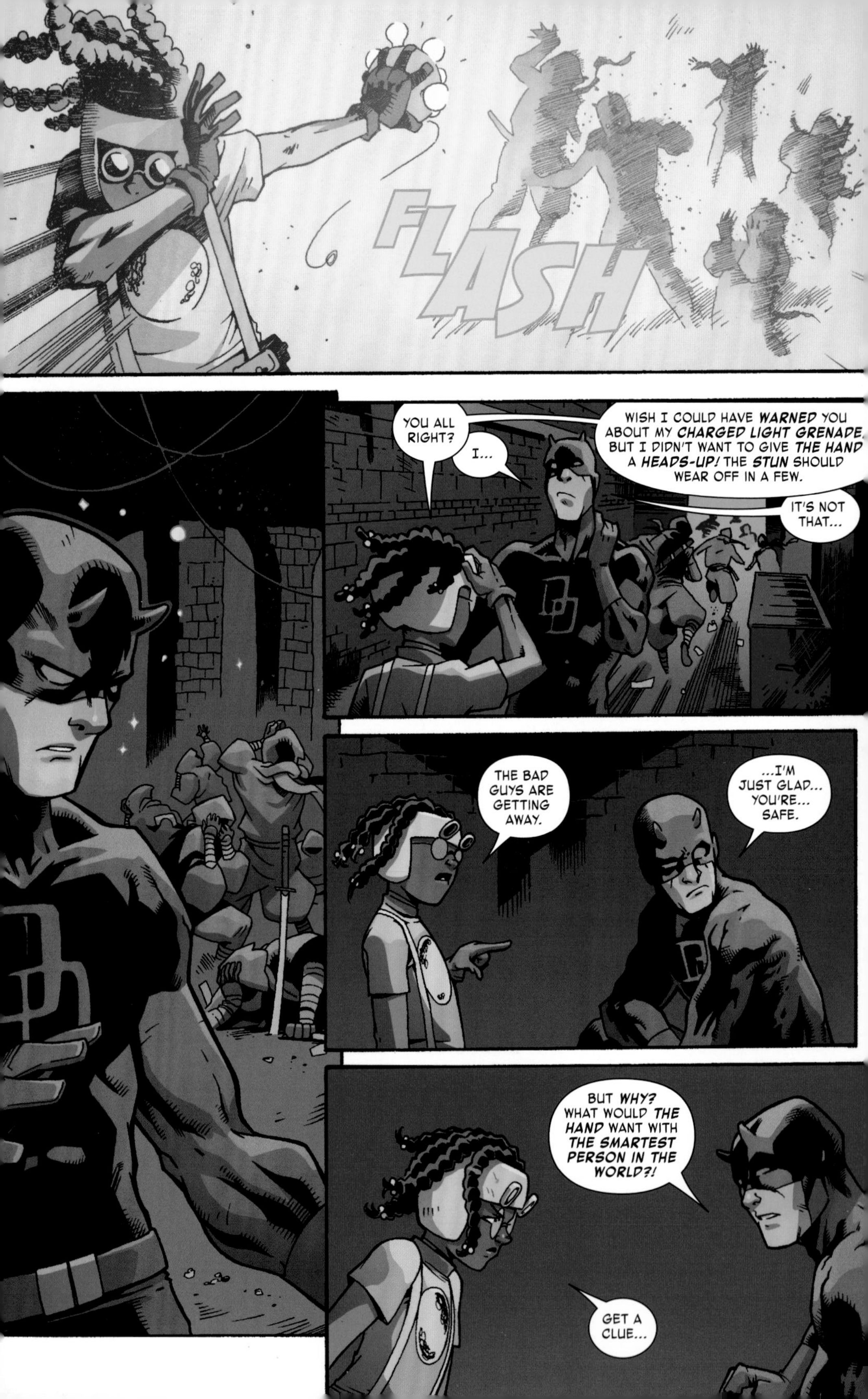
FLASH
YOU ALL RIGHT?
I...
WISH I COULD HAVE WARNED YOU ABOUT MY CHARGED LIGHT GRENADE, BUT I DIDN'T WANT TO GIVE THE HAND A HEADS-UP! THE STUN SHOULD WEAR OFF IN A FEW.
IT'S NOT THAT...
THE BAD GUYS ARE GETTING AWAY.
...I'M JUST GLAD... YOU'RE... SAFE.
BUT WHY? WHAT WOULD THE HAND WANT WITH THE SMARTEST PERSON IN THE WORLD?!
GET A CLUE...

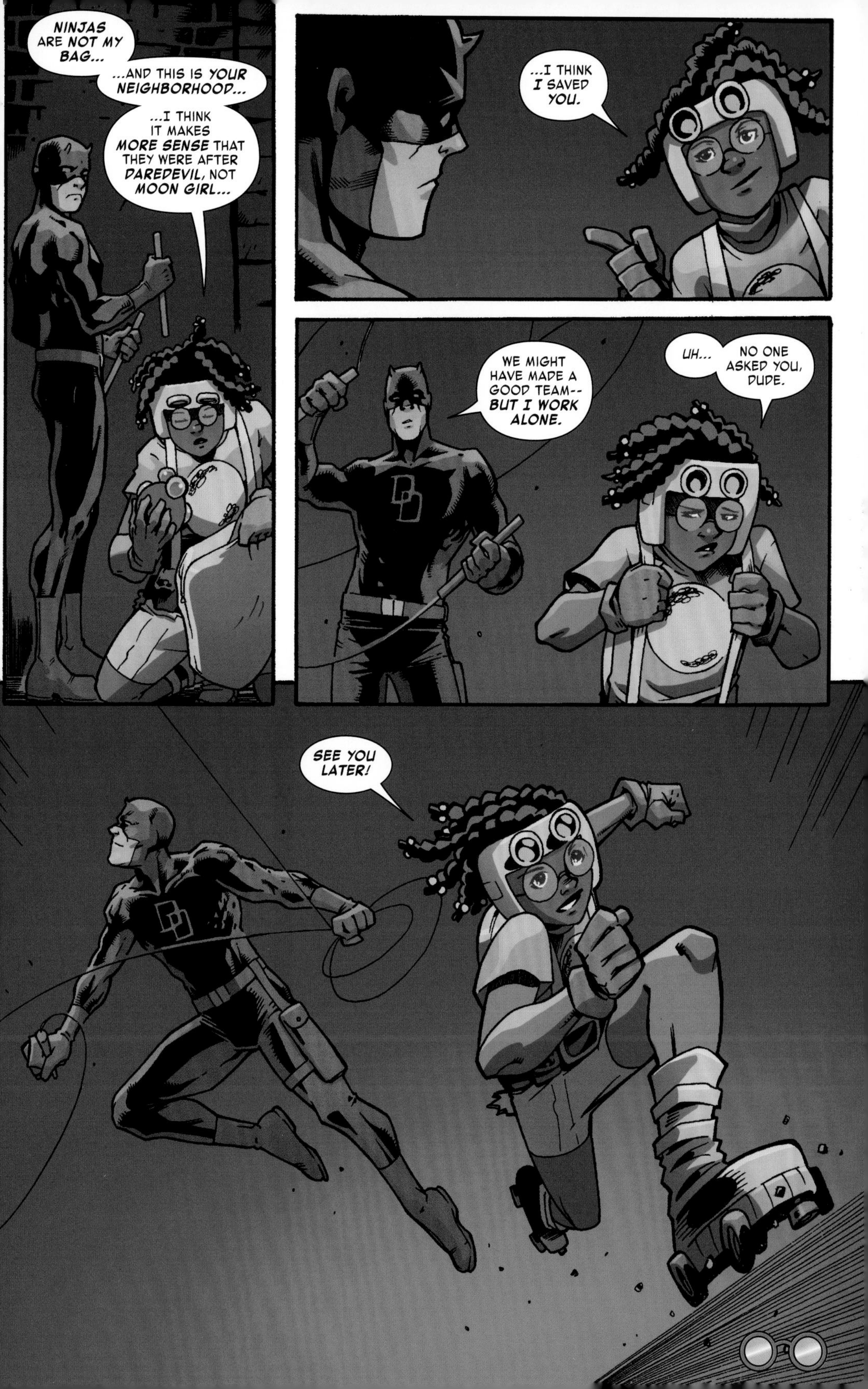
NINJAS ARE NOT MY BAG...
...AND THIS IS YOUR NEIGHBORHOOD...
...I THINK IT MAKES MORE SENSE THAT THEY WERE AFTER DAREDEVIL, NOT MOON GIRL...
...I THINK I SAVED YOU.
WE MIGHT HAVE MADE A GOOD TEAM-- BUT I WORK ALONE.
UH...
NO ONE ASKED YOU, DUDE.
SEE YOU LATER!

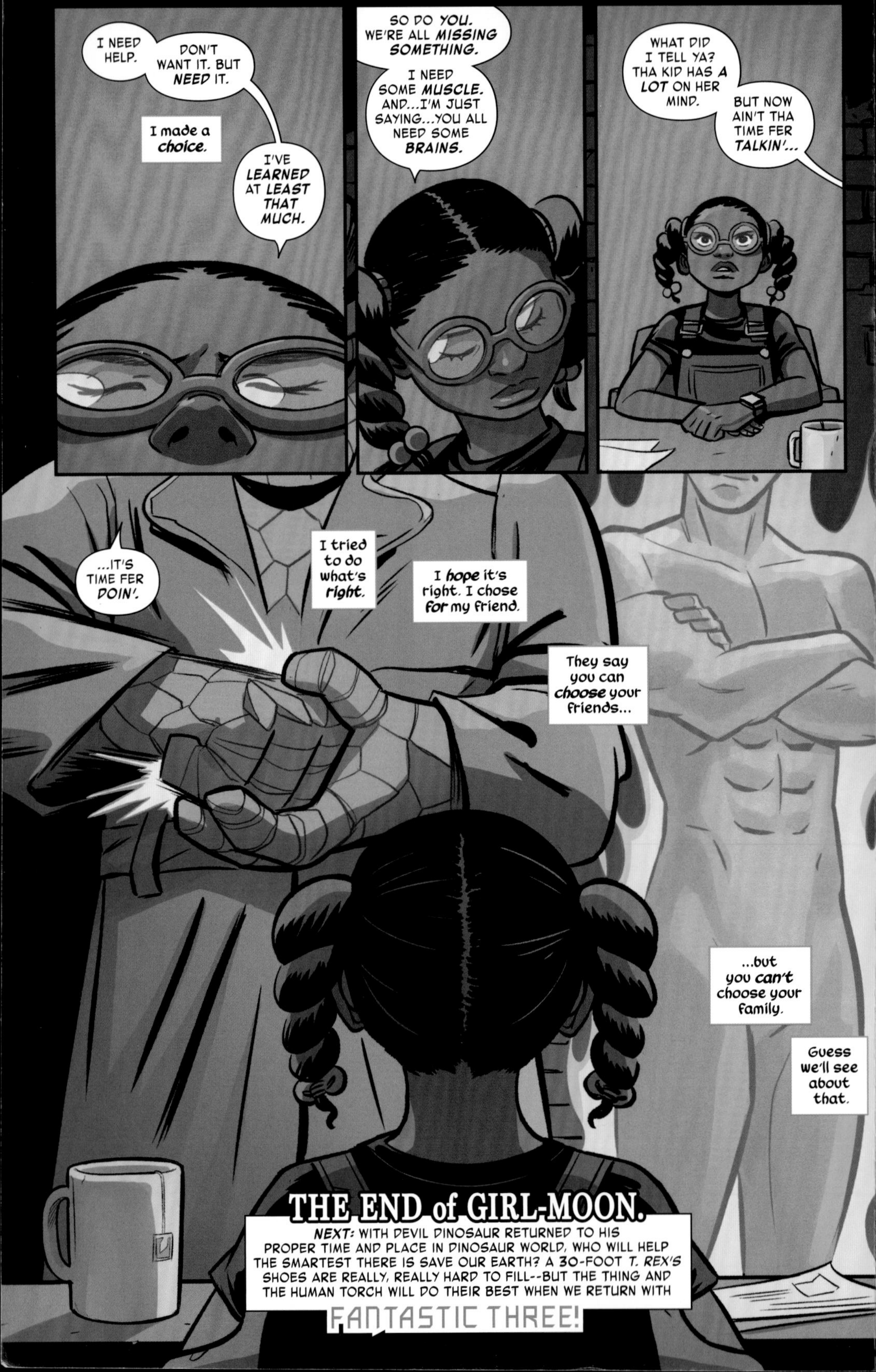
I NEED HELP.
DON'T WANT IT. BUT NEED IT.
I made a choice.
I'VE LEARNED AT LEAST THAT MUCH.
SO DO YOU. WE'RE ALL MISSING SOMETHING.
I NEED SOME MUSCLE. AND...I'M JUST SAYING...YOU ALL NEED SOME BRAINS.
WHAT DID I TELL YA? THA KID HAS A LOT ON HER MIND.
BUT NOW AIN'T THA TIME FER TALKIN'...
...IT'S TIME FER DOIN'.
I tried to do what's right.
I hope it's right. I chose for my friend.
They say you can choose your friends...
...but you can't choose your family.
Guess we'll see about that.
THE END of GIRL-MOON.
NEXT: WITH DEVIL DINOSAUR RETURNED TO HIS PROPER TIME AND PLACE IN DINOSAUR WORLD, WHO WILL HELP THE SMARTEST THERE IS SAVE OUR EARTH? A 30-FOOT T. REX'S SHOES ARE REALLY, REALLY HARD TO FILL--BUT THE THING AND THE HUMAN TORCH WILL DO THEIR BEST WHEN WE RETURN WITH
FANTASTIC THREE!

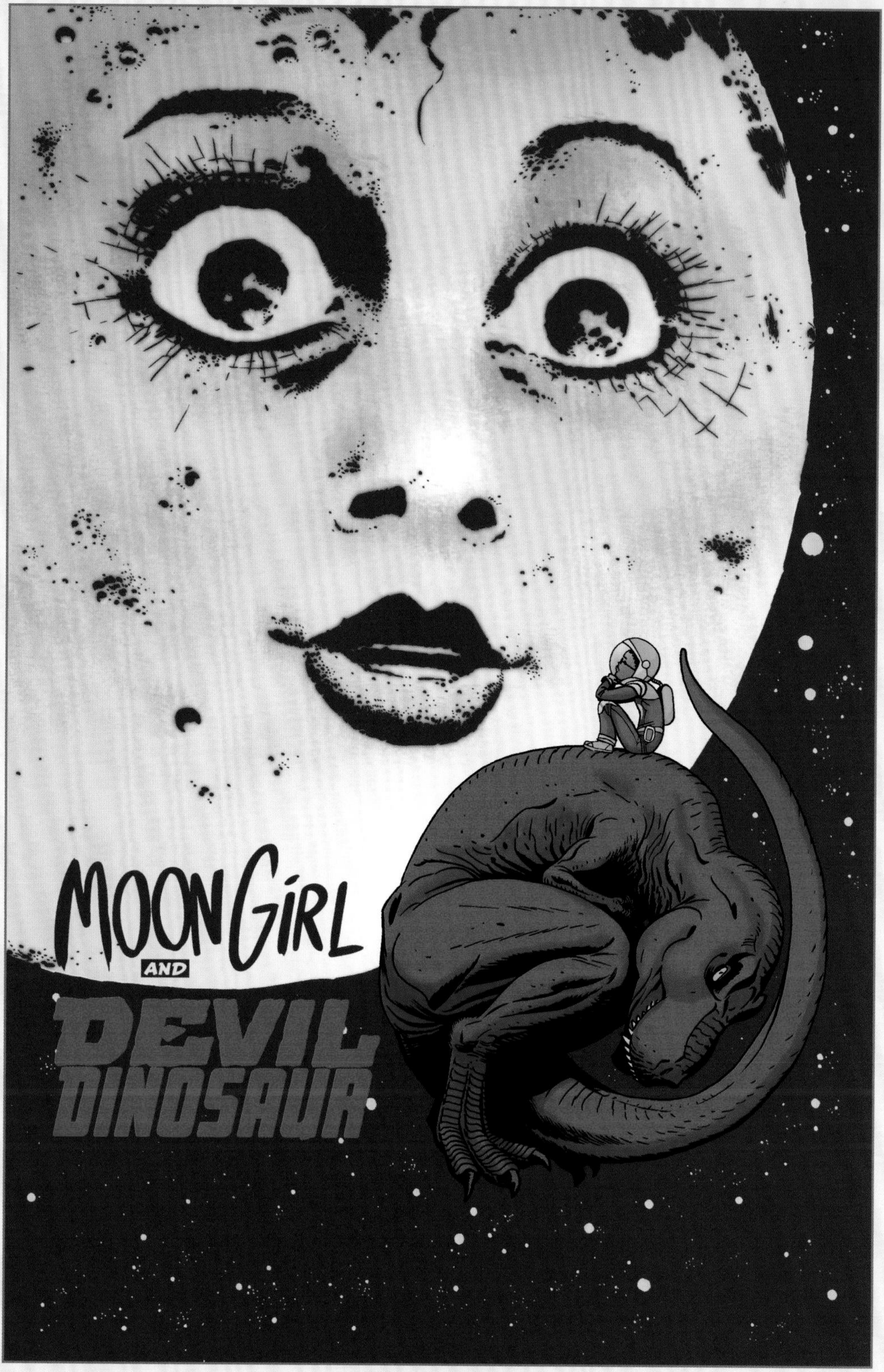
MOON GIRL
AND
DEVIL DINOSAUR

#19 VARIANT
BY MARCOS MARTIN

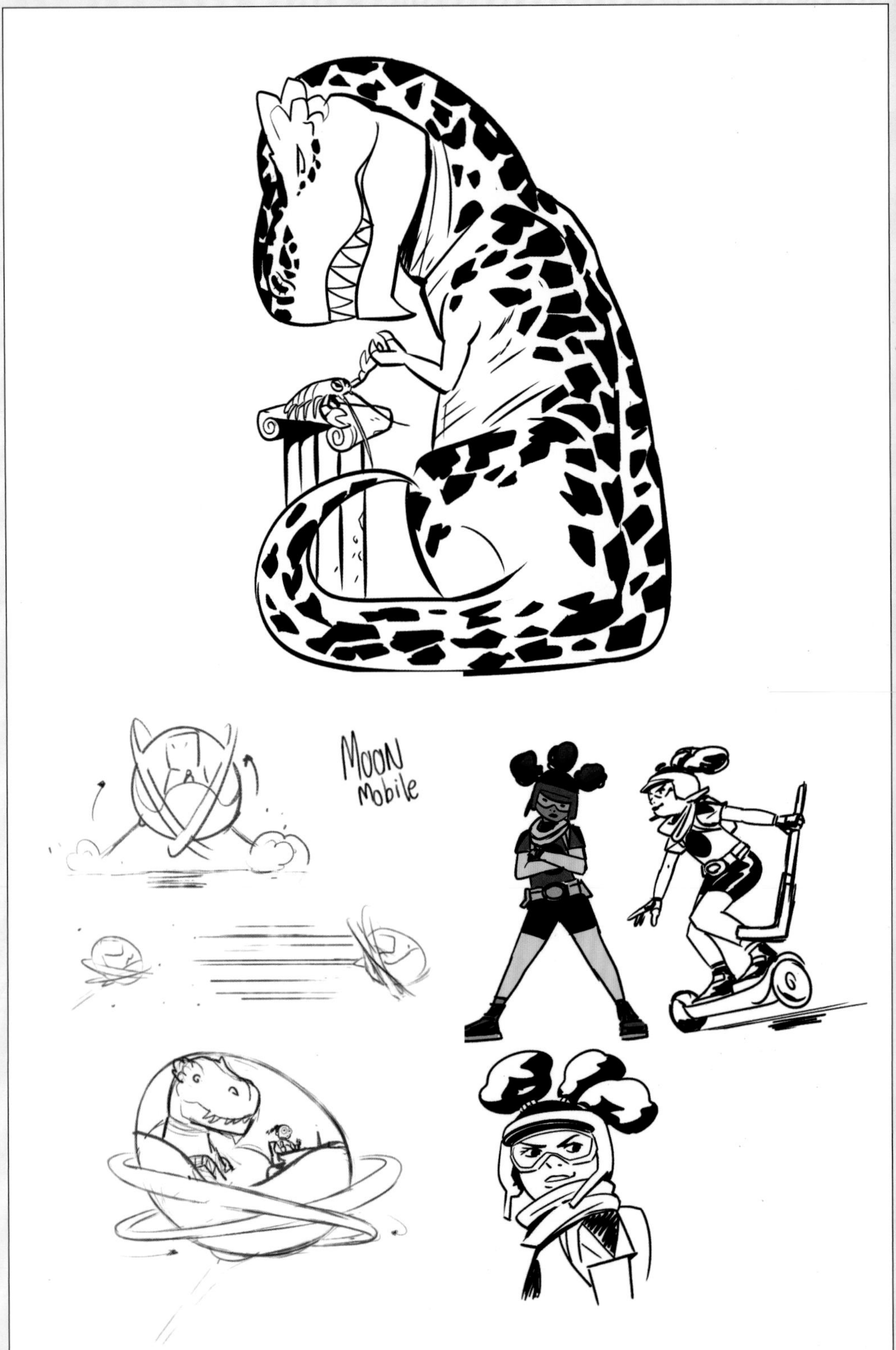
MOON Mobile

CHARACTER SKETCHES BY NATACHA BUSTOS

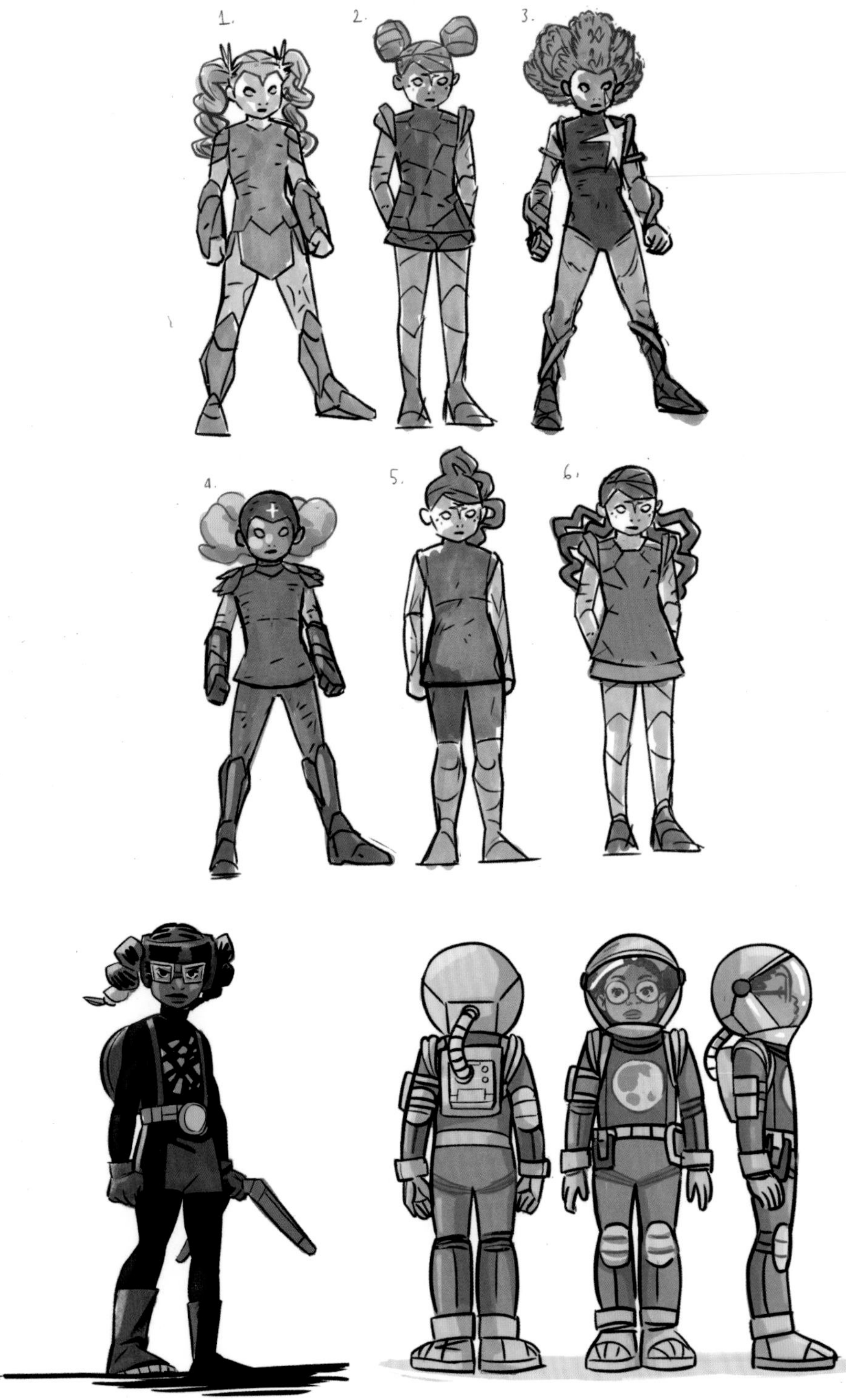
1.
2.
3.
4.
5.
6.

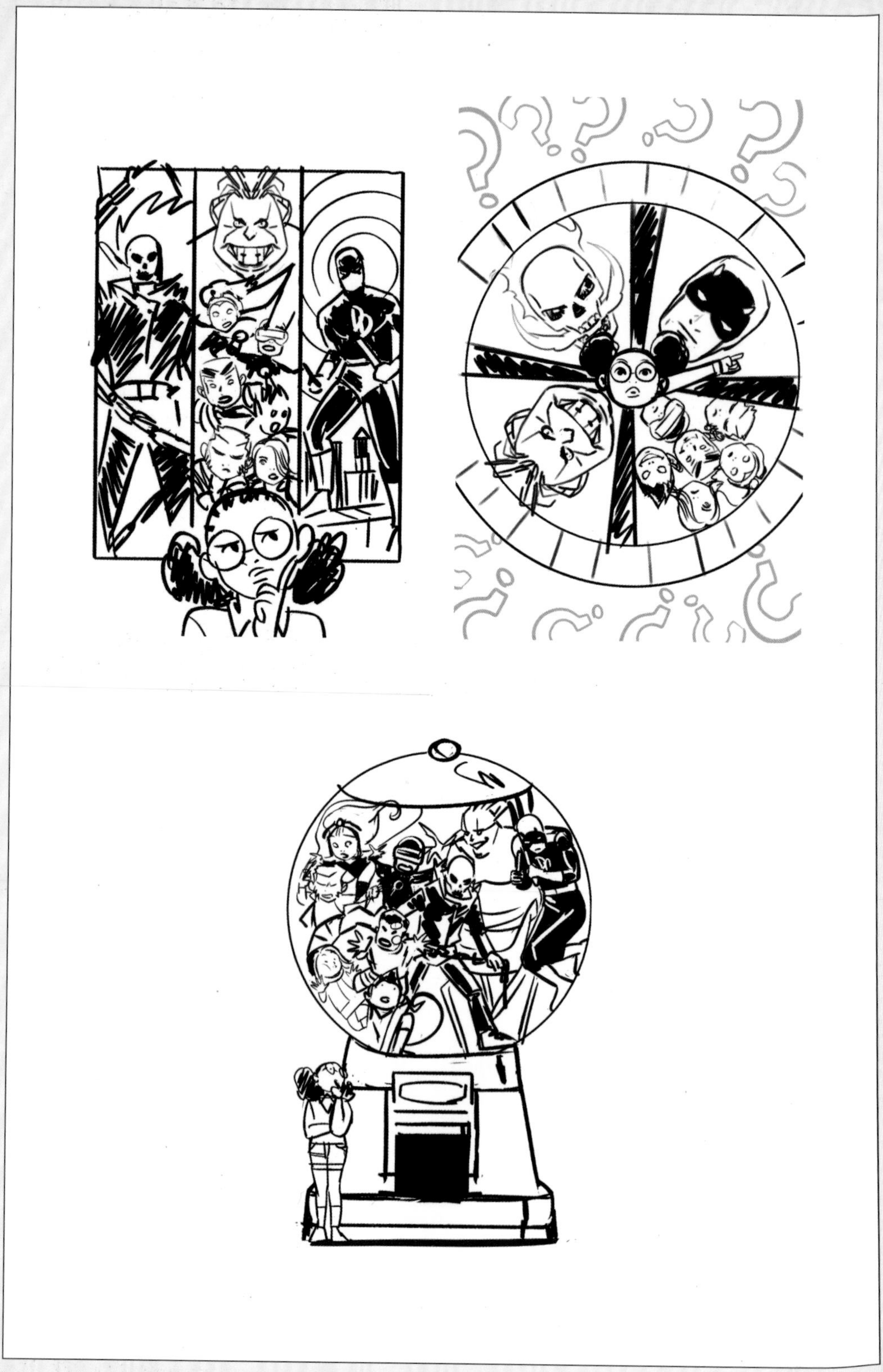

#24 COVER SKETCHES BY NATACHA BUSTOS